Despite All Odds:

A DREAM FULFILLED

Gladys Lawson

xulon PRESS

Copyright © 2007 by Gladys Lawson

Despite All Odds: A DREAM FULFILLED

by Gladys Lawson

Printed in the United States of America

ISBN 978-1-60266-467-8

First published in 2005 by:

Blackie & Co © Copyright 2003

A CIP catalogue record for this title is available from the British Library

www.xulonpress.com

Dedication

"My grace is all you need
for my power is greatest when you are weak"

(2 Corinthians, chapter 12, verse 9)

I read these words recently and smiled at their poignancy. I thought about the many days of weakness I had experienced while writing this book. The days when my vision was not so clear, the days I felt confused, unsure, tired, weak. As I sat and reflected upon these days the truth of these words resounded in my mind.

This book is a testament that God's Grace is all one needs, it is sufficient, and so I dedicate this book to God with thanks on my lips and praise in my heart.

Acknowledgements

To the first family I knew, my parents Mr and Mrs Lawson, my brother Richard, sister Liz and brother Tunde: I will always love you, and I pray that the blessings of God be with you always.

To my wonderful husband, and to my children Stephanie and Zachariah: You are precious and you know what? I wouldn't change a thing. Your understanding, patience and love have helped to produce this book and I thank you.

To everyone that has helped me: May the sun always shine on your face and the gentle wind of encouragement always blow on your back, may you come to a place in your life where you have peace, joy and happiness. And, may the smile on your face be a reflection of the love in your heart.

And finally to the loving memory of my Grandmother
— She was a beautiful, kind-hearted and strong woman —

Gladys Lawson-Adeyemi

Acorns into trees they grow

"And what do you want to be when you grow up Billie?"

Sitting back in my little chair I put my thumb under my chin and think. As usual It does not take my five year old brain long to come up with an answer.

"Well, I want to be a doctor or a lawyer and deep down in my heart I want to help people and make them happy. I want to buy a big house and take care of my family and friends...oh and for my *real* job, I want to write stuff like poems, songs, lots and lots of songs that mean something and help people and I want to be happy and in love like my mummy."

Everyone in the class looks at me as I sit there feeling important. Hoping I haven't missed anything out I give Mrs Taylor one of my big toothless grins.

"That's nice Billie dear, work hard and you can be anything you want to be..... anything at all. You have a lot of potential."

Nearly twenty years later the memory of that day still makes me smile, for her words have never left me. Looking back I realize, outside of my family, that was probably my first encounter with a 'dream maker'.

There are many 'dream makers' in the world. People who encourage you emotionally, give you that positive smile, helping hand, right words of inspiration when needed. They are the people that are placed in our lives to assist us, help us fulfill our destiny, our dream. The 'dream breakers' on the other hand are the exact opposite. Their role, to break up every plan, destroy every bridge, confuse every situation. To stop you fulfilling your destiny! In a battle between both, the 'dream makers' always win. So be smart, be a 'dream maker'.

REJECTION:
Turn down, Veto, Disregard

Nine letters when put together form the word rejection. A word that we live with each day hoping that it does not adversely affect us, does not wreak havoc on our emotions; in our lives.

So many words can be used to describe the word rejection: decline, refuse, say no to, are just a few of them. They more or less all boil down to the same thing and are used when people do not want something, they are not interested in something or they think that something is crap. You see I know the sting of rejection well.

I'm not bitter or resentful in any way. What we went through then has made us what we are now. It has taken so long to get Jamie out there, so long for other people to see what I saw at the very beginning. People see and want the glory now, they don't know the story, they can't live the story.

They don't know what we went through. How we had to put up with the 'dream breakers', the people that told us we were wasting our time. With criticism and insults from so many people inside the music industry, as well as outside. The people that told me I was 'flogging a dead horse' and to try another, more 'suitable', more feminine profession, the people that made fun of my belief in God. These are the very same people who are now telling me how right we were and how terrific Jamie's voice and my songs are.

If I had listened to them then, I would be nowhere now. Well, no, actually that's not quite true, but I would probably be on the way to being a lonely old person sitting in a rocking chair staring at my false teeth in a glass; dreaming of what could have been. What if ....

I refused to let that happen, refused to accept that I could not achieve my dream. Now I am here to say to anyone that wants to listen, never give up on your dream. Pray persistently, work hard and believe. Don't be reliant on people, they may and can let you down. Put your complete trust in God, be obedient to Him and as sure as tomorrow is the day after today, you will not fail. In fact you will see that Despite all odds your Dream will be Fulfilled.....

Billie Lewis
Taken from:
'Time and People Magazine'

PROLOGUE

Billie sits still as she stares out of the tinted window of the limousine in amazement. London, Japan, America, Monaco, she has seen this so many times but each time is like the very first, simply astounding. She is lost in the crowds of people that line the street, lost in the happy faces they pass by. She feels Jamie's hand squeeze hers, hears the voices of their American personal assistant and publicist in the background, but is totally captivated by the people outside the car. It has been reported on the news that some of them have been here as early as 6am this morning waiting to see the celebrities arriving at 6pm. Their car gradually slows down as it joins the queue of other cars whose occupants comprise some of the most renowned movie, music and money people in the world.

Billie lowers the window a little and looks out, the enormity of the event hits her full in the face and leaves her a little breathless. The car stops, the door opens almost immediately.

The crowds go crazy as Jamie emerges from the stretch limousine.

"Jamie! Jamie!" People scream from every possible direction. He smiles as he waves, glowing in the limelight. He then bends and assists Billie out of the car. The first they see of her are long elegant legs as she swings them out of the car. Legs, which have been voted the best in several magazines and given a six figure insurance value in a number of their polls, (all of which, Billie found too amusing to comment upon).

"Oh my goodness look it's Billie! Billie Lewis!" She smiles as she hears her name. Stepping out of the car into the warm Californian evening she smoothes the delicate material of her dress down over her slender limbs. Jamie places his arm protectively around her waist as the cameras click and flashes explode like crazy in their faces.

They are a handsome couple, Jamie in his tuxedo, which he makes look good and Billie in her designer dress, adding to her exquisiteness.

"Billie over here! Jamie! Billie!" Microphones seem to come alive as they are thrust in their direction. The security men are very good and keep everyone back so the celebrities and their entourage can make their way leisurely along the red carpet to the prestigious awards ceremony.

Having both previously agreed with their publicity and promotion people in London and America, they pose for as many pictures as possible, talk to the Press as well as shake hands with a number of the fans. They know that because of God, they owe their success to the fans. While the record people only look at this as 'good strategy' for promotion and sales, they on the other hand happily do it. They can never forget who have made them as popular as they are by buying their records. To them their fans are the real people, the people that matter.

"Hi Billie! Hi Jamie! Over here!" A popular reporter from a Network News Channel, shouts as he tries to get their attention above the noise of the crowd. "How are you guys? How does it feel both being nominated?" They stop in front of him and answer his questions then wave and smile into his camera.

Jamie recognizes a reporter from GMTV London a few yards away and gently steers Billie over to her. She is beside herself as Billie and Jamie smile, answer her questions and crack a few jokes with her; like the 'regular' unpretentious people they are. Over and over again she thanks them for talking to her and wishes them good luck for tonight. By now people are shouting for their attention from every direction. The flashes of the hundreds of cameras create a strobe light effect. It is pure crazy. Radio, regular TV, satellite TV, magazines, everyone wants to talk to the new English sensations that have taken America and the world by storm. They spend a few moments with an MTV reporter talking about the person they most want to see perform tonight and of course, their nominations.

"I hear you're a fan of both *Stevie Wonder* and *Lionel Richie*, Jamie, I bet you can't wait to see them perform tonight?"

"I'm really looking forward to it," Jamie replies smiling.

One of the meticulously dressed security men comes over to them, he speaks into his head radio microphone then discreetly advises them to think about heading inside with the other celebrities. Taking his advice they quickly pose for a few more pictures, sign some autographs and shake hands with a few more fans then make their way inside. Their friends, family and colleagues are already seated inside the grand hall.

To all and sundry, it seems as if Billie's smile is fixed permanently on her face. It is. For Billie is more than just happy she is exuberant. Her heart feels light and her head slightly bubbly and despite everything, she is determined to enjoy the evening. If anyone had ever told her years ago that she would one day be a guest at this awards ceremony and be a nominee, she would have laughed, hyperventilated and then laughed again.

"How did it all happen?" An American news reporter had asked this morning when they had attended a pre-awards interview.

Even now some people still look at them and think that it 'just' happened. That they are some sort of pre-packaged, overnight success. Some people do not believe them when they say it took time and persistent prayers, it took dedication and it took a lot of hard work, very hard work for that matter.

It wasn't that long ago a top music reporter had called Jamie *'a flash in the pan one hit wonder'* and condemned him to failure before he had even really started. He had accused Jamie of the crime of following that all too famous 'solo' road, of an ex-member of a previously successful group; of living an impossible dream. Billie's crime; *aiding and abetting him.* After six consecutive top ten hit singles and two triple platinum albums he had been forced to write several retract articles and like a number of other people, talk with a new set of lips.

Each day Billie wakes up she says a prayer, for she is so grateful to God for her blessings; she has an attitude of gratitude. She does not believe for one moment that she met Jamie by chance or because she was lucky as some people chose to think. She strongly believes that it was meant to be, the quality of their songs, the impact they have and the message they re-lay, is a 'gift' that is simply meant to be. Their songs have touched and changed peoples lives and are still touching many lives around the world.

'How did it all happen?' The question that magazines have offered large sums to publish. The sixty-four thousand dollar question, which, only a few know the true answer to. Even then, only one or two of those few, know the real facts behind the death and murder of two people that drive Billie and Jamie to push and aspire to reach heights that many would never dare to attempt.

Here, now, to all the onlookers they are the picture of happiness. The years of hard work, painful and bad experiences, deception, back-stabbing, jealousy, drugs and sex scandals, all a thing of the past. A past where failure brought friends, and success brought enemies.

They are living proof of the saying that 'Present happiness can sometimes ease a painful past'. They have been up against some very difficult times, but now they are happy; the present is bright and the future even brighter, so it seems.....

As they walk along the red carpet, Billie grows more and more conscious of the armed security people around them. She is conscious of Jamie's protective arm around her waist. They know the killer is still out there, they know he is psychopathic amongst other things and can strike at any moment. Being here is a chance they have taken and possibly the only way to bring the killer out before he kills again. Billie holds her breath as on cue two police officers disguised as a reporter and a cameraman rush towards them.

"Jamie, Billie, welcome to 'tinsel town' do you have anything to say to the folks back in England rooting for you?"

"Just thank you for your support," Jamie says and smiles.

The camera focuses on Billie, "I would just like to say hello to everyone and thank you," Billie says, she waves. As she lowers her hand, she quickly turns it around so the ring she is wearing is visible.

The coded message is sent to the killer!

Now, amid the lights, people and cameras of the paparazzi, amid the fervour of the event, they know, they are acutely aware that time is running out for the person the killer has abducted.

The words you have read so far were taken from Wanda Young's best-selling unauthorized biography about my life. My name is Billie Lewis and the words you are about to read are true and concise, for they are my words; this is my story.

CHAPTER 1

Every end has a beginning

Eye contact has not yet been made between any of the GUM (Genito-Urinary Medicine) waiting room's four occupants. In this room with walls adorned with posters advertising safe sex and HIV/AIDS awareness, they have no names, just numbers. The occasional sound of the page of a magazine or a newspaper turning every few minutes confirms to each of them that the 'others' are still in the room.

"327491 please," the nurse says.

The only male occupant of the room clad in painfully tight, bright blue leather trousers stands up and scurries out the room.

Taking a deep breath, the redhead looks up at the person who is sitting in one of the corner armchairs. The woman she glimpses is borderline chubby, has streaky blond hair and a lot of make-up on. That is all she sees before she is forced to lower her eyes and hide discreetly behind her magazine as another 'number' walks into the room and sits down. In five seconds flat a novel is produced by the new arrival, which she immediately places in front of her face, in a fruitless attempt to conceal her identity. To the imaginary onlooker, the picture of children closing their eyes and thinking that no one can see them is portrayed.

The redhead looks at the words in the magazine that she holds in front of her. Words that make up the title of two of the supposedly true stories featured in the magazine. *'My boyfriend seduced my mother, so I killed him'. 'My husband killed his mistress then tried to kill me'.* She shakes her head as she thinks about all the things happening in the world today. How, despite the increase in value of property and other material things, the 'market value' of the human life seems to be falling. Spiralling down to the lower lows.

She looks at the HIV/AIDS poster and grimaces as she thinks about the things she has done. The times she has had casual unprotected sex just to be popular or to make a new boyfriend stay with her. It never worked. Something tucked away in the side of her chair catches her eye, and she pulls it out. It is a health leaflet, she reads it: *'The sexually transmitted disease Chlamydia, has been linked to cervical cancer and infertility. It is on the increase as is Gonorrhoea, Syphilis, Genital warts and HIV/AIDS. They have all been found to have increased drastically in the last few years - more than 100% and rising – especially amongst young people. There is now a growing concern by the government...'* Grimacing she stops reading and puts the leaflet down, something stirs in her heart and she wonders if there is another way, a better way to life. After years of doing things the wrong way, surely there has to be something more. She turns the page of her magazine and looks at the pictures of the scantily dressed men and women. Her thoughts change. The embers of the flame that had flickered briefly in her heart start to fade. They do not die completely, they wait patiently for her to fan them again, stir them into life.

"Number 327498 please," the nurse calls.

The redhead freezes momentarily, then she bends her head to check the number on her card. Standing up she futilely pulls the red hair of her wig forward in an attempt to hide her face. Quickly she walks past the newcomer and the two other occupants in the room, she hopes they are not watching her. Behind the nurse, she walks down a long sterile corridor and into a room with a large green medical screen. The screen surrounds a long leather looking examination table covered with a length of green disposable paper towel. The aroma of bleach and disinfectant hang pungently in the air, they assault her nostrils making them tingle.

"Take your knickers off, lift your skirt up and lay down on there please," the nurse says pointing to the table.

She obeys quickly. She is still in shock and totally embarrassed about being here. An elderly female doctor walks into the room and hands something to the nurse. A trolley is wheeled over to the table where the redhead lays. The doctor extends no greeting to the redhead, no words of comfort.

"Umm.., sudden severe vaginal discharge and low abdominal pain," the doctor reads out the symptoms that have been written down. "Right, let's get started, knees up and legs apart please," she says pressing a switch on the wall. The adjustable light comes on and the nurse pulls it towards the redhead's lower body. The redhead feels hands positioning her and fingers touching her as the doctor and nurse continue to talk.

"We need to clean around the outside," the nurse says. Despite the verbal warning, the redhead's whole body flinches in response as moist cotton wool held in sterile forceps, touches her.

"It's just cotton wool and a mild disinfectant dear," the nurse says quickly squeezing the redhead's leg reassuringly, sensitive, unlike the doctor, to her discomfort.

"Take a couple of deep breaths and try to relax," the doctor says coldly to this year's 327,498[th] patient.

She obeys the command. Squeezing her eyes tightly she tries to ignore the instrument, the speculum, that is being expanded inside of her and the voices of the doctor and nurse. Instead she tries to concentrate on the different colours that flash across her tightly closed eyelids.

"Umm hmm, not good, looks like I'm going to have to take some extra swabs," the doctor says to the nurse and writes 'Query Pelvic Inflammatory Disease' in the clinical details section of the request form.

"Do you want a GC plate?" The nurse asks the doctor.

"Yes and a Trichomonas culture plus Chlamydia swab."

Suddenly the redhead is alert, her head starts to throb. She hears feet walk away and come back. She feels something gently prodding at her insides. As she listens to them talking, she feels the nauseous bile rising in her throat. For unlike the many women that have probably laid in this room in the exact same position, she knows and understands exactly what they are talking about. She knows that a GC plate is used to grow Gonorrhoea. She knows what all the other things are as well, because she uses them daily at work.

The speculum is removed. She lays there, eyes closed and intermittently holding her breath. The snapping sound of rubber gloves being taken off follows. As she lays there she tries to normalize her breathing. Feet walk away, a door opens and seconds later closes. Still she lays there.

"Are you okay to get up now?" The nurse asks.

Nodding she struggles to sit up, her unshed tears momentarily blind her. She feels a strong grip on her arm as the nurse assists her off the table.

"The doctor will see you in her office when you get dressed."

"Thank you."

"You need to fill out a consent form for an HIV test, and get a Syphilis test done as well. The doctor looked quite concerned and I really think you should get the tests done."

"HIV? AIDS?" Shock is evident in her voice.

Experienced eyes are adverted, "The doctor will explain everything dear, get dressed," she pauses, "I know the doctor seems a little brusque, it's just-, sometimes things can get so frustrating here. Thousands of people come in here every week to find out if they have a sexually transmitted disease. Chlamydia, Syphilis, Gonorrhoeae and HIV are all on the increase. Despite all the information we give out, all our efforts to educate, we see hundreds of more people now than we did a few years ago, some as young as eleven! Out of every 10 teenagers that come here at least 1 will test positive for a sexually transmitted disease. That is 10 for every 100 or 1000 for every 10,000. It's like something somewhere is blatantly not right!" She shakes her head at the disincentive nature of her work. She pushes the trolley against the wall and starts to prepare for the next patient.

Number 327498 sees the doctor then leaves the clinic clutching her bag. She has been told that she will get her results in a few days. Pending the results, she has to start a course of antibiotics because of what has been detected microscopically in the analysis of her samples. She has however, other things on her mind as she walks to her car with determined steps. Her heart is pounding, her head is pounding, and her feet pound on the pavement, as her pace increases her thoughts mock her. The brown autumn leaves on the pavement seem to take part in the assault as they mockingly dance in the gusts of wind, over and over they rise up and then fall down, pounding at her feet. The thoughts in her head play over and over again as the pounding grows louder.

"Where the hell is my car?" She says loudly as she stops abruptly and looks up and down the street. She turns round again and looks down the street, the sky seems to turn with her. Clarity is lost in her state of confusion. She walks back up the street and passes her car again.

When she eventually gets to the car she is on the verge of hysteria; everything seems to close in on her, squeezing the breath in her lungs into a tight knot in her chest. The pounding is all around her now, it has consolidated and taken the form of a rhythm of words; words that wash away all denial. What they can't wash away, are the lies, the betrayal and the pain she feels deep within her. She looks at her reflection in the rear-view mirror, her eyes look remarkably calm as she finally acknowledges the doctor's words that are making her head throb, making her feel physically sick:

"Do you or your partner have multiple sexual partners?" The doctor had asked.

"No," she had replied feebly, *"that is, no I don't and I don't think he does."*

"So you don't know about him or how many sexual partners he has, or sexual partners those partners have had, or currently do have? So, in effect by sleeping with him, you could be sleeping with as many as 30 or 40 other people. You could be playing Russian roulette with your life. Well, he needs to come in and get checked, there is no point treating you and not him, only for you to get infected again. Right, your results: you have a pungent discharge and slight decomposition of your cervical cells which could be due to a serious sexually transmitted infection, and you also have a bulky uterus which could mean you're pregnant or something else. The antibiotics I have prescribed will not cross in to the placenta if you are pregnant. We will know more once we have all the results back, until then, I seriously advise total abstinence!"

*　　*　　*　　*　　*

I sit and watch the animated lunch time discussion not really taking part. It is more out of a lack of interest than anything else. Every so often someone tries to pull me in but quickly gives up at my 'one-word' answers. The conversation around me is getting a little too loud.

"Will you just let me-"

"Man are you way off point," Roger says.

"Let him finish what he-"

"No he hasn't got a clue so why should I let him finish, why should I?" Roger interjects loudly.

As usual it's Roger Manning-Smith, one of our supervisors in the Microbiology Department, who is getting loud, nasty and not listening to anyone else. I sometimes feel that he uses his position as a Grade Two, Senior Biomedical Scientist, coupled with his good looks and tall physique, as some men use a flashy car or a beautiful woman to impress and sometimes intimidate others. I never get involved in laboratory gossip but I have heard it said amongst some of the female staff in the ladies toilets, that he is lacking in a certain area. They laugh at him behind his back and call him Mr SBS (Small Brain Syndrome), they say the only reason he was given the senior position is because his rich parents make regular large donations to the hospital. Rumour has it, that once, when he had accidentally overheard them talking about him, they told him SBS, apart from being an acronym of his grade title (Senior Biomedical Scientist), also stood for 'Solid, Big and Sexy'. Now, who would believe that you might well ask. I hear Roger did, with relish.

Personally, I don't feel that he is that bad, especially when you compare him to some of the other people in my department. I just find that sometimes he goes out of his way, almost to the point of pretending, to be crude, obnoxious and something else, something which I can't quite put my finger on, something still fluid, yet simmering on the verge of crystallization.

I feel like getting up and leaving as the argument is getting a little too heated and I am not in the mood to get caught up in it. A number of heads keep turning in the direction of our table.

"Look do you or don't you agree?" Roger asks.

"Well to be honest, I-," Nigel Elison starts to say.

"Cut the crap, do you or don't you?" Roger demands again.

"It's not that simple," Nigel replies, blushing slightly. He is a Grade Three, one grade higher than Roger, but for some reason always seems intimidated by him.

"Come on man, this is really getting arduous, wake up or is your brain having a private moment?" Roger says angrily, "if you are speeding and you jump a red light what is the first thing you do?"

"I, err, well-"

"You look around to make sure there are no 'Coppers,' no '5-0', right. It's a reflex thing, just like that," he says snapping his fingers loudly, "so do the same now please. Give me a bloody answer, go on take a risk, live dangerously for once."

"Look, I don't think this is going anywhere. I don't-"

"Think! That's your problem, you don't," Roger says rudely.

Nigel's eyes narrow and his blush deepens, "I don't think that you should expect thanks from everyone and as for the second issue, I personally think that until you experience the same thing, you can't really fully understand what someone else is going through-"

"BULL!" Roger interjects loudly.

Silence steps in, heads turn.

I look at Roger, I haven't really been following the whole conversation but I, like most people at the table, find his outburst a little over the top. Nigel literally goes from pink to red to crimson in seconds. I notice his jaw twitching.

"Excuse me," someone says.

"What the-," Dr. Colin Plowman, the new junior registrar, starts to say then looks at Nigel and stops suddenly.

"You heard me," Roger continues ignoring the objections of the others at the table. "Bull-bloody-shit, if I do something I expect thanks, *'mucho gracias'*. Now anyone who bloody says otherwise, is either a hypocritical scum or a twerp, full of it. For too long we have wrapped ourselves up in cotton wool, talking about feelings, wanting to experience before we relate, instead of just relating," he bangs his fist hard on the table as he speaks.

No one says anything, I look around the table, is it just me, am I the only one that is totally confused? I shake my head as I realize, no one is going to say anything, no one is going to stand up to him, as usual.

"Oh, you have something to say little Miss Songwriter?" Roger asks as he smirks at me.

"Who me?" I reply. The realization of my little head shake suddenly dawns on me.

"Who else writes songs Ms Billie Lewis?" He sneers at me, "who else thinks she's in the same league as *Diane Warren*? Who else thinks she has so much talent? Who else always has her head in the clouds and is always trying to be nice to everyone? Who-?"

"No I don't really have much to say," I quickly interrupt, sensing that he is getting a little carried away, "but, whether or not someone says 'thank you' for something does not justify you calling them, what was it? 'Scum'. That's the stuff that floats on the surface of dirty bath water isn't it?"

Roger claps his hands slowly and I struggle with the irritation that is building up inside me.

"And the meaning of 'twerp' is?"

"Look everyone is entitled to their own opinion, I can see your point but Nigel has a point as well," I say trying to pacify him and not get into the argument he seems to want.

"Oh does he? Please share your vast wisdom, do tell us Billie, what is Nigel's point exactly?" Sarcasm drips from every one of his visible pores. With effort and assisted strength I ignore the comical face he pulls.

"Take for example, someone who has just lost, say their mother, you can't really know what they are feeling deep down inside, if your mother is still alive. You can try to empathize, you can be compassionate but it's not the same as actually experiencing it," I say.

Heads nod in agreement with me but no one says anything.

"Here we go with the psychoanalytical words, the nitty gritty hypothetical solution. You always have to complicate things don't you?"

"What?" I am totally confused now.

"You always have a long answer to a short question don't you? I bet you were first in your class-work and last in sports when you were little. I can just see you, little Miss Perfect. Regular Miss Sensible, I bet you never burn your mouth when you check to see if the pasta is cooked? I bet your hairdresser is a man?"

"What?..., Why-?"

"Why is a very rhetorical word, don't you think so Billie? My mother used to say that why meaning the letter Y, has a very long tail. Everyone wants to know why. Why this, why that. Why does a boiled egg smell to everyone but the person eating it?" He smiles at me mockingly. He turns to Dr Plowman, "Man I just love innuendos don't you?"

I can't hide my amazement at his desultory behaviour, I look at him, "Pasta? Sports? Hairdresser? Boiled egg? Do you have a problem focusing on one thing at a time?" I ask not really understanding him. "Or do you just have very few pleasures which you don't like people taking away from you?"

"Pleasures? What pleasures? What are you talking about now Miss Know-It-All?" Despite the strange and confused look in his eyes he continues to smirk. I know I have to go, but I can't leave without answering him now, that would be rude.

"You know what I mean Roger, one of the very few pleasures you thrive on. Actually, it's probably the main one because it's a thing you do all the time," pausing for effect, I slowly pick my bag up and move my chair back a little, "in simple English, there isn't really one adjective one 'lone' descriptive word that sums it up. I'm digging deep here so bear with me but, irritating, overbearing and egotistical spring to mind. You are in your own little world and all you want to hear, is the sound of your own voice, your own opinions. The only time you listen to anyone else, is when they agree with you."

His smirk disappears and I stand up and walk out of the canteen. I can feel eyes boring into my back. I knew I should have left earlier, why hadn't I listened to myself? Each time I fall into the same trap with Roger, first he gets nasty and I jump in to defend someone, then he starts picking on me and criticizing me personally as well as my work in the laboratory. You'd have thought I would have learnt my lesson by now.

Standing in front of the shiny lift doors, I look at my reflection as I wait for the lift. My long curly dark brown hair, sun kissed, light brown complexion and hazel eyes fade, I see the image of me when I was seven or eight, running around with my cape, paper sword and newspaper hat. I was the 'defender of the down trodden', righting the wrongs of the innocent. 'Billie the Brave' I used to call myself. My brother Steve however, being a few years older than me didn't quite share my enthusiasm and used to call me 'annoying ant'. Smiling at my thoughts I reach out to press the call button again. My hand stops in mid air. I feel his presence before I hear him. He is standing behind me, a little too close and breathing a little too deeply.

"My, my, aren't we the feisty one Miss Billie Lewis?"

I don't reply, I don't turn around.

"That new doctor, thinks that you look like a cross between *Jennifer*, the girl in the 'Flashdance' movie, *Alicia* the singer, and *Kelly* from that hot group. How tall are you? 5ft 7in? 5ft 6in? mmmm, you're definitely fit," I feel him move closer, "I'm guessing, 36-24-36, um,um,um. I understand what Dr. Plowman means. I like the way you always dress, it's smart, tasteful, cool, just the way I like it, you never show anything. Keep me guessing."

"What are you talking about now?"

"My pleasures! Talking about my pleasuresss! I like an acerbic woman, man I can feel myself getting so excited at the thought of-"

"Say one more word and I'll have you for sexual harassment, just one more word," I dare him.

"Hey I was just kidding, come on Billie it's a joke can't you take a joke?"

"Yes Roger I can, when I hear one," turning I face him.

"Lighten up, the others don't mind."

"I do."

We stand, facing each other. Eyes locked in battle. Finally he backs down and looks away. He even looks a little embarrassed as he walks towards the stairs. I walk into the lift and press the button for the ninth floor. 'There is definitely something wrong with that guy', I think, shaking my head in disbelief at his sexist behaviour. I am in two minds; should I make a formal complaint about him or not? I go into the ladies toilets to calm down and think.

I pay no attention to the first slam of the cubicle door as I stand in front of the sink and run the warm water over my hands. Somewhere between the third and fourth slam my curiosity takes control and I walk round the corner to the cubicles to see what is going on.

"They lied, they bloody lied to me!" Phoebe O'Connor, a Grade Two, Senior Biomedical Scientist in the Chemistry Department, and, a good friend of mine, says as she slams the door again. Her face is red and contorted in pain.

"Phoebe! What's wrong?"

She freezes then turns and looks at me; her face is tear stained, shock and hurt shine from her brilliant blue eyes. She moves gingerly away from the door as one does when they've been caught damaging public property in private. Wiping the tears away from her face with the back of her hand she sits down on a chair near me and shakes her head, her chestnut brown hair falls across her face.

"What is it?" I ask again gently pushing her hair away.

"Seven years, for seven years I worked hard, I studied hard, they promised me the promotion, they said 'as soon as I passed my exams'," she mimics and shakes her head. "They said I would get the job, I believed them Billie but they never had any intention of giving it to me," she wipes her face again. I reach for a paper towel and hand it to her. She blows her nose.

"What happened?"

"We had a charade of an interview yesterday and today they say they are giving the job to someone from outside, but they promised it to me."

"The Grade Three position?"

She nods, "I'm leaving, I will not work for a bunch of people that promise one thing and do another, I feel so stupid, so small, I actually believed them Billie."

I stand for a moment looking at her not quite knowing what to say. I have never seen her like this before, she is always cheerful, always positive. Always so *'thank God the glass is half full'*. What words of encouragement do you give to someone who always goes around encouraging others, someone who's passion is going to different schools and conferences in her spare time. Speaking to children, parents, in short anyone; about unity, love and working together to promote peace, love and positive thinking. My mind goes blank but I sit down next to her knowing that I have to say something.

"Phoebe, you're stronger than this," I say putting my arm around her shoulder, "come on, we all have disappointments, what you need to do is learn from this and not give up, use this experience."

"Why? What's it all for? The system here is wrong, look at what happened to you last year with your interview," she blows her nose loudly then sniffs, "they didn't even tell you the date or time for the interview until the actual morning it took place, then the recruitment people lied and said they had."

21

"And what did you tell me at the time when I was ranting and raving about the injustice of it all Phoebe? You told me something valuable that day, you told me to *'trust in God'*, remember?"

She looks away.

"Why do we trust people Billie?"

I don't answer.

"Why do people lie?" She stares ahead, "why do they say one thing and do another regardless of who it hurts?"

"People let you down, you decide if you stay down. What have you told me so many times Phoebe?"

"What?" She asks. I see the confusion in her eyes.

"When I was lied to about the interview, when my mortgage broker tried to 'gazzump' me, when Wayne stole my songs and threatened to physically hurt me when I tried to stand up to him. When…," I pause and think of the many other occasions, "do you really want me to go on?"

She shrugs.

"You said that *'the truth will always come out. Lies come and lies go but the truth will always stand strong'*, remember?"

"I know I did, but this really hurts Billie, I feel this high," she holds her hand a couple of inches above the floor.

"You won't see it right now but it's for a reason Phoebe, the hurt will pass."

"All things happen for a reason. The whole interview was fixed. *'Where do you see yourself in five years?'* My manager asked during the interview, I should have said to him 'where you are now and doing a much better job'."

I watch the occasional fidget with the bracelet and continuous tapping of a foot. I sense that something else is on her mind.

"Apart from the job, is there something else bothering you?"

"Family stuff, the usual problems Billie. I grew up with it day in and day out, you'd think nothing would touch me now wouldn't you. But this job thing, my family thing, it's all getting a little too much."

I sit quietly, just being there for her if she wants to talk. I know about her background, from what she has told me, her years in Northern Ireland had not been that nice. Phoebe is Irish, her mother from a devout Catholic family and her father from an active Protestant family. There was so much friction between the families that when she was eleven, her parents, siblings and herself were forced to leave Ireland. Not however, before she had witnessed some terrible things; one being the death of a brother in a car bomb. Others, she has only ever hinted to me, but not gone into full details about.

"Remember Billie I told you about the time my mother's dad was ill and needed a kidney, and my father volunteered to get tested to see if he could donate?" I nod. "Then grandpa says, *'I'd rather die than be given a kidney from the likes of him'*." She shakes her head as if the event of fifteen years ago happened only yesterday. "Then it comes out that my dad didn't really want to do it and had just been pretending, he had just wanted to be seen to be doing the 'right thing'. Each Sunday they both go to church and say the *Lord's Prayer* asking God to forgive them as they forgive others, but they still have a grudge against each other. The irony of it all. Anyway now my grandpa's ill again and he wants to see us, but not my father or my paternal relatives. My father says, 'we will go only if he comes as well, because he is tired of the bad blood and will not take flowers to a funeral, if he never gave flowers or love to the person when they were alive'."

"I agree with that," I say.

"So do I, especially as I was the one who got him to see things that way in the first place, I had to get him to read and understand the true meaning of love as it is in the Bible. To love others as you love yourself. You know my father is a preacher, he has read the Bible from cover to cover three or four times, but only understood the true meaning of 'agape'- unconditional love, recently. Love that is not based on emotion, love that does not change with each torrential outburst of feeling. Love that is displayed not because of what you feel but regardless of what you feel."

Because of her turbulent past, Phoebe is what she calls a non-denominational Christian. At her motivational talks she often refers to herself as a born-again 'hybrid' of the Catholic and Protestant faith, as being 'both' with a heart full of love for God her neighbour and herself.

"Sometimes Billie, I wonder what it's all about, didn't my parents think about all these problems before they got married. Even now they act as if everything is all peaches and cream when there is so much undercurrent, so many shackles. So how do we fix something that won't admit it's broken?"

"A wise old woman said to me once that prayer can work wonders and I believe that never a truer word has been spoken," I say in an Irish accent.

"Hey, easy on the old," she says poking me in the leg, "yes I did tell you that Billie me old lass and you know what, thank you for telling it right back to me. Can I just ask though, where exactly is that accent from?" The twinkle is back in her eyes.

I think about *Frank McCourt's* bestseller 'Angela's Ashes', I try to recall some of the places mentioned in the book.

"Why lass can yous not tell 'tis from Limerick now," I say in my best Irish brogue. She laughs and shakes her head.

"I'm sorry about back then, the door and the language, I just felt so frustrated."

"I understand, I'm not sure if the door does though. It's probably feeling a little bit banged up right now?"

Her smile borders on embarrassment and she looks away. I start to laugh and she looks at me then starts to laugh as well. Still laughing, she reaches into her pocket and pulls a piece of paper out, unfolding it, she hands it to me.

I glance at her small neat handwriting, "What is it?" I ask.

"It's your poem, go on read it." I hear the excitement in her voice. "I've learnt it by heart now, test me."

I read the familiar words to myself as Phoebe says them aloud from memory:

"Wisdom - Happy is the man that finds wisdom

What is it I hear you say
For what exactly did you pray?
Was it for wealth?
Was it for health?
No, then what, oh do tell
You know I always wish you well.
Wisdom, you prayed for wisdom, why not wealth?
Why not prosperity and good health?

Wisdom, why, what on earth for?
When there is so much, so much more
You could have prayed for riches, luxuries the best
You could have prayed for happiness, health, and endless rest
Why did you ask for wisdom please do tell
I thought I knew you only too well.
Then, you look at me and in your eyes
I see something you cannot disguise
Your smile reveals to me the truth
For with the wisdom God gives, you cannot lose
With the wisdom from God you are truly blessed
And with it comes knowledge, riches and health in abundantness."

"Well done, you remembered every word," I tell her.

"Can I use it for my next talk Billie? I'm talking to a group of teenage girls this Thursday about the wisdom of a virtuous woman, the title is **'De-pressu-rize-me'**. I did a survey recently, did you know that girls as young as thirteen are being pressurized into having sex, they give in and become the eighteen year old Sexually Transmitted Disease patients and the twenty six year old and over, 'had too many men, now I can't get a man' sisters. I have the whole talk planned to make them understand that wisdom means if he really loves you he will do the right thing and wait."

Nodding I smile and listen to her talk. She is back to her old positive self, tears have been shed, her disappointment faced and now determination shines fiercely in her eyes. This is the person I know, the person that has told me so many times in the past, that a simple line is all I need to change a negative sign into a positive one. A simple prayer, can change a negative situation into a positive situation.

*　　*　　*　　*　　*

He is pacing.

Backwards and forwards he walks along the small landing of the spiral stairwell between the eighth and ninth floors. He is deep in conversation with himself. Each step is symbolic and carefully retraced.

His pacing picks up speed and he gesticulates frantically, he looks the picture of madness. Face twisted, eyes glazed, he continues his backward and forward journey.

He stops as suddenly as he had started, he stands dead still and smiles to himself.

"She smells so nice doesn't she? She's not like the rest that douse themselves in cheap perfume is she?"

"No she isn't like the others that cover up one nasty smell with another one."

"I agree with you both-"

He hears voices that are not his own, not part of his discussion with him and himself. They are coming from a lower level of the stairwell. He drops to the floor quickly, crouching he looks around him knowing there is no one there, but looking anyway. Quickly he makes his way up the final flight of stairs and walks through the connecting door. He whistles to himself as he remembers her smell.

"She smells nice, doesn't she?" He asks himself.

"I bet she feels nice as well," he replies.

"Understand she will be mine!" His third voice adds with spine chilling confidence.

CHAPTER 2

The three children are confused.

Ten minutes ago everything seemed normal. What could have happened in ten long minutes to change everything? What had their mother done wrong? Had she been naughty again? Was there blood on the walls again? They know that when the shouting and screams start they are supposed to leave the room and keep quiet. They know that if they keep extra quiet, the bad sounds don't last very long and they will not get hurt.

In their innocence they believed that this uncle was different from all the other uncles. They thought that he liked them, after all he gave them sweets and comics and took them out, he picked them up from school sometimes. They thought that he liked their mother and would not hurt her. Would not make her cry like the others nor make her shout at them.

Luke, the eldest, signals for the other two not to move, he goes to see if it is all right for them to come out from behind the wardrobe; their hiding place. The front door had slammed shut a few minutes ago, he hopes that uncle has gone. His heart pounds in his small chest but he knows he has to be strong and careful. Bravery and caution are two skills he had to master years ago while many his age were just getting to grips with Sesame street. They say that the memory of a child can be full of distorted facts and inaccuracies, but two fractured ribs and a broken arm, are not something that this child will ever forget in the years to come; not something his mind will ever distort. He walks down the familiar passage that seems bigger and somewhat strange, he stops outside a door. He can hear sobs coming from behind it.

"Mummy?"

The sobbing stops. There is no reply only an airy silence.

"MUMMY?" He says louder.

Slowly the door opens, his heart beats faster with every inch. He is terrified and cannot move. All he wants is his mother. He cannot look up, his eyes are fixed on the ground.

"Mummy?" He says in fear as the urine runs down his legs.

"It's okay, I'm okay, where are the others?" His mother asks.

"Hiding," he replies finally looking up. He sees the familiar presence of blood on her clothes and the bruises on her face.

"It's okay," she says again, trying to convince herself that he believes her. She stumbles towards the front door. As she passes the mirror in the hall, she glances at her reflection. 'Shit' she thinks, 'I'm going to have to phone in sick again'. She double-locks the front door, her head throbs and her hands tremble as she slides the bolt across and latches the chain.

She reaches for the phone in the hall.

"Hello, it's Sarah, I won't be in for the rest of the week, I'm not well. Can you tell Tina or one of the other supervisors please," she listens to the person on the other end talking. "Thank you," she says and replaces the receiver. She ponders for only a few seconds then picks the receiver up again and quickly presses the phone number.

"Hello, can I have the police I want to report an assault."

*   *   *   *   *

"I'm sorry but all tickets have gone, we're completely sold out," I say cradling the receiver next to my ear with my shoulder as I sort table cloth fabric out.

"Arrrr, can you please get me on the guest list, pleeassee," the male voice says.

"I'm sorry that's not possible."

"C'mon darling, try, I want to come down with a couple of celebrities, 'A' list celebrities."

"The guest list is full, I'm really sorry," I say for the twentieth time this evening. I listen patiently as he throws a couple of high profile names at me. I smile at his mention of *'U2'* because I know from watching the News that they are currently on tour but I politely listen anyway. I add his names to my imaginary celebrity guest list which is by now pretty impressive. It has *Westlife, Travis, Gabrielle, Lemar, Coldplay* and several high profile footballers, athletes, actors, supermodels and TV presenters on it. What has struck me several times this evening is how everyone seems to be using the same ploy. Originality seems to have died a death with most of the callers. Then again getting tickets is the aim, and name dropping the game.

"Sorry but the guest list is still as full as it was a few minutes ago," I say when there is a pause in the name dropping.

He mentions a few more names and I apologize again, after offering me three times the going rate for a ticket, which I refuse, he finally hangs up. I replace the receiver and turn the answering machine on. There is no point in taking any more calls tonight. This coming Friday is a ticket only event at my cousin Martin's nightclub, and the tickets have all sold out.

"Man I tell you, come Friday night this place is gonna be SLAMMING," Liam Lawal, Martin's resident DJ and good friend says as he swaggers past me. Enormous headphones hang around his neck and wires drag behind him. Shiny sparkles from the disco balls have attached themselves to his natural afro hair and glimmer there.

"You can say that again," my brother Steve concurs as he sits tuning the twenty five television sets that take up a section of the wall. He has set them up so that they will become one large screen on the night.

"Man come Friday this place is gonna be SLAMMING."

"You can say that again," Steve says again.

"Man come Fri-"

"Hoy-kay guys, enough all-ready," Trudi says holding up her hand and gyrating her head talk-show-style. I laugh. Trudi is Petrula Stanmore, fashion editor of a popular magazine, a really nice person and one of my closest and dearest friends.

We have all been here for over three hours now helping Martin with the final preparations for his opening. This is our second evening here and we have two more to go before Friday. Everything is more or less done, we are just adding a few personal touches and 'kidding' around. I try not to think that this is a reflection of our personal status, but the fact that Steve, Trudi and I are single, probably does play a part in our availability.

"Guys, guys, I want you to listen to this mix and tell me what you honestly think," Liam says walking over to his DJ booth next to the stage. In seconds the club is booming with loud music. We listen as Liam does his thing. He mixes 'old school' music from the late seventies and early eighties. This is the kind of music I grew up with because of my older disco dancing, 'Soul Train' brother, Steve. I watch as Steve lines up some chairs then proceeds to dance down the aisle of chairs, 'Soul Train' style. We all cheer him on and watch, I know that *Michael Jackson* would be real proud of him as he does the 'moon walk' back up the aisle of chairs. Who would have thought that the hours he had spent watching the videos when we were little, would one day pay off.

"Go Stevie, go Stevie," we all chant.

Trudi dances down the aisle of chairs next, her hair flying everywhere. She is 'head shaking' and 'cabbaging' amid cheers and claps. It brings back memories of when we were at university together.

"What's going on here? What is all this? You guys are supposed to be working and you three helping me out," Martin says pointing at his staff and then us. The music stops abruptly and we all look at him, he walks towards the chairs. "This should not be happening here, who started this?" He adds turning to me, the usual suspect. I try hard not to laugh, I know I'm not succeeding. Everyone is staring at him.

"But.., but Martin-" I pretend to protest weakly.

"You can't just come in here and start dancing like this, where do you guys think you are, some nightclub?" He takes off his jacket and flings it over a chair. "Now, next time you guys wanna get down, at least have the decency to call me." He has his hands on his hips as he speaks. I look at the people not believing that they honestly think he is angry. Some of the bar staff look a little unsure.

"Music please Liam," he says. The music starts and Martin starts dancing down the aisle of chairs.

I laugh as Steve, and then Martin, dance to *Shalamar's* song 'There It Is', index fingers pointing everywhere. It is absolutely hilarious to watch.

Trudi, the staff and I take turns in dancing down the aisle of chairs, that is, when Steve and Martin will let us.

*   *   *   *   *

"Said it's Friday night and the feelings light, gonna rock t'night ...oh oh oh. Said it's Fri..."

I smile at the song that someone walking past the laboratory is rather loudly attempting to recreate. The weekend mood is upon us all it seems.

Friday, a day that signifies the end of the week and is loved by most, except maybe, people that have to work on Saturday.

I walk back into the inner room of the Category 3 laboratory and turn off the safety cabinet. I tidy up and disinfect my work bench with the Hycolin disinfectant while I wait for the cabinet to shut down completely. As the noise of the cabinet dies down, I hear voices coming through the wall from the office next door. Although the voices are slightly muffled, I can make out what sounds like a man and woman talking and can just about hear what is being said.

"-You said 'you loved me'," the female voice says.

"So?"

"What the hell do you mean by so?"

"So," he says again.

"Do you know what I went through last Tuesday? Do you have any idea how embarrassing it is to have to go to a clinic for sexually transmitted diseases? Do you? I had to do an HIV test."

"Hey, I told you that has nothing to do with me."

"You're the only one I've been with."

"So?"

Silence follows then a muffled sound, like sobbing.

"Don't start that crap again," the man says loudly. His voice sounds familiar but I can't place it.

"There's someone else isn't there?"

"Is there?"

"At least have the decency to be honest."

"Decency? I didn't know you knew that word."

"Is there someone else?"

"There has always been someone else."

Something smashes hard against the wall, the voices get louder.

"Everyone said that you're a bastard, I should have listened to them, all I ever did.., all I ever did was love you. You said 'you loved me', you said that-"

"Hey I lied okay, so sue me why don't you."

I don't wait to hear anymore. Quickly I wash my hands and turn the lights off. Leaving the laboratory, I gently close the door and walk down the corridor towards the lockers that line the walls. I open my locker and get my things, then slam the door shut really loudly and wait a few seconds. I look in the direction of the office, no one comes out. Knowing that I have to walk past the office to get to the lifts, makes me feel a little uneasy. Taking a couple of deep breaths I make my way towards the lifts. As I walk past the office, the door suddenly opens, I freeze. Tina Foxton, one of the Senior Biomedical Scientists walks out.

"Hiya, I hear you're not coming with us tonight Billie, that's a shame," Tina says. She seems fine, all smiles, almost jovial, nothing like the broken girl I had heard a few minutes ago. In my confusion I find myself staring at her. "Billie, are you okay?"

"Yes, err.., yes I'm fine. Sorry what did you say?"

"I said that I heard you weren't coming out with us tonight."

"Yes, that's right I have other plans." Whoever is in there with her makes no attempt to come out. "Are you working late?" I ask trying really hard not to look over her shoulder into the office.

"No, not really," she smiles. A silent, heavily pregnant, pause follows. Birth does not seem to be forthcoming.

"Okay, I'm off, err.., see you then."

"Bye, Billie," she turns slightly and flips the light switch off in the office, closes the door and walks towards the lockers.

"Actually, hold the lift when it comes Billie, I'll be there in a second," she calls out.

I quickly look through the glass section of the office door, it is dark and there is complete silence. I turn and look at Tina who is pulling her coat on and frantically looking for something in her bag, she seems to be talking to herself or something in her bag. 'Something strange is going on here', I think as I walk towards the lift. A sudden weird creepy sensation comes over me at the thought of getting into the lift with her. Where is the man she had been talking to? Had there been a man in there? I remember a scene from the film *'Psycho'* and feel a shiver run through me.

The lift comes, it is empty. I hear her footsteps coming.

"Thanks Billie," she says as she walks past me into the lift. I follow her and quickly press the Ground button.

"Hold the lift," a chorus of voices say just as the lift doors start to close. Hands reach in and push the doors apart as I reach up to press the 'Open' button. Roger, Colin and Nigel rush in.

"Thanks ladies," Roger says moving towards me.

I smile at them and glance at Tina, she looks straight ahead and is nervously biting her lower lip. Roger reaches across my shoulder and presses the 'Ground' button of the lift just as I am about to do it. His hand sort of brushes against mine and as he pulls his hand back I feel it touch my shoulder. I move away from him. The lift stops on the third floor and two more people come in. Roger moves closer to me and I move away from him. I hear a soft chuckle then feel him move closer again.

The lift stops on the ground floor, and I have to restrain myself from literally clawing the lift doors open in my desperation to get out.

"Where have you guys been?" Chloe asks as we step out.

"Sorry, I had to work a little late," Tina replies running her fingers nervously through her hair, "are we all here now?"

"All except Sarah, she phoned in sick again during the week."

"Typical!" Tina says, "she is always off sick. I don't know why we bother paying her."

"She could be really ill you know," I say a little shocked at her coldness, considering that they are supposed to be good friends.

"Yeah right and pigs can fly, look up look up, OOPS you just missed one," she says pointing above my head. "Let's go guys, see you Monday Billie."

Chloe touches my shoulder and smiles. "Ignore her Billie and have a good weekend, see you Monday."

I smile at her then frown, "Your mascara's smudged a little on your cheeks. Have you been crying Chloe?"

"No," she says quickly and wipes her cheeks, "umm about Phoebe's talk, I know I said I would try and come with you but.. I.. umm, I won't be able to. I won't be able to go to church with you either."

"Okay, maybe another time. Have a good weekend."

"Bye Billie," she turns abruptly and walks away.

Frowning I watch her walk with the others in the direction of the wine bar. Turning to go in the opposite direction, to the car park, I almost collide into Roger. I hadn't noticed him lingering behind me.

"Are you sure you don't want to come out with us? I was really hoping to get to see you with your hair down tonight." He lowers his voice, "plus, I want to apologize in my own special way for the way I behaved the other day in the canteen." He seems a little anxious, a little too eager to please.

"Apology accepted and yes, I am sure about tonight."

"C'mon Roger," Tina shouts. I turn. She is standing by the revolving doors staring at us.

"Go with the others, I'll catch up," he shouts back not even bothering to look at her. She doesn't move, she just stands there and continues to stare at us. This does not seem however to bother Roger as I appear to be the only one that finds her behaviour a little odd.

"I have to go," I look at my watch, "have a good weekend and I'll see you Monday."

"See you Monday then," he says. He leans towards me, "Be good but if you can't be good, be careful, for me."

"Excuse me!" I step back.

"Joke Billie, it's a joke," he holds both hands up in a sort of exasperated manner and smiles. An uneasy feeling comes over me as I watch him walk towards the revolving doors. He strolls in a really cocky manner past Tina and through the doors, without so much as a glance in her direction. I stand and watch them walk separately in the same direction.

'Odd and odder', I think to myself as I wave goodnight to the security guard and walk out the other exit towards the car park.

* * * * *

Halfway home, a thought flashes through my mind. 'Is there something going on between Tina and Roger?'

"Nah," I say loudly dismissing the thought, knowing that Tina was the one that had coined the phrase Mr. SBS. 'Plus', I think to myself, 'she is in love with the mystery man that had been in the office isn't she? Then again had there been someone in that office?' The spooky feeling I felt earlier revisits me, as images of the imaginary *'Mrs Bates'* sitting in her rocking chair at the window talking to *'Norman'* creeps into my mind.

Ten minutes later, sandwiched between two cars, stuck in the usual evening bumper to bumper rush hour traffic on the A406, another thought runs through my mind, 'on what basis exactly had Tina coined the phrase 'Small Brain Syndrome', she hardly spoke to Roger at work.' I ponder on my thoughts as my eyes wander around and look into the other stationary cars. My rush hour companions look as tired as I feel. Something happens further down the road which allows us to move a couple of inches forward. I recognize a woman from twenty minutes ago as her car and mine stand side by side again. She smiles and shakes her head. I smile in return knowing that we will probably see each other again further down the road. Turning, I notice some people in a car in the other lane looking into my car, they seem a little confused. They see me sitting on the left in front of the steering wheel, nod to themselves and drive slowly past. As I watch the car move forward something catches my eye, I turn and look at the dark building that I have driven past so many times. It is a derelict house with many windows; a number of them broken, and graffiti covered walls. I see a man at a large window on the first floor, he is staring down at the cars, he looks odd, out of place in his black dinner suit, crisp white shirt and black bow tie. I notice a man and a woman walk past the building, look around in a somewhat discreet manner, turn around and walk back to the building. The man pulls open the front door, the woman walks into the building and he follows. Frowning I look up, the man in the suit has gone. The driver of the car behind me takes out his frustrations with the slow moving traffic on his horn. Startled, I look in my rear view mirror then in front of me, the car in front has moved a few feet forward. I follow it.

*　　*　　*　　*　　*

The man and woman rush up the stairs. Coldness and dampness reach out to them and try to engulf them. They ignore the vile atmosphere and rush into the room.

The room is full of people. No one speaks as they wait for the leader to come. A door slides open and the leader; a man dressed in a black dinner suit, white shirt and black bow tie walks in, everyone stands up. He walks to the front of the room and sits down.

"Does anyone have anything to report?" He demands.

Silence.

He pulls at his bow tie in irritation and frowns.

"I do not wish to repeat the question."

"No sir, nothing," someone says.

"Things are still developing sir," another quickly adds.

"I have brought some new people sir," a third person says.

"Good, where are the newcomers?"

"Err excuse me, I thought you knew everything?" One of the newcomers ignorant in the ways of evil asks, 'mock' plays happily among his words.

"Sshh," a few people chorus, they look in annoyance at the man who has asked the question.

Tension mounts and the panic levels soar as people look at each other. The silence is deafening, too loud to hear a pin drop.

"How dare you ask me that! Seize him!"

The man is dragged to the front and thrown on the ground in front of the leader. He raises a hand and pleads.

"I am sorry, it's just that I thought you knew everything. Please don't hurt me, I am sorry, I will do whatever you want."

"Yes I do know everything because I have people everywhere that listen to what people out there say and watch what people do, they write it down and come and tell me. I use that information against the people. For instance I know that you are struggling with certain beliefs, I know that every day you say you are broke, you are sick and tired, you are unhappy and worthless. I know how and when you got that scar on your cheek, I know what you did this morning. You are just what we are looking for, so I will not harm you. You have come here like the many musicians, actors, professionals and non-professionals before you, some wanting money, some wanting fame, some wanting earthly power but all wanting them quickly," he laughs. "Some come here physically, some by accident while dabbling in the occult, some have given up on religion because of our false prophets in sheep's clothing, our false prophets that can appear as angels of light, we send them out to confuse people by infiltrating the truth with our lies. People don't bother to find out the truth in God's Word so they stumble and cannot cope, as a result they want another way, my way." He looks at the man on the floor, "I will give you what you want and you in return, will give me what I want."

"What do you want?"

The leader looks down at his gold ring with the black diamond shaped like a heart. "Souls, I want souls, your soul and the many that you will help to make dark like yours, by revealing my ways to the weak, vulnerable, desperate people." He hands him a chain, "Take this, wear it as a bracelet on your wrist, never take it off, it will be our bond. Listen carefully, it serves two purposes: first, it binds you to me, it represents my mark on you. Second, with it you will get everything you want. Believe in it. Years ago people worshiped and believed in wooden images, today in ignorance people do the same thing, they say 'touch wood' believing that wood will bring them luck."

He laughs evilly, "Look at it as your personal piece of wood!"

A chain is given to each of the other newcomers.

*　　*　　*　　*　　*

Forty five minutes later, after the start of my bumper to bumper journey home, I walk through my front door. Drained, I sit down and listen to my messages. I have survived another week of hard work, stress, arguments, temper tantrums, politics and the usual abuse of power. All the ingredients of a modern day work place, which I do not particularly like. I am glad that it is Friday and I have two whole days before I have to go to back to work. It's funny but I never envisaged that I would end up working in a routine clinical microbiology laboratory when I had been at university. If I had, I would never have wasted my time studying for a first degree in Medical Microbiology for three years, a postgraduate degree for another two years, and doing a Management then a Counselling course. I honestly always thought that I would end up working for some big scientific organization with my name and the title 'Microbiologist' on the door. I'm not really a fussy or greedy person, any big 'mega bucks' blue chip pharmaceutical or food company would have suited me just fine. Now instead, here I am with all my qualifications, over qualified, over worked and under paid.

I keep telling myself that something has to change, that I have to go out into the world and do what I really want to do. Not some nine to five job that I don't like. One minute I seem to be 'high', full of anticipation ready to take a risk, the next minute I just seem to be trudging along 'safely' like everyone else going to work just to pay my bills and pay off my acquired debt.

I know that so many people out there seem to think that they should work in the field they studied or trained in. I used to be one of them. Over the past few months the urge to do what I really want has been like a bug in my system. I constantly feel that I am just wasting my time and that there is so much more to life than what I'm doing now. It's like I am not fulfilling my purpose. Weeks like this week, make me more determined and more aware that I should be doing something else. Something that I always dreamt I would do since I was little. My brain sighs and a few seconds later I hear the audible manifestation as it departs from my mouth. I have been at this particular point so many times over the past few months. Each time I get to 'this' place where I feel the scales tip more towards my taking a risk, leaving my stable job and doing what I want, reason rears its head and I pull back and think of the things that stop me taking the risk; mainly paying off my debts. Most people feel that risk equals normality minus stability. Unlike most people though, I have started to question just who determines normality.

I get up and turn the radio on, using the music as I usually do, to drive the conflicting thoughts out of my head. The words of the song playing catch my attention, they seem to stick in my head momentarily driving out all my other thoughts. I smile at the simple potency of the words.

There were times I felt so low
Had nowhere to go

You came and made me strong
Helped me carry on.
Thinking about you night and day
Thinking about the different ways
You changed my life around
I'm so glad I found.....youuuoooo....

I kick my shoes off and lay back on the settee resting my head on the cushions. Suddenly I am too tired to stop the sleep that is fast approaching, too tired to even go and get something to eat. 'I'll get up in five minutes' I think as I close my eyes and shift into a comfortable position. I hover a little, floating on soft clouds, before that warm familiar darkness called 'sleep' comes and carries me away...

...The atmosphere seems strangely tense. It is dark and I can hear sounds coming from upstairs, I place my foot on the first step then all of a sudden I am outside a door. The sounds are much louder and more ardent, my heart is pounding and my palms sweating as I open the door and look in to the room. A wave of nausea hits me as I stare in shock at Wayne in bed with a woman! I know who she is! They both turn and look at me. Wayne has a look of sheer contempt in his eyes.

"What did you expect, I get nothing from you." With that he turns back to the woman. I notice they are both fully dressed and I cannot seem to comprehend what is going on.

"Will you please leave," they both say. Quickly I turn and run down the stairs, to my horror I bump into Wayne at the bottom. Am I dreaming? This feels so real, his hand on my arm feels real and hurts. I am filled with a sort of dread, I am confused, my head feels like it is spinning, either that or the room is moving.

All of a sudden we seem to be in a different place, a different time and Wayne is in one of his moods.

"I hope it's not going to be one of those events where you go off and flirt with everyone," he says. "I can just see it now, you get there and do that thing you do," he takes a few steps away swaying his hips in a totally exaggerated manner then comes back to me and grabs hold of my arm again before I can move away.

"There's absolutely no chance of that happening Wayne, it's a children's party, who am I supposed to flirt with? my nephew or his four year old friends?" The humour in my voice is lost on him, as usual.

"What, you think it's funny do you? Me going out with you dressed like this, showing off your legs, all the men staring at you like you are some, some.., I bet you get a kick out of it don't you? Don't you? You and your stupid poems and rubbish songs, you think you're something special. You are nothing without me. No one will ever want you." He grabs hold of my other arm and shakes me really hard, then he slams shut the lid of my piano. I don't know why, but I feel like a five year old. I look down at the simple long dress I am wearing, it stops just above my ankles, not an inch of my body is exposed indecently and something inside me snaps.

"That's It! I've had it with you and your possessiveness, take your hands off me!"

"No one will love you like I do, no one, you hear me. If you leave me you'll never find anyone else that will care about you like I do...you'll end up sad, alone and miserable.. I will never let you go!"

I am screaming at him, he is shouting at me, I try to push him away. From the corner of my eye I see his fist fly towards my face. My brain screams a warning in protest as it tries to protect me, but my arm responds too late. Before it can rise and shield my head, I feel and hear a loud thud, suddenly I am flying across the room, scattering everything in my path. Seconds later I hear Wayne saying sorry over and over again. His voice is distant, faint and pathetic. He is kneeling next to me but sounds so distant. His voice is fading. I look down at the blood that drips from my nose onto the white carpet. I can't move, there is blood everywhere. Everything is red, everything hurts, everything is...ringing...

...I wake up with a start, a sob buried deep in my throat, something is ringing. For a few seconds my mind is completely blank and can't figure out what it is. It rings again, I look around finally realizing it is the phone. Picking up the receiver, I cradle it against my head. My heart is thumping, I see shadows move quickly across my wall and jump up. I suddenly realize that it is dark outside and all my lights are off. The light from the street lamp shines into the house and assisted by the trees outside, cast the moving shadows on my walls.

"Hello," I say. No one answers. "Hello, who is it?" Still no one says anything but I can hear someone breathing on the other end. The person sniffs twice but says nothing. I put the phone down and wait, nothing happens. A shiver runs through me, the dream was so real, so spooky. I must have been more stressed out than I realized to have dreamt about my ex-boyfriend. I haven't given Wayne Campbell a thought for so long. I don't understand the dream, I am confused. Wayne never hit me. He played with my mind, made me feel worthless by constantly criticizing me but he never hit me. What did the dream mean? I sigh and shake my head, after a few shakes I laugh at my feeble attempts to physically get my thoughts together and not think about Wayne. Like most people, I used to feel just that little bit more comfortable burying bad memories in deep holes in my mind.

My stomach starts to make a growling noise as it does when I am usually very hungry. The phone rings again as I draw my curtains. I turn on the light then pick up the receiver. Again the breathing, which isn't particularly heavy, the sniff but no words. I hang up. I pick up the receiver and press 1471, the caller has withheld their phone number.

One chicken salad and cup of coffee later, I sit back and think about everything. As the music plays in the background, the memories come out of their deep black holes and take me on a trip down memory lane.

I see myself staring out the window waiting for Wayne to turn up for a date, panicking; calling his mobile over and over again, thinking that something had happened to him when he did not return my calls or show up. I was young and I didn't understand then that it was all a power trip to him. A game. Sometimes, for days he wouldn't return my calls and I would work myself up into such a state. Wayne Campbell, a very handsome cover that concealed a sometimes very ugly, very emotionally cold content. He would criticize me, flirt with other women and throw it in my face. He would make me feel like nothing, like I was worthless. Then he would tell me that he loved me and no one would ever love me like him if I broke up with him. Needless to say, I was constantly confused. When he wasn't making me unhappy, I would think of sad things to make myself unhappy. Time and time again, I would have 'pity parties' with myself and cry myself to sleep at night. I would watch sad movies, eat and cry. I would have conversations with myself; in my head I would plan how if he said this I would say that and if he said that I would say this, I would work myself up in to a ball of frustration. It was as if I was in a place that I didn't want to be in, but I didn't want to get out of. Very confusing.

Constantly Wayne told me my songs were rubbish, that I was wasting my time writing them. Contrary to his words, he stole two of my songs and passed them off as his own. I couldn't understand why I let it happen, why I had invested money in his plans and ignored my own, because he had said my dreams were unachievable, my dreams were dead and should be put in a coffin and buried. Each time I got a rejection letter for one of my songs from a publishing company or agent, he would laugh. And each time it felt like a fresh nail being added to the coffin of my dreams.

Another thing I couldn't understand was why I had gone from a cautious, never owned a credit card, spender, Pre-Wayne Campbell, to a person thousands of pounds in debt, owing just about every major credit card company, Post-Wayne Campbell? Why had I lied to loan companies; just so that I could borrow more than I could repay, because Wayne needed the money for his business? When I first met Wayne, I didn't have low self-esteem, I didn't feel unattractive, I didn't come from a broken home. So why?

Had I been so desperate for love that I let it blind me? Let it take away who I was. I know a lot of people can identify with what I call my 'past sad mad situation'. In my attempt not to be alone I had dated Wayne. He made my life miserable and for most of our relationship I had felt so lonely and constantly wondered if I were not better off alone. I am being very open about my relationship with Wayne because I know that there are people who are going through what I went through then, right now and wondering, 'is there light at the end of the tunnel?'.

There is!

I will never forget the day I saw my light. I cried hysterically for hours that day; I was completely broken and in need of restoration and transformation. In sheer desperation and pain, I knelt down and begged God to get me out of the mess my life was in. My life then, which consisted of Wayne hurting me time and time again, and then saying that he loved me. Of me persistently lying to my family and friends, saying that I was fine while secretly I felt like I was dying inside. Looking back now I can see it all so clearly, see where I went wrong, what I should have and shouldn't have done. I know it is all hindsight now, but sometimes it really baffles me why I couldn't see it then. I know one day I will have the answer to that question, right now I am thankful for what I have. I am complete. It took some time, but I got my self-esteem and self-confidence back. I went to the gym and lost the two stones that I put on while I was with Wayne and just after I broke up with him. I did a counselling course and a management course to improve my career prospects and I have what I prayed for that day, I have inner and outer peace. I also have a deep longing to help others that are hurting as I once was.

I know that I will meet the right person one day. This may sound strange to some people but I even know the kind of person he will be. Metaphorically speaking, someone with the right kind of heart, someone with a good content and not just a handsome cover. I do wonder about the cover sometimes, I pray constantly that I will know it when I see it....

Smiling at my thoughts I get up and turn the music off. I jump slightly at the loud shrill of the telephone. I stare at it as it rings a few more times then reach for the receiver.

"Hello."

"Hi Billie, what time you coming down?"

For a few seconds I sit staring at the wall, I don't say anything.

"Billie, are you there?"

"Martin?"

"Yes, were you expecting someone else 'Tubbyless'?"

I smile at his use of my nickname, my heart warms at the comfort of his voice, "No I wasn't and about ten."

"Who are you coming with?"

"May I ask why you are asking?"

"Umm...no reason."

"No reason?" I question.

"No, not really."

"Not really? Umm.., are you happy with that answer or do you want to go fifty-fifty or maybe even phone a friend?"

43

He laughs in reply, rich bubbly infectious laughter and I feel secure in its familiarity.

"I'm going to pick Trudi Stanmore and Jennifer Harper up about nine at Jen's, is this information helpful to you?" He laughs again.

"Maybe, is Jen singing?"

"Maybe," I reply.

"So you have the song sorted?"

"Yep, sorted and ready to deliver."

"Good, see you later and don't forget, '80s dress code and it applies to all, including relatives."

"Right on man, I got my gear sorted, I am solid."

"Your gear? Right on? Solid? What era is all that from?"

"The '80s," I reply feebly realizing that I may be wrong.

"I don't think so, '60s hedging '70s more like." We laugh and talk for a few more minutes. I tease him a little about Jen and he teases me about my un-coolness and lack of knowledge of 'original hip' street lingo. I replace the receiver smiling, happy in the knowledge that my cousin is finally coming out of his shell and openly admitting, albeit with a little twist of his arm, that he has feelings for Jen.

When I was younger, my mother used to say, *'When you look back on the problem, in the future it won't look so bad, and you'll be able to smile as you wonder why you fretted so much.'* She always said this when I had a problem that to me at the time seemed so big. Sitting here now I smile, because looking back at my life, I know that I am totally free from the past now. No more pain, tears or sadness. My mother, God bless her, was right.

CHAPTER 3

The phone rings.

Dr Evan McIntyre swears softly to himself then reaches for his work mobile phone as he pushes his very young, very attractive, female companion away and lowers the volume of the television. It is late and even though he is on call tonight he had hoped that he wouldn't actually get called.

"Hello, McIntyre here."

"Doctor, I need help, help me doctor I can't stop thinking, it's driving me crazy."

He recognizes the voice of the caller immediately.

"Have you taken your medication?"

"No, I don't need medication I need help, you are a doctor, so help me."

The caller is pacing and becoming incoherent, backwards and forwards he walks, his head twitches a little.

"We have talked about this already, you need to take your medication if you want to get better." Dr McIntyre's voice is calm on the phone but he is worried.

"I want help, I need help to stop thinking about her, I don't need medication."

"Listen to-"

"NO YOU LISTEN, YOU HEAR ME," he shouts, spit flies out of his mouth, some dribbles down his chin. "It's late, it's dark I want help."

"Calm down, it's late, I know. Calm down and speak clearly," McIntyre says.

"Don't you tell me what to do," the angry voice screams at him down the phone, "don't you dare tell me what to do."

McIntyre takes a couple of very deep breaths to calm himself then tries again, "Focus and breathe, you need clarity and you need to be calm. Tell me what happened."

"I am paying hundreds of pounds of money so I can tell *you* what happened?" He snarls.

McIntyre coughs, he senses the caller is becoming intractable, he needs to turn his thinking around, re-focus him.

"OOPS, sorry there Doc, I stand corrected, my parents are paying you. Should have corrected me there. You know …," he pauses.

"I know what?"

"Why I thought you knew everything 'docky', I thought you were the greatest psychologist in the world. I actually thought you were smart because you have all those certificates in your office, all those dead trees sitting on your wall." He starts to laugh. Deep hysterical bursts echo down the phone and chill Dr McIntyre to the core. The laughter dies suddenly and silence follows.

"You still there doctor?"

"Yes. You sound a little bit calmer now. You're doing good, take some deep breaths and talk to me. Tell me what happened."

"Calmer! Are you nuts? You really think you've got me 'sussed' don't you? My parents pay you for this crap?" He stops pacing.

"Your parents want to see you well and so do I." McIntyre's voice remains calm, he knows this is the only way to get through.

"Right, my 'richy rich' parents, their only concern is that no one finds out that they have a 'loony toony' for a son."

"Is that what you think you are? Is that what you really think about yourself? I know you're calmer now, so think deeply and tell me, honestly, is that what you think about yourself?"

"No."

"Good, good," he says hiding his relief, "I didn't think you did. So where are your tablets?"

"Here, at home with me."

"I know you think that you don't need your medication sometimes but it does help a little doesn't it?"

"Sometimes."

"I want you to take one tablet, sit down, stay calm and wait for me, can you do that?"

"Yes."

"Good, I'm on my way."

Dr McIntyre picks up his jacket and rushes out the door ignoring the woman on his bed. He knows the caller will take the medication, he always does after his episodes, but he also knows he will need extra monitoring because the episodes are happening too frequently, in fact a little too frequently. McIntyre knows that the caller needs to be sectioned and should have been long before now. The objections of the caller's rich parents supported by large amounts of underhand payments to keep their name untarnished has overtly swayed him from doing the right thing. He stops to pick up a male nurse from the hospital for assistance, his mind somewhat occupied with his task ahead. He tries to keep his thoughts in perspective and not to focus on the extra money he will make for this particular call out. He has been over charging his private patients for so long now, it is difficult not to think about money. He knows he has to stop, he knows the quality of his work has deteriorated and he is only still in practice because of his past reputation. His past, where the patient was the cause, his present where the love of money has taken over his mind. The guilt that creeps into his mind dies a quick death. Its short life is washed away, exterminated by thoughts of bills, more bills and a lifestyle which has grown accustomed to him.

The caller goes into the bathroom to take his medicine. He opens the cabinet, takes a bottle out and closes the cabinet door. He fills a glass with water, puts one tablet into his mouth, then washes it down with the water. His blue eyes look into the mirror over the sink, his lips smile, her eyes look back at him, a third pair of eyes watch him.

*　　*　　*　　*　　*

The eyes looking back at me have totally transformed my face. I move closer to the mirror and the eyes move closer to me. I look really different, it's amazing what a change of eye colour can do.

"Billie you done yet?" Jen asks as she walks into the room, she stops and stares at me "oh my, oh my, blue contact lenses, you look incredible."

"It's not over the top?" I ask, touching my ginger wig.

"No way, no how. You look, how do you English folks say it 'brilliant', absolutely fabulous darling."

I laugh, "You ready?" I ask noticing that in the last five minutes she has changed outfits again. She has also added a beauty spot on her upper lip and brushed her dark wavy hair differently. I see a little uncertainty in her hazel-green exotic eyes.

"Umm, I'm not too sure about this top, I'll be ready in a sec."

"Okay I'll go and wait with Trudi, don't take too long I think she's getting a little impatient."

"Give me a couple of seconds," Jen says as she leaves the room. As I walk into Jen's front room Trudi snaps shut her compact mirror and folds her arms with attitude. 'Here we go' I think to myself trying not to smile, knowing that it will only add fuel to her embers.

Trudi, Jen and I have spent the last five years growing up together in so many ways. Despite our different backgrounds we have found a common ground where we bond. Even when we disagree we still respect each others opinion. As Jen often says in her quaint New York accent, 'we are sisters and cover each others backs'. Time and time again we have proved that this is true. Although there are times, like now, when Jen's saying is tested.

"What's she doing?" Trudi asks standing up and walking to the door, "JEN DARLING" she shouts. I smile and she wags a finger at me. "Jen you have exactly two minutes, then I'm gonna drag your little 'bee-hind' in here."

"Go sit on it!" Jen replies.

"She's gone and done it now, she has broken her own record. Normally she keeps us waiting for thirty minutes, but look at this," she raises her voice, "it's nearly an hour, yes ladies and gents, Jen has broken both the American and British records."

I start laughing and Trudi points her finger at me, "You know this is all because of Martin don't you?"

"Is it?"

"You know it is, what I want to know, is when will those two come out and get this thing on?"

"When they are ready, I suppose."

"Oh, and when will that be, if we leave it to them we could be talking about a long time."

"Long time for what?" Jen asks walking into the room.

"Jen you look great," I say looking at her outfit.

Trudi is staring at her with a look of total disbelief on her face.

"Jen that's the first outfit you had on this evening when I got here. You mean to tell me that I have been sat here waiting for you while you changed four times, then you put that jumpsuit back on."

"You got a problem with that?" Jen asks turning towards her a frown evident on her face.

"Who me? Oh no, no, no, you know what? Knock yourself out. I'm gonna sit and wait while you go change some more."

"Okay" Jen says turning towards the door.

"NO!" Trudi and I both shout at the same time.

Trudi picks up our jackets and moves menacingly towards Jen. "Move it or lose it," she says.

"Yeah, says who and who's army?" Jen replies.

"Now, now ladies," I say putting an arm around each one and escorting them both out the door.

In my car we listen to one of Trudi's tapes as we head towards the club. The singer is a new British artist called Leebeth who is already big in America and Japan and is starting to make waves in Europe. Her songs are really good, she has an exceptional voice.

"Listen to this next song Billie, it's called 'One Step At A Time'." Trudi says after the sixth song ends.

I listen to the words:

> ..*You're living a lie, living a lie*
> *Cos every day he made you cry*
> *I feel your pain, I see your shame*
> *Where do you turn who do you blame*

The words take hold of me and I find myself listening intently to the chorus.

I've seen it all before
No need to look no more
True love is always kind
Just seek it and you will find....
Gotta take, gotta take one step at a time.
Know when to start, when to stop,
when to leave the past behind..

I listen to the rest of the song, where it finishes something inside me starts. I don't know what it is. I have just listened to words that relate to me, words that constitute part of my life. I think about the songs I have written over the years and I know that they are just as good, just as meaningful and can one day touch someone's life, as this song is touching mine right now. An overwhelming feeling takes control of me as the realization hits me. I can't sit on the fence anymore, I have to do something more with my songs. The blast of a car horn, pulls me out of my thoughts and I look in my rear view mirror. Trudi and Jen turn around and look through the back window. The car behind me has its beam lights on which momentarily blinds me, I slow down. The driver horns aggressively again.

"What is his problem?" Trudi asks.

"I don't know, he probably thinks he is doing the Grand Prix," I say as I indicate, then pull over so he can drive past. In my rear view mirror I watch the car pull over and park behind my car. The beam lights are still on and I can see the outline of a man but not his face.

We all turn and look at the car then each other. Jen reaches across my shoulder from the back and presses the central lock button down. Without indicating, I pull out and drive down the road, the car follows. I slow down, the car slows down. I go faster and the car goes faster. I see a traffic light up ahead, the light is green as I drive up to it, I wait. The car behind horns, I still wait. The light changes to amber and the car behind continues to horn. My heart is pounding as I wait, seconds seem like hours. As the amber light goes out, just before the red light comes on I press hard on the accelerator and drive down the road leaving the car at the traffic lights.

"Slow down, he's not following," Jen says looking through the back window.

"What was all that about?" I ask.

"Probably some weirdo," Trudi says.

Paranoia sets in and I drive through back streets to the club. 'Trudi is probably right, it must have been someone with nothing better to do' I think to myself as I keep looking through my rear view mirror.

*   *   *   *   *

The party is nearly over and several lives unknown to their owners, set on the path of potential ruin. The man drinking has finished his tenth bottle of whiskey, and he smiles as he looks around at the people that have tried to keep up with him, and who on their fourth or fifth glass have given up. He smiles, because he knows, that he has succeeded in giving a number of them a hunger for alcohol which unknown to them, without deliverance, they will not be able to part with. He can hear the fights, feel the evil and the anger as people grow the way he wants them to. There is 'darkness' here, yet to the people; the smoke, the loud music and the unending flow of cocaine, LSD, heroine and Indian hemp is bliss. He looks at them lost in their stupidity, knowing that he would have freely given them the drugs and alcohol but they would rather pay for it, because they, believe like most people, that nothing is free. If only they knew!

A woman turns to him as two men walk in, two newcomers. He nods and she gets up in her revealing clothes and walks over to them holding two goblets. Two complimentary drinks; free drinks that they will 'pay' for. They smile and take them from her, she leads them upstairs, they follow her.

Roger watches the two men walk up the stairs with the woman. She had not seen him standing in the background. Not seen Nigel turn, catch his eyes and mouth for him to wait. The club is badly lit, he can just about see the outlines of people in the distance as he looks around. No one is dancing. There is a sense of coldness in the atmosphere and a reek of depravity. He walks slowly, he touches the wall from time to time, as his steps carry him further into and around the room. He can hear voices whispering, chanting, moving all around him, taunting and yet enticing him. He stops at a door and listens to someone inside talking.

"..It is going well, people are doing what we want. They have a God given choice to choose between good and evil and people are doing exactly as we want; they are believing our lies, they are choosing evil."

Voices in the room cheer loudly.

"We need to keep lying, keep tempting, keep deceiving, keep twisting the truth, keep putting up more strongholds in peoples lives then get them to believe the strongholds don't exist. In their ignorance we can continue to operate 'in' and 'through' their lives. When we keep encouraging people to do wrong they will think that it is good to do bad. Distract people, make them too lazy or too busy to find out the truth in God's Word. In their ignorance, let them keep fighting each other with wars and racism instead of understanding that their fight is not against flesh and blood but against evil powers and principalities, spiritual wickedness, against *us*. THEY MUST NOT FIND OUT ABOUT THE WHOLE ARMOUR OF GOD!

Frustrate their efforts, fill them with doubts, make them believe their gift is a curse, blind people to the truth. Let them envy and fight each other. Divide and conquer; it works all the time. Turn one set of people against another and watch them in their ignorance do our work, watch them destroy each other. Highlight all the destruction in the media, make people believe there is no hope." The spine chilling voice laughs and people cheer.

"We need more family problems, sibling rivalry, more fights, more hate, more drinking, drugs and depression, more hurt. Let the hurting people hurt others. When you hit families, you hit nations, everyone lift up your glass and drink to destruction."

"To the destruction of families, destruction of friendships and destruction of nations," the voices chant.

Fear rips through Roger's heart at the sound of the chilling laughter and sudden realization of what is being said. He panics. He leaves.

CHAPTER 4

The ambience is breathtaking as we walk into the brightly lit club. Despite my being here every evening this week prior to tonight, helping to get things ready, I am dazzled. The large disco balls that hang from the ceiling rotate and reflect different coloured lights everywhere. The large TVs are all tuned; they amalgamate into one screen, and show clips of 'Soul Train' and 'Top of the Pops' from the '80s. A lot of the people in the club are dressed in the style of the '80s adding to the feel. I smile as we head to our reserved table, an American football coach would easily feel at home here amongst all the shoulder pads. The whole scenario brings back a sense of 'wholesome' nostalgia. The introduction of a song starts as we sit at the table, people cheer.

'Friends, I've got friends....' A number of people rush onto the dance floor. I watch as they try to recreate the steps of 'back in the day'.

"I remember this song," I say dancing in my chair.

"Me too," Jen shouts smiling and bobbing her head to the music. A wistful look plays on her face. "Girlfriend, those were the days. I was ten or eleven but I was really into music then." We sing along to the rest of the song. The song comes to an end and I find myself staring at the amazing effect of the TVs as I watch a clip from 'Solid Soul'. Jen is constantly looking over her shoulder in the direction of where Martin and Steve are standing talking to a couple of ladies.

"Looking for someone?" I ask.

"Not really," she replies, "I just wondered where Trudi was."

"Powdering her nose, which can mean anything."

"Umm..," she says and turns back to look at Martin.

"Look who I bumped into in the ladies," Trudi says as she sits down. I smile and hug Phoebe and her sister Caroline.

"You both look great!" I pull out chairs for them to sit down.

"Blue eyes, very nice Billie," Phoebe says as she adjusts her shoulder pads.

A waiter stops at our table with an enormous bottle of low alcoholic pink champagne and some glasses.

"Compliments of the Manager," he says and puts the glasses down in front of us then proceeds to fill each glass. He fills my glass half way then pulls a bottle of orange juice out of his pocket and places another glass in front of me. He fills the glass with juice.

"Thanks John," I say, "how's it going?"

"Really well," he replies, "the non-alcoholic wine is going down a treat, it was a really good idea of Steve's."

"That's good."

"Let me know if you need anything else ladies."

"We will, thanks," we chorus.

I look around, the club is really lively, people are pouring in. I see Martin talking to some friends, I watch as people pass by him, some pat his back others wave. I watch as he greets people, a smile constantly playing on his face. He is really glowing in his success and I feel really proud of him.

It seems funny to think that this may never have happened. A couple of months ago Martin's father had been ranting and raving, because Martin, a qualified accountant, had refused to join the family accounting business full time. He had opted to set up his own business, 'A prestigious high quality nightclub with no drugs, drunks or decadence'. Somewhere that people can hang out without feeling harassed by depravity or, the need to conform to it. A place where young people can come and listen to Gospel music three times a week and see the live artists perform. Martin's mother, my mother's sister, my aunt, called me one evening because she wanted me to talk to Martin. I suspect, to talk him out of it.

"He always seems to listen to you dear," she had said in her upper class patronizing voice. I could almost hear her unsaid "why, I don't know."

Of course being the dutiful niece I went round to their house but ended up agreeing with Martin. I knew it was something Martin had always wanted to do, something he had talked about constantly when we were children. His father accused me of encouraging him and ended up exchanging harsh words with him, neither of them listening to the other. He then stormed out. I on the other hand was glad that he left without bringing my father into the conversation, a thing I felt he was well known for doing when our opinions clashed.

My parents live in Orlando, Florida. My father is Black and from West Africa and my mother is White and from England. Sometime ago I learnt that Martin's mum had actually met my dad first while he was at university in England. She had really liked him but he fell in love with her younger sister. My parents married, had my brother Steve and I, and were very happy, even though everyone including my aunt, had said it wouldn't work.

I sort of have a detached feeling about the whole situation. I think this is because I can write a book on what my parents went through in the late seventies as a mixed race couple. My mother has told me stories that can 'curdle' a fresh pint of milk in seconds. So I find it very hard to deal with when it comes from within the family.

I am glad that the closeness Martin, Steve and I share is not affected. We are like three very close siblings. 'Tub', 'Tubby' and 'Tubbyless', my mother called us when we were younger. Names we still use for each other now.

"Hello ladies." I smile as my brother's greeting interrupts my thoughts. His greeting, that is somehow intended for all of us, manages to find its way to Caroline. She blushes.

Trudi winks at me then turns to Steve, "Honey did the babies get to sleep hoy-kay?" I hide my smile with difficulty as I watch. I don't know which is more hilarious, the look on Steve's face or Trudi's attempt at a Puerto Rican/American accent.

"What?" Steve asks looking confused. He looks from Trudi to Caroline and back to Trudi, he frowns.

"Little Stevie Junior and little Shenaynay, don't mind my husband," she says touching Caroline's arm, "he sometimes forgets about our babies."

Caroline's look of shock speaks volumes.

"What?" Steve says again, "Trudi stop, now, please."

Jen and I start laughing as Trudi leans forward and explains to Caroline that she is joking, getting Steve back for a similar joke he had played on her.

"Ladies and gentlemen our first performance from the '80s is a real trip down memory lane," Liam says adjusting the volume of the background music. "Here to take us on the start of our journey are Lisa and Tony singing *Marvin*

Gaye's 'What's Going On'." The music starts and the duo start to sing. I sing along and dance as I sit and watch them.

"Billie you're up next," Martin says and nods towards the stage, "are you all set?"

"Yep," I reply "come on ladies, let's go."

Martin walks around the table, past Trudi and I, and helps Jen out of her chair, he says something to her and she smiles at him.

"Phoebe come with us, you know the song 'Ain't No Stopping Us Now' by *McFadden* and *Whitehead*, don't you?" I ask.

She nods.

"So let's go sing it."

"No Billie I can't, really, I don't know the words."

"Go on," Caroline says pushing her up, "it's karaoke, the words are on the screen."

Jen pulls and Caroline pushes until Phoebe gets up.

"I'll stay here and watch the bags." Caroline quickly says moving her chair firmly under the table.

"And, I'll watch Caroline watching the bags," Steve adds. We all look at him until the realization of what he has said makes him cover his face with his hand and laugh in embarrassment.

We get to the stage just as Lisa and Tony finish. Liam introduces us as 'Billie and the Billettes', he hands us a couple of microphones then presses the button on the karaoke machine. The music starts, we all sing the first few lines of the chorus. Trudi starts the first verse, she sings two lines then Jen sings the next two. Phoebe does the next two lines and I do the last two. Together we all sing the chorus. We are really getting into the vibe of the song, dancing in our platform shoes. I am about to start the second verse when the screen goes blank. The music does a solo act as it plays on without the words. I look at the others they look at me. I can't remember the words.

A voice starts to sing the invisible words. It is coming from behind us. We turn and look at each other while the singing continues. A man walks towards us, mesmerized I turn and look at our 'singer in shiny armour' as he walks on to the stage singing. He finishes the second verse and smiles at us then gestures for us to continue. We sing the chorus and finish the song. The crowd clap and clap probably thinking that it has all been staged. I clap for the mysterious singer who has disappeared.

"Did you see his cute dimples?" Trudi asks.

"Cute dimples? He is gorgeous," Phoebe adds, as we make our way back to the table.

"Did you hear his voice?" I ask.

"Voice? Billie didn't you see what he looked like?" Jen asks.

"Err.., not really, his voice sort of blew me away."

"His voice? That's it, girlfriend you need to get out more."

Martin isn't at the table when we get back so I go to look for him. I have to find out who that guy is. A lady wearing a red dress starts to sing *Karyn White's* 'Superwoman'. I pause in my search and listen to her. The original video is playing on the television screen and I feel a sense of nostalgia as I remember watching the video over and over again years ago. She finishes the song and amid the clapping I continue my search for my cousin. I spot Martin checking something in the bar, as I stand waiting to get his attention I feel something brush and then linger on my shoulder. I turn around immediately but no one is there.

"Looking for me?" Startled I quickly turn around.

"Martin! Yes I am, the singer who is he? Where is he from? How come I didn't know anything about him?"

"Whoa, slow down," he looks at his watch, "his name is Jamie Sanders and he'll be singing again in 10, 9, 8, 7, seconds. Let's go sit down and listen to him." He takes hold of my hand and pulls me towards the table.

*   *   *   *   *

He smiles to himself, he is invisible. No one can see him. He stood right behind her and caressed her lovingly and no one saw. He is sweating but that is okay, it isn't down to nerves, it is down to excitement. She has just sung a song to him telling him how she truly feels. She said with her own lips, her own beautiful soft lips that nothing can stop their love. He watches as her cousin leads her to the table. He hums the words she sang to him softly as he stands in the shadows watching her. He hums 'their' song.

*　　*　　*　　*　　*

Martin and I sit down just as the lights go down a bit and the music stops. Liam does not make any introductions and everyone seems to be looking around. The stage lights come on and there is complete silence as we all stare at the man sitting on a stool with his head bent. The introduction of a ballad starts and then the hairs on the back of my neck and arms literally stand up as I hear the voice again. I stare at Jamie Sanders as he sings so effortlessly, knowing instantly that he has a 'gift'. This is something that only a few people have. The ease with which he sings, the way the words pour out of his mouth is not to be confused with a talent. It is a gift, full stop. The range, the power, the tone, the projection of his voice is beautiful. He sings three songs and then stands up as the lights come on. The house comes down. My hands hurt from the clapping.

"He is really good!" Trudi says.

I turn to Martin, "Where did you meet him? Is he going to sing here again? Tell me everything. Now. Please!"

"Answer number one, he came in a couple of weeks ago when we had just finished renovating," he pauses.

"And?"

"He asked for the Manager and someone pointed him in my direction," he pauses again and takes a sip of his drink. I look at his glass then I look at him. He moves the glass away as if he has read my mind and smiles.

"Where was I?" I see the twinkle in his eyes. "Oh yeah, he said he could sing and that he had heard that I would have live 'old school' and 'new school' performances from time to time. He sang a couple of songs and I said that he could perform on opening night."

"So why didn't you tell me about him?" I ask.

"I would have but he cancelled a week later, he said he had other commitments, he only reappeared this morning."

The light that had come on in my brain earlier this evening is now glowing like a 200 Watt bulb. The words *'this is it, this is it'*, keep floating around my mind.

"Is he signed to a record label?" I ask.

"No he isn't, he mentioned something about being in a band in the past but that things didn't work out. I know he wants to do some original stuff, I told him to join us when he finishes his set."

Trudi runs her fingers through her hair, "Jamie is going to come and join us?" She asks.

Martin nods. "I told Jamie that you write songs Billie and that I would introduce him to you, maybe you can work on some original material together for him."

"You did?" Looking up I see Jamie walking towards our table.

"Jamie over here," Martin says and pulls up a chair so that Jamie sits between the both of us. He introduces Jamie to everyone around the table. I look at him properly as he smiles and says hello. He has dark blonde hair and blue grey eyes.

"And this is my cousin Billie, the one I told you about."

"Hi Billie."

"Hi, thanks for helping us out with the song."

He smiles and I catch sight of the dimples that Trudi had mentioned earlier. I smile back. He has a very attractive smile, one that reaches his eyes and makes you feel welcome, at ease, like pulling up a chair.

"So Jamie how long have you been singing?" I ask.

"Properly, for a number of years now."

"You've got a really good voice, at one point I actually thought you were miming, then I saw it was all you."

"A lot of people say that when they first hear me sing," his smile deepens.

"I hear you sing and what I hear is a little of *Luther Vandross, George Benson, Jaheim, Rick Astley, John Bon Jovi, Lemar*. It's not that you sound like anyone of them in particular, it's more like you're out there with them. Unique." I have his full attention, he is staring at me as one does when they can make perfect sense of someone else's logic.

"This may sound strange to you but I know that you are going to be big. You are going to be around musically for a long time."

He looks a little startled.

"Have you tried to get a record deal with anyone yet?" I ask.

"Not now, no," he pauses, "I was in a band a few years ago, we were signed to a label but things didn't work out," he pauses again. I think he is about to tell me more about his band so I wait.

"Martin said that you write really good songs Billie, songs with very strong messages, that touch the heart and need to be heard."

I smile, my cousin has made me sound like some award winning lyricist.

"My songs can mean different things to different people. Yes, most of them have a strong message but some of them are just good old fashion love songs."

We talk some more about music, about songs and artists like *Kirk Franklin, Karen Carpenter, Mary J Blige, Fred Hammond, Usher.* Now and then we join in the general discussion at the table but music seems to pull us apart from the others and towards each other. As Jamie and I talk about music I find myself opening up to him, sharing thoughts that usually stay in my mind.

"Music is such a powerful communication tool and I have a lot to say. I want to get my songs out there and make videos to go with them, videos that bring the lyrics to life." My enthusiasm is rubbing off on him, he looks really interested so I continue. "I want to discover new singers. There are so many people out there that are good singers, but can't break into the music industry simply because they don't know anyone, or they don't know where to start. In the old days record companies saw the potential in an artist, now record companies want an instant hit. No one wants to take a chance with new artists until they've made it, but how can they make it if no one gives them a chance."

He nods in agreement, "Catch-22. So are you in the industry now?" He asks.

"No, I'm a Microbiologist, I work in a hospital but I know a few people in the industry and I sort of co-managed a group before."

"Can I listen to some of your songs?" He asks.

"Sure I'll send you a tape," I reply. "Shall I send it care of an agent or a manager?" I fish for information.

"No, I don't have either right now." He puts his hand inside a pocket of his jacket, frowns, then pulls a piece of paper and a pen out. He writes on the paper. "This is my home address, you can send it here."

"Are you serious about working on some original material?"

"Very serious," he replies.

Something seems to be pushing me, telling me to take a step further in this direction. He has something unique, something that will be big and lasting. I can hear him singing my songs, I can see it clearly - 'The Big Picture'.

"Look if you are serious about taking your singing to another level, I'd like to manage you."

"Manage me?"

"Think about it, you 'naturally' have what it takes. Here's my phone number, give me a call, let me know what you decide," I say writing my number down on a napkin and handing it to him.

"I've just met you yet you have more belief in me than people that I've known for years. I don't know what to say."

"Billie has always had an ear for music," Martin says, "she always knows which singers have longevity and which ones don't, which ones will do well in those reality TV competitions. *Kelly, Ruben, Fantasia, Lemar, Will, Garreth,* she has got it right so many times. If she thinks you have it, take her up on her offer."

"She voted for *Lemar* twice," Trudi says, "actually come to think of it we all did."

"I voted for him three times," Jamie says and smiles at her.

I smile at Trudi then turn to Jamie, "Think about it Jamie."

He looks at me, his eyes are serious, "I honestly think I might just do that," he says.

*   *   *   *   *

His eyes narrow in frustration as he watches Billie and Jamie talking. 'Why is she talking to the singer?' He thinks to himself. Agitation sets in; he needs his medication but he also needs to speak to her, to let her know that he feels

61

the same. He takes a couple of steps towards the table where she sits then stops. In his mind he quickly rehearses what he will say. He is about to move forward again when a hand reaches out and pulls him back.

"What-the-hell-are-you-doing-here? Are you crazy? We're leaving, now." The hand pulls him towards the exit.

"Yes," he replies chuckling softly, "of course I'm crazy, I thought you knew, I thought our great minds were alike."

CHAPTER 5

J amie is deep in thought.

As he sits at the bar his mind replays the evening's events over and over again. Tonight has brought him out of his dark self-inflicted abode into a place he never thought he would return to. For three years he has lived a lie, he convinced himself that singing was part of his past, a past he never wanted to revisit. The temptation was always there but his will to resist was stronger, that is until tonight.

He picks up his glass and looks at the tonic water inside as he recalls the crowd cheering and clapping, recalls the buzz he had felt. A smile plays on his lips as he thinks about the beginning of the week when he had phoned Martin and cancelled tonight, making up an excuse about other commitments preventing him from being able to come to the club. Then something which he still can't explain happened today.

This morning he had not been able to find a set of keys. They were very important and he panicked trying to remember where he had last seen them. He recalled hanging his jacket up when Martin had asked him to sing on his first visit to the club. He knew definitely that up until that point, the keys had been in the pocket of his jacket. On the assumption that they had somehow fallen out of his pocket, he called the club. He was told that several sets of keys had been found a couple of days ago and were being kept at the bar. This had been his only reason for coming in this morning. It turned out that none of the keys were his. On his way out of the club he bumped into Martin and Liam, they assumed that he had changed his mind and come in to do the show. Before he could explain, one thing led to another, accumulating in the events of this evening.

Reaching into the inner pocket of his jacket he pulls out the set of 'lost' keys that had been there all the time. He had only discovered them this evening when he had been looking for a pen and piece of paper to write his address for Billie.

He smiles as he remembers Billie, he is glad that he has met her. There is something about her that he really likes. Meeting her tonight was like encountering a breath of fresh air after years of slow painful suffocation. A real person, full of enthusiasm and passion, a far cry from the fake and fickle people he was used to. His smile broadens as he remembers the way her eyes lit up as she talked about what she wanted to do. The way her enthusiasm had reached out and touched him.

"Jay-Jay, Jay man, I thought it was you."

The familiar artificially over accentuated, cockney accent throws him totally off balance, immobilizing him. It takes a couple of seconds for him to regain his composure. Turning around, he looks at the man who has placed a hand on his shoulder. The years have not altered Dave Pemberton's striking, dark, good looks one bit.

"Jay I caught your gig, man were you wicked or were yooooooun wicked, you still have the touch Jay-Jay, you still have the golden voice." Jamie smiles to himself, not at the complement but at its lack of sincerity.

"It's been a long time Dave."

"Too bloody long matey, too bloody long, where you been?" He asks as he pulls up a bar stool and sits down. "We've been looking for you everywhere, it was just by chance that I heard you'd be here tonight."

"Why have you been looking for me Dave?"

"Look buddy, I'm not gonna beat about the bush right. Marcus, the record boys and I are thinking of setting up again. Everyone is doing comebacks now, look around, we have to get on the bloody 'gravy-loaded' train Jay."

Jamie smiles to himself, if there was one thing that he would always remember about his past it was Dave's use of words. For someone that had gone to a very expensive private boarding school, his vocabulary was somewhat limited, crude and a little bit questionable.

"Last I heard Marcus was in America," Jamie says.

"He was, he's back in town now and ready to rock 'n' roll, get jiggy." He jigs a little, *Will Smith* style, to emphasize his point.

"I don't get it, the band is history now, why go back?"

"Look Jay, the past is the past I agree and we gotta move on, hang slack so to say but why give up the chance to make some dosh while we're moving?" He senses Jamie's reluctance to listen and quickly continues, "Ben wouldn't want us to act like a bunch of lemons when there's 'readies' to be made, dosh to gross. I know he wouldn't."

The stab of pain at the nonchalant mention of Ben's name is so intense Jamie can't believe it. He has tried to put the past behind him, tried to cover it with cobwebs and dust. Once in a while he even commends himself on doing a good job. Now here he sits with the past in front of him. He looks at the word 'Troyston' embroidered in gold thread on the breast pocket of Dave's jacket and listens to him going on about loyalty and true friends. A topic when push came to shove Dave knew nothing about, or did a very good job pretending he knew nothing about it. One never really knew with Dave. Ben on the other hand had been the exact opposite. Dave's persistent voice drones on in the background as Jamie's mind wanders:

The Auditions had been tough. Nothing at all like the TV reality shows. Two hundred thousand, five hundred and seven boys had responded to the advert in the National Newspaper. The record company however were only looking for four. After a gruelling three days, two hundred boys made it through to the first heat. Two hundred were placed into twenty groups of ten, Jamie and Ben were in the same group. 'Chinese whispers' had it that only one person would be selected from each group and then the finalists from the twenty. This exacerbated the situation within the groups and made the competition fierce and sometimes terrible, absolutely nothing like the reality TV competitions. Jamie and Ben's defiance to the competitive nature within the groups was obvious. They hit it off immediately, helping each other with different ideas for melodies and ad-libs.

After six rigorous weeks, the group 'Troyston' was formed consisting of Jamie Sanders, Ben Edwardson and step-brothers Marcus Cole-Pemberton and Dave Pemberton. Four young impressionable boys that to the record company, stood for one thing - 'big bucks'. It was never really about the boys. They were given a strict, controlling, dominating manager and housed in a prestigious area. Each had a car, even though two of them couldn't drive, and the green light to do what they wanted, in short be 'lads'. And be lads they were, everything was done for them. They were a bunch of good looking guys that could sing and dance and do what they were told with little or no resistance. They were ideal to the record label, right age, easily manipulated and hungry for the 'generational success' of the likes of the Beatles, the Jackson 5, the Osmonds, Bay City Rollers, New Kids on The Block, The Backstreet Boys, 'N Sync and one of Jamie's favourite bands U2.

Success came very quickly, they went straight to the top. They were everywhere and everything they endorsed sold, from scooters to clothes from clothes to male dolls. They were not allowed to have girlfriends or a close relationship with anyone, in fact their contract stipulated that they would be disciplined or even sacked if they contravened certain rules. They were constantly reminded of this. Having a girlfriend was a major contravention. Their fans, some as young as nine, had to see them as accessible. Available. So that they could fall in love with them, fantasize about them and of course, buy more records. It worked! They sold millions!

"Jay-Jay, man are you listening to me? Did you hear what I said?" Jamie looks at him and shakes his head. "Jay, the record label is offering us a deal man, a big deal. I'm talking about a lot of dosh here."

"Exactly what for?"

"What for? What for?" Eyes roll in a swanky manner. "For a bloody comeback. Come on man don't tell me you don't miss the money, the honey, the partays, the bootie calls? Those were the days, those were the days Jay my man." He dances in his seat carried away with his memories and the music they form in his head.

Jamie looks at him closely trying to see the man behind the mask. What he sees is a man who sniffs every few seconds, cannot control his shaky hands, continually scratches his thighs and arms, in short, a man who is way too hyper to be clean.

"Are you still using?"

"Nah man, not me," he sniffs "I don't touch the stuff anymore. Drugs kill." He sniffs again and looks a little uncomfortable, his eyes dart everywhere managing in their travels not to meet Jamie's stare.

Dave continues to talk aimlessly, he travels in and out of topics as he loudly reminisces about the many escapades they had gotten up to in the past. He pauses mid-sentence suddenly sensing that he has lost Jamie's interest, in desperation he grasps at a familiar tool.

"Look Jay I know that Ben would want us to continue, I know he would. He was a go-getter, remember when he-?"

"Ben is dead Dave and truth be told I don't think he would give a damn." Jamie stands up feeling a sudden tightness in his chest.

"Jay, buddy sit down, hear me out."

"There's nothing you or anyone can say. It's the past, leave it there and move on man," turning he walks towards the door.

Outside he takes a couple of deep breaths and tries to clear his head of the images that are bombarding his mind. As he stands leaning against his car he notices two men standing by a car about a hundred feet away. The shorter man is shouting and waving his hands at the taller man who is looking at the ground. He watches as the shorter man pushes the taller man to the ground and kicks him.

"Hey!" Jamie shouts, both men turn to him. "What are you doing?" A dark car with the head lights off moves towards the men and the man on the ground gets up. Both men stand by the car. The taller man pulls a knife out of his pocket and holds it behind his back. Jamie walks towards them. He hears the sound of commotion coming from the club and turns away from the men and towards the club.

"Jamie, wait. Sorry, excuse me, sorry," Dave says pushing past people. "Jamie come on man hear me out!"

"Watch it!-" someone says.

"Hey-," another person shouts as he steadies his drink.

"Sorry, I'm sorry." Dave says still pushing. He rushes towards Jamie, he is desperate and has to make him understand, the band has to get back together, he has to get some money fast to pay off his drug debts, or he could end up floating in the river Thames.

Turning away from Dave, Jamie notices that the two men and the car have gone, frowning he looks around.

"Jamie, I didn't want to have to tell you mate," Dave pauses trying to catch his breath, "I really need you on board here, Marcus needs you in on this, he's not well, this could be his last chance."

"What! What's wrong with him?"

He can see that he has Jamie's full attention now and in a way he is hurt and angry. Jamie always came through for certain people, like his precious dead Ben and even Marcus, but he never gave him the time of day. His anger fuelled by his drugged mind makes him talk and as he talks Jamie listens.

*　　*　　*　　*　　*

Driving home Jamie cannot stop the thoughts flooding into his mind. The dam has broken and the thoughts that have been buried away for so long, now, like untamed water, pour in.

'Ben', he thinks, 'rich beyond imagination at seventeen, dead at nineteen'. Tears pour down his face, pain rips his heart. He pulls into the drive of his house and turns the engine off. Resting his head on the steering wheel he sits in the car. Four years later the pain is still as raw as if it were yesterday. Sometimes he wonders if it will ever get better, pain is supposed to fade with time isn't it?

He has asked himself a million times over if he could have done something to prevent Ben's death. Why had he been the last person to find out that Ben had been on drugs. He had been the closest person to him in the group, his big brother in the big bad world, so why hadn't he suspected anything. Had he been too wrapped up in himself? The fact that their Manager and the record executives knew and covered it up, (according to some, actually supplied him with drugs) just to keep the group together and make more money from them, made him physically sick sometimes. He has locked a lot of thoughts out of his mind over the years and now as they flood back in, he hates it, he hates the vulnerability they cause.

He gets out of his car and slams the door shut with such force that the car alarm goes off. Mumbling irritably he turns the alarm off and walks into the house. His thoughts walk loudly beside him, they follow him.

"Remember the good times you had with him Jamie, never forget them. They meant so much to him." Ben's mother had said at his funeral but he found that the price of the good memories included the pain of the bad ones. So he found it easier not remembering.

Now, from out of the blue Dave shows up and wants the band to get back together. He knows he can never go back. It had cost him the royalties of two of the songs that he had co-written for the group, plus a clause which banned him from singing for two years, to get out of his contract with the record label. He has no intention of going back. He is older now and so much more wiser. Moving towards his bookcase his eyes linger on something. Losing the internal struggle, he puts his hand into his pocket and pulls out the set of keys he had thought were lost. Opening the glass cabinet he pulls out the photo album. As he turns the pages he smiles at some of the pictures. He hasn't looked at the photo album for nearly two years, he hadn't wanted to. Sitting down he looks at the clippings and pictures and re-lives each event.

> *Troyton's 'Christmas number one'.*
> *Troyston wins 'Best New Group' and 'Best Single'.*
> *Troyston number one again.*
> *Troyston's debut album goes triple platinum in four days.*
> *Troyston shines at BRIT Awards.*
> *Troyston take 4 MTV Awards.*
> He turns some more pages over, words jump out at him.
> *TRAGEDY HITS TROYSTON DAYS BEFORE GRAMMY!*

He looks at some of the clippings, reads the familiar words that he knows by heart *'Youngest member of the group Troyston found dead, two members of the group arrested for possession of drugs'.* His gaze falls on the last clip.

"It's my fault, I did this. I should have stayed with him." Words said by Jamie Sanders after he is found by police holding the body of dying member of Troyston. For a few seconds he is 'there', he is holding Ben in his arms and shouting, "WHY?", at him, over and over again. He can feel the life seeping out of Ben's body and he clings to his friend, trying frantically to keep him alive, but not knowing how. He had pulled the incriminating bag of heroin out of Ben's hand and put it in his own pocket seconds before the police had arrived. He shudders and stands up abruptly, leaving 'there' and returning to his present. He puts the photo album back and reaching into his pocket he pulls the napkin out. He

looks at the phone number written on it. 'There's no going back now', he thinks to himself as he picks up his mobile phone and stores the name and number onto it. He presses the 'save' button and Billie's name and phone number appear on the screen.

* * * * *

Dave walks unsteadily towards the sports car that is parked under some trees in the shadows of the night. His mind, still drugged, is working overtime. He takes a puff of the joint that he was not allowed to smoke in the club, then gently extinguishes the light against the trunk of a tree, saving the rest for later. He swears softly as he stumbles along the pavement. As he crosses the road and approaches the car, he quickly composes himself. Smiling he taps on the window of the car and waits. The window rolls down and the man inside the car looks straight ahead, after a few seconds he turns and looks at Dave.

"You are late, get in."

"I told you I could do it, didn't I say leave Jay-Jay to me, didn't I tell you he was in *my* bag, boxing in *my* corner, didn't I?" Dave says as he clambers into the car.

The man observes him coldly noting his hyper state of activity, the hand jerks, the leg twitches. He knows there is no point in asking if he is 'high' for he knows that Dave is too secure in his own denials. He found out, a long time ago that Dave lives most of the time in a world of his own, oblivious to the obvious.

"Has he agreed to the comeback, to re-unite the group?" The man asks emphasizing each word as he rubs the scar on his face.

"Yes he has, he said he'd think about it seriously, he said-"

"Think about it? You said it would be a sure thing."

"It is, man don't worry about it, it's a sure thing."

"You have sniffed and injected a quarter of a million pounds, you owe nearly half a million, some of which is my money. It had better be a sure thing, make sure you keep me in the loop."

"Sure man, Jay-Jay is my man and I'm telling you it's a sure thing," Dave says knowing that it will be, once that is, he can convince Jamie. "Why didn't you come inside the club? You were the one that told us he would be here, I thought you were going to come in and see him perform," he quickly adds trying to change the subject, "I would have hooked you up with Jay-Jay." Playfully he holds his fists up and punches the air, "Jay-Jay and me are tight." The man watches him as he shuffles about in the seat, babbling about the old days and how the comeback would be massive. He isn't listening to him, he has heard it all before, several times. He sits back and waits for him to finish. The reason he puts up with Dave is pure and simple, he knows that there is money to be made.

Dave knows the man isn't listening, he knows that it is all about the money, but he also knows not to let on that he knows. He plays the simpleton drug addict well, sometimes when he actually takes the drugs, a little too well. Four years ago this person sitting next to him had jumped to attention each time Dave walked into the room. Now their roles have been reversed. From being 'top-dog' Dave has become the 'under-dog', a thing Dave finds maddening, way beyond his comprehension. So, occasionally he turns to drugs to keep himself sane. He continues to babble about his next line of action and how much money there is to be made. He knows his words fall on deaf ears, but to his drugged senses, even though he is the 'under-dog', in a way he isn't, he still has the upper hand. The man still has to pretend to listen to him.

*   *   *   *   *

It's 4am and I am wide awake. The first day of the rest of my life started four hours ago. I have been home now for just under an hour and I have not been able to focus on anything but Jamie. I have retrieved every single song that I have written and recorded over the years from their various 'resting' places. l look at them now as they lay in CD and tape form on my table. Bursting with energy, I run upstairs to my bedroom and run back down with my CD/tape player. I listen to all my songs mentally selecting the ones I will record onto an audio tape and send to Jamie. My mind is buzzing away and I know from experience, that I will not be able to sleep if I don't sort everything out now. There is this urgency inside me. It is a strange feeling, one that I cannot fully explain. It is more than just connecting with Jamie. I feel like a cook that has been preparing a feast for

71

some time, but has had to wait for one last ingredient before everything is ready. It's as if his voice is that one last component that I have been waiting for. I feel light headed, high on life, excited, as I play some happy chords in C major on my piano.

It's like finally, I have an answer for the past few months of my emotional turmoil, my confusion regarding my work. Everything seems so clear, the past few months of my life has been a prerequisite for what is about to happen. After hearing Jamie sing and talking to him, I know now, emphatically what I want to do. Gone is the uncertainty, gone the clouds of fear, gone the doubt.

CHAPTER 6

Seymore Jenkins sits in the prestigious office of McKnight Records/Entertainments, located in Brentwood, California and waits. He is a little early so he doesn't mind waiting. He is also a very patient man. He has to be in his line of work. Seymore Jenkins is a Private Investigator. His clients include some of the rich and famous of California's influential residents. Fighting the urge not to smoke, he focuses on arranging his brightly coloured tie over his protruding belly while he chews vigorously on his nicotine gum.

His client enters the office. Seymore rises as the striking, tall, elegantly dressed man approaches the table. P.A. McKnight extends a hand and Seymore shakes it. They both sit down. P.A. looks at him with a somewhat guarded expression.

"Good afternoon err…" Seymore coughs nervously, rearranges his tie, then continues, "you'll find everything in here sir," he says as he slides the large sealed manila envelope across the magnificent glass table. "Everything including the last major withdrawals, deposits, times, places, meetings the lot," he sits back in his chair in the relaxation of knowing that he has done a good job. "I managed to get inside the warehouse where they store the pirated CDs, I saw him finishing a run. Everything is highly organised."

P.A. McKnight looks at the envelope and nods, he doesn't touch it. He hadn't wanted to go down this route at all, it had been a last resort, a thing that he wasn't comfortable with but knew at the time had to be done.

"There's some more stuff," Seymore says opening a notebook and taking out a brown envelope.

"Stuff?" Eyebrows rise inquisitively.

"I wasn't sure just how far you wanted me to go seeing as you only gave me her name," he pauses sensing a sudden surge of almost visible electrical interest. "Hopefully, with this information I have proved that my company is efficient and my reputation is intact."

*   *   *   *   *

Twenty minutes later P.A. sits in the back of his chauffeur driven car heading to his home in Beverly Hills. He opens the envelope, pulls out the folder and reads through the contents. Words confirm the suspicions he has had for weeks. He knows someone is stealing from his company, he knows 'sensitive' information has been sold to a rival record company and several of his artists' newly recorded material is already being sold on the streets; in form of pirated CDs. Now he knows who is behind it. The photographs of his business partner, William Mathias, having dinner with a notorious rival record boss; a man well known for his underhand tactics of bribing, bullying and blackmailing DJs to play the records of artists signed to his label. A man that launders money and has major investments and share dividends in the drug market. A man being investigated by the FBI for the mysterious deaths of two artists that tried to leave his record label. P.A. sighs as he looks at more pictures of William looking through a batch of pirated CDs, they speak the words the investigator left out in his report.

Angelo, the chauffeur, notices that his passenger is unusually quiet today. He decides not to play his niece's demo tape, sensing that now may not be a good time to solicit.

"Everything okay Mr McKnight?"

Eyes look at him in the rear view mirror, "Everything is fine Angelo, can you take the long route please."

"Sure thing."

Angelo turns the car around and takes a side road. P.A. looks out of the window as the car turns then makes its way along the roads of Beverly Hills. A picture falls from his lap, he bends and retrieves it. He stares at the picture then puts it in the brown envelope he had received it in, the envelope marked with an address and phone number on top of which sit the words 'Billie Lewis'.

CHAPTER 7

Her neighbours are used to the police dropping by at odd hours, but this visit seems different. The police car has been parked outside her house for over an hour and there is no sign of movement. Tell-tale curtains move as eager eyes wait to see what is going on and who, if anyone, is going to be arrested.

Inside the house the police are going over the statement once again with Sarah. It has been five days since she first phoned them to report the crime. She had refused to go to the hospital on the day of the incident because there was no one to watch the children. The police saw no reason in insisting that she go, because by the time they had arrived, Sarah had already taken a bath removing any form of retrievable trace evidence. This was proving to be a difficult case but the police were persisting with their investigations.

The children are in their bedroom, Sarah and the two officers are in the front room. She can see that they do not believe her, then again who would. If it hadn't happened to her, she probably wouldn't believe it herself. The male officer looks at his notes and then at Sarah.

"So madam you say that on the day of the incident you had an argument with your boyfriend, he stormed out and when you stepped out of your front door in an effort to go after him someone grabbed you from behind and attacked you?"

"Yes."

"And you did not see who it was?"

"No."

"Do you know who it was?"

"No, he was behind me, he…," her voice falters, "he…,"

"It was definitely a 'he'?"

"Yes."

"He wasn't the one who hit you though?" The female officer asks masking her exasperation well; with polite official coldness.

"No, that was my boyfriend."

The male and female officers exchange glances and a discreet head shake. The male officer, being more compassionate, tries again.

"I know it's been five days but I still think you need to get checked at a hospital madam. St. John's Hospital is near by."

"No, I work there, plus I've told you I can't leave the children here alone."

The front door bell rings as a voice accompanied by a lot of static relays some information on the male officer's radio. He gets up, winks at his female colleague then leaves the room. Silence is left behind as Sarah and the female police officer sit facing each other. The officer coughs softly as she sits looking at Sarah trying with difficulty not to be judgmental. In her line of work she has seen many similar cases but is no closer to understanding, having had no first hand personal experience, why women put up with the abuse or the beatings. Despite her attempts to be non-judgmental, she cannot help but think that women like Sarah are their own worst enemy. She flips through some notes that she has written down to try and help her be patient and understanding; then like a bull in front of a red sheet, charges forward, verbally.

"Sarah is your boyfriend possessive, jealous or suspicious? Did he start hitting you when you were pregnant? Has he isolated you from your friends and family? Has he ever threatened to kill, cut or disfigure you? Has he made you feel like you have no self-worth?" She stops reading from her notes and looks up at Sarah.

"No, err yes, I don't know. I'm sorry, why are you asking so many questions at the same time. I...," Sarah rubs her forehead in confusion, tears sting her eyes. She knows the police woman has already charged, prosecuted and sentenced her.

"Do you know what the latest statistics show? Two women die each day due to domestic violence. Every single day many women and some men are being abused by their spouses. You are just another number Sarah, a statistic, part of a survey unless you do something to make it stop, tell me the truth!"

"I really..., I don't..."

The female police officer sighs loudly and shakes her head, unbeknown to her she closes any doors that could have given her access to the situation.

"I think you should leave now," Sarah says. She stands up and walks to the door.

"Are you sure it wasn't your boyfriend that assaulted you?"

Sarah closes her eyes trying hard to remember. She recalls the unfamiliar piercing eyes staring at her, remembers a face that seemed to change right before her eyes, then everything going black.

"No," she finally says hoping this is the truth, "no it wasn't."

*   *   *   *   *

Phoebe is sitting at the back of the hall looking over her notes. I can tell from the smile she gives me that she is a little apprehensive. This I find very strange because she has given motivational talks for nearly two years now and I have never known her to be nervous in the past. I lean towards her sister Caroline, who is sitting in the chair in front of me and gently tap her shoulder.

"She looks a little nervous, is something wrong?" I ask.

"I think it's because my dad and maternal grandfather are both here," she whispers and discreetly points at the two men that sit at opposite ends of the hall. Grimacing I sit back as one of the organizers picks up a microphone and climbs up the steps onto the stage.

"Our next speaker is a lady well known at our conferences so she needs no introduction, but I'll introduce her anyway," he says. Everyone laughs. I watch with pride as Phoebe makes her way to the side of the stage. The introduction continues, "this is a lady who has been blessed with wisdom way beyond her years. Ladies and Gentlemen, please welcome Miss Phoebe O'Connor."

Everyone stands up and claps as Phoebe climbs up the steps and stands on the stage. She has a body microphone clipped on to the lapel of her jacket. I watch as she places her notes on the stand and moves away from them. Smiling she holds her hands up and thanks the audience. She waits. We sit down and wait.

"I'd like to ask a question," she says. There is complete silence. "Have you ever been lost in a familiar place before, lost right in the middle of somewhere you know very well?" She pauses and looks around. All her nerves seem to have evaporated as she places her hands on her hips and looks at her audience, the people she has already captivated.

"I have, so many times," she continues. She walks along the stage, the eyes of the audience walk with her. "I want to share one of those times with you. A couple of weeks ago I went to Oxford Street on a Saturday afternoon. Now we all know that this is a busy place in London on a Saturday under normal circumstances, but that day was extra busy because the sales had just started. There were so many people walking along the street, going in and out of shops. It was so packed that after about ten minutes I just wanted to get out of there, I felt trapped."

She pauses and looks around, her head slightly tilted to one side. "At one point I actually felt that the crowd was carrying me along, I was so boxed in and sort of just moving along so I wouldn't get trampled on. I felt that if I tried to side step to get out, I would bump into someone or trip someone up so I just continued walking with the crowd. This went on for a while all the way up and down Regent Street I think, I got so confused. When I eventually saw a small gap in the crowd on Oxford Street, I had to literally push my way out. After doing that I found myself in front of two large doors with so many posters stuck on them. I had two choices: go in and escape the crowd or keep walking. Naturally I walked through the doors. I was hoping for a little respite but I found myself in a departmental store and guess what?" She pauses as a few people laugh, "Yes, those of you laughing were probably there that day or have been somewhere similar, you guessed right, I walked smack bang, straight into another crowd of people." Phoebe uses her hands and body as she re-enacts the scene. "This time people were buying things and rushing around trying to get the bargains before someone else could. Picture it in your mind, picture the pushing, the shoving, the noise. Can you see it? Can you feel the buggies hitting your feet, feel the tension of the people as they fight over a pair of last season's designer jeans?" She looks around at the people as they nod and smile. She nods with them and smiles.

"Well, it was ten times worse than that," she says and everyone laughs. She waits for the laughter to subside then continues. "Anyway, I left the store and decided to go home, I was hungry, tired and my boots were scuffed with wheel marks from all the buggies. I knew it was time to go. So I left the store, got back in with the crowd and tried to make it to the nearest tube station. Now, I knew where I was, I knew where the station was supposed to be, but I had a problem, I didn't know how to get to the station. I walked along with the crowd of people in what I thought was the right direction, only to get to the end of the road and not see the station. I turned and walked back down the road against the mass of human traffic, and still I couldn't find the station. Yet I knew where it was, I had been to Oxford Circus hundreds of times in the past and had used the station, so I knew it existed. After walking up and down the street several times it got to a point where, in the middle of the crowd of people, I started to panic. I asked a couple of people where the station was and they pointed in the direction I had just come from. Not trusting them, I went round a corner and asked a few more people, they said to go in another direction, which I knew couldn't be right. You see I knew where the station was but, I couldn't find it." She pauses and looks at the audience. "You're confused aren't you? Stay with me."

Smiling she walks over to the stand and slowly opens a bottle of water and lifts it to her lips. She drinks from it and then slowly screws the lid back on. I know this is all for effect because I have seen her do this at a number of her talks.

"Where was I?" She asks rubbing her forehead, "oh yes, so there I was looking for something that I knew existed, but couldn't find. I walked further down the road and found an exit for the station but it said 'No Entry' so of course I couldn't go in. As I stood to one side, thinking whether or not I should just run down the stairs and hope that it would lead me to where I wanted to go, I saw two women carrying a buggy up the stairs with a baby fast asleep in it. I asked them if they knew where the entrance to the station was; they both pointed in different directions. I'm going on with this story a bit now so I'll cut to the chase. Eventually, after a little internal struggle I walked back in the direction I had come from. There were still a lot of people walking up and down the street but this time I didn't allow myself to get carried along with them or irritated at the crush. I didn't become part of them I just walked along with them and I looked for the station. I walked past the departmental store I had gone into and something caught my attention on the left, I turned my head. Suddenly there it was, the big round sign with the red, blue and white colours and the word 'Underground' written on it. At that point, I honestly knew what it felt like to see an oasis in the desert. You see I had walked up and down that same street several times; I had walked past the station several times. I knew where the station was, but I had let myself get carried along with the crowd of people." She looks down at her legs and brushes something off her trousers. There is complete silence as we all wait for her to continue.

"How many times have we let things or people carry us along the wrong path when we knew what the right thing to do was? How many times have we known where something was but have been blinded by crowds and not looked properly to find out where it actually is? I know I have, several times. See I think we all know right from wrong, we all have a sense of the truth but we let people and things around us cloud our judgement. We do what people say without questioning the right or wrong of the matter, we follow the crowd." She shakes her head as she looks around.

"For example, why do we hate? We hate because everyone else hates, we dislike, because everyone else dislikes, and we don't know why. We let ourselves get carried away with the crowd." She walks over to the stand and picks up a piece of paper but doesn't look at it. She folds the paper in half.

"Why do we follow what others do without our own reasons, why do we follow the crowd? The crowd may not necessarily be strangers, it could be a husband, a wife, a mother, a father or even an historical event. I have asked the question before, why do we hate? Is it because we were brought up to hate, because our families have taught us to hate or perhaps because hate is good. When do we say, 'enough is enough', when do we say 'I will not follow the crowd anymore if they are doing wrong'. When do we break free and decide to do what is right. When do we look around properly, open our eyes and stop walking past our tube stations. When will we be like that child that stood out from the crowd, spoke up and said that the emperor was naked!

Don't get me wrong, there are things that I hate and dislike. For instance, I hate getting home after a hard day at work and eating the first thing I see, which usually ends up being chocolate biscuits. I hate this because I eat them, they go to my hips, I have to go to the gym," she pauses, "I dislike staying out late on a weeknight if I have to go to work the next day, because I'll be too tired to work.

Being a Scientist, I dislike seeing people spit on the streets; apart from it being disgusting, I know it is a health hazard to others in terms of say Tuberculosis transmission and other airborne pathogens. See I have reasons why I dislike certain things. These are my reasons, they are not based on any one else's. I find it so hard to comprehend sometimes when people say they dislike or hate something for no apparent reason. When people decide to hate other people because everyone else hates them. When people hate someone because of something they have done." She looks at the folded piece of paper in her hand and folds it again, then she looks at the audience. "A wise Priest said to me once: *'hate the act, don't hate the actor'*. People do things every day that we dislike, hate what they do, hate the evil behind their actions, but don't hate them.

You know what a great 'gift' is? It is having the ability to love, no matter what. You see it's easy to love someone that loves you or that you really care about. The real 'gift' comes into operation when we have to love someone that hates us or someone that we may not like. It is only when we can truthfully do this from our hearts that we are using the 'gift'. When we go along with the crowd, we give that gift away, because love is a free will thing and in a crowd, there is no free will. A crowd carries you along, maybe to somewhere you never wanted to go. A crowd can block your vision so you can't find your station. A crowd can brainwash you.

The Bible tells us that there are many gifts from God but the greatest one is love. Jesus knows the importance of love, in the Bible He tells us about the greatest commandment which is to love God first with all our heart, with all our soul and with all our mind, and the second which is to love our neighbour as we love ourselves. A commandment is something we have to do, an 'act'. How many of us say we love God but then we do not do what we are supposed to do. We hate our neighbours, we hate ourselves, we follow the crowd and we never see our oasis. We choose to hate, knowing that hate consumes us, it can make us ill but we tell ourselves that it is okay, because everyone else hates. We refuse to forgive knowing that unforgiveness eats away at us but everyone else does it, so it's okay to do the same. We condemn people and then do exactly as they do, not realizing that in the process we condemn ourselves. We judge people, we readily point at the speck in their eyes, yet ignore the log in our own eyes. We forget that every time we point a finger in judgement, three fingers point right back at us." She lifts her hand and demonstrates by pointing.

"We have to learn to look at things and look for things, the right way. We have no right to judge people or hate them because they are different and because everyone else hates them. Even when people do things that we don't like or when a history of people have done things that we don't like, hate the acts, don't hate the actors. Don't misunderstand me, I know that there are so many injustices in the world, so many atrocities have happened. Let's propose for one minute that everyone loved one another in the first place and wished them well, do you think they would still have happened? We can't change the past but we can do something about the future. If we all care about other people as we care about ourselves, do you not think that the world would be a much better place? Evil would not have the hold that it currently has on some people, especially the children.

Children are very susceptible to their parents, especially at a young age. They see, like I did, their parents and grandparents preaching one thing and doing the exact opposite. Is it a wonder they are confused and rebel? We say the children are our future, yet what are they inheriting from us. A world where they are taught to be part of a crowd, part of 'our' crowd. I have seen two and three year olds using racist language. I have seen pregnant twelve year olds with their thirteen year old partners; 'babies' having babies. I have seen children carrying guns, selling drugs, drinking, smoking, cursing. What are we teaching the children? We readily jump on band wagons, fighting the 'cause', when we could have prevented the very same 'cause' by teaching our children the right things. We readily turn a blind eye to bullying in schools, homes, and at work, yet make an uproar when we hear about domestic violence, murder and abuse. Where do you think it starts?" She stops talking, she seems to be struggling within herself. She rubs her forehead with the back of her hand several times.

"I was bullied as a child and I hated it. I hated the fact that one or two children could make my life miserable. I wouldn't speak in class because they made fun of my Irish accent. I was about eleven when two boys brought a can of Guinness to school one day. They shook the can then opened it spraying the drink all over me and my books. They laughed and said their parents had said that all

Irish people get drunk on Guinness and are lazy. Who was I supposed to hate, the children or their parents? I ran home and told my mother. She was angry but she did something I will always remember and cherish. She told me to pray for them, to pray that they and their parents lose their ignorant ways and allow Jesus to come into their life and fill them with love. The next day, I went to school with my head held high. I went up to the boys and told them I had prayed for them and if they ever pulled a stunt like that again I would get someone big and strong to deal with them. I meant God, I don't know who they thought I meant. They ran off and never bothered me again or instigated trouble for me in class."

Everyone claps.

"Parents are supposed to discipline their children with love. Children need to be taught about 'Love' and 'Respect' or they end up either never finding their station or going to the wrong station altogether. They end up as part of a crowd, hating, judging, miserable and unfulfilled, just like us. They form gangs, 'crews', fighting over a piece of turf or an area. Often killing each other because they have no love or consideration for anyone. The same children that figuratively, would never fight for their country are ready to fight and die for a piece of turf, for 'street credibility' or respect, 'neighbourhood respect' or 'tower block respect'. Look around it's already happening right now, with little or no provocation, children are killing children. People teach what they know, so what do you think they will teach their children, better or worse. The fruit never falls far from the tree." The silence is deafening. I glance around and see the odd shake of a head, a hand wiping away tears.

"Charity or love, begins at home yet some people can 'pretend' to love the world and show absolutely no love to the people at home, their family. I say 'pretend' love because if love does not begin at home anything displayed outside your home is not real. We are fooling ourselves and our children who are our future. They emulate us, they dwell like us in ignorance waiting to fool their children.

A lot of the time we hide like our parents before us, behind pride, we say we are not going to forgive or love or listen to anyone. We try to find our underground by ourselves and we end up going backwards and forwards. We don't get anywhere because we get trapped in a crowd. We get trapped in tradition, trapped in religion, trapped in racism, trapped in the unforgiveness of a wrong that was not even done to us personally, but to someone in our crowd or someone in our history. In our ignorance we go around holding on to unforgiveness, we become blinded with hate and anger and we miss a very important fact, the fact that we may or may not be hurting the other person by not forgiving them, but we are hurting ourselves so much more. Forgiveness sets you free," she pauses and looks around, "unforgiveness eats you away, slowly but surely. Some of you may be thinking 'why is it so important to forgive?' Read Mark chapter 11 verses 22-25 in the Bible when you go home. God says we have to forgive others as He forgives us, when we pray. Blessings, answered prayers, only come with obedience." She pauses again and looks down at her hand then up again.

"You cannot love God and hate your brother! We say we know God, we love Him, yet we don't do what we are supposed to do. Proverbs chapter 18 verse 21 says: *the power of life and death are in the tongue.* How many people do we encourage with our words? Jesus said in Matthew chapter 12 verses 36-37: '*Men will have to give account on the day of judgement for every careless word they have spoken. For by your words you will be acquitted, and by your words you will be condemned*'.

Take a good look at the things you do and say because it is the same mouth we use to pray to God, we use to slander others, curse others, hurt others, gossip about others and then we wonder why God does not answer our prayers. We go around full of hate yet pretending that we love; forgetting that God sees past the charade of our actions. God sees our hearts. Black, White, rich, poor, we all have the one heart. White, Black, rich, poor, God loves each and every one of us the same." Her voice breaks slightly and she turns away from the eyes of the audience. I feel the tears well up in my eyes as I stare at her back.

"When will we see that it is only when we break out of the crowd and look properly for the right thing to do, only then will we find peace."

She turns around, "It's only then that we will find our own oasis. It may be hard for some people, I do not propose that it will be an easy task. Some people have had years of experience of doing wrong, so it will not be easy for them to automatically do right, but with God's help, nothing is impossible. To break out of the crowd we have to renew our minds daily, we have to let go of old habits, old destructive attitudes, old negative thinking, in short anything that God tells us to let go of. Ephesians chapter 4 refers to it as putting off or taking off the 'old man' that is the old corrupted self and renewing our minds and putting on the 'new man' which is created to be like God in true righteousness and true holiness.

God is the potter and we are the clay, so let Him do His work. Let Him mould us into what He wants us to be. All we have to do is ask Him, is that so hard?" She walks over to the stand, picks up her bottle of water and looks at it, but does not open it. "The path of the righteous gets brighter and brighter. If your path is getting darker surely it means it's time to change." She puts the bottle down.

"Is it so hard to change? We know that once we give everything to God and let Him do His work in us, then we will, by His Grace, be able to do what is right and leave our past mistakes behind. So why are we not doing it? Why do we pretend? We risk our future when we hold on to our past. When you drive a car you can't move forward and reverse backwards at the same time. To climb a mountain we must take that first step and to physically win a football match that first kick. It is only when we trust in God that we will find - there are no blockages on the road to change that cannot be dismantled with the Word of God.

You see if we don't make a move forward for change, take that first step, how will there be change? How will we love others as we love ourselves, how will we teach our children to be better than we were? We have to believe, trust and do the Will of God. How do we know His Will? His Will is in His Word," she lifts the Bible up. "Some people depend on weapons of mass destruction believing them to be all powerful. I depend on the greatest 'weapon', the greatest 'power' in the world, one which brings about *'mass construction'*, I depend on love. Love conquers hate and moves any mountain. I depend on love because I have read this Holy Spirit inspired book and it tells me, that God is love! People will tell you otherwise but you have to decide. Free will means that you make the choice. You have to take that step, break out of the crowd and find your Underground, your oasis. It starts in your *mind*, with faith, for it is only when you can conceive it in faith, that you will achieve it. Only then, for as a man thinks, so he is."

As she concludes her talk, she picks up the rest of her things from the stand. People clap and cheer. I join the people and stand up quickly wiping a tear away as I clap, and clap, and clap.

*   *   *   *   *

Weekends are notoriously known for going too quickly. One minute it's Friday the next thing you're going back to work on Monday morning wondering where the weekend went. Today is Wednesday and I am still wondering. Jamie hasn't called me yet and most evenings as I sit by the phone waiting, I wonder if he will. I have packaged, but not yet sent him, my songs; I am waiting for him to call. I pick up the package with his address on it and think about putting it in the post for him tomorrow. My phone starts to ring and I put the package down.

"Billie, hi it's me, guess what, you are not going to believe this," Trudi's excited voice says.

"What?" I ask frowning.

"I know someone who indirectly knows Jamie Sanders."

"Tru, how can you know someone indirectly?" I ask as I feel my senses become alert at the mention of Jamie's name.

"He is a friend of a friend's brother or something like that, have you sent the songs to him?"

"No, I'll probably do it tomorrow."

"Billie! You got the songs ready on Saturday, why haven't you sent them? He's probably waiting for them and thinking you were not serious."

"He hasn't called, maybe he is not interested."

"You're joking right? Did you not see the way he was listening to your every single word? Billie send the songs!"

"Tell me what this person said about him."

"No, send the songs."

"Trudi you called me to tell me something, so tell me."

"No, send the songs then I'll tell you. This information is too hot to waste."

"Tru…"

"Look, go out and put the tape in a mailbox now and I'll call you soon with my information. Oh, and the source works for my magazine. Billie this is hot stuff, this is explosive information I'll call you soon."

"Trudi wait…," the line goes dead. I know her so well, if I call her back she will not tell me anything. She knows me, she knows that I will not say I have sent the songs if I haven't. I pick up the padded package, my jacket and keys and leave the house.

As I walk down my street, I feel as though I'm being watched. My road is a very quiet one and most of the people have lived in the same semi-detached houses for years. When I first moved here after I sold my flat in South West London, everyone seemed to be really curious about me. A single young lady buying a house in a quiet London suburb. Since then I have come to know most of my neighbours, and we get on very well; they no longer think me strange as they once did. Although, some of them still find my preference of a 'left hand' drive Mercedes car a little peculiar.

My feeling of being watched intensifies as I hear the faint sound of music coming from a car radio. I look back at the cars lining both sides of the road. I notice a movement in an unfamiliar car parked a few doors away from my house. I try to recall if the car had been there when I had come home this evening. I am sure it hadn't. I don't recognize it. Something catches my eye and I look up to see Mr Evans who lives in the house across the road from me. He is looking out of his bedroom window in the direction of the car. He sees me and waves, I wave back. Quickly, I walk down my road and turn the corner. The mailbox is at the end of the next road.

I push the package addressed to Jamie through the small opening of the mailbox and quickly walk back to my house. My eyes are alert in the twilight as the street lights start to come on. Looking along the road I see that the car is still there. As I get closer, I can't hear any music, nor can I see any movement. I am sure that someone is sitting in the car but I have no intention of walking further down the road to find out. I get to my gate and open it quickly, keeping my eyes on the car. My front door key is poised in my hand and I open my door and rush inside, thankful for the security lock and alarm system my brother had fitted last year. I turn my lights on and go to draw the curtains in my front room. I look out the window. The car has gone.

* * * * *

It has been two days since I sent the songs to Jamie and he hasn't called me yet. I wonder if he has received the package. A thousand and two questions go through my mind as I sit in the laboratory reading my Gram stained slides under the microscope. What if he doesn't like the songs? What if he doesn't want me to manage him? What if...?

I push the questions aside and read the last slide. Just as I finish recording the results on the patient's form, my mobile phone starts to vibrate. I quickly pull off my gloves and answer it.

"Hello."

"Billie! Hi this is Jamie Sanders, we met at your cousin's."

"Hi," I say trying to conceal the excited shock in my voice.

"Err..., I got your songs yesterday afternoon. I've listened to them several times and I think they are all really good."

"Really?"

Silence.

"Yes, is this a bad time to call?"

"No, no it isn't. I wondered why you hadn't called before."

"I was waiting for the songs and I wondered why you hadn't sent them earlier in the week."

Silence.

"Do you want to..."

"Can we..."

We say at the same time, silence follows.

"I'd like to talk to you about you managing me, that is if you were serious."

"I was very serious Jamie, I am very serious." A smile spreads across my face as I try to keep the excitement at bay.

We arrange a day and time to meet at Martin's club. I put my phone back in my pocket.

In the form of, *Pele, Maradona, Best, Milla, Ronaldinho Beckham, Vieira, Ronaldo, Kanu, Okocha, Diouf, Henry, Van Nistelrooy, Rooney* and all the other great footballers, just after scoring a goal, but silently; I jump up and down, wave my hands in the air, run around my small laboratory shouting, "YESSSSS!..."

CHAPTER 8

"**J**amie was in Troyston?" I ask for the seventh or eighth time in as many seconds. My heart is pounding and I can feel the goose pimples forming on my arms. "Trudi, Jamie was in the group Troyston and you didn't tell me?" The phone starts to slip from my hand and I realize my palms are sweating and tighten my grip.

"Billie, breathe. Nice and easy, breathe in and breathe out, put your hand on your tummy and breathe, let the air in, feel your tummy rise and now, exhale."

"Jamie was in Troyston?" I ask and breathe deeply. "The group with all those hits four or five years ago?" I feel the need of a brown paper bag. "Why didn't you tell me?"

"If I had told you would you have sent the songs to him?"

"No."

"That my dear friend is exactly why I didn't tell you."

I can't believe it, trying hard to concentrate I try to picture the faces of the members of Troyston, my mind is blank I can't remember what any of the members looked like. I knew of them, everyone probably did, they were as popular as the 'Backstreet Boys', 'N Sync', 'Blue', but I recall there being something different about them. I remember something I had read years ago about them having the potential of being in the same league as the 'Beatles', 'Stones' and 'U2' if they had not tragically and prematurely broken up.

"Are you sure this friend of a friend's brother has got this right?" I ask.

"Billie I checked it out myself, I went into our music archives, double checked by going over to the BBC's music archives and then again on the internet. It's true."

"But, I'm meeting him today. I can't pretend that I don't know, what if he doesn't want me to know?"

"Well if you're going to manage him I would assume that he'd tell you."

"Manage him? How am I going to manage him? He was in Troyston, they were on MTV, at every single music award ceremony, they were everywhere. Tru, they were massive."

"So, he said that he likes your songs didn't he?"

"Yes but-"

"No buts, the lead singer of Troyston likes your songs and wants you to manage him. The End."

"Lead singer! Trudi you never said he was the lead singer," my heart starts to pound again.

"Didn't I, oopps."

"Is there anything else I need to know about Jamie?"

"Grab a pen," she says.

*   *   *   *   *

I have a couple of hours to spare before meeting Jamie, so I decide to visit a friend that lives near Martin's club, where Jamie and I will meet. I miss two turnings on the way to her house and have to turn back and start again. I'm usually very good at directions so I can only put it down to the news about Jamie. I breathe a sigh of relief when I eventually find her street, then make my way to the front of her house. There is nowhere to park in front of her house, so I park a few doors away and walk to her front gate. Pausing I look at the dark blue car parked directly in front of her house. It looks familiar, like the car I had seen parked on my road a few days ago. I take a mental note of the number plate, then open her gate and walk up the short path to her front door and press the bell.

"Who is it?" She asks from behind the door.

"Open and see," I say thinking that she is joking.

"TELL ME WHO IT IS OR I WON'T OPEN THE DOOR," she shouts.

"It's me, it's Billie," I say a little shocked at the tone of her voice. As the door opens I notice the chain is still latched.

"Billie, I'm so sorry," the door closes; she unlatches the chain and opens it.

"Sarah, are you okay?" I ask as I walk past her into the hall. I can hear the children playing.

"I'm fine, sorry I didn't know it was you."

"You've not been to work, you're not answering your phone, I've left messages on your machine, you haven't returned my calls. What is going on?"

"Nothing," she says walking past me and into her front room where the children are, "I've just been under the weather."

I look at the heavy make-up on her face and the telltale signs that she tries to hide with her bleached blond hair.

"What happened?" I ask

"What?"

"Your face."

"Nothing, I fell and hit my head."

"You fell? Where? When?"

"Don't give me the third degree Billie, I'm not in the mood."

"Sarah I just think-"

"Auntie Billie!" Luke, my adopted godson shouts. I turn just in time to catch him as smiling he rushes at me with his arms wide open. I pick him up and give him a hug. The other two children come over and stand looking up at me. I playfully hug them and swing them up in the air. As they scream and laugh, I look at Sarah, she seems worried and agitated as she constantly looks out of the window, she seems to be looking at the car parked in front of the house.

"Do you want to talk in the kitchen?" I ask.

She shakes her head and looks away. I focus on the children, joining in their card game and laughing as Luke the oldest, makes and then breaks the rules. Luke's father is a medical doctor, the son of a very wealthy Ghanaian Chief. He worked with Sarah years ago. I think that it is because Luke is mixed race like me, that I have a soft spot for him. He is such a loving child and much older than his years. Nick's father is a man that Sarah had met in Scotland. I don't know who Maddy's father is.

"Two of hearts, you lose," Luke says.

"But Luke you said two wins," Nick says, confusion knotting his little brows.

"Not now, that was then," Luke says sucking a sweet loudly.

"But-"

"You have to keep up Nick."

"I am but it's not fair, you're cheating."

"No I'm not, you're not concentrating. You are my swabling and anyway I don't cheat," Luke replies.

"What's a swabling?" I ask Luke.

"My teacher said a brother or sister," he replies.

"You mean sibling," I say and laugh.

"Aww, you did it again Luke," Nick complains.

"You were not concentrating."

"I am conce-training," Nick says.

"Luke, play fair!" Sarah snaps, interrupting Nick's objections. I see the look of hurt on Luke's face and say nothing.

As I sit here playing with three children that are the sweetest I have ever met, I suddenly feel very uncomfortable. I know that their mother whom I work with, is in an abusive relationship with a man whose identity she has kept a secret, and I don't know what to do.

As I drive towards Martin's club where I will meet Jamie I feel troubled. I saw bruises on Sarah's arms, neck as well as beneath the heavy foundation on her face. She refused to talk about them. I know I have to help, I can't just ignore it as everyone at work does. They talk about it in her absence, a few people actually sounding sympathetic while a few others laugh about it. Yet they totally ignore it when she is around.

A couple of months ago I saw a program on GMTV about domestic violence, there was a contact number at the end of the program which I wrote down and gave to Sarah. She took the number but told me to mind my own business. I phoned the number myself to see if there was anything that I could do, any advice they could give me to help her. I was told to try and support her, they said that the victim needs to admit that it is happening before it would stop. Most women are in denial or too scared to do anything about abuse.

The irony is, I know first hand just what she is going through. That is why I can't just do nothing. That is why despite her attitude I keep checking up on her, hoping that one day she will admit what is happening is wrong, and denial makes it worse. One day she will see like I did, that the worse thing one can do, is put up with abuse because they are afraid of being alone or afraid of facing up to the truth. The worse thing is to be afraid of the fear.

*   *   *   *   *

Jamie is waiting outside the club as I pull into the staff car park. He looks nice, casually dressed but smart. I am still not sure how to play things, should I just come out and say I know about Troyston or wait for him to mention it first? Should I say nothing if he says nothing?

"Hi Jamie," I say as I walk towards him.

"Hi," he says and smiles revealing the asset that Trudi or was it Phoebe had been fascinated with the other night; his dimples. We walk into the club and sit down at a table. There is an awkward silence as we sit facing each other. I see him looking at my hair and my face.

"Would you like something to drink?" I ask.

"Yes thanks, whatever you're having."

"Okay, two glasses of milk coming right up."

He smiles.

I get up and go over to the bar where one of the barmen is taking stock.

"Hi John, can I have two orange juices with no ice."

"Sure," he says putting his note pad down and going to the large glass-door refrigerator. He pours the drinks then picks up his pad ignoring the money in my hand.

"Here," I say stretching my hand towards him.

"It's okay Billie, Martin says you are not to pay for anything."

"I know but he's not here now so take it." He looks at the money and shakes his head and I refuse to pick up the drinks unless he takes the money.

Finally he takes it, "I'll bring the change over."

"Thanks John," I say and walk back to the table.

I place one glass in front of Jamie.

"Milk?" He questions.

"Orange flavoured," I reply.

He chuckles, "Spiked?"

"With water."

We laugh.

"Right," I say trying to sound confident, "I like your voice, you like my songs, I think together we can do good things." Jamie smiles and takes a sip of his drink. I can feel myself trying hard to keep my nervousness concealed.

"Here's your change Billie, for the record I'm only taking your money because Martin isn't here and you twisted my arm," John says. He places my change on the table and walks off. I smile at his retreating back.

"You pay for your own drinks in your cousin's club?" Jamie asks sounding a little bemused.

"I'm not supposed to, but this business is his livelihood."

"Talking about business have you managed anyone before? You said that you're a Scientist."

"I sort of co-managed and wrote songs for 'Nu-Force'."

"The group with 'the' Natasha Dubree?" He looks impressed.

I nod, "Nu-Force needed a lead singer and I brought Natasha to the table. She had just left another group at the time. I only co-managed, there were people around at the time who had more experience."

"I know most of their songs, which ones did you write?"

I look at him wanting to tell him the truth that has been buried beneath the layers of lies. Could I trust him? Should I trust him? Wayne had stolen the songs and claimed them as his own so everyone thought that he had written them. I was called a liar when I tried to tell the truth. I take a risk and trust him.

"Umm.., 'In too Deep' and 'I Don't Wanna Escape'," I find myself saying.

"What! You wrote 'In too Deep' and 'I Don't Wanna Escape' they both got into the top five in the singles chart. They were there for weeks and weeks! I thought Wayne Campbell wrote those songs."

"So do a lot of people but he didn't," I look away.

"That explains a lot."

"Such as?" I ask turning back to face him.

"Why he hasn't written anything half as good since those songs, which he claimed were his."

His comment catches me off guard and fills me with relief, as I look at him, my nervousness disintegrates and then disappears. I look into the familiar eyes of the man I had first met over a week ago. The man I had shared my dreams with. I smile at him as I feel the barriers of shyness and awkwardness fall away.

"Is that why you stopped co-managing, because Wayne Campbell stole your songs?"

"Not just that," I pause, "there were so many people involved with the group. It became harder and harder to get my ideas across, the old timers, the executives, were not open to new ideas, they didn't have a problem with taking my ideas and changing them slightly then using them though. The group's Manager, Poppy, was brilliant but the others just felt that I was reaching too high. Then I found out from the newspapers that Wayne and my cousin Natasha, were an item, they were photographed coming out of a hotel at five O'clock in the morning. I thought it was best that I left."

"Natasha is your cousin? Wayne and you?"

I nod in reply to both questions. I refuse to acknowledge the hurt I once felt at their betrayal. I sit back and wait for him to recover from the shock of my revelation and to close his mouth.

He coughs, "From the casual way in which you tell it, am I to assume that it's all history now?"

"All in the past. Forgiven and forgotten."

"How?"

"I am not going to lie, it was hard at first but when I realized that the hate, hurt, anger and unforgiveness were eating me away, making me ill, I let go. When it first happened I was constantly angry, aggressive and anxious, I pretended I wasn't but in my heart I knew I was. Then I realized I was harming myself, doing wrong things and thinking wrong thoughts, so I changed. I threw my plans of revenge, all 1001 of them, out of the window, put my trust in God and now I truly wish them both well. I have truly let go of all the sad memories."

"That easy?" He does not look convinced.

"No it wasn't that easy, at the time I didn't understand what was going on. Natasha was the one that got me going to church after I sort of stopped going regularly at university. I couldn't understand how as a Christian she did what she did, then one day I realized that God didn't make Natasha act the way she did. She made the choice to do it."

He nods slowly.

"Do you swim?" I ask.

"Yes."

"I used to swim a lot in school. I got my bronze, silver, gold and elementary survival medals. Have you ever swam the length of the pool in a straight line?"

"Yes, in the ones with the lane division ropes."

"What about one without the ropes?"

"In a straight line? Dead straight? Maybe not."

"I had this picture in my head. I had to swim across the length of a pool in a straight line to get my prize at the end which was something I desperately wanted. Imagine this with me, I'm a good swimmer but I had things in my past holding me back, trying to keep me at the start line. I had chains, shackles of hurt, anger, hate, things that I had to let go of. When I managed to break free from them, there were currents along the way that tried to push me off my course. Plans of revenge, of retaliations, of getting my own back. Further down, were people trying to pull me to the bottom of the pool. The dead weights that wanted me to stay as I was, stay in my state of anger and pain. They wanted me to keep on gossiping and assassinating the characters of the people that had hurt me. At the other end of the pool was the prize: love, joy and peace which I desperately wanted. So I had to focus, keep my eyes on the prize, press forward, completely let go of everything else."

"What happened?"

"I have love, joy and peace in my life now."

"You got the prize?"

"Yes thanks to God, I got the prize. The swim wasn't easy but what I have right now is great, more than worth it. In my heart I know I have forgiven them. I sincerely wish both Wayne and Natasha well."

"Were you and Natasha close?"

I smile to myself, "Once upon a time," I stare at my glass. "I guess she was the big sister I never had, she looked out for me. Once, a long time ago, my brother Steve, stood up for this little boy that was being bullied by four or five other boys. The bullies circled Steve and this other boy, I was on my bike and saw what was happening, so I jumped off my bike and stood in front of Steve and this boy and told the bullies that no one messed with my family. That they would have to come through me to get to Steve. I think I scared Steve more than them. Anyway, I stood my ground and Natasha came running over, she pushed me back and said that she would flatten anyone that laid a finger on me. Being older than me, she was much bigger. Steve pushed both of us back and walked towards the bullies, they ran away. I was about thirteen, we were very close. It's funny how evil works through people close to you, your family or friends. If a stranger had done what she did it wouldn't have hurt so much."

We sit facing each other, I wait for him to ask more questions. He doesn't.

"So Mr Sanders, tell me more about you. I remember you said that you sang in your church choir when you were little," I smile.

I'm not sure and I may be wrong but I feel he is searching for the right words. I wait for him to find them.

"I could tell from the way you looked at me in the car park that you know about Troyston." Again I am caught off guard at his perceptiveness, I wonder how he had guessed.

"How?" I ask.

"At the club when we talked you had this openness about you, today in the car park you seemed a little guarded."

"Did I now? I should have spent a few more minutes in front of the mirror practising how to be less guarded," I say practising in front of him now.

He laughs and despite myself I laugh as well.

Jamie tells me about Troyston. As he speaks I am taken along with him on a journey of quick success and gruelling work. A journey of amazing experiences, luxurious living and sadness. I notice his eyes light up as he talks about Ben and the good old early days. He tells the stories so clearly and concise that I feel as if I know everyone, as if I am there.

"A lot of people see boy bands and automatically think of drugs, wild parties and girls. It's not really like that you know."

"What! No parties?" I ask jokingly.

"We were young and it was really hard work. We had to tour, do interviews, gigs, sometimes it was 24/7. We practically lived in one hotel after another and didn't get to see our families for weeks. It used to get really lonely. Sometimes in the middle of a crowded party, I would feel so alone."

"Were you all close?"

"We got on well most of the time. Once in a while there were the arguments, usually right after some magazine published a poll that showed the fans liked one of us more than the others, or vice versa. The polls always seemed to change, we were constantly gauged against each other, that's why I never took them very seriously."

"One minute they build you up, next they tear you down, then if you are lucky they build you up again to tear you down," I say.

"Exactly, see for me, it was all about achieving goals, doing what I wanted to do and getting paid. Whatever they wrote never really bothered me that much. Ben was a lot more sensitive than he let on, some of the stuff really bothered him, some…," I see a far away look in his eyes, then silence.

"Were you happy?" I ask.

"Most of the time, yes. Then again I was happy within myself before I joined the band. Both my parents were youth ministers in a very big church, I sang in the church choir. All I ever wanted to do was sing. My family was and is my backbone, I have a younger brother and two adopted sisters, one from China and one from South Africa. They encouraged me, loved me, kept me sane, when things got really insane. Fame comes and goes but your family Billie, they last forever. See the band brought the fame and money, but money didn't bring the happiness or peace I had. You have to find those first, you have to find the peace and happiness from within, because no amount of money will bring that." I nod my concurrence. "So you've heard about Troyston, do you still want to take me on?"

"Umm," I say pretending to think, "as long as you realize that with me there will not be the wild parties and half naked women."

"Arrr, why?" He asks. He places a hand over his mouth but not before I see the smile that he attempts to hide. I play along.

"I've read about some of those women at those wild parties and in the music videos, you know what?" I lower my voice, "they don't really like half of the artists they work with. They 'clock' everything they do, when the clock stops, that's it."

"No!" He says in mock horror and laughs.

"I'm afraid so and as long as you're okay with a not-so-wild-lifestyle, I think we can come to some arrangement."

Smiling we shake hands.

We talk about contracts and different agreements then we move on to ourselves. I see the light in my eyes reflect in his as we talk and I know that this is the beginning of something big, much bigger than the both of us.

*   *   *   *   *

It has been nearly two hours since she left and he is tired and cold as he stands behind the shrubbery. A thousand and one and a half thoughts pump through his mind in no sensible order. What had she wanted with his family? Why had she brought sweets for his children? That was his job not hers. Why was she always interfering and giving Sarah ideas above her station? Making Sarah think that she is special and the children a blessing.

"Rubbish," he says loudly to himself. He looks around, his thoughts intensify. So what if the children were not all his, he helps to look after them, he cares for them. Now because Billie Lewis has interfered, Sarah has called in the police. If not for his 'associate', he would have sorted Ms Lewis out, but he had been told by his stronger half, not to touch her. His stronger half is crazy about the smell of her hair and likes to follow her around at night. A strong breeze blows, he shivers in response. He is cold and he is tired as he watches the house. He has a key but he knows that Sarah has changed the locks. He knows this because he had stood where he is standing now, and seen the locksmith come to the house and change the locks three days ago.

He hadn't meant to hurt her, why had he done it. His memory is a little blurred, it gets that way without his medication. He wants to go home but he knows he can't, he knows that a police officer will come and check on his family in an hour's time. He knows everything that goes on before it happens. He knows he is clever, in fact no matter what others think of him, he knows he is simply the

100

best. He hums to himself *'I'm simply the best, better than all the rest'* as he waits for the police officer to come and do the routine check.

*   *   *   *   *

Sarah stands in the doorway of her children's bedroom watching them as they sleep. They look beautiful, so peaceful and innocent. She is past wondering how she has got into this mess. Her children mean so much to her, yet she has exposed them to unimaginable danger. Her heart feels heavy as she watches them sleep knowing that they will awake to the reality of the mess she has created. 'What kind of mother does this to her children, what kind of dysfunctional, selfish mother am I?', she thinks as she covers her face with her hands and weeps. She needs help, she can't do this by herself. She falls to the floor as the tears fall from her heart.

"Please help me, please help me God. Please," she says over and over again quietly. It is only when her shoulders stop shaking, only when her silent sobs abate, does she realize that a little arm is placed around her shoulders. She looks at the face inches away from hers, the six year old face full of love and compassion.

"Mummy is going to make this right Luke," she whispers as she pulls him into her arms.

He nods, he has heard this so many times and even though nothing seems to change, she is his mother and he believes her.

CHAPTER 9

Outside a derelict warehouse: Downtown Los Angeles

Tyres screech, rubber burns, the car suddenly stops.

"William, I'm here, don't do anything stupid," Philip says into the phone held against his ear as he climbs quickly out of the car.

"WILLIAM!" He shouts. No one answers, he turns the phone off, throws it inside the car and starts running. He runs towards the building as people shout for him to stop. His heart is pounding but he knows that if he waits someone may die.

"What the..."

"Who the..."

"Mr McKnight? Philip, wait come back, everyone hold your fire, I repeat, do not shoot," the senior police officer, Lieutenant Drake, shouts and runs towards the building after him.

Breathing hard Philip pushes the door open and steps inside.

"William, it's me. Let Rosa and the baby go."

William Mathias walks towards him, he holds the gun against his face lovingly.

"Philip, my old roomy, my partner, my buddy, you came man, you came." William's words are alcohol assisted, slurry and disjointed.

"Put the gun down."

"My..., my baby and Rosa are here."

Philip walks towards him, he lowers the gun.

"What are you doing? You have half the police officers in LA waiting to shoot you. You have your wife and child held hostage and you are half stoned and drunk. What is it all about?"

"You don't understand, nobody understands P.A."

"Understand what?"

"You froze me out."

"You were stealing from the company, selling drugs, pirating songs that our artists worked their tails off to produce."

"I was gonna pay you back, honest I was. The drugs..., the fake CDs..., I know I messed up, but why did you call the police? When we talked you said you would help me."

"I didn't call the police, I-"

"He didn't, I did," Rosa says. She walks towards them. "I knew they were investigating you William, so I called them. If I hadn't, chances are, you'd end up dead in some gutter. Killed by the gangster you are doing your dirty deals with, your 'famous' bootlegging buddy. I tried to put up with the drinking and the drugs William, but the girlfriends, the stealing, the lying and the pain got too much for me."

"Rosa! You? You called the police?" He points the gun at her.

"What you gonna shoot me William? You gonna make our son an orphan? Because if you don't change you're gonna end up dead too."

"I'm sorry Rosa, those women they meant nothing, I am sorry. Please don't leave me."

She shakes her head, "I'm still leaving you."

Philip steps in front of her, "Put the gun down William."

They look at each other and William lowers the gun. Suddenly the door bursts open and ten armed police officers rush into the room.

"PUT THE GUN DOWN-"

"LOWER YOUR WEAPON NOW-"

Philip turns and sees several guns pointed at his friend.

William holds the gun up.

"Drop the gun," Philip shouts quickly, he hears the safety catch of a gun behind him being released and shouts again. Things seem to take on a slower motion, as William struggles to drop his gun, a police officer fires his. Rosa screams and Philip watches as William falls to the ground.

"ARRR! It's not loaded!" William screams as he rolls on the ground clutching his arm. "The gun is not loaded. I only did it for you Rosa."

Panic steps in, questions and orders quickly pursue.

"I told you to hold your fire-," the Lieutenant shouts.

"Ma'am step away-"

"Sir can you take her away-"

"Where is the baby?-"

"Paramedics-"

"Get a doctor in here, he is losing blood fast-"

"The gun wasn't loaded!" Rosa says in disbelief. Amid the pandemonium she walks over to William and looks down. "You dope-head, you couldn't even get that right."

Philip looks at Rosa and sees the hate in her eyes.

"You called the police? Why? We agreed not to."

"The line has been crossed."

"What line?"

"The line between love and hate. He made me cross it," she sees the confusion in Philip's eyes, "I loved him, now I hate him. He made me cross the thin line."

"When things were good and the money was flowing Rosa, where was this line? William has been the same since you met him. All he needed was help and love, not the rejection you gave. Not the affairs you had. You never crossed any line, maybe you were always on the wrong side. It's not too late."

She looks away but not before Philip sees the truth in her eyes. Philip walks past her. He picks up William's bloodied jacket laying on the floor.

"For better or worse Rosa, for better or worse." he says then follows the paramedics carrying his friend on the stretcher.

CHAPTER 10

I sit and watch as Jamie walks around my front room looking at the different pieces of African art that adorn my walls and bookcase. So many barriers came down the last time we met, I feel he is part of my extended family now. I feel neither shy or embarrassed around him as I did at our first official meeting. I hope he feels the same. I watch as he picks up the figure of a 'Palmwine Tapper' and turns it around in his hands.

"This is really nice, where did you get all this stuff from?"

"Mostly Nigeria in West Africa, I lived there for a few years with Steve and my parents. My father is from there and as you can see from Martin being my cousin, my mother is from here."

He walks over to the corner where I have a very large picture of a man wearing native 'Yoruba' attire and beating an African drum. It is a beautiful picture, full of vibrant colours. The first time I saw it I knew that I had to buy it. It had taken a lot of haggling over the price but I got it in the end. Apart from being very colourful, it is also very unique. You see the drum the man is holding is made out of solid bronze. The artist has used a lot of skill and imagination in this picture and as Jamie stares at it, I know the question that is about to follow. Everyone who looks at this picture asks the same question.

"How did they get the bronze to stick on to an oil painting?"

"It's welded on," I reply going into a little detail about the procedure with him.

"Umm, interesting," he says as he moves to my CD collection. I smile and pull out the list I have made of the things we need to do today from my briefcase. I watch as he inspects a rug spread out on the wooden floor of my front room. It has a central place because my parents brought it back from Mexico for me and I love my parents. He sort of half frowns then nods. I have no idea at this point if he is actually interested in my things or shy about being in my house. The thought of the latter causes me to chuckle to myself. As he moves towards a corner of the room with a large array of houseplants I feel it's time to find out.

"Now, if you have finished admiring my things perhaps we can get down to some work?"

"Why yes ma'am," Jamie replies.

He sits in an armchair opposite me and picks up a cushion.

"Are you okay?" I ask realizing that he *is* nervous.

"Fine, err, I'm fine, thanks."

"Okay, first of all I think I should tell you something; I don't know much about Troyston, I was never really attracted to any of the members, I don't know all of the songs they did, I don't have any T-shirts or tattoos, I…" I am trying so hard to keep a straight face that my face muscles start to hurt.

"What?" Jamie looks surprised.

"What I'm trying to say is, you can relax around me."

"I was trying to, then I saw you watching me as I admired your things. I saw you smiling to yourself."

"That's because I thought you were nervous," I say.

"I was," he replies.

We both start to laugh.

"You know what's a little bit spooky?" Jamie asks as he wipes his laughter tears away with the back of his hand.

"Apart from you, no," I reply.

"Having the same sort of humour as your Manager."

*   *   *   *   *

An hour later finds us in front of Liam's house. I double-check the piece of paper with the address written on it to make sure that we are at the right place. The three storey, one front door bell, detached house, looks very impressive. I don't know what I quite had in mind as a place of abode for my cousin's resident DJ, but it certainly wasn't this.

"Does he own the whole house?" Jamie asks as I park my car in front of it.

"To tell the truth I don't know, I only know Liam from the club. I know that he used to be a radio DJ."

We make our way down the short drive. I press the doorbell. After waiting for a few seconds I press it again. Liam opens the door.

"Hi guys, how are you? Come in come in, welcome to my humble home. The studio is upstairs." He closes the door and we follow him up the stairs to the first floor. His studio consists of a large, very well equipped soundproof room with two glass recording booths adjacent to each other in one of the corners. Microphones attached to extendible stands are lined up against one side of the wall and a drum set and two guitars the other.

"Okay, here is what we are going to do," Liam says without much ado, professionalism oozing out of his pores. "First, we record your backing music on this tape spool," he points to it, "while I'm doing that Jamie you can go into a recording booth and start to warm your voice up, when you're ready, I'll record your voice on top of the backing music, any questions?"

We both shake our heads.

"Are you cool with the songs Jamie, word wise, pitch wise, song wise?"

"Yes I'm fine."

"Okay so let's do this. Billie you can sit over here." He wheels a chair over to the large mixing board. "You'll be able to hear everything that Jamie will sing, if there are any changes you want or ad-libs you want included, excluded, let me know okay."

Nodding I sit on the chair. I watch as he moves buttons up and down on the mixing board. He presses buttons and flips switches as I stare at his skilled hands.

"Are you interested in this aspect?" Liam asks.

"What? The studio mechanics? In a way, yes. I'd like to know how to do the fine tuning of a song and how to use a 'Vocoda' to alter the singers voice and how to layer vocals."

"Looks like you know a lot already," he presses a button on the panel and we can hear Jamie's voice as he sings one of the songs.

"He's good."

"He's very good," I concur.

He waits for Jamie to finish the song then tells him to stand closer to the microphone and sing directly into it. Jamie does this and the power in his voice soars across time and space and dazzles us through the speakers.

"Nice one Jamie, very nice," Liam says as he adjusts some knobs on the panel. He connects some wires to another speaker and asks Jamie to sing again. This time Jamie's voice is much more clearer and twice as powerful. "Let's do it with some music, then we'll record."

"Okay," Jamie replies sticking a thumb up at us.

*　*　*　*　*

Over six hours later, the time it would take to fly to say, New York or Nigeria from London, we have a demo tape consisting of two songs. Without, I hasten to add, the fine tunings. Liam will do this tomorrow and let me have a copy of both songs on CD. I pay Liam for his time and work and wait as he writes a receipt for me.

"Martin said that you write lyrics," he says handing me the receipt. "I was wondering if you would listen to some music and see if you can come up with some lyrics?" He holds an audio cassette up. "It's all original stuff, produced by me."

I hesitate, a feeling of *déja vu* washes over me.

"I'll listen to it," I say shrugging, "see what I come up with."

"Thanks Billie, no pressure, I know you're busy."

*　*　*　*　*

I am engrossed in an internal struggle as we drive back to my house and to Jamie's car which is parked outside my house. 'Maybe I shouldn't have taken the tape from Liam,' I think to myself as I drive. 'No it will be okay, he wouldn't do a Wayne Campbell on me, he's a really decent person. But then again, you thought Wayne was a decent person didn't you, you nearly got engaged to him.'

"...Billie?"

"Sorry, did you say something?" I ask.

"I just asked if you were okay, you're a little quiet."

"I'm fine I was just thinking about something."

"Do you mind if I say something?"

"Go ahead."

"I know in our contract we have an agreement which states that you take care of all expenses until we get a recording deal, then you get 25%, but have you any idea how much we could be looking at money-wise, pre-record deal?"

"It could be a lot but a deal is a deal, plus I recoup all expenses anyway," I say wondering what exactly he is getting at.

"I just want you to know that if something needs to be paid for pre-record deal, then let me know if you are short, this is nothing to do with our contract."

"Thank you for thinking that," I say feeling touched.

"So what's on your mind, you went quiet after Liam gave you that tape." We are near my house but I need to talk right now so I pull the car over to the side of the road.

"Remember last week when I told you about the songs I wrote a couple of years ago?" He nods. "Well something similar happened when I wrote those songs. I was seeing someone at the time and-"

"Wayne Campbell?" He asks.

I nod, "He gave me some music and asked me to write some lyrics. The music wasn't that good, so I changed it and wrote the lyrics and gave it to him and," I pause and breathe deeply.

I can still feel the pain of his rejection and criticism, "he said that the songs were crap, that a ten year old could have done better, but he still took them. He actually acted as if he was doing me a favour. The next thing I know he flogs the songs as his and manages to bed my cousin in the process."

"So, you were thinking maybe the same can happen again, with the music Liam gave you I mean?"

"At first yes, I had this weird feeling of *déjà vu*. But Liam is nothing like Wayne and," I pause, "anything I do now involves contracts and copyrights."

"Smart lady, I knew there was a reason I hired you," he says light-heartedly.

I play along, "Really, I'm still trying to figure out why I agreed to manage you."

*   *   *   *   *

My head is throbbing. Not being one for phoning in sick; without a plausible reason, I decided to brave it, and came into work this morning. Now as I sit in the Clinical Bacteriology laboratory, I am regretting my decision. Jamie and I had talked for a couple more hours last night, then I dropped him off in front of his car. I thought it was really sweet the way he had waited for me to get inside my house, then wave to him from my front window before he had driven off.

"...Sarah, I asked you to get those plates twenty minutes ago, I need them now please," Tina says loudly, interrupting my thoughts. I look up and see Tina standing with her arms folded next to the bench where Sarah is working.

"I'll get them in five minutes," Sarah says very weakly obviously embarrassed. "I just need to finish subbing these cultures."

"Finish that later, go and get the plates now."

"I will get them, I really have to finish this it should have been done yesterday, it's a day late."

"What exactly does that have to do with me? If you can't keep up with your work or you're not well enough, then maybe you should take it up with the Manager. Now, go and get those plates."

Still really tired I walk over to Sarah's bench as she stands up.

"I'll get them, I need to stretch my legs anyway." I place a hand on Sarah's shoulder and gently push her back down.

"I think she should get them, She's the MLA," Tina says emphasizing the fact that Sarah is a Medical Laboratory Assistant, and therefore two grades lower than her. Of course, me, being 'Billie the Brave', 'the defender of the universe', sees the injustice and steps in to defend the wronged.

"Look Tina, I said I'd get them, Sarah is busy. So you have two choices, either you get them yourself or I get them."

She gives Sarah a look of pure hate and walks off. I turn to Sarah who is fidgeting with some paperwork on her bench.

110

"I thought you two were good friends once upon a time?"

She shrugs and looks a little embarrassed but in her loyalty to her old friendship, does not divulge any information despite her so called friend now behaving like an adversary. I find this commendable.

"I'll go and get those plates, ten packs of blood agar and five of McConkey right?"

"Yes, thanks Billie."

"Don't worry," I say, "I need to wake up a bit anyway and the cool air in the cold-room will do the trick." I try to suppress a yawn as I stretch, "It's funny sometimes how one becomes extremely brave when one is extremely tired." She smiles and I, yawning, head towards the cold-room where the Plates are kept.

The cold-room is a new addition to the department. It is a massive cold store room of approximately three hundred square feet, with two large doors on opposite ends of the room, appropriately called 'north' and 'south' doors. It had cost the department a huge amount of money and is still causing a series of executive arguments as to whether or not it was worth the amount it had cost.

Most of the arguments against it are based on the fact that most of its special features are too good to be true; or in plain English - do not work. For instance the two doors are supposed to work on some sort of trigger switch mechanism, if one door is open you are not supposed to be able to open the other door. If one door is open for longer than two minutes then an alarm will sound. In theory it all sounds good but in practice it doesn't work.

As soon as I open the south door and walk into the cold-room I shake my head and smile as I notice that the north door on the opposite wall is slightly ajar. I make a mental note to close it before I leave. I stand in the middle of the room where it is coldest, and breathe in and out deeply. After a very short while I can feel the tiredness slipping out of my system and the stimulating effect of the cold air slipping in. I look at the shelves that line the walls, shelves stocked with all the reagents and Agar plates used by the whole of the Microbiology Department. Things that need to be stored at a low temperature pending the time they are used. As I stand in the middle of the cold-room I wonder why people need to pop pills to wake themselves up, all they need is a few minutes in a cold environment to give them a 'jump start'. I am wide awake now and full of energy. I look around for the plates that Tina wants which are not where they are usually kept. I push boxes out of the way as I try to find the one I am looking for. I hear something fall on the floor in the distance, startled I look up, I hadn't realized that someone else was in the room. Roger appears from in between an aisle of shelves. I freeze hoping that he hadn't heard or seen me come in. The last thing I need right now is for him to start his weird behaviour. He places the box in his hands on a trolley, just as Nigel walks into the room. Nigel looks around suspiciously then closes the north door. He says something to Roger, I cannot hear what. Roger looks as if he is about to walk away when Nigel grabs his arm. I am shocked at the reversal of roles. Roger always seems to be the bully and Nigel the bullied.

"DON'T YOU TURN AWAY FROM ME," Nigel shouts.

Roger says something.

"What the hell do you mean?" Nigel replies loudly.

"He says he can't 'up' my prescription, something about me already being on a high dosage," Roger says loudly.

"Sod that. I want it today, do you understand?"

"Relax man I'll try-"

"Relax?"

It is as if I am on a movie set, I watch Nigel push Roger against the wall, watch as his body bounces off the wall. In a flash and with martial art precision, Nigel kicks at Roger's legs then puts an arm under his chin. He must be pressing really hard, because Roger's face turns red instantly. I watch amazed at Nigel's strength. Roger is around six foot and Nigel five six or five seven. What amazes me even more is that Roger makes no attempt to fight back.

"You go back and tell Mckee that I want my Prozac, S-Paxil and Valium. Do you hear me?" Nigel waves his free arm about as he shouts. He loosens his grip and Roger slides up the wall. Turning I walk along the back wall, I know from where they are standing they cannot see me. Slowly I edge towards the south door. I am a few feet away when I see the box containing the plates Tina wants. I know there is no way I can open the south door without them seeing me from where they are standing. I have no other alternative. I put the ear piece from my mobile phone in my ear. Picking up the box of plates, I drop it loudly on the floor and wait a few seconds, then get down on my knees and start to pick the pre-packed plates up. I examine them for damage then put them in the box. I hear footsteps coming towards me and start to sing and nod my head to imaginary music.

"...*Lean on me, when you're not strong, I'll be your friend, I'll help you carry on. For lalalalaa lalalalaa...*"

"Billie!" Nigel sounds shocked, "what are you doing here?"

I jump and pretend to look startled as they both tower over me.

"What?" I say loudly. I remove the ear-piece from my ear, "sorry, what did you say? I didn't hear you guys come in."

"I asked what you were doing here?" Nigel asks.

"Getting some Agar plates for Tina," I reply sounding surprisingly very calm.

Roger looks at the plates suspiciously then at me he looks remarkably composed. "How long have you been in here?" He asks moving towards me.

"A couple of minutes or less, why? Someone left the north door open, was it you?" I ask frowning and standing up.

I glance at Nigel, he seems different and is rubbing his arm as if in pain and looking like the harassed not the harasser. I play along with the scenario.

"Are you okay Nigel?" He looks at Roger with what looks like fear in his eyes and nods. I turn to Roger. "Have you been picking on him again? One of these days you're going to pick on the wrong person." I grab the box with the Agar plates off the floor and walk past both of them. Closing the south door behind me I breathe a sigh of relief as I lean against the door.

* * * * *

'What did she see? What does she know?' The questions plague his mind as he goes looking for her. 'What did she see? What does she know?' The voices asking the questions echo loudly in his head. He swipes his ID card, pushes the barrier forward then walks into the large library and looks around. His heart starts to beat faster as he sees her bent over some books at a corner table. He walks towards her. 'What did she see? What does she know? Find out, FIND OUT NOW-'

"Roger, can you give me a hand please?"

Startled, he turns towards the 'external' voice. The owner is holding a wooden flap of a bookcase up and clutching some journals under her arm. He glances at the figure seated at the table, then walks towards Tina, he takes the journals from her.

*   *   *   *   *

'Prozac, S-Paxil and Valium' I think to myself as I run my fingers down the index of a Medical Encyclopaedia. I know that Valium is used to either calm people down or by people who cannot sleep at night. People with insomnia. The other two, I have an idea, but I want to make sure. I read that Prozac is used mainly for depression and S-Paxil as an anti-depressant and for social anxiety disorders.

'Why does Nigel want these drugs, is he depressed?' I think to myself. I look through another book trying to get some more information. I hear someone call Roger's name and literally freeze. After a few seconds I turn slightly and see that he is talking to Tina. Reaching out I grab some books that someone has left on the table and place them on top of my books. I can feel the beginnings of a slight panic attack because I know that if he sees the books I am looking at, he will know that I heard what was said in the cold-room. Quickly I place my ear piece in my ear and press some numbers on my phone.

"Hello library," the voice says.

"Hello can you place an announcement for Roger Manning-Smith please, he has an urgent phone call and needs to come upstairs to the laboratory right away," I say into my mouth piece softly.

"You can transfer the call down here if you like-"

"No! I'm really sorry he needs to come up now, it's urgent."

"Okay."

"Thank you," I say. I turn my phone off and hope that she does what I have asked her to do, quickly. Turning my head slightly, I see that Tina and Roger are standing by the book shelves talking. He is looking in my direction. "Do it now, please do it now," I say softly to myself over and over again. I hear foot steps walk towards me and stop behind me. I don't turn. I continue to stare at the Microbiology text book in front of me.

"Studying?" Roger asks leaning over my shoulder. I hold my breath and wait for the librarian to page him. He sits down next to me and my heart starts to pound. "What's this?" He reaches for the book I am supposed to be studying. I know if he lifts it up he will see the others.

My mind starts to scream, 'What is she doing? Why-?'

"Will Roger Manning-Smith please come to the front desk, Mr Roger Manning-Smith, urgent please."

He stands up.

Breathing a sigh of relief, I turn and look up at him. He is staring at the book in front of me. He looks at me then turns and walks to the desk. I watch as he leans over and says something to the librarian and then walks out of the library. As soon as the doors close behind him I jump up and place the books I had been looking at back on their shelves. I take a couple of Medical Microbiology text books off the bookshelf and place them where I had been sitting, just in case he comes back. I have a strong feeling that he will.

*   *   *   *   *

I unlock the passenger door of my car and throw my bag onto the seat. As I walk around to the driver's side, a dark blue car pulls up next to my car. Roger lowers the window and looks at me.

"Drive carefully Billie, I don't want to hear any stories about you jumping any traffic lights tonight," he says.

I watch him speed off in his car.

CHAPTER 11

As I drive to Jamie's house I find myself constantly looking in my rear-view mirror. Roger's words play on my mind. Had he been the one in the car the night we went to the club? I think hard trying to remember if I had mentioned the incident to anyone at work, anyone that could have repeated it to Roger. No one springs to my mind.

I pull into Jamie's drive and park my car next to his. As I walk towards the front door it opens, Jamie and a man step out.

"Billie, how are you? I've heard so much about you," the man says. I look at his handsome face, his striking blue eyes, knowing that I have seen him or his picture before.

"Hi Billie," Jamie says, "this is Dave Pemberton, we were in Troyston together."

Smiling I reach out and shake the hand he has extended.

"Nice to meet you Dave."

"Nice to meet you Billie," he stands smiling down at me, I notice that Jamie is a little distant. "I was just going, I'll see you again Billie. Jay-Jay let's all get together soon. Do tea." I sense sarcasm and see Jamie's eyes narrow. Dave walks towards his car, opens the door and climbs in. He horns twice then drives off.

"Did you get the tape from Liam?" I ask.

"Tape and CD," Jamie replies as we both walk into his house.

"Have you listened to the songs yet?"

"No I was waiting for Dave to leave."

"Why?"

"He has been here three times trying to get me to rejoin the band. Says he is trying to re-launch Troyston and get on the gravy train. He can't seem to understand I can never go back to that life."

I understand and nod. "I have our contract here. Steve added the changes yesterday. Are you sure you want to go ahead with this?"

"You're joking right? Give me the papers and a pen."

$$* \quad * \quad * \quad * \quad *$$

"Play it again" I say really excited.

Jamie presses the rewind button and then the play button. We sit and listen to the songs again. It is not that often that cover songs sound better than their original version. Sometimes a song can sound different but equally good when sung by two different artists. Take for example the case of *Dolly Parton* and *Whitney Houston* and the song 'I Will Always Love You'. Once in a while however; the artist singing the cover song puts everything into it, taking the song to new heights, making it theirs. As I listen to the songs, I know that this is definitely one of those occasions.

$$* \quad * \quad * \quad * \quad *$$

"Trudi I think the make-up is a little too much," I say as I look at the foundation and lipstick on Jamie's face.

"I know it looks that way Billie, believe me it won't show. The light that we will be using will sort of deflect it. You see, because what you want is a large glossy postcard with a black background, we need to put a little more make-up on. Trust me, we do it at the magazine all the time."

I watch her walk over to Jamie and ruffle his hair again, then adjust his shirt. She walks back over to the camera and looks through the lens. She takes a couple of pictures.

"Jamie, can you put the other shirt on please," Trudi says.

"Sure, keep these trousers."

"Well you can lose them, if you want."

"Are you flirting with my artist?" I ask.

"No, Billie, I was only joking," she blushes and I hide the beginning of a smile as I look from one to the other. Trudi bends her head and concentrates on her work. She measures, she adjusts, she re-focuses her lens. I listen to the music playing and watch her work.

"That's it. It's done, these pictures are going to be good."

"When will they be ready?" I ask.

"I'll bring them round day after tomorrow."

"Good, thanks."

"Not a problem. He looks good in white, light blue and beige shirts on top of jeans, preferably blue jeans. Go for tight T-shirts because of his abs and I think dark brown, dark blue and if you want to be adventurous, dark green," she says matter-of-factly as she packs her things away.

"Is that right?" I ask and smile.

"Err…, yes…., I umm…, I believe so."

*   *   *   *   *

I hear the bleeper going off and I struggle to sit up. I am on call tonight. It is nearly two in the morning, because I was working on different strategies for Jamie I only went to bed an hour ago. Yawning I pick up my mobile phone and call the hospital.

I drive to the hospital to process the urine sample of a child with a high temperature and stomach pains. It is now after two and I clear my mind of Jamie, and concentrate on work. I park my car and walk into Accident & Emergency. I show the A&E nurse my identification badge and pick up the sample then walk towards the building that houses my department. I swipe my card and key in my pin number. The door opens and I walk into the dark, quiet, building. In the lift I look at the sample noting that it is a pale clear yellow liquid.

I walk towards the laboratory knowing that I will not be here for long and hoping that I will not get called out again. I turn the lights in the laboratory on and lock the door behind me. In five minutes I have examined the urine under the microscope for blood cells, bacteria and casts. I put a loop-full of the urine onto a plate of solid agar media, to grow anything that may be present, and incubate the plate in the 37°C incubator. There were no blood cells, bacteria or casts in the sample and I telephone the doctor who requested the test, to inform him of the results. I take off the disposable gloves, bin them, take off my lab coat, wash my hands and pick up my bag from the side office. The phone starts to ring as I am about to leave the laboratory. Thinking that it is the doctor calling to ask for another test I answer it.

"Hello."

"Is that the Microbiologist on call?"

"Yes," I reply.

"My name is Jade Naylor, Head of Security. We have had a report of strange noises coming from your floor, can you please stay in your laboratory until I come and get you and escort you out. Please don't panic, just stay in the laboratory with the doors locked."

"Okay," I say, panicking.

Five minutes later he knocks on the door, I check his identification through the glass panel and then open the door.

* * * * *

Holding the knife tightly in his hand, he watches as the security man walks with Billie to the lifts. His other half is getting crazier each day and he is worried. Gripping the knife handle he walks towards the stairs. He has to make sure that Billie gets home safely.

* * * * *

I sit back and look at the pictures of Jamie. They are really good, the make-up is barely visible. I choose five pictures and write the words *'Jamie Sanders - Who I Am Not'*, in white ink on them. I put a picture, an audio tape and a short artist blurb or biography into a large Jiffy envelope. I address the envelopes to the heads of the Artist and Repertoire or A&R, at SONY, EMI, ARISTA, XZEL and VIRGIN records. I wait for the replies.

* * * * *

While I wait for replies, I set a schedule for Jamie. He has a lot of spare time as he only works part-time as a voluntary vocal coach, with a children's choir.

Having managed his money shrewdly during his Troyston days he does not need to work. He asks questions as I go through the schedule with him.

"Why dancing lessons now?"

"It is better we do it now so that when we get the call from a record label, you are up to scratch. If you have your craft together now, when opportunity knocks, you will be ready," I reply.

"Doesn't the record company take care of this though."

"Theoretically they do, from my short time with Nu-Force I know that in most cases the artist pays the bill. The record label will try to recoup most of its expenses. What they can't recoup, they write off as a tax loss anyway."

"You know about all that? When I was with Troyston we didn't have a clue. We were given so many things we didn't stop to think that one day we would have to pay for them. Nothing was free, we had to pay for the cars, the plush flats, the expensive clothes and the one thousand and one other little things. We were all so young and naive at the time, we thought that all the things we got were 'freebies'. I only found out recently that for the first year when we sold tens-of-millions of records, we were in debt. Troyston in debt!" He chuckles softly and shakes his head in disbelief.

"It has happened to so many artists in the past, it probably will continue to happen to many more in the future. I hope and pray it doesn't happen to us. I don't think it will."

"You sound confident."

"I am, very confident. I have checks in place to ensure that things are done properly and money is properly managed. Accountants to check the accounting of my accountants. Regardless of all that, what we need to do is be sharp at the start. You saw in Troyston that there are no freebies, everything in this business has a price tag attached. So instead of complaining like a lot of artists about the record company getting all the money, we do what smart groups like 'Simply Red' did, we go for a smaller up-front payment and larger royalties. I believe in your abilities Jamie and I am trusting in God to help me with mine. Are you with me on this?"

There is no doubt in his eyes, not even an iota of uncertainty whatsoever.

"Yes," he replies.

CHAPTER 12

W orking with the colours that Trudi has suggested, I watch as Jamie tries on some of the clothes that he has brought round to my house.

"See what I want, is for you to be ready to go. Have your own style of clothes, your own look. In Troyston there were four of you so you could disappear and still be visible. As Jamie Sanders you are on your own, you have to be comfortable with yourself before people feel comfortable with you. You have to express your own style, I don't want anyone tampering with what you want to be. When you don't have your own identity, people can try and make you into something they feel you should be and not who you really are. People who are supposed to work with and for you can try to control you when you are not confident about who you are and what you want to achieve. They can slap a label on you. Fortunately, I don't see you like that."

"So how do you see me?"

"Elegant, casual and very confidently stylish or panache as they say now."

"Panache, I can do panache. I am what 'they' call a regular Mr *Je Ne Sais Quoi,*" he says and laughs. Tastefully he sits down and crosses one leg over the other.

"They?" I query. "So you have it err.., but, can you dance?"

"To be confidently stylish or have panache, I must be able to dance?" He asks.

"No, but I can see you need help being confidently stylish, I just need to know if you need help in the dancing department as well," I say laughing. He stands up and turns my radio on, *Kirk Franklin's* latest song is playing, he increases the volume and nods his head to the music. He starts to dance. Impressed I watch him. He is good.

"Now you're not just going to sit there and watch are you?" He asks. Smiling I get up and dance with him.

We are still deep in plans a couple of hours later. It is late and I am making dinner for us while Jamie looks through one of my books containing all the top forty hits of the '80s.

"That smells good, what about this one?" He asks pointing to a song that was number one for five weeks.

"Not quite you," I say.

"What about 'Trapped'?"

"By *Colonel Abrams*?" I ask.

He nods and hums the chorus.

"No one has done it recently, it could be a maybe," I say as I put the plates on the table. We jump in and out of topics.

"Did you check with Martin?" He asks.

"Yes, he is going to have a word with a few people he knows who own clubs. Hopefully in a couple of weeks you'll be doing a few showcases so you can get the feel of being out there on your own."

"Sounds good and that looks good."

"Let's eat," I say.

*   *   *   *   *

It has been three weeks since I sent the tapes out and I have not got any replies yet. I have done follow-ups with a phone call but apart from a couple of rude negative responses, nothing. I find that everything I do now is centred around music. I watch all the music channels on cable and I keep a constant eye on the music charts. I have amassed a lot of information from the internet. I know how the music and video charts are compiled by the Official UK Charts Company. I know how many singles were sold weekly by all the number one artists in the two previous years.

I also know that compared to what is out there in the charts now, the two songs that Jamie has done are on the same par if not better. So what I can't understand is why the record companies are not banging on my door. Why a few people that I know in the music industry, whom I have asked to listen to the songs, are now avoiding my calls. I was so sure when I started that this was going

122

to be a piece of cake, that once the A&R people listen to the songs; they would see what I saw, feel what I felt.

I know that it will happen, I just don't know when. Sometimes I feel like shouting from the roof-tops at them, "Can't you see that this is going to be big…, huge…, massive…."

*   *   *   *   *

"Natasha I need a number."

"Who is this?"

"I'm hurt, after how many years together, you don't recognize my voice?"

"Wayne?"

"I don't have time for games Nat, I need a phone number."

"Whose?"

"Billie's."

"You want me to give you my cousin's phone number after what you did to her? You're joking right?"

"No Natasha I am not joking and there seems to be a little lapse in your memory darling. You should have said after what 'we' did. Look give me the number now or I will come round and get it."

"I don't have it Wayne, even if I did I wouldn't give it to you and no my memory is still intact, you came on to me, remember?"

"We have been through this so many times. Now is not the time for playing the blame game or for fake loyalties. We were together for two years, not one day did I hear you say no to me. Not when I came on to you or when we were in her bed. Give me her number Natasha."

"Why, you need her to write some more 'hit' songs for you?"

The silence is tense.

Wayne puts the phone down and gets out of his car. He walks to the dark green front door and rings the bell.

The door opens slightly, Natasha's head appears, she is still holding the phone against her ear. Seeing Wayne at the door she freezes and drops the phone.

He pushes her front door in ignoring the fear in her eyes. He grabs hold of her arm, and pulls her kicking and screaming into the house.

*   *   *   *   *

"…Look Billie love, don't take this the wrong way but do you really know what you are doing?" Dave asks me on the phone.

I grimace at his patronizing voice. He has phoned me several times and I have no idea where he got my phone number from. Jamie categorically denies giving it to him. I sigh, the last thing I need is the voice of gloom, doom and discouragement.

"Yes Dave," I say in a really cheerful voice, "I know exactly what I am doing."

"You don't seem worried."

"There is nothing that worrying can do, so what is the point of worrying?"

"You are a strange 'bird' you know, you got Jamie listening to vocal lessons on CD, touching his diaphragm, breathing funny and saying 'arrrrrr' everywhere."

"That's just to help him breathe properly while he sings. I know what I'm doing."

"Do you? Jamie is part of Troyston, that's who he is, you can't make him something he is not. Now there is a lot of money to be made if we put the band back together and tour. We would have sell out gigs everywhere and if you know anything about this business, which you obviously don't, the rule of thumb is that we will pick up at least 70% of the tour fee. Unless he writes his own material as a solo artist he won't make 'didly squat', 'nada', you know I'm right."

"Jamie is Jamie. He was part of a group now he needs to prove himself as a solo artist. I am trying to get him out there with a new and different image, his audience has changed, he has changed. Speak to him Dave, listen to him when he talks about his dreams, it's obvious what is in his heart."

"Typical woman! I'm talking about money here and you are going off at a tangent talking about heart and feelings. Wake up Billie, this is the real world,

124

fairy tales are for the weak. I need Troyston back together, now are you in with me? I could make it worth your while."

"What!"

"I need you to agree with me that Jamie should -"

"But I don't agree with you. Jamie needs to fulfill *his* dream. To do that he needs to perfect his skills, work hard, write songs and prepare for the success that will come. Success that will involve *him* doing personal appearances, going on tour to Europe, Japan, America, making great records, signing publishing deals. The money will come but it's not just about money."

"What drug are you on Billie? Are you sure you're not hooked on some dud supply? So what is it about if not the money? I really think that you should cut your losses now, you're obviously on a road to nowhere."

"I know what I'm doing."

"Do you? Are you really sure about that? Are you sure that you're not holding him back? Not allowing him to move forward?"

"Of course I'm not holding him back," I reply shocked and hurt at his insinuation.

"That's what you say, maybe he would have moved a lot further and faster with a geezer managing him, have you thought about that?"

"I don't think so Dave, there are a lot of artists out there now, especially male solo artists. You have to play the market, I want Jamie to come out when the competition is a little lighter."

"I don't agree, I think he needs to jump in there and slog it out with the other singers, the 'Robbies', the 'Ronans', the 'Wills'-"

"He will, when the condition and time is right-"

"Oh and when will that be, when you pray about it?"

"Dave, can you not see it?"

"See what?" He asks.

"You really can't see it, can you?" I sigh. "Sometimes Dave, you have to stand still to move forward. Jamie will be out there with them on a different level anyway. His music is different. His sound is different, it's more Contemporary R 'n' B, Soul, Contemporary jazz with a hint of Pop."

125

"Yeah right and my name is Davinia and I'm the lead singer in an all girl band."

"What?"

"I feel that your head is in the clouds and the light air up there is affecting you and your judgement. I know someone, in fact a number of people that could easily take Jamie off your hands. They would pay you double what you have invested already, easily. This one guy in particular, a veteran in the music world, a real 'hard-nose' geezer, has let it slip that he would pay you as much as four times what you have already invested, for Jamie's contract. Everyone agrees with me that a geezer would manage him differently, be a lot more 'butch' about it, get things done. Even Jamie."

"What?"

"You have to admit you have a soft touch about things."

"No I don't, I just believe that it will happen. I don't disbelieve that and I never will. So I tend to see the people that say negative things now as not realizing the potential here. *John Denver, Elvis* even the *Jackson Five* were rejected when they first started out. Come to think of it, I don't think that many really good 'evergreen' artists, were not rejected when they first started out."

"What you think that Jamie…"

It suddenly dawns on me that I am wasting my time, "Look Dave I have to go, bye." I replace the receiver and sit back in my chair. I don't normally let Dave get to me but today he has succeeded. I pick up my car keys and bag, and leave the house.

*   *   *   *   *

"Hello gorgeous."

I smile at the 'body building' owner of the gym and shake my head at the large platter of chicken and the two huge glasses of yellow milky fluid on the counter in front of him. His protein fix, he calls it. A lot of food, I call it.

"Hi Gary, have you seen Jamie?" I ask.

"Cardiovascular," he replies and takes a big bite of chicken.

"Lunch?" I ask.

"Snack," he replies smiling. "Billie tell Steve and Martin that the new equipment and weights we talked about have come. I'll be setting it up today, they can come down from tomorrow and try them."

"Will do," I head towards the cardiovascular section at the back of the gym. I find Jamie cycling away and listening to something on his personal CD player. He sees me and pulls his headphones off.

"Billie! What are you doing here? I thought you said you trained this morning."

"I did. I need to talk to you Jamie and I need you to be honest."

"Okay," he climbs off the stationary bike and walks with me to the front of the gym. He sits down at the table and wipes the sweat off his brow, I sit down opposite him so I can see his face.

"I had Dave on the phone a few minutes ago, he-"

"He was going on about things not progressing, right?"

"Yes, has he spoken to you about it?"

"Only over a hundred times. Look Billie, Dave has it in his head that if we get Troyston back together, have this big comeback, we can cash in. It's not what I want and it's not what I'm going to do, he knows it, so he's trying to work on you. Get you to pull out of our contract."

"I don't believe him! He said that even you agreed with him."

"What exactly did he say to you?"

"The usual, I won't be taken seriously because I'm a 'bird' and that I may be holding you back, that maybe you would have progressed a bit more if I were a geezer."

"I take you seriously, believe me I wouldn't be in this gym if I didn't, if I wasn't scared that you'd kick arse. Namely mine."

I smile.

"Billie, remember when we first met at Martin's club? You said something to me, you said that I was out there with *George Benson, Rick Astley, Jaheim, John Bon Jovi, Luther Vandross and Lemar.* You said that I was unique as well and that I was going to be big. No one has ever said anything like that to me before, even when I was in Troyston."

"You were listening?"

127

"I have never stopped listening to you, you say things that are beyond the here and now with so much confidence. I have never heard you say a word against anyone. There is something in you that makes me a better person. Something in you that shines. Do you understand what I'm saying?"

I nod.

"We are a team, a good team, I'm not looking for any other players, boss lady."

"Boss lady?"

He smiles, "Dave has a lot on his plate right now, I don't know why he keeps calling you. I still haven't found out how he got hold of your phone number."

"How is it going with his drug rehabilitation?" I ask.

"Slow, very slow. He won't admit that there is a problem. He can be very convincing sometimes."

"Hang in there."

He nods.

*　　*　　*　　*　　*

I smile as I listen to Dave on the phone. It has been two weeks since he last called. I listen and I say the occasional, "umm". He is obviously on a mission and I sense his frustration growing as he talks.

"No offence darling but you really think that record bosses will deal with you. Apart from the obvious, you being a 'bird', you haven't really got a clue have you?"

I breathe deeply, savouring the oxygen in my lungs before I answer, "Dave I have an understanding of how the system works, I have co-managed a group before and my being a lady has nothing to do with anything."

"Yes but-"

"No buts Dave," I interject, "everyone wants a piece of something good. It wouldn't matter if I was a man, woman, boy or girl. If I have something really good then people will be interested."

"Excuse me for pointing out the obvious but you do sound a little naive. DJs won't work with you, promoters will take the piss."

"How do you know?"

"I just know."

"How?"

"I've seen it happen, time and time again darling. This is a rat race, you have to be in it to win it, you are either in or out."

"In what exactly Dave? A race or hanging out with rats?"

"What?"

"Look Dave no disrespect, this is going to happen and right now I really don't need any negative vibes around me anymore. You have your views but I know that Jamie is too good for this not to happen. I'm going to have to go, I have to get to the gym. Take care and I'll talk to you soon. Bye." I hang up.

I do the best thing one can do for negativity, I draw a line of action through the negative line and make it a positive. My line of action - I make five more copies of Jamie's demo tape and package them. I address the envelopes to five more record companies and put stamps on the packages. On my way to the gym I stop at a mail box and slot the packages in.

*　*　*　*　*

Dear Billie

I am writing in response to the demo that you recently sent to us. Having listened to it we have decided that it is not suitable for our current repertoire.

However please do not hesitate to send any future projects that you feel may be of interest.

Finally I apologize for the delay in responding to you and for sending a photocopied letter. I receive a lot of demo tapes/CDs every day and I am unable to respond to everyone with a personal letter.

Good luck and best wishes.

Yours sincerely

I read my first letter of rejection again. Since I got it two days ago I have read it over ten times. When I first got this letter I was angry, then upset, then confused. I thought that there had been a big mistake, a mix up of tapes of some sort. It was not until I had played the tape that came with the letter that I realized they were rejecting Jamie. I phoned the record label and asked to speak to the sender. To my surprise his secretary came on the line and said that her boss was too busy to talk to me, and didn't feel the need to anyway. She suggested in a round-about-way, that I try another profession as she didn't think that I would do well in this one, because I felt the need to question her Manager's professional decision. She also added that I was lucky to even get a written reply; as most record companies just chucked bad material like mine, into the bin. Without waiting for me to respond she hung up.

I put the letter back into my kitchen drawer and go to prepare some more packages, to send out to more record companies. I can almost visualize Dave smirking at me, almost hear his words: *'I told you so darling'*, *'you're a bird'*, *'no one will take you seriously'*. I smile to myself, my comfort is in the knowledge that he is wrong. Just for Dave, I add a couple more packages.

*   *   *   *   *

"Phoebe if you don't do it now, when will you do it?" I ask.

"I'm not sure if it's ready, last time I sent it out I got so many rejections, I nearly packed the whole thing in."

"That was two years ago, the book has changed since then, you have changed. Believe me I have read your book twice. It is going to be a best seller."

"Thanks Billie, you always have this way of recharging me, saying the things I need to hear when things don't look too clear."

"I say it as I see it, plus, I blame this wise old woman who taught me well," she laughs.

"Right, that's it, I'm going to pray and then send a synopsis and three sample chapters out tomorrow."

"Do you pray specifically for things or generally?" I ask out of curiosity.

"Both," she replies.

"I read my Bible and a prayer guide every day, as well as pray generally. I thought that with that, anything that is meant to happen will just happen. I thought that if you have faith that is, believe and don't have any doubts then it will happen."

"That is true but I have always found Billie, that the best things happen when I pray about them specifically. I ask God to take control of the situation, and He gives me the best result. More than I asked for in the first place."

"Really?" I ask a little confused.

"Let's say for example, you want to make something that requires lots of different parts. You also need energy to make this thing work and a lot of energy to make it last."

"Okay."

"Which would be better, putting all the parts together and making this big thing, then giving it energy, or, taking each individual part and giving each part energy, and then putting them together to form this big thing and giving it some more energy?"

"Giving each individual part energy, putting them together and giving the big thing some more energy," I say.

"Exactly," Phoebe says, "I find it's like that with prayer, when you pray generally and then specifically as needs arise, you find that: (1) you are praying a lot more and (2) your prayers are more focused. It's something I've learnt recently and I find that it works."

"Did you pray when you sent your manuscript out the first time?" I ask.

"No, I rushed around doing everything by myself. I didn't get anyone to proof-read it. There were so many spelling and punctuation mistakes, as you saw when you read it then. Not long ago, I read a couple of books about the power of prayer and my life literally changed overnight. I read about how Jesus prayed constantly about everything, and how important talking to God constantly through prayer is. Now I pray generally as well as specifically for His favour. I don't do anything without praying first. If you look at the book of Proverbs in the Bible, the source of wisdom, it says in Proverbs chapter 16 and verse 3: *Ask the Lord to bless your plans and you will be successful in carrying them out.* I do that now every day in prayer with thanks and as each prayer is answered I continue to give thanks to God and I continue to pray that I do His Will. Try it and see. Have you heard about **P.U.S.H**?"

"Push? No I haven't. What is it?"

"It's an acronym which stands for 'Pray Until Something Happens'. One thing I have learnt Billie, and I tell it to everyone now, is this. Never look at a problem as bigger than God. When you do that, it's like you are saying that God cannot help you. You are actually putting a limit on what you think He can do, and He will never give you more than you can handle."

"I have never looked at it that way, I always thought that things happen when God wants them to."

"That's true but I think that there is more to it. I think that when you have complete trust and believe that nothing is impossible with God, then your expectations are placed completely in Him. We know that God knows what we want before we ask for it, but we still have to ask Him. That is when we know, that something did not happen because we made it happen, it happened because we trusted not in our own abilities but totally in His ability. Basically we need to focus on God not on our problems. Does that make sense?"

"Yes actually it does, my grandmother used to say the same-"

"Is this a private meeting or can anyone interrupt?" Nigel asks startling us. He is standing in the door way of the tea room staring at the ground. I wonder how long he has been there, I look at Phoebe, she shrugs.

"Err.., no Nigel you can come in and use the tea room we were just going back to work anyway," I say standing up.

"I didn't come to use the tea room, I came to give Billie a message," he says. I wait, he continues to stare at the ground and does not say anything.

Phoebe jumps up, "Sorry is it private, I'll go."

"No it's not private, someone called Jamie or Jaming or something like that called. He wants you to call him back."

"Thank you Nigel," I say.

Finally he looks up. He has a strange far away look in his eyes.

"I told him not to call you again," he turns quickly and walks away leaving me staring after him in shock.

CHAPTER 13

I listen to the words of *Helen Baylor's* song 'Hunger For Holiness' on Premier Christian Radio, as I sit in my front room. It has been six months since I sent the first demo tape out, six months of planning, hard work and more planning. I have tried everything, now after twenty eight rejection letters, some of them from really high profile people in the music industry; a number of pessimistic phone calls from Dave, I sit in front of all my plans, rejection letters, returned tapes and CDs. I wipe away my tears. Internally I push away the doubts hovering, waiting to take root. Externally I push everything on the table to one side, I place a piece of paper and a pen in front of me, bow my head and pray.

I pray for wisdom and God's guidance. As I sit on the floor in my front room with my head resting on my knees I ask God to show me what to do. I have tried everything and nothing seems to have worked. Six months ago I thought that within a few weeks we would have a breakthrough, I was so sure. Now I realize that it may take a little longer than I initially thought. The presenter on the radio reads a verse from the Bible: Proverbs chapter 16 and verse 3. As I sit quietly with my eyes closed the words take hold of me, I feel a sudden warmth, slowly it flows through me. Peaceful reassurance takes hold, and from somewhere deep inside I know, with God's help it *will* happen. I open my eyes and from deep within the realization hits me. In the last six months I have done exactly the same thing over and over and over again, and expected a different result. I pick up a pen and some paper. With calmness and peace I write my new 'changed' plans down. I make my vision real.

* * * * *

He sits with his head bent, his whole body is still. He is focused on one thing as he sits waiting. His eyes are shut and silently he prays for Divine favour, he asks God to bless his work, to give him success.

"Mr McKnight, they are ready now."

He stands up and walks behind the secretary into the large conference room.

She introduces him, "Gentlemen, Mr Philip McKnight."

"Good afternoon Gentlemen. Shall we start?" He says taking the initiative. He places his folder on the table and sits down. The five men seated around the table look at each other and then at him.

"Mr McKnight I have been nominated as the spokesman today and I start by welcoming you and thanking you for coming to Florida at such short notice. My colleagues and I have looked at your proposal and feel that it is a very generous one."

"What have you decided?"

The spokesman clears his throat, "We have spoken to our financial advisors and accountants, they have assured us that with your European merging bids, this venture will be a huge success. I take it you have signed the contracts with your partners in Europe?"

"Yes, I have the signed paper work here," Philip says handing the folder to him. The spokesman looks through it, and then passes it on to the man seated next to him.

"Mr McKnight, we know that there has been a lot of bad publicity involving your ex-partner. We know that you were vindicated and your company cleared of involvement."

"That is correct."

"We also understand that your ex-partner, who is currently serving a prison sentence for drug trafficking, will have no claims whatsoever to your company or this deal."

"None whatsoever."

"Congratulations Mr McKnight! We have ourselves here one of the biggest deals in the history of music involving the new DB Byte and the legal down loading of music and music videos from the internet amongst many other new things, congratulations."

*　　*　　*　　*　　*

"SURPRISE!" Trudi and Jen chorus on my front door step taking me completely by surprise.

"What's going on?" I ask looking from one face to the other and then at the paper bags containing foil food containers in their hands.

"Oh we just thought that as you've been too occupied to go out recently we'd take you out to eat," Trudi says pushing past me.

"Then we had an even better idea, so here we are," Jen adds.

"So you both thought you'd take me out to eat at my house?" I ask as I close the door.

"Exactly, let's eat while it's hot. Jen can you get the plates please, Billie can you get the glasses."

"Yes ma'am," Jen says pulling me into the kitchen.

"Have you spoken to Martin recently?" She asks as she opens a cupboard and takes out some plates.

"Yes, I spoke to him yesterday. Why?"

"Nothing," She says vaguely and walks out of the kitchen. I follow her back into my front room. Trudi is sitting back reading through my new plans. I cough and she looks up smiles and continues to read. I cough again and she looks up.

"Oh, sorry," she says putting the papers down, "I like the way you have written everything down Billie. It makes it more real. How come you have two different sets of plans?"

"The first set, the one on the lined paper is something I did months ago. They are the things I wanted to happen, things I spent months trying to make happen."

"Let me see," Jen says putting her plate laden with food on the table and picking up the papers.

"So what are these then?" Trudi asks.

"Those plans are the plans I wrote down after praying for wisdom and direction from God. I was sitting here one evening listening to Premier and praying about everything, asking the 'why' questions and getting a little emotional when I heard something on the radio. It was like a direct Word in season. A number of thoughts came to my mind and I had this strong urge to write everything down so I wouldn't forget."

"The second set of plans are really detailed and clear. It's amazing because even though they look similar the second set feels real," Jen says.

"I felt the exact same thing when I read them, and I know they will happen because God always makes provision for your vision when you trust Him and even though it may not happen when we want it to, it will happen," Trudi says.

"Delay does not mean denial," Jen adds.

"Amen to that," I say "It's the power of prayer, it's amazing what prayer can do," I sit back, we eat and talk.

"What's Jamie schedule like this week?" Trudi asks casually as we pack the food containers away and take the plates to the kitchen.

I feel a weight behind the question, "How do you know he has a schedule?" I smile and Trudi tries to conceal her embarrassment.

"I've seen it, remember when I took the pictures?"

"Yes, I remember when you took the pictures."

"He was looking at it then."

"His schedule?" I ask and wink at Jen. We start to laugh.

"Don't make me come over there," Trudi threatens.

"Okay, okay, he has dancing lessons, vocal training and fitness training for now."

"He's taking them very seriously," Trudi says to herself.

I don't laugh.

* * * * *

As we head to the ice cream palace in Jen's car I wonder why I have agreed to come with them. After the meal Trudi said she felt like some ice cream and because I didn't have any at home, they had insisted on going to get some. I had hoped for an early night today. Managing Jamie and working full time is beginning to affect me. I always seem to feel tired.

"We are here sleepy head," Trudi says pulling me out of my light, well earned luxuriate doze.

We sit down and drool over the pictures of the different deserts on the menu and those that are displayed on the walls. I look at the picture of the slice of double chocolate cheesecake served with a double scoop of vanilla ice cream and chocolate sauce tenderly. I order one scoop of chocolate ice cream without the cheesecake or chocolate sauce. A waitress finishes taking our orders just as a mobile phone starts to ring. I smile as I notice that nearly everyone in the restaurant checks their phone. The ringing continues.

"Billie."

I look up, "Yes."

"Err, I think it's yours," Trudi says.

I quickly reach into my pocket, and pull out the phone that is still ringing.

"Hello."

"Hello, can I speak to Mr B. Lewis please?"

"Mr Lewis, no you've made a mistake it's Miss Billie Lewis and she is me. How can I help you?"

"My name is Jasmine Peters, I work for XZEL Records."

My heart starts to beat rapidly and I hold my breath as I start flapping my hand up and down. Jen and Trudi stare at me. Jasmine Peters continues, "I received the demo tape you sent and I have listened to it a number of times. I love the voice. Does Jamie have any original material?"

"We are working on some."

"Can you send me something that shows his voice projection. The songs you sent are covers and I want to hear how he handles something that hasn't been done before."

"Okay."

"I look forward to getting something soon then Billie."

"As soon as possible," I say.

She gives me her office phone number and her mobile phone number and tells me to call her as soon as the song is ready, then she hangs up. I look from Jen to Trudi and then at my phone.

"Oh my, oh my-" I struggle to get the words out.

"Who was that?" They both ask.

My heart is pounding with excitement as I tell them.

*   *   *   *   *

As I listen to Jamie sing the words of a song I wrote three years ago I am overwhelmed with emotion. This is a song I had written when the hurt in my life was so severe, that I honestly did not think that things would ever get better. I will never forget the day that Jen had turned up on my doorstep three years ago, and asked me if I was really happy. She waded through my hostility, coldness and desperate need to be alone that day, to indulge in my tearful self pity, and said something that I will never forget. She said, *'I see pain in your eyes Billie, pain that I know. Even when you smile. It's hidden so well that the others don't see it but I do. You are pretending to be happy and in love, but one thing I do know now is that love is not supposed to hurt.'* That was when I wrote the song. It was my way of healing as well as telling other people what I had been told. *'If a person loves you they don't intentionally hurt you'*.

"What did you think Billie?" Liam asks, "personally I think it's excellent, I think you guys are going to blow XZEL Records away."

I smile and nod my head as he continues to ask me questions, then answers them himself in his excitement. I notice that Jamie is reading something in my song book. Liam's front door bell rings and he excuses himself and leaves the room. I walk over to the booth where Jamie is still reading something and knock on the glass door.

"Err Billie, umm…, I was just looking at some of your other songs," he quickly closes the book and stands up. A piece of paper falls to the ground.

"What's that?"

"What?" He asks looking at the paper then back at me.

"Jamie, that piece of paper just fell on the floor. What is it?"

"Oh, this," he bends and picks it up, "it was in your book. I know you only gave me your book so I could practice 'Love Is Not Supposed To Hurt' but I started looking at your other songs and this one was folded away at the end of the book. I'm really sorry I didn't realize that it was personal until I actually read it." He holds the paper up. Frowning I take it and unfold it. I look at the words on it and then read them:

INVISIBLE PAIN

Chorus
No one sees it
but I can feel it

138

No one sees me when I cry
all I do night and day is lie.
It's an invisible thing
but believe me it's real
and alone some of us never heal.........

Verse 1
So how did this start
when did I first let you break my heart
Was it when, was it when I tried to pretend
that the pain was a lie, that the pain would soon end.
Each time you hurt me you take me so low
I can't tell anyone it feels like I have nowhere to go.
It's all insane, I'm living a lie I can't explain
So caught up, so wrapped up, in this invisible pain.

Chorus

Verse 2
Sometimes there are no bruises
No marks or contuses
No one can see my scars inside
I don't let them in, within me I hide
For me it's hurtful words, what is it for you?
Go on be truthful that's the only way we'll make it through.
Let's not put up with this hurt and silent abuse
Let's not keep making excuses after excuse.
See, I'm breaking free of these shackles, breaking free of this shame
I know now that I don't have to live with this invisible pain....

Chorus to fade....

"Billie? Billie are you okay?"

"I'm fine, really I'm fine," I say staring at the words on the paper; remembering the day I wrote them.

"Guys," Liam says from the door. We turn to the door, he is standing in front of someone, "this is Bryronni, she is England's answer to shall we say an 'early' *Britney*, I have to play a couple of tapes for her and her manager downstairs. I'll be back in 10 minutes."

"Hi guys," Bryronni says shyly.

"Hi," we chorus.

The door closes and I am left alone with Jamie and my song.

"Is this about your abusive relationship with Wayne?"

I grimace at his bluntness.

"Some of it, some of it is just about anyone going through the same thing in a different form." I walk back over to the mixing board and sit down. Jamie follows then sits next to me.

"Did he hit you?"

"No, he was too smart for that, he played with my mind which can be just as bad. I was young and sort of believed him when he said he would never let me go or if I broke up with him, I wouldn't find anyone else, I would end up alone, sad, and miserable. Sounds so stupid now but for some reason, at the time I really believed him, I was so…., scared."

He puts an arm around my shoulder and pulls me gently against him. "How did you get out of the relationship, emotionally I mean?"

"Divine intervention. The bubble burst and I saw him for the control freak he was. I never looked back. In a way it's made me realize that I don't have to settle for just anything, that's why I haven't."

"Now I see why you are so strong."

"Things, experiences happen for a reason, they happen so we can learn, grow stronger and help others," he raises his eyebrows and I see the question in his eyes. I explain, "When you have an experience you are supposed to learn, when you learn you grow, when you grow you can help others. That is the reason for the experience."

"Hemingway?" Jamie asks and smiles.

"No, Billie Lewis after a lot of help," I reply returning his smile. He pulls me into his arms and hugs me. At first I freeze, then I realize that his hug is a hug of reassurance. I breathe deeply and hug him back. I think I will feel embarrassed when he lets me go, I don't.

"When you get established I want you to sing this song."

"Are you sure?"

"Very sure, I'll just re-write some of the lines, add a 'bridge' and maybe a third verse, then it's yours."

*　　*　　*　　*　　*

Producing an original song is very hard work. As I sit with Liam in his studio for the third consecutive evening this week I see just how much work it takes. It seems as if Jamie has sang the song over a hundred times in twenty different styles. Tonight we are doing the backing vocals with a lady called Sade. I sit and listen as Liam harmonizes the two voices together. I watch as Jamie and Sade joke about in the recording booth during a five minute break and smile.

"Okay let's do it again," Liam says, "when you get to the last word of each line of the chorus raise your voice a little. This will help me harmonize the vocals to the music, thanks guys." Sade and Jamie give him the thumbs up sign.

I listen and learn. I watch everything Liam does on the mixing board. I notice that Liam is a word perfect producer, every single word has to be clear and sound perfect.

Three hours later we have finished. Liam says that he will need a couple more days to do some mixes and final touches. Jamie and I make the mistake of asking him to do it in one day.

"One day! One day? You cannot rush a professional, was *Beethoven* rushed? Is *Andrew Lloyd Webber* rushed?"

"No Liam," Jamie and I chorus, realizing our mistake.

"You know my policy."

"Anything that leaves this studio must sound good," Sade says.

"Exactly, I'll give you a call as soon as it is ready. I'm going to put it on CD and audio tape. A CD will look and sound better."

"Thank you Liam," we chorus again.

He smiles.

CHAPTER 14

I hear someone calling my name but I am too tired. I feel someone touch my hand, my head jerks upwards. I have been dozing in one of the armchairs at the back of the library. My heart is racing as I glance at my watch. I look around. Nigel is sitting in an armchair in the opposite corner of the small alcove, that I have sought refuge in. He is staring at me.

"Late night?" He asks.

I don't answer, I'm sure I felt someone touch my hand.

"I tried to wake you, nothing seemed to work. What were you up to last night then?"

I glance at my handbag on the floor and back at him.

"You should be careful with your bag, you never know who could be up to what these days," he gets up and walks away.

I pick up my bag and look through it. I am so tired it is unbearable. After three nights in the studio and two nights of being on call prior to that, I am washed out. I don't know how long I can keep this up. I cannot do both jobs and I know which one I want to do.

* * * * *

I get the phone call from Liam two days later. I feel his excitement on the phone. "Billie it sounds hot, good, BRILLIANT."

"When can I pick it up?"

"I'll bring it to Martin's club tonight, you are going to be there aren't you?"

"Yes, what time will you be there?"

"Seven."

"I'll see you there. And Liam, thanks."

* * * * *

We are all at our usual table in Martin's now hugely successful club, talking. I haven't yet told Jamie that the song is ready I want to surprise him. The club is full because Martin has a group from the early nineties performing live tonight. I discreetly give Liam the thumbs up signal and he makes an announcement. Next the introduction of a song plays and I watch Jamie's mouth fall open as he listens to the song. Liam is right the song sounds really good, really brilliant.

As we listen to the last note fade everyone at the table starts to talk at once, everyone is excited. 'Jasmine Peters has to like this' I think to myself as I get caught up in the excitement with everyone else.

*   *   *   *   *

I am excited and at the same time, a little apprehensive as I slot the tape into the laboratory cassette player and press the 'play' button. I stand back with a number of people in the laboratory and listen to Jamie sing. I smile as I hear a few excited whispers of admiration. Chloe, Tina and Nigel are standing together. They are talking about something and not listening. The song ends.

"It sounds good, Billie," Roger says, a few of the others concur. Chloe and Tina are still talking; I feel a little hurt that they did not bother to listen, especially as they were the ones that asked me to bring it in and play it. I take the tape out of the player and put it in my pocket.

"Have you heard that new song by Brian Turner?" Chloe asks Tina as I walk past them back to my bench.

"No not yet," she replies.

"Err, Billie that sounded good," Chloe says. I turn and smile at her, I see something in her eyes and I realize that she does not mean it.

CHAPTER 15

"**W**hat's all this about you and XZEL?" Dave asks, walking into Jamie's front room carrying a large bottle of mineral water. No 'hello Billie', no 'how are you Billie?'. I look up from the plans I am working on not really wanting to tell him.

"They want an original song," I say reluctantly after a while.

"Have you got one?" He reads my plans over my shoulder.

"Yes, I have a copy here."

"What are you writing?"

"I'm updating the plans I made for Jamie, dancing lessons, vocal training, arranging dancers, working on more songs. Stuff like-"

"Whoa, what makes you think you will get that far. What if no one likes the song?"

"Have you heard it?" I ask.

"No, but-"

"Let me play it for you," I walk over to Jamie's player hoping that he gets back from the gym quickly. I don't really like being around Dave, his criticism is his one constant. Surprisingly the only positive thing his constant criticism does is, make me more determined to succeed. I slot the tape in the player and press the play button. As the song plays I watch Dave closely for his reaction. Even though he is quick to conceal it, I see shock in his eyes.

"Not bad," he says, "needs a bit more base though."

"We are doing a few more mixes, I'll let the producer know," I walk over to the player and take the tape out.

"Do you mind if I borrow the tape, I can play it to some people I know from back-in-the-day."

"Err…," I hesitate, "I can get a copy to you, this is the master copy. I still have other record companies that I want to send copies to."

"Other record companies? I thought it was only XZEL that requested an original song? Which other record companies?" He demands.

A little shocked at his tone, I decide to proceed cautiously.

"I just took out some insurance in case XZEL are not interested, I sent a copy of the song to a few other record companies, here and abroad."

"It's a good song, I still feel you need a man doing all the networking, managing Jamie and making any deals. No offence darling, but I still don't think that a bird, err.., sorry, lady, is needed. You got your head screwed on well Billie, but even a bloke like me, will get a better result. No offence."

"No offence taken," I say watching as he opens a bottle puts some tablets in his hand then quickly puts the bottle back in his pocket. He puts the tablets in his mouth and drinks some water. Even though his hands are quick I notice that the tablets are not regular painkillers. I also notice that even though he is making an effort to conceal what he is doing, he is doing it openly. It suddenly dawns on me that he never takes the tablets when Jamie and I are in a room. I wonder why. His mobile starts to ring, he quickly answers it.

He listens, looks at me strangely then walks out of the room.

*   *   *   *   *

"Did you get the tape?"

"No, I tried but she wouldn't give it to me," Dave replies.

"I want that tape and a copy of every other song she writes."

"That may not be possible, I-"

"Dave, I want the tape."

"She will not give it to me."

"Then steal it."

"Steal it!"

"I want to know everything she is doing."

"She doesn't trust or confide in me, how will I-?"

"You promised me Troyston, you failed. You still owe me money which I will not fail to collect; maybe a few broken bones will expedite my collection, or maybe I'll pay a visit to your step brother Marcus in hospital. I could follow you there and in your presence get my boys to break some of his bones."

"Please, look..., I..."

"I want her songs Dave, my company needs them."

"I can't do it, I can't steal her songs, she-"

The caller hangs up.

Fear grips Dave as he stares blindly at the phone.

*   *   *   *   *

"Is that Billie, spelt BILLY?" The male Scottish accented voice on the phone asks.

"No, spelt BILLIE," I reply.

"Okay I'll let her know you called, as I said, I was told that she is in a meeting now, she should be finished in an hour or so."

"Thank you, please tell her it's urgent, I've left five or six messages this week already."

"Will do."

Slowly I put the receiver down, I massage my temple. I don't understand what is going on, I personally gave Jasmine Peters the CD of the original song two weeks ago. Each time I call I am told she is in a meeting and will call me back but she never does. I know two weeks is not a long time but you either like a song or you don't like it.

There are thoughts at the back of my mind which I try to keep at bay, thoughts which I try to convince myself, are not relevant to this situation. As hard as I try the thoughts keep popping up.

*   *   *   *   *

"Hello, can I speak to Jasmine Peters please, my name is Trina Catrella from the New York office," I say disguising my voice.

"Hold on Ms Catrella, I'm transferring you."

Seconds pass, I hold my breath.

"Hello Jasmine here how can I help?"

I hang up and walk back to my car. I ask myself the question that everyone else has asked me during the last six weeks, *"What is going on?"*

I have made so many phone calls to Jasmine Peters' office and left so many messages, but she has not returned any of my phone calls. Not even to acknowledge receipt of them. I have had to walk around with a positive attitude for weeks knowing that something fishy was going on but not knowing what.

As I sit in my car parked opposite XZEL Records I stare at the building. All those times I was told she was in a meeting or she had just left the building were probably untruths. 'Well Ms Peters two can play at that game.' I think to myself as I get out of the car.

* * * * *

As I walk past the receptionist I smile confidently at her, I walk towards the lifts. She does not call me back, I don't think she even saw me. I have no idea which floor Jasmine's office is on but I am determined to find it. I walk towards the first lift that comes with the other people waiting. It is small and we cannot all fit inside so I step back and let some of the other people go in. I glance at the other people still waiting, they all look confident, I suddenly feel unsure about what I am about to do. I turn towards the reception and take a few steps then turn and walk back to the lifts. I stare at the floor as I think about what I should do.

"Are you okay?"

I look up at the elegantly dressed lady that has asked me the question, she looks familiar.

"Sorry?"

"I don't mean to pry, it's just you look a little nervous and you remind me of someone."

"Who?" I ask.

"Me," she replies and I look at her with confused eyes.

"I'm sorry, my name is Gladys and I manage a singer. Last year I was so frustrated with the way things were going and all the negative response I was getting from people in the music business. I was so fed up with some of the 'independent' con men that tried to rip us off with their friendly extortion tactics, don't get me wrong there are some really good independent record labels out there. Anyway, I snuck in here armed with some songs my artist had done. I didn't know who anyone was or where to go. Thanks to God the first office I walked into had this list of names and job descriptions on the wall. I managed to get the right people in here to listen to the songs. They signed my artist that week."

"Your artist?" I gasp, "you're LeeBeth's Manager!"

She nods, "it's really difficult to get into this building, you've come this far, don't turn back."

I am about to ask her if she knows Jasmine Peters when a lift comes, the door opens and I walk into the lift with Gladys and the other people waiting. Everyone gives their floor 'order' to the person pressing the buttons. I stare at the ground and say nothing.

"That's a nice brooch, unusual," Gladys says.

"Thank you," I smile as I touch the birthday gift Jamie had given me.

"I like the way they make them nowadays, don't you?" Realizing she is purposely making light conversation with me to help ease my nervousness, I smile and nod as I listen to her.

The lift stops on the fourth floor and she smiles at me, mouths "good luck" and walks out. I look at the number panel by the door, there are only two more floors left. I am the only one left in the lift. Keeping my finger on the 'door open' button I look out at the row of doors that line the two walls.

"Are you looking for someone?" A Scottish accented young man, casually dressed in jeans and trainers asks.

"Err, no I'm going to an office on the sixth floor," I say smiling as I move back into the lift and press the button. He walks into the lift as the door begins to close. The lift ascends.

"Umm, you don't work here do you?" He asks, sucking loudly on a sweet; reminding me of Luke.

"How do you know?" I ask.

"Call it a hunch."

The lift doors open on the six floor and I look out at the roof of the building, at the numerous sun chairs and tables.

"There are no offices on the sixth floor, but you can't tell from outside," the man says, "let's start again, my name is George Contanalis and I work on the fourth floor in A&R. You are?"

"Billie Lewis and I am looking for Jasmine Peters' office."

"Billie spelt BILLIE?" He questions.

"I've spoken to you on the phone haven't I?" I ask completely surprised as I remember having a couple of very short conversations with him on the phone.

"Two times, I work with Jasmine."

"I want to see Jasmine, I know this may sound stupid and unheard of but I want a straight answer from her about the song and my artist, and if she is not interested I want my CD back."

"She's interested all right, as I hear so are a number of other record labels. That's why she is giving you the run around. She's trying to figure out who wrote the song, so she can, shall we say, borrow it. If it's a hit she'll pay a little compensation, if it's not, everything gets buried. If she can swing it she'll try to get Jamie signed to her and then peddle him off to the highest bidder."

"What! I wrote that song and Jamie is signed up with me."

"You wrote 'Love Is Not Supposed To Hurt'? That's twice in one day you have impressed me. You have guts coming here to see her, many wouldn't. I found out a few days ago that she has done this a number of times and got away with it. I'm only telling you all this because I don't agree with it and I'm leaving. A word of advice, off the record, what ever you do stay away from Patchwork Records."

"The independent record label?"

He nods

"I got a letter from them a few days ago, then the manager, Derek Brown called and said someone had passed Jamie's demo on to him. He said that if I paid him three thousand pounds he would sign Jamie to his label."

"Did he tell you that the major record labels wouldn't be interested in Jamie? Or that the majors will short change both of you?"

"Yes, how did you know?"

"Don't fall for it, he and Jasmine are a tag-team, they have a good cop-bad cop routine. She co-owns Patchwork records with Brown. She frustrates you here and Brown sucks you in there."

Stunned I stare at him, "How is she able to do this and why?"

"How? Because none of the artists have ever had the balls to confront her, then again no one is able to get hold of her on the phone. She is good at her job so the management here turn a blind eye to her 'shinanigans'. Why? The money, the prestige and the greed, the list is endless, have you got time on your hands."

I follow George along a corridor on the fourth floor of the large building that houses XZEL Records. He stops in front of a door and knocks, I wait behind him.

"Jasmine, Billie Lewis to see you," he says. I hear a door in her office slam and for a second I think she has bolted out of the room. George moves aside, as I walk past him he smiles and discreetly holds a thumb up. I smile back.

"Billie! How are you? How did-?"

"I am fine thank you Jasmine."

She looks nervously at a door beside her large desk and back at me, "So Billie, how are you? I was going to call you today to talk about the song and Jamie."

"What about the song?" I ask.

"Nothing, it's really good. I just wanted to know who wrote it, if they have any more songs. You know."

"No Jasmine, I don't know. Explain it to me."

"Err, I was going to call you," she reiterates weakly.

"I gave you the song six weeks ago, I have left so many messages for you."

"I know, I know darling, I have been so busy."

"Busy? You acted like we were friends when I gave you the CD. All I asked then was if you liked it or didn't like it, you let me know. You said you would call me without fail the next day. That was six weeks ago." I emphasize the time period again.

"I was going to call you Billie, you know how it is with work. It's been so unbelievably busy darling. They expect me to work twice as hard as the men. It's such a dog-eat-dog world."

"Is it? It's funny that was why I actually thought that as a woman, you of all people, would understand how hard it is in this business. How no one wants to open a door to you, no one wants to give you a chance. You are just like the rest, actually you're worse! You must have gone through what I am going through now at one point. People constantly reminding you that you're a woman, people not wanting to give you a chance. Yet instead of giving a 'sister' a break you go out of your way to keep me down."

"Billie you are absolutely wrong, I was going to play the song for my boss and a few other colleagues and then call you."

"It's been six weeks, how long would it have taken to do that?" I look at her and she looks away, I see the truth in her nervous movements. "It gets very lonely at the top when you try to keep others down so you can rise up."

"You have got this whole thing wrong Billie, my colleagues are here, I'll play them the song and call you tomorrow."

"Play it for them now," I say calling her bluff.

"Now? Err, I need to schedule a meeting, err.., make sure everyone is there."

"You know what, don't worry about it. If you had felt the song was worth it in the first place you would have done that already. You obviously don't think that it is up to scratch."

"Oh but Billie I do, I was hoping to find out who wrote the song and if they have any more songs." I sense from her anxious eagerness that this is the first true thing she has said since I walked into her office.

"Why?" I ask.

"So that we could have err…," she pauses.

"Jasmine, I wrote the song. I know that you have your own ideas and plans, but before you set them in motion know this. I have taken out a copyright on that song and all my other songs; so if I so much as hear this song or anything similar anywhere, I will sue you." Her mouth falls open, I continue, "I want the CD I gave you, now please."

She opens a drawer, reaches inside and pulls out the envelope I had given her. Her hands shake as she holds the package up to me. I take the package from her and open it to make sure that it is the right CD. As I pull the CD out of the envelope the picture of a man I have never seen before falls out. On it are the words *'Thompson Turrell - Who I am not'*. I shake my head as I look from the picture to her, and back again at the picture. Not only had she planned to steal the song and my artist, she had planned to steal my idea and use it for someone else.

"Billie it's not what you think. I have to keep coming up with new things, new ideas. Look we could work together, forget Jamie, ditch him, let someone else pick up after him, stop flogging a dead horse. You think about number one, you, think about what we could do with you and your song."

"What?"

"I can get Jamie signed up with my management team, they have years of experience, you and I could work wonders with your song, we don't need Jamie in on this. Come on Billie, I need a break, you know how it is?" She begs.

"My heart bleeds. I'm not angry, I thank God. I'm so glad that we never signed up with XZEL records. You know something Jasmine? You'll never know just how glad," I put the package in my bag and leave.

*   *   *   *   *

"I can't believe it. Billie has changed completely."

"You heard it all then?" Jasmine asks looking at her boss, who emerged from behind the door next to her desk, seconds after Billie left.

"Every-single-word Jasmine, she has really grown up, it's unbelievable. A few years ago Billie wouldn't say boo to a ghost, now she has taken on the one and only 'hard woman', Jasmine Peters and won. Very disappointing Jasmine."

Fuming Jasmine slams her desk drawer shut. She looks at Wayne Campbell not sure what to do now, "At least we know that she wrote the song," she says.

"I knew that the first time I heard it," he replies.

CHAPTER 16

I have not told Jamie what happened in Jasmine Peters' office. I simply said she did not like the song, and that I was trying other record companies. The incident at XZEL has taught me a good lesson and I know that in my future dealings with any record company, I will follow certain guidelines. I don't believe that this is a dog-eat-dog world, I believe that people with a hidden agenda, try to make it look like that, so they find comfort in their wrong doing. If only people realized that no matter what, 'right' always wins, they would think twice about doing 'wrong'. Fight harder to resist the temptations.

*　*　*　*　*

"Billie wait," I stop and turn at Phoebe's voice. She rushes up to me and pulls me into the tea room. Most people have gone home already but she looks around making sure the room is empty then she screams. My heart stops then quickly restarts as I look at her.

"I got this today Billie, read it," she eventually says when she comes up for air. I take the letter from her hand and read it. My eyes stare at the words:

'We love your book, we would like to publish it as we are sure that it will...'

I stop reading the letter and scream. There are tears in my eyes as I hug her.

"Phoebe this is brilliant! Thank God! This is so good."

"I got a call from the American publishers, they are going to simultaneously publish it there. They want me to come over for the promotion next month. They are talking about a movie and me writing the screenplay and script with their people over there."

"A movie?" I ask, excitedly stunned.

She nods, I see tears in her eyes, "If you had not encouraged me Billie I would have given up."

"No you wouldn't. You prayed and your prayers have been answered," I say hugging her again.

"To think, if I had got that grade three job then, I wouldn't have been able to do this. It's a dream come true, a blessing." We look at each other and count to 3.. then scream and scream and scream.

*   *   *   *   *

The loud screaming of the train on the tracks as it rushes forward to its destination does not disturb Jamie. He is asleep in the seat opposite me as I read the newspaper, we are on a train to Leicester. From time to time I look up at him and smile as he snores softly. I turn the page of the evening newspaper and words jump out at me making me catch my breath. 'Appoint To Disappoint' by Phoebe O'Connor is number one for the second week on the best sellers list. There is a short synopsis of the book and a brief biography about the writer. They are calling her book a phenomenal success. I smile as I read the book's review.

"What are you looking so pleased about?" Jamie asks.

"Phoebe's book is still number one. According to this she has several chat show appearances here and in America-," my mobile starts to ring.

"Hello."

"Billie, hi it's Steve. How's it going?"

"Fine, we're on the train heading to Leicester. We should be there within the hour or so."

"Listen, I know I probably didn't sound as positive as I should have and I know you and Jamie have put a lot of hard work into this..."

Silence.

"Steve?"

"Umm.. 'Tubbyless', what I'm trying to say is sorry. The last thing you need right now is for me to be over cautious. I know you know what you are doing, you're also my little sister and I still feel I have to look out for you."

"I understand."

"Just take care and all the best sis. I love you."

"I love you too, see you when we get back and thanks."

I put my phone in my bag and fold the paper. I pull out the map of our intended journey and look at it.

I have taken two weeks annual leave to do this and despite all the initial opposition I was determined to go ahead. Determined to stop doing the same thing over and over but to try something different.

With Martin and Liam's help I have booked Jamie to appear in five clubs starting tomorrow. Our first stop is a club in Leicester. From there we are going to Manchester, Blackpool, Liverpool and finally Cardiff. Five clubs in five different locations.

A lot of people, especially Dave, thought that I was reaching too high too quickly. I tried to explain that this is right and the timing is right as well. I want to get Jamie out there, get him to the public. Every time I went over my plans with people they were knocked down. Dave was the worse. So I stopped going over my plans.

Jamie welcomed the idea of doing the clubs and stood up to anyone that knocked it. I am so happy that he can see what I am trying to do. In a band you can get lost in the crowd. There is so much going on that your personality and character can be hidden. As a solo singer it's all about you on stage. You are on your own so if you can't handle it with small crowds you will have problems with larger ones. This is a promotion as well as a character building expedition. I am hoping it will go well.

*   *   *   *   *

"Ladies and gentlemen, lads and lasses make some noise for Jamie Sanders. You saw the flyers, heard the adverts on the radio, now here he is all the way from London." The crowd of about one hundred people cheer as Jamie walks onto the stage. I have all three Digital Audio Tapes or DATs with Jamie's backing music on in my hand. I hand the first one to the DJ as Jamie woos the crowd.

"Are you having a good time?"

"Yeahh!" They chorus.

"C'mon you can do better than that people, are you having a good time?"

"YEAHH!" They chorus again, much louder this time around.

"Good, good," he nods and I tell the DJ to start the music. He starts the first song. I don't know what to expect but no one is dancing and I do not know if this is a good thing or not. I watch as a couple of very hefty bouncers walk around the club. They talk into their head microphones and then walk up to a man, take hold of each arm and walk him towards the exit. The first song comes to an end and there is complete silence. I hand the DJ the second DAT just as the crowds erupt into cheering.

The DJ leans towards me, "Billie that was the business."

The intro music of the next song starts and Jamie starts to sing. I look around at the audience as some of them start to dance while others just stand and stare as Jamie dances. I like them am mesmerized at his dancing.

The DJ pulls off his head phones and holds it up to my ears.

"Listen to that Billie, that is one powerful voice Jamie has," I listen and nod professionally.

I tell the DJ to mix the final song into the one playing as I hand him the final DAT. The introduction of 'Love Is Not Supposed To Hurt' starts. Jamie stands still and 'ad libs' on top of the soft music, then he starts to sing. At the end of the song the crowd clap and cheer as he smiles, waves and thanks them.

I collect the three DATs from the DJ, thank him and go to meet Jamie in a room behind the stage.

"Well?" I ask walking into the room smiling.

He moves quickly across the room, picks me up and swings me around, "It was great. I can't believe it Billie. Tonight was great. UNBELIEVABLE!"

*   *   *   *   *

We received similar responses in Manchester and Blackpool. Tonight we are in Liverpool and Jamie will be on in ten minutes. I talk with a couple of DJs by their booth while Jamie gets ready in the changing room provided. This is a much bigger club than the other three he has performed in. I have been told that tonight three hundred people were originally expected, but word has travelled from the other clubs and the management has been told to prepare for five hundred people.

The dance floor is packed, the DJ lowers the volume of the music.

"Hiya all," he says loudly, "we got a lad all the way from London city for you tonight and I know you heard that he's good, that's why y'all here." The crowd cheer and clap in response. "Well here he is, Jamie Sanders, give him a big Liverpudian welcome people!"

Jamie walks on to the stage amid the clapping and cheering. I give the DJ the first DAT as Jamie starts to talk. He gives the nod and I tell the DJ to start the music. Three songs later the crowds are cheering, clapping and asking for another song. Jamie looks at me across the crowd. We do not have any more music. I mouth for him to sing Joe's 'I Wanna Know' without any music, 'a cappella'. He has recorded a paraphrased version of the song with Liam, I know he sings it well with or without music. He raises his hand and the audience go quiet. I tell the DJ to increase the volume of Jamie's microphone and not to play any music.

Jamie starts to ad-lib, there is complete silence as he sings. His final notes releases an outpour of clapping and cheering such that I have not heard before.

"Let's hear it for Jamie, people," the DJ shouts. The noise is deafening as I collect the DATs and go to the changing room.

*   *   *   *   *

We are still buzzing from the response of the audience as we walk to the taxi that will take us to the hotel. The assistant DJ that had been so nice to us earlier, is talking loudly to another man. As we get closer it is impossible not to hear what he is saying.

"...Man I'm sick of these White dudes cashing in on Black music, a Black dude wouldn't get half as far, even though he may be twice as good," the assistant DJ says.

"That's not true, if you want it badly, if you are pertinacious, you'll get it, no matter what colour you are," the man says.

"Perti-what? For real man, how many Black or Asian brothers, with real talent, are stepped over, because some White dude like Jamie, fits the bill and they don't."

"What?"

"How many?"

"You are off point man, what's wrong with you? Are you drunk? When did you start thinking like this man?"

"Like what?"

"Like this? You are White, your wife, my sister like me is Black, so where is all this anger coming from? I thought that you were at peace with colour."

We watch as they pour vodka into their beer cans and drink from them then start to laugh.

"At peace with colour? Where did that come from? Man this cheap stuff must be good," the assistant DJ says. He holds the bottle of vodka up. They laugh and playfully push each other.

"No matter what you say, Jamie can hold a note, his voice is grade A," the man says, "and Billie is a true professional they both have credibility."

The assistant DJ nods reluctantly, "You can't tell me there is nothing going on between those two though. If I had a Manager that looks that 'hot' she would be managing all of me, career, body, bed, you name it, she got it," he says.

"Rubbish! They are close, but I don't think there is anything going on, it's almost like they are related the way they act around each other, like a brother and sister."

"Yeah right, did you see the figure hidden under those clothes. Related or not I wouldn't mind giving her-"

Jamie coughs and both men turn. Standing there with my mouth half open I look at the person I had thought was really nice.

"My Manager and I find what you have just said about her, disrespectful," Jamie says moving towards the assistant DJ.

"Jamie! Billie err.., I didn't mean to be..., see what I meant..."

"I think you owe my Manager an apology."

"I just said what people think," he replies defensively as he takes a step towards Jamie. I stare at them not sure what to do.

"No you didn't, you said what your sick mind thinks. I'm not going to ask again," Jamie walks right up to him. He steps back and lifts his hands up defensively.

"Billie I'm sorry. Really, I'm sorry."

I nod.

We ride in silence to the hotel. I reach into my bag, pull out and hand Jamie the key to his room.

"I knew there was a reason I asked you to go to the gym," I say as the taxi stops in front of the hotel, "and I knew it just wasn't so you could get *'Peter Andre'* abs."

"Well actually I was counting on your *Tae Kwon Do* skills, if things went pear shaped."

"Jest not," I say laughing as I show him some moves in front of the hotel. He tries to repeat them and falls down. The doorman probably thinks we are drunk as we laugh and swing our hands and feet around. We are, drunk on the beauty of Life!

* * * * *

Like the other venues Cardiff was a success. The DJ in Cardiff like the other DJs had invited us back promising us a fee in addition to the accommodation we got this time. He arranged for us to do two interviews while we were there, one with a popular magazine and the other with a local newspaper. At this point I don't feel that we will go back to the clubs, Jamie has succeeded beyond my imagination. He can carry his own as a solo artist anywhere and anytime.

On the train heading back to London, I look out the window as Jamie reads a book. I see all the evening lights shining through the window. I remember the light in my head the first day I had met Jamie. I remember the big picture.

'Faith' I think to myself, *'believing in the things you cannot see as if you can see them'*. The lights fly past in the distance. We have one more stop.

* * * * *

"Why are we here again?" Jamie asks.

"I just want to show you something," I reply, "come on, there's dinner at Martin's club afterwards, he's trying out a new chef today." We walk into the wine bar that doubles as a nightclub with live performances every Saturday night. I pay the entrance fee for both of us and wait for Jamie to be frisked for weapons by a burly bouncer almost twice his size. I raise my eyebrows when I see that the bouncer is looking at me. He smiles and tells us to go in. We walk into the main hall. We look around and immediately notice the difference between this club and Martin's. This place looks like something that should have been shut down years ago.

"Don't worry we're not staying long," I say and I smile as I see the instant relief on Jamie's face. We walk towards the stage.

There seems to be some sort of technical hitch with the music; a man is walking up and down shouting at the engineers that are rushing around trying to rectify the problem.

"DO YOU KNOW WHO I AM? DO YOU?" The man shouts arrogantly, "I have played Wembley, Earls Court, Radio City, Mall of America. I don't need this mess. Get the music started, don't just stand there, MOVE."

Music starts, the man picks up a microphone and starts to sing. Most people in the audience are not listening to him. I take Jamie's hand and pull him right next to the stage.

"Isn't that-?" Jamie starts to ask.

"Yes it is," I answer before he finishes the question.

"He had a number one hit late last year didn't he?"

"Yes he did and a number seven in the middle of the year."

"What happened to him?"

"Fifteen minutes of fame went to his head. I don't know for sure but I heard that after two hits he thought he was untouchable and could do what he wanted. His record label couldn't handle the pressures he brought, sales fell, so they dropped him. Fame doesn't last long when you don't handle it properly. Some people don't, they let it fill them with arrogance, egotism and pride, they forget why it was given to them in the first place."

He nods and together we watch as the man finishes his song, hardly anyone claps for him. He immediately starts to sing another song; his old number one hit.

I watch Jamie as he stares at the man, he has a pensive expression on his face. His eyes are literally glued to the stage. The man on stage finishes the song, he throws the microphone on the floor as if in disgust, then walks off the stage.

The room starts to vibrate almost immediately with the sound of 'garage' music. We quickly make our way out of the building and back to the car. On our way to Martin's club I notice that Jamie is deep in thought. I don't ask him what he is thinking, because I know that I am thinking the same thing.

* * * * *

My eyes are glued to Phoebe's face.

Jamie, Steve, Trudi, Martin, Jen, the new chef and I all stare at the large television screen in Martin's club as we eat. We watch in fascination as Phoebe talks about her best selling book live on America's number one chat show. Her hair and clothes have changed but as soon as she starts to talk, I know she hasn't.

"So Ms O'Connor-," the show's presenter starts.

"Please call me Phoebe."

"Phoebe, I have read your book and so have most of the audience. It's an amazing book," the audience clap. "Why 'Appoint To Disappoint' Phoebe? Where did the title come from?"

"When I first wrote it I didn't have a fixed title, I used to call it 'the book' or 'it'. Last year I asked Billie, a dear friend of mine, to read it. The first thing she said when she saw me the next day was: *I read the first four chapters and I agree, why do we put people in places in our lives instead of God and then we get upset when they let us down? When will people see that the arm of flesh will fail but absolute reliance on God will always lead to total victory.* That was when it came to me, we appoint people in our lives only for them to disappoint us. We expect too much from people and too little from God."

"Very interesting and very true. What has drawn a lot of people to this book, is the way you have written it, and the way that even though it is a story dealing with people, it also deals with real social problems and the answers. How did you think of that?"

"Truthfully, I prayed for wisdom. I got the idea of writing each chapter as part of a whole but also as an individual. I tried to, in story form, deal with a new issue in each chapter."

"You did an excellent job Phoebe, well done. One of my favourite chapters is Chapter Six, where Ellen the teenage daughter is having problems at school and is being pressurized by her girlfriends to break the rules, and her boyfriend to start having sex. She is talking to the School Counsellor who tells her something that I love, something I wish I had been told as a teenager. I'm going to read a section from this chapter. Before I do I'll tell you something about Ellen ladies and gentlemen. She is sixteen, going through the whole growing-up-thing and is afraid of the changes. She has been caught with drugs at school, her parents called into school and she is currently in with the School Counsellor; a very wise, meek and compassionate woman. This is what the School Counsellor, Mrs Islehower, tells her." She opens to a pre-marked page and reads:

"Ellen I have just spoken to your parents, you may not believe me but I do understand what you are going through, I've been there. I know that right now everything feels and looks so confusing. You have been told to do one thing at home, which, when you get to school doesn't seem to cut with the 'cool' children. You're afraid of not fitting in but you're also afraid of losing yourself and your family's love if you do. Right now the smallest thing is intensified into the most significant. You do not care about the important things because they are not significant to you, right?" Ellen nods. "I am not going to give a sermon to you Ellen, but what I am going to do is say this, I know your parents and I know that they want the best for you. Like every single student in this school and every child in this world, you have potential. So the question is, what do you want for yourself? To find the answer to that, you have to look beyond the fears you have of not fitting in, not being cool, not having a boyfriend and look at what is in your heart.

What do you want to do?

Fear can take you to lows that you do not need to go to. It can make you do things that a few months down the road you will ask yourself if it was worth it. The worse thing that you can do is be afraid of your fears. Face them, embrace them in the knowledge that 'perfect Love casts out all fear', for only then will

162

*you conquer them. Don't let them paralyse you or change you into something you are not. The word FEAR to me is an acronym, it stands for **F**alse **E**vidence **A**ppearing **R**eal, it's not something that should have any control of your life or take away value from your life. Do you understand?"*

Ellen nods as tears form in her eyes, "I don't want to sleep with Tommy, I know it's wrong, I'm afraid of not fitting in, I.., the drugs are.." her whisper of a voice falters.

"We all want to fit in with others Ellen, sometimes this involves losing a bit of ourselves. You can only give to others out of the well of your self-esteem. You can't give what you don't have. Drugs take away your self-esteem, they can leave you stealing, begging or selling your body for money," Mrs Islehower pauses and looks at Ellen across the table. She is fidgeting and looking at her hands. After a few seconds Ellen looks up. Mrs Islehower continues, "Have you heard about the circle of 'no' life?"

Ellen frowns and shakes her head.

"It's where people hope for something, they grow up dreaming of good things and try hard to fill their lives by themselves as they grow. Nothing works and they die without fulfilling their destiny, their dream. They die leaving two pieces of paper behind, one with the date they were born and the other with the date they died, a birth certificate and a death certificate. That's all, because their lives never touched anyone else's.

Make your life count Ellen, don't just be two pieces of paper. Be a book! Have pages of wisdom, love, goodness, happiness, joy and truth inside. Let your pages touch other people.

We all have what I call a 'God space' in all of us. Some people fill theirs with drink, drugs, women, money, men, pets or other things. Things that take all their love so that they have nothing left, they are empty, they have no reason in their lives. If the answer was at the bottom of a beer glass, in the drugs, in the casual sex or in money why hasn't it been found there after all these years. Why are people still looking for an answer? Still looking for a reason?

The truth is that only God can fill that space. Ellen when you fill that space in you with God, when you seek Him first, focus on Him, only then will there be reason in your life, only then will everything else make sense. Only then

Ellen. You're not too young, start filling your space now. You see anybody can do anything, so you be somebody and do something," the presenter pauses and looks at Phoebe and then the audience.

"That is deep, don't you all agree?" The audience clap and nod their heads, some of them have tears in their eyes.

"I have heard that for each chapter you have a little message."

"That's correct, in that chapter, what I am trying to show is that people, young and old, respond so well to encouragement, yet most people continue to use criticism when trying to get people to change or do better. We all need to use more encouragement. Use words that build up, not tear down."

"That's so beautiful. I know we need to go into a commercial break soon but before we go can you tell me about the iron story?"

Phoebe laughs, "Oh my, the iron story. I have been asked this question so many times after I mentioned how I used things that have happened in my life to write the book. The iron story is a true story and it is really about an iron. I used the story to try and describe how used and neglected a married female character in the book felt. So much so that when another man starts to pay her a little attention, she welcomes it. Life at home for her is not good. She actually starts by saying that she is sick and tired of being sick and tired, and she uses my iron story to explain to her husband exactly how she feels. How like a lot of women, she feels neglected, misused and un-loved. The only romance in her life is from novels and movies. She can't understand why her husband whom she loves finds her so unattractive and takes her for granted, while she sees admiration in the eyes of other men. I guess what I am trying to say to both men and women is take care of what you have or you may lose it. Communicate honestly with each other. I have lost count of the number of marriages that have broken down because the husband never told the wife that he loved her, never showed any affection. The wife became hostile and cold due to a lack of love, and the husband confused, because every time he asked if something was wrong, she said no. Relationships are ruined because of a lack of care, a lack of nurture. People go from one rela-tionship to the other taking the same baggage along with them. They look for younger versions of the older models which, when they get, may look and feel good for a while but in their hearts they know the truth. They know that it is not the same as that old love.

Anyway this is the iron story as it happened to me and as I said before, it is really about an iron:

I once had an iron and I would use it and not take care of it, not bother to pack it away properly. Each time I used it I noticed that the cord got more and more twisted, and the surface more dirty. I did nothing about it, I continued to use it without cleaning or taking care of it. One day I was in a hurry and I needed to iron a specific dress I had to wear. So of course I plugged the iron into the wall, put the switch down, but the light did not come on and the iron did not get hot. It didn't work. The cord was so twisted that some of the wires inside were exposed in certain places. I rushed out to buy another iron but all the shops were closed.

I bought a new iron the next day, one with all the latest fancy gadgets. With my new iron I did something different, I took care of it, each time I used it I waited for it to cool down and then I would wrap the cord around the base and stand it upright in the corner. You know something, that iron is still working today, but it is not the same as my old iron."

The audience clap.

"You used an iron to highlight an important issue?"

"I find that people respond better when you use everyday examples to relate to things."

"That is so true. You know what else I really like about this book ladies and gentlemen, it's the way Phoebe has incorporated idioms into the story. Take for instance when Mr Wilson in Chapter 2 says to his wife that she is wasting her time trying to change their son. He says," she opens the book and reads: *"Maggi May you are just wasting your time woman, I keep telling you that you are banging your head against a brick wall with that boy." Maggi May Wilson turns to her husband, unflustered by his words, unflustered by his idiosyncrasy and says, "You know Trevor, I can either give up on him like you have, and treat him like your father and mother treated you, with coldness and no love. And, maybe one day he will sit with his wife talking about giving up on his own son, or, I can change things with God's help, I can keep on banging. Maybe, just maybe,*

165

when I pray and bang my head hard and long enough something will happen, even brick walls fall down if you bang them hard enough." She closes the book.

"We are definitely going to a commercial break now, ladies and gentleman join me with Phoebe O'Connor when we return. I leave you with this, taken from her international best selling book 'Appoint to Disappoint'." She opens the book at another pre-marked page and reads: "*We all say the grass is greener on the other side, we think that when we go to that other side we will be happier with our greener grass. What we need to do is look after the grass on our own side, fertilize it, trim it, water it. Only then will we be able to see what the people on the other side can see. That the grass is just as green, if not 'greener', on our side.*" The presenter shakes her head, "Wisdom," she says and smiles. "This is not just a book for adults or moms and dads this is a book for young people as well. Young people go out and get this book and learn. Join us after the break viewers."

We watch as the audience clap, Phoebe smiles.

*   *   *   *   *

Since meeting Jamie, I have always known that this day would come. I read through my resignation letter one more time then put it in an envelope.

I knock on my Manager's door, wait a few seconds then walk into his office.

"Billie, how are you? Is everything all right?"

"Fine thank you. I want to talk to you about my job. I have decided-"

"About your job Billie, I have spoken to the Divisional Manager and we have both agreed. We want you to have a senior position. We know that last time you didn't get the senior's job when you should have. We feel as we felt then, that you are more than capable."

"Thank you," I say really astonished, "but I actually want to talk about-"

His phone starts to ring as I pull the letter from out of my pocket. He answers the phone. I turn away as he talks, a colourful scarf catches my eye. It is hanging from a drawer of a desk in the corner, a desk that I know Roger uses every day.

166

My Manager says something and then listens, he covers the mouth-piece with his hand and asks me to excuse him and pop back later.

Still holding the letter I walk out of his office. 'Why is it that now I want to leave I am being offered a promotion' I wonder as I walk back to the laboratory. I don't dwell on the thought for long because I know that like Phoebe if I was meant to stay here I would have got the senior job when I applied for it. I am not sure who it was that said 'little-big-things' have a way of distracting you just before a big breakthrough, especially when you are destined for something bigger.

*   *   *   *   *

Jamie is at Liam's studio working on some new material. We have six original songs and four cover songs on CD now and I have sent out samples of our new material to a number of record companies. I am supposed to be with Jamie tonight, but I cancelled earlier on because of something that has been running through my mind, and eating at my thoughts all day. My car is being serviced so I am driving Jamie's Jeep. As I struggle a little with the gear stick I wonder why I didn't take the automatic BMW he had offered to me yesterday, instead of this. I drive down the street and past the house, there is nowhere to park on the street so I turn right at the bottom of the street and right again. I find somewhere to park on the street behind, at the back of the house. I walk down the alley way connecting both streets, it is dark and the trees at the entrance play with the street lights, throwing shadows on the walls. At the end I turn right. I climb over the low wall, instead of walking it's length twice, and ring the door bell.

"Who is it?"

"Sarah, it's Billie. Open the door."

The door opens, I walk in, "Where are the children?" I ask.

"Asleep. Billie what's going on? Why are you here so late? It's quarter past ten."

"What's going on? What's going on? You tell me Sarah, exactly what is going on?"

"I don't understand?" She says as she walks down the hall. I follow her into her front room and close the door.

"The last time I was here I saw a scarf hanging in your hallway. Very bright colours, looks very much like the one I bought you for Christmas. I saw the exact same scarf hanging out of Roger's desk drawer today. I saw a blue car parked in front of your house, the same blue car parked on my road and the same blue car being driven by Roger recently. Coincidence? I don't think so."

"You don't understand Billie don't get involved, Roger-"

"Roger and Nigel have a Dr Jekyll and Hyde thing. Why are you involved?"

Expressions flow across her face in quick successions, shock followed by denial and then resignation. "I didn't know at the time, Billie. Roger is not a bad person on his own, it's when he is around Nigel that he acts err-"

"Weird," I finish.

"Billie I'm serious, stay out of this. You can't help me," her defeatist attitude makes me boil.

"How many times have I been here, how many times have I asked you what was wrong, begged you to confide in me?"

"What do you want from me, huh? You come here at this time and start asking questions. What gives you the right to-?"

"Those children give me the right, Luke, Nick and Maddy, you give me the right. I care about you all. That's why I'm here. That's why, when I see the hurt in your eyes I feel hurt."

"Look no one cares about me, I'm on my own. I've been on my own for a long time. I know what they say about me at work. I've heard it all before, *single mother with three children by three different men, so desperate for it that she has boyfriend after boyfriend and no husband, so desperate that she lets them beat her up*'. No one cares about me."

"I care."

"Why? You don't know what I'm going through, you have no idea how worthless I feel sometimes, how I feel so desperate for love and affection that I-"

"That you think it's all right to take the abuse as long as you have someone in your life. That you let him hurt you because he says he loves you. You are scared when he comes around and scared when he doesn't. Sometimes just to get his attention, his love, you get thoughts in your mind about throwing yourself down the stairs or something worse, just so that he will stop hurting you, feel sorry for what he has done and maybe, really love you. Maybe Change." The story of *my* life unfolds.

"How did you know?" She whispers. The wall starts to crack, at last, affirmation.

"I know because I have stood at the top of those stairs and looked down and wondered, what if?"

"You? But you're different, you're beautiful, you're smart."

"I'm human just like you, I have felt the pain of rejection. I know what it is like to think that you are totally in love with someone and have that person hurt you, belittle you. What it's like to think that you can change someone that didn't want to change.

As for the people at work you're right, they do say things about you, they say things about me, and you can bet they say things about each other. Forget the 'he said', 'she said', 'they said' gossips. What matters is what you say about yourself! That's what counts! When I look at you, I see a wonderful person, a mum who has three beautiful children that she loves and that love her. A lady who is looking for love and affection from a man, the problem is, you have so much love to give, but sometimes you don't give any to yourself. You're looking for your purpose in a relationship with a man. People can help you fulfill your purpose but you can only get your purpose from God. You think I don't understand loneliness and what it can make you do. It's not my place to judge you or anyone-"

"Everyone else does Billie, you might as well," she interjects defensively.

"Sit down Sarah, I'm going to tell you what someone told me," I see the resistance in her eyes and she sees the determination to get through in mine. She sits down.

"There was a man drowning in the sea and he prayed to God to rescue him-"

"What has this-?"

"HEAR ME OUT!" I interject loudly, "he called out to God to rescue him. As he was calling out a man in a small fishing boat came along. He stretched out his hand to the man drowning and said 'Take my hand, I will help you', but the man in the water said that he was waiting for God to help him. So the man in the boat left. Two other people came along to help, and the man drowning sent them away because he was waiting for God. Eventually the drowning man drowned. He died wondering why God had not rescued him. Sarah, God sends people to help others, that's how He works. Don't you understand?"

"So, who's there for me? Who has He sent to help me? Why am I always alone Billie? Why-?" She turns away slightly. "Why do I always-?" Her voice breaks and she starts to cry. Tears fill my eyes.

"I'm here Sarah, I've been here for some time. Trying to reach out to you."

Her shoulders shake, I move towards her and gently put my arm around her. I let her cry her river.

I hand her some tissues and she blows her nose and smiles at me weakly. "I'm sorry, I feel so hopeless Billie. It's like I have done so many wrong things and I can't find a way to get out of the cycle. Someone said to me once 'Cast your cares and worries upon the Lord', how do I do that?" She sniffs.

"By letting go of them. Pray, ask God to forgive you and to help you. Give everything that you cannot handle to Him, every worry, every problem, every hurt, past and present. When you let go of them, you will have peace in your heart and you will not have to go out looking for happiness and peace in a person."

"That's what Phoebe said before she went to America. She said *only the Prince of Peace, the owner of true peace, can give real internal and external peace*."

"Sarah it's going to be okay," she nods, reaches into the pocket of her trousers and pulls out a piece of paper.

"Remember this? It's the number you gave me when you tried to talk to me about domestic violence. I've kept it for months, too scared to use it. For some reason I've had it in my pocket all this week trying to get the courage to phone." She stands up and walks over to the phone. I watch as she presses some numbers and then talks.

I've always wondered why I went through what I did with Wayne. For years I never understood why. Now as I watch Sarah, it all makes sense. I know that my experience has made me understand what she is going through. It has given me the tenacity to hold on and not get offended at her attitude and give up on her. It has made me look beyond the situation and at the solution.

*　　*　　*　　*　　*

Weeks ago I started doing what Phoebe suggested, I started praying more and praying more specifically about things especially for wisdom and discernment. Asking in my prayers to have a giving heart and to help whoever God wanted me to help. I find I have become a lot more sensitive to things and situations now. So much so, that as I now sit with Sarah in her front room I suddenly have this overwhelmingly, urgent feeling to leave. Not just leave, but get everyone out of the house. I feel like a fish in a bowl. Each time I turn my head, the room seems to move, the feeling is growing stronger.

"Sarah, get the children, pack some things and let's go."

"I don't understand, the children are sleeping Billie, go where?" She looks at my face and jumps up, "something's wrong, what is it?"

"I don't know, just do it. You can stay at my brother's place. Do it now." I start to shake a little.

She rushes out of the room, I follow her. My heart is beating fast but I feel remarkably calm as I help her put the children's clothes in a bag. I grab some toys laying around and put them in the bag as she goes to get some things for herself. She is back in less than five minutes with a small bag. Together we wake the children up, to my surprise they are alert as soon as we gently shake them. They do exactly as we tell them. It is almost as if they are used to being woken at night. My heart hurts at their lack of sluggishness and their keen survival instincts. Four year old Maddy grabs hold of her comfort blanket, tucks it under her arm and quickly puts on her shoes and coat without moaning or asking a question.

Sarah walks towards the front door with Maddy and Nick, I follow with Luke and the two bags. I watch as she lets go of Nick's hand and lifts her hand

171

up to open the front door. My brain screams as I watch, it's like everything is happening in slow motion.

"No, not the front door," I say heading towards the kitchen, "I'm parked on the other street, behind the house. Let's go through the back door and out the garden gate."

I manipulate the two bags and Luke's hand then open the back door and look out. I walk through and wait for Sarah who is carrying Maddy and holding Nick's hand to follow. She closes then locks the back door and we walk quietly through the garden, over the toys laying in the grass. I feel the dampness of the grass on my feet and the coolness of the gentle wind on my face. I look down at Luke hoping he is not too cold. He is wide awake and confident in his stance. I open the garden gate and again wait for Sarah to pass through. She waits while I pull the gate shut. I take the lead and walk down the alley way to the Jeep. I hold the key chain up and press the button to open the door, nothing happens. I press it hard again and to my horror the alarm goes off. The noise is deafening and the hazard lights start to flash. Quickly I press the button again, nothing happens, the noise starts to attract some curtain movement. In a panic I press the button twice. The noise stops as suddenly as it had started.

"Quick get in, the doors are open," I say as I help Luke into the front seat. I fasten the seat belt around him then throw the bags onto the floor under his feet.

Sarah puts Nick and Maddy in the back and then climbs in next to them and slams the door. I climb in, start the engine and drive. It is not until a few minutes later that I realize I have not turned my headlights on.

*   *   *   *   *

"They are fast asleep. Thanks Billie. I don't know what happened back there but right now I feel safer than I have felt in a long while. Thank you but are you sure your brother won't mind?"

I shake my head, I do not try to understand what happened in Sarah's house. I just know that it was the right thing to do. As I make something for us to eat Sarah sits and watches. She looks very pensive as she sips from a glass of water.

"Why do you work in the hospital as a laboratory assistant?" I ask trying to get her mind off her thoughts.

"What? Oh, err.., sorry I was miles away. Why do I work in a hospital? I trained like you as a Microbiologist. I was a section senior in another laboratory."

"I heard about that but I didn't want to ask because you never talked about it."

"It was a long time ago and it was not that nice an experience. I worked for a Manager that was a bit weird, he would say one thing and want another thing done. I couldn't understand a word he said sometimes. I heard rumours that he used to be an alcoholic, I think he was a little depressed and I really felt sorry for him at one point, but then he started behaving strange. He was never at work, he was always travelling, I think the company just paid for him to have one holiday after another. When he did come in, he went out of his way to find fault with everything all the time. I think he didn't like me and felt threatened by my qualifications."

"It must have been really hard working there?"

"Believe me it was. I have worked for a number of managers in my time, but he was the worst. We had some really young girls in the department and he would call them into his office one at a time for meetings, and I would catch him staring at their breasts. The photocopier was right by his office and you could see him openly doing it. My skin used to crawl and I lost respect for him, I didn't trust him. He probably noticed that I wasn't comfortable around him. There was a really nice old lady working in the department, he would constantly make fun of her, to her face and behind her back. One minute he was really condescending towards her, the next openly rude.

He would tell me to make sure I kept the junior staff in check, make sure I was tough on them, stop them from talking and then he went around being 'Mr Nice Guy'. I didn't do it and after a while everything I did was wrong. He acted like the department was his own little empire, he had his little spies that reported everything to him. In return he did things for them." A smile breaks out on her face, her first smile all evening. "One day he rudely asked me to update a proposal he had written and presented to his boss, he was upset because his boss had rejected his draft. Each time I drafted something he would reject it just to frustrate me. So I copied something he had written in our departmental prospectus, word-for-word, and gave it to him. He read it and then said it was rubbish," she starts to laugh.

"What did you do?" I ask, not able to conceal my shock.

"I showed him the prospectus, he went bright red with embarrassment and started to stutter. Anyway I worked a few more months but his constant mood swings and nasty attitude started to affect me so I left. Best thing I ever did." She puts the glass of water down and takes the vegetables on the chopping board over to the sink.

"Billie are you sure your brother won't mind us staying here?" She asks again as she washes the vegetables.

"No of course not, he is in America visiting my parents." I watch her as she chops up some vegetables. She is confident, relaxed. For the first time since I have known her, I see the absence of fear in her eyes.

"Do you ever wonder, what it's all about Billie? Why we go through certain things?"

"Yes, I think it's mainly to help us and others. Take for instance your previous job, at least you know how to treat people and not behave like your Manager. How not to make other people feel worthless, just so you can feel good about yourself like he did."

She nods, "Why do some people have so much in the world and others nothing though Billie?"

"I think that everyone is here for a reason, we all have something that we are supposed to do. We also have gifts and talents to help us fulfill our destiny or purpose, our reason for being here. Like I said before, I think people are meant to help others, people with money are supposed to help those without. God blesses people so they can help others, spiritually or financially."

"It doesn't happen though."

"That's because some people who have, forget that they once did not have. You see it all over the world, the famous actor, footballer, singer or rich person, they put all their confidence in their abilities, in their money. They think that it's all about them and not about their purpose. What they have goes to their heads. After a while they lose their heads, the money they have may still be there, but they don't enjoy it anymore. They start to look for something else, something that will give them a bigger 'buzz' or a higher 'high'. They have large luxurious beds but are not able to sleep, food from every country in the world in their refrigerators, but no appetite to eat it."

She frowns, "I don't understand that, they have the gifts, talents or money, so surely they can choose what they do with them."

"Look at it like this Sarah, if you make something to do a job, it's about you and getting the job done not about the thing you made."

"True," she says, "go on."

"See, if the job was not important you wouldn't have made that thing in the first place. So it's about the job not the thing you made."

Her eyes light up and she smiles "The maker is God and the job, bringing people to salvation?"

"Yes!" I say smiling, "how did you know what I was talking about?"

She chops a few more vegetables, "I heard something similar at a church I went to last week," she pauses mid chop, and looks at me, "don't look at me like that, I know that you've been trying to get me to go to church for a long time."

"Look at you like what?" I ask as I quickly move my hand across my face trying not to smile.

She smiles.

"I'm listening," I say.

"At church the lady preacher talked about Joseph, you know Joseph and his coat of many colours?"

I nod.

"How what Joseph's brothers planned for evil God used for good. She said people think that Joseph's life was just about him having dreams and the ability to interpret dreams. She said, that was his gift, and not his purpose or destiny. His destiny or purpose was to bring his family out of Canaan and into Egypt, to prevent them starving during the famine; and by doing that, prevent their death and the death of many other people. She asked, what would have happened if Joseph had kept his gift to himself? Or maybe charged people for its use to prosper himself. Or taken all the glory and given none to God, because that's what people do today with their gifts."

"Exactly," I look at the dish in my hand, "you know, when I was nine we performed the musical 'Joseph And His Coat Of Many Colours' at school. I have read that story a number of times but I never really looked at it that way."

"It really makes you think doesn't it Billie?"

I nod.

* * * * *

I can hear someone calling my name. I turn around and cover my head with the blanket. I hear a gently persistent tap on the door and sit up.

"Who is it?" I ask.

"Billie it's me," Sarah replies.

I get out of bed and open the door. Sarah is standing in the hall, she looks scared. I notice her mobile phone in her hand.

"Billie, the police just phoned me. My house was broken into last night, it was vandalized."

"What!"

"My house was broken into around 10.50pm. It was them, they wrote their initials on the wall." I see fear replaced with confusion in her eyes as she stares at me. "If you hadn't come, if you hadn't turned up last night like you did…"

CHAPTER 17

Dear Billie

Thank you for your demo tape. We would like to meet with you and Jamie. Can you call my secretary on the number above to arrange a suitable time for yourselves.

Best Wishes

Pete Wilson
Assistant A &R Manager
Vigil Records

I stare at the letter, amazingly my hands are remarkably steady. The rest of me is trembling with excitement. Vigil Records are not only very big they also have some of the hottest artists signed to them. I read the letter again. It has been 11 months and 6 days since I met Jamie. Nearly 48 weeks of holding on and believing that one day things would happen. I pick up my phone and dial Jamie's number. His phone rings twice then his voicemail comes on.

"Jamie. Hi, it's me, call me as soon as you get this message. I just got a letter from Vigil Records. Call me!" I hang up. My phone starts to ring almost immediately.

I grab the receiver, "Jamie?"

"Hello can I speak to Billie Lewis?" The male voice asks.

"Hello, sorry I thought you were someone else, sorry. I am Billie Lewis."

"Hi Billie, my name is Francis Wells and I work for Digital Records. I got the demo you sent and I would like to meet you and Jamie."

I don't say anything. I hold the phone to my ear.

"Hello, Billie are you there?"

"Yes, umm…, yes, I am, sorry you said Digital Records?"

"Yes that's right, I'm the A&R Manager."

"Manager?"

"Manager, Head, it's all relative nowadays."

"Oh."

"I'm sorry, is now not a good time to talk?"

"It's fine, I, it's just that, I…," I stop talking.

"Why don't you have a word with Jamie, whenever you are both free within the next few days, give me a call and let's have this meeting, yeah."

"Okay that will be fine Mr Wells."

"Please call me Francis. Have you got a pen?"

"Yes."

He gives me his mobile number, I write it down and thank him for calling. My head is spinning. For months nothing, now two 'major' record companies are interested. I pick up the phone and dial Jamie's number again. His voicemail comes on again. "Jamie, call me, it's urgent. Vigil and Digital. Call me."

I put the phone down and jump up and down with excitement.

Almost immediately my phone starts to ring, 'it has to be Jamie' I think.

"Hello," I say making sure that it is him before I start to scream. My smile literally freezes and my excited scream dies in my throat as I listen.

With trembling hands I put the receiver down, grab my bag and car keys and run out of the house.

* * * * *

Twenty minutes later I run down the hospital corridor still not sure how I managed to drive here. I see the sign for the intensive care unit and run up the stairs two at a time. "Please let him be all right, please don't let him die," I say over and over again as I run down the corridor. The first thing I see when I push the door to the ward open, is Martin sitting in a chair with his head in his hands. I stop and look at him, taking a deep breath I walk over to him.

"Martin, how is he?" I ask.

The eyes that look up at me are red and puffy and for a minute I cannot breathe.

"His heart stopped twice, now they say he is stable but critical."

I let out a sigh and sit down next to him placing an arm around his shoulders.

"He will be fine, we have to be positive, where is your mum?"

"She's in there with him, I needed to get some air, he…, he's attached to so many tubes and wires, I couldn't stay in there."

I nod and get up, "I'll go and see what's happening."

Nothing, not Martin's words or having seen patients in the Intensive Care Unit of the hospital I work in, has prepared me for the sight of my uncle laying in a bed attached to tubes, wires and machines. Martin's mum is sitting in a side room, as I walk towards her I see she is sleeping. I walk back towards the bed and stare at my uncle, tears fill my eyes as I sit down next to his bed. 'Why now?' I think to myself. 'Now, when things were just starting to get better between Martin and his dad.'

I still cannot explain why I did what I did, I just did it. Some weeks ago Jamie and I had been listening to some songs at his place trying to get another 'cover' song for him to record. He played a song called 'The Living Years' by *Mike and the Mechanics*. As I sat listening to the story of a man and his father unfold, I knew it was the story of Martin and his dad. I didn't want their relationship to end like the one in the song so I went and bought two copies of the song, and sent one to my uncle and one to Martin. I sent a little note with each tape saying *'Please listen with your heart'*, I disguised my handwriting so they wouldn't know it was from me. I prayed that the song would touch them in some way. Break down the walls of silence, the lack of communication and affection. Break the cycle that passed from one generation of men to the next. Each generation forgetting that they were brought up without the affection they craved for from their father, forgetting their vows not to repeat history. Instead, acting exactly like their fathers, and wondering why their sons could not relate to them.

The song worked. A couple of days after I sent it, Martin's mother called. She sounded as if she had been crying. She thanked me for sending the tapes and tried to explain how, she had attempted to get Martin and his dad closer for years;

but to no avail. She ended up breaking down completely. I can still hear her sobs in my head. I wonder how she had known it was me that sent the songs.

I hear a gentle sigh and turn, "Billie, is that you dear?"

"Yes auntie, how are you?" I walk over to the side room, sit next to her and place an arm around her. I feel her collapse against me.

"Oh I'm fine, thank you, the doctor gave me a sedative."

"What happened?"

"One minute he was fine, the next he was clutching his chest and complaining of a sharp pain. They said…," she breathes heavily, "they said his heart stopped twice." I can feel her shaking in my arms and I feel ill. All this pain now that could have been so much love then. I think of the number of times I had avoided visiting my aunt because I knew my uncle would be home. As I sit here, I feel thoroughly ashamed of myself.

Steve walks in with the doctor and Martin. The doctor pulls up a chair and sits in front of Martin's mum.

"As I said before, he is critical but stable at the moment. Hopefully he will not get any worse."

"Will he recover fully?" My aunt asks.

"We have to wait until he wakes up to tell. We will be able to run some tests and see how he responds to stimuli." He explains a few more possibilities to us then leaves.

Steve's phone starts to ring as a nurse walks into the room.

"I'm sorry sir, you have to turn that off once you leave this room. We don't allow the use of mobile phones on the ward." Steve smiles and nods his head then answers the phone. He speaks briefly then hands the phone to my aunt.

"It's mum," he says quietly to me.

"Thank you," my aunt says, then listens. "We should know by tomorrow. I'm fine, all the children are here," she listens, "I will call you tomorrow or sooner if there is any change. I love you too, bye Anne."

I feel a lump in my throat as I listen. I have never heard my aunt speak to my mother with affection before. I walk out of the room and towards the bed. I stand by it and look down at my uncle. I ignore the tubes and machines and wires and gently take hold of his hand. I speak softly almost to myself.

"I'm sorry I avoided you for so many years, I thought you didn't like me because I'm Black. I heard you say once when I was nine or ten, that you couldn't stand uncle Neville and his sort, I thought it was because he was Black that you said that. I'm sorry for not asking or saying anything and for not seeing beyond what I wanted to see. Please make it, so I can tell you myself. Please God let him make it, let us all get through this and come out stronger." I squeeze his hand as tears pour down my face. I remember when we were little, the times Steve, Martin and I had done naughty things; my uncle had always come to my rescue saying that they were boys, and should have known better. Even when I had instigated things. He had bought me my first piano when I was seven because I told him I wanted to write songs. He had insisted I go for piano lessons. He was always nice to me, yet after I heard him say the thing about uncle Neville I shut him out of my life. I look down at his hand that I hold and notice that he is holding my hand as well.

"That normally happens when someone is in a coma," the nurse attending him says. "It's a reflex thing. He will be all right, his complexion looks much healthier than it did earlier."

I smile at her, praying that she is right.

Six hours later there is still no change, my uncle is still critical but stable.

"I really think that you should all go home and rest, we will let you know if there are any changes to his condition," the Sister says with years of experience in her voice.

"No, I can't leave him, I won't leave him. Children you go I'll stay," my aunt says.

"No," I say.

"I think that you all need to try and get some rest so you'll have strength for tomorrow," the nurse says.

"The nurse is right," Steve says taking control, "come on auntie, you're going to feel terrible tomorrow when he wakes up and you're too tired."

"But Steve-," my aunt starts to protest.

"I'll take you home, stay at your house and bring you back early tomorrow."

"Okay dear," she resigns.

"Is that all right with you Martin?" Steve asks.

Martin nods.

My aunt turns to the nurse and grabs hold of her hand, "You will let us know if he wakes up in the night?"

"I will personally phone you, please don't worry."

"Thank you."

Martin has not said much in the last few hours, I notice that his hands are shaking as we leave the room. I reach out and take hold of his hand and squeeze it reassuringly. We walk in silence down the corridors and out of the hospital, to the car park.

"Thank you all for being with me today, I know that I can be a bit, well you know, but today has shown me that I couldn't wish for anything better than the three of you." I look at her with new eyes. Grief has warmed her heart and brought her out of her cold shell.

Steve smiles, "Right I will take Martin and auntie home, Billie, do you need a lift?"

"No, I drove down, my car is over there."

"I drove down as well, I'd better drive my car back," Martin says as he pulls his car keys out of his pocket.

"I don't think you should drive Martin," I say taking his car keys from his hand which is still shaking."

"Why don't you leave your car here and take Martin's car home," Steve says to me.

"Okay, I'll drop it off at the house tomorrow morning when I come round." I hug my aunt, Martin and Steve and watch as they walk towards Steve's car.

Half way home in Martin's Porsche, his car phone starts to ring. I slow down and pull the car over to the side of the road.

"Hello."

"Hello, can I speak to Martin please," I recognize the voice.

"Jen?"

"Billie?"

"Jen, something's happened."

"Is Martin okay?" I hear the panic in her voice.

"Martin's dad had a heart attack, he's in hospital."

"Oh no, they were just starting to work things out. I was going to visit with my parents in Manhattan tomorrow but I'll get the first flight I can from JFK airport back to London now. I'll see you tomorrow."

I put the phone down. I'm tired and hungry. As I drive home I say a prayer for my uncle and aunt. I pray that things do not end up with 'if only'.

*   *   *   *   *

The first thing I notice when I walk into my front room is the light on my phone flashing. I have eight messages. I look at the phone for a few seconds knowing that I cannot let anything else in right now. I walk past it, turn the lights off in the front room and in the hall and go to bed.

*   *   *   *   *

The simultaneous ringing of my phone and front door bell drag me out of my sleep. I stumble out of bed in a panic, and rush to the phone hoping it is not bad news.

"Billie, it's Jen. I'll be at your house in an hour, I'm leaving the airport now, wait for me."

"Okay," I put the phone down and walk to the door. I see Jamie through the spy hole and open the door.

"Something is wrong, what is it?" He asks staring at my rough and crumpled slept-in clothes. He follows me into the front room. "What's Martin's car doing here? What's happened? I called you over a dozen times yesterday."

I slump into an armchair and tell him.

"What time have you got to be at the hospital?"

"I have to go to Martin's house first, what time is it now?"

"6.30."

"In the morning?"

He nods, "What time did you get to bed?"

"I don't know, I'm so hungry."

"I'll get something sorted."

I can feel myself slipping in and out of sleep as I sit in the chair. Startled, I jump as I hear something bang in the kitchen. I get up and walk to the kitchen; there are pots and pans on the cooker, eggs, bread and coffee on the table.

"Go and take a shower, I'll make some breakfast."

Showered and dressed I sit on my bed and comb my hair. I hear the front door bell ring.

"I'll get it," Jamie shouts.

Jen bursts through my bedroom door seconds later, "Billie, how are you? How are Martin and his mom? Have you heard anything from the hospital?"

"I'm fine and no I haven't heard anything."

"Jamie let me in?"

"He got here about an hour ago, look do you want to shower and have something to eat, then come with me to Martin's?"

"Yes please."

Jamie knocks on the door, "Breakfast is served ladies."

As Jamie and I tidy the kitchen up I suddenly remember Vigil and Digital Records. "Jamie, did you get the messages I left about the record companies?"

"Yes, but let's deal with them later, we need to get to Martin's and then the hospital, right?"

"But…"

"No buts, hurry Jen up and let's go, this is important."

"Okay," I turn to go, stop and turn back, "thank you."

CHAPTER 18

Thirty minutes later I park Martin's car in the drive of his parents' house and walk up to the front door with Jamie and Jen. I ring the bell and Steve opens the door. He ushers us inside and pulls me to one side. I see the concern in his eyes.

"Can you go talk to Martin," I nod and run up the three flights of stairs to his room. I knock on the door, he does not answer. Turning the handle I push the door open and call his name. He is sitting on his bed staring at the wall.

"Martin, we are going to leave for the hospital in about thirty minutes, you need to get ready."

"Ready for what?"

"Martin you-"

"Ready to see him die?"

"That's not going to happen."

"You know that for sure Billie? I don't."

"What I know is that you can choose to stay here and feel hurt and angry or you can get up and believe that he will get better and walk in that belief."

"What if I do that and he doesn't get better, that's what scares me, what if I walk in my belief and he still doesn't make it?"

"At least you tried, at least you will know for the rest of your life that you tried, you didn't give up. Sometimes things don't always happen the way we expect them to but no matter what the outcome we should never give up on our belief. If we do that, we have nothing."

He looks away and shakes his head "All those tubes, all those wires, I don't think that I can take it again today."

"Look past the tubes and wires, look at your father laying on the bed and love him anyway."

"She's right Martin, you need to get ready," Jen says. We both turn and look at her. I didn't hear her come into the room.

"Jen! When did you get back?" Martin asks. He gets up from the bed but does not move towards her.

"This morning. Martin I'm so sorry about your dad but you have to get ready and go to the hospital, for your mom, your dad and for you."

I move towards the door and Jen walks towards the bed, she touches my arm as we pass each other. As I step out of the room and turn to close the door I see Martin move across the room and hug Jen. I watch as they stand holding each other, then I close the door and walk down the stairs to the first floor. I knock on my aunt's door.

*   *   *   *   *

As soon as we all walk into the ward, we are told that nothing has changed from yesterday. The nurse looks at us and I can tell that she is a little concerned.

"The doctor will be here soon, you can all stay in the side waiting room. Only direct family members will be allowed into Mr Palmer's room."

I watch as my aunt arranges his bed sheets and brushes his hair gently backwards with her hand. She touches his face lovingly. I leave her alone with him and go back and join the others in the waiting room. We don't say much to each other, it's like we draw strength from each other in our silence, in our patience.

Two hours later it is as if I am on the set of a movie. I see the nurse move over to my uncle's bed and then I see her press a button on the wall and rush out of the room.

"What's going on?" My aunt asks jumping up and rushing over to the bed. A loud ringing noise starts as the light on one of the machines starts to flash. We all jump up and rush into the room. My heart is beating so fast I cannot breathe properly.

The doctor rushes into the room.

"Right everyone move back please," the doctor says.

"What's happening? Will someone please tell me what is going on?" My aunt asks as she attempts to push the nurse out of the way.

186

"Mrs Palmer, please move back, you need to go into the other room so we can do our job."

"But he is my husband, I want to know."

"Please Mrs Palmer."

"Mum come on, let them do their job," Martin places his arm around his mother's shoulders and brings her back into the waiting room. The nurse closes the door, leaving us in the room, we are all full of anxiety.

Ten minutes later the doctor walks into the room, his face is expressionless.

"Mrs Palmer your husband has regained full consciousness. We have done some preliminary tests and the results look good. I don't think that we will need to operate. You can go and see him now for a few minutes."

Martin takes his mother's hand and leads her into the room. I see the relief on their faces that I feel in my heart.

*　　*　　*　　*　　*

It is a week since my uncle was admitted here. I walk down the familiar corridors knowing that my visits here will soon come to an end because he will soon be going home. I have come to do what I promised I would. I greet the nurses whom I have come to know so well and walk into my uncle's room.

"Billie, how are you?"

"I'm fine, how are you?"

"Tied up," he says pointing to the wires and the machines that he is still connected to. I smile and place the flowers I have brought into a vase.

"Come and sit over here," he says pointing to a chair next to his bed, "so you have finally decided to leave work now have you?"

I nod.

"Good, you always wanted to write songs and poems plus you are good at it, so follow your heart."

I am shocked. I thought he would say that it was a bad idea. Martin is right he has changed.

"When you were unconscious I prayed that you would get better, and I promised that when you did I would talk to you."

He sits up a little, "Was it the day that you held my hand and talked to me? I saw you standing by my bed and talking to me. I tried to squeeze your hand but couldn't manage it."

I stare at him amazed, "Yes it was that day."

"I didn't hear what you said then, but I'm listening now."

I breathe in deeply, there is no turning back, "When I was little I heard you say something about uncle Neville and his sort and I thought that you didn't like me, so I avoided you and now it doesn't matter. You're my uncle and I love you."

"Neville? When?" I see from his face that he is confused, "the only time I remember having an argument with Neville was fourteen or fifteen years ago when he tried to get your dad to lend him money for a business idea. I knew he was going to use it to gamble, so I told your dad not to give it to him. I said I didn't like his sort because he was a gambler and played on the good nature of people like your dad. You thought I said that because he's Black?"

I nod.

"Why?"

"I thought you didn't like Black or mixed race people."

"What! That's not true. Your dad has done so much for me Billie, I wouldn't have made it this far if he hadn't prayed with me and for me nearly every day. When I started having problems with my business he helped me, when Martin wouldn't work with me, he tried to help me understand, that I had to let him live his life but I wouldn't listen. Then someone sent me a song a few weeks ago and I understood everything your dad has been saying. I regard your dad as a brother, I always have. I talk to him practically every day."

"I didn't, I didn't know, I …"

"Billie, you were my little princess, you could do no wrong in my eyes. It really hurt me when you started avoiding me, when you wouldn't come round." He closes his eyes, "All those years wasted. Why didn't you say anything to me?"

I shrug, I have no answer.

"I would never do or say anything to hurt you or any other member of our family. What did your dad say?"

"I never told him, I never told anyone."

"You kept this to yourself since you were nine or ten?"

I nod.

"Billie," he says softly.

I know that I have hurt him and I feel sad.

"Can we please start again?" I ask.

He raises his arms and holds them open. The scales in my eyes fall away and I see something I have not looked for in his eyes for a long time, I see love. The coldness is no longer there; it may never have really been there in the first place. I get up and move into his arms.

*　　*　　*　　*　　*

"If you need anything, anything at all let me know Sarah."

"Billie, the children and I are fine in our new home. I found a part-time job not far from their school, so everything is fine, really."

"Okay but just let me know, anything."

"I will, is your uncle back home?"

"Yes, and he's doing really well. He's planning to take my aunt to visit my parents in Florida next month. Things are good."

"That's great, what about Jamie?"

"He is fine. Right now I am waiting with Trudi while Jamie is trying on some clothes in the changing rooms. We've been to all the major shops on Oxford street."

"Is this for the meetings?"

"Yes, we have a meeting with two record companies this week and one next week."

"I'm glad things are working out at last Billie."

"So am I."

"Take care, I'll talk to you soon."

"Okay, kiss the little ones for me, I'll try and come down before the end of the week."

"I'll let them know."

"Bye"

I put my mobile phone back in my bag and wait for Jamie to appear. When he does emerge from behind the curtains, I am really impressed. He looks like a model. The clothes Trudi selected for him are fashionable and elegant. He looks as if he has just walked off a page of *'GQ'*.

"This one is a definite," I say to Trudi who is busy looking at some more shirts.

"I concur," Trudi says holding up a shirt, "what about this?"

"Looks good."

"Jamie is handsome and he can sing. He doesn't need to walk around half-naked for anyone to buy his record." She hands the shirt to me and walks over to Jamie with a T-shirt in her hand. She holds the T-shirt up against his chest. Jamie places a hand on top of hers, she blushes and removes her hand. I watch as she ruffles his hair slightly, then uses her fingers to comb it to one side. For a moment they seem lost in each other. What I feel right this moment as I watch them, is not shock, it's not even surprise because I know that Trudi sort of liked him from the first time she saw him. I know that she has gone out of her way to help with his appearance by letting us use her magazine's store discount card. She has suggested twice that I let her do a feature on him in her magazine to promote him. Jamie drops something and they both bend to pick it up. I smile as it suddenly dawns on me, yes she does like him, and from the very beginning she never doubted, she never once said that it couldn't be done. She saw the big picture too.

*　　*　　*　　*　　*

He watches her drink her coffee. His eyes narrow as he looks at the very short mini skirt she is wearing, at her legs which are over exposed and her cleavage which leaves nothing to the imagination. He frowns as he wonders what has happened to the 'treasure hunt' and why has it become the 'norm' now to find the treasure before the hunt even starts. He does not like women that feel they have to show more than is needed to be seen. He does not like women who constantly feel that they have the right to inflict their lack of morals on the world.

190

She finishes her coffee, picks up her folder and walks towards the door. A number of eyes walk with her. She senses that she is being looked at and intentionally adds a little more sway to her hips.

His mind clears and he becomes focused as he gets up pays his bill and leaves. He follows her down the road keeping a respectable distance. She turns the corner at the bottom of the road and he loses sight of her. He does not increase his pace. As he turns the corner he sees her opening the large gates of the school and shutting them carefully behind her. He crosses the road and walks to his car which he has parked opposite the school. He waits for the school to close. As he waits he goes over his plan again, he knows Ms Mini Skirt, he knows her type. He is confident that she will fall for it, hook line and sinker.

*　*　*　*　*

"Billie, what do you think?"

I look at the skirt suit that Trudi holds up and whistle.

"It's really nice," I say feeling the fabric. We are in another designer boutique and the clothes here are exceptional.

"Good, I thought you would like it. I think you should wear it for the meetings. You can change your blouse and wear it anywhere, work, church, outing, it's an all-rounder."

"Me? No, we're here to get Jamie stuff not me."

"You and Jamie are a team Billie, sure they like his voice, they like it even more singing your songs. The companies are interested in both of you, so you both have to knock them off their feet."

"Umm, I'm not sure."

"Sure you're sure. It's sorted anyway I've put it on the card so you only have to pay a third of the asking price. Try it on with these," she says holding a blouse and a pair of shoes up."

I look at the price tag on the suit, mentally divide the amount into three and don't wait for her to ask again. I really like the suit. Minutes later I walk out of the changing room with the suit on. I notice a couple of people staring at me as I walk towards Trudi.

"Wow! Jamie, over here," she shouts. Jamie walks over, he is wearing an elegant suit. He does a double-take and I laugh. I feel very self conscious as people in the shop keep looking at me. Trudi lifts my hair off my shoulders and pins it on top of my head. She turns me around and I am really shocked at the elegant lady looking back at me in the mirror.

"Record guys, be prepared to be blown away," Trudi says looking at both of us, quietly confident in her abilities, "be very prepared."

CHAPTER 19

On cue, Ms Mini Skirt walks out of the school building. He watches as she opens the gate, walks through it and closes it. She walks towards him. He walks towards her, on a collision course. He holds his breath and as she walks towards him he braces himself. He holds up his A-Z, and when she is a few feet away he increases his pace. He slams his body into her. She lets out a cry and falls to the pavement, winded. Her folder falls out of her hand and a few of her papers spill onto the ground.

"I am so sorry," he says helping her up and quickly retrieving the papers for her, "I am so terribly sorry, I wasn't looking where I was going. Are you okay?"

She looks up at the very tall, very handsome, very well-spoken young man behind the slightly tinted glasses and nods. He gently takes hold of her hands and checks them for cuts and bruises. He continues to apologize and smile at her.

"Really, I am fine thank you," she finally says not in a hurry to pull her hands away.

"Look can I buy you a drink or something, I feel so terrible about this, I was looking for Crenshaw Nursery and Junior School."

"Crenshaw? It's just down there, I work there."

"You do? What a coincidence!"

"I'm Lorna."

"Nice to meet you Lorna, look let me buy you a drink, there is a nice wine bar/coffee shop, around the corner," he quickly says not divulging his name.

"Pertonio's?"

"Yes, I go there all the time, do you know it?"

"I go there nearly every day!"

"What another coincidence!" He says taking hold of her arm.

"Come on it's the least I can do."

As they walk down the road the sound of her white stiletto's clicking on the pavement start to irritate him.

They place their orders and he unleashes his charm.

"Do you want to come back to my place?" Lorna asks totally captivated by the handsome young man. He freezes with disgust.

"Err..., maybe. Let's have something to eat first."

As they eat he flirts with her, she places her hand on his leg. He can feel his irritation rising and battles to keep it down.

"I'm just going to powder my nose," she says and stands up, "I will be right back, unless that is you feel like coming along." She leans towards him, pressing herself seductively against him.

He recoils internally, externally he smiles, "We have all night, we don't need to rush."

"My kind of man," she smiles. She turns and walks towards the toilets. Roger looks around, no one is watching him. He reaches across and opens Lorna's bag. Her identification badge is in a side pocket. He takes it out and looks behind the picture. Sure enough the PIN is written on a post-it-note which is stuck on the back of the card. He smiles at his successful stake out mission. After watching her carefully for several days, he suspected that it was the PIN she checked each morning on arriving at the school. He puts the card in his pocket. He is still looking in her bag when she returns from the toilet.

"What are you doing in my bag?"

"I was err, checking to see if you had any condoms, I don't have any at my place."

"No I don't, I don't carry them around with me, I ain't cheap y'know, I ain't no 'slapper'."

"I know but I can't wait any more. You know what, I'll go and get some at the petrol station around the corner. Wait here for me." He pulls out a wad of fifties from his jacket pocket, her eyes bulge at the sight of them. He hands her six notes, "Hold on to this in case the waiter thinks that I am going to do a runner. I've ordered some more cocktails. I'll be back soon," he blows her a kiss and gets up.

"Hurry back," she says.

Outside the wine bar he waits to see if she will open her bag. A waiter places two cocktails in front of her, she places her bag on the chair without looking inside.

He runs down the road in the direction of the school. Using Lorna's card and PIN he lets himself into the school. He has been here a number of times in the past to pick the children up, and knows where everything is. Quickly he makes his way to the office.

He turns his torch on and shines the light on the filing cabinets. He opens a drawer and looks through the files. He finds the one he is looking for. He smiles to himself, he is simply the best. He picks up a piece of paper and writes the name of the new school of his children. "I will see you soon Luke, Nick and Maddy. Real soon," he says softly to himself.

He chuckles at his cleverness as he puts everything back in place and leaves the office. He is still chuckling as he walks back to the wine bar.

"Did you get them?" Lorna asks looking excited.

"Yes," he says pulling the condoms out of his pocket and showing them to her.

"Your place?"

"No, I can't wait, go into the toilet and wait for me, leave your bag here, I'll tell the waiter that I am taking it to you if I am stopped. Go on I can't wait."

"Okay," she says jumping up and walking towards the toilet.

He looks around and then slips her identification badge back into her bag. He places the bag on the chair, gets up and leaves the restaurant. 'What's wrong with people nowadays, what has happened to common decency', he thinks to himself, 'she didn't even know my name'.

Anger surges through him and Lorna is forgotten in his silent rage. He walks to his car talking softly to himself.

"I've got my family back. You hear me Billie, you tried to take them away but I've got them back."

*   *   *   *   *

"It's going to be fine," Trudi says as I inhale deeply and exhale slowly. I look at my reflection in the mirror and breathe deeply again. Trudi stops arranging my hair and looks at me.

"It's finally happening Trudi, and I am so nervous."

195

"You and Jamie have worked hard for this, you have what? Twenty, twenty five songs recorded? That's nearly two albums worth of material Billie."

"I know, it's not the songs," I pause, "you know when you pray for something and it finally happens?"

She nods her understanding, "You feel like you can't breathe, overwhelmed, happy and a little bit nervous?"

"Yes," I say loudly at her apt description, "I'm so thankful as well and I keep getting really emotional."

"Give a good singer a badly written song and it will sound bad, give a not so good singer a well written song and it will sound good. You have a good singer singing well written songs, the result, they sound fantastic! Embrace it all Billie. You always say things happen for a reason, this is the reason for all the things that have happened in the past. This is the reason! In less than two hours you have your first meeting with a 'major' record company."

*   *   *   *   *

"Hi Billie, Jamie," the pretty petite lady says as we walk out of the lift and onto the 7th floor of the building that houses Vigil Records. "My name is Tracy Banks, I am Pete Wilson's assistant, you are both very welcome," she shakes our hands and smiles at us.

"This way please, Pete is using one of the conference rooms."

We follow her down the carpeted corridor. I look at the impressive gold and platinum record discs on the walls and the pictures of some of the artists signed to Vigil. Tracy knocks on a door and walks into the room. We follow her. The room we enter is as long as it is wide, there is a large mahogany table just off centre of the room surrounded by high back elegant mahogany chairs. A huge man adorned with numerous gold necklaces, bracelets and rings, that I assume is Pete Wilson, is seated at the head of the table. He stands up as we walk towards him.

"Jamie Sanders and Ms Billie Lewis, at last, nice to meet you both, I'm Pete Wilson," he shakes Jamie's hand then mine. As we shake hands I feel his hand grip mine tightly, I see his eyes wandering over my body; I pull my hand away.

"Tracy, drinks," he orders rudely

"Yes, umm.., sorry, what would you like?" Tracy asks us blushing with embarrassment.

"Nothing thank you, I'm fine," I say

"Water please," Jamie says.

"The usual for me, gin with no T and no ice," Pete demands.

Tracy walks to the corner of the room and returns almost immediately with some drinks.

"Right, Jamie, Billie, I have listened to all the songs you sent in, I like what I hear," he nods and rubs his hands together, "so tell me about you Jamie. Who are you?"

I turn and look at Jamie hoping that he is not nervous. I smile as I listen to him confidently tell Pete about himself. We have both agreed that we would say nothing about Troyston. He says nothing.

"Billie?"

"Yes."

"Tell me about you?"

"I write songs and manage Jamie," I say not really knowing what else to say.

"How many of the songs did you write on this list?" He asks sliding a sheet of paper towards me. I pick it up and look at it.

"Eleven," I reply and put the paper down.

He whistles, "Have you taken out copyrights?"

"Why?" I ask.

"I know someone that is in the market for some songs. He would buy the rights from you, lock and stock. I'm talking about a lot of money, enough to pay off all your debts and more."

"What!"

"Think about it Billie-"

There is a knock on the door, Tracy jumps up and rushes towards the door. A man says something to her and she tells him that we are in the middle of a meeting. I notice that Pete looks uncomfortable and I can only put it down to the interruption.

"I'm sorry about this guys, you'd have thought that the person could read the bloody 'do not disturb' sign on the door," he exhales slowly and sighs. I turn as Tracy rushes back to the table. She looks very nervous as she whispers something into his ear.

"He is past his sell by date, he hasn't had a hit in a while and his slip has been showing for months. No hits means he is 'history', he knows the rules of the industry. I don't have the time for him or his antics anymore. The sooner we drop that sack of potatoes the better, we need to get some 'fresh meat'." Pete says arrogantly in response to what she has told him.

I try to hide a frown as I wonder who he is talking about.

"Sing 'Love Is Not Supposed To Hurt' for me," Pete says loudly, "Tracy play the song but hike up the music."

Jamie sings and I sit back and listen, I look from Pete to Tracy. 'Assistant A&R Manager' I think to myself. I don't know why but I feel a sense of 'Jasmine Peters' in the air. Jamie finishes singing the song.

"Great, bloody great," Pete says gleefully rubbing his hands together.

"I think that-" Tracy starts to say.

"Fantastic," Pete says interrupting her, "I'm sold. So let's talk about the kind of image we would be looking at. You have more than enough material for an album, I am happy with that."

"Image wise, we were thinking of elegant, but casual. Sort of what he's wearing now," I say.

He looks at Jamie, "I don't know, umm.., we have professional image consultants here, who know what they are talking about, so we'll see what they think. Me, I'd recommend tight trousers, open shirt to show off the abs. The kind of stuff that sells, sex, sex and more sex."

"I think that the image consultant people would like Jamie's look now it's very appealing, he looks really good," Tracy says.

"Personally, with my years of experience, nearly twenty of them to be precise, not that we're counting, I don't think so," Pete says rudely interrupting her.

"What direction will you be taking his image and will we have a say, will our ideas be listened to?" I ask.

"We will take things on a need to know basis, we know and you don't need to," he laughs, Jamie and I frown.

Someone knocks on the door and before Tracy gets to it, pushes it open and walks in. My mouth falls open slightly as I recognize the singer Brian Turner.

"Wilson, I need to talk to you, now," he stands by the door.

Pete is red faced as he splutters, "I'll be with you shortly-"

"What part of 'NOW' did you not understand?"

Pete stands up and rushes to the door, he ushers Brian out and closes the door. I look at Tracy who is staring at the table.

"What were you going to say Tracy?" I ask.

"Which time?" She asks and smiles weakly, "oh it wasn't much, I was going to suggest that Jamie not have one look. That he can do some things really dressed up, and others casual. Sort of dress to suit the song, because your songs are different. Not have just one image but constantly keep changing it, reinventing it; if it can work for footballers, it can work for singers."

Jamie and I look at each other and then at her.

"That's a really good idea," I say.

"He won't listen though."

"But we will," Jamie says, "do you mind if we keep it?"

"No, please use it." She tells us about the different looks for the songs. We listen as she describes colours and background effects for photographs.

"Right, where were we? Where were we?" Pete asks as he walks in a really cocky manner back to his chair. "Image, we were talking about his look and the way we want him to look, weren't we?"

I nod, "Tracy was telling us about some of her ideas, we think they sound really good."

"She can tell me about them later," Pete says in a dismissive manner. "Now let's see, we need something that will get the ladies hot don't we Jamie?"

"Do *we*?" Jamie asks. I know him so well now and I can tell that he is being a little, just a little, sardonic. I smile reassuringly at Tracy. I sneak a glance at my watch, I don't feel comfortable here at all. The fact that we have a meeting with Digital Records this afternoon does not play a part in my eagerness to get out of here. If this were our only option, I would still feel as uncomfortable as I do now. Pete is talking about the album and how many singles will be released in the first instance. As he talks I hear a glibness, a lack of sincerity in his words.

"Bear in mind that we want you both on board, any questions?"

"How long before the album is ready, considering we have a number of songs already?" I ask.

"As long as it takes, one year, two years," he replies.

"Who decides what goes on the album?"

"We do."

"No discussions with us?"

He looks at me in a strange way, he seems to be trying to convince us that he is thinking. "No," he eventually says, "we are not necessarily obliged to put any of your songs on the album."

"What!" Jamie says, I hear the shock in his voice.

"We may be steering you in a totally different direction, say rock," he holds a hand up and waves his first finger and 'pinky' at us, flashing what is known as the rock 'n' roll sign to some and the two horn demonic sign to others. "Or maybe even 'Indie' pop."

"Rock? 'Indie' pop?" I query totally shocked.

"That's not to say that we will be doing that or we won't be using your songs Billie," he quickly adds defensively. "We can always come to an agreement can't we Billie." He winks at me. I sense a hidden innuendo.

We look at each other in uncomfortable silence.

"What type of contract would we be looking at?" I ask.

"You know about the different contracts?"

"Yes."

"We would have to take that to the legal department."

"I am not talking legalities, I'm talking album deals here. Are we looking at a one, two or a five album deal?"

"I err, I have to.., I have to find out from the A&R Manager. I think we would be looking at nothing less than say two."

"Over what period?"

"Oh, two, three maybe four years, most likely four years."

"What?" I ask. I am trying with great difficulty to sit through this meeting let alone believe what he is saying. "Four years for two albums? Who –"

There is a loud knock on the door, Brian Turner walks back in.

"I've had enough of waiting Wilson, you guys are talking to new artists when you have done nothing for me recently. I have brought millions to this shit hole, now you think that you can just discard me. I hear rumours flying around that you are thinking of dropping me. I read articles in the newspapers, and you sit there trying to get new artists in the front door while you kick me out the back. You don't even have the decency to tell me to my face. Get out here now Wilson. I don't know who you guys are, but take it from me, these people either use you and pocket all the money, or 'shelf' you. If you have a few lousy sales they stab you in the back. WILSON, OUT HERE, NOW!"

Pete gets up and rushes out of the room. He closes the door but we still hear the shouting and the swearing.

I glance at my watch again. I nudge Jamie's leg with mine and point to my watch. He nods.

"Tracy, we are going to have to leave."

"I honestly don't blame you."

"No, it's not that," I say pointing to the door, "we have to get somewhere and we are cutting it a bit fine."

"Okay, I'll tell Pete."

As soon as she leaves the room I turn to Jamie, "Well Mr Sanders, I don't think that we need to place any orders for any tight trousers just yet." We try really hard to laugh quietly.

Tracy walks back in, "Err.., I told him you have to leave now and he said he would call you. As you can hear, he is a little distracted."

We thank her and she escorts us to the lifts via another door.

"Your idea about Jamie's image is a really good one."

"Really?"

"Really."

"Thanks."

"Thank you for your time Tracy."

*   *   *   *   *

"How long do we have before Digital?" Jamie asks.

I look at my watch, "Just about an hour."

"Well, what did you think about Vigil?" He asks. "I hope Digital is better. That's all I can say, I really hope that they are better."

CHAPTER 20

The song fades then ends, Francis Wells turns the player off and looks from Jamie to me, and back to Jamie.

"Excellent. That's what I said when I first heard it and that's what I am saying now." We both nod and wait for him to continue. "I have played the tape to our French and Italian partners and they are just as excited."

Someone knocks at the door and Jamie and I exchange glances and grimace. The door opens and a lady walks in pushing a trolley in front of her. Francis gets up and helps her to bring it inside his office.

"Thanks Velma, we were just listening to the songs. Billie, Jamie I'd like you to meet my assistant Velma Conuche. Velma, Billie Lewis and Jamie Sanders."

"Hi," she says. "I left a message for you on your answer machine last week Billie. It is nice to meet you." She has a Colombian accent. I know it is Colombian because I attended a short management course with someone from Colombia a couple of years ago.

"Nice to meet you."

"Right, I am starving, I have not had a chance to stop and eat all day. Please join me," Francis says. He picks up little plates and obviously not prepared to take no for an answer, hands the plates out. I get up and walk to the trolley that is laden with cakes, biscuits, crisps, sandwiches, soft drinks, tea and coffee.

We sit and listen to some more of the songs and eat. I feel very relaxed. I can tell that Francis Wells is a very astute person, I can also tell that he is a decent person as well. Although Jamie and I have no pre-arranged signals, I sense that he is comfortable here.

"As you have probably already gathered from all our phone conversations, I definitely want to sign Jamie to our label. Even though I will send a copy of the tape to our new American company, I have the final say. Billie how do you feel about working in our song writing department part-time?"

"Me?"

"We understand that your main job will be to manage Jamie. Velma thought that we could tap into your abilities as well."

"That's right Billie, I have listened to your songs several times and I think that you have an ability which we could use. A way of using simple words to talk about complicated issues." Velma gets up and puts a tape into the machine and presses a button. We all listen to the song. It is one I wrote a couple of months ago called 'Need To Be Loved'. I listen to Jamie's voice sing the words knowing that he has done a good job. When the song finishes Velma continues.

"I have spoken to some people in our song writing department and played a few of your songs to them. They say they would love for you to work with them whenever you can."

"You can think about it Billie. I can see that you are surprised, so without trying to overtly sway you, the job does comes with a very nice on-site office," Francis adds.

"Thanks, I will think about it."

"Okay at this point I can say that with Jamie we would be looking at albums."

"What options would we be looking at?" I ask.

"Options?" Francis asks a little guarded.

"One album with the option of say, two or three albums?"

"Definitely. Though we would have to look at a time frame as well as options."

"What about up-front payments?"

"What did you have in mind?" Francis asks. I can see that he is looking at me differently now.

"Low up-front payment with a larger royalty percentage."

Francis and Velma exchange glances then look at me.

"Can I ask, just out of curiosity, why? You see most artists that come in here want a large up-front payment and a smaller royalty percentage."

"I am hoping that with a smaller up-front payment we will be given certain rights as well as a larger royalty percentage."

"Rights? Such as?"

"Having a say with regards to Jamie's image, what goes on the album and what his videos are about," I say and hold my breath as both Francis and Velma stare at me.

"Interesting, very interesting. Jamie you are one lucky man that this lady is 'batting' on your team. Okay Billie, now that I probably have to write a special contract just for you guys, is there anything else you want?"

"Umm.., can I have a copy of the contract say, a week before we sign and can I have your word that we can make changes, within reason, if needed."

"Within reason?"

I nod and watch him.

"Velma can you knock up a contract for Billie's perusal, ASAP."

"Sure," Velma says writing something on a piece of paper.

"Once everything is signed we will start talking promotion. We have people on this site that deal with all the promotion work."

"We will be looking at the normal things first" Velma says flipping through her notes. "GMTV, This Morning, The Lottery, Openings, Showcases. Basically as you know the success of a new artist is very dependent on promotion. I have lost count of the number of times you see a video on The Box or MTV over and over again, and a few weeks later the song is number one in the national singles chart. A lot of money will be spent on getting Jamie out there. I understand Billie that you have done some clubs up north. That's good, we will ride on that wave, get him up there again. Leeds, Liverpool, Manchester, Birmingham, as far as Edinburgh. The more people see an artist, the more the artist is remembered, especially one that can sing really well and looks as good as Jamie," she smiles at him. He smiles back.

"I think that Jamie looks good in what he is wearing now," Francis says looking at him. "Of course we have fashion consultants that will work with you."

"So we will definitely have a say?" I ask.

"You will have a say. You do understand that the interest of the company will come first though? We will not tell him to wear a taffeta G-string or anything like that, but at the same time he cannot dress or behave in such a manner that we are discredited."

"Obviously," I say.

"Do you have an agent Billie?"

"No, not yet."

"We have a list of people that we can recommend. See, we pride ourselves on being one of the few companies that actually supply an agent if needed. The agents we recommend are from our PR department, they have both your interest at heart as well as the interest of the company. They do a good job, we've not had any complaints." He talks some more about the company, and what strikes me as I listen is the way he talks as if we are already a part of the team.

"How about we take you round and introduce you to some of the people here?" He asks.

"Okay," I say.

"Great!" Jamie concurs.

Thirty minutes later we stand by the lifts and talk.

"Thank you both for coming in," Francis says as he shakes our hands. "Velma will have a copy of the contract sent to you, just for you to look at Billie, you can show it to a lawyer, let us know about any possible changes and we will take it from there."

"Thank you," I say as euphoria sets in.

*　　*　　*　　*　　*

Outside the building Jamie and I stand facing each other. One year, two weeks, and one day after we first met. For a minute it is as if we are both lost in our own thoughts. Then I look up at him and he looks down at me. He is shaking his head as if in disbelief.

"What just happened in there?"

"I don't know," I say, "but I know that they are going to send a contract to us, ASAP." My heart is beating really fast.

He closes his eyes and I cover my face with my hands.

"God thank you," I say as I notice my hands that were confident a few minutes ago, are now shaking.

Jamie grabs hold of me, "ASAP," he says, "ASAP."

"YEAHHHH....," we both shout as he swings me round and around and around.

* * * * *

He waits outside the new school for his children. It is nearly home time and he knows that they will soon come out. He holds the bag containing the comics and sweets tightly in his hand as he waits. He cannot wait to see the look of surprise on their little faces when they see him.

"Excuse me sir, what are you doing here?" He turns and finds himself looking at a police officer.

"Sorry?"

"I asked what are you doing here? We received a phone call from a member of staff who seemed to be concerned about a man loitering by the school gates. A man fitting your description has been seen loitering at these gates for nearly an hour."

"Loitering? Me?"

"You are the only one here. Are you a parent?"

"Yes of course I am."

"Who are you here to pick up?" The police officer pulls a notebook and pen out.

"Err.., well actually, I am here to pick up my nephew and niece. My sister's children."

"What are their names?"

"I err.., I...,"

"Their names please sir?"

"I err...,"

"Right, do you mind coming with me sir?"

"With you? Where to?"

"The police station, come along sir." The police officer takes the bag from his hand and opens it, he sees all the sweets and comics inside. 'Classic', he thinks grabbing hold of him and leading him to the waiting police car.

* * * * *

"Mummy, mummy, guess what? There was a man outside the gates today and he had a big bag of sweets and was trying to steal children," Luke says to his mother as soon as she walks into his classroom.

"What?" Sarah asks, turning to the class teacher, "what happened?"

"There was a man loitering by the school gates this afternoon. One of the teachers noticed him and called the police because she was a little concerned. That's why we are asking parents to come into the classrooms today." She lowers her voice, "He had a bag of sweets and comics so the police think his intention was to try and lure a child-"

"Comics and sweets?" Sarah asks. Her heart starts to race, she tries to control herself. 'It can't be him' she thinks to herself. 'He doesn't know that the children are in this school.' She helps Luke to put his coat on and tries to ignore thoughts that bombard her mind. Despite her efforts she cannot ignore the fact that Roger used to bring comics and sweets for the children. Or the fact that he used to hang around the school gates waiting for them in their old school.

She takes these facts to the headmistress, knowing that the children would once again have to change schools.

CHAPTER 21

"**A** toast to Billie and Jamie," my uncle says lifting his glass of orange juice up.

"Billie and Jamie," everyone choruses.

I smile as I look at the people who have come to Martin's club to celebrate with us; I am so happy that Jamie's brother and sisters have come. Even though we have not yet signed the contract, the deal is as good as done. We did not go to the meeting with the third record company because we both felt that Digital was right for us. Jamie had said that he didn't want to get into a position where too much choice would cloud his judgement and I agreed. My uncle and aunt, like my parents had been over the moon when I told them about the record deal. I watch now as my uncle talks to Jen. They are both smiling. He looks years younger and so full of life.

"Billie, you are sure you don't mind looking after the club tonight?" Martin asks.

"Of course I'm sure."

"Thanks."

"Your dad looks so happy, every time I look at him I feel so glad inside."

"So do I Billie, believe me, so do I."

*   *   *   *   *

As I sit in Martin's office going through the final draft of the contract someone knocks on the door.

"Come in."

Delroy, Martin's head bouncer walks into the office, "Billie there's a guy by the bar from New York, he's looking for Martin."

"Did he say why?"

"No, just that he flew into London today and decided to stop off here and see Martin before going back to New York."

209

"Thanks Del I'll go and have a word with him."

I get up and walk through the vibrant club with Del to the bar.

"This is Martin's cousin, Billie, she is running things tonight," Del says introducing me to the man.

"Hello I'm Jason Alexander, I went to university with Martin. I haven't seen him in a while. I heard about this place from a friend of a friend of my wife's, and thought I'd check it out while I'm in London," the man says. He extends his hand towards me. I shake his hand and smile at him. His voice is amazing and sounds so familiar.

"Martin is out with his parents and girlfriend. I can take a message for him."

"Thanks, it's not really that urgent or anything, I'm here for a couple of days so I'll probably catch him at home," he looks around, "so he finally did it? For years he talked about setting this place up. It looks even better than I thought it would be, wholesome." I smile knowing exactly what he means.

"Do you know if he is still going to set a place up in America?"

"Yes he is, he's looking for someone based over there to set it up with," I reply

"This sort of place is needed in America. It is clean and wholesome, it will build up young people instead of pull them down. Someone in America said that he has Gospel nights, where the only music played is Gospel music, is that true?"

"Absolutely," I reply "three times a week."

"That is incredible, he always said he would do it, he always said he would go against the grain. I am blown away with this."

I stand staring at Jason knowing I have heard his voice before.

"Billie, is everything okay?"

"Sorry, I don't mean to stare at you, it's just.., I have heard your voice somewhere before. Are you a DJ in New York?"

"Busted," he says and smiles, "I was hoping for Incognito."

"Not possible, not with your voice."

He smiles modestly.

"You have that day time radio show don't you?"

"Yes I do."

"Throughout my last visit to New York I listened to you every day on the radio. You have done so much for new talent. The way you play the songs that no one wants to take a risk with, and then as soon as the song is played, and everyone likes it, the other DJs latch on. I really admire you. I can't believe I'm standing here talking to you. I didn't know you knew my cousin, it's really nice to meet you," I stop talking realizing that I am rambling.

"Thank you Billie, I'm glad you like the show and what it stands for."

"I do, I really do. Actually can you do something for me? Give me a few minutes I'll be right back," I rush towards Martin's office.

Rummaging in my bag I find and pull out an audio cassette with 'Love Is Not Supposed To Hurt' recorded on it. I rush back to the bar. "I really hope you don't mind, I respect your taste in music and if you really don't mind can you listen to this song. If you feel it's good enough, play it on your show, if you don't put it on the shelf."

He takes the tape from me, "I'll listen to it, I can't promise anything else."

"That's all I ask."

"You won't get offended with the outcome if it's not favourable?"

"No, no I won't. A few months ago rejection was rampant and I had to learn to deal with it. I think you'll like it."

"Confidence runs in your family I see. Okay I'll do it."

"Thank you."

"Can you tell Martin that I'll give him a call tomorrow." He puts the tape in his pocket.

"I will and thanks Jason."

*   *   *   *   *

I can hear a lot of chatter coming from the tea room, as soon as I walk in it stops. 'What's going on?' I think to myself. I look around the room at the people sitting in the armchairs. I smile at some of them and they smile back. 'Is it me', I think and walk towards the fridge.

"I hear you're leaving soon Billie, is it true?" Tina asks.

"Yes I am."

"When?" Chloe asks.

"In a few weeks," I reply.

"I honestly never thought your music thing would take off," Tina says. "I was just saying to Chloe before you walked in that I am really surprised. Chloe agrees."

"Oh does she?" I ask looking at Chloe, "I didn't know that."

She looks down at her charm bracelet and moves the chunky things that hang from it around. She does not look at me.

"I think it's just taken us all by surprise," Chloe says, "I never actually thought that you would get this far."

"Good job you didn't tell me months ago that you thought I wouldn't make it, you always sounded positive when we used to talk then."

"It's not that I'm not positive, it's just that I look at you as just Billie, a technician. It will take a lot of getting used to, seeing you as something else other than a laboratory technician."

"Will it?" I ask, she doesn't answer.

"Is it true that you were offered a senior position here?" Dr Colin Plowman asks.

I nod as I look at him. He looks different, he has dyed his blonde hair jet black. He stands up and walks over to the fridge. I realize that he is nearly as tall as Roger and look up at him.

"I had hoped you and I..., err, this place won't be the same without you Billie."

I wonder what he means. I cannot remember having had more than a handful of very short conversations with him since he started his medical rotation in the department. Frowning I look at him again, his eyes look dark and menacing but his mouth smiles at me. I feel my skin crawl and step away from him.

"I read an article about you and Jamie in a magazine," he says and sniffs loudly.

"Which magazine?"

"Oh some magazine I don't remember the name, I read so many of them."

"What did you read in this magazine?"

"Something about the type of male film stars you like. Would you like to go out for a drink and talk about things?"

I don't have a clue what he is talking about, "No thank you Colin," I reply.

He frowns, "Is it true that you would never go for a drink or a casual date with just anyone, that you are waiting for the right guy?"

I literally freeze and look up at him.

"I never said that in any magazine. Where did you hear that?"

"You look like that kind of person-"

"Colin!" Tina says loudly. Startled I turn and look at her. She gets up and walks towards us.

"Move Colin," she says.

"Sorry Tina-"

"Just move, go and sit down somewhere and stop being a nuisance," she says rudely.

Colin moves quickly out of the way and she puts something in the fridge.

"Good luck Billie," she says and walks out of the room.

Chloe is still sitting down. She quickly picks up a magazine and holds it in front of her face ignoring me. Colin sits down and smiles at me but does not continue the conversation. I open the fridge take out my small bottle of orange juice and close the door. I walk past Colin and sit down in a chair as far away from him as possible. I pull out a novel from my bag and look at the writing on the pages. Chloe has put her magazine on her lap, she appears to be reading it intently and does not look up or say anything to me. I feel a little hurt by her behaviour. Until recently we used to talk a lot to each other. Now she has shut me out and I don't know why, she won't tell me. I asked her a few questions about Roger and Nigel some weeks ago, I didn't go into detail about what I had seen in the cold-room. She told me to mind my own business. Now, I don't know if she is angry because I asked her the questions or if she is just envious of the fact that I am moving on. Each time I try and talk to her she cuts me off, I am beginning to suspect that it has nothing to do with my questions.

When it was all just a dream and I was still working, dreaming and doubting my abilities, it was okay with her but now my dream is becoming a reality it is a problem. She used to encourage me in the past and I really thought that she was a 'dream maker'. Now as I look at the blurred words in the book I am holding I realize for the first time that 'dream breakers' can pretend to be 'dream makers'. They pretend to support you and when things are difficult you may believe that they are your friend. As soon as things start to get good you realize that the friendship was never real. That they never wanted or hoped that you would rise up above a certain level. That, in fact, they did everything in their power to help you stay down. Dead-weights! There are people like this everywhere, 'Friends in Failure', supporting you in your dreaming, yet hoping your aspirations, your dreams, are never achieved.

My advice: Pray to God for wisdom and discernment, then *use* your God given wisdom and discernment to stay on the path of your purpose. And, pray for the 'dream breakers', pray that they see the 'light' and change.

CHAPTER 22

Tonight is my last night on call. My bleep went off ten minutes ago at eleven thirty, and I am driving to the hospital to process a sample. 'After tonight no more getting paged late at night or early in the morning any more' I think to myself as I look for somewhere to park my car.

I finally managed to speak to my department manager last week, and despite his generous offers aimed at changing my mind, I handed in my notice. I have three more weeks to work here and then that's it. I can't wait.

I park my car and walk into A&E to collect the urine sample I have been called in to process. The nurse looks at my identification badge and hands me the sample. I check the name on the container with the one the doctor had given me on the phone and thank the nurse. I walk out of A&E and towards my building. There is an eerie silence floating around as I swipe my ID card along the security pad attached to the wall in front of the building. I key in my PIN, the door opens and I walk in. I notice from the lights above the lifts that both lifts are on the ninth floor. As the person on call tonight, I had been the last to leave the department. I don't understand why both lifts are there. I press the call button, nothing happens. The lights above both doors indicate that both lifts are still on the ninth floor. I turn towards the stairs.

Slightly out of breath I climb the last flight of stairs. I place my hand on the door handle and rest a few seconds, just as I am about to pull it open, I hear a noise. I look through the glass panel of the door, I can see that the lights I had turned off before I left this evening, are now on. The lift doors are held open with large yellow clinical waste bins. I walk down a flight of stairs and call the hospital switch board. They connect me to the security office.

I hear something fall above me and despite being told by the security man to come back downstairs to the entrance of the building and wait for him, I walk up the stairs. At the door, I look through the glass panelling again. I can see a hole in the wall, there is a piece of the wall laying on the floor and what looks like small bottles standing in racks in the hole. 'What is going on?' I think to myself. I see a shadow moving towards the hole, I hold my breath and watch. Nigel walks up to the hole and takes a rack out and puts some bottles into the rack. I hear Tina telling him to hurry up. I turn and quietly walk down the first flight of stairs.

Roger watches from where he sits on the next flight of stairs leading to the tenth floor. He watches as Billie quietly stands looking through the glass panel. He says nothing as she turns and walks down the stairs. Tina and Nigel rush through the door seconds later.

"Was there someone else here just now? Was someone looking through the glass panel?" Nigel asks.

"Yes," Roger replies.

"Who was it?" Tina asks.

"Me," Roger answers.

*   *   *   *   *

When I get to the sixth floor, I start to run. I hear voices from one of the floors above, but don't bother to look up. On the ground floor I rush through the doors and almost collide into someone. I jump back as hands grab hold of me.

"Miss Lewis?" The man in a security uniform asks as he steadies me.

"Yes."

"Are you okay?"

"I err, yes, I'm fine. I thought I heard something when I was on the stairs. I panicked."

"Okay, I'll go upstairs with you now."

I look at the sample in my hand, I don't want to, but I know that I have to go back upstairs and process it.

"Will you stay upstairs with me until I finish this please? I won't take long," I hold the sample up.

"Sure," he says.

He walks to the lifts and presses the button. "I don't think the lifts are...," I stop talking, amazed I see from the lights above the lifts that they are both descending.

"What's wrong with the lifts?" He asks.

216

"Err, nothing," I reply as I notice his comical expression.

The doors open simultaneously. I peer inside both lifts, they are empty. We walk inside one and the security man presses the ninth floor button. Slowly the lift ascends. I step back and let him move forward when the door opens. The first thing I notice as I walk out of the lift is that all the lights are off. Frowning I look around, half expecting someone to jump out at us.

"Right, you get started on that while I look around."

"Actually can I come with you, then you with me?"

He appears to hesitate, "Sure," he finally says.

I process the sample in under a minute, phone the results through and leave the laboratory with the security man. As we walk towards the lift I pause and look at the place in the wall where I had seen the hole. I can't see anything there now. There is no evidence of there ever being a hole.

"Are you okay Miss Lewis?"

"I'm fine," I reply following him to the lift. I hear something crunch and we both look down.

"What the…?"

"It looks like glass," I say, "It wasn't there when I left around nine, and the cleaners did this whole floor around seven this evening."

He presses a button on his radio and makes a request for some more men to come upstairs and search the ninth floor and then the rest of the building. While he is talking on his radio I look at the wall, my eyes move along it trying to see if the hole had been further along than I had thought it was. Something shiny on the floor catches my eye and I move forward. I bend and pick up a small glass bottle. It has an agar slope in it with what looks like some bacteria growing on it. On the bottle are written the words *Salmonella enteritidis, Campylobacter jejuni, Vibrio cholerae*. I frown as I look at the bacterial concoction.

"Are you all right?"

"Yes, I found this on the floor."

"What is it?"

"It's a culture of three bacteria that cause diarrhoea and mixed together like this, if ingested, can be very lethal. It's strange, why would someone put three very harmful bacteria on the same slope?"

He shrugs and I assume that he does not really understand the significance of my question.

"Experiment?" He queries.

"Not that I know of, especially not with such lethal bacteria. It's not something that a Microbiologist would do," I say frowning.

*   *   *   *   *

Sometimes when a story comes to an end, the odd twist of the tale or unexpected occurrence, happens to extend the story. My story here has come to an end. There are no twists in the story of my working in this hospital, no unexpected occurrences that can make me stay any longer. If I could leave right now I would.

Patients' samples arrive and I watch as staff in white laboratory coats rush to the specimen reception area. Trained hands sort through the samples placing them in sample bins labelled with the sample type on them. In less than a minute everyone walks back to their bench with their sample bins. This happens five times a day, five days a week.

As I sit working hard in the laboratory I pause for a while and look around at all the other staff. In the midst of all these people, I feel so lonely.

"Billie, phone," Chloe shouts down the laboratory to me. I get up and walk towards the office.

"Hello."

"Miss Lewis, it's Pete Wilson here from Vigil Records, how are you?"

"I am fine thank you," I say surprised that he is calling me at work, even more surprised that he knows where I work and the phone number.

"Good, good. I was just wondering if we could have another meeting. We were err..., interrupted the last time we were together and I just wondered if we could get together at say 5pm tomorrow?"

"Tomorrow? Umm..."

"I will not take up a lot of your time, I just want you to meet the A&R Manager. He really likes your songs and wants to meet with you. We were thinking about the options you are interested in."

"Options?"

"Yes, regarding the low up-front payment and the larger royalty percentage. We think we can come to some arrangement."

I freeze, I never discussed any options with Pete Wilson. He tells me that he is willing to pay an initial up-front payment which is almost double what Digital have agreed to, and give us a larger royalty percentage. I am stunned. 'How did he know about the figures I have been discussing with Francis Wells?' I think to myself.

"Hope to see you tomorrow Billie, wear something a little more 'talent' revealing," he chuckles. "We have a surprise for you and I know you will not get another offer better than ours. You can't, so don't be naive. Think about Jamie's career and make the right decision. You wouldn't want things taken out of your hands now would you? Can I suggest that you drop the goody two shoes, girl next door image Billie, you are a vibrant woman. Use what you have to get what you want, take a look at the dark side of life, you may like what you see. Why trust in what you can't see," he laughs, "I can make you rich and famous, think about it."

He hangs up and I stand staring at the receiver. I put it down and walk back to my bench. 'What was that about?' I wonder.

I try and concentrate on my work but my mind is working overtime and I can't concentrate. 'I have to phone Jamie and Francis Wells as soon as I have a break' I think to myself. I look around the laboratory, I wish I was somewhere else.

"Billie, phone call," Chloe shouts down the laboratory again ten minutes later. I quickly get up and walk towards the office.

"Hello, Billie it's me," Jamie says, "sorry about calling you at work, this is important. I just got off the phone with Pete Wilson, he asked me to come to Vigil Records and meet with his Manager."

"Did he say anything about money or contracts?"

"Only that he has spoken to you and they are prepared to pay a bigger up-front payment and royalty percentage, he also said something about a car. He asked about our personal contract, if it was legally binding, whether or not it could be easily dissolved. He said that you and he both agree that I need to be managed differently."

"What! I can't believe this, he is lying. He just called me about ten minutes ago, offered me twice the amount that Digital are offering up-front and a larger royalty percentage. I don't know how he knows what Digital have offered us."

"There's a leak."

"A what?"

"Someone in Digital is 'feeding' Vigil and maybe other record companies information for money."

"They do that with new artists?"

"Anyone they think will sell."

"That's a good sign then, if they think we will sell."

"Not necessarily. Some labels do it only to stop other record labels from signing an artist. They don't actually have the new artist's interest at heart. They only do it to stop the competition."

"I don't understand that. What do you mean by competition?"

"Take for example a really popular female singer or group that are already signed to a label. It will not be in the interest of the record company if another artist that sounds similar to theirs comes along. Competition wise, sales wise. So what the label may and can do is quickly step in and sign up the new female singer or group to avoid another label signing them and any competition."

"Then the new artist will be competing with the old one on the same label. So how do they work that one out?"

"By putting the new artist on the 'shelf'. They keep them from being signed by anyone else, but don't really promote them, so they don't compete with their existing artist."

"This is all above board?"

"Depends on where the board is placed."

"Right, I'm going to get to the bottom of this. What time did he tell you to get there?"

"4pm."

"He told me to get there at 5pm."

"They are obviously planning to work on me first then. Divide and conquer."

"Leave this with me Jamie, they are not going to work on anyone. I'm going to call Francis right now. We still absolutely agree, Digital, right?"

"Definitely."

"Good, I'll call Francis then I'll call you back." I put the receiver down and stare at the wall. 'Is there nowhere where things are done properly anymore?' I think to myself as I let out a deep sigh.

"Are you okay Billie?"

I turn around, Roger is standing behind me. "Yes I'm fine thank you."

"Late night?"

"No, why?"

"I just heard that you were on call last night, that's all. I wondered if you had any late call outs."

"No, not too late. I'm going for an early lunch," I say walking past him. I stop as I remember something someone had said this morning. "I heard you left your wallet at home and need to borrow some money Roger." I hand him a ten pound note.

"You want to lend *me* money?"

"Yes, if you need it."

"Thanks Billie, I really do need it, I've asked everyone but no one would lend me anything. Thank you I'll pay you back tomorrow," he says and takes the money.

*   *   *   *   *

As I walk past my Manager's office I look inside. He is sitting at his desk. I knock on his door and walk in.

"Billie, everything okay?"

"Yes."

"I heard you had a little scare last night."

"Not really, I just thought I heard some noise when I came in to process a sample. Have you got a few minutes?"

"Yes, what's on your mind?"

"I know I said I would work for three more weeks but I have a lot of annual leave to take so I have decided to leave earlier."

"How much earlier?" He asks.

"End of this week," I reply.

*   *   *   *   *

Francis Wells sounds genuinely surprised about the offer from Vigil Records.

"I don't know what to say Billie. This sort of thing does happen once in a while," he sounds a little cautious and I wonder why.

"I have talked it over with Jamie, we had another label that we were going to meet with but we cancelled after we met with you. We have both decided to go with Digital."

"You have? Right!" From cautious, he now sounds surprised.

Silence.

"Francis?"

"I'm still here. Sorry, no one has *ever* said that before. They usually just go with the highest bidder. That or everything becomes one big haggle. I am totally shocked at what you just said. You know what Billie, I'm going to match Vigil's offer."

"What?"

"I'm going to match them, can we get this contract signed?"

"Okay," I reply completely stunned.

*   *   *   *   *

"What do you think Steve?" I ask.

"It looks okay, very okay actually."

"Jamie?"

"Looks good."

"Let's do it then," I say.

Someone knocks on the door, we turn as the door opens. Francis Wells walks back into his office.

"How's it going? Is everything okay Steve?"

"Fine."

"Billie?"

"Yes."

"Jamie?"

"Okay."

"Good, let's sign then."

*　*　*　*　*

The atmosphere is very relaxed. We are now a part of Digital Records, soon to be a global company called - McKnight Digital Entertainments or Records (I don't think they have decided yet). It is company policy to have a small party when a new artist signs to the label. This is our party. Jamie is signed to the company for a three album contract with the option of five albums. We have a say as regards his image, songs and videos. We also have a six figure up-front payment and a very good royalty percentage. I have a part time contract with the company in the song writing department. I can work there when I have the time because I insisted it say in my contract, that Jamie is to come first. Francis walks over to me, he looks at me, smiles and shakes his head.

"Off the record Billie, you are one tough and shrewd business woman. This contract of yours has caused me many sleepless nights."

"Has it?"

He nods, "I still can't believe it."

I smile, "Thank you for being honest when I called to ask questions during the week."

"Not a problem, I knew you would go and check the legalities for yourself with your brother, after you mentioned that he is a lawyer."

"I did."

He shakes his head again, "I tell you, you are something else, you have definitely impressed the big guys in America. I hear Mr McKnight himself of McKnight Records/Entertainments asked to see a copy of your contract."

"Is that good or bad?" I ask smiling at him.

"Good," he says. He winks at me, then goes to help Velma with the wine. I look around the room at some of the other artists signed to the label, artists that I have only ever seen in the past on 'Top of the Pops', 'CD:UK', and other television shows.

"This is the start of something new," I say to myself as I look around. Before meeting Jamie, I was in debt, because of loans I had taken out to help Wayne. After meeting Jamie I accumulated a little more debt because I had to take care of all the bills. One day several weeks ago I was seriously contemplating re-mortgaging my house or borrowing some more money from a loans company because the bills were piling up. I opened a note book which I use during church services to record important things and something caught my eye. It was something that I had written the year before. It said: *'I am a lender and not a borrower'*, and that once I trusted in God and did the right thing, whatever I did would be blessed. That day I decided not to borrow any money or to re-mortgage my house, I decided to trust in God. Emotionally, it wasn't easy, I had a lot of liabilities and no assets. More money going out than I had coming in, even after I made several cut-backs.

Each day I would get letters in the mail offering me one credit card or another, one loan with 0% interest or another. I was tempted to give in and borrow, but each time I looked at the tempting offers the words: *'I am a lender and not a borrower'* would flood my mind. I threw all the letters away, concentrated on writing more songs and kept the fire of trust and hope burning daily.

Now, a few weeks later, I am debt free and have a substantial amount of money in my bank account. Now, thanks to God, I have no liabilities and several assets. Now I can help Sarah and her children properly as I have always wanted to. Now I can send some money to my parents, even though they don't need it, I can still send it. I have paid off my mortgage. I am no longer a borrower. Now I can also do something that has been in my heart, I can increase my giving to my church and the children I sponsor in third world countries. As I mingle with the artists, a number of actors and several professional footballers present, I am so thankful that 'now' has come.

"Everyone can I have your attention," Francis Wells says holding his hands up. "As you know these gatherings are to welcome new artists onboard. Today we are welcoming Jamie Sanders and his Manager/Songwriter Billie Lewis." Everyone claps.

"As is custom, I will now ask them both to come and say a few words." He turns to us, "It can be about each other, experience thus far or something about yourself. Billie," he beckons to me.

I walk towards Francis and look at the people in the room. I hope that I am doing a good job concealing my nervousness.

"Umm, I just want to say thank you all for welcoming us. I would also like to say thank you to Jamie for not looking back, for sticking with me when things were cloudy and...," I pause and look at Jamie, "once in while you meet someone who has so much clarity in their heart, everything they do is clear. Some people hide or pretend so you never know what's going on in their mind, you only see what they want you to see. Jamie has shown me that when you have goodness in your heart you can't hide it. It will always come out," I smile as everyone claps.

"Jamie," Francis beckons him. He walks towards us.

"What can I say, thank you for all coming today. I am really excited about being here. Umm, about my Manager. I have a Manager that saw things at the very beginning. Things I had only ever dreamt of. The first day I met Billie she made me feel confident that I would make it. She made me see things differently. Her faith never wavered and made mine stronger. She is like a sister, mother, aunt, all rolled into one. As a guy you can get a lot of flak having a young lady as your Manager. I would put up with anything and I wouldn't change a thing."

I join everyone and clap. Right on cue, 'Love Is Not Supposed To Hurt' starts playing in the background.

CHAPTER 23

"I can't believe it, you really did!" Dave says as he stares at me in amazement. "A Three album deal with the option of five?"

I nod.

"You signed yesterday?"

I nod again and watch as he takes a bottle out of his pocket, opens it and takes some tablets out. I say nothing as I watch him put the tablets in his mouth and wash them down with water.

"Are you okay?"

"I'm fine, I have a headache that's all. Well, well, well, good on you Billie. I really mean that. Digital are merging with McKnight and together they will be worth about seven times Vigil and XZEL put together."

"How do you know?"

"I still have contacts. How come you were so sure about everything, so sure that it would happen? It's like you were waiting for a set time, like you knew not to rush things. How?"

"Prayer, faith," I reply getting up, "I'm going to get something to eat, do you want anything?"

"No, I'm good."

I walk into Jamie's kitchen and look in his fridge for something to eat. I hear something and turn. Dave is standing at the door. I turn back to the fridge and continue to rummage around.

"Good to hear that Marcus is doing well isn't it?" I ask referring to the third living member of Troyston, Dave's step-brother.

"Umm," Dave replies.

"You know, when you were talking in there just now, I noticed something different about you?"

"Oh."

"Your language and your manners were different."

"That could be due to you taking me and the world by surprise. I never thought you could do it see. I thought that you being a 'bird', you wouldn't be able to pull it off," he walks into the kitchen and sits down at the table.

"I know you much better than you give me credit for. Cut the crap Dave, stop the *Ali G* talk, Jamie is not here."

"What are you talking about?"

"I am talking about you wanting to get the band back together and because of that, trying to knock every single thing I did down. I'm talking about you popping those pills. I'm talking about Marcus and the fact that even though he is your step-brother, Jamie seems to care more about him than you?"

"Oh well, now that's Jamie for you, he cares for everyone else doesn't he?"

"Everyone else? You think that he doesn't care about you? Why would you think that?"

"Marcus is sick, he goes to see him nearly every other day, I don't know, let me think, that could be the reason!" I hear anger beneath the sarcasm in his voice.

"Marcus had a tumour, it could have been malignant. Shouldn't you be thanking God that it wasn't?"

"There is history that you know nothing about Billie, so stay out of it."

"History? Well right now, will be tomorrow's history, so why don't you write a different ending?"

"No, no, no, do not use any of your gospel theory on me," he says holding his hands up, "the others may want to be closer to their big maker in the sky, me, I think I'll wait a few more years."

"Gospel theory, that's a good name for the truth. The problem with you though, is if you keep doing the cocaine, the other drugs and the heavy drinking, you may not have a few more years."

"Yeah, right, whatever," he says.

"Dave, don't lose your tomorrows, don't waste-"

"Look, Stop trying to kid a 'kidded' Kidder and stop quoting your stupid quoted quotes. Believe what you see and not what you want to see, for once just once, be realistic."

"But not everything you see is real Dave."

"Here we go, I've seen so much crap in the world, what makes you think that there is something better?"

"Hope, faith, knowing the Truth."

"Wake up Billie! The coffee's smelt, drunk and finished."

I take a deep breath and blow out slowly as I try to ignore the contempt I hear in his voice.

"Okay, those tablets you're taking, what are they?" I ask changing the subject.

"Why?" He looks confused.

"Are you ill?"

"Why?"

"Every time I am here I see you taking tablets, you always do it when Jamie is not here so you obviously don't want him to know. So, my question is, why?"

He doesn't answer, he just sits at the table staring at his hands. I walk out of the kitchen and into the front room, his jacket is still hanging on the chair. I walk over to it and put my hand in the pocket. I feel and then pull out three bottles containing tablets, and read the labels.

"What the hell are you doing?"

"Why are you taking these?"

"Give them to me, who do you think you are? How dare you go into my pocket."

He moves quickly across the room, grabs my arm and we wrestle a little as he tries to pull the bottles out of my hand. I let go of them and step back.

"I am tired of you showing up when you know that I am here and Jamie is out. Each time you come here you pop pills in my presence. Do you want me to help you? Is that it? Is this some cry for help? If there is anything I can do to help I will."

"Help me? How can you help me? You think you are something special don't you? You get Jamie a record deal and now you think you can do anything." I am shocked at the menacing tone of his voice, he talks as if he hates me.

"No, I don't think I can do anything but I may be able to do something," I breathe deeply not fully understanding why he hates me so much.

"If I need help I know where to go, is that clear?" His face and menacing finger are inches away from my face.

"No."

"What?"

"I said no. Jamie may fall for your crap, your foul language and bad attitude, personally, I don't have time for it." He moves back a little, he looks stunned. "I have put up with months of you undermining me, phoning me and telling me that I was stupid, telling me that because I was a 'bird' I wouldn't get anywhere. You tried to coerce me, bully me, to sign Jamie's contract over to you and your associate. Constantly you criticized me, constantly you made fun of me but I refused to yield. I am not going to yield now, is that clear? I have never been rude to you or disrespected you publicly or privately and I am not about to start now, is that clear?"

He does not answer, he stands staring at me. I see the shock in his eyes. I wait for him to say something, he doesn't.

"Okay, you don't want to talk to me, that's fine by me, I'm no expert but I've worked with patients taking those tablets Dave and you are not taking them properly."

"What tablets?" Jamie asks.

Startled I turn around, Jamie is standing by the door.

"What tablets?" He asks again as he puts the bag in his hand

down and goes to close the front door.

"Dave is taking headache tablets, they are really strong and he hasn't had anything to eat," I reply not looking at Dave.

"Good job I got some food on my way back then," he picks the bag up and walks towards his kitchen. We follow him.

"How's Marcus?" Dave asks nervously.

"Good, he asked after you. Said he expected you down last weekend."

"I got tied up, I'll go this weekend," Dave says as he turns the kitchen television on. I watch as he moves around the kitchen getting plates out. He does not look at me. I shake my head. My mobile phone starts to ring and I pull it out of my pocket and answer it.

"Billie, it's Sarah, I just want you to know that I am going to change the children's school and I may be moving house."

"Why? What's happened?" I ask walking out of the kitchen and into the front room.

"I'm not sure, there was a man arrested at the front of the children's school last week. He was loitering at the school gates for nearly an hour."

"Do you know who it was?"

"No, I phoned the police station he was taken to, from the description they gave me it may have been him. I haven't allowed the children back to the school since it happened."

"Are you okay?"

"A little scared but we have a police officer checking up on us each night."

"Good, look why don't you stay at my brother's place again? He won't mind. I would say stay at mine but when I resigned I gave a couple of people my address, so it may not be that safe."

"Are you sure?"

"I'll come and get you tomorrow."

"Thanks Billie."

"I'll see you tomorrow morning."

"Okay."

I put the phone back in my pocket, sit down on a chair and massage my temple. 'Why would Roger go to the school? How had he found the school? What is going on here?' I think to myself as I start massaging the back of my neck. 'Roger? Dave? What is it all about God? I need help, please help me as only You can, please. What do You want me to do with Dave? Walk away or help? Help me to be strong, help-'

"Problem?"

I don't look up, I don't answer Dave. I sit with my eyes closed and continue to pray silently. When I open them I am surprised that Dave is still there.

"I'm sorry, I went over the top. You don't deserve the crap I dish out. It's one thing having people on the outside trying to break you and Jamie up, it's worse when you have to put up with people like me on the inside," he says.

I nod. The words in my head are jumbled and not properly thought of, so I do not say them.

"Are we eating now?" Jamie shouts from the kitchen. I walk back into the kitchen.

"I think I'll go home Jamie. I'll see you tomorrow."

"Why? What's wrong?"

"Nothing," I look at Dave as he walks into the kitchen with his jacket in his hand, "I just need to get something sorted out."

"Billie, please don't go yet, you were right, I need your help."

Dave pulls out a folder from his jacket and hands it to me.

"What is it?" I ask.

"My medical notes."

"What's going on?" Jamie asks. He walks over to Dave.

"Billie and I had a fight just before you came."

"A fight! What about?"

"About these," Dave says holding the bottles of tablets up.

"What are they?"

Dave does not answer.

"Dave, what are they?" Jamie asks again.

He does not answer.

"Billie?"

I don't say anything.

"Somebody say something?" Jamie says and I look away.

"They are my umm…, tablets err…, combination therapy, medication for…, HIV/AIDS."

CHAPTER 24

"You were right Billie, I was taking those tablets in front of you on purpose. I thought that if you asked what they were, then I could ask you to have a look at that." Dave says pointing to his folder. "Jamie said that you worked, err.., used to work in a hospital laboratory, I thought that if you didn't know what everything meant then you could ask someone, a doctor, I….," he looks away.

I pull out some chairs, "Let's sit down," I say.

Jamie moves all the dishes to one side and I open the folder and pull the papers out. The first thing that catches my attention are the different hand writings on the pages and the different names of the doctors.

"I don't understand, why do you have so many doctors?"

"I umm, I don't stay with one for that long. A lot of them are private. If it got out that I was HIV positive the media would have a field day. 'Where Are They Now Special - Ex Troyston Member HIV Positive'," he laughs nervously.

Jamie and I do not join him.

"Why didn't you tell me?" Jamie asks.

"You were busy, I didn't want to bother you."

"Bullshit Dave, why didn't you tell me?" I sense the hurt in his voice. I don't look at them, I continue to read the different reports not wanting to get in the middle of old issues, of history.

"If I had told you, it wouldn't have mattered, you wouldn't have cared." Dave says defiantly.

"Why do you always do this? You did it when we were in Troyston and you are doing it now. You want someone to act like they care while you act like you couldn't care less. Why the pretence?"

"I don't understand-"

"Yes you do, you understand very well exactly what I am talking about. You want people to feel things for you that you never show. You've always acted like you never cared about me, about Marcus or about Ben. You shut us all out and

232

then expected us to understand things you never said or showed. You act like no one cares about you, like you're all by yourself and then when people treat you that way, you get angry and hurt."

"When have you ever cared about me Jamie, it was always about Ben and Marcus, never me. You always did stuff together, you…," his voice falters

"YOU SHUT ME OUT, YOU 'STONE WALLED' ME, YOU'RE DOING IT NOW," Jamie shouts.

There is a long drawn out pause, I look up from the papers take a look at their faces and look down again.

"You're right, I shut you out."

"No," Jamie says sarcastically.

"Jamie," I say hoping he can see the pleading message in my eyes for him to listen.

"You guys never understood, I had issues before I joined the band, things I couldn't talk about. The fame and fortune we got didn't make me the way I am, it only magnified what was there in me already. At times I felt that I didn't have any control over anything. We couldn't do this, we couldn't do that, we couldn't take a pee without someone knowing what we were doing," he pauses and I look up. Jamie is staring at him as if he is seeing him for the first time. "I took drugs, different kinds. I took stuff to help me relax, I took stuff to help me sleep, I took stuff to wake me up and stuff to help me make it through the day. I couldn't get too close to you guys because I couldn't let you see the shit that was in my head. I was so insecure, so messed up Jamie, really messed up. That's why I skipped rehearsals, that's why I always went off on one for the slightest thing, I was messed up."

"You never acted like it, sure you behaved a little arrogant and weird but I didn't know you had so many problems."

"I was forced to create this 'bad boy' imagine, this 'life and soul of the party' image for myself that was so hard to maintain. No one really knew what was wrong with me, I didn't even know half the time. Ben tried to help once."

"Ben?"

"He found me in the car park after an awards ceremony, I was crying and cursing because a reporter had criticized me in his magazine. He stayed with me until I calmed down and promised not to tell anyone what he had seen."

"He never told me," Jamie says softly.

"That was Ben, he always did what he promised."

"He was like that."

"Solid," Dave concurs.

I look at both of them, lost in the same happy but sad memories. I wait for them to return from their journey down memory lane.

"What can you tell from the paperwork Billie?" Jamie asks leaning towards me.

"It's a little confusing?"

"In what way?" Dave asks.

"In all the information written down, there is no mention of the day you were tested. When did you get tested for HIV?" I ask.

"Tested? Isn't it there? They have done so many blood tests I honestly can't remember."

"No, all the blood tests they have done are for certain white blood cells. They have tested your CD4 and CD8 levels."

"CD4, CD8, what are those?" Jamie asks.

"They are a type of white blood cell."

He frowns, "A type?"

"Blood is made up of different cells, mainly red blood cells and white blood cells right?" He nods. "The red blood cells mainly carry oxygen around the body and carbon dioxide to the lungs, the white blood cells help the body to fight infections. There are a number of different types of white blood cells that have different functions. Neutrophils, Basophils, Eosinophils, Monocytes and Lymphocytes-,"

I stop talking as both Jamie and Dave look completely confused. I pause and think of a simple way to explain things.

"Okay CD4 and CD8 cells are a type of white blood cell called Lymphocytes. The CD4 is also called a helper cell. It helps the body to fight against infections. It is also the main cell affected by the Human Immunodeficiency Virus or HIV.

The virus destroys the CD4 cells, this is why people with HIV that progress to AIDS lose their ability to fight infections that would not be a problem in a healthy person." I look from Jamie to Dave they both nod. "They become more susceptible to infections or immuno-compromised, meaning that their immunity is compromised. I don't understand your medical notes though, come to think of it why do you carry them around with you?"

"I don't want them falling into the wrong hands, so I tell the doctors that I might be travelling, they let me have them. What is it you don't understand?"

"In most hospitals, if a patient has been tested and found to be HIV positive it would say so in their medical notes. There would be a test result and date of some form. You have notes that say nothing about you being HIV positive, just your lymphocyte count results. Have you had any infections with any opportunistic micro-organisms?"

"No...., wait there was the time I got arrested for possession, after I was released on bail I had to go to a drug rehabilitation centre. I stayed there for two weeks. The day I was released I got high and drunk and crashed my car. I ended up with a broken leg and fractured arm. I spent a week in the hospital and got MRSA; an iatrogenic nosocomial infection they called it."

"MRSA? Iatrogenic?" Jamie queries.

"MRSA is an acronym, it stands for Methicillin Resistant Staphylococcus aureus," I answer. "It's a bacteria that is resistant to a number of antibiotics, it infects people in hospitals mainly, hence its classification as a nosocomial or hospital acquired infection."

"And iatrogenic?"

"It means caused unintentionally by medical treatment."

He nods

"Apart from that Dave, have you had any infections with parasites?"

"Parasites?"

"Yes, like *Toxoplasma Gondii.*"

"No," he says and frowns.

"What about fungi or bacteria?"

"No."

"I know I seem to be repeating myself but have your doctors ever spoken to you about *Cryptosporidium, Pneumocystis Carrinii or PCP, Mycobacterium Avium-Intracellulare* or MAI, any viruses?"

He doesn't answer immediately he seems to be thinking.

"No," he eventually says.

"Have you been treated by a doctor for anything recently?"

"No."

"One thing that strikes me as odd is you CD4/CD8 ratio. See, look at this value here," I say pointing to the most recent test "In immuno-competent people or healthy people there are more CD4 cells than CD8 cells. This means that the ratio of CD4/CD8 is high. In HIV/AIDS patients the ratio is inverted, this means that there are more CD8 cells than CD4 because the CD4 cells have been destroyed by the virus. Your CD4/CD8 ratio is high, so it doesn't look right."

"When exactly did you do a test and when were you told that you were positive?" Jamie asks.

"Umm.., I was with this girl before joining the group. Before Marcus's mum and my dad got married. She died of AIDS a year before the band broke up. I went to the hospital and told them that I suspected I had HIV because of what happened. I did a lot of tests and was placed on medication."

"I think you need to go to a hospital and get re-tested. The day you did your first blood test, were you okay? Were you ill?" I ask.

"I was recovering from really bad flu, I remember still having a cold when they took my blood. Why?"

They both look at me with questions in their eyes, questions that I cannot answer.

"I think you need to get tested again and take it from there. From these notes your CD4/CD8 ratio looks like that of a healthy person. You need to do an HIV test," I say placing my hand on top of his. In my heart I pray for him.

"I'll take you to a private clinic tomorrow," Jamie says.

*   *   *   *   *

Dave stayed at Jamie's house last night. It is as if years of pain were washed away in minutes yesterday and I think of one of the many promises that God has given us: *I will restore the lost years.*

Today they are both going to a private clinic where hopefully Dave will be able to have his HIV test done. I have arranged to meet them at the clinic this afternoon. This morning I am helping Sarah unpack her things in my brother's house. I know she feels a little awkward, she has asked me several times already if I am sure Steve will not mind. I arrange the children's toys around the room, trying to make her feel more at home but I can see as she lingers by one of the beds, she still needs convincing that she is not being a burden. I cannot begin to fathom how she must feel, having lacked true affection from adults for so long and now to be bestowed with so much.

"Sarah you can stay for as long as you like, I spoke to Steve and he says he'll stay with Martin while you stay here."

"I feel as if we're putting him out of his home."

"You know Steve, if he didn't want to do it he wouldn't."

"That's true," she says and smiles.

'At last', I think to myself. I grab hold of her arm and lead her into the front room where the children are sitting and watching cartoons on the television. "See, they've made themselves at home already. You do the same."

"Thank you so much Billie, I am so grateful for everything."

"It's okay, have you told the police that you will be staying here until the refuge can re-house you?"

"Yes, they said that they'd check on us at night."

"Good, I've filled up the fridge and freezer so you don't have to go out much. Actually maybe you should stay in for a few days. I'll pick up some DVDs for the children. Has Luke got his cards?"

"That was the first thing he packed," she says smiling.

"How is he doing?" I ask. I know that he is aware of what is going on and has probably been for some time. The other two are still young.

"He's doing really well despite all the moving around and changing schools. You know what he said the other day?"

"What?"

"He said that when he grows up he wants to be a person on the phone that helps people with problems. I guess he sees the change in me each time I talk to the people at the domestic violence unit on the phone."

"You have a winner there, you know that don't you?"

She nods her head and I see tears in her eyes.

"You know what, I'll divert my phone calls and stay here for a few days with you. I'll go and get the things for the children now."

"Thanks Billie, for everything."

* * * * *

I climb up the stairs and walk into the elegant building that houses the private clinic. I feel the plush carpet under my feet and sort of float across it to the receptionist's desk.

"Hello."

"Good morning how can I help you?"

"I am looking for a friend of mine that came in for a test."

"Name?"

"Dave Pemberton."

She checks a register, "Down the corridor, first door left."

I walk down the corridor and into the room. Dave is sitting on a chair and Jamie is talking to him. Dave's head is bent and his shoulders are shaking. A lady is sitting in front of them talking to Dave. I walk towards them and look at her badge, she is a counsellor.

Jamie looks up, he has tears in his eyes, he smiles.

"Hi, how did it go?" I ask

"He just got the results."

"Dave?"

His shoulders stop shaking and he looks up and stares straight ahead then looks at me. His face is wet with tears and I hold my breath.

"They did the test twice Billie, and they were both negative."

"Thank God!" I say kneeling by his side and putting my arms around him.

"They are running some other tests while I am here, Hepatitis A, B and C. I should have the results in an hour or so. I think they said my haematocrit level or value is a little low."

"It means you may be anaemic. We just need to get you eating right and taking iron tablets, don't worry about that," I reassure him.

"I don't understand, how can it be negative, I…,"

"Sometimes Dave things happen, we don't understand them, but we appreciate them, and we thank God for them," the counsellor says.

CHAPTER 25

V elma places a number of files in front of me and then proceeds to do the same to Jamie. This is our first official meeting and we wait for Francis to start.

"Right, in these files Velma has prepared different schedules. We have a schedule for several photo shoots for a number of magazines, promotional pictures, posters and flyers which will start tomorrow. This afternoon you have a slot in the recording studio, a meeting with our public relations people, and an in-house photo shoot. Correct me if I am wrong, Velma these schedules are for the first three months?"

"That's right, basically we know that you will have a certain way of doing things, so this is a guide. Even though I say it's a guide, the things listed should at one time or another, within the three month period, get done, preferably in the order in which they are listed. Okay?"

Jamie and I nod.

"We have twenty five recording studios in this building and another fifteen down the road," Francis continues, "you will both get a proper induction so don't worry. We may send you to work with a private studio if we feel that it is needed for new material." He looks at some papers and places them to one side then picks up some more.

"Schedules, what we have found with schedules is that they enable the studio time to be used properly, and everyone knows what everyone else is doing. According to this one you are in the studio this afternoon. We want you to record 'Love Is Not Supposed To Hurt', we will get it mixed and then in five days time start work on the video."

"Five days?" I ask, really impressed.

"Yes, we need to get the video made and then played on The Box, Smash Hits, MTV and all the other music channels. We already have someone who will meet with you both the day after tomorrow, to go over the different 'treatments' first, and then the final story boards for the video. He knows that you have a say so don't worry Billie you won't have a fight on your hands. At this moment we are looking to release the first single in twenty one days."

"Right," I smile.

"Francis and I have had a word with a few image consultants, a couple of them were at your welcome party last week. Anyway, Jamie you will be glad to hear that they both felt you looked good in what you were wearing, and are looking to work with that look. About the idea to change your image with each song, it sounds good," Velma says.

"When we finish here, Velma will take you down and introduce you to Charles Parker, he is the PR guy who will be working with you. He will write up a short biography for Jamie. He has been told that he cannot divulge anything about Troyston without your say so."

"Thank you," Jamie says.

"So that concludes our first of many meetings. You both have my phone numbers, call if there is anything you need to know. Remember, the door to Velma's office is always open. Feel free to pop in any time," Francis says and smiles at Velma's comical expression.

* * * * *

"For each studio we have what we call a log-in system," Velma says. She looks from Jamie to me, to make sure that we understand, "Basically it tells us who has used the studio and for how long. It is mainly for accounting purposes. You both have connecting cards with your own personal identification number or PIN. Each time you need to use a recording studio, you have to have an engineer. Most of our artists have a particular in-house engineer that they constantly work with. My advice is to try as many engineers and producers as possible, because they all have their different abilities. Any questions?" Velma asks.

"No," Jamie and I reply.

"Good, let's have some lunch, work starts this afternoon."

* * * * *

The last note fades and I look up at Aidan who is staring at me. I am not sure if he is nervous or suspicious. He is the engineer/producer that has been working with us for over two hours. Jamie has just left to go and get ready for the in-house photo shoot, and I am going over the final version of the song with Aidan.

"What do you think?" He asks.

"There's something missing. Keep that version, can I show you some chords on the keyboard? The original version has something else."

"Sure."

Aidan gets up and I sit in front of the keyboard, "In the middle, just before the 'bridge', the chord of notes on that version falls too low. The base in general is not that loud. Listen to this."

I play some notes on the keyboard first, then I add a baseline and play the notes again. "See what I mean, done this way it makes the 'bridge' jump up and hit you."

"I get you, drum loops, bigger base," he smiles for the first time since we started this afternoon and nods, "give me a few minutes and I'll play it for you again."

"Okay," I say. I sit and watch him place head phones on then press buttons and move levers up and down on the mixing board. He then plays some notes on the keyboard. I watch his confident hands, the way his head bops up and down to the music and the seriousness on his face as he moves between mixing board and computer. He knows his trade.

"Listen to this, of course it's not finished but what do you think?"

He presses a button and I listen. I notice the louder baseline and stronger sound. Just before the 'bridge', the chords pick up and the 'bridge' hits hard. As I listen, my smile grows wider and wider. When the song fades my face has an enormous smile on it. A smile which must be contagious because I see it on Aidan's face.

"That's it, that's the feel."

"I know what you mean, it's large."

He saves the song on the computer and pulls out some blank CDs to download it on to.

"You know when I first heard that I would have to work with you today, I thought that you might be bossy, used to getting your own way."

"What! Me, bossy? I have not got a bossy bone in my body. Why would you think that?"

"You know how people have preconceived ideas about others, I probably preconceived it."

"Or you heard in the 'grapevine' about Jamie's contract."

"Maybe," he says and smiles, "actually it was that."

"Look, I just want to do the best I can."

"You're cool," he says nodding his head. His mobile phone starts to ring and apologising he answers it. I try not to listen to what he is saying, I look through some of the CDs on the table.

"I am really busy, now is not a good time…"

I watch as he starts to scratch his head and tap his foot rapidly.

"I will be late but I will try and make it. I know I said the same thing last week but I will try…"

He listens some more then stares at the phone in amazement.

"She hung up on me! I don't believe it," he presses some buttons on the phone frantically and then holds it to his ear. "Voicemail," he says and puts the phone on the table. I watch as he rubs his face and shakes his head.

"Are you okay?" I ask.

"Yeah, my wife just gave me an ear full and hung up on me. I've been working late trying to finish off a lot of work, I haven't been home the last couple of nights, I've been doing the 'graveyard' shift. She thinks I'm fooling around. But it's cool, I'll call her later."

"Your wife? It sounded like you were talking to a friend."

"What?"

"Have you not heard that song 'Say My Name', I know it's none of my business, so excuse me because I'm going to poke my nose in, albeit in a non-bossy way. When you speak to her on the phone, say her name. That way she will know that you are not with someone else. If you work late or all night, phone her in the morning and wake her up. Call her to say you're thinking about her or just plain call her. Just now when you were talking to her, you sounded guarded, closed, how can she look in and trust you and what you are doing, if you are not open with her on the phone. I'm a woman and I'm just telling you what I would want. Try it."

"Phone calls, saying her name, is it really that important?" He looks perplexed.

"She hung up on you, I think it is to her, I know it is to me."

"Thank you Billie, I never thought all that stuff was that important," he reaches for his phone.

I walk towards the door, "All the best Aidan."

"Thanks."

* * * * *

I look at my watch again. I can't believe that this photo shoot has taken nearly four hours and six changes of clothes. I feel sorry for Jamie, the lights shinning on him are so hot that the make-up girl has to constantly wipe his damp brow. I never realized how much hard work went into getting the perfect picture. Everyone around acts like this is normal while I fidget a lot.

"We have what we need," the art director finally says, "that's a wrap, thank you everyone." A few people clap.

I smile at the look of relief on Jamie's face which he quickly masks, "At last, let's go and get something to eat," I say quietly to him.

"Give me two minutes to get out of these clothes."

* * * * *

We walk down the corridor to the lift that will take us down to the restaurant on the first floor.

"You know how when you start to do certain things you can get hooked Jamie?" I ask.

"What things?"

"Anything, take you for instance..," I stop and look at him.

"What?"

244

"I think you're getting a little too comfortable with all that make-up on, I can't help but feel a little bit concerned. Has Trudi noticed any of her make-up missing recently?"

"Oh no! I forgot to take it off. Why didn't you tell me? I can't believe you let me walk out of that room with all this stuff on."

I am laughing so hard at his futile attempt to wipe it off.

"OOPPS, you've smudged your mascara, I have some in my bag, here let me fix that for you honey."

Jamie starts to laugh. He takes hold of my face and wipes some of the powder and lipstick onto my cheeks.

"No, stop it," I protest, laughing I try to push him away.

One of the photographers walks down the corridor towards us, we try to control our laughter and act cool.

"Hi," he says.

"Hi," we say back.

"Billie you have make-up smudges all over your face," he says.

Jamie and I start laughing again.

CHAPTER 26

Iam a little nervous today. We have Jamie's first press conference which Charles Parker from the public relations department has arranged. After we will go and look at the location for the video with Raj Patel, the director/producer. We were both impressed with his 'treatment'. He had so many ideas for Jamie's video, ideas that I never contemplated, his storyboards for the song were visually spot on.

"Right, Billie, Jamie, it's Q and A time guys, questions and answers! The reporters are in the other room," Charles says. He claps his hands gleefully, "They have a list of the questions that they may ask. You need to bear in mind that the list is just a guide for them. They can in effect ask anything. You don't have to answer everything. I will step in if they ask anything that is way over the mark," he lowers his voice conspicuously, "like Troyston okay," he adds. He holds a copy of the list of questions up.

Jamie nods, I look at the questions. There is nothing here about Troyston which I hope means that they will not ask Jamie anything about those days. I watch as Charles flutters up and down the room briefly then opens the door to the conference room and beckons us. I'm not sure about him, I get the feeling that his words don't come from a warm source. I breathe in deeply and blow out slowly as I follow Jamie into the room.

I still don't know why I have to sit here next to Jamie on the high table, but I do it and smile. Trying my hardest not to look nervous is not an easy job, especially when there are forty or so reporters staring at me, and about ten or so video cameras recording my every move.

"Okay guys can we take the first question and please bear in mind that we have copies of Jamie's biography to hand out later," Charles says.

There is a massive eruption and cameras start to click, light from their flashes momentarily blind me. I blink as a reporter stands up and asks a question. I can hardly hear him, I listen to Jamie's reply.

Jamie is like a fish in water, he answers the questions and jokes with the reporters.

"Jamie, we heard a few of your songs earlier, your voice is different, who has inspired you? Who did you listen to when you were younger?"

"*Nat King Cole, Ray Charles, Elvis, Michael Jackson, Paul Simon,* a lot of the old Motown artists. I didn't really listen to one type of music. I was exposed to a wide range at a very young age."

"How would you describe your type of music? What is your genre?"

"Music for everyone. I don't really have a definitive word or genre. I have a wide range of songs with different flavours. R and B, contemporary pop with a bit of soul as Billie says."

"Billie," I freeze. "You wrote a couple of songs that 'lived' in the top five a couple of years ago, do you think that this will happen again?"

I look at Jamie and he shrugs and shakes his head slightly. Charles is staring at the table, he does not look up and I realize that he has told the reporters what he said he wouldn't.

"I hope that the songs I have written, and will continue to write for Jamie, will do well?" I say.

"Do you both have the same taste in music Billie?"

"Yes and no."

"Jamie when will your first single be released?"

"In two weeks."

"Do you plan to tour?"

"In the very near future yes."

"Who would you most like to go on tour with?"

"A number of people."

"Would you like to see yourself as a pop idol Jamie?"

"No, definitely not. I'm no idol and I don't want anyone to see me as one. I hope people will like my work. I hope the songs I sing will touch people and leave a lasting impression."

"What's it like having Billie as your Manager?"

"Great, she keeps my feet firmly on the ground."

"You are both very attractive, do you have a romantic as well as a professional relationship?"

"Unfortunately Billie has a preference for the tall, dark and handsome sort. I have tried to dye my hair," he shrugs and laughs. We all join him and I playfully pinch his arm. "Plus she supports Arsenal and I support Man U." We both laugh as a couple of reporters loudly voice their support and some their opposition for either team.

"I read somewhere a couple of weeks ago Billie that your ideal man would be a combination of *Keanu Reeves, Denzel Washington, John Travolta* and *Will Smith,* is this true?"

I smile and shake my head, "I was asked what sort of look attracted me to a man, to which I replied, 'it really isn't about a look'. The reporter then gave me a list of ten names and I chose those four." I stop, having nothing else to say about the matter.

"Billie, where do you get your inspiration from?"

"From life, from people, I write about things I see, things that lift people up and make them realize that 'hope' is not just a word."

There is a pause and I watch amazed, as some of the reporters write what I just said down.

"I heard that you lost two stones not long ago Billie. Is there a weight loss book in the pipeline?"

"No, there is no need to go down that route. If you really must know I relied a great deal on self-motivation and will power. I went to the gym, jogged, ate balanced meals and drank lots of water."

"It certainly paid off."

"Thank you."

"Why water?" Another reporter asks.

"A friend of mine has beautiful skin, she drinks two litres of water a day. So I started drinking a lot of water."

He nods and writes something down.

"Err.., excuse me Billie, Pete Wilson here Vigil Records, have you read what Jasmine Peters is saying about your underhand antics?"

I freeze, I don't have a clue as to what he is talking about.

"No," I answer warily.

"Is it true that you went to XZEL Records uninvited and you were thrown out?"

"No!"

"Is it not true that you were later offered a lucrative recording contract for Jamie which you turned down because they were not in the least bit interested in your songs?"

"That's not true," I reply.

Jamie and Charles are frowning.

"Is it not true that Jasmine Peters went out of her way to help you, even though it nearly cost her job, yet you rejected her offer, telling her that this is a dog-eat-dog world and you were going to the highest bidder."

My heart is pounding, "Mr Wilson, I don't know where you got all this information from but none of it is true."

"So tell us, what is the truth?"

"I have no comment regarding any of those allegations except that they are lies. The truth will be revealed in due course. This is Jamie's interview so I think that we should concentrate on him."

The silence is loud, it deafens.

"Jamie what is it like singing by yourself now and not being part of a band?" A reporter asks breaking down the silent wall.

Charles is looking at the reporters and contradictory to what he had said earlier does not step in.

Jamie clenches his fist and waits, I can only assume for Charles to say something.

"It's fine," Jamie says eventually and smiles.

"I am so sorry to have to stop things right now, my mobile is vibrating which means that we have to leave. We have to get to the other side of London in less than forty five minutes. Thank you all for coming. I am sure that Charles can answer any more questions. I was told earlier that the refreshments are ready in the next room. Thank you," I say and stand up

"Thanks," Jamie says.

We walk out of the room.

"Guys, guys, I had no idea they were going to ask those questions?" Charles says rushing after us.

"You had no idea! Is that why you didn't step in Charles? That explains it, you were in shock weren't you?" I ask.

"I…"

"That was out of order Charles and you know it," Jamie says.

"People are asking questions they are inquisitive, they want to know about who they will be spending their money on. This Jasmine Peters angle and the Troyston angle will sell records *and* magazines which will help sell more records. Let's capitalize on it because you can't stop it happening."

"It's not about stopping it, the information about Troyston is out there, we just don't need to lead them to it. But it's more than that Charles, it's about you giving us your word. I don't care what lies are spread about me by Jasmine Peters. We had an agreement with you about getting Jamie recognized as Jamie Sanders a singer, not Jamie Sanders ex-Troyston member trying to make it off the back of past success. You sat at the conference table and agreed with us."

"Look everyone is doing it, there is no shame in using past success."

"Exactly, everyone *is* doing it, that's why we wanted to be different. You know how they set you up for a fall when they find out that you're from a band trying to go solo, or, an actor from a popular television soap trying to sing. You need to go back in there and make sure nothing about Troyston comes out."

"But…"

"No offence but I mean it Charles," I say.

Fuming he walks back into the conference room.

"Let's go to the video site and leave him to it," Jamie says taking my arm.

*   *   *   *   *

"Billie! Jamie! I'd like to introduce you to an old friend of mine, this is Rupert Truman the III, a renowned director both here and in the States. He owns RT Video Productions and Prestige Movie Makers and according to the latest magazines is worth millions. Rupert, Billie Lewis and Jamie Sanders," Raj Patel says.

We say our hellos and shake hands. After a few minutes of small talk Jamie walks over to the dressing room with Raj. Rupert tells me about Raj and about a few antics they got up to at university. I smile as I listen to him.

"So Billie, I've heard a lot of good things about you. This is your artist's first video right?" He asks.

"Yes"

"Raj was telling me how good some of your ideas are, very un-mundane and refreshing. I'm in the Bahamas shooting three videos next week."

"That sounds nice," I say.

"Have you ever been there?" He asks.

"The Bahamas? No, not yet."

"Beautiful place, I have a house there."

"That's nice," I say. I sense a little arrogance in his voice.

"So Billie, tell me about you."

"Me? What do you want to know?"

"Do you like cars?"

"Cars?" I frown.

"I happen to own a Lambogini, a Ferrari and a Porsche. My latest acquisition is the new Jaguar, it's a beautiful toy. I have a passion for fast cars and," he looks straight at me, "beautiful women."

"Oh!"

"I have to go soon, I have a meeting with the president of Independent Television Advertising. Did I mention that I was going to the Bahamas to shoot a couple of videos?"

"Yes, three videos. You just mentioned that," I try, with difficulty, not to smile.

"Would you like to come along?"

"To the Bahamas?"

"Yes."

"With you?" I query. Not knowing why I have a need to get the facts right.

"With me, we could brainstorm ideas among other things."

"You don't know me."

"Hopefully I would get to know you there."

I look at the nice looking man in front of me and shake my head in astonishment.

"Thank you but no thank you," I say.

"Maybe I'll look you up when I get back then."

"Maybe I don't want you to look me up when you get back."

"I can help advance your career, put in a good word with a number of people. You would be up that ladder in no time."

"Thank you but no thank you."

"Playing hard to get? I can work with that."

"I'm not playing any-"

"It's okay Billie, I like to chase sometimes, it intensifies the excitement of the catch."

"Don't bother starting the race, you are not going to catch anything."

"Umm.., you never know."

"Look Mr Truman, you may be a friend of Raj's but that does not give you the right to come onto this set and think that you can proposition me or any other female here."

He genuinely looks shocked, "Women usually jump at the chance of a free holiday. What is your problem? You're not into guys?"

I ignore his last 'over used' comment, "Maybe you need to take a look at the women that jump at the chance, and then, maybe take a longer look at why? Then ask yourself, who's fooling who." I turn and walk towards the dressing room.

*   *   *   *   *

"Oh no," I say softly as my phone starts to ring. I glance at the clock. It is nearly midnight and I have an early start tomorrow. The phone keeps on ringing and reluctantly I reach out and pick up the receiver wondering who is phoning so late.

"Hello?"

"BILLIE IT'S ME!" A voice screams down the phone. I climb back into my skin and steady my heart as I realize who it is.

"Jen! I thought you were in New York with Martin visiting your family?"

"I am, I am, Billie guess what?" She says and I quickly sit up.

"Jen?"

"You're not going to believe this, so sit down. Jason Alexander played your song on the radio this afternoon in New York. Since then he has had over-, are you sitting down?"

"Yes," I say jumping out of bed, my heart pounding.

"I know you're not, anyway, since this afternoon he has had nearly two hundred calls requesting that he play the song again. His phone lines were jammed. Billie did you hear me? JAMMED!"

She screams again and I feel tears in my eyes.

"He likes the song?" I ask.

"Likes it? He loves it." I hear Martin's voice in the background telling Jen to calm down and give him the phone.

"Billie," I hear the excitement in his voice, "I just spoke to Jason, he loves your songs."

"Songs? What do you mean Martin? I only gave him one."

"Apparently the tape you gave him had three other songs that you wrote and Jamie recorded. People are phoning his radio station about 'Love Is Not Supposed To Hurt', they want to know where they can get a copy to buy. It's crazy Billie."

I hear Jen shouting in the background, "Thank God, Thank God, I knew she would do it, I knew it, yeahhhh!"

"Get some sleep Billie, I'll call you in 'your' morning," he says referring to the time difference.

"Okay, thank you Martin, I am in shock, I can't…, I don't know…," my voice breaks.

"Remember when we were little and you said that you wanted to touch people's lives with songs and make them think?"

"Yes," I reply.

"I wanted to own a place where people could meet, hang out and not be categorized and Steve wanted to help people legally that didn't have money."

"We were going to grow up and make a difference. Make a mark. I remember we always used to say that we wouldn't let anything hold us back," I say.

"We said that by God's Grace we would make our dreams come true didn't we?"

"True till the end," I say as I remember the three of us; average age of eleven, sitting in my garden talking about our tomorrows.

"This is it! This is it Billie!"

CHAPTER 27

No one on the set has said anything about the song being played in New York and I don't say anything either. I told Jamie, when we were in the car this morning coming to the set, that Jen and Martin had phoned and said that the song had been played on the radio a couple of times in New York.

It is still early morning and the set is being arranged. Francis wants the video finished today and has promised to send some help down if we need it. I spot Raj by the camera and walk over to him while Jamie heads to the dressing room. Yesterday Raj had asked my opinion about most of the things he did. He showed me how to avoid shadows, maximize the light and play with the camera. Rupert had left the set almost immediately after our short discussion yesterday. I don't know if he has mentioned anything to Raj, I act on the presumption that he hasn't.

"Good Morning Raj"

"Billie! Good morning, good to see you. Today we're going to do the car scene, club scene and outdoor scene. Look at the monitor when I stand here do you see any shadows?"

"No."

"What about now?"

"Yes, really big ones."

"I thought so. When we have more than two people standing here and *blocking* they will cast even more shadows."

"What about if we did the scene in the shadow?" I ask.

"In the shadow?"

"Yes, under the trees over there by the building. The shadows are already there so the people won't make any more shadows when they move around, sorry when they are *blocking*." I use his terminology.

"Billie you little flower, that's it! People come this way please, we're going to shoot the first scene over there under the trees. We need to maximize the natural light and use the artificial lights so let's move things now."

*   *   *   *   *

"Everyone quiet please!" Raj says. "Scene 5, Take 1" an assistant shouts and claps the clapper board down in front of the camera. I have learnt that this is called slating and is used to sync picture to sound as well as inform people what the scene and take is.

"Three, two, one, action!" Raj shouts.

The music of 'Love Is Not Supposed To Hurt' starts and I watch Jamie walk under the trees. In reality he is taking very small steps but it looks like he is strolling. I look around totally overwhelmed at the number of people here. Apart from the actors taking part in the video, there are the camera people, photographers, recording people, a wardrobe person, make-up people, three security men, Raj who is directing and producing, his two assistants, two gaffers, catering people, Jamie and me. Nearly forty people to make a four minute, maximum five minute film. I am really overwhelmed. People are coming and going and it is hard trying to remember who is who, and who is doing what. I look around the area that we have cordoned off from the public, people are standing outside the area watching what we are doing. I smile to myself as I watch a woman and a little boy of about five years standing by the tape. The boy looks really excited, he is jumping up and down. He probably thinks that we are shooting a 'James Bond' film. I focus on the camera and watch the dancers and Jamie perform.

"That's it. Excellent," Raj says taking off his base ball cap and wiping his brow with the back of his hand, "let's have a break, we have two more scenes to shoot today," he claps.

Everyone is smiling as they head towards the catering trailer. I walk over to the woman and little boy who are still watching. They have been there for nearly three hours.

"Hi, I noticed you earlier, my name is Billie, we are shooting a music video here. Would you like to come and meet the artist?"

"Yes please," the little boy says. I ask their names and take them both past a security man and on to the set.

"This is Jamie Sanders, this is his video for his first single. Jamie this is Thomas and his mum Debbie."

"Hi," Jamie says. He shakes their hands and shows them around with me.

"Can I have some writing on a paper?" Thomas asks.

"He means your autograph," Debbie says.

"My autograph, wow you are the first one I am giving my autograph to in a long, long, time Thomas. This is a special autograph."

Jamie takes some paper from a clip board and writes something down and signs.

"Can I have yours?" He asks me.

"Mine?"

He nods and I write a little message on the paper and hand it to him. We introduce them to the people on the set, get them something to eat and drink from the large mobile canteen and then escort them off the set ten minutes before we are ready to start again.

*   *   *   *   *

We have one more scene to do and then it will be a wrap. Everyone works together to change the video set as the sun sets. It has been a long day, but no one complains. I like the feel here, I like the solidarity. No temper tantrums or nastiness.

Francis Wells strolls on to the set, I didn't know he was coming down and Raj looks surprised to see him as well. They talk briefly and then he walks over to me. I wonder if he has heard anything about the song being played in America. A thought suddenly crosses my mind, 'Would it affect things here?', I don't know much about the music laws in different countries but I hope that people will not record the song off the radio and not bother to buy the single.

"Will you ever cease to amaze me?" He asks.

"What?" I ask.

"Don't give me that innocent look, I have been bombarded with phone calls from America requesting the song. How did you do it Billie?"

"I gave a copy of the song to a DJ from New York weeks ago, Jason Alexander."

"You know Jason Alexander?" He sounds impressed.

"Not really, he went to university with my cousin, he came to 'Martin's', that's the name of my cousin's nightclub-"

"Your cousin is Martin Palmer, the owner of 'Martin's'?" Francis interjects, "I tried everything to get tickets for the opening night. This woman kept answering the phone and saying that all the tickets had gone. I tried everything!"

"Err.., did you?" I grimace.

"They were like gold dust, sold out weeks in advance. Your cousin is the owner? Your cousin is Martin Palmer?"

I nod.

"He knows Jason Alexander?"

I nod again.

"Well, Jason obviously felt what everyone else is feeling about the song. I've had people in California on the phone requesting copies. Do you know how many years it takes some British artists to break America? Or how many really good artists never achieve transatlantic success?"

"Not really."

"Many, many."

"That many?"

"Digital merging with McKnight Records/Entertainments will open the doors for our artists, in America and world wide, but it will still take time. You however have opened a whole set of doors all by yourself, well done. We're going for an earlier release date over there and then promotional tours here and there."

"Really? How early?"

"Next month."

"Next month?"

He nods, "By the way have you heard of Levin and Barrat?"

"The movie makers?"

"Yes the 'A' list movie makers, they want to use your song for the sound-track of their next Blockbuster which is coming out very soon."

"They what! Levin and Barrat? 'Love in not Supposed To Hurt'? Oh-my-goodness."

He smiles, "That is not all, they want you to do a cameo."

"Me? I'm not an actress."

"They saw the interview you did recently and like your look. Levin says and I quote: *Billie Lewis has the look of inspiration.*"

*   *   *   *   *

We shoot the final scene quickly. I am in a daze. I know Raj asked me a few questions during the shooting of the last scene and I know that I answered him but I cannot remember what I said. I am buzzing with excitement and even when Raj says we will do an additional scene with strobe lights, I just smile. Francis has sent a few more people down to help because of the newly added urgency. I smile as I watch people moving around filming the 'making of the video'.

I help to pack away the things that we have finished with. They will go back to storage and come out again to be used for another video. I stack some chairs and carry them over to the van to be loaded. I push some of the chairs already in the van back to make space for more things. As I lower my hands, my wrist bracelet attaches itself to my hair. I can't move my head without my right hand following.

"Let me help you with that," a deep husky American accented voice says. I turn slightly as he tilts my head to one side. "You are going to have to turn completely so I can see." I turn and face him, my eyes rest on broad shoulders in a leather jacket on top of a white T-shirt.

"Thank you," I say to his chest.

"No problem," he replies.

I recognize the 'twang', "West Coast?" I ask as he tries to release my hand.

He chuckles, "How can you tell?"

"My godmother lives in California and you sound like her."

"How so?"

"When you said no problem just now, you emphasized the 'prob' not the 'lem'." I realize that I am almost resting my head on his chest and try to move back.

"Hold still," he says.

I feel his breath on my forehead and freeze.

"Not that still," he adds.

Embarrassed, I laugh, "Have you done it?"

"It's done," he says.

I step back and look up at him, "Thank you," I say staring at him. He stares back and doesn't say anything.

"You're welcome," he replies eventually, "you might want to keep your hand and hair at a distance when you wear that bracelet."

I nod, clear my throat but don't speak as I look at him. He is casually dressed in a white T-shirt, jeans and leather jacket. His eyes are deep brown, very warm, very striking and set in a handsome naturally tanned, well groomed face. I wonder why I had not noticed him earlier. We stand staring at each other, I wait for him to speak. He doesn't.

"Are you working on the set? One of the actors?" I ask.

"I'm just helping out, I'm with the American team."

"American team?"

"McKnight Records/Entertainments, we merge officially with Digital next month."

"Oh."

"You're Billie Lewis, right?"

I nod.

"Francis Wells pointed you out to me fifteen minutes ago."

"Oh. You are-?"

"P.A. your cell phone," a man talking on a mobile phone says, and hands him a ringing phone.

"Thanks Kenny."

Kenny smiles at me then turns and continues his own conversation.

"Please excuse me for one minute Billie, this won't take long."

I stand and watch as they both talk on their phones. I know that I should go and help with the rest of the things but for some reason I just stand and watch.

"I'm sorry about that, where were we?"

"P.A.?" I ask.

"Philip Anderman," he replies.

"So Philip Anderman, did you say that you were part of the extra help that Francis said he was sending?"

"Extra help?" He frowns, "I umm…"

"Billie we've finished come and see!" Raj shouts excitedly.

"I have to go. Thank you for helping me earlier."

"No problem," he says and smiles. I return his smile.

"Nice meeting you."

"Nice meeting you, Billie."

I turn and walk to where Raj is standing looking at the monitor. Raj presses the replay button and I look at the monitor. Through the corner of my eye I see Philip, Kenny and Francis walking towards a car. As I stare at the monitor, I wonder who Philip Anderman is.

CHAPTER 28

This is it. The screening of Jamie's video will commence in two minutes. Nearly everyone is seated in the large elegant conference room waiting. All the people that have been involved in making the video are here as well as other invited staff members and press people. The door opens and Francis Wells, Velma, Philip Anderman and two men walk in. I recognize one of the men as the man who had handed Philip the mobile phone the other day. They sit at the back. I watch as Philip looks around the room, he sees me and smiles. I smile back.

I turn and look at Jamie as he fidgets with his watch.

"Are you okay?"

He nods.

"It's going to be good."

"Now I know what you meant when you said that in Troytson I was visible, but lost in the crowd. I feel like a one-man-band."

"I bet now you're happy you went for all those dancing lessons? The times I had to drag you down there Jamie."

He starts to laugh, "Remember Claude? Remember the time he made you do that two hour routine with me?"

I recall Jamie's dance instructor and start to laugh with him. Jamie tries really hard to control his laughter. I wipe the laughter tears from my eyes as the lights are lowered. The video starts and there is complete silence. I watch the story of my song unfold and I find my laughter tears being replaced with emotional ones. I watch the sadness fade, and then the happiness come in as the message that love is not supposed to hurt comes to life. The choreographed final dance scene ends. The room erupts immediately with clapping and cheering.

"I told you," I say quietly to Jamie as he hugs me.

"Director, speech, speech," people chorus.

Raj stands up as the lights are turned back up, he walks to the front of the room. Everyone starts to clap again.

"Thank you, thank you. I just want to say that the team that worked on the set were brilliant. I know I have worked with most of you before and so you are hearing this again. Well done. Working with Billie and Jamie was as new to me as it was to you, I didn't know what to expect. What I got, were two people who are so humble and giving. Jamie is a sensational singer, an absolute professional and a polished performer and Billie is…," he pauses and I hold my breath, "Billie is…, she knows exactly what she is doing, she listens and her ideas are so simple and so effective, yet you wouldn't have thought of them in a million years. She has such an eye for detail.

I couldn't believe it when Billie went to the spectators and brought a little boy and his mum on to the set, because she felt that they had been standing there watching for a couple of hours. Jamie and Billie took them around during the break period, when everyone including myself, were actually having a break, and showed them the set. I didn't expect that. I have worked for a number of record labels and you get so used to the 'me, me, me' syndrome. The 'ism or 'I, self, me' phenomenon. It comes as a shock when you meet people like this. People that put others first. Billie, Jamie, I had a brilliant time working with you both and I hope we can do it again soon."

We all clap as he walks back to his seat.

Music starts and everyone seems to start talking at once. There is a lot of congratulating and hugging. The doors open and some ladies wheel in large trolleys laden with food. In my emotional excitement all I see are the magnificent colours of food on the trolleys. The colours look beautiful.

"Billie, terrific, what can I say," Charles says patting my arm, "I haven't spoken to you since the interview. Did Jamie tell you that they didn't print anything about," he lowers his voice, "you-know-what?" He winks.

"Yes Charles he told me and I checked."

"Of course you know that I can't hold them off for long, they are animals."

"I'm sure you'll manage Charles."

His smile depicts confidence and importance. "You know me, I'll try my best." He walks over to a female singer and starts gushing, I breathe a sigh of relief.

"Billie!"

I turn, "Hi Francis."

"Let me introduce you to some people from McKnight Records/ Entertainments in America." He escorts me across the room to where Philip and the other men are standing."

"Billie this is Kenny, Marcel and Philip."

"Hello," I say and shake their hands.

Philip shakes my hand and smiles at me, "You didn't shake my hand the first time we met."

"That was because we had not been formally introduced," I say smiling at him, "I'm old school."

I see amusement in his eyes as he smiles. I stand for a few minutes and listen to their comments about the song and video.

"Can I get you something to drink Billie?" Philip asks.

"Orange juice, thanks," I reply. I watch him walk to the table.

"So Billie, I hear things are going to get really busy for you both," Kenny says.

"Yes that's right, during the promotion of this single we will be working on more songs for the album. We have decided which single he will release next and we are planning the video for that. We have tours and local showcases planned here then according to Charles Parker in Promotions we have showcases in Milan, Spain, France, Germany and Czech. It's quite busy."

"That's really good to hear. I hear the song is already in a number of European charts. It's good strategy to go there," Marcel says.

"Here's your orange juice," Philip says handing me a glass.

"Thanks."

"Do you want to sit down?"

"Okay."

The others are talking and do not join us as we sit at a table nearby. As soon as we sit down, I regret moving away from the others. I find that I don't have anything to say. I don't know who this person is and I don't know what to talk about. I don't know if he senses my nervousness, I don't look at him, because every time I try to look up, he is staring at me.

"I'm staring, I'm sorry, am I making you nervous?"

Startled I look up at him. His eyes look so gentle.

"Yes," I say smiling, "in a spooky sort of way."

He starts to laugh and I laugh with him.

"What do you like to do?"

His question is unexpected and I don't answer right away.

"I like to relax, watch old movies."

"Which ones?" He asks.

"I like period dramas and comedies."

"Period dramas?"

"Like 'Pride and Prejudice', things along that line."

"No kissing, no violence."

I look at the comical expression on his face and laugh.

"I also like a lot of the *Abbott and Costello* comedies."

"You're joking! *Abbott and Costello*?"

"You like them as well? I've watched most of their films."

"Who's on first base?" He asks.

"What?"

"No. What's on second?"

"Why?"

"No, Why's on third."

We start to laugh at the old *Abbott and Costello* joke. The laughter dies slowly and I look up and find that he is staring again.

"Err.., excuse me but you're doing that staring thing again."

He smiles and I smile and place my hands on the table.

We talk about old films, music, food. We laugh a lot. As we talk I notice that he listens intently, it is almost as if for him, no one else is in the room. I like the way he uses his hands to describe things. I like the way that once in a while when his hands are on the table next to mine our hands don't touch. Some soft music starts playing in the background.

"So you're 'old school'?" He raises his eyebrows and smiles. "Just for the record, for how long would we have to be chaperoned or meet in a crowded place, before I could say ask you to dance?"

"Not that long, we're looking at two maybe four, less than six."

"Weeks?"

"Months," I reply.

We laugh.

"Are you seeing anyone?" Philip asks. I look at him, surprised at his question, he looks a little nervous but very serious. "I don't mean to pry, it's just that nowadays relationships are not what you think they are, there's a lack of substance. People are so busy playing games and jumping into things that they don't seem to bother to ask questions. Important questions I mean. What do you think?"

"Yes."

He looks surprised, almost scared and I wonder why.

"You're seeing someone?"

"What? No I meant yes, I agree with what you said. No, I'm not seeing anyone," I reply. I see something that looks like relief in his eyes. "Are you?" I ask and hold my breath.

"No," he quickly replies.

Silence, comfortable silence.

"I think Jamie might be trying to get your attention, he's looking over here."

I turn, Jamie smiles but says nothing.

"I have to go, I'm giving him a lift home. It's been nice talking to you." As I push my chair back Philip gets up and pulls it out.

"Thank you," I say standing up. (Who said chivalry is dead?)

"No problem."

We smile at each other.

"Goodnight."

"Would you...," he stops.

"What?" I ask.

He doesn't say anything and I look up at him and wait.

"Would you like to come to dinner?"

I shake my head, "I don't think so, but thank you..."

"Not with me, umm.., I will be there but so will ten or so other people. I know you don't know me so umm.., we won't be alone. This is not coming out right. It's because you're staring at me."

"I'm not," I smile.

"Would you? My cousin will be there and his wife Angela."

"Your cousin?"

"Kenny. I didn't tell you that Kenny and I are cousins?"

"No."

"We're cousins, same Hawaiian grandmother."

"Your part Hawaiian?"

He nods, "One third Hawaiian, one third Italian, one third American and one third African American. Some of the thirds cross."

I smile.

"Please come, I know we don't know each other that well yet but we have to start somewhere."

"I umm…"

"Francis will be there."

I feel my heart race in a way I have never felt before and all of a sudden for some strange reason, I don't feel uncomfortable.

"When?"

"Next Wednesday. I'm in California until Monday."

"When are you travelling?"

"Tomorrow."

"Oh."

"Wednesday?" He asks.

"Okay Wednesday then, I'd better go."

"May I..," he pauses and shakes his head. "Can I call you before then? Your phone number is on the video shoot program."

I nod.

"I'll call you tomorrow Billie."

CHAPTER 29

I can't believe that in two days Jamie has done twenty one interviews. At one point it seemed never-ending; television, radio tours, magazines and newspapers, all one after another. I tried to stay in the background for most of them but time and time again I was asked questions about the song, about the hint of a relationship between Jamie and I, about where I get my inspiration from. The one thing I found amusing was that the same questions were asked time and time again.

Today is interview number twenty two. It is 6.30am and Jamie and I are waiting for the make-up ladies for the breakfast television show. I was only told yesterday that they wanted to talk to both of us. We were both in the studio until 2am this morning and I know that I will need a lot of make-up to hide the tired circles under my eyes.

"Coffee, I need coffee," Jamie moans.

"I'm yawning in my sleep Jamie."

"Yawning in your sleep?" He smiles, "Tired?"

"Really tired, we have to reschedule some of our schedules and take proper time off each week or we're going to burn-out. I need an assistant, I didn't realize I'd be doing these interviews with you. It's six thirty in the morning. How many hours sleep did we have?"

"Two and a bit. I'm going to go and look for some coffee."

"I'll come with you," I pull myself off the chair. We walk down the hall. At the end we turn right and walk down another hall. I hear the sweet sound of banging pots and pans in the distance. At the end of the hall we walk through the double doors into a large canteen. There are people seated at tables eating breakfast.

"Sit down, I'll go and get them," Jamie says. He walks over to the large urns manned by women in white uniforms.

"Hello."

I look up at the man standing by the table, "Hello," I reply not knowing who he is.

"My, my, my, don't we look tired," he says.

"That's because 'we' are," I reply.

"Late night?"

"Late, busy, working, music, take your pick."

"Do you need 'something' to wake you up? Do you wanna try some good stuff?" Un-invited he sits down.

"What?"

"Something that will have you flying in minutes."

"Excuse me?"

"I've got some good stuff, it will have you doing the marathon in five minutes."

'Flying? The marathon?' I think to myself and frown, my senses are alert, my sleep depravation disappears.

"What stuff?" I ask

"Amphetamines, grade A stuff."

"You're joking right?"

"No"

"Do I look like a pill popper?" I almost shout.

"Hey lady they don't have a look," he quickly stands up.

"What's going on?" Jamie asks as he places the two cups of coffee he is holding on the table.

"He just offered me some pills to wake me up."

"What! What do you think you're doing?"

"Look I just supply a demand, celebrities come in here all the time needing a little jump-start. Sorry, my mistake, I thought you needed a 'lift'." He walks away from our table, stops to pick up his bag, and then walks out of the canteen.

"Is it me or is that normal? Should we tell security?" I ask.

"Unfortunately it's normal in some places, but I wouldn't have thought a place like this would have people like him here."

*   *   *   *   *

I am wide awake now and the make-up lady is adding a few finishing touches to her near perfect work. She unclips my hair and arranges it on my shoulders commenting on how lovely it is. I smile and look at Jamie as he sleeps in the next chair. He is exhausted but we have to do this interview and then two more, and a showcase this afternoon. We had a late session at Liam's studio booked for tonight, which I have cancelled, because I know he needs to rest; tomorrow is just as busy. As I look at Jamie sleeping it becomes clearer what Ben must have gone through. Ben was seventeen when Troyston were first successful, how would he have been able to cope with the gruelling tours, interviews and showcases at that age. The pressures of success.

I find it hard going from place to place, answering questions, some of which should not be asked in the first place, smiling, watching what I wore, watching what I said. Earlier, when that man had asked if I wanted those pills I had said no instinctively, but how many people like Ben have said yes. How many people take pills to wake themselves up and then pills to make themselves go to sleep when insomnia sets in. I never knew Ben, but I feel a sadness for him and for the many like him. The many who start with pills and end up using 'hard' drugs.

Heroin, crack, cocaine and LSD users may all have heard the same words initially, *'do you wanna try some stuff?'*.

I recall something I read not long ago, it was written by the renowned Psychologist, Dr Willard Kettering: **'If you have the will-power to take drugs you have the will-power to say no to drugs.** *For it takes will-power to inject heroin, snort cocaine, sample crack and LSD for the first time; not knowing how it will affect you. Most users that I have spoken to, were scared, a little apprehensive and required a certain amount of will-power the first time they took drugs.'*

'Poor Ben' I think to myself 'he probably didn't stand a chance at that age.'

*   *   *   *   *

I sit and watch Jamie sing the song again due to the large number of people that have just woken up and turned on their television in the last ten minutes. They missed Jamie's earlier live performance and phoned in to request that he sing the song live again. As I sit with the two presenters during Jamie's live performance I look around the set. I do a double-take as I see the man that had offered me pills in the canteen. He is wearing a suit and holding a clip board. I still have my microphone on so I cannot talk. I pick up a piece of paper from the table and write on it, 'Who is that man in the dark blue suit?' I hand the paper to the female presenter. She writes something down and hands the paper back to me under the table. I lift it up slightly and read:

'That's the producer of the show'.

CHAPTER 30

"The young American lady was brought in about two hours ago sir. She wouldn't speak at first. She sustained severe cuts and bruising. Said she was on a date with someone and she thinks he drugged her and tried to attack her," the police officer says reading from a note book.

"What!"

"She gave us your number and insisted we only contact you. She was very adamant about this."

"Thank you, has she been to hospital? Seen a doctor?"

"No sir, she refused. We have had our station doctor take a look at her but she refused to go to hospital. She seemed to be very concerned about newspaper reporters and not wanting any paparazzi to know."

Philip massages his temple and thinks, "Can I use your phone? I left my mobile at home."

"Yes sir, you can use the one in the office. Do you want to see her first?"

"No I need to make a phone call first."

He walks into the office, picks up the receiver and dials.

"Hello."

"Kenny, it's me. Sapphire is in the police station."

"Again?"

"Again."

"Give me the address. I'm on my way."

* * * * *

He walks into the room where Sapphire sits waiting for him. She is pulling at a blond tress and staring into space. She hears the door close and looks up.

"I knew you would come Philip, I know that even though you say you are not in love with me, deep down inside you may be."

"You can't keep doing this, one of these days you are going to get hurt really badly. Why are you doing this to yourself?"

"I don't understand Philip, I'm beautiful, I'm a Supermodel, everyone thinks that I'm beautiful but you don't want me. You tell me you don't want me when everyone else says they do."

"I thought we agreed that we would be friends. You left me nearly three years ago remember? For one of my friends."

"Only because I thought that it would make you jealous. But he dumped me after he found out about the 'adult' films I did. You are the only one that never judged me Philip...., I only went with him to make you jealous. "

"Jealous? Love is not jealous Sapphire, plus we only went on three dates, we were never really in a relationship."

"It was a relationship to me, but you never wanted me."

"We didn't have time for each other, you were always in Europe on one fashion shoot or another, I was busy in America. It didn't work then and it won't work now. Things have changed, I have changed," he says gently.

"It would have worked if you had tried harder, it can still work if we try to make it work."

"No, it won't work, back then I let a lot of things slide, now things have changed, things are different."

"You're referring to the drugs aren't you. You know I only took them because of the pressures of work. It's hard being a model, staying skinny, trim and beautiful all the time."

"It's hard being anyone, but you still have to try and I wasn't referring to the drugs."

"You said on the phone that since we went out, there hasn't been anyone else. That must mean something?" She says clutching at fragile straws.

"It means that I'm tired of the pretence, tired of casual relationships. I want more and I don't want to settle for less."

"This isn't just about you being a Christian and not sleeping with me is it? It's more than that?"

"It's about change Sapphire about me doing the right thing."

She looks at him, "You're not still in love with that dream? You think you'll meet that girl again and she will fall in love with you? Is that what you think? I'm here why can't you love me instead of a dream?"

"It's not that simple."

"I can change Philip I know I can. I'll go for treatment."

"That's good, but do it for you, not anyone else."

She starts to cry. Philip sits down next to her. He does not comfort her or touch her. He has been told by her therapist that for her, such actions are confusing. She has the tendency to misconstrue such actions.

They sit side by side, without touching, waiting for Kenny.

CHAPTER 31

Tonight is the launch party for 'Love Is Not Supposed To Hurt'. Steve, Martin, Jen, and Trudi are here giving us support. A lot of the other artists signed to the label and some that are not, are also in attendance.

"Where is he?" Jen asks referring to Philip, whom she and Trudi are very keen to inspect, sorry I mean, to meet.

"I don't know, he said that he would make it. He has probably been held up somewhere," I look around the room.

"Ladies and gentleman," Francis Wells says as he walks onto the stage. Most of the people in the room turn towards him while others, mainly the reporters and cameramen carry on talking. Francis picks up a microphone. "Ladies and gentlemen and reporters," everyone stops talking. "Thank you," he smiles, "we are all here tonight for the launch party. This is a new thing, because the song that we are launching is already in a number of charts based or pre-ordered sales." Someone in the audience whistles. Some people start to clap. "You hear of a song doing well on the first day of its release, or even in the first week; well this one has done extremely well before its release. So without much ado I present Jamie Sanders performing his smash hit 'Love Is Not Supposed To Hurt'."

Jamie walks onto the stage and some young girls in the room, who won tickets to be here tonight on the radio, start to scream before he opens his mouth.

"Oh my," Trudi says grabbing my arm, "look at them."

"Hi, thank you all for coming," Jamie says. The girls start to scream hysterically again and I look at them amazed.

Jen shakes her head, "Youngsters of nowadays," she says, "tell me we were not like that."

"We were not like that," I say. She pinches my arm playfully.

The music starts and Jamie ad-libs. He takes his voice higher than the music and projects it towards his audience with such virtuosity. His passion is amazing to watch. As Jamie sings the girls are quiet. They stare at him mesmerized.

As soon as he finishes they start clapping as do the rest of us. I watch and wait and sure enough seconds later they start screaming.

"I better get Jamie to sign some autographs for them," I say to Trudi and Jen. "I'll be back soon, if you see a tall dark handsome man with really nice eyes that will be Philip. He said yesterday that he was definitely going to come."

"Yesterday?" Trudi frowns at me, "you said he called you from America two days ago?"

"He did."

"You told me he called you three days ago," Jen queries.

"He did," I reply.

"So theoretically, what you are saying is that he has called you every day since he went?" Trudi asks.

"Yes, practically, umm.., twice some days," I reply and smile.

"Look at that smile Trudi! I've never seen it before!" Jen quips.

"Ooooh," they both chorus and then start to giggle. The teenage girls start to scream again and I look from them to my two friends giggling at my expense and wonder.

"Just look out for him, I'll get Jamie to sign some autographs."

"We'll keep watch," Trudi says, "please just sort the noise."

I grab some pictures and walk towards the girls, "Hello ladies, my name is-"

"It's Billie, arrrrr..," one of them screams. I stand there in shock as the others join in and start screaming.

"Ladies, calm down, I have some pictures here and I was going to get Jamie to come over and sign them for you."

"Jamie's picture, arrrrrrr..."

"Calm down we won't be able to do this if you keep screaming, there are a lot of other people here."

"OK, OK, OK," they chorus.

I count ten teenagers in all, I usher them to a corner of the room and go to get Jamie.

*　*　*　*　*

"And your name is?" Jamie asks.

"Chantelle."

He writes something on the picture and hands it to her.

"My name is Kim, can you write to my darling Kim."

"No, darling Kim, I will write to dear Kim," Jamie says.

"Okay Jamie," she turns to the others "he called me darling, arrrr-" she looks at me then stops. "Sorry Billie."

I am trying so hard to keep a straight face. I'm sure I wasn't like this when I was their age. I think back to my 'Top Of The Pops' days, I recall my mother telling me to stop the screaming and shouting each time someone I liked came on the show. Okay maybe I was.

"Done," Jamie says turning to me, "can we give them each a free CD?"

"I think so, I'll go and check. We should be able to take ten Promotion CDs out of the box for the radio DJs, there are hundreds in there."

"I'll go," Jamie says leaving me with the teenagers.

"Okay ladies, while Jamie goes to see if he can get you some gifts, why don't you all tell me how you won your tickets."

"I won a pair on Radio 1 yesterday morning. I had to go with my mum to the radio station to collect them. I gave a ticket to my best friend Esther," Chantelle says putting an arm around the girl next to her.

"That's nice."

"What about you?" I ask pointing to a girl at the back.

"My mum answered a question on the radio and won two tickets. She gave them to me and my sister," she answers shyly.

I listen as the others all share their exciting stories.

"All right ladies look what I was able to find," Jamie says putting a box down on the table. He pulls out some posters, CDs and little gift wrapped boxes.

"What's in the boxes?" I ask leaning towards him.

"Apparently they're little bottles of perfume that were used in a video. Francis says they can have them."

"That's so thoughtful."

"Thank you," he replies

"No, I meant of Francis."

Their faces light up as we hand them the gifts. You can tell that they hadn't expected it.

"I went to a launch party a few weeks ago and we never got to talk to the artist let alone get anything. This is really brilliant, thank you," Chantelle says.

There is an extra box left. I pick it up.

"You said your mum won the tickets and gave them to you and your sister?"

The girl at the back nods.

"Give her this as a thank you," I say smiling at her.

*   *   *   *   *

"Billie don't look now, there's a man across the room that has been staring at you for over ten minutes. He's tall, with dark hair…," Jen stops and looks over my shoulder in a rather overt manner. I turn to look and she squeezes my arm. "I said don't look. He's handsome and has really deep eyes," she continues to look over my shoulder.

"How can you see that from here?"

"Billie," I turn. Philip is standing behind me.

"Hi"

"How are you?"

"Good, how was your flight?"

"It was okay. You look great." He stares.

I smile, Jen coughs.

"Umm…, this is Jen a very close friend of mine."

"Hi Philip, how are you? We've heard a lot about you. It's nice to meet you at last."

"We've?" He questions and smiles.

"Yes, Trudi, she's the one over there talking to Jamie. Martin, Billie's cousin, he's over there talking to Francis, I think that's his name. Steve, Billie's brother is over there."

Philip nods.

I don't feel embarrassed that Jen has just hinted to him that all my nearest and dearest are wondering what he is like. I want them to meet him. Maybe it's early and I am being a little wishful but I hope that they like him.

"I've noticed that she keeps staring at me like that...,"

"What?" I ask.

"Philip said that sometimes you seem to go into a world of your own and just stare at him like you were doing just now."

"What? That's not true."

"You just did it now," Jen says.

"I was looking over there, he just happened to be in the way."

"What were you looking at?" Philip asks.

"That," I say pointing past him.

"Like I said Jen," he takes hold of my hand, "she just stares."

I laugh with them.

He does not let go of my hand.

* * * * *

My nearest and dearest have all met Philip. They seem to like him. I noticed Steve look at him strangely but I put it down to brotherly protection. Philip seemed a little nervous about meeting them initially, he is more relaxed now as we sit at a table.

"I'm sorry I was late."

"It's okay, you came, that's what matters."

"A friend of mine had a problem so I had to go and help."

"Is your friend okay now?"

He nods.

"I'm going to be staying at Kenny's house for a couple of days, my friend needed a place to stay, so I let them have my place."

I sense there is something he is not telling me but I don't ask.

"So, how have the interview schedules been since we last spoke?" He changes the subject, his eyes are filtering information.

"Still hectic," I reply, "why the sudden change of subject?"

He looks at me and for a moment I cannot be sure but I think I see a guilty look in his eyes and I wonder what it means.

*   *   *   *   *

"Thanks for the lift Kenny, nice meeting you both, I'll call you tomorrow Billie. Goodnight all," Jen says.

"Goodnight," we reply.

Kenny drives to my house. Soft music plays on the car radio and I stare out of the window in the back of the car. We all seem lost in our separate thoughts now that Jen, the main speaker, has gone.

"Are you okay?" Philip asks.

I look up, he has turned in his seat and is looking at me.

"I'm fine thank you."

"I told you I was staying at Kenny's for a couple of days," he seems a little nervous and I feel something is wrong.

"What's wrong?"

"Nothing, why?"

"You said your friend was staying at your place and you are staying at Kenny's." I notice Kenny looking at me in the rear-view mirror. "You've told me three times this evening. Is there something wrong with your friend?"

"She was beaten up this afternoon."

"She?" I ask. Again I get the strange look from Kenny. "You never said it was a she. Is she okay?"

"It's a she, yes she is okay, she needed a place to stay, but I'm not staying there. That's why I'm at Kenny's for a couple of days, she'll be staying at my place with a friend." His eyes are no longer filtering.

"What house number Billie?" Kenny asks.

"Number seven."

He parks the car behind my car, Philip gets out and opens the door for me.

"Goodnight Kenny, thanks for the lift."

"Not a problem. Take care Billie, I'll see you tomorrow."

We walk up my front path in silence and I stop at the door.

"Thanks," I say.

"Are you upset Billie?"

"No, not really. I don't know what to feel. I suppose I don't really know you that well."

"What? I told you because I want our relationship to be honest. I could have not said anything. Look here's Kenny's home number call me there," he puts his hand in his pocket pulls out a card and pen and writes something on it.

"No it's not necessary, you're right you could have not said anything," I say. He hands me the card, I take it reluctantly. "Look, I am still working on the presumption that what you said the other night is true. You're not seeing anyone."

"That is the truth, I…, you're the only….," he looks away.

"I'll see you tomorrow," I say a little nonchalantly not wanting to read more into him than he is willing to write.

He takes hold of my hand and looks straight into my eyes.

"If I told you how I felt right now, I'd probably scare you. I don't want to rush things. I can wait. Believe me, there is no one else."

His eyes are so intense, I catch my breath, I can't speak. I nod.

Moments pass.

I turn, open my front door and walk inside, "Goodnight."

"Goodnight," he replies and walks back down the path.

*   *   *   *   *

"Why did you tell her about Sapphire?" Kenny asks almost as soon as Philip opens the car door, "was she upset?"

"No I don't think so but I think she would be really upset if she ever found out one day."

"Is she still coming tomorrow?"

"I didn't ask, but she didn't say she wasn't. Actually she said see you tomorrow, so I guess she is. I'll pick her up at eight."

"Are you okay?"

"No," he sighs and rubs his eyes, "No I'm not, I've never felt like this before Kenny, ever. I'm nervous, I'm scared, but I'm so sure."

"That's a good sign, believe me, that's good."

CHAPTER 32

As I rush around in my attempt to get ready, my hair falls down on my shoulders again. I glance at the clock, it's too late to try and pin it up again, it's nearly 8pm. I pull out the hair pins and brush it down.

Today has been really busy; three interviews, two showcases followed by a long session in the studio working with a new female singer on a modified production of a *Madonna* song. After that I was in the song writing department with a popular female trio, working on some new material for them. I only got home thirty minutes ago.

The front door bell rings and I quickly glance in the mirror at my appearance then go to open the door.

"Hi," Philip says walking in, "you look really nice."

"Thank you, so do you, and you're right on time."

"Actually I got here ten minutes ago. I sat and waited in the car so I wouldn't appear too eager."

I laugh and lead him into my front room.

"I'll be ready in a few minutes."

"Take as long as you like," he says walking around and looking at my things. He stands in front of the large painting on the wall and looks at it. I prepare the answer to his question in my mind.

"Did you get this in Lagos?" He asks.

I take a couple of seconds to re-adjust my mind and answer him. He does not ask the question which every single person who has looked at that picture has asked, no, he asks a question that no one has ever asked. Smiling I run up the stairs to get my handbag and add the final touches to my make-up.

* * * * *

"You won a national poetry award when you were seven?" Philip asks as soon as I walk into the front room a few minutes later. His voice is full of intrigue.

"How did you know?" I ask, surprised.

He lifts up a folder that had been in my bookcase.

I nod, feeling the tug of my modesty strings.

"The Spider by Billie Lewis Aged 7 years, this is really good," he says. I stand in astonishment as he reads my poem out aloud.

> *"The spider spins a web so high*
> *through the trees and to the sky*
> *From afar it waits, hiding, waiting for a catch*
> *The little bugs, the flies, they are no match.*
> *'Not long' he thinks as the wind makes his web sway*
> *"There, I said it", he rushes towards his brand new prey.*

You were seven when you wrote this?"

"Yes, seven nearly eight, I did it at school, we were learning about spiders at the time."

"Come and sit down, tell me about some of these poems."

"Which ones?" I ask as I sit next to him.

"Start with this one, I read it earlier." He turns a page and I look at the words.

I Am Loved As I Am

I may not be who you want me to be
I may not see the things you see
but am I really that different? Do you think I am strange?
Is there a part of me you would like to change?

Stop for a minute, don't be in such a haste
rushing around like you have no time to waste.
There really is not that much difference between you and I
we all have faults, cover them up though we try.

But wait, maybe there is a slight difference.
What? You ask - what can it be?

Well, when you look in the mirror what do you see?

Because when I look I see eyes full of love, a heart full of joy
secure in God's love which no one can take away or destroy.
Look, can you see it, can you see what I do?
No, then turn away, turn towards, look again, see it now?
Yes, He loves you too.

"I wrote this one in stages, I wrote the first part when I was 15 or 16. I was living in Nigeria with my parents and brother. Some of the girls at school thought I was something that I wasn't. They used to look at me and say I was really pretty. They expected me to act a certain way, 'nasty' camouflaged as cool, which I never did. See, I never looked at myself through their eyes, I looked at myself through mine. This poem just reflects what I see when I look in the mirror, Me. I wrote the second part a few years ago it was after I met a man at a Christian barbecue. I had volunteered with some other people in my church to join members of other churches in the community, organise and run a Christian outreach. We made burgers, hotdogs and salads and invited people in the community to have a free lunch and get to know more about God. I was in charge of putting the ketchup on the burgers and handing out the drinks. A man came to the table and as I put the ketchup on his burger and gave him a drink I said: *'God bless you and enjoy your meal'*. He replied: *'I don't deserve God's blessings because when things were good for me I didn't acknowledge God, so why should God acknowledge me now that things are bad and I am an alcoholic?'*." I pause.

"What happened?" Philip asks.

"I explained to him that God's ways are not like ours. God is love and it is His nature to love. I told him that God loved him as much as me and the only difference between us was that I knew it and he didn't, that my smile was a reflection of that knowledge and my peace and joy the security of it. I introduced him to one of the lead organisers and they sat down and talked. About twenty minutes later he came up to the table, he had tears in his eyes and he thanked me. He said that he never knew until that day how much God loved him and what Jesus had done for him. I don't think that I will ever forget the look on his face."

I look up at Philip, he is staring at me. I smile, he smiles back. Moments pass. He coughs and turns a page.

"I read this one earlier as well," he says.

I look at the poem and smile fondly.

"Read it," he says softly.

I look at him, "I …umm."

"Please," he says wading through my embarrassment.

The encouragement in his eyes captivates me.

I turn and look at the poem, I read it.

"Hope

My pessimistic friend says that I am a joke
That I am too optimistic because I am called Hope.
We were once 'one' before but he made a choice one day
To remove me from his life, now he lives in a hope-less way.

He blames me for the pain and misery he suffers from all the time.
I have tried to tell him to change because his choices are his not mine.

You see I am what is considered a good thing
I have lost count of the many joys and anticipated blessings I bring.
There are so many people that look forward to a brighter day
So I am constantly called upon to show them the way.

I work hand in hand with a wonderful loyal dedicated friend
His name is Faith and he is strong, resilient and does not bend.

All good things come in threes so I am told
That probably explains why we have a third partner who is so glorious and bold.
He is the greatest of the three of us, full of passion and so strong
There is nothing He cannot do, and when you repent He forgives your every wrong.

His name is Love and He is truly the Great of great
Our mission: I, Hope, have Faith and with Love we operate."

"When did you write it?"

"Years ago," I reply.

"You have a wonderful gift of writing and communicating. It's amazing how you break down the truth into such a digestible form."

The years of criticism and rebuff are soothed by his words. His eyes reflect his sincerity and admiration. I stare at him. He turns a page, I hear him gasp and look at the poem.

"I've read this in a magazine before! I didn't know it was one of your poems."

"It was published last year in 'Music and Lyrics' and the year before that, in the 'What Next' magazine. I didn't use my full name, just Billie."

"Billie! I remember," he nods.

"Read it," I say impulsively.

He sits back and lifts the folder up.

I sit back and listen to him.

"Unforgiveness Eats Away

Day 1.

For how long do I have to smile and pretend all is okay?
Forgive and forget, while he continues to talk to me this way.
He always tries to tell me what to think, what to do.
It irritates me though, knowing some of what he says is true.

Let it not be said that I am bitter or hold a grudge in any way.
For I know the consequence of unforgiveness, I know it eats away.
So I am not angry neither am I sad.
Even though he upset me, I'm only a little bit mad.
Day 2.
I don't feel too good today,
I feel incomplete in the strangest way.

This morning when I tried to stand up, my legs had disappeared,
And, where they once stood a gap had appeared.

Anyway, let me continue from where I left off the other day.
I was talking about unforgiveness and how it eats away.

Maybe I should call my cousin and try and make amends.
Or, maybe call a couple of my estranged childhood friends.
Hold on, why does it always have to be me,
that picks up the phone to say 'I'm sorry'.

So what if they've apologized, they were wrong that's for sure.
On second thoughts, I don't need them anymore.
But I'm not angry, neither am I sad.
Even though they upset me, I'm only a little bit mad."

He moves closer to me and turns the page, "Finish it for me," he says softly.
I take the folder and rest it on my lap.

> *"Day 5.*
> *As the days go by I keep more and more to myself.*
> *I've tried not to worry, but now, I'm concerned about my health.*
> *First went my legs, then my arms, torso and neck.*
> *Now, I suspect my head has gone but I have nothing with which to check.*
>
> *Day 8.*
> *I'll continue from where I left off the other day.*
> *Remember? I was talking about unforgiveness and how it eats away.*
>
> *Now as my lonesome eye rolls around in my bed.*
> *I can conclude, that I am indeed without a head.*
> *I can also conclude that, yes, I was angry and yes I was sad*
> *and yes, all those people did make me very very mad.*

Foolishly, I let my power to forgive and love unconditionally stray,
*I held on to **bitterness** and pride, I let unforgiveness eat me away.*
I'm so sorry, where are my manners, I forgot to introduce myself to
you
I'm Carlos, Kemi, Ranjit or Sue, recognize me? That's right, I may
even be you."

"When I first read this poem I was having a problem with someone I worked with. It really spoke to me Billie. It made me realize that I could either stay as I was and let the whole bitter situation stay alive and eat at me, make me ill, or I could forgive, let go and be whole and free. I remember this one time I had the opportunity to get even with the person and I never took it, that's when I realized that I had really forgiven. It's funny how the people that say revenge is sweet are left miserable after they get revenge," Philip says.

"That is so true," I say, "people buy into the lie that revenge is sweet then wonder why after they get revenge they have a bitter taste in their mouth. It took me a while before I understood that we have to forgive others as God forgives us, and vengeance belongs to Him not us, when we try to get back at people it really destroys us not them."

He nods, "At one point I was emotionally tied up in hate, shackled to hurt and unforgiveness, then one day I listened to a message at church about God's love and that message changed me. I remember feeling so free afterwards. I guess that was why I was drawn to this poem the first time I read it."

"Free! That's how I felt when I wrote it. I had just forgiven my cousin after months of being angry and hurt with what she had done. It's funny though because after I had written it, I worked with a woman that constantly found fault with what I did and I used to get so angry with her. She was a lot older than me but she seemed to be so envious. Anyway I was looking for something one day and I came across the original draft of this poem. I read the words and I felt all the anger and unforgiveness in me die. I started talking to her and I found out that she was having problems at home and that was why she acted the way she did at work. If I hadn't read the poem then, I probably wouldn't have bothered. You're right, I too remember feeling so free," I smile.

He closes the folder, "A lot of research has found that pent up anger, bitterness and unforgiveness, can cause serious health problems. That when people let go of these negative emotions they actually get better and feel better. Letting go sets them free. What is it they say? *Forgiveness is the gateway to healing and good health!*"

"I've heard that; I also know from my own personal experience of letting go and forgiving, I was set free from pent up anger and irritation. The freedom is a really good feeling isn't it?" I smile.

"The best," he concurs.

Moments pass.

He is quiet, so I look up at him. It suddenly dawns on me that we are sitting really close to each other. He is staring at me again. I see his head move towards mine, I frown, I panic, I move back a little. He smiles and nods. I feel his fingers touching my hair and then on my face. I notice his fingers are trembling and I feel my breath catch at the back of my throat.

"You are so beautiful," he says softly, "and I am so nervous."

I look away and I feel his fingers move under my chin and gently turn my head back. I feel his thumb under my bottom lip, he tilts my head up and I look at him. He leans forward and kisses my forehead then moves back.

"We should go," he says softly.

"Okay," I say breathing out a sigh of relief as I stand up.

He puts the folder back and holds out a hand towards me. I take hold of it and we leave the house.

* * * * *

The restaurant is large and very impressive. We are seated around a large table, I have been introduced to everyone. They all seem friendly. Kenny's wife Angela and Francis' girlfriend Sofia are nice.

"Are you okay?" Philip asks again, attentively.

"I'm fine," I reply turning to face him. I place a hand reassuringly on his and smile at him. He places his other hand on top of mine and squeezes. He leans towards me.

"What type of flowers do you like?" He asks softly. I feel his breath on my cheek.

"Colourful ones," I reply and he laughs.

The food is served and jokes are flying around the table. I feel like I do with Jen and Trudi, really comfortable. I listen to the stories and jokes that are shared about the good old days and I laugh with everyone else. I am very aware of Philip sitting next to me and I feel happy inside that I am here with him.

Suddenly I hear some commotion and look in the direction of the noise. I recognize the singer Brian Turner in the distance. He is shouting at a waiter and waving his hands in the air. A lady walks towards him as if she is trying to calm him down, he pushes her away and shouts at her and then throws plates on the floor. I watch with the others at my table as he is escorted out of the restaurant.

"Isn't that his wife?" Someone on a nearby table asks.

"Yes it is. I read in the newspapers this morning that he has been dropped by his record label," someone on the same table replies.

I turn back to our table as the waiters hurriedly walk around the restaurant stopping at each table to apologize for the disturbance.

*   *   *   *   *

"…Yes we did go for counselling before we got married, and I think it was the best thing we ever did," Angela says and I look up realizing her accent is Canadian.

"Why before your wedding though?" Maria asks.

"It's part of the conditions in the church that we got married in and as I said it was a really good thing."

"Most counsellors help with problems that happen after you get married so what did your counsellor help you with?"

"A lot. We had two Professional Christian Counsellors. The most important thing they taught was that God ordained marriage and all marriages need to be submitted to Him to succeed. They explained how people who have excluded God from their marriage and try to go-it-alone usually end up failing. God has His role and the couple theirs. We went for six lessons, we were also taught about the different expectations in marriage, how to deal with things that may happen and how to treat each other. What men expect and what women expect. They teach you how not to look to a person to give you purpose, but to find your purpose before-hand. Usually people say that two halves make a whole and you have to go around looking for your other half. In pre-marriage counselling they teach you that you have to be a whole first. You have to be complete and then when you are complete, you are ready for a relationship, ready to give out of your completeness. When you are a half looking for your other half you are never complete and cannot give fully in a relationship."

"I don't know if I could do that," Maria says.

"I think it's a good idea," I say.

"Why?" Clifford, Maria's boyfriend asks me.

"It's based on wisdom."

"Wisdom?"

"With the high divorce rate in this country and worldwide I think that anything that helps prepare people for marriage is good and wise. Everyone wants a marriage that will last but are they prepared to put themselves last in a marriage."

"How do you mean?" Maria asks.

"In a marriage, if both parties put the other first and themselves last, it can only be a win-win situation, because they will both have their needs met. I think that women want real affection, love, to be treated right and security. I also think that men have wants as well. Men want to be respected as the head of the home, loved and taken care of. Selfishness, pride and emotional coldness cannot survive in a good marriage."

"Exactly, that's exactly what you're taught in pre-marriage counselling!" Kenny says.

"Women and men are different and I think it's a way of helping you to understand the differences," Louise says, "Angela and I have talked about this a number of times and I wish I had gone before I got married. It probably would have stopped me getting divorced after two years of marriage." I look at Louise, she is an attractive lady, I had thought the man she was sitting next to was her husband or boyfriend. He doesn't look embarrassed so I assume that he is just a friend. "Billie is right, women want affection, they want a kiss, a hug, a cuddle, reassurance that they mean something and are not just there for sex. They want a relationship no matter how much they pretend that it doesn't matter and they are okay with certain arrangements. Most women want the whole nine yards," she pauses and I notice that everyone seated at the table is listening.

"I'm sorry, don't mind me," she says blushing as she realizes that we are all waiting for her to continue.

"Please, go on," I say.

"I was just going to say, that it seems that our wires have gotten so crossed up with all the pretence nowadays. We move in with a boyfriend thinking that things are on an equal footing and that we are okay with everything. We wait, some of us for years, waiting for them to ask us to marry them, so scared of even mentioning the subject for fear that we will drive them away. We turn ourselves into good little 'I don't need a piece of paper' housewives.

Women are the ones that wait for the men to pop the question while they try to convince their family, friends and mostly themselves that things are cool as they are. I just think that women need to think a little bit more.

We did a survey in our magazine on how many couples who initially lived together, actually ended up getting married, and I tell you I was shocked with the results."

"How many?" Philip asks.

"Less than 20%."

"What happens to the other 80%?" A man sitting two seats away from me asks. I think his name is Thomas.

"Some of them don't get married at all they continue to live together, I think that was about 15%. The remaining 65% met someone else and got married or moved in with someone else. It just makes you think. According to Angela and Kenny, the counselling course they went on, did not approve of couples living together. So when they got married, it was a new and exciting thing and they were prepared for it mentally," Louise says. She picks up her glass and takes a sip of her drink, "It's like a present. If you have a present for someone and you give it to them before their birthday and they open it, come their birthday, it won't be a surprise will it?"

"You make it sound as if it's only the women that have a rough deal, it works both ways," Thomas says.

"I know it does, but let's be honest, in most cases unless the woman doesn't want to get married, she is usually the one thinking about her biological clock ticking away and hoping that the man asks her to marry him. Or she is usually the one who pretends things are okay with them being co-habitants surrounded by their confused 'modern' children, when secretly inside she is tired of being a bridesmaid and not a bride," Louise says.

"I think somewhere along the line communication has gone out the window. People don't talk about how they really feel anymore. Everything is kept inside, yet we expect the other person to know what we want, how we feel," Thomas says.

"You're right, you're absolutely right Tommy," Louise says.

"You are not going to believe what I saw the other day on this TV programme," Monica says. She has not said much all evening, I turn towards her as does everyone else.

"This man was talking about relationships between men and women and he said that women want so many different things from one guy and that guys want one thing from so many different women. Now guys is that true? Tell me it's not."

"You know that's not true darling," her husband Ian says. I see that he is trying to hide a smile. Clifford is openly smiling.

I turn and look at Philip. He is staring at his glass.

"Dis is not true Francis?" Sofia asks in a heavy Spanish accent.

"No sweetie-pie, it's not," Francis replies smiling at her.

Philip smiles at them and I wonder why.

"Sometimes what is seen as the 'norm' or the right thing, is the wrong thing which has been made to look right, dressed up like the wolf in little red riding hood to fool people. We're supposed to be with one woman, so if you go with different women for one thing you are basically shallow and led by the wrong head," Kenny says.

I look at him with a new found respect as I nod in agreement. Clifford looks embarrassed.

294

"I agree to an extent Kenny," Clifford says, "but I think that before you settle down you should shop around. Plus if you don't, how will you ever get to understand women?"

"Maybe if we concentrated on understanding the woman we are with instead of every single woman, it would help. If we stopped having several girlfriends while we look for a wife, it would free up some women. Plus a 'Shopaholic' is not cured by wedding bells. If they shopped around before, chances are they will shop around after. If not with cash, then with a credit card," Kenny says.

"Credit card?" I ask Philip as the others talk.

"Buy now, pay later," he replies.

"Oh."

"Good job I have everything I want, everything I need to understand right here," he says softly placing his hand on top of mine. I look up, our eyes lock and I feel something stronger than emotions. I can't move, I don't want to. My heart is pounding and I know that if I look away it will slow down but I don't want to look away.

"Philip? Billie? Are you having any dessert?" I look away, feel the pounding subside and answer the question.

* * * * *

"Thank you, I had a really nice time," I say as I sit with Philip in his car in front of my house.

"You're not just saying that, were the topics not too sensitive?"

"Nope, I like honest talk about relationships."

"Personal honest talk or just general group discussions?"

"Both," I reply.

"What do you think about our relationship Billie?"

I think about his question and do not answer immediately. I know in my heart that I have asked for the right person and that I will know him when he comes. There is a peace I feel when I am with Philip, even when I speak to him on the phone, which is now a daily, sometimes twice daily, occurrence. I inhale deeply and speak honestly.

"Potential."

"I'm thinking serious potential," he says, "very serious. Do you believe that God answers prayers?"

"Yes I do," I reply a little surprised at his question.

"So do I. He has answered mine."

*   *   *   *   *

"I'll call you tomorrow Billie," Philip says. We are standing in front of my front door.

"Okay."

"Thanks for coming with me."

"Thank you for inviting me, I had a good time."

He lifts my hand up to his lips, kisses it gently then releases it.

"Tomorrow," he says softly.

I nod.

My phone starts to ring as soon as I close the front door. I rush into the front room and pick up the receiver.

"Hello."

No one answers, I can hear soft breathing. "Hello," I say again.

No reply.

I walk over to the window, Philip is getting into his car. He is holding his mobile phone against his ear. I smile.

"Philip, is this you? It's not tomorrow yet."

"Who is Philip?" A harsh voice says. Startled I drop the phone.

296

CHAPTER 33

"**W**elcome back listeners, we are still here live with Jamie Sanders," the DJ says.

"Hello everyone," Jamie says.

"So listeners, as promised you can call in and ask Jamie some questions, he has agreed to answer most of the reasonable ones," they laugh and I smile.

"Look at all these lights flashing Jamie, let's take caller on line 3," he presses a button. "Go ahead please caller."

"Hello, my name is Mickey and I just want to say that I bought a copy of Jamie's single yesterday and it is absolutely brilliant. Nowadays with all these senseless songs going around, it is a relief to hear an important message like this in a digestible form. It's good for the youngsters as well to hear this sort of message. Where did the inspiration for the song come from Jamie?"

Jamie leans towards the microphone, "My Manager Billie Lewis, she wrote the song a couple of years ago and I think she felt like you that this was an important message for people to hear."

"Can you tell her and I know she must have heard this several times before, it's a good and very strong song."

"I will, thanks for calling Mickey," Jamie says.

"Can I just add at this point callers that it is now officially official, 'Love Is Not Supposed To Hurt' is on every single major and minor play-list in this country. It has broken down barriers and is being played on Christian, Pop, Rock, Country, Jazz, Soul and R'n'B stations everywhere. Congratulations Jamie."

I smile as I listen through the head phones.

"The song has been queued listeners, don't panic, we'll take a few more calls. Line 7 go ahead please you're live on air," the DJ says.

Glancing at my watch I see that Jamie has to answer questions for a few more minutes and then we have to go to a signing at a record store and a recording session. After that I have to set up interviews for a personal assistant in the next few days, Charles has already done the adverts for the position. I can no longer accompany Jamie to all his promotional events, I have so much to do that it is no longer possible. I know that there is something else that I have to do today and I flip through my organizer. The word 'dancers' jumps out at me and I remember. I have to organize an audition for dancers for Jamie's new video within the next few days. There is another radio interview pencilled in for this afternoon and a magazine shoot. For a few moments I push everything aside and think about Philip. I enjoyed the other night at the restaurant with his friends and our conversations on the phone since them. I am happy. Since Wayne, I hadn't wanted to go out with just anyone. Philip is different, he is like a friend and so much more. I don't feel shy around him, I can tell him anything. I close my eyes and smile at the lightness I feel in my heart when I think of him.

"You have been smiling like that all morning," Jamie says interrupting my thoughts, "has this got anything to do with a certain young man?"

"It may have, have you finished?" I ask.

He nods, "What next boss?"

"Record signing on Oxford Street, recording session at Abbey road, followed by work, work and more work. Let's go Sanders."

*   *   *   *   *

Jamie is in one of the studios upstairs working on 'Invisible Pain' with Aidan, his third single to be released before the album. I sit in the office that I use most days in the building and look at the list of the names of people that I have to interview. Someone knocks on the door and I look up.

"Come in," I call out.

"Hi," Philip walks into the office smiling. His right hand is behind his back.

"Hi, what are you doing here?"

"I have been thinking about you all morning, how has your day been so far?"

"All the better for seeing you, what's that?" I ask.

"What?"

I get up and walk round him but he turns, "Oh this," he says holding up a bunch of colourful exotic flowers.

"They're beautiful, they're…"

"Colourful," he says handing them to me.

"Thank you," I take them and look up at him. I feel tears at the back of my eyes and blink a couple of times. "No one has ever given me flowers like these before, thank you." Impulsively, I lean towards him and kiss his cheek. He turns, his lips brush mine.

He jerks his head back quickly and coughs, "I'll err.., see you later Billie."

"Okay."

I watch him leave.

*   *   *   *   *

I go over the itinerary with Charles. Jamie and I will be going to New York in two days to promote 'Love Is Not Supposed To Hurt'. I look at the list of places we have to go to and notice that Jason Alexander's radio station has not been included, even though I had specifically asked that it be. Frowning I turn to Charles who is telling me about the people we will meet and the type of questions to expect.

"Charles, why is Jason Alexander's radio station not here?"

"Err.., I don't think it's high profile enough. You guys are only there for a few days. I've got you guys on all the major radio, TV and magazine slots. Do you know how long it takes to get 'Radio City Music Hall' in New York or 'Carnegie Hall'?"

I shake my head.

"A long time but I," he points at himself, "got you in there. On the way back you stop off in Minneapolis, Jamie will do a live showcase at the Mall of America."

"Thanks Charles, I know you've worked really hard, but I want to fit Jason's radio station in as well, we can make the time to visit him."

"I don't think so, you have a prolific schedule, we need to keep you both high profile. You as well as Jamie will be doing a lot of the interviews. The

Americans look at you guys as a package, so you will be in high demand. I hear 'Invisible Pain' is going to blow people away so we need to get you both visible before it happens. People want a face to go with a name."

I look at the schedules again. I know that I cannot reshuffle pre-booked times but there has to be a lunch that we can skip so we can visit Jason's radio station. A time slot jumps out at me and I show it to Charles.

"No, I don't think so."

"Why not?"

"You need to get from Brooklyn to Manhattan in that time. These timings are all worked out with great precision, right down to minutes and seconds. I take my job very seriously Billie."

"Charles I've been to New York several times, if we get stuck in traffic we'll take the subway."

"I don't think it's a good idea."

"Okay, how about you tell these people that we will be an hour late," I say pointing to the scheduled record signing in Manhattan.

"Why must you change things Billie. You're in a Premier team stop acting like you're still playing for a third division club."

"What?"

He rolls his eyes, "What's so important about this Alexander guy anyway?"

"I sent Jamie's demo to so many radio DJs. No one would touch the song. DJs that I knew personally wouldn't return my calls, they avoided me like the plague. Jason Alexander didn't do what he did because of my cousin or me, he listened to the song." Charles leans forward and I think I see understanding in his eyes. I forge forward, "he was the only one that took the chance and played the song on his radio station. That was the first air-play the song got in America and things snowballed from there. I can't forget that."

"This is the music business, you can't get emotional here. Feelings obscure clarity! People use people and move on, you have to get with the programme Billie. You have bigger fish now, there's no time for small fry. He has served his purpose, move on."

"What kind of mentality is that?"

"The survival mentality. Anyway he phoned and I told him you guys couldn't make it."

"You what! How dare you do that? Look you have to run things past me, you can't decide for me or Jamie. Did he leave a number?"

"No. Look you may be playing with the big boys now but I still have to do my job."

"What are you talking about? Why do you always try to undermine me?"

He doesn't answer, he sulks and sits back in his chair and I am reminded of our last disagreement where he had insisted that Jamie drop his clean image and get into a fight at a club. He had even arranged for an actor to start a fight with Jamie and a couple of his own paparazzi friends to happen to pass by and capture everything on camera. When we said no he quickly suggested that Jamie smash up a hotel room or act really difficult in a public place so he would be seen as a 'bad boy'. Again we said no. We also said no to his idea of Jamie dating a notorious actress and having fights with her in public as well as his idea of Jamie being conveniently photographed leaving a hotel with a married woman. He sulked throughout the remainder of the meeting.

"All I'm saying Billie is that it is important you go to all the places on the list."

"We will go to all these places but we will also meet up with Jason, now unless there is some unethical reason why we can't, company policy or something, that is what we will do."

"There's no reason apart from time."

"So if we do it in our own time, it's not a problem?"

"No," he says reluctantly.

"Then we'll do it in our own time."

*   *   *   *   *

Desperate times call for desperate measures. I know that sometimes, actually most of the time with Charles, it is as if I am constantly banging my head against a brick wall. My prayer recently has been that the brick wall comes down

301

because until it does I am resigned to keep on banging. I press numbers on my mobile phone and hold it to my ear.

"Hello, Martin, can I have Jason Alexander's phone number?"

"Sure, let me get it," I hear the sound of papers being moved around and I visualize Martin in his office looking for the number under his piles of invoices and other paperwork. "How's it going?" He asks.

"Good, we're in New York in two days and I want to see if we can stop by Jason's station."

"Here it is."

I write the number down.

*   *   *   *   *

"Hello can I speak to Mr Jason Alexander please I'm calling from London."

"Hold the line ma'am."

"Hello, Jason here."

"Hi Jason , it's Billie, Billie Lewis, Martin's cousin."

"Billie! Hi, how are you? I called a few days ago to talk to you, I spoke to someone called Charles."

"I only got the message that you called about ten minutes ago. We will be in New York in two days, can we stop by your radio station for an interview?"

"Can you stop by? You're kidding right?"

"No."

"I have had my secretary call, I have also called only to be told that you and Jamie were going to be in New York for about two or three days and are booked solid."

"We are but we're free on the day we arrive, what about then?"

"Give me the details and I'll start advertising now. This is great, thanks Billie."

"No, thank you."

*   *   *   *   *

"I'll let you know, thank you for coming," I say. The lady smiles and walks out of the office. I have interviewed five people already and I have not seen what I am looking for in any of them. I don't want someone that just comes in to do a 'nine to five' job and is in awe of recording artists. I need someone that is used to seeing an artist at work here and on the television or in a movie, and is not intimidated by that. Someone that does not mind going that extra mile. I wait for the next person to come in. After a few minutes when no one knocks I get up and walk to the door. A man is seated with his back to me, I see his scruffy long hair and trainers. He is sucking loudly on a sweet.

"Hello, are you here for the interview?"

"Err.., yes. Sorry I was late. I'm just filling in this form," he stands up and turns towards me.

"George? George Contanalis?"

"Yes that's me. Sorry, do I know you?"

"Jasmine Peters, XZEL records, over a year ago?" I see recognition in his eyes.

"Billie Lewis, Billie, spelt BILLIE," he says.

I smile and nod, "What are you doing here?"

"I left XZEL about ten months ago, a whole bunch of us did. I've been working freelance. I saw the advert and decided to give it a try. I didn't know it was working for you, the advert said to contact Charles Parker."

"Come in."

He sits down opposite me, I pick up his application form.

"So you want to work as a personal assistant and according to this an agent?" I ask looking at his form.

He nods confidently.

"Tell me about you George?"

"I've worked as a personal assistant for a number of years. I am hard working, reliable and loyal to my employer. I am also a person that believes in doing what is right and treating people with respect. When it comes to loyalty and compromising my beliefs I will not compromise."

I nod, "We have a one year contract with an agent that works for the record company. What I am looking for is a personal assistant as well as someone with ideas that will work with our current agent and eventually take on more of their responsibilities."

"I can do that Miss Lewis."

"Convince me. Without my artist having to jump into bed with every single female, have torrid affairs with notorious actresses, singers or models. Without him destroying public property, shooting up drugs or being a royal pain in the butt. How would you negotiate to get my artist noticed and keep him noticed?"

"There are over a million other ways Miss Lewis, have you heard about the 'Charlie and the Chocolate Factory' approach?"

"No"

I listen as he goes into detail.

Twenty minutes later I give George the job for a trial period of four months. I think that this is the best way to see if he can do it, as well as if he really wants to do it. Sometimes the two don't always tally.

*   *   *   *   *

It is late afternoon and Trudi is in the middle of her interview with Jamie for her magazine. She has taken several pictures already of Jamie modelling her choice of clothes and a cameraman is now recording her questions and Jamie's answers. I smile as I wonder if she like so many other reporters, will ask him about his personal life. It is no longer a secret amongst close friends and a few others that they are dating. The record company's PR department, I suspect mainly Charles Parker, has asked him to keep it quiet so that record sales will not be affected. Jamie has agreed to do this up until the end of the year.

I help Trudi's assistant to pack away some of the clothes already used.

"Excuse me Billie, Francis asked me to give you this," one of the A&R assistants says handing me a fax.

"Thanks, is Francis back from Italy?" I ask.

"No, he will be back tomorrow."

I read the fax. Francis wants me to pick up the confirmed American tour dates for Jamie. He has asked America to fax them to Mr McKnight's secretary's office. The American tour is due to kick off straight after the European tour in two months. I signal to Jamie that I am going upstairs and make my way to the lifts. I cannot believe how much work we have done today, in fact I cannot believe how much work we do every day. Signings, interviews, television, radio and more signings. I hope George will be able to cope.

According to the fax Mr McKnight's office and his secretary's office are connected and are on the sixth floor. I have never been up there and have no idea where exactly they are on the sixth floor. I get into the lift and press the button, the lift ascends. A few seconds later the doors open, I immediately notice the difference as I step out. This is where the executive offices are housed, where the money is counted, where the movers and dealers of the music world communicate. A man elegantly dressed walks towards me. 'Armani or D&G' I think to myself as I look at his suit, 'definitely Gucci or Prada' I think as I look at his shoes.

"Excuse me I'm looking for Mr McKnight's office. Do you know where it is?" I ask.

"Sure, go down the corridor, all the way down and it's on the left," he says with an American accent. I thank him and follow his instructions. I walk down the corridor and about half way down I notice that none of the doors on either side have names on them. I walk to the end of the long corridor, turn and walk back down slowly. Suddenly a lady comes out of a room with papers in her hand a few feet ahead of me. I am just about to call out to her when she opens a door opposite and walks through it. I continue to walk back down the corridor hoping that she will come out again. As I walk past the room that the lady has come out of I notice that the door is slightly ajar. I peep inside. Two men are sitting at a table in a large spacious office. I cough to try and attract their attention. They both turn. I recognize Kenny immediately and smile as I push the door open.

"Hello, how are you?"

"Good, how are you Billie?"

"Fine, I just need a little bit of help. I got this fax from Francis Wells, it says I need to pick up the American tour confirmations from Mr McKnight's secretary."

"Mr McKnight?"

305

"Yes, that's what it says, I don't know who he is or what his secretary looks like. I met a man by the lift and he said that Mr McKnight's office is on the left-hand side. I don't know which one."

"Mr McKnight?" He says again. I notice he looks confused.

"There are no names on the doors," I say.

"They are working on that, err.., let me go and check if he is in. Please sit down. Joe can you excuse us please."

"Sure boss."

I sit down and wonder why he looks confused. I look around the office and admire the decor. Kenny walks back in with Philip behind him. I stand up and smile.

"Hi! What are you doing here? Did Kenny tell you I've been walking up and down the corridor looking for Mr McKnight's office. I got a fax from Francis saying that I have to pick up the American tour dates from Mr McKnight's secretary. The problem is I don't know who Mr McKnight is or what he or his secretary look like. I'm thinking he must be old to own his company but I really don't have a clue." I stop talking when I see the strange look that had been on Kenny's face now on Philip's.

No one says anything and I start to feel strange. I look from Philip to Kenny, they are both staring at me.

"Is something wrong?" I ask.

"Billie, I thought you knew?" Philip says.

"Knew what?"

"I'm Philip McKnight."

CHAPTER 34

I stand there with my mouth half open and in complete shock.

"You said you were Philip Anderman," I whisper as waves of hot and then cold emotions flow through me, I shiver.

"Philip Anderman McKnight, P.A. McKnight," he is staring at me and I don't know where to look. I feel so stupid, so embarrassed. I have thought about him, day-dreamed about him and I didn't even know his last name. Come to think about it I don't know that much about him.

"I...,umm.., I need the dates," I finally manage to say.

Kenny hands me some papers, "Billie are you okay?"

"I'm fine, thank you," I say trying unsuccessfully to smile.

I look at Philip and then the list, "I'd better go," I turn quickly and almost collide into the lady that had left the office earlier. "I'm sorry," I say not waiting for her reply. I close the door behind me and walk quickly down the corridor.

"Billie wait!" Philip calls just as I contemplate running down the corridor and hiding somewhere. I don't turn around. I keep walking.

"Billie please wait a minute," he grabs my arm and turns me around. "I honestly thought you knew who I was."

"Well you thought wrong," I say not looking at him. I can't look at him. He touches my cheek then puts his fingers under my chin and lifts my head up. I feel hurt and confused.

"Billie, I would never do anything to hurt you, never."

I don't know what to say, I struggle to stop my eyes flooding.

"I have to get to the recording studio."

"Can we talk later?"

I look away.

"Please Billie," I hear the urgency in his voice and nod.

I hear the lift doors open and turn towards the lift. I quickly walk inside. I know he is standing there and looking at me but I don't look up, not until the doors have closed.

*　　*　　*　　*　　*

Hot and cold emotions have run riot through my body and have finally left me numb. I sit on a bench on the veranda next to the recording studios and think. I would give anything to go home and hide under my blanket. At the back of my mind there is a niggling feeling; if I had not bothered to ask his full name or what he did for a living, what did that say about me. Jen and Trudi are now in relationships, am I feeling so left out that I am just going for the first person that comes along. I beat myself up some more then jump in and start defending myself. He said his name was Philip Anderman, how was I supposed to know that McKnight came at the end. This has nothing to do with Trudi and Jen, things feel right with him and I know that if he is the one, things will work out.

"I really like him," I hear myself say. I let out a long sigh, I just said 'like' and not 'liked'. I still really like him but I can't face him again. Not yet anyway.

*　　*　　*　　*　　*

"Did you get them?" Jamie asks me.

"What?"

"The tour dates."

I feel something in my hand and look down. "Yes, here they are. George, the guy I told you about, is starting tomorrow so we'll all go over them then. How did it go with Trudi?"

"Good. Aidan is running late."

"Who?"

"Aidan, our main engineer/producer."

"Oh," I nod not sure if he asked me a question or not.

"Okay, what's going on?"

"Nothing, why?"

308

"One minute you're over the moon, the next you're confused and not listening." He sits down on the bench next to me and puts an arm around me. "Talk to uncle Jamie, sugar."

I smile, "Have you ever felt really silly?"

"Err.., in what way?"

I don't answer.

"Okay, the reason for the big grin on your face these last few days has been Philip. I'm taking a very long guess here, a very long guess, I'm assuming he is the reason for the long face."

I nod, "I went upstairs to get the dates from Mr McKnight's secretary on the sixth floor because Francis sent me a fax. I walked up and down the corridor because the doors have no names. Then a lady came out of an office and I walked up to the door, and Kenny, Philip's cousin is in the office with another man." I stop and look at Jamie who looks as if he is making sense of everything.

"I explained to Kenny that I was looking for Mr McKnight's secretary and I didn't know what she or Mr McKnight looked like. He looked at me as if there was something wrong with me then said that he was going to check if Mr McKnight was in. He came back a few seconds later with Philip. The other man left the office."

"The other man is Mr McKnight?"

I shake my head.

"Mr McKnight wasn't around?"

"No, Philip is Mr McKnight. Philip Anderman McKnight."

I cover my face with my hands and Jamie whistles.

"Philip Anderman, the guy you went out with the other night is Mr McKnight, the owner of McKnight Records/Entertainments?"

"Yes and I didn't know his last name until now."

"Can I ask a question?"

"What?"

"You really like him, right?"

I nod, "So?"

"What do you mean by 'so', look you are a beautiful woman even though you don't readily acknowledge the fact. You didn't know who Philip was but you liked him right. You liked him for himself! I remember the first time you saw him you thought he was an 'extra' on the set."

I nod as I recall telling Jamie at the time.

"But-"

"No buts, do you know how many guys dream about meeting someone that would just want them for themselves, not for who they are?"

I put my head on Jamie's shoulder and think through his logic.

"I saw you this morning Billie and just like the last few days you looked really happy. If you like him and you get on well with him, what exactly has changed about him other than you now know his last name?"

I know what Jamie says makes sense but I still feel silly.

"He said, he thought I knew who he was," I say softly looking down at my hands.

"There you go, he didn't set out to make you think he was who you thought he was, he thought you knew who he really was all the time." Jamie is teasing me now. Trying to make light of the situation so I don't feel so bad. "It's just a misunderstanding. If he makes you as happy as you were this morning, then you go girl," he says in an American accent as he clicks his fingers left to right and back again, talk-show-style. We both start laughing.

"Thank you Jerry, err.., Jamie."

"Anytime ma'am. Take care of yourself and…"

"Each other," I finish and we laugh.

"Come on let's get some work done then go home," he says and pulls me up gently. We walk into the studio.

"Are you going to see Philip tonight?"

"No," I quickly reply.

"Don't leave things hanging for too long, talk to him."

"I will, maybe tomorrow or the day after."

"If you're free tonight why don't you come round to Trudi's for dinner? She invited me and I'm inviting you."

"I don't know…," I hesitate.

"Maybe I didn't make myself clear, dinner at Trudi's tonight."

I smile, "Thanks."

Aidan walks in minutes later, full of apologies. We start work on a new song.

* * * * *

I watch as Trudi rushes around her kitchen preparing dinner and I take another sip of my diet coke.

"Slow down Tru, it's only me, I'm happy with baked beans on toast," she smiles and walks over to me, she looks at me and narrows her eyes. It is almost as if she is inspecting me. I don't pass.

"Billie I think you need to go and freshen up?"

"Why, do I smell?" I ask and sniff my armpits.

Jamie walks into the kitchen, he has showered and changed.

"Trudi says I smell," I tell him.

He frowns and then smiles, "I don't smell anything that bad," he says as he sniffs around me.

"I didn't say you smelt, I said go freshen up. Go on."

"Jamie, help," I say.

"I'm sorry boss, no can do, I want to eat."

"That's it, you are doing three new songs tomorrow and I'm going to set Charles on you."

"I've laid out something for you in the studio flat, I know you will like it," she says.

I am hungry and I know like Jamie, that the quickest way to get fed is to do what Trudi says. I rush up the stairs and into the bedroom/studio flat, in the loft that Jamie uses sometimes whenever we have late nights in the studio or a very early start in the morning. I decide to go the whole nine yards and take a shower. I quickly dry myself and put on the dress that Trudi has left on the chair. It is comfortable and elegant. I don't bother to think why we have to dress up for dinner. I put a little lipstick on, brush my hair and run down the stairs, prepared for battle if she doesn't relinquish the food now. Just as my foot touches the bottom step the door bell rings.

"I'll get it," I shout. I smile as I think of ways I can wrestle her and get something to eat.

The smile on my face literally freezes as I stare at him standing on the door step.

"Who is it?" Jamie asks behind me.

Philip is smiling, "From the look on your face I guess you didn't know I was coming?"

I don't reply.

"Hi Philip," Jamie says as if they are old friends. He gently pulls me back so Philip can come in.

"Hi, I didn't know which colour wine you both preferred so I got a couple of bottles of both," he hands Jamie a box containing several bottles of wine.

"Thank you very much," Jamie ushers him into the front room and I watch in total amazement as Trudi walks into the room and he kisses her on the cheek.

"Dinner won't be long Philip," she smiles, "please make yourself at home." She pulls me into the kitchen. I turn round and see that Philip is staring at me.

"Trudi what's going on?" I ask before she closes the door.

"Sshh," she says, "he'll hear you."

"Why didn't..."

"Would you have come?"

"No."

"That's why."

*　　*　　*　　*　　*

The meal looks and smells delicious. Jamie blesses the food and we eat. I am conscious of Philip sitting next to me, but my hunger takes priority over my nerves, I relax and eat.

"You don't drink that much do you?" Philip asks looking at the juice in my glass.

"I umm..."

"Billie it's me, I'm the same person, I just have a new last name." His voice sounds so gentle. "Why don't you drink that much?"

I breathe in deeply as I look into his eyes, "I can't, I have a low alcohol tolerance level."

"How did you find that out?"

I smile and tell him. He starts to laugh and I join him.

"Don't laugh it wasn't funny when it happened. I drank one glass and I was sick for nearly two days afterwards."

The ice breaks. He takes hold of my hand and smiles as he apologizes for laughing then starts laughing again.

*   *   *   *   *

"-And 1992?" Philip asks holding a question card up.

"*Whitney Houston - I Will Always Love You,*" Trudi says.

"*Michael Bolton - To Love Somebody,*" I say.

"*Nirvana - Smells Like Team Spirit* or something like that," Jamie says.

"One more round for 1992," Philip says.

"*Boys To Men - End Of The Road,*" I say.

"*En Vogue - Free Your Mind,*" Trudi says.

"I Don't Know - I Can't Remember," Jamie says and we start laughing at his comical expressions.

I sit back and enjoy the atmosphere as we play games and laugh about things that happened when we were growing up. I don't want the evening to end. We take trips down memory lane and back again as we talk about films, music and life.

*   *   *   *   *

"Thank you both for inviting me. I had a really good time," Philip says.

"You're welcome, we must do it again, soon," Trudi says.

"I'd like that."

"So would I," I say smiling.

I hug Jamie and then Trudi. "Thank you" I whisper into her ear. She smiles.

"Have you any plans for next Sunday?" Philip asks.

They look at each other and shake their heads.

"Why?" Jamie asks.

"It's my nephew Danny's birthday, Kenny's little boy, and I'm having a small party for him in the afternoon and a small get together afterwards for adults. I'd like it if you could come."

"Thanks, we'd love to. Jamie and Billie are back from New York on Friday, so it should be okay. Right guys?"

We both nod.

"Good, here's the address. I'll see you on Sunday," he writes his address on the back of his business card and hands the card to Trudi.

"Thanks for taking Billie home," Jamie says.

"No problem," he replies putting his arm around my waist.

*   *   *   *   *

"Drive carefully," they both say as we wave from the car.

Philip drives in silence and I find myself looking at him from time to time.

"Can we talk, there is a place that stays open all night. It's not far from here. It's called Pertonio's." He drives for a few more minutes in silence.

"What do you want to talk about?"

"Us. The past."

"The past?"

"You don't remember me do you?" He asks.

CHAPTER 35

W e sit facing each other in Pertonio's, I stare at him waiting for him to continue the conversation he had started in the car. I am a little apprehensive. I watch as he orders two coffees. The waiter fusses around for a while and then he leaves.

"Philip?"

"I was at Kenny's graduation five years ago. I saw you then, you had longer hair with little beaded plaits in front. You had a cream dress on and you were the most beautiful girl that I had ever seen."

"Kenny's graduation? Five years ago?" My heart is thumping as I try to remember.

"Your brother Steve and Kenny graduated from the same law school. You came down with your family for the graduation ceremony, I was there with mine," he is speaking softly and staring at me intensely.

"Steve and Kenny? I didn't know they went to the same law school."

"You don't remember me then?"

"No," I reply.

"As soon as you walked into the crowded hall I couldn't take my eyes off you. You seemed to be taking care of everyone. I remember you were seated at the end of the row. I saw you get up, walk out of the hall and come back with a glass of water for your grandmother, and then you looked around. I thought you were looking at me. I remember holding my breath. You got up again, walked to the back of the hall and escorted this old Chinese man who was standing at the back of the hall to your chair. Then you went and stood at the back of the hall where he had been standing," I shiver as I remember doing exactly what he says.

"All I could see when I looked at you was this beautiful person inside and out, nothing like the people I moved with at the time. Back then I had so many 'fair-weather' friends, it was one party after another. We were young with so much, yet so little," he looks away.

"Philip?"

He turns back and smiles at me, "I begged Kenny to introduce me to you, he wouldn't, he said that I should get to know Steve first."

"I can't believe it."

"That was the first time I saw you."

"The first time?"

"Am I scaring you?"

"A little."

"What happened this morning scared me a little. I feel like I need to get everything out in the open now."

"Go on."

"It was a couple of years ago, I was just leaving Tilly Ann's house in New York."

"My goddaughter?"

He nods, "You know she has four godparents, well she's my goddaughter as well."

"What!"

"Her dad and I are good friends. I got into New York the day before the christening party and celebrated with her family, I stayed the night, but had to leave the next day on urgent business. You were parking your car when I was leaving in the back of a cab. You had this huge white furry toy animal in your arms. I saw you as my cab drove past and I nearly told the driver to stop, so I could get out and talk to you but I didn't know what I would say."

The waiter places a tray on the table and unloads the coffees. I look at Philip while he is distracted. He smiles at the waiter and I know that he is telling the truth.

"Enjoy," the waiter says and walks away.

"I called Tilly Ann's mom the next day, to find out how she knew you. She said you had gone to the same university, she also said that you had just broken up with a boyfriend and that you had hired a car in New Jersey, driven to Chicago and returned that morning after a week of driving around America."

I pick up my coffee and take a sip of the hot black fluid. It burns a little, it wakes me up a lot. I remember something that Jessica, Tilly Ann's mother, had told me a couple of years ago.

"Jessica told me that someone had called asking about me. She said she had told the person to wait a while and then call."

He nods and smiles, "She said that if I approached you then, you would turn me down because you were getting over a bad relationship."

"I remember her saying that the person had called her a lot."

"I called her every night for a week and a half," he smiles.

"I don't know what to say, that's everything, right?"

"That's everything, but…" he pauses.

"But?"

"I told you at Trudi's that I studied business and Kenny studied law, I started McKnight Records/Entertainments then Kenny joined."

I nod.

"We had another person join us as a partner a couple of years later. An old college friend of mine. Not long ago I found out he was taking money from the company and selling information, amongst other things. I had to get proof, so I hired a private investigator. The only reason I'm telling you all this is because the private investigator mentioned in passing, that he could locate anyone I wanted, he was trying to advertise his abilities." He takes a deep breath and I wait for him to finish, "I umm.., I gave him your name, just to see if he could really do what he claimed."

"You did what!"

"I know this probably makes me look like some pathetic, desperate, lonely man. I was going through a lot then and I really wanted to hear something about you. Jessica said that you had changed address and were yet to give her your new address. I don't know why I did it, I had this notion that I would call you and things would somehow fall into place. The private investigator got me the evidence I needed against my partner and he also gave me an envelope with a picture of you inside. Your address and phone number were on the back of the envelope. After he gave it to me, I was so embarrassed I put the envelope away."

"I-umm..," I sit back as I try to take everything in.

317

"Billie, my heart is already involved in this relationship, it has been for some time. I just want you to know everything. I don't want you finding out something when I'm planning our wedding service and trying on wedding suits. If you don't want to see me anymore now, I can just about handle it. Later when you start to feel the way I do and I feel a lot more, I don't know if I could. Do you understand what I'm saying?"

I nod slowly.

"And?" he asks. I feel the weight behind that one word. I look at him as a multitude of emotions wash over me.

"I know what I am about to say may sound strange but since we're being honest, I suppose if I had met someone or in your case seen someone, and I wanted to meet them again but I didn't know how and the chance that you had arose…," I ponder and reflect on everything he has said.

"Billie?" He whispers.

"I would probably do the same thing."

"You would?" Relief floods into his eyes

"Probably."

He closes his eyes and breathes in deeply then exhales.

"Is there anything you want to know about me?" He eventually asks, his eyes are so gentle. I shrug, not having prepared a list of questions, I ask the ones that pop into my head.

"How old are you?"

"29 in a few months," he answers.

"I'm 25."

"I know, third of February."

"What do you like to eat?"

"Anything, what can you cook?"

"Anything. What's your favourite colour?"

"Truthfully, yellow."

"Yellow?" I make a comical face.

"When I was really young I remember seeing the sun set from my grand-ma's house on the beach in Hawaii. It was such a brilliant yellow colour, since then I've always liked yellow. What's yours?"

"Blue."

His eyebrows go up.

"Seven is my favourite number," I quickly add.

"Blue?" He makes a comical face and smiles.

"I like blue. Have you got any brothers or sisters?"

"One brother, Simon Patterson McKnight and one sister, Simone McKnight, they are twins, both younger, both in America with my parents."

"I don't know what else to ask you."

"It's just you and Steve right?"

"Yes, he's a few years older than me."

"You are both really close aren't you?"

"Very close. He always used to come to my rescue when we were little, he still does. Back then I would get in the middle of arguments, I would stand up to bullies who picked on my friends and just before things got out of hand I would get someone to go and get Steve. He would come running to my rescue, sort of like the bionic man. Dedededee..dededede..dedededee," I move my arms in slow motion.

Philip laughs as I make the bionic sound and lift a teaspoon up.

"I used to watch that years ago," he smiles.

"Steve and I watched every episode in the eighties, re-runs."

Still smiling he holds out his hands and looks at me. I look at his hands and then his eyes. His eyes are gentle and trustworthy. I place my hands in his. I listen as he tells me more about himself. I tell him about myself, my family, my writing. We talk about our faith.

* * * * *

"I read that most of your songs are about people, is that true?"

"Yes."

"I was really impressed when I heard that you had written 'Love Is Not Supposed To Hurt' it's a really good song."

"When did you hear?"

"About a week after you signed with Digital. Kenny was in France doing some legal work with the Digital company there, tying up loose ends for the merge. He phoned me one afternoon and all he said was: '*Billie Lewis, just signed her artist, Jamie Sanders to Digital Records UK, I have a copy of an interview she did in Cardiff, it has pictures of her and Jamie. Philip, it's her!*'. I couldn't believe it, the last I had heard about you from Jessica was that you were working in a hospital laboratory. I was on the phone to Francis the next day. He was full of praises for you and Jamie. He told me what happened with Vigil Records and how you had both already decided to stick with Digital. I was really impressed. Integrity is something that is not that common in this business. I asked to see a copy of your contract after I heard about the terms and conditions you had requested…"

I smile modestly as I listen to him.

We are still at Pertonio's and it is nearly morning. The clouds have released the moon once again and it now shines brightly in the sky which is starting to get lighter. I cannot believe that we have sat here talking for so long. I am not tired and I don't think that it's due to all the coffee I have drank. I feel something in my heart for Philip, something that I have never felt before. I don't know if it's real because I have nothing to compare it with. I do know that I want it to grow and to last.

"We had better make a move," Philip says looking at his watch.

"Where are the toilets?" I ask.

"You mean the bathroom," he teases.

"No I mean the toilets," I say.

"Down there, through the door and on the left."

*   *   *   *   *

I look at my reflection in the large glass mirror. My cheeks feel flushed and my eyes are very alert. I have to be in the studio this morning, but I am free in the afternoon. George is starting today, so I'll be able to delegate some things to him. I hear footsteps walk past the door. I open the door and walk out. Something catches my eye and I turn in the direction the footsteps had gone. I can see a man's leg clad in dark trousers and shoe, sticking out. The rest of his body is hidden behind the wall. I am sure I have seen Philip in a pair of similar shoes.

"Philip, is that you?"

"Who's Philip?" A familiar harsh voice asks and I feel the hairs on the back of my neck stand up. The walls seem to move and I freeze momentarily and then rush through the doors in the opposite direction back into the restaurant.

"Billie, what is it?" Philip asks rushing towards me.

"There was someone in the hall when I came out of the toilet, he startled me."

"Miguel," Philip calls the waiter. He asks him to go and check. He pulls me into his arms. "You're shaking," he says as he holds me.

"No one's there Mr McKnight," Miguel says, "I found a cigar stub on the floor and the fire exit door is open. I don't know, this place is busy, it could be anybody."

"Thanks Miguel," Philip says.

I look down at his shoes. He is wearing the same shoes I had seen a few seconds ago and dark trousers.

*　　*　　*　　*　　*

"You are sure you're okay, Billie?"

"I'm fine, my brain is probably over stimulated."

"I'm going to come in and make sure that everything is okay."

"Really, you don't have to."

Philip takes my key from me and opens the door. He turns the light in the hall on and starts to look around. I close the front door behind me. 'Maybe I shouldn't have told him about the strange phone call or the car parked on my road' I think as I see the look of concern in his eyes.

"I'll check upstairs" he says as I check my alarm system. All the lights are on indicating that nothing has been tampered with. I smile as he walks down the stairs.

"Thank you Philip."

"You are sure you're going to be okay?"

"I'll be fine, the alarm is set, any problems and I'll call the police and then you."

"What are you doing tomorrow, err.. later on today?" He asks looking at his watch.

"I'm in the studio around ten thirty this morning until one in the afternoon. Why?"

"I want you to listen to a group of four guys for me and tell me what you think. They caught one of your radio interviews a few days ago and they would really like to meet you."

"Who are they?"

"Really good singers, I met them a couple of weeks ago, I think they just need the right material and style. Can you do it?"

"Sure, what time and where?"

"Say two in the afternoon in my office or in one of the studios on my floor."

"Okay."

"I'd better go. Call me if you're concerned about anything and I'll come down."

"Okay, I will."

He moves closer to me and pulls me gently into his arms.

"I know I keep touching your hands and holding you, I'm just trying to convince myself that you are really in my life. I have dreamt about this for so long, it still feels unreal."

I pinch his arm.

"Ouch," he says and pulls away.

"I'm real," I say and smile.

CHAPTER 36

The session in the studio went very well. We have two mixes and an original version of 'Invisible Pain'. We have also just recorded an up-tempo song called 'Mind Games', which Jamie and I wrote together and which I am very excited about. We are going to New York tomorrow morning and I have to make sure that Jamie's clothes and accessories are packed for his live performances as well as both our things for the interviews. George is seeing to the biographies, DATs, pictures and hotel arrangements. He also has to sort out Jamie's bookings for when we get back. I walk towards the dance studio where the auditions are taking place today for dancers that will be used in Jamie's new video as well as on some of his European tour dates. I stand by the door and listen, I can hear Charles talking 'at' the dancers. I have never met someone who went out of their way to abuse their position as he does, before. He acts as if it's his right to trample on people because, as he has shared with Jamie and myself on several occasions, when he was coming up through the ranks he was trampled upon many times.

"We don't waste time on time-wasters! If you can't dance then please do us all a favour now, and just go, leave, vamoose. I don't have any time for people that think they can dance and then come and display rubbish. I do not suffer fools or time-wasters likely."

I walk into the studio and smile at the people.

"Good morning, my name is Billie Lewis and I'm sure that Charles has put you up to speed with what is required."

I look around at the nodding heads.

"Good, we're looking for roughly ten really good dancers. We need people that are quick and can easily pick up a routine. We have a choreographer called Claude LeMardes coming in any minute now. Jamie will be here in about thirty minutes. All the best."

As if on cue Claude walks in with his music box, "Billie darling, how are you sweetie?"

"Good, Claude, really good. You?"

"So-so darling, so-so."

I sit back. After a few minutes of introductions Claude divides the forty five dancers into three groups, gets them to stick name tags on their chests and goes through a routine with them. I watch as Claude's skilled, perfectly toned body performs. He is nearly forty eight but dances like a twenty year old. Some of the young dancers have a hard time keeping up with him. I know how he works and I know he is watching them in the mirrors. They think he will sit back and watch them perform some Grande finale at the end then choose. Usually by this time he has made up his mind.

I notice that a big Asian girl with the name Sunita on her name tag, is getting all the moves right. I smile as Claude does a few strange turns and she immediately gets them right. She is about three stones over weight but she can really dance. I notice some of the slim girls sitting down are discreetly pointing at her and laughing.

"Okay next group please," Claude says and goes through the exact same moves with them.

Jamie walks into the studio with George in the middle of the routine. Heads turn, eyes try to catch his attention. I smile to myself as I see hair being flicked off shoulders and fingers running through hair.

"How's it going?" Jamie asks me.

"Good. How did it go with you guys?"

"Fine, George has set the official website up, he's a dab hand."

I smile at George, he blushes.

The third group go through their paces as we watch. Charles leans towards me, "What do you think?"

"I'm going with the Asian girl, Sunita."

"The fatty? Duhh! She's a little bit overweight isn't she?"

"I know but she can dance and you can see she loves what she is doing, she has passion."

He sighs and shakes his head, "Billie I keep telling you, you can't allow sentiments in this business," his voice is patronizing but I don't rise to the bait. I let it dangle.

Claude asks all the dancers to perform the routine together. I notice that some of the attractive females have moved towards where we are sitting, and are constantly smiling at Jamie. I shake my head and decide to burst their bubbles before they start the routine.

"Can I just say something before you all start. The way this will work is, I will choose one person, Charles over here will choose one person and Claude will choose the other eight. Jamie is just observing he will not be choosing anyone."

Almost immediately the girls who have moved to the back, move to the front to be next to Claude. Charles walks over to me as the music starts.

"Errr.. thank you," he says bewilderment evident in his eyes.

"What for?" I ask.

"Not treating me the way I treat you, the way I deserve to be treated by you. You and Jamie are not like most of the other people here you are both different. I'm sorry about my comment yesterday, I heard in the grapevine that you didn't know Philip McKnight was the boss." I blink in shock as I watch him walk back to the table and sit down. I try to remember what he had said yesterday, something like: *'I was playing with the big boys now'*, I hadn't understood what he was talking about then and had not given it a second thought, putting it down to part of his normal dogmatic abnormal behaviour.

I turn to the dancers and watch them perform, I give them a hundred and ten percent of my attention. Most of them have forgotten the moves. I look at Sunita, she is in a world of her own as she does all the steps. I watch as the others start to copy her. We clap at the end of the routine. Claude asks fifteen people to come out and he shows them another routine. I watch as they practice, Claude tells them the different names of the dance steps as he does them.

"Okay, everyone, 'Wobble', one two, 'Pop', go, go, go, 'Rock' five six, 'Hitch kick', break a move…., and freeze," Claude shouts.

I know that these are the people that Claude has seen that have picked up the first routine very quickly. I watch as again Sunita shines.

*   *   *   *   *

"Sunita Singh," I say and she jumps up screaming.

"John Robins," Charles says.

Claude calls out eight more names.

There is more screaming and laughing.

"Well done, thank you all for coming. Remember Claude is in charge," I say. I gather my papers together and get ready to leave.

"Excuse me Miss Lewis," I turn to see Sunita standing there, "thank you, I just wanted to say thank you for giving me this chance." She rubs her knuckles together nervously. "I know, left to the others, I wouldn't be in. Thank you. This is something that I have wanted to do for so long, and, every time I went for an audition I was turned down because of my weight." Her voice falters and I squeeze her arm, "I was at the point of giving up. I tried for years. People take one look at me and don't give me a chance, they say I don't fit in with the others, I get discouraged and eat too much."

"Don't listen to what people say if it doesn't encourage you. People like to box or categorize others, it makes them comfortable. Some people are not meant to fit in a box with others. Some people are meant to be beside the box or on top of the box or even just there to make the box look more attractive. You're a good dancer Sunita, you make the box look good." She nods modestly, "don't give up. Some of these dancers have done a number of music videos and from what I have seen today, you are the best one here. If you hang in there you're going to go places."

"I won't give up, thank you," she says then joins the others.

*   *   *   *   *

I step out of the lift on the sixth floor and walk towards Philip's office. Kenny walks out of his office, he turns, sees me and stops. I feel embarrassed and I quickly try to hide it as I walk towards him.

"Hey, Billie how are you?"

"I'm fine," I look away.

"Don't."

I look up at him a little confused.

"Don't feel embarrassed on my account. I've got name tags printed for Philip now so it won't happen again." I laugh and he gently squeezes my arm. "I'm glad you guys sorted things out, he really panicked when he thought he had blown it. He's waiting for you in the recording studio, two doors down."

"Thanks Kenny."

"That's okay."

*   *   *   *   *

I knock on the door and walk into the large studio.

"Hi," Philip says walking over to me. He introduces me to the group and I shake hands with the four members.

"You look better in real life than you do in the magazines..."

"We have read so much about you, you have come a long...,"

"It must be great realizing your dream..."

I stand back and look at them as they all talk at the same time. Four completely different guys, average age of twenty. Greg is Black, Ryan is White, Leon is Chinese and Dillon is Indian. I don't remember if Philip mentioned how they came together.

"Okay let's get started," Philip says walking towards the player.

The music starts, I watch the four guys come alive musically as they dance and sing. Their voices harmonize well but I think the song needs to change a little. The music fades and they all look at me, expectantly.

"Umm.., I like your voices, I think that they go well together. The song is good but when I listen to it I hear only one thing, sex." I walk further into the room and sit on a stool in front of them. "Words are really important and the right words used properly can make what started off as an average song, a really good song. Your song has got a good feel and strong hook, but I think that if you change a few words and the presentation, it could mean the difference between a good song and a really, really good song." I look at their faces to see if my logic makes sense to them.

"Go on," Philip says encouragingly.

"In the chorus you say 'I want to bump and grind you', why not just say, 'I want to love you'. I know you want to be raunchy, but sometimes if you want to capture a bigger audience you have to play with your words. Some people will always interpret what you say the way they want to anyway because they have a way of projecting what they want onto things. Other people just want to kick back and listen to a nice love song without too much sex thrown into their faces. I know that I get tired of seven, eight, nine and ten year old girls singing songs with rude lyrics that they don't understand."

They nod.

Be honest, Philip had said this morning. I comply. "Another thing, you all have really good voices and I think that you should all sing a major piece of the song. That way you show your versatility. A lot of people like me are tired of seeing ten people in a group with only one person singing all the time. I think that a group where everyone sings, or contributes, is much stronger and has a greater chance of sticking together and greater productivity."

"Like *Boys II Men*?" Greg asks. I nod.

A question pops into my head, I think about it and then ask it.

"Why do you think that groups break up?"

"Money, greed, pride," Dillon says.

"Power struggles," Ryan adds.

"Feeling inadequate," Leon says.

"All of the above," Greg says.

I smile, "You're right all of those reasons and a few more. Dillon, why money, greed and pride?" I ask.

"People forget that they started with nothing and when the money starts coming in they don't want to share, they become greedy. Pride steps in, pride comes before a fall."

I nod, "Why did you say power struggles Ryan?"

"Everyone wants to be the leader, no one wants to be the follower, so you have groups with everyone doing their own thing."

I nod, "Leon, why did you say feeling inadequate?"

"If the group members don't let you sing much you feel that you are not really valued."

"Greg?"

"All of the above plus one member may feel that there is more out there as a solo artist and neglect and forget what they already have," he says.

"There, you have just gone over how easy it is to break a group up and what you need to do to avoid doing this. Let's take for example a birthday cake with icing, candles, name of the birthday person, the works. Now what do you think is the most important thing or things that make up that cake?"

"The icing," Ryan says.

"No, the candles," Dillon adds.

"But you can't make a cake without butter," Leon says.

"You need all of those things," Greg says.

"Not really, think about it because that's where people make mistakes," I say looking at them. "People want to be the icing on the cake or the candles glowing. Some people want to be the writing on the cake. All the visible things that are not really necessary. They become dispensable because they are not part of the key ingredients. To be a major part you need to be eggs, sugar, flour or butter because without any one of those things, there is no cake." I continue to look at their faces as I wait for what I have just said to sink in. "When you're part of the main structure you don't undermine yourself and others don't undermine you. You are just as important as the next person."

"So do you think that every member of a group should sing?" Greg asks.

"No, I think that if every member of a group has a really good voice and that voice fits in with the particular song, then they should sing. In some groups you have a singer who also writes, and a writer who sometimes sings. Look at the *Lighthouse Family* were *Paul* writes most of the songs and *Tunde* sings. Now that's unity at work. There are so many groups out there that are 'solid' because the members all contribute."

"How come you know so much about groups?" Ryan asks.

"Have you worked with a group before?" Greg asks.

"Yes, some time ago. I also manage someone who was in a group, plus I did a bit of work on human nature during my First degree at university. It involved knowing how the human mind works."

Philip's mobile phone starts to ring, he pulls it out of his pocket and turns the ringer off.

"As a group or individually what is your greatest fear?" I ask.

"Rejection," they all chorus.

"Everyone says that. I don't think any artist, if they are truthful, will say they were not rejected by a record company. Rejections will happen but look past them and work even harder."

"I read the article you did in the *'Time and People Magazine'* about rejection, it was really good," Dillon says.

"Thank you."

"How do you deal with rejection though?" Leon asks.

"By staying focused. By not letting rejection knock you off your path and keep you off. If this is the path you truly want to follow, you must face the rejection and move forward to the next level. I used to work in a laboratory and I used to think that I was overworked, then I came here and I realized that I wasn't. I work ten times harder here. The only difference is that because I love doing this I find that I am prepared to work hard. That's what you have to decide, is this what you really want to do, if it isn't then everything will be difficult. This has to be your dream, because you can't live someone else's. Some days you may have to get up very early in the morning to do a photo shoot, do a radio interview, record a song with a certain producer like *Dr Dre* or *P Diddy,* or work with song writer/producer *Babyface*, because that is the only slot they have available for you. If this is what you really want to do, then yes, you'll be tired some days and exhausted on others, but you'll do it because there isn't anything else that you'd rather do. I have worked with people who thought that they wanted to sing, but when push came to shove, they couldn't cope with going to the studio three or four times a week, with practicing on their vocals, or with being disciplined with their weight and fitness."

"People condemn the music industry for packaging artists, making them have a certain look. Do you think that we should conform to the image out there or not?" Greg asks.

"A very debatable and good question. I personally believe that people should have their own look, one they feel comfortable with. I also believe that people should learn from others and not judge them. Look at the discipline, fitness levels and health that some artists have without popping pills, doing drugs or smoking. Yet people sit back like couch potatoes, stuff their faces with food and criticise, judge and condemn them. Instead of learning how to take care of themselves, how to eat right and exercise. Today many people are overweight, they have heart disease, diabetes, so many other problems because they let food control them instead of controlling what they eat, instead of doing things in moderation. Children are obese because they copy their parents or are 'toys' in the hands of the food, drink and sweet advertisers. As music artists you are out there influencing a lot of people especially children. Set the pace! Touring, doing gigs, being on the road takes it out of you so you have to be fit in this business you can't afford to crack or have bad days. You have to be healthy and smart, learn from others that do the right thing, do you understand?"

They nod.

"Have you heard the story about the shrewd manager?"

"No," they reply. Philip smiles.

"There was a manager that was accused of wasting his boss's money. His boss confronted him about it and was on the verge of firing him. This manager went to all the people that owed his boss and called in their debts. He asked the man that owed say eight hundred thousand pounds to pay four hundred thousand pounds and the one that owed one hundred thousand to pay eighty thousand pounds. In so doing he was counting on the fact that if his boss sacked him he would be on good terms with these people because he had saved them money, and they would sort him out. When his boss saw what he had done he commended him for acting shrewdly." I look at them.

"That was really smart of him," Greg says.

"Exactly, see we have to be shrewd in this world, we have to be wise. I find that people tend to judge or condemn others and not see what needs to be seen. There was a song a couple of years ago called 'A Better Way'."

"By *Clarkson*?" Dillon asks.

"Yes. It was a really good song, now *Clarkson* are a big group, they have been around for years but they did something which I didn't understand. They had that uproar because they wanted their song to be played on certain music channels and not others. They said as Christians they didn't approve of these other music channels and what they represented. As a Christian myself I found that on one hand I respected their decision but on the other hand I didn't agree with it, I didn't think it was wise. You have a beautiful song telling people about a better way of life and the people that need to hear the message are watching the channels that you don't want the video played on whereas you want it played to people that already know."

They nod, they understand.

"Being shrewd means looking at what is going on, praying for wisdom and using the wisdom you get wisely. You don't have to copy what others do, but don't be 'blind-sighted'. Don't copy the lifestyle, attitudes or hype, look beyond that, never do anything to cause someone else to fall. Be disciplined, the key to success is perseverance. Look around see the 'common denominators' in successful people, which are: a dream, determination and graft also known as hard work. Look at *Tiger woods, Michael Jordan, Whitney, Usher, Alicia, Bill Gates, Anthony Robbins, Richard Branson* and the many others, look at their history, look at the work they had to do to succeed, be it mental or physical.

Overnight success usually ends as it started, overnight. The success that lasts, is due to faith, hard work, dedication and a dream that you can feel. When everyone else thinks you're aiming too high or you're crazy, you know what you feel. You know that the dream is real so you push forward." I look at them and they look at me. I see something new in their eyes. I see respect. I follow through.

"Can I suggest some changes to your song?"

They nod in unison. Philip holds his 'vibrating' phone up and indicates that he needs to take a call outside. I smile and nod.

"Can you sing it again, I'll record it. Then I'll make some changes and record the new version."

"Okay," they chorus.

*　　*　　*　　*　　*

I listen to them sing again and record the song. I listen to their individual voices. I smile as I notice that this time they sing the song in a less raunchy manner. When the song finishes I move them around and give them different lines to practice. I change the lyrics a little and listen to them sing the new version. I make them go over it again and then record it. I am amazed at the difference and at the quality of their voices. Philip has not come back, so while we wait, I log on to the computer and show them a song I wrote a couple of weeks ago for the song writing department, called 'Only What You Wanna Hear'. I hum the melody for them and let them look at the lyrics. I sing the first verse line by line getting them to repeat each line. Leon sings a line from the chorus in a high voice and I feel goose bumps on my arms.

"Sing that again," I urge him. He sings it and again the goose bumps re-form.

"Okay," I say as I swing into motion. "Ryan you start with the first two lines." He sings them and I nod.

"Greg, next two lines, at the end of your second go 'soul'." He sings the lines understanding exactly what I mean by 'soul'.

"Dillon next two lines please." He sings them.

"Okay Leon, chorus, exactly as you did before."

Leon sings.

"Can you all do the last line of the chorus together, harmonize your voices. Then Ryan go straight into the second verse and Greg and Dillon follow, then Leon do the chorus. For now all of you take the 'bridge' and harmonize your voices."

They sing the song through twice, and I hit the record button on the player without letting them know on their third take.

Philip walks back in as they finish, "How's it going?"

"Good," I reply, "listen to this."

I rewind the tape and press the play button. The music of their song starts and I see the look of surprise on Philip's and then their faces as they listen. The song ends and the room is silent.

"That was great! I can't believe that is the same song," Philip says amazed.

"I can't believe that's us," Ryan says.

"This is the first time you rehearsed this version of your song. Think of when you've practised it and you're all more familiar with the changes. You will sound great," I say. "Now listen to this," I press the play button and the song

'Only What You Wanna Hear' starts. I watch them as they listen. The song ends, they look really astonished.

"Where did that come from?" Philip asks.

"Billie," they chorus.

"It's incredible, it sounds really good," he looks at me, "you just showed it to them now?"

I nod, "They sound really good don't they?"

He nods as he looks at me strangely, "Play it again, I can't believe that in the time it took me to take one phone call you got them to do so much."

"They are fast learners," I say and press the rewind and then play button. We listen to the song again.

"Leon?" Philip says shaking his head, "that's you?" Leon starts to laugh, the others join him.

*   *   *   *   *

I look at my watch "I have to go, guys before I go I just want to say that you sang 'Only What You Wanna Hear' really well." I pause. "It's your song if you want it."

They all start talking at once. Thanking me and thanking Philip for asking me to come. A name pops into my head and I look on as they talk and jump about in excitement.

"Kaleidoscope," I say.

"What?" Philip asks.

"A name for them, Kaleidoscope, changing colours, changing patterns."

"I like it," Philip says.

"So do we," the boys chorus.

*   *   *   *   *

"You were great in there, you have real 'people knowledge', and a gift of encouraging people," Philip says as he walks me to the lift. We can still hear the excited voices coming from the studio.

"I'm happy to help."

"You have taken a bunch of guys that were starting to feel dejected and turned them around. Thank you Billie." I see the seriousness in his eyes.

"You're welcome," I say and step into the lift. "Oh, and no prob-lem," I add just before the lift's doors close.

CHAPTER 37

She picks up the keys and climbs out of her car. She looks up at the building. Even though she knows he isn't at home, she is still a little apprehensive. A man walking a dog passes by her, he looks at her as she stands by her car. He notices her strange red coloured hair and the way she quickly turns away from his gaze. She waits for him to reach the bottom of the road, then she walks towards the building.

Her hands are sweating as she climbs up the stairs to the first floor. She walks across the communal landing and stands outside a front door. Quickly she looks over her shoulders making sure that she is alone. She opens the front door and steps into the flat, closing the door behind her.

Her attention falls on the sparsely decorated living room. It looks un-lived in. She walks around the room, there are no photographs or pictures on the walls, no *objets d'art* anywhere. She walks out of the room and down the narrow hall. The hall has rooms on either side, she ignores them. She walks straight down the hall and into the kitchen. She looks around, the kitchen is clean and empty of essentials. No cooker, no fridge. There is a door facing her, under it she can see a light. The knowledge that she is alone in the flat, gives her confidence. Her confidence carries her across the kitchen to the door opposite. She pulls it open and freezes. The room is small and windowless. On the walls are pictures. Every single section of the walls are covered with pictures. She feels the bile rise in her throat as she stares at the pictures of missing and murdered people. She sees the words 'YOU ARE MINE' written boldly in something red, something that looks like blood across the pictures at the bottom, pictures of people she knows. She picks up a piece of paper laying on the floor and reads what is written on it. She shudders at the sick, depraved words. Slamming the door closed she rushes to the hall where she had seen a phone. Panting and gagging for breath she picks up the receiver and dials a number. The phone rings, the answer machine comes on.

"Billie, it's me. When you get this message please call me. Sarah and...," she pants, "..danger. Call me, it's Chloe. You were right..., I'm sorry I should have listened…" she hears the sound of rushing wind. She may even have heard the sound of a bone crushing thud.

She does not finish the sentence. She does not finish anything. She never heard him creep up behind her. She probably never felt much pain. She is dead before she hits the ground.

CHAPTER 38

I look around my front room, everything is in place. I have checked the house, all the windows are locked and the back door is locked. The light on my phone is flashing. I see that I have nine messages. I don't have time to listen to them, Jamie and George are waiting for me in the taxi. I quickly press the button on the side of the phone and pull the micro tape out. I replace it with a spare tape that I keep on my bookcase. I will listen to my messages later on my Dictaphone. I still carry a Dictaphone around with me everywhere I go, because I never know when a song or a melody will pop into my head. I look around one last time and quickly leave.

*   *   *   *   *

"I can't believe this. I started work two days ago and I am going to New York today. I can't believe it," George says as we sit in the taxi heading towards the airport.

I see the excitement in his eyes and smile. He has cut his hair and according to him, taken his wife's advice and smartened himself up. I look through the itinerary of the trip. There is so much work to do and I know that I will need him. I was surprised that Charles went along with the suggestion that George come along, immediately it was out of my mouth. I make a mental note to get Charles an 'I Love New York' T-shirt. He likes wearing colourful T-shirts with his fashionable suits. I look out of the window at the other cars carrying people and luggage, all heading towards the airport and I think of Philip.

The taxi stops in front of the departure section. George takes control and I smile to myself. He indicates for a porter to come over with a trolley and then helps the porter load the bags onto the trolley. Jamie and I are wearing dark glasses so I don't expect anyone to recognize us. I am wrong. As soon as we walk into the building I notice heads turning in our direction.

"What's going on?" Jamie asks.

"I think it's called recognition," I say as we walk behind George and the porter.

"That's Jamie Sanders!" I hear someone say and look in the direction of the voice. Without warning someone appears in front of us and starts taking pictures. I jump back, startled a little. Jamie puts an arm around me and guides me around the photographer.

"Billie can you take your sunglasses off please?"

"No I'm sorry we have a flight to catch in less than an hour."

"Please just one picture, c'mon guys."

"Sorry, we're really in a hurry" Jamie says.

We walk with George and the porter to the checking in section. I reach into my bag and pull out our passports and hand them to George. From somewhere not too far away we hear screams and the sound of many running feet.

"Jamie, Jamie," voices shout.

I turn, there are about a hundred teenagers running towards us screaming and waving their hands. It is all happening fast but for some reason it feels as if it is happening in slow motion. George and Jamie grab me, an airline official runs towards us grabs Jamie's arm and shouts at the porter to follow him. At the same time about ten security men rush towards the girls. From standing at the checking in counter, in less than ten seconds I find myself standing in a secured room behind the counter with Jamie, George, the airport official and the porter, who, looks the most shocked out of us all.

"I'm sorry we were not outside to meet you, we heard that you were coming, but we didn't know about the girls until a few minutes ago. Are you all okay?" The official asks.

"We're fine thank you," I reply.

"Just so that you know next time, there is a celebrity entrance that you can use."

*   *   *   *   *

"I can't believe I'm in first class. I just started work two days ago and I'm in first class, flying to New York," George says. I see mischievous amusement in his eyes and I know that he is up to something.

"George?" I query.

He laughs, Jamie and I look at each other a little confused.

"I'm sorry guys, it's just you've both looked so serious since we met up this morning and I was trying to get a smile."

"So travelling to New York is no big deal to you?" Jamie asks.

George turns to face him, "No."

"You've travelled there how many times?" I ask.

"About ten or twelve," he replies.

"So all that and I quote 'I can't believe it!', was to try and get us to smile?" Jamie asks.

George turns to him, "Well, sort of."

"How did you think it would work?" I ask.

George turns to me "I thought that-"

"Did you not think that you could have tried another way?" Jamie asks.

"I just thought-"

"Like a joke?" I ask Jamie.

"A joke is good," Jamie says to me.

"Maybe George doesn't know that we like a good joke."

"Maybe not, he's only been with us a couple of days."

By now George who has been looking from Jamie to me and back to Jamie like a tennis spectator, has started to look confused.

"Gotcha," Jamie says and we laugh at the comical, confused, expression on George's face.

*　*　*　*　*

"Ladies and gentlemen this is your Captain speaking. We will be landing at JFK international airport, New York, in five minutes. Please make sure that your seats are in the upright position, tables are folded away and your seat belts are fastened. Thank you once again for flying with us, we hope you had a good flight. On behalf of myself and the cabin crew, thank you."

*　*　*　*　*

"Miss Lewis?"

"Yes."

"My name is Paul Duyfrey. I'm from McKnight Records/ Entertainments." He holds up his identification badge. "I'm here to take you to the hotel. Once you collect all your bags ma'am would you all kindly follow the signs to the exit. I will be waiting for you there."

"Thank you," I say

"I'll go and make a start with the bags," George says walking in the direction of the conveyer belt. Jamie and I follow him. From somewhere in front of us I see bright lights and I hear the sound of a number of people talking at the same time. George is in front of us and he keeps walking. We follow him. He stops suddenly and turns to us.

"There are people here that seem…"

From behind him we see what looks like over two or more hundred people rushing towards us.

"What the…," Jamie starts to say.

"They must be here for a celebrity," I say.

"RUN!," George shouts. From behind him we see TV cameras and hear the girls shouting, "JAMIE, JAMIE."

"I'll be all right, I think they're only interested in Jamie," I say to George, "I'll get the bags-"

"ARRRR... IT'S BILLIE," someone shouts.

"RUN BACK UP," George shouts running towards us with the camera men and girls right behind him. We turn and start running. Paul is in front and I call out to him. He turns and rushes towards us.

"In here quick," he says opening a side door. As soon as George runs in he slams the door and pulls out a mobile phone. We watch as he presses some numbers and speaks to someone. We can hear a lot of voices outside the door.

"We'll be out of here in five minutes," Paul says to us reassuringly.

* * * * *

Less than five minutes later, there is a knock on the door. Paul knocks twice. The person knocks twice again and Paul knocks once. Jamie and I exchange amused glances.

"It's okay, the cavalry have arrived," Paul opens the door and walks out. We wait. Silence follows. He walks back in smiling.

"It's all clear, the girls have been escorted outside the airport by security. You are safe to come out." We quickly walk out and go to get our bags. Paul takes us to the exit where the car is parked.

*   *   *   *   *

As soon as we step out of the airport, it is as if a dam has suddenly broken. There is an out-pour of thunderous noise, almost deafening. Gone the quiet calmness of frustrated travellers, gone the noise of children running around and parents shouting at them to come back. From all around us, pour the screams and shouts of people being held back by burly security men. I look up in shock and see placards with Jamie's name on them and posters rising up and down as the people carrying them jump up and down in excitement.

"This way, quick," Paul says.

"JAMIE, JAMIE, JAMIE," the people scream.

We rush to the car and climb inside. The doors close and I hear the click of the central lock. There is a bang on the boot of the car and we all turn to see about five girls banging on the boot and screaming. We watch as two men rush towards the car, grab the girls and pull them away.

"What is going on? How did they know that Jamie would be here today?" I ask Paul as the car starts to move forward.

"I think they put two and two together, we saw you guys leave London on the news here, they knew, like everyone else that you were coming to New York. I guess they knew it was just a matter of which flight."

I look at Jamie and George, "Are you both okay?" I ask.

Jamie nods, George sits staring through the back window with his mouth open. I think he is in shock.

*   *   *   *   *

"Jason!" I smile and hug him. He hugs me back.

"Billie, thanks for coming. We saw on the news just now that you guys were mobbed, welcome to New York. Are you all okay?"

"We are fine thank you. Jamie this is Jason Alexander, Jason, Jamie," they shake hands.

"Nice to meet you Jamie."

"It's good to meet you at last." Jamie says.

"This is George our personal assistant."

"Nice to meet you George." They shake hands.

"Nice to meet you Jason," George says.

"I thought we'd take some photographs, do my show and meet some of the artists that are trying to break into the music world here. My wife and I would like to take you all to a Broadway musical later. I hope you don't have any other plans for tonight?"

"No, as I said on the phone, we start our schedule from tomorrow morning," I say.

"Good, let's go."

*   *   *   *   *

"…I just wanna know, how did you both do it? How did you keep on keeping on when nothing was happening and the hard-nosers were putting you down?" A man sitting in the front row asks. We are recording in a conference room of Jason's radio station, talking to artists and their managers, people that are trying to make it in the music world. People who are where we once were.

Jamie looks at me, he lowers his voice, "Do you want to go first?" He asks, I shake my head.

"I just asked my manager if she wanted to answer your question first because she is the one that kept pushing when the doors kept closing. She is the one that had to put up with the rejection letters and the 'cold calling'. Throughout the 'dry' period as we call it, she never gave up. Her faith is strong and her determination resilient, through our close association some of her strength has definitely rubbed off on me. I know some people don't believe or understand this but I am telling the truth, Billie prays about everything. She wakes up early every day and prays. Through her, I learnt to pray. I learnt to ask for guidance, that if this was the Will of God then it would happen. We worked hard, even on the days when we didn't feel like sitting and working in the various studios until two o'clock in the morning, we were given the strength to do it. So, we know that it happened, because we prayed, we believed and we worked hard. We all know how hard it is to break into the music business and even when you're in, it doesn't guarantee that you'll make it, that you'll have longevity. It's hard to get in, but so easy to quit. I know Billie will agree, giving up was never an option for us was it Billie?" He sits back.

"No it wasn't. I think that Jamie has covered everything. So can I just quote a few inspirational words from an unknown poet. These are words I read years ago, words that I turned to in the 'dry' period: *'You can never tell how close you are, it may be near when it seems afar; so stick to the fight when you're hardest hit - it's when things seem worse that you must not quit'.*

I believe that we go through things to make us better people, to prepare us for the future. The things we go through should not determine what or who we are because we are just passing through them, to come out stronger. When we give up and refuse to go on how do we know that the record deal, the breakthrough, the thing that we have been waiting for, is not just around the corner, waiting for us to step through the trial period. If you don't keep on pressing forward, if you give up, you'll never know," I look at the heads nodding in agreement.

"Hello, my name is Vance Grady, I manage a group of three guys, we are really struggling to keep things going right now amid all the rejections. I am starting to wonder if this is what I should really be doing. Did you ever have any doubts Billie?"

"Yes I did, I had loads of self doubts about what I should be doing, this was before I met Jamie. I sent my songs and poems out to a number of places, no one was interested. Someone would say something unpleasant about my songs or poems and I would think, 'they're right Billie, give up, no one is going to want to read anything you write'." I smile, "I never doubted God, I never doubted the fact that if I trusted in Him, put Him first in my life, then no matter what I saw happening around me, what was said about me or my work, I would be successful in what I did; the head and not the tail. It sounds easy but it wasn't, I have sat where you are, I know what you are going through. Trust, hope, abiding, are words of power when you use them the right way and for the right purpose. They will get rid of the doubts and keep you strong."

A lady jumps up, she looks very anxious, "My name is Yvette Marshal, I am a Gospel singer, what if you're not sure you're doing the right thing though? What if you've waited for so long and the doubts start to come? What if everything around you seems to be stopping you? You see people singing songs about hate and violence with multi-million dollar record deals and all you want to sing about is love but there are no record deals in sight. You start to wonder if this really is the right thing to do. I've cried buckets full of tears, I've been disillusioned, confused, hurt-" she sniffs loudly and appears to be struggling to hold her tears back.

I smile reassuringly at her, "I went through a period like that Yvette, writing inspirational songs and poems and wondering why no one seemed interested. Why poems that I didn't understand and songs that had no meaning were being received and mine were not. I was working as a scientist in a hospital and I had utility bills to pay, as well as a mortgage and a number of other debts. I got to a period in my life, a cross-road. I knew that I wanted to write songs, to make videos for my songs, but, I knew if I stopped working I would have no money coming in. Jamie mentioned earlier that I pray a lot. I pray all the time and I pray for and about, everything. I went through some tough times, everything seemed to be against me, trying to stop me, but I always knew it was for a reason and that I would come out a better person.

Anyway back to your question, I had a lot of doubts about my ability, I had been around people who told me my songs were rubbish and a small part of me started to believe what I was told. I'm so thankful though that the rest of me doubted what these people had told me. The rest of me started to pray for guidance and for things to happen, to show me what I should do. Not only that, but to let me know how to do the things. I had a really bad week at work and it was a Friday evening, it was that day that I started to sense things around me change. That was the Friday I knew I was going to go for it with my songs. I was going to get them sung, get them out there. I was going to look for someone to sing them. That same Friday about three hours later, I met Jamie at my cousin's club.

Even after we got together it seemed as if everything was hell bent on stopping us, stopping me from fulfilling my dream. Then I heard a scripture on the radio: Proverbs chapter 16 verse 3. I believed in the words and I stood on them. The rest is history. Faith moves the mountain Yvette, so stand strong because faith *will* do it." She smiles through her tears. I get up and walk over to her, I hug her. "Hang in there Yvette, hang in there," I tell her.

People start to clap. Jamie waits for the clapping to die down.

"Now you see why I call her - boss lady," Jamie says. Clapping turns to laughter. "She has something that we all have but don't all activate, she has faith," he pauses, "when the doubts come into your mind, and they will, think of the reasons you want to do what you want to do. People have different reasons for doing the same thing. There has to be commitment and a love for the thing that you want to do, not the money connected with it, a love which can withstand any doubt. If you have that, then, the doubts when they come, will only last a while but you will be more determined to fulfill your dreams, more committed to hang in there and withstand anything," I nod in agreement and clap with everyone else as I walk back to my seat.

"Billie, how do you cope with writing songs and managing Jamie?"

"I wrote a lot of songs and poems during the years I worked full time, before I met Jamie. It's something I have always done. In terms of managing Jamie, things have all fallen into place and we work really well together. He calls me 'boss lady' and I call him -," I pause for effect and pretend to think, "- Jamie," everyone laughs.

"Hello, my name is Benson and I manage a singer. Do you ever disagree? I read that Jamie said that you keep him grounded Billie. How do you do it?"

Jamie smiles and I sit back and let him answer.

"Billie is down to earth. She has made me see that whatever I have has been given to me for a purpose and it is not all about me. I'll give you an example, I was on a schedule when we started and I had to look after my voice, practice new songs, go to the gym. Anyway one night I went clubbing with an old friend and I got home really late. The next day I had to go to the studio to do a new song. I hadn't practiced properly and I was really tired. There were several people there as well as Billie and the engineer. I warmed up by singing the song twice and then recorded it. I thought I had done a really good job and a couple of the people in the studio thought so too. They voiced very positive remarks, said the things I wanted to hear. I look at Billie and she is frowning and I am thinking 'on no'. She tells the engineer to play the song for us to listen to it. Then she takes it to pieces and points out areas that were flat and off key. The people in the studio who thought it had sounded great, didn't know where to look. She knew I hadn't practiced properly and she just said the truth. She made me listen to her sing the song again, practice it over and over and then after a couple of hours of hard work she said, and I will never forget: *'I can buy it now. Always remember Jamie, sell what you honestly know you can buy.'* She keeps me grounded and she tells me the truth. You have to stay grounded in this business, you get offers and propositions thrown at you from so many directions, so you have to surround yourself with positive people that tell you the truth. You have to stay true to you! I learnt a valuable lesson that day, one that has stayed with me," he smiles. "You can so easily buy into the 'hype' of this business, take my advice, don't. Remember, hype leads to pride, and pride comes before a fall."

A lot of people nod and clap, I join them.

"Hi Billie, I write songs as well. Where do you get your inspiration for your songs and what do you think about the songs out there now?"

"Mmmmm, my inspiration. I get my inspiration from people and life. I write about what I know, either first hand or through other people's experiences. I think that music is a very powerful tool and should be used wisely. There are some really good songs out there now, but there are also some really bad ones. If you notice though, most of the good songs are always copied or sampled and you can listen to the original ten years later and it still sounds good, they withstand the test of time. The bad ones live very short lives."

"What do you think makes a good song Jamie?"

"I think that a good song is one that you can listen to ten or twenty years later and you don't ever have to wonder why it was produced. It is ageless, timeless," he answers.

"Hi Billie, hi Jamie, my name is Reanna and I am from Boston. I am a struggling writer. I know that you have both spoken about praying and trying to do the right thing in rough times. I read a poem recently by *Jacques du Burmage* called

'Make time to listen, only then will you hear'. Have either of you read it? Did it inspire you? And how do you hear from God?"

"I haven't read that poem," I reply. "Have you Jamie?" I ask.

He shakes his head.

"Can you remember any of the lines?" I ask. "Maybe I can identify with some of the writer's ways."

"Oh I know it all by heart."

"Can you recite it to us?"

"Of course, *'Make time to listen, only then will you hear'* by *Jacques du Burmage.*

The Word of the Lord is very clear
It speaks healing, redemption, answered prayer.
Often times I have been asked how else I hear
Draw close and the many other ways I will share.

How do I hear?
In many ways.
Be it a gentle whisper or a loud bang
A sudden hot and cold feeling or tremble of my hand.
Be it a caressing, mild or gentle warm breeze
A flood of peaceful emotions that weakens my knees.
Tears may fill my eyes when I hear the answer to my silent prayer
From the lips of a stranger, a brother or a peer.
I smile when people wonder or mock how I hear
People that do not listen to, pray to or even fear.
The One that created everything and everyone.
The One that gave His beloved, begotten 'Living' Son."

We all clap.

She looks around at the people in the room and smiles.

"I can identify with some of those ways," I say. "I would probably add to that list, a warm reassuring, peaceful feeling in my heart. A conviction that I am doing the right thing." She nods.

"Hello Billie I'm from California and I just love your accent, I read some of your poems a few months ago and I had no idea until recently that you had written them. I'm sorry I'm going on here, my question is why did you stop writing poems?"

"I haven't really stopped. I still write poems. I had two new ones published recently. I don't write that many now because I'm busy but it's something that is part of me, something that I will always do."

"May I just say something?" A young lady asks.

"Sure," Jason replies.

"My name is Camille, I don't have a question, I just wanted to say that I have read 'Unforgiveness Eats Away', 'Patience', 'I Am Loved As I Am', 'Your Will Not Mine' and 'Wisdom'. I know you have written many more poems Billie. As you can probably tell, I like poetry. One thing that always strikes me about your poems is that I don't need a Thesaurus or Dictionary by my side when I read them." I see a few heads nod in agreement with her. "You write simple, straight-forward powerful words that make sense Billie. That's what I wanted to say."

The audience clap and I smile my thanks.

"When will the album be released?"

I indicate for Jamie to answer.

"The album will be out hopefully early next year or sooner. We have two more singles that we will release first."

"What did you do during the 'dry' period that you talked about? How did you keep yourself from being discouraged?"

Again I indicate for Jamie to answer.

"We did a lot of work. We kept positive. During this period we recorded twenty two songs?" He looks at me and I nod my agreement. "So we didn't give up. Billie sent me to the gym, dance lessons, vocal training. We worked then, in preparation for now. When you don't keep busy you start getting bitter and resentful. You may even miss your opportunity because your frame of mind is not right, not receptive."

"Billie I read that you are a scientist, when did you decide that you were going to write songs?"

"I think from the age of about five or six I knew that I wanted to write. I remember telling my class teacher at the time that I wanted to write songs, I also gave her a list of other professions, but I was so sure about music. For a while I let things slip and I did what I thought I had to do, and not what I wanted to do. Then I met Jamie and knew for certain what I really had to, and wanted to do. To me this is a dream come true and I am so grateful to God for everything."

"Thank you for answering the questions, can we just take two more questions, then we have to go," Jason says.

"My name is Benny, a lot of us here have had a few bad experiences with people in the music industry is there any advice that you can both give?"

I lean forward, "Be careful what you sign, read everything and make sure you understand the small print. If you don't, take it to someone who does. Don't get carried away by the 'lifestyle' you see on TV and sign your life away."

Jamie hesitates then leans forward, his face wears a pensive but serious expression, "Some of you may have heard stories of record labels cheating artists, putting artists on the 'shelf', getting artists to sign contracts that tie them up for years, of executives in the music industry getting artists hooked on drugs to control them. Of recording artists being killed, ending up as fatal casualties in the wars between record labels. These stories are all true! Don't jump into the canoe without a paddle. If it looks too good to be true, it usually is. Pray for wisdom and use it wisely!"

All the heads in the room nod in agreement, everyone claps.

"Excellent advice! Can we take one more question please?" Jason asks.

"Hi, my name is Michelle and I am a singer, this is more of a request than a question, can Jamie please sing a song."

Everyone claps, Jamie nods. George ever the professional quickly takes the DAT containing the backing music for the song out of his bag and hands it to Jason's engineer.

I sit back and listen with everyone as Jamie sings 'Love Is Not Supposed To Hurt'.

* * * * *

The Broadway show was spectacular and dinner afterwards really nice. We stand outside our hotel and wave to Jason and his wife Carey who have just dropped us off. I am tired and we have a very early start tomorrow. I know that by hook or crook, we will all be up early and at the first scheduled function on time. I am not prepared to face the wrath of Charles Parker if we are not. We make our way to the lifts.

"Miss Lewis, you have a message," the receptionist calls out as we walk past. I walk over and from behind the desk he lifts up a huge bunch of very beautiful flowers. I hear Jamie whistle behind me, I stare at the flowers in shock. They are so beautiful. He hands me a small envelope. I open it and read the message: *'Missing You' Love Philip.* My heart stops and starts almost immediately, I smile and look at the flowers.

*   *   *   *   *

The two days did not flash past, neither did they go by slowly. They were so full that I am still amazed at what we did in so short a time. Charles had been right there was no way that we could have gone to Jason's radio station during the two days. We were so busy, it was one event after another. I remember being at Coney Island for a record signing, passing Borough Park, Fort Hamilton and Prospect Park to get to Grand Army Plaza in Queens for another record signing, and then going to Willets Point Shea Stadium. From there we went to Manhattan for a television appearance. The next day was just as busy. We did a television show in Manhattan first, then a radio show in Harlem and a magazine shoot in the Bronx. From there we went to the Queens Corona Plaza for a signing and a live radio show. We had to rush through the streets of New York to get to China Town for a record signing and then Times Square for a live television show, then 'Radio City Music Hall' and 'Carnegie Hall' for live performances.

The same type of questions were asked during most of the interviews, and the same answers given each time. The Memorial concert and the American launch party for the single were really good. Jamie was up late recording two new songs with an American producer, while I slept on a couch in the studio. On our way back to London we stopped in Minneapolis where Jamie sang four songs to thousands of people at the Mall of America. It was excellent!

Now as we head to our various homes, I speak for all of us, we are totally exhausted. Jamie slept on the plane and George is asleep now as we drive through the wet windy London streets.

"Jamie, Philip's nephew's birthday party is this Sunday."

"We'll be there. Do you want me to come and pick you up?"

"No, I'll find my way. You have the whole of tomorrow off."

"Time off? What was that?" George asks.

"Tomorrow, we're all probably going to be jet lagged so no work tomorrow," I say.

"Okay, I just need to start tracking the song in the charts here and the rest of Europe, check on the Japan dates, confirm the showcases lined up and the photo shoot for Monday and then I'll rest," he says and puts his head on the window and closes his eyes.

CHAPTER 39

"Sarah you don't have to do this I was going to have Cornflakes for dinner," she ignores me and continues to get pots and pans out of the cupboard.

"Cornflakes?"

"I've slept all day, I'm starving but it was a toss between cornflakes and a take away. Cornflakes won."

"Look I don't mind cooking something and the children wanted to see you."

"Are you sure you don't mind?"

"I don't mind, now get a chair and sit down before you fall down and tell me all about New York. Was it really like what was shown on the television? Did you really have to run from all those screaming girls?"

"And screaming guys," I say, she starts to laugh.

"Auntie Billie the phone is ringing," Luke calls out.

I go into the front room where the children are watching cartoons on the television and pick up the receiver.

"Hello."

"How are you?"

My heart warms at Philip's voice, "I'm fine, thank you for the flowers they were lovely."

"You're welcome. I don't know why but for some strange reason I can't seem to walk past a flower shop without thinking about colourful flowers," he chuckles softly as I laugh. "What are you doing this evening?"

"Resting. My friend Sarah is here with her children. I was thinking that I'd ask her to stay the night and then come down with her and the children for the party tomorrow."

"Good idea. Did you get my message?"

"No."

"I have to pick something up near your house, I'll drop by."

"Was that the message?"

"Yes."

"See you later then," smiling I put the receiver down. I look at the phone, the light indicating that I have a message is not flashing. Frowning I look at the phone properly. There is no tape in the slot and the answer machine has been turned off. I think back to the day we went to New York, I know that I put another tape inside the machine when I had taken the old one out. I look on the table around the phone. I check the book case. Nothing.

"Luke, did you see an answer machine tape?"

"Tape?" He asks, "no, what does it look like?"

"Like the tape I got you with the player for your birthday only smaller," I reply.

"No, I didn't see one and Nick and Maddy didn't play with the phone, they only played with the radio and television, but I told them to stop."

"It's okay Luke, you go back and watch TV, I must have taken it," I watch as he goes back and sits with his siblings in front of the television. I feel a slight tension in my forehead as my frown deepens and I run up the stairs. Inside my room I pick up my bag and tip the contents onto my bed. The old tape falls onto my bed along with everything else. I rummage through the things looking for the new tape, which I know, I placed in the telephone. I pick up the old tape and my Dictaphone. I never got round to listening to my messages in New York, because we had been so busy. I slot the tape in the machine and press the play button.

Message 1: I listen to Jen tell me that she and Martin are thinking about going to Florida to visit my parents and his parents who are currently visiting mine.

Message 2: the caller does not leave a message.

Message 3: Martin tells me what Jen has told me.

Message 4: Jamie tells me that he will be coming early to pick me up for the trip to New York.

Message 5: Francis Wells voice says hello-

"Billie your phone is ringing," Sarah shouts from downstairs. I turn the Dictaphone off and put it in the drawer of the side table by my bed. I reach in the drawer and take out another micro tape for the answer machine and go down-stairs to answer the phone.

* * * * *

"It was nice meeting you Philip," Sarah says.

"Same here, I'll see you tomorrow. Happy birthday Luke."

"Thank you, it was four days ago. So I'm eight and four days now," Luke says proudly.

"That old?" Philip asks.

He nods.

"I'll see you tomorrow."

I walk with him to his car. We tower above his old classic Porsche. I look at him and then the car and shake my head.

"What?"

"Oh nothing, I was just thinking about men in general and their little toys."

"The car huh?"

"Yes, the car. You're six foot plus, how do you fit in it?"

"Come with me," he pulls me around to the passenger side and opens the door. I climb in and sit down. I am impressed with the leg room. He walks round, climbs in, sits back and stretches his legs, comfortably, "Any questions?"

"No, I can see that even though it is low, it is quite comfortable. There is one thing though, where will the children go?" I look at the back of the car. He does not answer and I turn to him.

"Children?" He asks softly.

"I..., err..., I was joking."

"I've really missed you," he says and takes hold of my hand.

"I thought about you a lot," I say surprising myself at my complete honesty.

He smiles, "For a while there I thought that I was going to have to resort to other measures to get you to tell me how you feel. You know that this is not a casual thing for me don't you?"

I nod

"I have never felt this way before Billie."

I smile and hold his hand tightly. I don't feel embarrassed any more, I feel that I am looking at someone who is and will always be a part of my life. I feel secure in that knowledge.

* * * * *

I tidy up the breakfast things in the kitchen while Sarah takes care of the children. I am happy that they are here and that they spent the night. Sometimes people like me who live alone can get selfish, wanting everything in a certain place and done a certain way. We don't want interference. With Sarah and the children here, I see that there is more to life than perfectly arranged things. I don't mind children's toys laying everywhere and the noise. I see things differently, I see that true love for others covers a multitude of sins. What do I mean by this? We all have faults, things which we do that are wrong, but when you really care about other people you don't look at what they do or do not do, you care about them regardless. I still don't know the whole story about Roger, Nigel and Sarah, I know she feels I will be in some sort of danger if I know everything, so she is still keeping things to herself. I know from something which Luke said this morning, before he was quickly taken upstairs, that she has spoken to Roger recently. I don't let my thoughts stop me from doing what I can and will do for her and her family. I smile as I hear Maddy laughing upstairs. I finish the cleaning and climb up the stairs. Halfway up the stairs the door bell rings. I turn, run down the stairs and open the door.

"Philip!"

"Good morning."

"Good morning Mr McKnight," I reply.

"I'm going to church, do you want to come?"

"Church?"

"Yes," he says smiling.

"Of course I'd like to come. Give me twenty minutes."

"You have twenty five," he says.

"Can we come to church?" Luke asks.

"Sure, if your mom says it's okay," Philip replies.

Luke runs up the stairs, "Mum can we go to church with uncle Philip and auntie Billie?" He shouts.

*   *   *   *   *

Luke, Nick and Maddy walk into the church's Sunday school. They have been to this church before and know where everything is. I smile as they rush over to the other children and start talking.

"I can't believe that we go to the same church? A friend of Billie's and mine, Phoebe O'Connor, told me about this church years ago when she was trying to get me to go to church. Her dad preaches here," Sarah says to Philip, "I know that the children and I have only been here a few times but I don't remember seeing you before."

"I usually go to the afternoon service when I'm in London. They have a branch in California that I go to regularly. So you know Phoebe? Her dad is taking the service this morning. I haven't met her yet but I've read her book. It's really good."

A smartly dressed lady usher appears and directs us to the fourth row from the front, we sit down.

The choir starts to sing *'As The Deer Panteth For The Water'*. Everyone claps when they finish. I turn and look at Philip as he claps. He smiles at me.

A man wearing a suit and holding a large Bible, some papers and a large transparent plastic jar, walks onto the stage. I recognize him immediately, Phoebe's dad, Pastor O'Connor. He places his Bible and papers on the pulpit and the jar on the floor and looks around.

"Let us pray," he says.

*   *   *   *   *

"-Turn with me to one more reading. Luke chapter 10 verses 18 and 19 says:- *Jesus answered them 'I saw Satan fall like lightning from heaven. I have given you authority to trample on snakes and scorpions and to overcome all the power of the enemy; nothing will harm you'."* He closes the Bible.

"We have been given authority, power, dominion over evil." He looks at us as we sit looking up at him. "My questions today are: Do we really know the power we have as children of God? Do we walk in the knowledge of that power? Do we ask God for the knowledge? Do we know, really know the power of God's Grace?

The answers are, No. A lot of us don't know. A lot of us perish because of the lack of this knowledge. Those that do know try to walk in the knowledge but they let things hold them back. We are told that we have authority over the power of the enemy but we give our power to the enemy and let the enemy hold us back and keep us in ignorance." He tilts his head and looks around and then brushes something off his trousers, I see where Phoebe gets her mannerisms from.

"How do we do this? You ask. We do this every time we give in and do wrong, every time we give in to temptation. Every time we walk away from the Word of God, away from living a spiritual life and live a life controlled by the flesh. Every time we walk in anger, hate, jealousy, bitterness, unforgiveness, racism, greed, judgement, pettiness, lies. Every time we walk in the things listed in Galatians chapter 5 verses 19-20. Go and read it when you get home."

He holds a very long piece of paper up, the paper has a lot of writing on it. "This is an example of a very incomplete list of things that take away our power. We cannot walk in the power we have been given if we are still holding on to any of these things. The enemy knows this so he works to keep you in situations that will allow anger, bitterness or hate to stay in your life. He strives to allow sisters in the church to walk in jealousy, pettiness, suspicion of other sisters, and brothers to walk in pride, arrogance and resentment. Why are we envious of what other people have when we don't know what they went through to get it? We are supposed to live by the Spirit exhibiting the fruit of the Spirit which is love, joy, peace, patience, kindness, goodness, faithfulness, humility and self-control." He shakes his head.

"We have the choice to do what God wants us to do which is the *right* thing or follow evil, there is no middle ground. We know that God's way will lead to life and the evil way will lead to death. Yet we still do what is wrong, myself included. In 2nd Peter chapter 1 verses 5-8, there are seven things we are told to add to our faith, seven things that will help us to live effectively and productively. Goodness, knowledge of God, self-control, patience, godliness, brotherly kindness and love. When we don't add these things to our faith, we are unproductive and ineffective in our knowledge of Jesus, we hold on to our past sins and we have no power. In our ignorance we cannot see, we are blind but we pretend to the world that all is well.

There are so many powerful machines today, so many hi tech, extremely expensive machines, that do things that seemed impossible a few years ago. Let me digress a little, imagine for a few minutes a machine that can read your mind and see what is in your heart. A machine that you stand in front of, and in seconds, it tells you everything about you. Such a machine would be worth, what? millions? billions? trillions?"

Some people nod, others verbally agree.

"No such machine exists, a polygraph or lie detector cannot see what is in your heart, it cannot read your mind. Truth serum will not work if someone does not know they are lying, if the lie has become the truth to the person. But wait a minute," he appears to be thinking, "umm…, read our minds and see our hearts?" He clicks his fingers, "GOD DOES THAT!"

He looks around and smiles.

"God does that! He sees our hearts, He knows what we are thinking. He does not cost trillions, He is free. Read Hebrews chapter 4 and verse 13."

Clapping and cheering erupt and resound around the room, he waits for it to subside.

"For years I held on to unforgiveness, hate and bitterness, I gave in to temptation. My wife and my children tried to make me change. Just for a little peace in the house, I pretended that I had changed, but my heart hadn't. Yet I pretended so well, that after a while, I believed my pretence and ignored what was in my heart. I forgot that God sees our hearts and our motives. I did good works or deeds, I counselled people, prayed for people, went to peace meetings but I did all this with evil in my heart. I would pray the first half of Psalm 51, verses 1 - 9 to be precise, I avoided verse 10 and continued doing wrong," he shakes his head.

"My wake up call," he shakes his head again and turns some papers over. "My wake up call did not come in the form of flashing bright lights or a loud voice, it came in the form of something that I understood, a poem called *'Change Your Heart'*. Let me read it to you."

He picks up a piece of paper:
"There are things deep inside that you effectively hide
Everyone around you thinks you're a saint and more beside
There are thoughts in your heart you do not share
For if you did your true appearance all would fear.

People around you think you're so good
If only they could see your heart, if only they understood
You act 'Church' all day but in your heart you plan
Revenge, evil discrimination, bigotry, towards anyone you can.

You store up hate and bitterness inside
You struggle with anger, jealousy and rebellious pride
If you were to die right now everyone would be sure
That you would be knocking on Heaven's door.

For they have all seen your generous displays of love and giving
And, they think that you are consecrated, full of holy living
But, you know the truth which has not set you free
You know your heart is not where it should be.

Dear friend God sees our hearts and He judges accordingly
He sees what man cannot see, way beyond 'externality'
He sees the hate, bitterness and pride
He sees all the lies that from man you continually hide.

And so when the time comes no matter how much you pretend
Unless you repent and change, in darkness you may end

Think hard, pray harder and don't let this be your fate
Don't let the last thing you see be the 'closed' Heavenly gate.

How is it you think I recognize your heart and all you do?
It's simply because not long ago I did the same things too
So change your heart while you still have time
It's not easy but with God it's possible, I know, for He helped me
change mine."

He puts the paper down and looks at us, "The day I first read this poem was the day I stopped living a lie. The day I broke free of chains which had held me captive for years. The day I let go of hate and anger that was buried deep inside of me, that had become part of me. The day I fell on my knees, cried out and begged God to take control and help me change."

He pushes the plastic jar with his leg, "God is good! The next day a miracle happened. After nearly thirty years of living in conflict with my father-in-law I picked up my mobile phone and called him, at exactly the same time my wife handed me our house phone. My father-in-law for the first time in nearly thirty years wanted to talk to me. After nearly thirty years of religious conflict we settled, we found peace, the peace, love and joy that is in Jesus brought us together. I was released from so much hate, I .. " his voice falters, he wipes his tears.

He bends and picks up the plastic jar, "Do you know how they used to capture monkeys years ago? They used to put nuts and bananas amongst other things in a large transparent jar or container with a narrow opening that was stuck to the ground. The monkey would put its hand inside the jar to pick whatever was inside up." He takes the list that he had held up a few minutes ago and puts it in the jar. Next he puts his hand in the jar. "The monkey would hold on to whatever was in the jar and try and pull its hand free," he does the same, "the monkey would pull and pull, refusing to let go of the contents in its hand." Again he does the same, "The monkey did not know that to get free, all it had to do was let go of the contents in its hand," he lets go of the paper. "Unclench its hand and then pull its hand free," he does exactly as he says and pulls his hand free. He puts the jar down and looks around.

"That is how we get caught, how we forfeit our power, we hold on like the monkey. We hold on like I once did, to unforgiveness, hate, anger, everything on that list and the many more things that are not. We don't let go. We get trapped in sin, we lose our power to overcome. You see while you are caught, the enemy makes you think that there is no way out. You feel so guilty, so ashamed, you think that God will not hear you if you pray, so you don't pray. You don't know that all you have to do, is let go. Do you understand what I'm saying? All you have to do is let go. It may look difficult, it may even sound difficult. It's not. That is just a lie that will keep you with your hand in the jar; keep you caught, keep you trapped.

Nowadays there are so many people in the church and outside the church who are confused like I was; who are caught. To everyone else they pretend all is well, they forget God sees everything, and to Him, we cannot pretend," he looks at his notes.

"The enemy works by dividing and conquering anyway he can. The Church is the body of Christ. There is one body, so why do we still have Black churches and White churches, or four small churches all residing in one building independent of each other. Why do we have so many denominations all fundamentally saying the same thing but at the same time holding on to their differences, using these differences to condemn others and justify themselves. Looking at 'specks' in other churches and ignoring the 'logs' or 'poles' in theirs.

We need to know that unless we unite and draw strength from each other, we are divided. The enemy will always try to highlight the differences in the churches and lowlight the similarities so as to divide and conquer. The body of Christ cannot be divided. God works through His people; a 'united' people, to preach the Gospel. Imagine what would happen if God's churches unite, stop the arguments, and walk in His Truth displaying His Love. The enemy would be defeated. Our actions allow the enemy to cause division.

We need to recognize the things that we are doing which are wrong, and ask God to forgive us, we need to forgive others, we need to do what we know is right in God's eyes not our own. We all know right from wrong, no matter how we try to pretend that we don't.

We need to love people from our hearts regardless of colour, race or creed, whether we agree with them or not. When we walk in the love that God has given us then, that love will cover a multitude of sins. People will always hurt us, will always abuse us. Always try to get us to hurt and hate others. Whatever they do, don't agree with them, but love them anyway, let the love you have cover their sins. Pray for them, don't judge them. Don't love their evil deeds, hate that, but, don't hate people. Hate doesn't make them change, it will make them worse. Love may not make them change but I tell you now at least it will not make them worse. *Abraham Lincoln* said: *'The best way to defeat your enemy is to make him your friend'*. Why? Because he knew what I found out, that hate destroys the 'hater' more than the 'hated', but love builds.

What we say, what we do, comes out of what is in our hearts. A lack of love for other people comes out of a heart where there is no true love. So no matter how much you preach or say you have faith or pretend to do good, it means nothing if there is no true love in your heart, read 1st Corinthians chapter 13 and verses 1-3.

We have to renew our minds daily, change our thinking. We come to church on Sunday, have a mid week service on Wednesday, and read our Bible now and then yet there is no change in our hearts, no love for others, no passion for God and doing the right thing. If there is no transformation! Then we must ask ourselves, 'What is the point?'

Some of us pretend and some of us try to be holy. We ask, 'What Would Jesus Do?' We wear 'WWJD' bracelets and pendants. We read the Bible and find out exactly what Jesus would do, yet we don't do it. We go around pretending to love yet walking in greed and in envy of each others gifts. We say 'God show me Your Will', God's Will is in His Word. Read Romans chapter 12."

He turns a paper over "You see people outside the church are tired of people inside the church talking the talk, but not walking the walk, of church folk being listeners of the Word but not 'doers' of the Word. Faith comes by hearing, and hearing by the Word of God. Faith without works is dead. Your lack of good works, or deeds, show the level of your faith and ultimately whose voice you are listening to.

People are asking, *'Where is the love?'*, *'Where is the evidence of God in our lives?'*. They are tired of knocking on our doors looking for love, only to be told to go away because we are busy doing unnecessary works or deeds, that make us look good. They are tired of the lack of character and integrity or righteousness they see in us. Tired of us quoting scriptures and not living them. We preach 'at' people already living in their own little hell, we forget that it is the Holy Spirit who will convince people not us. We say to these people, 'change or you may end up in eternal hell'. They say: 'Hello, we're already there, we are already living a hellish life'. All they want, is to see a demonstration of the love of God in us reaching out to them, helping them to seek for a way out of their situation, a better way of life, a life with God.

I know there are a number of pastors and church leaders here today, can I just say please, please, please, don't be like the leaders of Jesus' day, the people He said were externally clean but internally unclean, whitewashed tombs. Don't get caught up living the life of a movie star. Don't gain the whole world and lose your soul, don't cause others to fall. Yes God prospers people but He blesses us to be a blessing to others with our finances, talents and time, not to take advantage of people, use and abuse them. Never forget in the midst of your much to help whoever God tells you to help. We are charged to take care of *His* sheep. His sheep must be fed the Word of Truth. So we need to do just that and let *His* name be glorified always. God is God, you are His creation, stop glorifying in yourself, stop thinking that it is all about you. It is not, it never was and it never will be. God must be worshiped in spirit and truth.

I want everyone here and those people watching at home or listening to me on the radio to think for a moment, what do people see when they look at you? Do they see the image of Jesus? Do they see His Righteousness and His Love? Do they hear His Truth from your lips. Judas Iscariot betrayed Jesus, the Bible says that Judas went to the people in the temple and offered to betray Jesus for thirty pieces of silver. How did the people in the temple know to trust him? He could have been a spy. There must have been something in him that they recognised because the same thing was in them. What do people see when they look at you? Jesus said in John chapter 13 verse 35:- *'By this all men will know that you are my disciples, if you love one another'*. We have to love one another and people have to see this or they will not know who we are and we will blend in with the crowd."

He nods and I watch as two men and a little boy walk onto the stage. The men are carrying two large containers with something in them, the little boy is carrying a small container with something in it.

"I'd like to introduce you to this wonderful little boy here. Stephen, come over here son," the little boy walks towards him. "His name is Stephen but he also has another name. It is a Nigerian 'Yoruba' name, *Oluwaseun*. Directly translated it means; 'God thank you'. His sister's name is *Oluwatobi* which means 'God is great'. You can tell that there is a love for God in this family can't you?" Some people clap their hands, others verbally agree. "Now this little boy is six years old and the other day he told his mother something in the presence of his eight year old sister, his mother told my wife, and my wife told me, and I will now with his permission, tell you. He said, and I quote: *'God is a coat and the devil is an evil, bad, wind. When you take your coat off the devil will blow you about'*." I hear the gasps in the audience, I smile. "From the lips of a six year old child. *Oluwaseun*-God thank you. In the book of Proverbs chapter 22 and verse 6 it says:- *'Train a child in the way he should go, and when he is old he will not turn from it'*. His parents are definitely doing a good job. Now he has a little demonstration that he is going to do with his dad and his uncle.

The two men start to fill the jar that Phoebe's dad had placed on the stage earlier with what looks like sand from their containers. They fill it to the top and stop. The little boy moves forward and tries to pour his sand, which is a different colour, into the jar, it spills on the floor.

"When we fill our hearts with bad things, with hate, racism, bigotry, anger, there is no space for love," Phoebe's dad says. The little boy looks frustrated as he continues to pour the sand. "This is how evil operates, when we let it, it fills us so we have no space for goodness. In our ignorance we think that we are doing the right thing." One of the men picks up the jar and empties some of the contents into a bin. He places the jar back on the stage and gives the little boy another container of sand. The boy pours the sand into the jar slowly, he smiles as it all goes in.

"Turn to God, pray, renew your minds daily. How do you renew your minds? By reading the Word and growing spiritually. By letting go of things, of thoughts, of actions that keep you trapped in sin. Don't just talk the talk, walk the walk. Stand on God's Word and His Word will stand with you. The power is in the Word of God.

We all have things inside us that we need to let go of, empty ourselves of. We try so hard to do it by ourselves and constantly we fail. We make New Year resolutions; new month resolutions; new week resolutions and nothing happens. We need to try another way. We need to start filling ourselves with the right things, daily; weekly; monthly and yearly. These right things will increase in us, change us and, drive out the bad or wrong in us. Try it. It worked for me. Change occurs when something is done differently," he turns to the men and little boy that have finished clearing the sand away and are walking off the stage.

"Thank you gentleman and thank you Stephen."

I feel Philip move his leg next to mine, I turn smile at him and turn back to Phoebe's dad. He is drinking some water that was probably placed on the pulpit before we came. He holds the half full glass up and looks at it, "We put water in juice or squash to dilute it, don't we? Have you ever thought that you are not just diluting the juice, you are also diluting the water? Don't compromise your life, don't listen to the lies of evil and dilute the truth. The enemy is a liar and he will try to dilute your faith with lies, when you succumb you give him your power. What power, you wonder? When you know the Truth, you have power, use the power to defeat the enemy. Don't live in the lie of defeat when we have already been given the Truth of victory. Lies cause division, the Truth, unity to conquer. Over the years 'unity' has suffered great attacks, one of the main instruments used has been man made laws. A group of people not happy to conform to the Truth of God's Word break away and form their own group living lives based on lies. You cannot add or take away from God's Truth, to do that is to live in un-truth."

He puts his hand in his pocket and pulls it out. He lifts it up, his finger and thumb appear to be holding something very small.

The choir start to hum the song *'Amazing Grace'* softly in the background as he talks, "All we need is faith. Faith as small as a mustard seed. This is a mustard seed. If you have faith as small as this and do not doubt but walk in obedience to God, victory will be yours. Water your mustard seed with the Word and see it grow into a big tree. Have faith and let your actions speak of your faith."

The choir sing beautifully and softly, *'Amazing Grace'*.

"Can everyone close their eyes and bow their heads. Is there anyone here today who has not yet made that commitment to God, who has not yet invited Jesus Christ into their life as their Lord and Saviour? Remember it's not about doing things in pretence, because God sees everything. And, it's not about forcing people to do what they don't want to. Read your Bible, look at the life of Jesus Christ, everything He did, He did with love not force or quarrels. He gave us a choice. When you make this commitment, you are asking for the forgiveness of your sins, you are repenting. In 1st John chapter 1 and verse 9 we are told that:- *God is faithful and just to forgive us of our sins when we confess them and to cleanse us from all unrighteousness.* Cleanse us from all our past wrongdoing. When you repent and invite Jesus Christ into your life, you are letting go of your past sins and becoming *born again* into a new life, a life with Jesus Christ as your saviour. A life where your new born again spirit is supposed to be in control of your mind and body and all three are in-line with God's Will.

Salvation is by God's Grace. God's Amazing Grace, simply means He gives us what we *do not* deserve. He is such a wonderful awesome God that in all the wrong we do, He is merciful and does not punish us in the way we *do* deserve. He waits for us to turn back to Him, to repent. Know this, time is not standing still but moving, running out. The door will soon shut and no man will be able to open it.

So you search your hearts, are you ready to take that step forward and let go of sin? If you are, then come forward and let us pray together, the prayer of Salvation."

I hear people move towards the front, my eyes are closed and my head bent. I feel the person sitting next to me stand up. I don't open my eyes or lift my head up as Sarah squeezes past my legs.

He continues, "John chapter 3 verses 16 and 17 says:- *For God so loved the world that He gave His one and only begotten Son, that whoever believes in Him shall not perish but have eternal life. For God did not send His Son into the world to condemn the world, but to save the world through Him.*

Romans chapter 10 verse 9 says:- *If you confess with your mouth 'Jesus is Lord' and believe in your heart that God raised Him from the dead, you will be saved.* After we pray I want you, when you go home, to continue to pray. Ask God to lead you, let His Holy Spirit guide you. Read John chapter 3, chapter 14 and chapter 15. Pray for discernment, wisdom and understanding. You have to know and live the Truth because only the Truth will set you free. This is not just a church event, this is 'the' way to abundant life. God is not just the God of Sunday, He is the God of every day, every hour, minute and second."

People continue to move to the front. The choir sing *'I Surrender All'* softly and beautifully.

"Please repeat aloud the following prayer: **Dear Heavenly Father I am sorry for all the wrong things I have done in my life. Please forgive me and cleanse me. I confess that Jesus is Lord and I believe in my heart that You raised Him from the dead. Please come into my life and fill me with Your Holy Spirit and be with me forever. Create in me a new heart Dear God and be LORD over my life now and forever. Thank you Father. Amen."**

CHAPTER 40

Philip stops his jeep outside two large wrought iron gates covered with balloons of every imaginable colour. I hear the excitement in the children's voices at the back of the jeep. I watch as he presses a button on the side of the dash-board and the gates swing open.

"Wow," Luke says.

'Wow', I think.

He drives up a winding path and I catch my breath as I see a large house up ahead. It looks a little like a stately home.

"You live here?" I ask.

"Yes," he says. I note his modesty. He parks the Jeep in front of the garage and turns the engine off. "I'll show you around later."

"Wow," Luke says again and I smile.

"Do you live here by yourself?" I ask.

"Yes and no, it's like an open house. I have a very large family. My paternal grandparents had six children and they had children. I got this place so that anyone could come and visit or stay. Do you think it's too big?"

"Not really, I haven't seen inside yet."

"I really hope you like it Billie," he says and walks ahead.

I look at the cars parked in the drive. I can hear the voices of children coming from around the back. Luke, Nick and Maddy run into the house after Philip. Sarah walks with me into the house. As soon as I walk in, I notice and feel the warmth. Sarah and I walk down a large hall-way and into a reception room. The room is elegant but lived in. I look around liking what I see.

"Billie!" I turn and smile at Kenny. I walk into his open arms and hug him back. Smiling I introduce him to Sarah.

"Where did Philip go?"

"He went upstairs to change. Come out into the garden, let me get you both something to drink. What would you like?"

"Orange juice, please," I say.

"The same, thank you," Sarah says.

We step out of the back of the house into the little park which Kenny called the garden. It is so big. There is a large bouncy castle in one corner and a clown entertaining some children next to it. A number of children are running around on the basket ball court. Tables and chairs are set up at the other end under a large canopy. Angela is sitting under the canopy with her feet resting on a chair. I walk over to her with Sarah. She stands up as we approach her.

"Hi Billie." We hug and I introduce her to Sarah. She hugs Sarah. "Let's sit down, in about an hour we are going to be rushed off our feet."

A man walks over to us with two glasses of orange juice. He places them down on the table

"Two orange juices ladies," he says and sits down. Noting his Canadian accent I look at him and then Angela.

"Billie, Sarah, my brother Simon."

"Hello," I say extending my hand.

"Hello Billie, I've heard a lot about you, man is Philip a very lucky guy to have you," he takes hold of my hand and squeezes it. I smile politely and pull my hand away.

"Simon," Angela says, I sense the warning in her tone.

"Hello," Sarah says.

"Hello Sarah," he replies.

I take a sip of my drink and watch as some more people arrive. Sarah's children are running around with the other children. I notice that Maddy keeps glancing at us from time to time, diffidently. Sarah says it's for reassurance. As soon as she sees Sarah, she starts to run around and play with the other children. I turn to see Jamie, Trudi and Dave walking towards us. Luke has also seen them and runs towards them. I watch as Jamie turns and catches him then swings him in the air. He puts him down. Luke hugs Trudi and shakes Dave's hand then runs off back towards the other children. I smile and look at Sarah. She is looking at her hands and twisting a ring I have never seen before, around on her finger.

"Hello," Trudi says shaking hands with everyone as I introduce her. Dave does the same. Jamie shakes hands with everyone but me. I reach out to shake his hand and he pulls me to my feet and hugs me.

"You okay?" He asks.

I nod, "You?" I ask.

"I'm okay," he replies, "still a little jet lagged."

I turn to Dave, "How are you?" I ask.

"Thankful, getting better and better each day."

"That's good."

To my surprise he pulls me into his arms.

"Thank you," he says softly.

"Any time," I reply.

"Billie did George get hold of you this morning?" Jamie asks, "he said that he tried to leave a message but your answer machine wasn't working."

"No, I haven't heard from him. Is there something wrong?"

"Something about the Japan dates moving forward."

"I'll call him later."

"Would you just look at those two?" Angela says laughing.

I turn in the direction she is looking at, Philip and Kenny are wearing frilly aprons and setting up the barbecue area. I smile as I look at Philip. A little boy of about four or five is standing by him. The boy is holding a disposable plate and a fork in his hands.

"Oh look Philip has a customer already," Angela says.

I watch as Kenny brings a tray piled high with burgers and sausages out.

"Oh look there's one they did earlier, isn't that just so cute," Simon says sarcastically.

I look at him and then Angela, she looks as if she is trying to stay calm. She stands up, "I'm going to give them a hand, Billie can you come with me please."

"Sure," I stand up.

"Food and drinks are inside, Philip is our resident DJ, hopefully the music will soon start. Please make yourself at home and have a good time," Angela says to the others. I notice that Simon is frowning as he looks at her.

She is a little agitated as we walk towards the barbecue stand.

371

"I'm sorry Billie, he is my brother and I love him to bits, but since his girl-friend died in a car accident, he blames everyone. He is so angry with everyone and it hurts because he is such a lovely guy. He seems to take pleasure in upsetting me and the rest of my family all the time. It's as if he wants us to feel his pain over and over again. Let's slow down, or better still, let's go over to the children, if Kenny sees that I'm upset in my condition, he'll flip and tell Simon to leave and I don't want that."

"Your condition?" I ask.

"I'm pregnant," she replies.

*   *   *   *   *

I watch Angela attend to some of the children. Philip and Kenny are dishing out burgers and sausages to some of the other children. They now have a few other men helping. I watch as they professionally and diligently add different things to the plates as each child walks alongside the table. Jamie and the others have gone inside as Angela suggested. Simon sits by himself at the table under the canopy.

Maddy does not want to go and get something to eat, she stands next to me as I help Angela. She keeps looking around the garden.

"Maddy are you hungry?"

She nods shyly.

"Do you want me to take you to get something to eat?"

She nods vigorously.

"What do you want, a burger or a sausage?"

"Both please," she replies

I take her hand and walk slowly with her towards Philip. We get in line. I watch Simon walk towards Angela. He stands in front of her running his hand through his hair. They talk. Holding Maddy's hand we move further down the line. I watch as Kenny puts his spatula down and moves towards Angela and Simon. Philip holds him back. I turn back to Simon and Angela. They seem to be deep in discussion. I watch as they hug each other.

*   *   *   *   *

"Can I help you ma'am?" Philip asks Maddy.

"Can I have a burger and a sausage please," she whispers shyly.

"Coming right up ma'am in just a few minutes," he says to her. She nods.

"I like the frills, they suit you," I say smiling at him.

"You weren't hoping to get food from here I take it?"

"Why?" I ask.

"You do not make fun of the chef and, expect to get fed."

"Chef? Is there a chef here?" Playfully I look around.

"That's it madam you are on bread and water."

"Good thing I know burger maker number two," I say winking at Kenny.

"Do I detect a 'sassy' note in your voice?" Philip asks leaning towards me smiling. I lift up my hand and measure my 5ft 7inches height against his 6ft 1inch.

"Nope, no 'sassy-ness' here," I say laughing.

Simon walks past us, Philip takes a swig from a bottle of Cola and puts it down. I notice him look at Simon strangely. Kenny walks over to Angela.

"Okay Maddy, your burger and sausage are ready. Here we go," Philip hands her a plate with food.

"Thank you," she smiles.

"Thanks Philip," I say taking Maddy's plate from her and holding her hand.

"Do you want anything Billie?"

"Maybe later," I smile. I take Maddy to a little table where the other children sit and help her to sit down. I check her hands as I have seen her mother do, to make sure that they are clean and then I place the plate in front of her.

"Hold on," the Microbiologist in me says. I reach for some wipes on the table and clean her hands properly. Then give her a fork knowing that she will use her fingers.

"What do you want to drink?"

"Fizzy orange," she says tomato ketchup already all over her fingers and face. There are no more unclaimed drinks on the table so I walk to the house to go and get one. I look on the worktops, in the fridge and in the utility room. I can't find any drinks.

"What are you looking for?" Simon asks startling me.

"Fizzy orange or any other drink for a child," I reply.

He walks past me and opens a cupboard door, "I put them in here so they wouldn't clutter up the place." He takes a couple out and hands one to me.

"Thank you," I say reaching for the drink. I take it but he doesn't let go. He looks at me strangely.

"You look familiar, so much like…," suddenly he moves towards me and touches my hair and then my face, "you even feel like her," he says.

I move back, "Stop it!" I push his hand away and turn to leave.

"Billie! Wait, I didn't mean…, please wait, look," he reaches into his pocket and pulls out a picture, "look" he says. I hesitate and then take it from him. I look at the picture of a pretty girl with masses of curly hair. She is standing on a rock, there is sand all around so I am assuming she is at the beach.

"It was taken in LA, on Santa Monica beach last year a few weeks before she died. You look so alike, you could be sisters. I'm sorry about just then," he breathes deeply. "Every day is so hard for me, it really-, I-," his voices falters, "people are sympathetic, they are sorry but their words mean nothing to me, she's gone. When I see people carrying on all around me as if nothing has happened, I just think that it's wrong. Sometimes I can't breathe, the pain is so strong and I feel like I'm suffocating with grief and then someone asks me if I'm hungry? If I want a cup of tea?" He holds his hands up as if in disbelief and moves away from me. He runs trembling hands through his hair.

"Sometimes people don't know what to say to comfort your heart because there isn't much that they can do or say. So people do what they know, they try to comfort your body," I don't know what else to say.

He turns and looks at me strangely and talks softly almost to himself. "People tell me to pray and that they will pray for me. I can't seem to make them understand that it's too late, she's dead, what is there to pray for?" He sits on a stool at the breakfast bar and stares at the picture. I walk over to him and sit on another stool.

"People handle things differently Simon, people feel pain differently, it doesn't mean they don't feel it. Maybe what they're saying is that when we can't face things by ourselves, that is when we need to pray and ask God to face them with us. To comfort us."

He sits staring straight ahead, after a while as if he has just heard what I said he nods.

I sit quietly with him.

*　　*　　*　　*　　*

I feel a surge of warmth as I watch Philip flip the burgers. I feel myself shiver as the warmth takes over the cold in my heart and drives it out. I am helping Angela serve ice cream to some of the children. I watch as Danny runs backwards and forwards between Kenny and Angela. He is so cute it is hard not to smile and look at him wishfully.

"Don't go all dreamy, Danny is a handful," Angela says as she watches him run around the garden. "Sleepless nights, potty training," she says smiling with pride.

"It's worth it though, isn't it?"

"Definitely and absolutely," she replies.

"I want chocolate please," a little girl says looking at the empty container in my hand.

"We don't have any more chocolate ice cream out here honey, do you want strawberry?" Angela asks.

"Ummmmmm…, maybe," she replies.

"Try some," I say putting a little bit in her plastic bowl. She tries it with her finger and gives me a big toothless grin.

"It taste like strawberries and chocolate." I look at the ice cream and then at the spoon I had used to serve it. The spoon has a little bit of chocolate on it. I bend down and kiss her forehead.

"I'm sorry, it's my fault." She smiles again and then runs off with the ice cream. Two minutes later she comes back with two little boys and a girl.

"Can you play baseball with us again?" One of the little boys asks me.

"Sure, as soon as I finish doing this I'll come over."

The four of them stand in front of me whispering to each other and pushing each other forward. I frown.

"Can we have chocolate ice cream or strawberry ice cream and a kiss please," they chorus and start giggling.

Angela looks at me and starts laughing.

"Not funny, I'm going to get some chocolate ice cream."

I search frantically in the freezer.

"Are you the lady giving strawberry ice cream out with a kiss? Can I ditch the ice cream and have two kisses?"

Playfully I shake my head.

"What about one and a half kisses?"

Smiling, I close the freezer door and turn to face Philip.

"You heard about that?"

He nods.

"What is half a kiss?" I ask.

He leans forward and kisses me gently on the lips. He rests his forehead on mine and looks into my eyes, "That was a quarter kiss," he says and I laugh. He kisses me gently again.

"Are you having a good time?" He asks.

"Umm.., there was a slight occurrence with a burger guy thinking he was a chef but I handled him pretty good."

Laughing he pulls me into his arms. I put my arms around his neck and hold him. I feel his hand stroking my hair, for some strange reason I think about the pain that Simon is going through. The thought of Philip not being there suddenly scares me.

"Are you okay? Baby you're shivering," he says softly.

"I'm fine, just hold me," I feel his arms tighten around me and close my eyes.

*   *   *   *   *

"He dribbles, he scores," Philip says bouncing the basketball around a friend and then throwing it towards the hoop. "Yes," he shouts as it goes in. I watch and clap with the children and other spectators as he high fives Kenny and the two other guys on his team. The children are cheering as the men run up and down the court passing the ball. It's like being at a professional NBA game and I laugh at the way some of the wives and girlfriends cheer louder than the children in their support. Someone blows a whistle and the players walk off the court. Philip walks towards me.

"I'm impressed," I say and he smiles.

"Can you play?"

"Sure, it's like netball, right?"

He takes my hand and guides me onto the court. He picks up the basketball and hands it to me.

"Okay Miss Lewis, show me what you've got."

I bounce the ball a couple of times and dribble around him as I move towards the hoop. I aim, I shoot. The ball hits the side of the hoop, I jump up and down and cheer for myself.

"Err.., it's supposed to go through the hoop," Philip says in bewilderment.

"I know but at least it touched the hoop," I say laughing.

He picks up the ball and throws it to me, "Let's do a little one-on-one. The ground rules are-"

"The rules are there are no rules," I shout and run towards the hoop. I lift the ball over my head and lean backwards in preparation. I feel hands grab hold of me from behind and arms lift me off the ground. Still clutching the ball I turn and look at Philip.

"What are you doing?"

"You said no rules, drop the ball."

"No."

He turns so we are facing the house and not the hoop.

"You don't drop the ball you don't shoot."

"What? Put me down, you're cheating."

"Are you going to drop the ball?"

"No."

His arms tighten around me and I hold the ball away from him and try to wriggle free.

377

"What are you guys doing?"

We both turn.

"Kenny help me! He's cheating, he won't let me go."

"Kay, she said no rules and she 'travelled' with the ball."

"I what?"

"You 'travelled', that's not just a rule that's a no-no."

"What?"

"No rules, oh well," Kenny says and turns away.

"Wait Kenny, don't go!" I start to laugh, "please don't go, don't goooooooh," I sing loudly. Philip starts to laugh. In the distance I see Angela laughing at us. She has a camera in her hand. I watch as she raises it and points it at us.

"Okay I'll drop the ball," I say finally.

*　　*　　*　　*　　*

"-and this is the music room," Philip says. I stand back as Luke walks into the room. I follow him. There is a large piano sitting in the corner of the room, it still has bubble wrap around its legs.

"I didn't know you played?"

"I don't, not really," he takes hold of my hand and leads me towards it. "What do you think?" He asks.

"It is beautiful," I reply.

"Try it," he urges, "the acoustics in this room are fantastic."

I sit down in front of it and he lifts the lid up. I press a few keys and sit back amazed at how well tuned the keys are. Luke walks over to us and takes hold of Philip's hand. I play a song that I have written for my uncle called, 'I Never Knew You Loved Me'. I have the chorus and half of a verse. I hum as I play. I press the final note and look up. Luke claps, Philip stares at me.

"That was great!" Philip says.

"Thank you kind sirs," I say smiling at them.

*　　*　　*　　*　　*

Luke and I walk with him as he shows us the rest of the house.

"This is my room, it doesn't have a shower so I tend to use the one in the gym upstairs. You know how we Americans love to shower."

"Actually I didn't know that," I say

"Didn't you?"

"Nope."

He opens the door and I look inside a large, very manly, plush room. Luke runs in and climbs on the bed. He bounces a little, then climbs back down. We watch as he walks through a door.

"Auntie Billie there's a toilet and bath in here," he calls out, "can you both wait for me please, I need to go wee wee."

Laughing, we wait for him.

"Why don't you put a shower in here?"

"I will one of these days. I travel a lot and each time I get round to doing it something more important comes up," he looks at me, "do you like the house?"

"Yes, it is really nice. It looks big from the outside, but it is really nice and homely inside."

"So you could live here?"

"Yes I could," the words are out before I have time to think.

"That's good to know."

We stand looking at each other, I feel a lightness in my heart and I look away. My eyes fall on something on a table by the door. I pick up one of the leaflets and read it. It is an advert for volunteers for a homeless shelter.

"Do you help the homeless?" I ask.

"Yes, that's the shelter I work at, it's a really nice place."

"I'd love to do something like that. I've always said I'd do it when I had the time. Can I take this with me?"

"Yes of course you can, I can take you down there and introduce you if you want."

"Okay, I'd like that, I-"

"I've finished and I washed my hands with soap," Luke says running towards us.

"Luke let me show you my games room upstairs. You're going to love it."

"A games room, wow," Luke says. Smiling I follow them.

*   *   *   *   *

Salsa music starts and someone taps my shoulder. I turn and smile at Dave standing behind me holding out a hand and dancing.

"You can dance to this?" I ask.

"Yes I can and I hear you can as well."

"Okay then let's go," I say. The music is fast and we soon get into step. I laugh as we dance, I can't believe how good he is. I did a few dance classes at university and I put the steps I learnt there into practice.

When the song ends, I find that I am really sweating.

"Excuse me," Philip says and Dave steps aside. I smile at him and turn to Philip. The music changes tempo and Philip pulls me into his arms as gentle music fills the room and soft lyrics are sung.

"You changed the music?"

"I wanted to hold you," his arms tighten around me.

"Who is this singing?" I ask.

"*Taral,* the song is called 'Don't Let The Feelin' Go Away'."

"I like it," I say resting my head on his shoulder and listening to the lyrics. I feel his hand gently caressing the back of my neck.

"Look," he says softly.

I turn. Kenny, Angela and Danny are dancing. Danny has an arm around each of his parents.

*   *   *   *   *

"Everyone, I just heard yesterday that a young man celebrated his birthday five days ago. Can we all get up and sing happy birthday to him when I bring him in," Philip says.

"Billie?" Sarah whispers.

"I didn't know anything about this."

The lights are turned down and Philip walks to the centre of the room with Luke. Angela walks towards them with a large cake, the light from the eight birthday candles glow. I look at Luke's face, his mouth is opened in astonishment and his eyes are happy and shining. I look at Philip as he smiles at the look on Luke's face.

"Happy birthday to you…," he starts to sing. We all join in.

*   *   *   *   *

I climb into bed, then get back out again. I have forgotten to bring the faxes which George sent earlier, upstairs with me. It has been a long day and I know that I will have a busy one tomorrow. My mobile phone starts to vibrate and I pick it up. I have a text message. I press the button and read the message: *'Sleep well, Love Philip'*, smiling I send him a reply.

Sarah and the children are asleep in the other two rooms, I creep over the noisy floor boards and tip toe down the stairs. I don't bother to put the lights on because I know where I have left the paperwork. I walk into the front room and pick the papers up, I stop dead in my tracks. Sarah is talking on her mobile phone to someone. She talks very quietly, but I can hear her.

"I'll call you tomorrow, take care and be careful Roger."

She listens.

"I will, bye." She turns and almost collides into me as I stand holding the papers.

"What's going on?"

"Billie! I didn't hear you come down. Going on? Nothing," she looks guilty and my heart falls.

"Sarah, you were talking to Roger. The Roger who hits you, who vandalized your home."

"He called me and I didn't want to wake the children or you, so I came downstairs to talk."

"Does he know you are here?"

"No, he doesn't know where we are."

"Sarah?"

She sits down on the chair and looks at her phone.

"He has been phoning me for weeks. I didn't hear from him for a few days and I thought that he had finally got the message and left me alone." She breathes deeply and stares at the phone, "He called me yesterday and said that he had been beaten up and was in hospital. He didn't say who had done it. He said he was sorry and was going into a rehabilitation clinic for drug and alcohol abuse. He phoned me from there just now. He is scared and he thinks that they are after him."

"Who are *they*?" I ask.

"He wouldn't say. He said it's better if I don't know."

She puts her head in her hands and starts to cry. I don't know if she is crying for Roger or for herself. I don't comfort her or say anything. I hand her some tissues.

"It's all a mess Billie. It's all a mess," she blows her nose.

"What is?"

"Me, Roger, Maddy."

"Maddy?"

"Yes poor little Maddy?"

"Why? What has this got to do with Maddy?"

She looks at me with hurt, fear and panic in her eyes.

"Roger is Maddy's father."

CHAPTER 41

Sarah has gone to bed.

I can't sleep. I have looked at the faxes, confirmed the times and now I am pacing up and down in my room. I don't know if Roger is telling the truth. If he is, I don't think that it is the complete truth. What I don't understand is why hasn't Sarah mentioned his phone calls before. 'How can Roger be Maddy's father?' I stop pacing, my thoughts make me feel uncomfortable. I really want to talk to Philip but it is too late to call him. 'Maybe I can dial his number and let it ring a few times, if he doesn't answer, I'll call him tomorrow', I think to myself. I open my bedside drawer and pull out the piece of paper with his home number on it. My eyes are drawn to my Dictaphone, I pick it up and decide to finish listening to the messages instead. I press the play button and listen to Francis Wells talk about tour dates and videos.

Message 6: -

My mobile starts to ring and I stop the Dictaphone and quickly answer it, not wanting to wake the children up.

"Hello," I whisper.

"Hi, I couldn't sleep. I thought I'd let it ring two or three times, if you didn't answer then you were asleep and I'd call first thing in the morning," Philip says.

"Actually I was going to call you and do the same thing!" I say putting the Dictaphone back in the drawer.

"So why didn't you? You don't have to play hard to get, I respected you from day zero," he teases.

"I really was."

He chuckles and I smile.

"Glad you came today?"

"I'm very glad I came, I know stuff about you which I didn't know yesterday."

"So why were you going to call me before I called?" He asks throwing my thoughts off balance as usual.

"I umm…, it's just umm…," I pause.

"You know you can tell me anything don't you?"

I tell him my thoughts.

He tells me to continue with what I am doing, to be supportive, loving and non-judgmental.

*　　*　　*　　*　　*

I watch mesmerized as Kaleidoscope rehearse for the merger party that will take place in two days. Their dance moves and their vocals are top grade. Their performance is unbelievable. They finish their first song. I watch them sing 'Only What You Wanna Hear' and I am really blown away.

"That is going to be a number one," Jamie says.

"What?"

"That is going to be a number one song," he repeats.

"Is it?" I ask trying to sound distracted. I look around the room and catch George's attention. He indicates that everything has been set up and leaves the room, I get ready.

"Jamie, I'm not sure but it looks like George is signalling for you to go out there."

"What for?"

"I don't know, maybe you need to go over there to find out."

"You and George have been acting strange all morning."

He doesn't get up.

"You are just too lazy to go over there and see what he wants."

He stands up, "Me? Lazy?"

"I still don't see any movement in that direction Mr Sanders."

He laughs and walks across the room. The television people rush in. They stand behind a screen. Jamie walks back in, he is frowning.

"Billie, George isn't out there."

"Oh, isn't he?"

"Jamie you're on," the director says.

"Billie, what's going on?"

"What?" I ask and shrug my shoulders.

Jamie walks onto the stage, his music starts and he sings.

The television people start to film him. Everyone who George has kept outside, including the reporters disguised as cleaners, pour into the room to watch. As soon as he finishes singing, the presenter of one of the top music shows walks onto the stage with two discs in his hands. Jamie has a look of utter shock on his face.

"Jamie Sanders I'm here to present you with this award for Best Male Newcomer and this second award for Outstanding Achievement from the 'M' Music Awards."

Everyone cheers and claps. Jamie looks so embarrassed. I have tears in my eyes as I watch him get something which he truly deserves.

"That's not all Jamie," the presenter says, "I have just received confirmation that 'Love Is Not Supposed To Hurt' is the new national number one song." The room erupts with noise. People are clapping, cheering and shouting, I eagerly join in. It is a good thing to be part of a record label that has number one songs. We all know that with so many artists out there, the competition between labels is strong.

I had heard the rumour that Jamie could be number one, but my source wasn't sure because the UK charts company were still counting the number of sales and internet downloads for the week. George and I hug. He hands me a piece of paper, 'Love Is Not Supposed To Hurt' has sold in excess of 300,000 copies in four days. George has written a small note under the number: *'Still selling like hot cakes'*.

"Billie!" Jamie shouts from the stage "I can't believe you didn't tell me, I thought this was to present you with an award." He starts to laugh, probably at the look of total confusion on my face.

"What! Is Billie Lewis here? I have an award for her. Where is she?" The presenter asks. Someone hands him another disc. I literally freeze, no one had said anything to me about this.

"She's right here!" George shouts. I turn in shock, he is standing right behind me smiling. Everyone turns and starts clapping and cheering as he pulls me towards the stage. I can see Jamie laughing and feel people pat me on the back, and say well done as I am pulled past them. I can't believe it. I am still in shock as the presenter hands me a disc for writing the song that has done so well in such a short time.

CHAPTER 42

Most people probably think that when you have a number one song in the charts, and have been given a number of awards, things get easy. They don't, they get harder, the workload almost triples over night. There are so many interviews, parties, charity functions, television shows, radio shows, children's Saturday shows and magazine interviews to do. Yesterday Jamie did three television shows and we had two magazine interviews and an MTV party to attend. The next few days will be just as hectic. As well as doing the shows, we have to work twice as hard to get the album out quickly so that it can utilize some of the momentum of the single. The schedules are becoming tighter and constantly changing. No two days are the same anymore, sometimes it is nice and sometimes it can be daunting.

*   *   *   *   *

My phone rings. I pick up the receiver and hold it against my ear. I glance at my bedside clock. It is four in the morning.

"Wakey wakey the 'City of lights' beckons you Billie."

"What?"

The person laughs, "Billie, it's Charles. You are booked on an emergency flight to France. We just heard that the song is number three in the charts there, and has a chance to be number one if Jamie can do a live performance. They want you both to present an award at a music award ceremony and do a few guest appearances there."

"What? When?"

"Today! Jamie is on his way to your house now. This is good strategy Billie, good strategy," I replace the receiver and stumble out of bed.

My mobile starts to ring, I quickly pick it up and answer it.

"Billie, I'm in a cab and I'm half an hour or so from you. The flight is in two hours," Jamie says, he pauses, "Billie I've just seen something in yesterday's newspaper, it's a disclaimer by XZEL Records regarding Jasmine Peters. Did you see it?"

"No, what does it say?"

"Apparently several artists and song writers have taken legal action against her, they say that she has stolen and sampled their songs without compensating them. XZEL have denied all knowledge of her fraudulent activities and have sacked her."

* * * * *

On our way back from France we stop off in Ireland for a live show. Jamie sings two songs and then we make a mad dash to the airport to catch a flight to Manchester. An artist I know Jamie admires is in the middle of his UK tour and is performing at Manchester's number one spot tonight. I managed to get some front row tickets and backstage passes. I want Jamie to meet him, to see how when success is handled properly, it endures.

The hall is packed. We wait with the rest of the audience for the show to start.

"Ladies and gentlemen give it up, make some noise for the British man of Soul Music!"

* * * * *

Tomorrow is the party of all parties in the music industry. Tomorrow is the merger party, it will be the official merge between Digital Records and McKnight Records/Entertainments. Even though it is being called a merger, McKnight is actually taking over Digital. The new multi-million dollar company (it will now be an American company) will be called McKnight/Digital Records. Philip has been so busy, I haven't seen him these last two days.

Jamie and I will be going to Japan for seven days. The song has done so well over there that dates have changed several times and they want us out there as soon as possible. The date for the release of Jamie's album has moved forward, so we are working on our old and new material. We will present twenty two finished songs of which fourteen will go on the album. We have been given a release date for the album, it is a week after we get back from Japan. I am working on a new song while Jamie, George and Kofi (George's new assistant) are attending a welcome party for a new girl group that has just been signed to the label.

I play a few notes on the keyboard and write some words down. I can hear a melody in my head which is very catchy, it plays over and over again and I know that it will make a good hook. I start the song from the top changing words as I go along. I get to the chorus and add the catchy melody changing the hook slightly, making it 'stick'. I know that if people like the hook, they will like the song. A lot of song writers know that once they have a good hook, they have a good song, one that will 'reel' the listeners in.

*   *   *   *   *

"Hi."

Startled I look up.

"Hi. You look very smart, meetings?"

He nods and loosens his tie, "That song sounds familiar."

"It's the one I played at your house on your new piano. The one I hadn't finished, I've added a few changes to it."

"Is it finished now?"

"Yes, do you want to hear it?"

He nods and sits down.

I play the introduction music and start to sing the words of 'I Never Knew You Loved Me'. I finish singing and play the 'outro' music then stop. I look up at him, "What do you think?"

"That was great. I'm not just saying that Billie, it was really, really good. I didn't know you could sing like that."

Apart from singing when I am teaching Jamie a song, I have never really sang in front of anyone else before.

"Thank you Mr McKnight," I say feeling a little modest.

I get up and walk to my bag where I have left a package, pick up the package tied with a large colourful ribbon and hand it to him.

"What is it?"

"Something I've been carrying around since yesterday."

I watch him undo the ribbon and pull off the wrapping. He opens the box and looks at the record inside.

"I don't believe it, how did you know?" He holds the *Donny Hathaway* vinyl record up and looks at the back.

"Remember some months ago when you took me to Pertonio's. You said you liked to collect old vinyl records, I recall you mentioning that one."

"You remembered?"

"Yes."

"Where did you get it from?"

"I know someone who has a market stall in Notting Hill Gate. He sells old vinyl records. I asked him to keep a look out for me the day after you mentioned it, he got his hands on it a couple of days ago."

"You care about me don't you?"

I look at him not sure if he is asking a question or stating a fact.

"I care about you very much. There's a card in the box."

He rubs his forehead and frowns, "*To Philip, all my love Billie*," he reads. He stares at the card. I can't be sure but he seems a little agitated, "What do you…? How do you…?" He stops and looks past me. I turn as the studio door opens and Kofi walks in.

"Billie we're all going over to the coffee shop across the road, we…, err… Mr McKnight, hello, sorry I didn't realize you were here."

"Hi," Philip says.

"Do you want to come Billie?"

"No thanks. You have a good time."

He smiles and closes the door. I turn to Philip. He is staring at the record in his hand.

"What are you doing for the rest of the day?" He asks. I look at my watch and then check the log book for the studio.

"Someone else will be using this studio soon. I've finished this song, so I am going to go home."

"Come out with me. It's been a few months now 'old school', I must have passed the induction?"

"You have with flying colours. Where do you want to go?"

"The National Gallery and then I'll cook you dinner."

"The National Gallery?" I'm surprised.

He nods.

"Okay but how about I cook you dinner."

"Okay, I just need to make a quick phone call to a friend of mine, then I am all yours."

CHAPTER 43

I listen to Philip talk about Leonardo da Vinci and Bellini as if he studied art history. This is another side of him I never knew existed. We leave the Sainsbury wing of the National Gallery and walk towards the West wing. I look at the different paintings amazed at the gifts that so many people in the past had. He takes my hand and leads me over to a painting by Michelangelo. I listen to Philip talk about the man and the ceiling which he had painted years ago. About how long it had taken him and how dedicated he had been. We look at the other pictures and then make our way to the North wing. I pull him gently over to a picture of Rembrandt and look at the dark colours that make the picture. Philip tells me how he had died without much money and in poor health. I look at some of his other pictures, now worth so much money. Money he probably didn't have in his life time. He takes my hand and we walk to the East wing. At once I notice the vibrant colours and the light hearted pictures. He pulls me towards a picture by Gainsborough. I look at a man standing next to a woman in the picture. There are some dogs in the background. The leaves on the ground indicate autumn to me. We look at the works of Monet and Van Gogh and Philip tells me a little of the history about the artists and the pictures.

"How do you know so much about these paintings and the people who painted them?" I ask.

"I read a little about them at university. I always wanted to come here and see some of these pictures first hand. Look at this one."

I feel my heart fill with warmth as I listen to him. I find myself looking at him and seeing another side of him, one like the others, I like.

*   *   *   *   *

"Excuse me madam, excuse me sir, good-day to you both, we have some poems here which we are asking people who visit the gallery to read for us. They are supposed to be special poems which indicate different things in different people. Will you read one?" A man with an Australian accent asks.

I look at Philip and then at the man who is asking us to read the poem. He is wearing the blue gallery staff blazer.

I shrug, "I don't mind," I say. He hands Philip a piece of paper and Philip holds it out towards me, I look at the words of the poem titled: **'Do You Love Me?** Yes I do'....

"According to the instructions the lady starts the first four lines; written in bold, and then the gentleman, the next four," the man indicates the different sections on the paper.

"Okay since madam doesn't mind, I'm game," Philip says.

I read my section of the title, **"Do You Love Me?"**

Philip reads his section, "Yes I do."

I read:

> *"Is this love?*
> *Is this real?*
> *Can you explain to me*
> *Exactly how you feel?"*

> Philip reads:
> *"I would climb a mountain, sail any sea*
> *I would do anything, please believe me.*
> *My love for you is real and totally true,*
> *There is nothing for you I would not do."*

I hear something in his voice that rings true, I read:
"You say love conquers all
Love makes one strong
Love turns everything right
And sees no wrong."

I look up at Philip, he is staring at me as he says the words on the paper:

"Yes I do say this for I believe it true
I was divinely blessed, the day I met you.
In you I have found the strength to conquer all
My love for you rights all wrongs, big and small."

I am captivated by his presence, by the words he either knows already or has learnt very fast. I look at the paper, at the last verse which I have to read.

"Read it, please," Philip says softly.

"Forgive me my sweet
For questioning you.
You see I have to be sure
that your love is true."

I stare at the paper. I don't look up at him.

"Billie," he says softly. I look up, he reads the final verse.

"My precious my sweet believe me when I say
You are the only lady that has ever made me feel this way.
For the rest of my life, I will love you and be true
Now that you give me your all, this and so much more will I do."

I am breathing but with difficulty as I look at him. I have been fighting something that I know is true. There is no one in the world that I would rather be with, yet a part of me feels unsure about him. '*How do I know for sure God?*' I hear my heart ask.

The man looks at us and smiles.

"Arrr, that was so romantic, and wait for it," he runs his finger down a chart of some sort, "yes I can confirm that you have scored 100%. Congratulations, you are both meant for each other, there is no one else for both of you so I can confidently say, sir, madam, it's love."

"I know, I just want madam to know as well, to be absolutely sure about me," Philip says. His eyes are intense as they search mine.

My breath catches in the back of my throat at his words, my answer.

"I'm sure she knows now Mr McKnight, I ...."

I look from Philip to the man and back at Philip again, something suddenly feels a little rehearsed.

"Do you know each other?" I ask suspiciously.

"Err..., I.., I have never really seen Mr McKnight in a while..., that is before today, umm, I saw him....,"

"What!"

"Here please take a copy each, free of charge," he quickly hands us each a copy of the poem.

"You know him?" I ask the man.

"Do I?"

"You said Mr McKnight"

"Did I?" The man asks.

"Yes you did, twice."

"P.A. man help me out here!" He says with an American accent.

Shocked I turn, Philip is slowly tip-toeing down the steps.

"Hold it right there P.A.," I tell him. He stops and turns around.

He is laughing.

"I didn't tell him to say all that stuff Billie."

"You set this up? You...," he stops laughing and grimaces then starts to run. Laughing I run after him.

* * * * *

I know he is watching my every move as I prepare dinner, and I smile to myself, because I am secretly watching him as well.

"I like that," he says suddenly.

"What?"

"I like the way you clean up as you go."

"That's thanks to my mum."

"It's good."

I smile.

"Ow!" He says as he stands up.

"What is it?"

"My back hurts. It must have happened when you insisted that I piggyback you all the way to the car as a punishment."

"I'm a little confused, are you saying that I'm heavy?"

"No, I'm not saying anything, my back sure is talking loudly though," he pretends to rubs his back and winces dramatically.

Laughing I throw a T-towel at him, he catches it then playfully chases me around the kitchen with it.

The food is almost ready, I watch him open a bottle of wine. He takes two glasses out of the cupboard and pours some wine into one. He holds the glass up to me, I shake my head. I don't feel like drinking wine. He opens the fridge and takes a carton of orange juice out. He pours the juice into the second glass and hands it to me. I smile and thank him.

"When I was little my family and I lived in Hawaii for a while. I used to go over to my maternal grandmother's house a lot. I used to love her food, she made dishes with fish and chicken that were unbelievable. A few years ago she was taken ill and we all went to Hawaii to see her. She thought she was going to die so she started praying for the family and giving out her final blessings and she said something to me. She said that since I was little I loved her food," he smiles and I wait for him to finish, "she prayed that I would be wealthy and generous, that I would always do the right thing in God's Eyes and that I would find true happiness with the right woman. I remember asking her how I would know the right woman. She looked at me and said, *'she will take care of you with her heart and without you asking. When you hold her it will not be about lust, it will be about love'.*" He touches the box containing the record I bought for him.

"Did she die?" I ask.

"No, it was a false alarm. She's still alive, still cooking," I smile, glad that she is alive, because I know he loves her.

"My paternal grandmother died in Nigeria a few years ago. She was half Brazilian and half Nigerian. She was a strong woman, she had so many sayings, like: *'the fact that it is called common sense does not mean it is common to every one'* or *'a successful person does not have two heads, neither do they have two minds about their aspiration. The two things they do have are faith and determination'.* Steve and I would crack up at her 'one liners' like: *'how can one size fit all when all are not one size!'* or *'that's the proud look of a foolish man!.'* I smile. He smiles as he listens.

"She used to call me *Omo mi,* it's Yoruba, it means 'my child'. She would tell me things about life and how to always try and do the right thing. I remember once when she was showing me how to cook something, she said that there was a 'probable' myth which had been going around for a long time. It said: *'the way to a man's heart, is through his stomach'.* She said that the way to a man's heart is through his heart. That if he loves you, he loves you. That there are men who have been happily married for 30, 40, or 50 years to women who cannot boil an egg. She had this twinkle in her eyes as she spoke and I knew there was more to come, so I waited for her to continue. She was adding spices and mixing and tasting what she was cooking and I waited patiently. She looked at me and smiled and said: *'but just in case, I'm going to show you Omo mi, how to capture the heart and the stomach'.* She taught me how to make a lot of Nigerian and Caribbean dishes. My mother and maternal grandmother also taught me how to make a lot of English, Spanish and Italian dishes, between all three of them they made sure I was well balanced. They always said that food must look good as well as taste good," I put the plates and dishes with the food on the table.

"That's Jollof rice, this is just a stew, that is Jerk chicken and these–"

"Those are plantains," he finishes.

"Correct," I say handing him a serving spoon and a plate.

"How do you capture the heart?" Philip asks.

"By being yourself and giving love and respect. Never giving what you would not like to receive."

*   *   *   *   *

He is cold as he sits waiting in his car for the man to leave Billie's house. He has to get the tape in her answer machine, he has to see what she knows. He hopes that she does not know anything. If she had listened to the tape, she would have called the police and questions would be flying. Since there are no police snooping around the hospital, or his home, there is still a chance she has not listened to the tape yet.

There is a sharp tap on his window, startled he jumps. He turns, an old man is standing beside the car. Slowly he winds the window down. The old man's dog leaps at the car door and barks, startling him again and causing him to jerk away from the window. The old man does not restrain the dog. He senses that all is not well with the stranger.

"Excuse me son do you mind moving your car?"

"Is there something wrong?"

"Yes, you are blocking my drive, I can't get my car out."

"I'm sorry," he says. He starts the car and drives down the road. He looks in his rear-view mirror as he drives, and sees the old man staring at his car. He wonders if the man is taking note of his number plate, panicking he increases his speed.

*   *   *   *   *

I feel the first stab of pain and nearly double over at the intensity. I place the plates I have been carrying on the table and sit down.

"Hey I thought you were helping me-? Are you okay?"

"It's just stomach cramps," I say blowing out slowly.

"Stomach cramps? What's wrong? Indigestion?" He crouches in front of me and takes my hand.

"No, I think the painkillers I took earlier are wearing off, I need to take some more. I'll be fine."

"Why are you taking painkillers?"

I look away as another stab of pain rips through my stomach.

"Period pain. I need to get my painkillers," I try to get up.

"Where are they?" He pushes me gently back onto the chair.

"In the cupboard over the sink." I feel tears fill my eyes as the pain gets worse. It is not normally so bad and I know it is because I have been really busy and have not been eating and resting properly. I feel like throwing up, I'm glad

I didn't drink any of the wine. I swallow hard a couple of times and breathe deeply.

"Here," Philip hands me the brown bottle and a glass of water. I uncap the bottle, take two tablets out and quickly swallow them down with the water.

"Is it normally this bad?" He looks worried.

"No. Look I'll tidy up later, I need to go and take a shower and lay down. You don't have to stay."

"I'm not leaving you like this. Go and take your shower, I'll tidy up here. Do you have a hot water bottle?"

I nod and tell him where it is.

I walk down the stairs and into the kitchen. It is tidy. Philip is not there. I turn and walk into the front room. He is watching the television. He looks up and smiles.

"Are you feeling better?" He asks.

"Yes I am, thank you."

He holds up the hot water bottle. I take it and sit down next to him, at a distance. I place the bottle on my stomach.

"Are you nervous?" He asks after a while. Stunned at his perception I look at him but don't answer. "I am," he says.

"You?"

"What, you think that because I'm a man I don't get nervous around you?" He touches my cheek gently. "What I want right now is no way as important as what I want in our future. So...,"

I look at him, "What?"

"I am controlling myself as you seem to do with such ease."

"Do I now?"

"I think that we need to get comfortable with each other."

"Comfortable? How?"

"How about we start by you moving closer to me and me promising that I won't jump on you," a mischievous smile plays on his lips and I smile. I move closer. "After we're hitched the promise is definitely null and void," he says softly, his lips rub gently against my ear. Stunned I move away, I look at his

398

smiling lips and serious eyes. Laughing he pulls me back next to him. "Until then you can relax around me," he says. His eyes are gentle.

We watch an *Abbott and Costello* movie. He places an arm around me, I feel him gently massaging my back. I hear him laugh softly at the film and I smile as I watch the film with him.

"Thank you," I say softly after a while.

"No problem, do you feel better?"

I look at him, "Yes but I meant thank you for umm…"

"I know," he kisses my forehead, "do you need anything?"

"No, I'm okay, thank you," I rest my head on his shoulder.

I open my eyes, it's nearly 7pm. I feel the dull edge of the pain but it is not as bad as it was. Philip is laying on the sofa beside me asleep, my head is on his chest, his arms are holding me and I feel the 'throw' covering us. The television is still on and it throws lights and shadows around the room. I look at Philip and struggle with the lump in my throat, I have never experienced this gentleness and kindness. Even in the early period of my relationship with Wayne when it should have been a familiar feature. I remember a time in the past when I had stomach pains this bad. Wayne came round unexpectedly, he saw another rejection letter for one of my songs and laughed telling me he had told me so. Then he sat using the internet for hours because his had been disconnected. He saw that I wasn't feeling very well but never asked what was wrong or how I was. Yet when he had the slightest headache I was expected to drop everything and take care of him. I shiver slightly at the memory and close my eyes. I feel warm lips kiss my forehead and arms tighten around me.

"Are you okay?"

"Yes," I whisper.

"You were shivering, are you cold?"

"I umm…"

"I'll always take care of you," Philip says softly. He pulls the 'throw' off him a little and over me. He gently rubs my back with one hand and holds me with his other arm. His gentleness and lack of shyness at showing his feelings is fascinating to me and I stare at him. He looks at me and smiles, his eyes are so gentle and caring. Suddenly there is a searing warmth I feel in my chest as I look into his eyes which are inches away from mine, it's my heart, melting!

"If you need me to get you anything Billie just ask."

I nod and close my eyes, I hold my tears of astonishment back.

It's a lie! All men are *not* the same!

*   *   *   *   *

He drives down Billie's road again and parks his car a few houses away from hers. The car is still in front of her house, so he knows the man is still there. He swears softly to himself knowing that he cannot go into her house now. He looks at the keys to her house in his hand. Keys that he had taken from her bag in the hospital, several months ago and duplicated. Angrily he throws the keys into the glove compartment of his car.

CHAPTER 44

My phone rings, it's nearly 11pm, I smile as I reach for it. I know it is Philip phoning to see if I feel better and to tell me that he has gotten home.

"Hello."

"Hi," he says, "how are you feeling?"

"Much better thank you. You're home, right?"

"Right."

"You sound strange, what's wrong?"

"Nothing really, it's just…," an eerie silence flows down the line. I wait for him to continue, "someone hit my car from behind at a set of traffic lights near your house."

I sit up, "Are you okay?"

"I'm fine. Are you okay?"

"Philip, what is it?" I hear a noise downstairs and jump up. "Hold on one second," I walk to the door of my room and listen. I can't hear anything. "Sorry I thought I heard something go on."

"The guy driving apologized then he said something about knowing you and Sarah. Something about working with you at a hospital. He seemed a bit strange. It's as if he was following me from near your house, then hit me on purpose."

"Describe him?" My heart beats faster.

He describes Nigel.

*   *   *   *   *

"Are you okay Sarah?" I ask trying not to unnerve her.

"I'm fine Billie, really. Roger doesn't know where I live."

"What about Nigel?" I ask not telling her what has just happened to Philip.

"Nigel? No, he doesn't know anything about me."

"Roger wouldn't have told him?" I push.

"No, definitely not Billie."

"Please just be careful, I can't tell you not to take Roger's phone calls, but I can tell you to be careful."

"I will, I promise Billie I will."

*   *   *   *   *

I can't sleep. I've phoned Philip twice to make sure he is okay, I have thought about everything, and now I can't sleep. I turn on the television in my room and watch the news. I listen to the headlines half watching the different clips.

"...We have just been informed that the badly decomposed body of a young woman has been found. The woman has not yet been identified. We will report more about this incident when we have more information."

I stare at the television knowing that something is not right. My mobile phone starts to bleep indicating that the battery is low. I go downstairs to get my charger and phone Sarah.

She is fine.

As I replace the receiver I notice that the tape in the answer machine is missing. I look around the room for it. I go to check the front door then the back door, they are both locked. I don't understand.

I sit down in an armchair, rest my head in my hands and pray.

*   *   *   *   *

No one notices the man in a white male nurse's uniform pushing another man in a wheelchair. He smiles as people open doors for him without asking him any questions. His face constantly twitches due to a lack of his medication. He pushes the wheelchair through the final doors. He taps the man in the chair who has been pretending to be asleep. The man gets out of the chair. Together they walk towards the room that they know Roger is in. The man that had been in the chair pulls out a knife and opens the door. Roger is in bed. Quickly he walks over to the bed. He holds the knife up and brings it down with brutal force. He

402

does it again and again. The other man is standing by the door, he can see that something is not right.

"Wait," he says walking over to the bed. He pulls the covers back. Together they look at the pillows on the bed.

*   *   *   *   *

Roger watches them from the small balcony outside the window. He knew they would come. He had anticipated that they would find out when the nurses changed shifts, find out there was a time period between the nurses coming and those going, when anyone could slip in and out. In preparation, during this period for the past two nights he has stayed outside looking into his room from the window. He watches now as they leave the room. The tall man leaves first pushing the empty wheelchair. Nigel takes one more look around the room, he looks at the closed 'barred' window, he takes a couple of steps towards it then abruptly turns and leaves the room.

CHAPTER 45

Excitement has saturated the atmosphere and is condensing in droplets everywhere. Today has finally come, the main event, the merger party. According to a number of magazines it is the party of all parties, the party of the year that signifies the change of modern music and the music industry.

I look at the list of all the things we have to do today. Jamie and I try to postpone the things which can wait. We have gone over the performance times with George and Velma. All the artists signed to both labels pre-merger will perform tonight, both American and British. I notice Jamie fidgeting with the strap of his watch as we sit in the large newly refurbished canteen of our record label.

"Something is wrong, what is it?" I ask.

He looks at me as if he has been caught doing something wrong. Now I know that something is up, "What is it?" I ask again.

"I'm going to ask Trudi to marry me," he quickly says.

"Marry you! That's fantastic Jamie. That's brilliant."

"You think so?"

"Of course I do."

"What about the promotion people? The label?"

"I'll handle them don't worry about that. I'm so happy for you. Trudi is fantastic." I feel the tears form in my eyes, "You will both be so happy. I know you will." We hug each other tightly.

"Excuse me, err..., Billie? Billie Lewis?" I pull away from Jamie and turn to the familiar voice. My mouth falls open as I look at Marvin, the lead guitarist for Nu-Force. "Guys it *is* her, it's Billie," he shouts. I jump up and turn as Leki the drummer, Peterson the percussionist and Ralph the lead male vocalist rush over to us. I hug Marvin and the rest of the guys and we all start to talk at once. I introduce them to Jamie.

"Where is he?" I ask referring to their Manager.

"Billie Lewis, you don't look a day over 17," a booming voice says. I turn and smile as I hug him.

"That means I've aged. You used to say 16 Poppy."

"You're still beautiful. In fact more so, if I were twenty years younger?"

"You'd still be married to your beautiful wife."

"Never a truer word said," he laughs loudly.

We all sit and talk about old times. The things we did, the things we didn't do and the fights we had.

"Jamie, this lady was young when I met her. She had just finished university but she brought ideas to the table that I couldn't believe. They were so bold, yet every single one of them worked. You are very fortunate to have her as your manager."

"I know," Jamie says.

"There was this one time I will never forget. We were looking at the group's image and their songs. Some people were suggesting that Natasha wear a low cut, really sexy, somewhat sleazy outfit. One of the record executives even made a wise-crack about the outfit assisting Natasha's vocals. He said that it would make the songs sound better. Well Billie here wasn't having it. She walks into the meeting with two audio tapes and smacks them on the table and says...," he pauses for effect and places his hand on his waist, *"One of these tapes was done with Natasha wearing the low cut top and 'micro' mini skirt, and the other with her wearing normal clothes. If you can pick out the one with her half naked and tell me it sounds better, then hey Poppy let's go for it."*

I cover my face and laugh as I remember that day.

"Don't laugh," Poppy says wagging a finger at me.

"What happened?" Jamie asks.

"I chose the wrong tape, the executive chose the wrong tape. In fact everyone chose the wrong tape," he starts to laugh and sets everyone else off.

"What are you guys doing here?" I finally ask.

"We are doing a song with 'EZ Flow', one of the rap artists signed to this label."

"I've worked with him. He is really good, I did a couple of choruses for him and his posse about a month ago. I never knew just how hard rap artists work perfecting their art until I worked with him. He is so down to earth and very passionate about rap and 'hard hitting' lyrics. Which song are you doing with him?" I ask.

"He's sampling your old song 'In too Deep', he wants the group to perform live with him tonight. There is talk of the new mix being a big hit," Poppy says.

"That's great! I didn't know anything about this, so where's Natasha?" I ask the question that up till now, no one has hinted there is an answer to. I notice the glances being exchanged and for a while I am taken back to years ago, when she was seeing Wayne behind my back and everyone knew except me.

"Guys it's okay, that was then, this is now. I've tried to talk to her a couple of times, I left messages but she never returned my calls."

"Upstairs waiting in one of the reception rooms," Marvin says.

"Thanks Marvin," I stand up, "I'm going to see her. I'll see you guys later."

I climb up the stairs and go to do something I have not done for nearly four years. I go to talk to my cousin face to face.

*   *   *   *   *

I pause at the door and look at the woman sitting in the armchair thumbing backwards through a magazine. I smile to myself, I do exactly the same. Natasha's mother was forever trying to get us to read a magazine from front to back when we were younger. Apart from the vibrant blonde streaks in her brown hair, she still looks the same. She looks up as I walk in and I see a number of emotions in her eyes. I pick up on the shame and discomfort.

"Hi Natasha."

She stands up, the magazine falls to the ground, she retrieves it.

"Billie! Err.... hi. How are you? You look great."

"I'm good Natasha. How are you?"

"I'm okay. It's been a while. I didn't go downstairs with the others because I thought you wouldn't want to see me."

As I walk towards her, I remember us playing together when we were little. She always wanted to sing and I wanted to write songs for her to sing. I remember us picking fights with Martin and Steve. She used to stand up to them for me. She always used to say that it was her job to look after me because she was older. I cover the remaining distance between us and hug her. I feel her freeze momentarily, then she hugs me back.

After years of silence we talk. I ask her why she hadn't returned my calls or responded to the pleas for a reconciliation that I had made through Steve and Martin. Why she had eventually shut Steve and Martin out.

"I thought you hated me Billie. I thought because of what I had done you wouldn't want me around and I was too ashamed to face Steve and Martin."

"I didn't hate you, I have never hated you. I was hurt. Not so much about Wayne, he made my life miserable. It was the fact that you knew I wrote those songs, and said nothing." I see the shock in her eyes. It looks real.

"Wayne said that you had given him those songs. You never said anything about them to me, so I thought it was true."

"I never gave them to him, he said they were rubbish but took them anyway. I thought you knew and went along with it."

"No I didn't know! Billie I'm so sorry I hurt you. I was jealous of what you had, your gift of writing songs and poems. After the group had its first hit and everyone wanted to know me I started acting stupid and arrogant. I never went to rehearsals or the gym when you said because I thought I knew better than you. I hurt you and I am so sorry." I see tears in her eyes. "I wanted to call you, so many times I picked up the phone to call, but I was too embarrassed. I got pregnant for Wayne, I was desperate to hold on to him. I miscarried. He said I was useless and stupid." Her tears fall and I feel sad for her.

"I didn't know Nat, I'm sorry."

"I'm so sorry I hurt you Billie."

"That's the past. Are you happy now? Are you and Wayne still together?"

"No and no, he never stopped loving you. I was just easy sex. He doesn't respect me like he respects you. Sometimes the whole thing makes me laugh, I thought I could take him and keep him by jumping into bed with him. You never slept with him, and you're the one who he has always wanted, the one he loves and respects." I look at her, the tears continue to roll down her face. "I always make a mess of things, how can anyone love me? No wonder no one does." She speaks the familiar disparaging, negative words of Wayne Campbell. Words that

407

only the Grace of God was able to emancipate me from years ago. I cancel her negative words by speaking positive words of encouragement to her.

"You are my cousin Nat. I love you, I always have. Whether you and Wayne get back together or not, you are still my cousin. I couldn't get rid of you when we were little and you used to go around picking on anyone who was mean to me, and come to think of it, some that weren't."

She smiles.

"I can't get rid of you now Nat. You are still that unique person with a heart full of love that I always looked up to."

"Really?"

"Really," I say.

She nods. She accepts herself.

*   *   *   *   *

"Everyone is talking about this new singer," I say to Jamie who is getting ready for his performance in ten minutes.

"Who?" Jamie asks.

"I'm not sure about the name, he has a current number one single and I'm hearing good things about his album, so he must be good."

Jamie smiles.

"Nervous?" I ask.

"A little," he replies holding up his shaking hands to show me how steady they are.

"Relax, show those people what we've been talking about for nearly two years. You're good. No, I take that back, you're the best. I'll see you at the table later."

"Okay. Thanks boss."

"No problem."

I smile as I walk back to the table. I have noticed that I use Philip's words and expressions more and more. I look around at all the glamorous people here tonight. Four television stations are filming this merger party and there are so many reporters and photographers present.

"Billie!" Charles says walking towards me, he has an arm around his fiancee and a hand on his hips. He opens his jacket and flashes the colourful T-shirt I got for him from New York, "I'm looking hot tonight."

"Sizzling," I say laughing with them.

"Hey beautiful," a husky voice says, "where are you going?" I smile and turn around, Philip is standing behind me.

"Back to my table over there," I say pointing to the middle of the grand room.

"I'm over there," he says and points to a table near the front.

"Ah ha, preferential treatment. That's where all the big shots are, all the 'who's who' in the music world. I think I'm gonna have to have a word with the management."

"I'm listening, or do you want to go somewhere a little bit more quiet?" He asks and moves closer to me.

"Here is fine, I don't mind airing my opinions in public."

"What about your dirty laundry?" He asks and I start to laugh. The atmosphere is full of happiness, the happiness is highly infectious.

*   *   *   *   *

Trudi, Jen, Martin, Steve, Claude, Claude's friend Maxine, Dave and I sit and watch Kaleidoscope perform. They are spectacular. Each time I watch them, they get better and better. They finish their song, wave and bow as the audience clap. A photographer starts to take pictures of us. We smile and pose for him. We apologize and shoo him away as soon as Jamie walks onto the stage. Trudi takes hold of my hand. The music for 'Love Is Not Supposed To Hurt' starts, the audience clap. Jamie sings the song and we all watch with pride. The song finishes and I think that the music for 'Invisible Pain' will start immediately. Instead Jamie starts to talk.

"Ladies and gentlemen, the next song I want to sing is also written by my Manager, Billie Lewis. It is a special song and I am honoured that she has allowed me to record it. I hope the words touch you as much as they did me when I first read them in the recording booth of a studio months ago."

Tears flood into my eyes, the lights are lowered and the music starts. I feel Trudi squeeze my hand. Jen hands me some tissues. I look at them not realizing that my tears have actually fallen. I touch my wet cheeks and quickly take the tissues from her. Apart from Jamie and I, no one here has heard the completed song before and I hold my breath intermittently as Jamie sings, I'm not sure what to expect. He finishes singing the song and I wait. I hear a gentle rumble at first and then the thunder of clapping and cheering. My heart starts to pound.

"Thank you, thank you so much. Ladies and gentlemen the person that put the words together - Billie Lewis. Billie where are you?"

"She's over here," Philip shouts, "spotlight please." He pulls me up and as the spotlight falls on me he moves back.

People start to clap.

I stand there saying, "Thank You," over and over again. Philip places a large bunch of colourful flowers in my hands and kisses me on the cheek.

*   *   *   *   *

I place the flowers down on a table in the ladies room and dab some cold water around my eyes.

"Oh, those are absolutely beautiful," a lady says admiring them. I watch as she touches the petals and smells them. "They remind me of home."

"They are lovely aren't they?" I say smiling at her.

She smiles and looks at her reflection in the mirror. I take the bunch and divide them into two.

"Excuse me, these are for you," I hand her the flowers.

"No I couldn't, really I couldn't," she says.

"It's too late now, I've already divided them. Enjoy them."

"Thank you very much. That's really kind of you."

"That's okay, bye," I leave and walk back to the hall.

Jamie is sitting next to Trudi when I get back to the table.

"I can't believe you did that Jamie Sanders."

"It was Philip's idea as well," he says smiling.

I sit down and watch the rapper 'EZ Flow' perform with Nu-Force. The song still sounds good and the rap enhances it. I notice that Martin and Steve do not say anything about Natasha so I say something.

"I spoke to Nat today and everything is okay."

"Are you sure?" Steve asks.

"Very sure."

"Is she still seeing Wayne?" Martin asks.

"Right now I don't think so, but it doesn't matter, it never really did." They both nod.

The song finishes and we clap.

I feel someone caress my shoulder gently and turn.

"Billie I want you to meet someone," Philip says taking hold of my hand. He helps me up and leads me across the room, "Please don't be nervous."

"Why would I be nervous! Who is it?" I ask as I follow him.

"My mother," he replies.

I almost trip over. Nervously, I follow him to his table.

Angela and Kenny are at the table, I smile at them.

"Mom I want you to meet Billie, Billie this is my mother." The lady turns around, I smile at the lady that I just gave half my flowers to.

"What a nice surprise! It was Billie that gave me these flowers," she points to the flowers on the chair next to her.

"Good evening Mrs McKnight, it's really nice to meet you."

"I've heard so much about you Billie and it is really nice to meet you at last dear."

Philip pulls out a chair for me and I sit down and talk to his mother. She wears gracefulness and humility like a cloak, and as we talk I see something of Philip in her, I see that the 'fruit' has not fallen far from the 'tree'.

CHAPTER 46

We have two hours before we are due at Liam's recording studio to work on the remix of 'Invisible Pain' and 'Mind Games'. Jamie has just finished a photo shoot. I have just finished two interviews; one for a woman's magazine and the other for a poetry magazine. Philip is in Florida on business. Jamie and I have something very important to do now.

*   *   *   *   *

I park the car outside the school and Jamie and I walk through the gates. The play has already started so we walk into the hall quietly and sit at the back. I laugh with the other parents and feel a sense of pride as I watch Luke act the part of shepherd number three in his school's Christmas production. The play ends and the audience of parents, teachers and family friends stand up and clap.

"Aunty Billie! Uncle Jamie!" Luke screeches jumping up and down on the stage. He waves at us, we wave back, people in the hall stare at us. I see the recognition in their eyes and smile. Sarah is sitting in front she waves at us and we wave back. The headmaster of the school walks to the front of the hall and everyone is quiet as he speaks. As soon as he finishes the children rush off the stage to their parents. Luke rushes over to Sarah as Jamie and I walk through the mass of children and parents towards them.

"Excuse me are you Jamie Sanders?" A lady asks.

Jamie nods and the lady smiles then rushes off.

"I was a shepherd. Did you see me?" Luke asks excitedly.

"We saw you, and we heard you say all your lines. Well done Luke," Jamie says ruffling his hair.

"Thanks for coming," Sarah says smiling, "he has been so excited all morning telling everyone 'my adopted godmother her name is auntie Billie and uncle Jamie the singer are coming'," we laugh.

"Excuse me can I have your autograph?" The lady who had rushed off earlier asks. She is holding a piece of paper and a pen. Jamie takes it and writes his name. She hands the paper over to me and I sign it. I notice a lot of the people in the room staring at us now and I tell Jamie quietly that we will have to leave soon.

"How are the other children now Luke, have they stopped picking on you?" I ask.

"All except him," Luke says pointing at a ginger haired little boy, "he picks on everyone." I look at the boy standing with his mother and father. I watch as he pushes the other children that move near him. His parents see him push the other children and actually hit a few, but they say nothing, they actually ignore him.

"I've spoken to his mum, but she's in denial. A lot of the other parents have complained, the teachers say they are watching him," Sarah says shrugging. "I asked Luke if he wanted to keep his distance from him, but he said that he wanted to continue being nice to him, that he didn't mind if he was nasty in return. Luke's Sunday school teacher taught the children not to repay evil for evil. She read 1st Peter chapter 3 verses 8-13 to them a couple of weeks ago and he has really taken that to heart."

"Doing the right thing is not always easy," I say.

"Tell me about it Billie, it really hurts when Luke is being nice and another child treats him badly."

I squeeze her arm gently, "Luke will come out on top, don't worry about it." She nods.

"Children say good-bye to your parents now, it's time to go back to your classrooms," the headmaster says. We watch the children quickly get into their lines. Sarah is helping the children in Luke's class to change their clothes, she walks behind the line with a few other mums. We wave at Luke as he walks back to his classroom and then at Sarah as she follows.

"That's the singer, Jamie Sanders!" Someone says as Jamie and I help to stack the chairs and move them to the back of the hall with the other parents.

"Is that his girlfriend?" Someone asks.

413

"No that's his Manager, she writes his songs and she was in that classy fashion magazine the other day, apparently she has great legs."

"Excuse me, can we have your autographs?" Someone asks just as Jamie and I start to make our way to the door. Our plan of a quick get-away starts to fade as I hear the distinctive voice of the headmaster call out to us to stay and have a cup of coffee. Smiling we turn round.

*　*　*　*　*

My door bell rings and I put the papers I have been looking at for over an hour down. I ask my uncle who I am speaking to on the phone, to hold on while I get up and go to see who is at the door.

"Nice jeans," he says looking at my knee ripped jeans.

"Philip! When did you get back?"

"Just now, I don't feel too good," he leans forward kisses me on the cheek and walks in carrying a small suitcase. He places the suitcase by the stairs and walks towards my front room.

"Err…, what's wrong?" I ask closing the door and following him down the corridor and into my front room.

"It's so cold," he says and sits down, "I was driving home with the heating on high when I just started to feel really cold. I wanted to see you."

"You've just got back from Florida. It's slightly hotter there than it is here in December," I rub his cold hands gently. "Let me finish talking to my uncle and I'll get you something hot to drink. He was going over my accounts with me and we were checking some stocks," I point to my laptop. I pick up the receiver and apologize to Martin's dad. I tell him that I will call him tomorrow and thank him for his help. I smile as Philip picks up the bowl of chopped fruits which I had been eating, and starts to eat them.

"What's this?" He asks looking at a piece of paper.

"A list of charities, Christian events, Church ministries I partner with, and children I help in Africa, South America and Asia."

"Financially?"

"Financially and with my time."

"And this?"

"Standing orders, I was just going over them to make sure that my monthly tithes and offerings are in line with what I earn. When I worked in the hospital I was on the same salary most months, but with what I do now, it varies."

He looks at the list and then at me pensively.

"So you feel under the weather?" I ask taking the list from him and putting it away with my other papers. I close down the windows on my computer, turn it off and place it by the side of the sofa.

"I need some TLC."

"The group?" I ask smiling. "Have you eaten?"

"I got a take out from a pancake place in Florida."

"A take out, you mean a take-away?"

"No, a take out, I took it out of the restaurant."

"A take-away, you took it away from the restaurant," I tease, he laughs softly, lays back on the couch and closes his eyes.

"See, that's why I want to be around you," he mumbles softly.

I go upstairs and get a blanket and some pillows for him. I pull off his shoes and make him comfortable then I make a phone call.

"Philip wake up. You need to eat something."

He opens his eyes and sits up. His eyes are red and I can tell that he hasn't rested properly for some time.

"How are you feeling?"

"Tired."

My door bell rings, I go to answer it.

"Hello Su Lee, he's in the front room, go through," she carries her black bag into the front room. I close the door and follow her. Philip is laying down again.

"Philip, this is Su Lee, she does massages and herbal therapy," he opens one eye and looks at her and then me.

He frowns, "Massage?"

415

"Yes, she will give you a massage, but first you have to have a soak in the bath for about ten minutes to loosen your joints. Trust me you'll feel much better afterwards."

"I'll go and get the bath ready Billie," Su Lee says walking out of the room.

"Massage? Soak in a bath?" Philip asks sceptically.

"She is really good, by the time she has finished and you have something to eat and sleep, you'll feel much better in the morning. You can stay in my spare room," I smile as he nods and reluctantly stands up.

*   *   *   *   *

I knock on the bathroom door, "Philip are you okay?"

"I'm fine, this feels great."

"I'll make you something to eat. Su Lee says that you should come out in about five minutes."

"Okay."

*   *   *   *   *

"Ow, ow, ow, ow," Philip says as Su Lee massages his back.

"Your muscles are too tense," she says, "you need to relax."

I watch as she works for twenty more minutes massaging and pressing muscles as she gets them to relax.

"There, it's all done. Your muscles feel much better."

She packs her oils and creams away in her black bag and I show her out.

"So how do you feel?"

He sits up, bends his neck and twists his back from side to side.

"Actually I feel much better," he sounds surprised.

"She gave me a prescription for you. I can't read her writing. Hold on, I think I can just about make out the letters in this word. R and then E, this looks like an S and this a T. Does that mean anything to you, does it sound familiar?" I ask showing him the paper.

"R.E.S.T," he spells, "Rest?" he says.

"Yes that's the word 'rest'."

* * * * *

After Philip has eaten I take him to the room which he will sleep in. I have changed the sheets and put his suitcase in the room. I hand him a hot water bottle, a glass of water and two Paracetamol tablets. He puts the tablets in his mouth, washes them down with the water, gets into the bed, lays down, curls up and falls asleep almost immediately.

* * * * *

I finish my morning sit ups and stretches and make Philip a cup of tea. I smile as I make it, because I have never actually seen him drink tea. What if he is a morning coffee man? I climb up the stairs with the cup and a fresh hot water bottle. I tap on the door. There is no answer. I push the door open. Philip is still sleeping. I put the cup of tea down on the night table and lift the covers up and feel for the bottle.

"What are you doing?" He asks sleepily, startled I freeze.

"I'm looking for the hot water bottle. I have another one here."

He hands me the cold one and I hand him the hot one.

"Thanks," he says.

"I put a cup of tea on the table there."

"Thanks."

"Are you okay?"

"Much better."

"Do you want something to eat?"

He nods.

* * * * *

417

I walk up the stairs twenty minutes later with a tray of toast, eggs, juice and coffee. I knock on the door and walk in. He is sitting up in the bed. He looks a lot better and I tell him so. I place the tray on the bed next to him.

"Thanks Billie."

"No problem," I say and leave.

*   *   *   *   *

I check on him thirty minutes later. He has eaten everything and is fast asleep. I pick up the tray and place it on the floor then cover him properly with the blanket. I touch his hair, his lips, the dark stubble on his cheeks and look at him. I have never felt this way before!

*   *   *   *   *

My fingers run over the keys of my piano and I hum my thoughts. I stop and write some more words down. I look at all the words I have written in the last three hours. I press the record button on my tape recorder; play the piano and sing the song from top to bottom.

"That's really good, what's it called?" Philip asks.

I turn the tape recorder off and look up at him.

"Sorry, did I wake you with the noise?"

"No. What's it called?" His eyes are intense.

"Your Hand Is On My Heart," I reply and turn back to the piano, "are you hungry?"

"Yes I am. 'Your Hand Is On My Heart'. When did you write it?" He sits down on the stool next to me.

"Today, what would you like to eat?"

"Anything. Who is it about?" He turns and faces me. I feel that he already knows the answer.

"Is pasta and chicken okay?"

"It's fine. Who?"

"You."

He does not say anything and I stare at the words in my book. After a while I turn and look at him. His eyes are closed. I touch his hand and he opens his eyes slowly and takes my hand in his. He looks at me and I feel the words before he says them.

"I love you," he whispers.

CHAPTER 47

"**D**rive carefully," I say.

Philip fastens his seat belt and turns to face me, "I will and don't forget to thank Su Lee for me. I feel like a new man."

"Umm…, you look the same to me."

"Come here."

I bend towards him and we kiss, lightly. I pull back and look at him. His eyes are closed and his lips slightly parted. I feel the familiar flutter in my heart.

"That's it, I'm going to have to go and meet with your parents soon," he jokes, "according to Steve, it's the introduction followed by the engagement and then the wedding."

"You've been speaking to Steve?" I'm surprised.

"I wanted to let him know that my intentions towards you are very honourable. You don't mind do you?"

"No, of course I don't."

"I'm a bit nervous about meeting your parents."

"Trust me, they'll love you," I assure him.

*　　*　　*　　*　　*

I walk back into my house and close the door. The first thing that hits me, is the absence of his presence. The house seems so big and empty. I run up the stairs and into the room that he slept in last night. He has tidied everything up. I look at his shirt laying on the bed and a copy of the USA Today newspaper laying on the bedside table. I pick up his shirt, hold it to my nose and smell it. In my heart I know that he is the one.

*　　*　　*　　*　　*

As soon as Philip walks through his front door he senses that something is not right. Lights are on which shouldn't be and he can hear movement in the kitchen. Cautiously he walks towards the kitchen. He waits just outside the door and listens. He sees a little league baseball bat that belongs to Danny propped against the wall. He picks it up quickly and pushes the kitchen door open then rushes inside.

"Philip!" Sapphire exclaims and stares at the baseball bat.

"What are you doing here?" He asks her.

"I was making you something to eat," she replies indicating the food on the table. He looks around his kitchen, at all the used pots and pans laying around in a mess.

"How did you get in?" Philip asks.

"You gave me a key the last time I stayed here. Is something wrong Philip?"

"Yes Sapphire, something's wrong. Give me the key."

"Why?"

"I don't want this to happen again. I could have hit first and asked questions later. Give me the key, now."

She reaches into the pocket of her skirt, pulls out a key and hands it to him.

"Do you have a copy?"

She hesitates and looks at him.

"Look I don't have time for this, give it to me," he demands. She reaches into her pocket again and pulls out another key. He shakes his head as he looks at the table laden with food. He looks at the tight red top and short skirt she is wearing.

"You're going to have to leave Sapphire."

"Please, I need a place to stay, just for a few nights, my flat is being decorated, I won't be in the way, I promise."

"I'll take you over to your friend's place."

"I don't want to stay there, I want to stay here. I'm trying to be the person you want Philip."

"I don't want you to be the person I want, be the person you want to be," he looks at the food, "I've already eaten, you can have something if you want, but we both can't stay here," he turns to leave.

"Philip wait. I will do anything you want, please don't tell me to go."

"I don't want you to do anything," he pauses feeling the start of a tension headache, "look it's late, so you can stay here one night, and one night only. I'm going to stay at Kenny's tonight."

"Where were you? I have been here since yesterday."

"At a friend's house."

"Friend? Male or female?" She smiles at her attempt of a joke. She thinks she knows him so well.

"Female," he replies.

She stops smiling.

*   *   *   *   *

He bangs on the door. There is no answer. He bangs louder.

"Go away," she says more concerned for the children than herself. She does not want them harmed any more.

"I need help, open the door."

"No, if you don't go I'll call the police."

"I really need help, I wouldn't have come here if I didn't. Please Sarah open the door."

She stands behind the door shaking, "Go away Roger."

He bangs louder.

*   *   *   *   *

He continues to bang on the door.

"Go away!"

"Sapphire, open this door now."

"NO!" she screams.

"What do you think you're doing?"

"LOVING YOU," she shouts.

"This is love? You lock yourself in my bathroom and threaten to take an overdose. What kind of sick love is this?"

"The one that will make you notice."

422

Philip bangs on the door again. She frantically looks around the room. She opens a drawer and puts the pills inside then closes it.

*   *   *   *   *

I feel light headed, happy, full of energy. I look around my bedroom for something to do. Everything is tidy and all my paperwork has been done. The thought of a workout creeps into my mind and I pick up my boxing gloves. I put one on and then remember that I was supposed to put a new string on the second one. I walk over to my bedside table drawer and look for the spare string. I see my Dictaphone and pick it up with the string. I press the rewind button down for a few seconds and then the play button, and put it on the bed, I sit down and thread the string through the glove.

Message 6: I hear shallow breathing and wonder who it is, then, "Billie, it's me. When you get this message please call me. Sarah and…, danger. Call me, it's Chloe. You were right…, I'm sorry I should have listened…" I hear a bone crushing thud and jump up, my heart is beating so fast, I gasp for air. The glove falls to the floor, bounces then rolls across the room. I can't move. I stare at the Dictaphone.

Message 7: There is an airy silence, I can hear someone breathing. The person does not leave a message. I hear a sound and turn around slowly. The room seems to turn with me. I try to control my breathing. 'Move' my brain screams at me. I feel tears flood my eyes and I start to shake. I hear a soft voice say 'Billie I've got you, let's move'. I look around the room, no one is there. I take a deep breath and run down the stairs. I pick up the phone and dial.

"Hello, this is the Metropolitan Police…"

*   *   *   *   *

"I'm asking for the last time, open this door. Let's talk."
"No, just go away Roger. Stop banging."
"I'm going to stay here banging until you open the door."

"That's it, I'm calling the police," she presses the number twice, on her phone. Her finger hovers over the number.

"You do that, call the police, but think, if I found you so can they," he keeps banging loudly on the door. In frustration he tries to push the door in with his shoulder, "They will find you Sarah!"

*　*　*　*　*

Again he pushes the door in with his shoulder. Sapphire is screaming for him to go away. He does not comply. He pushes again and again with his shoulder. The door vibrates. He can see that it is starting to move. He continues pushing. The door gives a final shudder and then flies open.

*　*　*　*　*

Anger gets the better of him and he kicks at the door. The door shudders after two kicks. It flies open on the third kick. He walks into the flat. Sarah is standing against the far wall. He walks towards her, she sinks to the floor, helpless and afraid.

*　*　*　*　*

He grabs her arms and pulls her up, "Did you take any pills?"

She shakes her head and tears pour down her face as she looks at Philip. Sapphire sees the look in his eyes and finally knows as he does, that she needs help.

*　*　*　*　*

My phone rings twice. As I reach for the receiver it stops. I look at it hoping that it is the police phoning back.

It rings again. I pick up the receiver on the second ring.

"Hello is that auntie Billie?"

"Luke! Darling are you okay?"

424

"Can you please come auntie Billie. My mum sounds like she is dying," my heart stops. In the background I hear screams and children crying.

"Luke I'm on my way, go and stay with Nick and Maddy."

"I'm with them now, we are hiding in the back."

I start to shake again and I can feel tears in my eyes, this time I don't freeze. I grab my bag and keys and run out of the house.

I drive down the dark streets not knowing. I don't know if Sarah is dead, I don't know if the children will be hurt. I struggle to stay calm, focus on the roads and draw strength from my previous prayers.

My mobile phone rings and I grab it thinking that it is Luke.

"Hello, Miss Lewis. This is the police, we are outside your house. We received a call from you."

I tell then where I am and where I am going and why. They radio for someone in Sarah's area to get over to her house immediately. I put the phone back on the seat and continue to drive.

*　*　*　*　*

The light has been red for nearly a whole minute. It is late, it is dark why a whole minute.

"Will you change!" I say loudly to the traffic lights as I massage my temple. I can feel panic rise in my chest. I pick up my phone and dial Philip's number.

"Hello," a female voice answers. The light changes and I quickly look at the number I have dialled.

"Hello," the voice says again.

"Err.., hello, my name is Billie, is Philip there please?"

"No, he's taking a shower in his room and we will be having an early night."

"This is an emergency, someone.., has.., can you tell him to-"

"I guess you didn't hear me Billie, I said we are going to bed."

The phone goes dead.

*　*　*　*　*

425

Philip walks into his bedroom.

"What are you doing in here?"

She doesn't answer.

"Was that the phone I heard?"

"It was a wrong number. I thought that maybe if we actually slept together maybe you would change your mind about us."

It is beyond him and he shakes his head.

"I don't want to sleep with you Sapphire. Why do you do this to yourself? What can I say or do to make myself clear? You know what, that's it! I'm taking you to your friend's house tonight, let's go."

"Philip, relax, just have a drink for old time sake, if you want me to go, then I'll go, one last drink." She holds out a glass containing a light brown liquid to him. He looks at it but does not take it from her. In desperation she moves towards him and lifts the glass to his lips knowing that if he drinks a little bit of the fluid heavily laced with Rohypnol; one of the many drugs used in date rape, then he would be hers. Her evil plan: sleep with him and get pregnant, but just in case she doesn't get pregnant tonight, sleep with him and then sleep with someone that looks like him until she gets pregnant, then, pass the baby off as his. She knows Philip is a man of integrity and will stand by her. In her convoluted mind her plan will work, parental testing is not an option that needs to be considered at this point, neither is the fact that Rohypnol has had a hand in an increasing number of mortalities.

He notices something and pushes the glass away, frowning he walks over to the phone. The wire has been pulled out of the wall. He holds it up, looks at her and shakes his head. He pushes the wire back into the socket in the wall and immediately the phone starts to ring.

"Hello."

"Hello?"

"Billie?"

"Philip?"

"Billie did you just call me?"

"I called about five minutes ago, I was told that you were going to have an early night. I must have pressed re-dial by mistake. I'm sorry I called, I don't have time right now."

"Billie what's going on?"

He listens and then puts the receiver down.

"Get your things."

"Philip I…"

"Sapphire, someone could be dead. How selfish do you need to get before you realize. Get your things. I'm going out, I'll drop you on the way with or without them."

* * * * *

I don't bother to stop at the next set of red traffic lights. I slow down, look around, then drive past them. I hear my tyres screech as I come to a stop outside Sarah's flat. An ambulance and a police car are already parked outside. The flashing lights press a panic button in me, I run up the path quickly.

"Excuse me Miss, are you the one that called the police?"

I nod.

"We were told that a little boy called for an ambulance, but we can't get him to open the door."

"The children are hiding at the back, they probably can't hear the bell," I say as I press Sarah's mobile number on my phone. Luke answers the phone on the first ring.

"Luke it's auntie Billie, I'm outside can you come and open the door please darling."

"I'm coming," he says. I catch my breath and choke back my tears as I hear my eight year old adopted godson tell his brother and sister to stay down, keep quiet and wait for him.

Seconds later we hear him pulling things away from the door.

"I'm coming," he keeps saying. I glance at the paramedics and police officers who sympathetically shake their heads.

"Luke son, move back from the door and we will try and push it open now," one of them says.

"Okay"

Two of the men push hard and the door flies opens. I stare in amazement at all the different pieces of furniture that have been used to barricade the door. The paramedics rush in. I grab Luke and hold him to me.

"It's okay auntie Billie, don't cry."

I take a deep breath and pull myself together.

"Where are Nick and Maddy?"

"At the back. Come I'll show you."

The paramedics are in the front room, they have closed the door. I walk with Luke to the back of the flat, to the box room. The door of the room does not have a handle and unless you knew the room was there you wouldn't find it. He presses the door, it springs open.

"Nick, Maddy, auntie Billie is here. You can come out now."

The children come out. They are dressed in their pyjamas.

"Where's mummy?" Maddy asks.

Luke looks at me, he doesn't say anything.

"Maddy, your mummy is not well, some ambulance men are taking care of her. Can you all go and change and I will go and see how your mummy is doing."

They nod and I take them to their room and tell them to wait for me in the room once they have changed. I walk to the front room. I can hear the paramedics talking about how bad it looks and I take a deep breath and push the door to the front room open slowly.

Sarah is laying on the floor in the recovery position. There are bruises on her face but she looks like she is asleep. The paramedics are still talking and I turn and walk towards them not understanding what they are doing behind the sofa. I freeze as I see the blood on the floor. I turn back to Sarah, she is not bleeding. I turn back and move towards them. I stop and stare as one paramedic gives the kiss of life to someone laying on the floor, a man. The other paramedic is pressing the man's chest, giving him CPR.

"Who is that?" I ask.

Professional hands do not stop working, "We don't know love. The lady has a head injury. This man has been stabbed." I look at gloved hands covered in blood pressing the man's chest.

"I think we've got it. Yes, definite pulse, weak but definite."

They stop and get up. I look at the face of the man laying on the floor. The face of Roger Manning-Smith.

*   *   *   *   *

"Can I go now?" I ask.

"We understand that you are tired and you want to be with the children, are you sure you can't remember anything else Miss Lewis?" Inspector Jack Freeman asks.

I shake my head, "I'm positive. I've told you everything I know."

"This person who left the message on your answer machine, Chloe Davenport, have you seen her or heard anything from or about her recently?"

I close my eyes and shiver as I think of the panic in her voice and the loud bone crushing thud I had heard.

"No I haven't," I reply.

"Were you close friends or just work colleagues?"

"Were?" I query.

"Sorry are you?"

"Sort of, we worked in the same department."

He looks at some papers, "Did she..? Does she take drugs?"

"What sort of drugs and why are you asking me?"

He looks at me a little strangely, "I'm sorry, this is probably not the right time."

"Right time for what?"

"We have a file on 'a' Chloe Davenport. It may or may not be the same person. We have your description of what she looks like, so we will work on things and keep you informed."

I nod.

"The children will be staying with you?"

"Yes, I have to go to Japan in a few days, but they will be with my brother," I pause and rub my temple which is now throbbing. "I need to get a nanny to help Steve watch them while I'm away," I say quietly to myself.

"I'll take you to the children, do you need a lift home?"

We stand up.

"Yes, I left my car at Sarah's…," I stop and look away.

"It's okay, we'll get someone to drop your car at home for you tomorrow."

I turn to leave the room, "One last thing Miss Lewis," I turn back to the Inspector, "Chloe Davenport, does she wear unusual jewellery? A red wig?" He asks.

"Jewellery, yes, she always wears a charm bracelet. It has chunky things hanging off it. I have never seen her wear a wig. Why?"

"I just wanted to know."

"Okay."

"Thank you Miss Lewis."

* * * * *

I climb out of the police car and bend to help the children out. The police officer pulls two bags containing the children's clothes and toys out of the boot. I take my house keys out of my bag and lift Maddy into my arms. Nick clings to my leg and Luke stays by my side. We walk up my front path.

"Billie!" I turn to see Philip close the door of his car and walk quickly up the path, "what happened?"

I don't say anything. He takes the key from my hand picks Nick up and walks to my front door.

"Are you okay Miss?" The police officer asks looking at Philip suspiciously.

"Yes thank you, I'm fine. I know him. Thank you for helping me with the bags."

Philip puts Nick down on a chair and walks out of the room. He walks back in carrying the two bags. He puts them on the floor.

430

"Let's get them to bed, then we can talk," he picks Nick up and takes him upstairs. I follow carrying Maddy and holding Luke's hand. We work together and have the children tucked up in bed in twenty minutes.

* * * * *

I stare at the specks floating in front of my eyes and listen to Philip talk on his mobile phone. I sense the urgency in his voice as he talks, but I don't look at him. I hear him tell someone to move Sarah to a private room as soon as possible and to make sure someone stays with her. He stops talking. I don't look at him.

"Billie?"

I don't answer. I don't want to stop watching my safe floating specks, I don't want to come back into a world of stabbing and beatings and defenceless children.

"Billie talk to me."

"What about?" I don't look at him.

"Anything, just talk don't keep it inside and let it do damage, let it out."

"What do you want to hear? I saw a man laying in a pool of blood with a knife in his chest, is that what you want me to talk about? I thought Sarah was dead. Is that what I'm supposed to let out?" I feel the tears falling down my face and I start to shake. Philip stares at me, "I have always looked for good in people. For a little speck of light that would illuminate the darkness in people. I can still hear the message on the answer machine that Chloe left, I can still hear the thud sound, like bone breaking, the police think she may be dead or into drugs. Maybe I could have helped her, maybe if I had taken the time to listen to the things she never said. Roger may die. Sarah is in a coma. Where is the light Philip?"

I feel arms like steel bands hold me as I cry.

"It's okay, it's okay Billie," I hear the sadness in his voice.

431

CHAPTER 48

I take a sip of the tea and sniff. I feel deflated, like a balloon which has suddenly been untied. I am limp because of the lack of air, but relieved, because the knot, the tension has been removed. Philip is sitting opposite me. I smile at him weakly.

"Have you ever watched really good boxers like *Ali* or *Lewis* train with a sparring partner?" He asks.

I shake my head, confused.

"During the training the sparring partner has to give the boxer a good workout. He has to hit him like a real opponent. The boxer has to watch properly to see where the blows are coming from. Each blow aimed at him prepares him for the next, he sees where it comes from. He measures the angle and checks the wind-speed, so he knows when to duck out of the way, when to block it or when to take it.

The blows in life prepare us, so that when 'things happen', and they will, we can stand in faith. And when it comes again, maybe in a different form, shape or size, like the different blows of the sparring partner, we will be prepared and able to deal with it."

I look at him, I understand clearly, I nod.

*　　*　　*　　*　　*

"Inspector Freeman?"

"Miss Lewis. I have just looked in on your friend."

"Is she okay?"

"Concussion and slight delirium the doctor said."

"What about Roger?"

"Mr Manning-Smith? I believe his condition is stable."

"I brought some things for Sarah, I'd better go and see her."

"Can you tell her that I *will* be back." He walks out of the hospital and I walk to the lifts. 'He is not telling me something', I think to myself as I wait for a lift to come.

I knock on the door and walk into the private room that Philip organized yesterday for Sarah. The private nurse is sitting at the foot of her bed and Sarah is laying down and staring at the ceiling.

"Billie," she says weakly.

"I'll go for a short break," the nurse says standing up, "please page me when you want to go and I will come straight back."

"Thanks."

I sit down next to the bed and look at Sarah.

"How are the children?" She asks anxiously.

"They're fine, Philip is looking after them. Jen and Martin are going over to his house later to pick them up and take them out."

"How is Luke?"

'Traumatized, scared, confused' I think, "He's okay," I say.

"I'm sorry for pulling you into this mess that I call my life. I thought if I kept quiet, it wouldn't touch you. That I could protect you from them."

"Who?"

She looks at me, "From Nigel, his partner and the trouble that Roger has got into." I watch as tears fill her eyes, "Billie please be careful, please don't let anything happen to you or Luke."

"Me? Luke? What are you talking about?"

"I can't remember everything but I know it has something to do with this person that Roger knows. He has an evil side to him. You have to be careful, you have a lot of work to do and a lot of people to help…, Luke… you…. part of Joshua generation. Millions of men, women and children.. all over the world loving and serving God not for what they can get….but because they genuinely love Him. Love God… with all their heart,.. soul,.. mind and might…love God. People that seek God's Face not just His Hand. When you seek His Face… He will show you… His Hand. You must be careful Billie, you must be careful." Desperate and agitated she tries to sit up and I gently push her back down.

"You need to rest Sarah, please lay back and rest."

She is on medication to stop her brain swelling. Although she is a little delirious now, the doctor says that her prognosis is good. I look at the monitors, the drip and Sarah. I take her hand, close my eyes and prayerfully thank God that she will survive.

*   *   *   *   *

"I really don't feel up to going to the promotion party Philip."

"What about the movie premier?"

"I'm sorry," I shake my head, "why don't you go?"

He looks at me and I feel that I have hurt him.

"If you don't want to go we can do something else. Martin and Jen want to take the children to some theme park tomorrow, so they're keeping them overnight. Tell me what you want to do."

I shrug.

"How about I introduce you to the people at the homeless shelter? I was going to stop by there later today."

"Okay."

We drive in complete silence. I notice Philip glancing at me from time to time when the car stops at a traffic light or zebra crossing. I don't feel like talking. I listen to the music on the car radio and try to figure out what is going on. I don't want Philip involved in the mess, but I can't walk away from it.

"We're here."

I look up, I hadn't even realized that the car had stopped.

"Okay, where is it?" I ask looking at the buildings for a sign above a door.

He doesn't answer.

I turn, "Philip, what's wrong?"

"I should be asking you that."

"I don't understand, what is it?"

"Since that day, you haven't really been open with me. Is it because Sapphire was at my house?"

"Sapphire! No of course not."

"So why didn't you ask what she was doing there? Why have you not said anything about it?"

"Do you love me?" I ask.

"Yes!"

"Would you go out with someone else behind my back?"

"No!"

"Is there anything going on between you and Sapphire?"

"No!"

"So it's okay then."

"That's it! No tantrum?"

"No. I see the same tenderness in your eyes all the time. No matter how much a person tries to pretend just to get their own way, there comes a time, when the pretence will slip, when you see the real motives behind the facade. You don't have any. You have never pressurized me to do anything I don't want to. Because of that, with you I can be myself, I don't have to pretend and I respect you for that." I stop and smile at the relief I see in his eyes.

"I thought you had assumed that there was something going on, you've been really quiet."

"I didn't assume anything, I just did a little bit of deductive reasoning."

"Deductive reasoning?" His eyes narrow.

"Yes, Sapphire said you were in your room taking a shower. I know that you have to take your showers upstairs in the gym, because you haven't had a shower installed in your room yet. Hence, deductive reasoning."

"So you knew this all along?"

"Yes."

I smile as the corners of his mouth starts to curl, amusement floods his face and then laughter erupts.

"I'm sorry, I've been a little quiet, I've been trying to figure things out with this whole Sarah, Roger, Nigel issue. I have a pen and piece of paper in my head, but every time I look at the paper, it's blank. I don't want you to get caught up in things. I-"

"Hey everything that affects you, affects me, okay?"

I nod and put my arms around his neck. We hold each other, I feel his lips on my forehead and close my eyes. For a while I close out the world as we sit in silence and hold each other.

*   *   *   *   *

Philip shows me around the shelter and introduces me to people along the way. I look in the two sitting rooms, the large clean kitchen and the dining room. I meet some of the volunteers and the manager. I am impressed with the unity, the way everyone works to try and make life just that little bit better for someone else.

*   *   *   *   *

"Mr Grace, I'd like you to meet Billie."

I smile as the elderly man turns around slowly with the aid of his Zimmer-frame and smiles at us.

"Philip, how are you son? So this is Billie? How are you?"

"I am fine thank you sir." I say to the elderly man. I look into his deep brown eyes and see kindness.

"Sir? No one has called me that in a long while," he extends his hand and I shake it. "Come and sit down Billie and tell me about you."

I sit down and Philip goes to talk to some of the other people. I tell Mr Grace about me and he listens and asks questions. I ask him about himself and he tells me.

"Philip is a good man Billie. He comes here often and he is very generous to this shelter, and a number of others. He is someone who has been blessed with a lot and his first line of thought is helping others. His heart is right." I nod in agreement. "Did he take you upstairs to the rooms Billie?"

I shake my head, "No, not yet."

"Get him to do that. It used to be an empty space but as soon as Philip saw it, he got planning permission, got builders in and turned the whole of upstairs into rooms with showers for people like me. So a lot of us that used to sleep on the streets, homeless people, can come here and have a room to stay in with our own shower, our own dignity. While it was all being built, he opened his home to us," he smiles and I smile back, "he has provided conveniences for us that I know he hasn't gotten round to providing for himself. Do you know the importance of doing for others before you do for yourself?" He pauses and I wait for him to continue, "I wish people knew Billie, if only they knew."

I look at Mr Grace, and it suddenly dawns on me, he is telling me something important, something I need to know. He has wisdom in his eyes and I feel a warmth spread through me as I listen....

"Can you get me a glass of water Billie?" He asks after a while.

"Of course," I get up, "can I get you something to eat as well?"

"Have you got any chocolates?" I see the twinkle in his eyes.

"No I haven't but I can see what they have in the kitchen."

"Okay thank you Billie."

"I'll be right back."

As I walk to the kitchen I pass a room. Inside Philip is sitting with two elderly men watching them play draughts. I watch him laughing with them as they dramatize each of their moves. He looks up, smiles at me and holds out his hand. I walk into the room and take hold of his hand. He introduces me to the men playing and then takes me to the kitchen.

"Can Mr Grace eat chocolates?" I ask Philip.

"Yes but a special kind, he has to watch his sugar intake. So what do you think of this place?"

"It's nice."

"I like it. I like helping people who don't feel they have to pay me back."

"How long have you been helping here?"

"Just over a year now."

He opens cupboards and pulls pots and pans out, "I have to help cook dinner for twenty five, can you give me a hand?"

"Of course. Let me just take some water and some fruit to Mr Grace then I'm all yours," I get a glass and fill it with water.

"Fruit? I thought you said he wanted chocolate."

"I know a place where they do some really nice low sugar chocolate 'treats'. I'll get him some tomorrow and bring them round."

"He was right."

"In what way?"

"He said I would fall in love with the right girl."

CHAPTER 49

The last person enters the dark cold room and closes the door separating the people inside from the noisy fancy dress party outside. He locks the door and quickly joins the others.

"I have called this meeting because I am disappointed with your efforts, disappointed with your lack of achievements. I told you to stop this happening. I said do everything and anything to stop this," the leader says, his voice is harsh and angry behind the mask he wears.

"We can only use what we were given. Our tools are not strong enough," a man feebly replies.

"SILIENCE! Do not come to me with excuses. Look for weaknesses. All humans have weaknesses. They are always concerned with the external enemies, wars, fighting, hatred. They never bat an eyelid about the enemy which lives inside them, they leave themselves open, full of weakness. You must strike when they are vulnerable and unprotected."

"Weakness?"

"How many times must I tell you. It starts with a bad, sad or mad thought, an act of un-repentance in the heart. When these things are not checked or corrected it develops, it grows, it pulsates, it festers until it becomes sin. When they are in sin they cannot bear good fruit, gone is the love, joy, peace, patience, kindness, goodness, faithfulness, humility and self-control. Because they choose to do wrong, they have no cover, they don't pray, they are too lazy to read God's Word. They forsake God's Will and revel in their own will. They are outside the boundary, the hedge. Attack then, you don't need an 'open door' to get in, use any available 'cracks' they have or any 'tiny holes'. When they are obedient to God, the door is closed in our faces. We have to make them disobedient, we have to distract them from God's Word, tempt them with lust, money and false power. Keep people ignorant of the ways of God, keep them living in the flesh and not in the Spirit, confuse them.

When they walk in the Spirit we cannot touch them, when they stand on His Word the door into their lives is closed and we have no power over them. So we need to gear up and do whatever it takes to make them give in to sin, this will open the door to us and allow us to cause death, decay and destruction in their lives. Billie Lewis must have a few 'cracks' we can work on."

"It is not that easy with this one sir, she covers herself with prayer, praise and thanksgiving every morning and throughout the day. She wears the Whole armour of God. Her cracks are quickly covered with prayer when she repents. She cannot be touched."

"Then touch someone near to her who is not covered in prayer. Someone who is not as strong as her."

"We have tried, but she covers them in prayer as well, she is always praying for people. She is very altruistic and encourages people to be the same."

"Do something, make this stop! Make the message of joy which she talks about stop. She is telling people, *'the joy of the Lord is their strength'*. That obedience to God brings joy to God, and that gives the obedient person strength from God. I want you to lie, increase fear and decrease faith. Billie and others like her are telling people, *'in God all things are possible'*, that according to 2nd Timothy chapter 1 and verse 7: *'God has not given His people the spirit of fear; but the Spirit of power, and of love and of a sound mind'*. We have to stop this!"

Someone moves forward, fear radiates from his eyes, "We have tried everything," he shudders and stares at the ground. He is afraid of the man in front of him, but that fear is nothing compared to the fear he has felt during his rampage of futile attacks on Billie Lewis and the millions of people like her. The people of God that are protected by His angels and have their eyes fixed on Jesus as they press forward. Nothing in his job description had prepared him for this. He breathes deeply, "She does not 'just' go to church, she pleads the blood of Jesus Christ on herself, family, friends, everything! She does not repeat empty words in her prayers or use long eloquent meaningless words. She knows the redemptive, protective, delivering, healing power of the blood of Jesus Christ. The power of the name of Jesus and the power of the Holy Spirit and uses them effectively. Her prayers are based on God's Word and she lives the Word of God daily. She knows that Jesus is the only way, the truth and the life, and she is telling people, she is contradicting the lies we have spread over the years. She is telling people to read

John Chapter 15, to abide in Jesus. We can't get near her. We can't stop her," his whisper of a voice falters.

Others start to talk, some voice their complaints.

The leader stands up, he raises a hand indicating that all must be silent or pay the price for the lack of silence. He speaks.

"For years we have made people use the Word, the Bible, out of context, we have caused confusion with our lies and false prophets. For example we have told them to resist the devil and he will flee. We have hidden from them the Truth, which is, that it is only when they submit to God like the Bible says, that they can then resist the devil and he will flee. Now she and others like her, are telling people to submit to God, read the Bible and pray. For years we have hidden ourselves in traditions, false religions and culture. Now she is exposing us, making people aware that we exist and telling them how to get rid of us by turning to God, believing in God and living a life of righteousness. She and others are telling the truth, that love fulfills the law, that people are now under Grace, that God so loved the world He gave His only begotten Son.

Think! Do you know what damage will be done to our kingdom of darkness if her songs get out, if her words get out to more people? Our years of hard work will crumble, it will fall like dust and be trampled upon. If her poems are read and understood by more people, we will lose them. She writes about unforgiveness and how it is bad. If people start to forgive others, then walls will be mended and wars stopped. People will not fight each other any more. They will not hate or live and grow in anger. They will not be narcissistic. Then all our work is lost!

She writes about love, that if people do not love their brother who they can see they cannot profess to love God who they cannot see. She writes about doing the right thing, about nobody being a mistake in this world and everybody having a purpose. For years and years we have made people believe they are nobodies, and she writes poems and songs telling them they are not just 'anybody' they are in fact uniquely and wonderfully made, they are 'somebody' and God loves them," he looks around his anger has reached a pinnacle, the atmosphere changes in response.

"If more people in the world read her poems and listen to the words in her songs that tell them to listen to each other, and to love…" He walks slowly around the room. "What will happen to the years of hate we have taught, the

441

racism we have spread, the families we have broken, the children we have stolen, the abuse, the fear, the evil we have spread? All will be lost." He turns around quickly, his anger explodes, some of the unoccupied chairs fly across the room and shatter against the wall.

"THIS IS A BATTLE! DO YOU UNDERSTAND? WE ARE FIGHTING FOR SOULS!" More empty chairs fly across the room.

"God loves His children He wants them saved. Our job is to stop that happening by encouraging people to sin and do what is evil. This way we get their souls. The message that Billie Lewis is spreading has to stop. It must stop. Get people to criticize her work, attack her character, make fun of her and her faith in God. We own most of the newspapers, magazines and radio stations, we control numerous people, use everything to attack her and her work."

"We have tried, something always happens to stop our attacks or make us flee in several different directions. We fall into our own pits, when we attack her we are attacked with our own attacks," a man says.

"TRY OTHER THINGS! USE PEOPLE TO STOP HER!!!"

"We have put people around her to give her bad advice and to demoralize her, she prays and people come who give her the right advice. We have tried to interrupt her prayers, but most of the time she prays in languages we don't understand and we cannot distract her, no matter how hard we try. None of our attacks work. Her protection is greater than our destruction. She is a child of God and our weapons cannot harm her, or any of the people she prays for."

"I have given each and every one of you worldly success quickly. Success that you did not earn, did not work for. Don't give me defeat. I have given you many disguises, use them."

He walks towards a man and points at him. The others watch horrified.

"Do something or lose everything I have given you."

The man starts to stutter, "I..I...I tried to sign… Jamie Sanders to my record label and 'shelf' him, I tried to break up Sanders and Lewis, I tried I really tried-"

"Enough excuses, do something or lose everything!"

Pete Wilson gets up and quickly leaves the room.

*　　*　　*　　*　　*

I pick up the receiver and press some numbers.

"Hello can I speak to Gladys please."

"She is in the middle of a meeting, can I take a message?"

"Yes can you-"

"Hold on, it looks like they are coming out. Who's calling?"

"My name is Billie Lewis."

"Hold on Miss Lewis," I hear voices in the background.

"Billie! Hi, I am hearing good things about you. How are you?"

"I'm good, how are you Gladys?"

"Really good, thanks to God."

"I know you're busy, so I won't beat about the bush. I was told not to do this now, but something happened this morning and I feel that now is a good time for the next song I want to do. I also happened to hear you were looking for a contemporary gospel song which confirms my feelings. I have a song and an idea for the video."

"I'm listening."

"It's a song called 'I Choose You Lord', it will have really big instrumentation, similar to 'the wall of sound', heavy baseline, the works. LeeBeth does the first verse. It is about a young girl asking questions about life and looking for answers. I have the words but we can change some of them. We will use a full choir for the chorus, Jamie still works with a really good choir, consisting mainly of children, that we can use. Jamie does the second verse which is about looking for love, for peace and seeing beyond reality and more than the eyes can ever see. They do the 'bridge' together and then go on to the short third verse. The chorus will be very loud, both vocal and instrumental wise. As I said, I'm thinking a 'full band'. The words for the chorus are:

> *I choose You Lord*
> *Way above everything*
> *I choose You Lord*
> *There isn't a single thing*
> *That I would rather do*
> *Than stand and worship You*

443

(Lower instruments)
Because when all is said and done
When everyone has come and gone
(lower the music even more, bring in drums boom boom boom)
I can stand and I can say (x2 echo)
Each and every daaaaaaaay.....
(Silent seconds, low drums)
I choose You (yes I do, yes I do)
I choose You."

Silence follows. Gladys does not say anything. I wait.

"I just had to sit down Billie before I fell down. No one apart from me, my husband and a Hollywood film writer knows what I am about to tell you. Not even LeeBeth. I got a script from this American film writer. He wants LeeBeth to sing a theme song for this movie which he is going to produce. He has also written a part in the movie for her. The movie is about the choices we make and a follow through of the consequences of these choices. It's about the things we choose to do with our life. It's loosely about three men with derivatives of the same name like Edmond Terrance Goodstone, Ed Terry Stone and Eddy Trent Donstone, something like that. Anyway it follows their lives and the choices they make, good and bad, and the consequences of the choices. When I read it I got goose bumps, I was crying, I was shouting with joy. It has so many twists and turns and really brings to light what Jesus said about the first being 'last' and the last 'first'. It is something I have a passion about, because God knows, before I accepted Jesus Christ as my Lord and saviour I made so many mistakes, so many wrong choices. This movie means a lot to me, it will help a lot of people. Your song is so apt, I love it! Billie I have tears in my eyes. I love it, it fits right in. When can we meet?"

"Tonight?"

"I am cancelling all my meetings for tonight. You bring Jamie, I'll bring LeeBeth. This is fantastic. This could be the theme song Billie. No, this *will* be the THEME SONG!"

CHAPTER 50

I drive down Philip's drive, turn my car around and park it near his garage. I watch him through my rear-view mirror come out of his front door and walk towards my car. I smile as he walks to the left side pauses and then turns around and walks to the right side of the car. He opens the door and I laugh at him.

"Good morning Miss Lewis, remind me again, why it is you drive a left hand drive car in London."

"Good morning Mr McKnight. My reasons ... umm, I like to be different. Then there is the consistency, it's easier for me to drive in America and Nigeria, however, the most salient reason...," I pause, "I got this car cheaper in Europe and it came with the steering wheel on the left hand side," he laughs, kisses me on the cheek and sits back.

"Thanks for giving me a ride in this morning Billie."

"That's okay, have you arranged for someone to come and fix your car?"

"Yes, they're going to come and sort it out later. For some strange reason the brakes felt really weak this morning when I drove it out of the garage. It happened with the jeep a couple of days ago, so I took that in for a service yesterday."

"No one can get in here and tamper with your cars can they?"

"No, why?"

"Are you sure?"

"Absolutely," he frowns and looks at the gates as we drive past them. I notice him looking in my side mirror as the gates close.

"So what's in the bag?" He asks.

"It's a piece of low sugar, low fat, home made chocolate cake for Mr Grace."

He chuckles, "You made it last night?"

"This morning," I say smiling, "he's a really nice man."

* * * * *

"Thank you both for this," Mr Grace says looking into the paper bag and smiling at us.

"It's for after breakfast Mr Grace," I tell him. He pulls his hand reluctantly out of the bag.

Marrebel, a residential worker at the homeless shelter, is making breakfast in the kitchen. She puts her head round the door and says loudly, "After breakfast Mr Grace, I'll be watching you. Philip can you help me get something from on top of the cupboard please."

"Sure," he says and goes to help her.

I smile at Mr Grace.

"This is home made isn't it?"

I nod.

"God bless you Billie, thank you so much for this."

"That's okay and God bless you too," I turn to leave and I feel his hand on my arm.

"Billie, don't believe everything you read in the newspapers. Don't let what you will read in them affect you. Be active, not reactive. Sometimes the only way into our mind is through the things we read or through false evidence appearing real. Whatever you see happening around you, however strange it may seem, don't be alarmed, don't panic!"

I nod not quite understanding his words.

"You read your Bible don't you?"

"Every day."

"You pray?"

"All the time," I reply getting more and more confused.

"Read the 6th chapter of Ephesians verse 11 to the end as soon as you can Billie."

"The Whole armour of God?" I ask.

"Yes, understand this because you will always be successful if you do. *'Greater is He in you Billie than he that is in the world'*."

I nod.

"Philippians chapter 4 verse 13 says-"

"*I can do all things through Christ who gives me strength.*"

"Exactly, you have a mustard seed of faith in you. You have the ability to tell a 'mountain' to move and it will move. Pray always and when the time comes, you will know what to do. Don't let what you read in the newspapers affect you. Go with your heart Billie. Your heart is protected, your opportunities are many."

"I will," I say. My confusion has suddenly disappeared, I search for it in my mind but it has gone. I turn to leave then turn back to him, "When I was younger in Nigeria, an elderly man using a walking stick, walked past my grandmother's house then stopped. I was sitting on the stoop, he turned walked back to me and said that my opportunities were many and that I was to-"

"-you were to take all of your opportunities as they came and make good use of them, not waste them. That if you trust in God, He will show them to you when they come and how to use them properly," he finishes. I smile at him and he smiles back. I don't feel shocked that he knows what was said to me nearly fifteen years ago. Even though he is White and the man who had spoken the words to me originally, was Black, somehow I knew he would know.

"That message has been sent to so many people in the world Billie, yet only a few like you, trust in God and make use of their opportunities," he looks past me and I turn. Philip is waiting by the door.

"I have to go. Goodbye Mr Grace, I'll see you later."

"Goodbye Billie."

Just before I step out of the door, I turn. Mr Grace is standing and looking at me. I lift up my hand and wave; like the elderly man when I was younger, in exactly the same stance, he waves back.

CHAPTER 51

I drop Philip off at the front of the building then drive around the side and into the car park located in the basement of the building.

I think about Mr Grace's words as I wait for the lift. A loud bang startles me and I look around wondering where the noise came from. I feel a sharp harsh unnatural breeze on the side of my face and turn in its direction, goose bumps form on my arms. A dark shadowy figure moves quickly a few feet away. As I stare in the direction it has moved, wondering what it is, papers on the floor start to move around as if carried by a spiral gust of wind. They rise up and fall down, I turn and press the call button of the lift again as I contemplate taking the stairs. The light in the hallway starts to dim then go bright as if struggling to stay alive. I sense a change in the atmosphere, I can hear voices in the distance chanting, but I don't understand the words they are saying. Thoughts flash through my mind, 'Is this a special effect scene in a video?', 'Is this really happening?', 'Am I in someone's dream?' I flush the thoughts out and look at the papers flying wildly around, at the light flashing on and off, and at the dark shadowy figures that now boldly move around. In my mind I take hold of my fear and cast it away. I stand my ground, reach into myself and take hold of some words. *'Greater is He in me than he that is in the world'* and *'God did not give me a spirit of fear but of power, love and a sound mind'.*

"Peace, be still!" A voice in the distance says loudly.

Immediately the papers fall to the ground, the light stops flashing, the voices stop chanting and the shadowy figures disappear. Stunned, I look around me everything has gone back to normal. Instinctively I quickly turn and press the call button of the lift again, the door opens immediately. A man dressed in a black suit and crisp white shirt steps out, he stares at me, I look at him. His eyes are vacant and cold, they do not heat up when he smiles.

"Miss Lewis are you down here?" Someone shouts.

I turn to see one of the security men running towards me.

"Are you okay Miss Lewis?"

"What?"

"I saw you drive in on the security camera then I saw things flying around weirdly and heard some strange voices on one of the other cameras, when you didn't come up in the lift I came down to see if you were okay."

"I ..umm, you *saw* things flying around? You heard?"

"Yes *I* did, but my partner didn't."

I stare at him.

"Did someone come out of that lift?" He asks.

"Yes, a man, he's over there."

"Where?"

I turn, the man in the black suit has gone.

"He was standing there a few seconds ago." I start to panic.

"Come with me, I'll escort you upstairs. Don't panic."

I walk into the studio a few minutes later, I do not fully understand what happened in the car park. The security man made sure I was safe but offered no explanation. I make a mental note to go and talk to him later and thank him for his help.

Jamie, George and George's assistant, Kofi, are in the studio. I look at their faces and know something is wrong. Jamie hands me a couple of the many newspapers laying on the table.

'Jamie Sanders, Ex-Troyston member. All the ingredients of a flash in the pan one hit wonder'. I look at the other papers with varying forms of the same headline, one slightly different catches my eye *'Jamie's Troyston 'wonder' days: threesome sex scandal'*. The story says that Jamie went to a sleazy hotel to look for Dave Pemberton who had missed two rehearsal sessions, he found Dave in bed with two prostitutes. There is nothing in the story to indicate that Jamie was found in bed with two women. I shake my head at the misleading words. Another story catches my eye: *'Jamie's Manager Billie Lewis-Miss hot legs; flogs a dead horse as she aids and abets him?'* I pick the paper up and read the article, I feel my blood start to boil but amazingly I feel calm, I toss the paper aside. Compared to what happened in the basement ten minutes ago, this is a walk in the park. I take charge.

"We are going to have a meeting with A&R and PR, we're going to prove these people wrong," I say calmly pressing numbers on my mobile phone.

*　*　*　*　*

"-this has nothing to do with me or my department, we didn't leak this to the press, I promised Billie we wouldn't do it and we didn't. Anyway you know I follow the rules of public relations and the first one is, if you get wind of something not so good, coming out in the newspapers, and it can't be avoided, do it yourself. Get your story out there first," Charles says vehemently. "I knew nothing about this. But, this deed has been done, now we need to see how we can turn this around and use it positively for Jamie and Billie," he adds. I silently celebrate the absence of the dogmatic man and welcome that of the pragmatic one that Charles has become.

Francis Wells, Velma, Charles, George, Malcolm Wexley from sales, Jamie and I are seated around a large table in a conference room connected to Francis's office. The newspapers are on the table. A few accusations have been made by Malcolm, but so far no answers revealed. I know someone has gone to the Press but I don't know who. As I listen to the denials and accusations, I am reminded of Mr Grace's words this morning. *'Be active not reactive. Don't let what you will read in the papers affect you'*. Philip and I had been the first outsiders in the shelter this morning, the newspapers had not yet been delivered. 'How did he know?' I ask myself. *'Be active not reactive'*, that's it' I think.

"I don't think it has anything to do with Charles or anyone in his department. Can I suggest that we call a press conference for this morning," I say.

"Why?" Francis asks.

"To tell our side."

"Everyone agreed with that?" Francis asks. Everyone except Malcolm says yes. I watch as he rubs the scar on his cheek nervously and constantly avoids eye contact with me, I know who has talked.

"Okay," Francis says and stands up, "keep me in the loop."

*　*　*　*　*

450

I wait for everyone to get up and head towards the door.

"George have you got a minute?" I ask.

"Yep," he turns, walks back to the table and we sit down.

"You're always talking about your contacts and how you know everything in this business because of them."

He nods.

"I need a favour from your contacts."

"I'm listening," he opens a notepad and places it on the table, "imaginary invisible ink," he says holding a pen up. I ask him the questions, he writes them down. I watch as he reads them to himself and then tears the paper out of his notepad and into little pieces. "I'm on to it," he gets up and walks out of the room.

*　　*　　*　　*　　*

I stand just outside the conference room by the large slightly opened doors and look in. I watch Jamie and Charles as they answer the questions. The reporters are hungry, watching them is like watching a group of vultures waiting to pounce on a potential prey. They circle around and around with their questions trying to extract the life out of their prey before they land. Malcolm looks nervous as he sits at the long table with Jamie and Charles.

"Jamie why didn't you want people to know that you were in Troyston?"

"To avoid a media circus, exactly what's happening now," Charles answers.

"Surely *Jamie*, you must have known that the public would find out," the same reporter asks emphasizing clearly whom he wants to answer the question.

"It was never a hidden fact, only one that we chose not to capitalize on," Jamie answers.

"What exactly do you mean by capitalize?"

"Use the success of a big band like Troyston to enhance me."

"Is it true that it was your Manager's idea?-"

"Where is your Manager?-"

"Why isn't she here?-"

The questions pour out, the vultures move in.

"Billie, I got something!" George whispers. He hands me several sheets of paper. "I just heard that some television and radio stations have picked up the story," he adds.

"That's all we need."

"I'll go and see what else I can find out," he says and hands me my jacket.

"Thanks George."

While Jamie and Charles hold the fort securely I read the information George has given me.

*　*　*　*　*

I wait for one of the PR assistants to set up another microphone next to Jamie, as soon as it is ready, I walk into the room. Heads turn and cameras click all around me. I smile confidently and walk towards the reporters. I look at the press identification cards on the reporters and make my way towards the three that I want.

"Mr Waverly! Hello how are you, I'm Billie Lewis and I read your article this morning. *'Flash in the pan one hit wonder'*- what can I say," he looks shocked, I shake his hand.

I turn to a lady and gentleman sitting in the front row and make my way towards them. I can see the look of surprise on Jamie's face.

"Miss Hallen and Mr Rinker how are you both? I'm Billie Lewis and I have *read* a lot about you both. Nice to meet you," I shake their hands. I walk to the long table and sit next to Jamie. I tap my microphone to make sure it is working.

"Hello and thank you all for coming. I am sure that you have heard and understood the reasons why we chose not to advertise Jamie's past, we wanted to get Jamie out there on his own merit. As Jamie said, we didn't want to capitalize on the past success of Troyston," I wait for an outpour of questions, none come, I have taken them by surprise. Now I understand Mr Grace's words - *'be active not reactive'*.

I look around, "I have read a number of the newspapers this morning and two articles really stick out. I read the 'Hallen Rinker' article. I have to admit it

452

wasn't that bad, it lacked clarity and meaning but it wasn't bad. I also saw there was a phone number advertised asking people who know Jamie or myself, to call with any gossip or dirty information about our personal lives," I smile and shake my head as I look at the papers which George had given to me. "I know you have a few questions for me, I also have a few questions. Mr Rinker and Miss Hallen, if you are in the public eye and you are an alcoholic who beats his wife and physically abuses his children, and someone knew this and decided to phone Hallen and Rinker, or any of the other celebrity gossip numbers, would this be acceptable Mr Rinker? Or if someone stole clothes and shoes and was arrested a couple of years ago for that as well as prostitution and someone knew and phoned one of these numbers, I wonder, would that be acceptable for you to print Miss Hallen?" I look at Hallen and Rinker. They are both flushed with embarrassment.

"You see, if I had information like that, this is what I would do with it," I pick up the papers and tear them in half. "I wouldn't, because of money, allow myself to be associated with things like that. Things which could hurt someone unnecessarily and generally bring someone down."

I turn, "Mr Waverly, hi I'm Billie Lewis, we met just now," he looks scared as I smile at him, "I read your story. You said that Jamie has all the makings of a one-hit-wonder and you have compared him and his debut single to, and I quote you: *'Nena - 99 Red Balloons, Boy Meets Girl - Waiting For A Star To Fall, Carl Douglas - Kung Fu Fighting'*. I know these songs, I'm sure when they were hits, no one called the artists, one-hit-wonders at the time. Jamie has only released one song so far, how does he qualify? Talk to me after his album, maybe then I will listen."

Charles picks up a newspaper, "According to your article Mr Waverly, no one from a successful boy band makes it as a solo artist. My question - has anyone told *Ronan Keating* or *Justin Timberlake* this? Maybe you need to go and have a word with them, clear up your confusion," some of the other reporters start to laugh. I smile at Charles who continues, "*Sting, Phil, Luther, Michael, Lionel, Paul, Seal,* I can go on and on with names of singers who were in successful groups and went on to become big successes themselves." Some reporters nod in agreement.

I strike while the iron is hot.

"Does anyone have any questions?"

Silence.

The questions start.

"Billie, what do you want for Jamie? You don't want Troyston mentioned is that it?"

"No that's not it," I breathe deeply, "please don't get me wrong, I'm here because I manage an excellent artist. He was in a band, yes, his band was successful, yes. Now he is a solo artist and a very good one. So, now I would like you to go by what you see him do, not by rumours and sordid manufactured 'phone-in' stories."

"You don't agree with phone-in stories then?"

I don't answer.

"The act of telling people to phone you and paying them for some story which may or may not have an ounce of truth, but is laced with lies, discredits journalism," Charles says. I look at him and he smiles at me.

"Billie, do you have anything to add?"

"I think Jamie and Charles have answered your questions."

"We were told by Pete Wilson that it was your idea to keep Troyston secret Billie, is that true?"

"Yes it is true," I glance at Jamie, he frowns, "when I met Jamie I knew that he had potential and I thought that if we mentioned Troyston, it would take his 'individuality' away from him."

"Is that true?"

"No, of course it's not true, but it's what you want to hear isn't it? Do you want the truth?"

"Yes."

"The truth is, we felt it would be better if Jamie Sanders earned the respect of the fans. He was in Troyston almost four, going on five years ago. He is now a solo artist. He doesn't need his past reputation to succeed in his present or future. The information about Troyston is on the internet, accessible to everyone. We did not hide anything."

"What is going to happen next Billie?"

"Jamie's next single will be released soon, we will be going to Japan in the next few days and 'Love Is Not Supposed To Hurt' is still at number one, so Jamie will be doing a lot of guest appearances."

"What is the name of his next single?"

"We are still waiting for a decision to be finalized."

"Do you think that the current comments in the newspapers will be detrimental to sales?"

"No I don't?" I say.

Malcolm from sales says nothing, he sits staring at a chain on his wrist, rubbing it nervously. He is mumbling something to himself.

"Thank you all for coming. Please check with my department for press releases. Thank you," Charles says.

* * * * *

"Miss Lewis, can we have a word please?" Mr Rinker asks.

I look at him and then Miss Hallen and nod.

We walk to a corner of the room.

"Yes?" I ask.

"Those things that you mentioned, err.., where did you get the information?"

"A phone call and I didn't even have to pay anyone," I reply looking from him to her.

"Every single newspaper does the same thing. That is how papers are sold. I think you are being a bit naive here Miss Lewis," Rinker says.

"Do you? So if I were to, in my naivety, phone your rival newspapers with the information I have about you and they pay me, it would be okay? See unlike you I wouldn't be exaggerating or speculating!"

I see the panic in both their eyes, they start to protest.

"You throw the first stone at others, you criticize others and yet your own lives are full of worse things. Don't worry about me, I'm not going to lower myself to your standards. If any phone calls are made to your rival newspapers, it won't be from me," I say remembering Mr Grace's words again.

"We are doing a good thing here, we expose people, mainly celebrities who get caught doing something. It is newsworthy! It is good that the public know about them. We can't always draw a line, because sometimes there is no line. Sometimes the good guys get caught up in the net with the bad."

"I think you've been reading too many of your own articles and watching too many 'C' list 'shelf stacker' movies. This is real life," I say trying hard but having difficulty understanding the callousness of some media people. "Someone has a drug problem and they're trying to get help or an alcohol problem which they are desperately battling with. They need privacy to mend and stay focused. When you publish things in their vulnerable state, the only option they think they have is to go back into the drugs or the alcohol. So forgive my naivety, but whatever happened to doing the 'right thing', where along the road did it fall off the back of the lorry?"

Silence.

They have no answer.

CHAPTER 52

The music plays and this morning's Press Conference has been temporarily forgotten, blocked out by the excitement in the studio. We are mixing an up-tempo song called 'Not From These Lips', using a vocoda and new voice layering technique. Claude is dancing in a corner of the large studio, he is practicing moves that he will show to the ten dancers waiting downstairs.

Someone knocks on the door, Claude opens it, Charles walks into the room. He looks a little unsure of himself which I find strange.

"Hi all, err, Billie can I have a word with you and Jamie."

"Sure," I say. We follow him outside and shut the door.

"Good news, they have all agreed to kill the story on one condition."

"Kill the story?" I ask.

"They are not going to proceed with it."

I am a little confused, "They have already written it, how can they kill it?" I ask.

"You know like in the case of the butler, where the story was in the papers every day for a while and then not. I know there are no similarities I'm just using it as an example."

Jamie and I nod.

"Well as from tomorrow they will not write anything else about Troyston. Two of the papers have actually agreed to say that we want Jamie to earn his merit as a solo artist, as have *Ronan* and *Justin* and for the fans to assess him as a solo artist. The others will just go back to writing about Jamie Sanders and what he is doing now. The radio and television will follow the papers."

I smile.

"What's the condition?" Jamie asks sceptically.

"They want an exclusive of your next video. Live coverage, release, the works."

"Not possible," I say now understanding the look on his face, "I have promised that to MTV. All morning while every single television station and radio station has been deliberating Jamie's future, while the bookies have been taking bets on him being dropped, MTV have supported him by not talking about his past and encouraging their viewers to look at him and his accomplishments now. They are getting the exclusive of 'Invisible Pain' once the video is done."

"Is there anything else we can give them?" Charles asks.

"We've just finished a song, Claude is going to show the dancers downstairs the moves and I was going to film everything and use it for the video of the song. They can film and take pictures of that."

"Brilliant, Billie, I owe you one. Thanks."

*　　*　　*　　*　　*

The cameramen and reporters are setting up at the back of the dance studio, as the dancers and Jamie rehearse the steps with Claude. Music to the song is booming in the background and Jamie mimes the vocals. I watch Sunita, as usual she is the first to learn the new steps and even goes out of her way to teach the others, when she is supposed to be on a five minute break.

"Okay everyone, we've been at this for nearly two hours, we're going to take it from the top, then have a break and then get down to some real work," I say and signal for my cameraman to start filming. I tell him to film the reporters and cameramen at the back of the hall as well. To move the shots between the dancers, Jamie, Claude and them on my cue. I sit back and watch the monitor as the music begins. We capture different angles, different facial expressions, the sheer energy of the fast steps. At the end everyone is sweating, Jamie looks as if he has poured a bottle of water over his head. I feel the excitement of the song and the energy behind it.

"That was great everyone, well done," I say to the dancers as they take a break. "We are going to Japan in a couple of days, when we get back we will be doing a few shows in England and a few spots in Europe. We definitely want you all with us, that is those of you that can come. Everything will be arranged by George and Kofi."

They all start to talk at once, I hear the excitement in their voices. I listen to the questions they ask and I indicate for George to answer them each time.

"Jamie will be doing a song with LeeBeth, we will need some dancers for the video," George says.

The excited voices grow louder, I pick up a few, "LeeBeth, wow," and some, "I can't believe it, she's really 'popular' as well." I smile at their excitement. I feel it too.

*　　*　　*　　*　　*

On my way home I stop at the security office.

"Excuse me I'm looking for the young man that was working here this morning. He didn't tell me his name. Can I see him please?"

"Young man?" The security officer asks.

"Yes about twenty five or twenty six, brownish hair and grey eyes. He was wearing the same uniform as you have on."

"Sorry Miss there isn't anyone that works in the security section that fits that description."

"He helped me this morning, he said he saw me on your security camera drive into the building and came to help me. I just want to thank him again."

"I've been here since seven this morning and Tom, Carl and Nnamdi are the only other three guys on the day shift this week. We are all over forty, no one fits that description. Another thing, we don't have any security cameras that can see people driving into the building!"

CHAPTER 53

Today is my day off. I don't get many, so I am determined to use it wisely. Jamie is resting because tomorrow afternoon we will make the long trip to Japan. Philip has a number of meetings today and I will see him later. I put the last chocolate chip muffin into the plastic container and close it. I pick up the two large plastic containers, my keys and leave the house.

* * * * *

"My, my, my, Billie what have you got there?" Marrebel asks when I walk into the kitchen with the two large containers. I place the containers on the table.

"It's my day off so I thought that I'd help here."

She looks at me strangely and smiles, "You should be resting but decided to bake cakes and come to help in a homeless shelter?"

"I can rest on the plane tomorrow, you need help. What do you want me to do?"

* * * * *

"This is lovely Marrebel," Mrs Cotterell, the assistant manager says taking another bite of cake.

"I know, I had some earlier, Billie made them this morning."

"She's such a sweet girl isn't she?"

"I know. I just hope that she is 'real'. How does one know?"

"Well, 'real' and fake look alike, fake can disguise itself as 'real', but 'real' like real love always shines through, it is stronger and it lasts. You can tell 'real' from it's 'fruit', it's character. She is 'real'."

"She will need strength," Marrebel says.

"Give her what you can, God is with her."

Marrebel nods as she watches Billie washing the dishes in the kitchen. She silently prays, asking God for discernment. She watches Billie turn her head and smile as she tries to blow some of her hair out of her face. Her hands are covered in lather from the washing up liquid. Billie shakes her head then uses her arm from which soapy water drips, to push her hair back. Her hair falls forward again and she starts to laugh at herself. Marrebel's heart suddenly races and she catches her breath in her throat, she looks at Billie laughing, she sees a bright light illuminating from her, shining and glowing. She blinks and shakes her head. The light has gone leaving behind the answer.

* * * * *

All the lunch things have been washed and I have tidied the kitchen. Marrebel likes everything in order so I make sure that I comply. We will start to make dinner in three hours. I go to find Mr Grace.

"How did it go?" I turn, he is standing behind me.

"How did you know?" I ask.

"Come with me Billie. You have a lot of work to do. A lot of people to help," I follow Mr Grace into the dining room of the homeless shelter. I look around the room which was almost full a few minutes ago, it is now empty, "Sit down Billie, let's talk."

* * * * *

"-What did your grandmother say when you told her you had seen that man?" Mr Grace asks. I think back to that day, it has never faded in my mind.

"She asked me what the man's name was. I told her. It was a Yoruba name, a name from the west of Nigeria. She looked shocked then she called my father to come to the front room. She told him what I had told her. They had a quick discussion by the door, they tried to act calm, but I could see that my dad looked a little scared. I heard him tell my grandmother that maybe I had misheard the man's name because that particular man was dead. My grandmother told him not to panic, she called me into her room, sat me down and said *'people come into*

461

our lives for a reason, to help us fulfill our destiny, our God given purpose'. She made me understand that I would pass through people's lives doing the same thing. That, I was to treat people better than I would treat myself, do things for people and not expect anything in return, put people first and love them regardless of what they do. Not to hate anyone, hate the evil they do because that is the devil working through them, but not hate the person. She said I was to always focus on God, that things may happen to try to un-focus me. I remember her describing a camera lens and telling me how the lens could not focus on two things at the same time. That, if I focused on any problems, then I would not be able to focus on God as well. She said that *'the eyes are like a lamp for the body. If the eyes are focused on God the whole body will be full of light but if the eyes are focused on evil, then the body will be full of darkness'.* She told me to always focus my eyes on God.

She said the greatest power on the face of the earth is love, but people don't know its power. People are being lied to," I stop and look at him.

Mr Grace smiles at me and I feel the warmth in his eyes.

"She taught you well Billie. She was a wise woman. Do you know what your purpose is? What do you have a passion for? What burns in your heart? Why you are here?"

"To help people," I say immediately, "to write words which touch and change lives and make people think about the things they do.

To open people's eyes to the injustice and lack of love in the world. To help people know and understand that there is a better way of life, a life where God needs to be first and then everything else will follow. I have always been drawn to what the apostle Paul said in 1st Corinthians chapter 9 verses 19-22, he said that *'he had become all things to all men in order to get the gospel across to them and save some'.* I personally want to use all I can, and do whatever it takes with my songs and poems to get the gospel out there and reach as many people as possible all over the world."

He nods, "When did you know that?"

"When I was little, I always wanted to help others, I lived in Nigeria and I couldn't understand why some people had so much, and others so little in such a rich country and nothing was being done about it. It's not just there, I have walked along Melrose Place and Rodeo Drive in Los Angeles, California, and seen so much wealth walking along the streets, yet two blocks away people are living out of shopping trolleys and boxes. In London people are sleeping on the streets in winter and others are spending more money on their pets than on another human being. It's like in Paul's letter to the Romans in the Bible, there just seems to be no regard for God, no love for others."

"Romans chapter 1 verses 18-32," he closes his eyes and nods, I wait for him to open them. When he does I feel a stab of pain in my heart at the pain I see in his eyes. "You are right Billie, the greatest power in the world is love. *For God so loved the world that He gave His only begotten Son.* Love conquers all but the enemy doesn't want people to know this, so the people that allow him, are kept in ignorance," he sighs softly. "When a myth is told or a fable, a ghost story or fairytale, people readily believe. The truth of years ago is ignored, the truth that Jesus Christ full of might yet meek, walked on water, calmed the storm, fed the hungry, healed every kind of infirmity and defeated the devil." He smiles suddenly, "Did you read Ephesians, chapter 6 and verse 11?"

I nod, "I read that and then the whole six chapters."

"Do you know who the enemy is?"

"Yes."

"Do you understand that it is not a fight against human beings but against the wicked spiritual forces?"

"Yes."

"Do you know that you have victory already, but it is a daily battle to walk on the right path?"

"Yes this is why we have to pray and wear the whole armour which is talked about in Ephesians," I reply.

"Exactly! We are told to put on the Whole armour of God so that we may be able to stand against the evil tricks of the devil. The belt of truth, the breastplate of righteousness, shoes that we must wear to preach the gospel of peace, the shield of faith, helmet of salvation, sword of the spirit which is the Word of God and at all times we are to pray. This is the Whole armour of God.

People in the world are confused, they know the truth but they are comfortable in their sin so they choose to ignore it. People like you are coming up with the truth in their hearts. A lot of things have happened to try and stop you, but you have kept your faith and trusted in God for everything so the attacks of the enemy have not been successful."

I look at him, "Attacks?"

"Yes Billie, there have been many. Each one aimed at stopping you from fulfilling your destiny. Did you have any car accidents when you were younger?"

"Yes, two."

"Direct attacks," he says. "Subtle attacks will come in the form of people criticizing you, discrediting your poems and your songs or anything you write because the evil in them recognizes the truth you write. The truth that they don't want anyone else to know."

"Why?"

"There are many people who will be touched and changed by the words you write. So you have to keep praying and trusting God and write the words which He gives you. People will always criticize you when you write the truth, but write the truth anyway. What you write will help some people and offend others, not because they are really offended, but because the darkness in them will not leave without a fight."

I nod and try not to show that I am a little scared by his words.

"Do not be afraid Billie, remember always, *'Greater is He in you than he that is in the world'*. There is Power in the blood of Jesus!"

I nod, "Why are there so many bad things, evil things and lies in the world? I see things happening and I know that they are lies and bad, but people can't seem to see it."

"People in the world are comfortable in their little cocoons of problems, hurts, grief and sadness. They want to worry, they want to get angry and hate. They think they don't, but they do. You see they have the power to stop but they don't want to use it. Until they use their power, they continue to live in perverted situations which this world says is normal. The evil one is loose in the world, he only has the ability to touch people who give in to him. Everyone has free will, they can choose to do what is right or what is wrong. When you do something wrong and don't repent, don't ask God for forgiveness, then you open the door for the evil one and his workers to come into your life, you create room for them. They move in, they take up residence in your heart. Right and wrong or evil cannot dwell in the same place. So when people let evil move in, right moves out. The truth which evil does not want people to know is that once you truly repent of the wrong-doing and ask God to forgive you, the evil is driven out and the right can move back in. Once you drive the evil out you must fill your heart with the right things or you leave the door open for evil to return with many other forms of evil and you end up in a worse state."

"Matthew, chapter 12, verses 43-45," I say.

He nods, "The enemy has filled the world with lies. People are slaves to these lies. They are trapped in bondage that only the truth can break."

"Jesus said: *you will know the truth and the truth will set you free. He is the Truth the Way and the Life,"* I say.

"This is why people like you are coming up, to tell the world about the truth of God and about the lies of the enemy. To make them see that it is wrong to love themselves more than the truth, wrong to worship the creation and not the Creator. It is wrong to be in awe of proud, rich or famous people, of local gods and traditions and be in lack of awe of the one true God. People like you will work together and do what Jesus told us to do, spread the truth to everyone in the world. Tell the people that have hardened their hearts and don't want to believe that it is only God that can take their heart of stone away and replace it with a heart of flesh. When they believe, when they trust and when they surrender to Him." He pauses for a second then continues.

"The sheep know the voice of the shepherd and in God's time they will hear and listen. God has started to bless you, but you must know that when God begins to bless you, the enemy will use whatever he can to stop you fulfilling your destiny Billie. The devil will offer you cheap gratification, the pleasures of a brief moment in exchange for the privilege of fulfilling God's will, he will say that his way is easier because spiritual growth doesn't just happen, you have to work at it daily. Don't fall for it. Pray to God for wisdom daily. The Holy Spirit will help you. God will guide you and place the people in your life that will assist you. Those that will help you and those that you will help."

"The security man!" I gasp.

He nods.

My thoughts suddenly fall on Philip.

"You will marry and have beautiful children. They will be children of God, protected and blessed. Good 'fruit' from a good 'tree'."

I feel tears fill my eyes and I smile at him through them.

"How do you feel?"

"Truthfully, blessed that I can do what I'm doing, knowing I am doing what God wants me to do."

"It is well Billie, it is well."

* * * * *

"I've been trying to get her to go home, maybe you can help," I hear Marrebel say. I stop drying the dinner dishes and turn wondering who she is talking to. Philip walks into the kitchen.

"Hi, what are you doing here?"

"I have been called to take you home."

"I've nearly finished, I…"

"Ar ar ar ar," he says taking the towel from my hands, "sit down, I will finish it."

I sit down and watch as he washes his hands then dries and stacks the dishes.

"Have you packed for tomorrow?"

"More or less," I reply.

"You know, 'more or less', 'not really', 'yes and no' are very confusing English expressions. The other day Marrebel said someone was acting 'willy nilly', then she put a plate of food down in front of me and said 'tuck in', I look down at my shirt and she points to the food."

I think about the words, when you think about it they don't really make sense. I start laughing at them, laughing he helps me up.

"Everything's done here, let's go," he says.

* * * * *

Philip parks the car in front of the departure building of Heathrow Airport. I look around thinking that any minute now someone will come along to tell him to move his car. Jamie climbs out of the back, he walks to the boot of the car and opens it.

I turn and look at Philip, "Thanks for the lift."

"No problem," he says and looks at me.

"That's everything," Jamie says closing the boot.

Philip and I climb out of the car.

"Thanks Philip," Jamie says extending his hand.

They shake hands, "All the best," Philip says.

I don't really like goodbyes and I try to make light of the matter, I offer him my hand. He starts to laugh and takes hold of it.

"I'll take care of her Philip," Jamie says. Philip nods. "I'll wait for you inside Billie, bye Philip and thanks for the lift."

"Bye."

I turn to Philip and wrap my arms around his neck, he hugs me.

"So it's true then?" He asks softly.

"What?"

"What they say about women, hugs and tactility."

"It is for me, so remember in the years to come, I need two or three hugs a day, some hand holding and some kisses thrown in for good measure would be nice." I say and snuggle closer. "I'm going to miss you Philip." I feel his arms tighten around me.

"I'm really proud of you Billie, you know that don't you?"

Shocked I pull back and look up at him.

"You know, I dreamt of this success for years, I prayed and prayed that it would happen. Now that it has, it is so much better than what I dreamt. One of the reasons is because of you," I caress his cheek.

He turns his head and kisses the palm of my hand.

"I'll be back in seven days."

"I know you will, it's just.., Billie it's like a part of me is-"

Suddenly a flash goes off and stunned we both turn. Four photographers take more pictures. Philip steps in front of me and holds his hands up.

"Mr McKnight, one more picture please, one more picture of you and Miss Lewis kissing," Philip shakes his head.

"Miss Lewis how-," a microphone is thrust in front of me.

"I said no, gentlemen, now Miss Lewis has a flight to catch so if you don't mind."

He reaches a hand back towards me and I take hold of it. Some security men rush forward and stand between the reporters and us. Philip leans towards me while the security men push the reporters back. In the commotion he kisses the top of my head and tells me to quickly go inside. I squeeze his hand and slip into the airport.

* * * * *

We unfasten our seat belts and sit back. Jamie keeps looking at me and smiling. I don't know if the smile is for me or if he just happens to be smiling every time he looks at me. The flight attendant brings us some magazines and newspapers, Jamie puts his to one side and turns to face me.

"Well?"

"Well what?" I ask.

"Did he? Are you?"

"What Jamie?"

He frowns, "You do know that he loves you?"

I nod as I tread cautiously with my thoughts and wait for him to say what is on his mind.

"I just thought that maybe I'd be hearing the sound of more wedding bells, maybe a joint wedding with Trudi and I."

I smile at the thought but I don't want to get carried along with his euphoria and jump into something too quickly, I....

"You're not listening."

"Sorry."

"What is it?" Jamie asks.

"Nothing, I umm-"

"Philip is a great guy. Did you read the interview he did in the 'Integrity' magazine?"

I shake my head, "No."

"Apparently he rarely does personal interviews, he only did this one to promote a 'half-way' home, for the rehabilitation of young offenders which he supports. It was a really good interview."

"He didn't say anything about it to me."

"I watched this American programme on TV the other day. It was about people having their homes renovated free of charge because they couldn't afford to pay for it. A team of expert builders and interior decorators help people to improve their homes and have a better quality of life. The team also go to third world countries and work with local communities to build houses, schools and churches free of charge. I was sitting there at the end of the programme really moved by how people were helping others when the end credits came on. Guess what? P.A. McKnight is the executive producer of the programme."

"What!" I am stunned.

"For who he is, what he has achieved and the way he behaves to people, there is no doubt Billie, he is a great guy. Besides you and Philip have the 'bond' anyway."

"The 'bond'?" I query.

"The 'bond'," Jamie retorts pouring some more cola into my glass and orange juice into his, "is something that Trudi and I learnt about in one of our pre-marriage counselling classes. It is the thing that people look for, they jump into bed with each other thinking that it will be there. Afterwards they find that it was never there in the first place. People mistake it with sexual chemistry. When that fizzles out, there's nothing left. Things are too casual nowadays, and what happens is that people don't know each other personally, but physically they know about hidden tattoos and warts which no one else does. Relationships have become a valueless game. The man calls the woman when no one else is around and he wants sex. The woman thinks she is a modern woman and can play just as hard. If that was the case, why does she end up feeling used and hurt. People don't bother to find out if they 'bond' with each other first. The 'bond' is unbreakable it is respect, unity, love, right, all rolled into one."

I stare at Jamie not able to hide my admiration.

"Jamie Sanders you never stop amazing me."

"Miss Lewis, Mr Sanders would you like a hot towel?" The stewardess asks.

*   *   *   *   *

"Billie, Billie," the voice pulls me out of my sleep, pulls me away from the words of Mr Grace whom I had been thinking about. I turn and try and get back into my thoughts and into the things which I have to do. "Billie."

I open my eyes Jamie is standing up and looking down at me.

"You need to stretch, we will be landing soon," I frown at him and pull the cover over me. "Up boss lady, come on I told Philip I would look after you," he pulls the cover off me.

I sit up and force my feet into my shoes which feel a size smaller. I get up, pick up my bag and walk to the toilet.

*   *   *   *   *

Twenty minutes later we have cleared Customs, collected our bags and are walking through the arrivals suite. I am walking behind Jamie. He stops suddenly and I walk into him.

"Hey," I say stepping back.

"Sorry. Look over there."

I look in the direction he is pointing. There are about forty or fifty girls holding pictures of Jamie and other artists, standing behind a barrier. The other passengers walk past us, some of them look at us and then at the girls.

"I don't understand this, we're a day early, no one knows we're coming today," I say.

"Excuse me, Mr Sanders? Miss Lewis?" A very smartly dressed Japanese man asks. He is carrying a piece of paper with our names on it.

"Yes."

He stands straight then bows, "My name is Tony Yamamoto, here is my identification card." Jamie looks at the card then hands it to me, I look at it then hand it back to Mr Yamamoto. We bow.

"George said he would call you at the hotel."

My guard lowers at the mention of George's name.

"Why are those girls there Mr Yamamoto?" I ask.

"It is all part of the publicity, they must have been tipped off by someone."

"How long have they been waiting here?" Jamie asks.

"Since morning," he answers, "most of the other artists have used a side exit to avoid them."

I turn to Jamie, "Feeling up to signing some autographs?"

"I was thinking the exact same thing," he says.

"Mr Yamamoto can you come with us in case we need a translator."

"Of course, but please call me Tony, Miss Lewis."

"I will only if you call me Billie."

Smiling he agrees.

*   *   *   *   *

"Jamie, thank you, thank you," I hear over and over again and I am happy Jamie is doing this. Someone taps me on the arm, I look down into large beautiful eyes. She is about eighteen, she says something in her language. I take her book and hand it to Jamie. She taps me again.

"No, no," she says and says something in her language again.

"Tony, please can you help me."

"What is the problem?"

I put my arm around the girl, "She gave me her book and I thought she wanted Jamie to sign it but when I handed it to him she said no. The girl says something to Tony, he says something to her, then he takes the book and opens it. I look at it, Jamie has already signed it. I look at Tony confused.

"She say she read in a magazine that you wrote the song 'Love Is Not Supposed To Hurt'. She say when she read the words of the song then listened to it she was able to get out of a very bad relationship. Now she is back at school and studying to go to higher education," I stare at her. She says some more things to Tony and starts to cry. "She say she thanks God for you and people like you. She also read your poem 'Irrespective' and it made her realize that she is not

471

unworthy of God's love because of all the bad things she had done in the past. That God loves her."

I feel my eyes fill with tears and I smile at her. I take her book, write a message in it and then sign it.

CHAPTER 54

Tokyo located in Japan.

Japan known as the land of the rising sun.

You hear and read so many things about this magnificent maze of a city. It has been described as many cities within a city, as an exciting collection of cultures incorporated yet distinct. It is a place you can describe only after you experience it first hand. I sit back in the car driving us towards the hotel and experience it; the game capital of the world. Tall magnificent buildings, fast cars, bright lights, advertisement boards, brightly lit signs written in Japanese and English capture my eyes as we drive through the city. The streets are teeming with people of various ages dressed in different forms of traditional, English and brightly coloured innovative personalized attire.

"I have to take you to the theatre later for rehearsals," Tony says. I turn and smile at him. He hands us backstage passes and a small mobile phone each for the duration of our stay. He shows us how to use them. They are so light and have so many features. I learn the basics but do not bother, unlike Jamie, to go into detail about the finer features. I leave them to talk about photo and video messages and all the other hi-tech stuff while I look out of the window again, at the tall buildings, the people and the cars we pass.

* * * * *

Tako, one of the hotel porters, escorts us to our rooms. We walk behind him along the plush carpet which lines the corridor of the fourth floor. He stops in front of a door, puts the bags down and inserts a card into the door. We follow him inside. Our rooms are a luxurious three bedroom suite. I look around and take in the sheer luxury of everything. All of the bedrooms have en-suite bathrooms. The sitting room is large and full of colourful flowers. There is a card on the table next to a large vase of flowers. I pick it up and read it.

'Missing you already. Love Philip xxx'.

"Dum dum de dum," Jamie hums over my shoulder. Smiling I put the card in my bag.

"Get some rest."

"Yes ma'am," he walks to his room. "Dum dum de dum," he hums again loudly.

*   *   *   *   *

I finish applying my make-up and pick up my bag. I can hear Jamie talking on the phone in the sitting room. He is talking to Trudi, his voice is soft and I hear the word 'darling', used as it should be, an endearment and not a tool of conde-scension. I walk into the room, Jamie smiles and holds up his hand indicating that I give him five minutes. He has showered and changed, he looks really nice. I put my bag down and go to look out of the window. The phone on the table starts to ring.

"Hello."

"Hi, miss me?" Philip asks.

My heart warms at his voice and I smile, "Hi, yes."

"How's everything going?"

"Good, the flight was okay, the hotel suite is great."

"Have you met Tony Yamamoto?"

"Yes, he's really nice."

"He's a good guy. He'll look after you," he sounds confident.

"You've already told him to do that haven't you?"

"Busted," he says and laughs.

I laugh with him.

*   *   *   *   *

The first concert is today and we have been at the theatre for hours, sound checks have been done, now we are going through the dance routine. Tony is constantly at my side as I get everything set up. The dancers watch the film I recorded with Claude in England, we have decided that Jamie will perform 'Not

474

From These Lips' tonight. Most of the dancers speak English, but I do not take it for granted, that all of them do and I ask Tony to help me go over things to make sure everything is clear. They practice the steps and after an hour they have mastered them. I search my medium sized vanity case which holds all the DATs, videos, and audio tapes and pull out the video of 'Love Is Not Supposed To Hurt' and slot it into the machine. I explain that I want to bring the video onto the stage in the form of mini slots. With Tony's help, in less than three hours everything is set to go. I have a finale which I want to do and I explain to the dancers what it is.

* * * * *

In thirty minutes the first show will start. I can literally feel the tension in the air as the three other English and two American groups wait behind stage with us. I watch as egos come out and show off. There is a lot of food and drink on a table by the far wall. The food has been ignored but a number of the artists have already reached full capacity on the drink.

I look out into the theatre, the audience are pouring in. Suddenly from some-where backstage, down the long corridor with all the dressing rooms we hear screaming. Nearly everyone behind stage rushes in the direction, Jamie and I take a few steps and stop as two Japanese girls fly out of a room and fall onto the floor, fighting and screaming at each other in Japanese and English. They start to rip at each others clothes, some of the male artists start shouting words of encouragement, goading them on. A frantic assistant organizer tries to get past the men looking at the scene. I watch as she tries to push through and is given the famous, 'don't you know who I am?', 'don't touch me' look. Some of the other organizers rush towards the crowd of artists and try and get them back towards the stage. The fighting girls are literally carried away by two 'Sumo-wrestler' like, security men.

"Come on please, nothing more to see," Mr Shimosato says. He is the person in charge, I notice that the artists who know who he is move quickly.

Music starts to pour out of the speakers. We were told this morning that this means filming has started. The first act goes on in ten minutes. Some dancers are on the stage entertaining the audience. Some photographers are backstage taking pictures of everyone. Tony walks towards us with a film crew and two reporters. He introduces us and they take our pictures and ask us questions. We answer one question after another. I watch the first act walk towards the stage. The four girls and two boys are very popular and the audience cheer and clap as they walk onto the stage. From where Jamie and I are standing, it is as if the flashes from the hundreds of cameras have a strobe light effect.

"Thank you Jamie, thank you Billie," the fourth set of reporters say, they bow and we bow back. An American group are on next. They are ushered towards the stage. As the group walk past us the drummer winks at me. I look away. He has been winking at me all day and I am beginning to think that there is something wrong with his eye. Tony goes to get the dancers.

I turn to Jamie, "This is it. This is the reason for all the hard work I've put you through."

He nods.

The dancers walk towards us as the American group start their second song. I tell them to gather round and I talk to them. I encourage them, I tell them to do their best, and as long as they know it is the best they are doing, it will be good enough for me.

"Group hug," I say in Japanese. We all move forward and hug.

Silently I pray that everything will go well.

"From London we bring you Jamie Sanders"

I hold my breath as Jamie squeezes my hand then rushes onto the stage, the dancers follow slowly behind him. They take their positions. The audience scream, clap, shout, and cheer as Jamie stands on the stage, it's electrifying. The music starts and the noise gets louder. As soon as Jamie starts to ad-lib the noise dies. Everyone listens. From where Tony and I stand we can see the dancers and Jamie clearly. He starts to sing the first verse of 'Not From These Lips'. It is a new song and the audience are not familiar with it, but I can see from their faces they like it. They dance along to the song as Jamie and the dancers give an excellent performance.

"He's good," Tony says.

"I know," I concur.

The music stops and everyone starts to clap. The music for 'Love Is Not Supposed To Hurt' starts, everyone is quiet. Jamie looks around then does something he has not rehearsed, something that is so him. He walks to the edge of the stage and touches the hands of the people. Everyone is silent as he starts to sing right next to them. They sing the chorus with him. The dancers stick to their rehearsed steps. As soon as the song ends the audience erupts with clapping and cheering.

"Thank you, thank you," Jamie says in Japanese as he waves.

The music for 'Invisible Pain' starts and Jamie moves to the side of the stage so that the dancers can act out scenes for the song. The dancers have changed clothes in stages so it was not noticeable.

A man and woman walk to the centre arguing in Japanese, the spotlight falls on them. Initially I had wanted them to speak in English but after a few attempts, I decided the message would be clearer in Japanese. The man says some really nasty things to the woman, he constantly belittles her, she falls to the ground crying. The next scene: a group of people all dressed in different school uniforms walk onto the stage, the spotlight is taken off the couple and falls on them. Jamie starts to sing the first verse of the song. In the group a smaller person is being bullied. The smaller person is a woman dressed up as a boy and wearing glasses. People in the group are calling the boy names and pushing him. He is crying and walking in front of them while they prod him with a stick. As Jamie starts to sing the chorus, the actors freeze. I hold my breath, my heart is pounding and I am sure Tony can hear it. Jamie ends the chorus and starts the second verse. The dancers silently continue to act as he sings. When the song finishes the audience erupt. It is amazing to watch. Jamie and the dancers walk off stage amid shouts for him to come back on. He obliges, taking the dancers with him. They wave and thank the audience then they run off the stage.

I hug him. I smile as I feel him shaking. 'This is bigger than both of us' I think to myself. 'Much bigger'.

*   *   *   *   *

I really feel like leaving this party. After the long day I have had, I am tired. The room, situated on the 52nd floor of this very popular hotel, is packed with singers, actors and supermodels. The supermodels are here for a special fashion show. I look at my watch and then Jamie.

"I'm tired," he mouths.

"Ten minutes," I mouth back and yawn.

A tray laden with sushi is placed on our table.

*   *   *   *   *

Sapphire looks at the curly brown luxuriate hair, okay body and natural beauty, that is Billie Lewis. She looks at the person Philip has passed her up for and with anger burning in her she looks for a way of getting back at Philip. She sees a drummer she knows and beckons him over. She hands him a pill and tells him to put it in a drink. She promises him a reward. He looks at her long legs and her low cut dress and quickly goes to do what she asks.

*   *   *   *   *

"Billie, how's it going? Can I get you another drink? Is it cola?" Before I can answer he picks my half full glass off the table and whisks it away.

"Hello mine is a lemonade," Jamie says feebly to the man's retreating back.

*   *   *   *   *

He gets the drink and puts the pill in it. Nervously he shakes the drink to make sure that the pill has dissolved. The drink is dark so he holds the glass up to the light to be sure.

"Looking for something?" A man standing next to him asks.

"Err.., no," he replies and nervously walks with the drink back to the table.

*   *   *   *   *

He places the drink in front of me, I look at the drink and then him. He looks nervous and I frown.

478

"Thank you," I say. He stands there watching me. I don't touch the drink.

"Drink up," he says and walks away.

"Billie! I thought it was you," I turn, Simon, Angela's brother is standing behind my chair. Smiling I stand up and take hold of both of his hands that are extended out to me.

"Hi! How are you?"

"Good, much better."

"You remember Jamie?"

"Of course, Jamie how are you? I caught your performance. It was brilliant."

"Thank you," Jamie says, they shake hands.

"Sit down, join us, we're going to leave soon but please sit down a while," I say.

"I'll be back soon, I'm going to phone Trudi," Jamie says standing up.

Simon sits down and I smile at him. He looks much better than the last time I saw him which was at Danny's birthday party.

"What are you doing here?"

"Working, I work for an IT company in America with branches in Japan. I come here once a month. It's good to see you again Billie. How's Philip?"

"He's well. I spoke to him today."

"Are you going to drink that?" He asks looking at the glass.

"No. The guy who brought it looks a bit..," I lift a hand up and rock it from side to side, "I don't trust him."

"Good, you are right not to trust him, I saw him put something in it." Simon says moving the drink away from me.

I freeze and stare at him, "He put something in my drink?"

"I saw him talking to Sapphire earlier, next he came up to you and took your glass, got a drink, dropped a pill in it and started shaking it about and looking at it under the light. I know that Sapphire is an old friend of Philip's, so I can only suspect she gave the guy whatever it was that he put in it."

"Where is Sapphire?" I ask curious to see the person I had spoken to on the phone.

479

"Over there in the blue dress," he says. I turn and look at the tall blond haired lady in a very bust hugging, low cut, short blue dress. The very same person who has bumped into me twice tonight and given me a number of really nasty looks. Now I know why. I ignore the annoyance which I feel and look at my drink.

"Too much flesh can put you off," Simon says. He picks my glass up and hands it to a passing waiter. He says something to him in Japanese.

"He is going to get rid of that and not give it to someone else?"

Simon raises his eyebrows, "Maybe we should tell him to give it to Sapphire."

"No, that would make us just like her."

"You think so?"

"I know so," I reply.

I look towards the door and wonder what is keeping Jamie.

"You remember the day we met at Philip's house Billie?"

"Yes."

"That..., that was a really bad period in my life," I nod understandingly, "I was on the verge of killing myself that day." I stop nodding. He smiles, "For months nothing worked. I was a walking mass of pain and I couldn't handle things anymore. My life was a dark pit and I couldn't see any light at the end of the tunnel. No one understood what was happening in my head, even I didn't understand. It was a mess. Poor Angela, she tried everything. When I saw you, saw the resemblance I couldn't believe it. I touched your face and you pushed me away," he has a distant look in his eyes. "I don't know if this makes sense to you or not, but what you said that day, was like a light in my darkness," he looks at me. "You were in the garden with Angela when Philip came into the kitchen, he asked me if I was okay, if I had eaten something. He said something about having made something special for me on the grill, something he knew I liked, a 'Chilli corn-dog'. Then it hit me, like a bolt of lightning, what you had said about people not knowing how to take care of your heart, so they do what they know, they try to take care of your body."

I nod.

"I lost it Billie, I completely broke down, I started crying. Philip was shocked, I was shocked. The last time I had cried was the day she died. I let go

480

of a lot of anger that day and made room inside me for comfort. The light gets brighter each day," he rubs his eyes and smiles.

It is a sad smile but one full of potential.

* * * * *

"Nice hotel," Simon says as he bends and looks out of the car window, "five star, impressive."

"Where are you staying?" I ask.

"In the four and a half star hotel around the corner," he replies. Jamie and I laugh. Simon smiles. He *has* really changed.

"Thanks for the lift Simon," Jamie says as he opens the door and climbs out. He opens the front door for me. I thank Simon and climb out.

"Billie, you did well back there."

"What?" I bend down and look at him.

"You could have gone over to Sapphire and kicked arse tonight, but you obeyed a higher order. A much better one."

I continue to look at him.

"Love your enemies and do good to those who hate you. Hate can't harm you when you love Billie! Goodnight."

CHAPTER 55

"**I**give you ground breaking information and you say you can't print it. What kind of gossip column are you running Rinker?"

"The truth is, we have a gagging order if you can call it that, on these two, they've agreed to give us some exclusives and in return we have to write about what we see now, not about their past."

"I guess I'm going to have to go somewhere else, I just thought I'd offer Rinker and Hallen the first pop, that's all."

"I think you'll find that most of the major newspapers are doing the same," Rinker says.

"I have some information on what really happened to Ben Edwardson and why Jamie Sanders took the blame. As for his manager, she's been photographed with that record boss, Philip McKnight. I have dirt on him."

"Pete, my hands are tied mate, I really can't touch Lewis or Sanders. Give me what you have on McKnight?"

He starts to divulge everything, Rinker makes notes. Ten minutes later Pete Wilson puts his receiver down, and Rinker picks his mobile phone up. He cannot write the story himself, but there is nothing that says he cannot sell it.

* * * * *

The phone is ringing in the other room. I wait, thinking that Jamie will get it. It stops ringing and I turn around and try to go back to sleep. I feel myself falling gently back into sleep, when suddenly the ringing starts again. Climbing out of bed, I drag myself into the sitting room and pick up the receiver.

"Hello."

"Billie it's George, how are you? How's it going?"

"George!"

"Billie, we're on the news, turn the television on," Jamie shouts from his room.

I tell George to hold on and quickly turn the television on.

"What channel?" I shout.

He comes rushing out of his room clad only in pyjama bottoms and takes the remote control from me. He presses a number and steps back. I watch a clip of Jamie's performance and the interview we did before he went on stage.

"Who's on the phone?" He asks.

"On no," I pick the receiver up, "George, are you still there?"

"Yes, they showed the performance on the television over here today. Followed by your interviews with some reporters. Since then the phones have been ringing non-stop. Francis Wells is sending a film crew down to work with you guys. He wants them to record shots for promotion here, Europe and in America. I've got some more Japan bookings for you. I'll fax them now."

"Okay, but don't book anything after our final scheduled date, we both want to be home for Christmas."

"Right, but you have over twenty extra booking requests. I'll clump them together, it should work. Might be a good idea to have conference interviews, radio tours. Get everyone in one place asking questions together, saves you doing it over and over."

"Sounds good, err.., George, have you ever been to Japan?"

*   *   *   *   *

"Thank you Billie, thank you Jamie," they bow and we thank them and bow in return.

"I've lost count, was that the fourth or fifth set of reporters?" Jamie asks.

"The seventh," I sit back and massage the back of my neck. Tony walks into the sitting room with another set of people.

"Billie, Jamie these are the reporters from the television station. They want to film as well as take pictures, is that okay?"

I nod, stand up, shake hands and bow. Our make-up artist checks her earlier work, she adds a few touches to Jamie's foundation and brushes my hair. We sit on the long sofa while the reporter sits opposite us, the cameraman, microphone man and light man stand around us. The interview starts.

The phone starts to ring in the middle of the interview. Tony answers it. I watch as he writes something on a piece of paper. I have started to fidget and I know this is a sign that I am tired. I have been asked the same questions over and over again since morning and I am tired now, actually I'm exhausted. I try to remember whose idea it was to get me talking in these interviews, I can't remember if it was Charles' or Francis' idea. I remember the person saying something about Jamie and I being a package and people saw us as a team. I make a mental note to gradually start sitting on the bench when we go back to England, start delegating more. As I sit here answering questions, my mind wanders to all the other things I need to do. There are two concerts tonight and I need to watch the rehearsals, I need to phone Philip and find out how Sarah and the children are. The phone rings again and Tony answers it again. I think of Mr Grace and the things we talked about.

"…Billie?" I look up, everyone is looking at me and I realize that the thing hanging in the air is a question, waiting patiently for its partner, the answer.

"We need to go to the theatre soon," Tony says.

I cannot hide the relief on my face at his words I look at my watch. "Yes I was just thinking that. Sorry what was your question?"

*   *   *   *   *

The gym and swimming pool are on the tenth floor. I step out of the lift in desperate need of a workout to relax me after yesterday's interviews, the two shows and some more interviews. I follow the sign in the hall and walk down the corridor. I have left my phone in my room and told Jamie and Tony that I will be back in an hour. Jamie is doing an interview which I have excused myself from. I push the double doors open and walk into a large room equipped with every piece of equipment known in the gym industry. Open mouthed I turn and look at the different machines all neatly arranged and colour co-ordinated. I don't know where to start and feel a sudden nostalgia for my 'simple' gym back home. I walk towards the treadmill section and decide to make a start there.

"Stop it, get off me!" A female voice says and I turn and look around. There is no one in the room.

"You owe me bitch, this is payback," a man says. I get off the treadmill and walk towards the voices. I hear something rip, the sounds are getting louder.

"Stop, no...," I hear the sound of a hard slap and rush towards the door from behind which the voices are coming. I push it open. A man, the drummer from the group, the one that had given me the drink the other night, is struggling to undo the belt of his trousers. He is laying on top of a woman whose top has been ripped. She is trying to push him away, he raises his hand and slaps her.

"WHAT ARE YOU DOING?" I shout.

He stops and looks at me. I see the shock on his face then the instant recognition.

"Billie! What are you doing here?" He sounds drunk.

"Get off her."

"Just go away I'll be done soon. She owes me from the other night, this is payback."

"She said no," I feel the adrenaline pumping in my veins and I grab hold of his long greasy hair and pull.

"Get off her now or I *will* hurt you."

"Oww, shit, let go, not the hair, don't pull my extensions out."

He gets up and staggers towards me, he stops in front of me.

"Why do you care about her, she's trash, supermodel or no supermodel, she's 'porn' trash." He walks out of the room and I look at the woman who is crying softly, she is laying on the floor rolled up in a ball. Her back is turned towards me.

"Excuse me, umm, come with me I'll help you."

"Go away, will you just 'get lost'. I don't need your help."

I reel back in shock and stare at her.

"I can't leave you here like this, plus he might come back. Is there anyone I can get to help you? Can I take you somewhere? Do you want me to call the police?"

"No, no police, no paparazzi. Just go! I don't need your help."

I stand there looking at her knowing that I can't leave her. Her top has been ripped to pieces and her jogging bottoms are in the corner of the room, she is still wearing her knickers. I untie the sweatshirt tied around my waist and walk further into the room. I hand it to her. She takes it and throws it across the room.

"I said go away, please just leave me alone. I don't need you or your help." She 'swears' at me as if articulating her point.

I look at her and the sweatshirt and I struggle within myself. I have a strong feeling in my heart, the feeling is telling me not to leave her. 'She doesn't need my help though, she wants me to go.' I think to myself.

'Don't go, stay with her, she needs Me, she needs Peace.'

"If that's what You want me to do, I will stay."

"What?" She asks.

I look at her, suddenly realizing that in my 'mental' dialogue I have spoken some words aloud.

"I know you don't want me to stay, left to me I would probably leave but I am being told not to leave you."

"Being told? By whom? It's just you and me here. Who are you talking to?"

I don't answer, I stand and wait half expecting her to use more profanity and laugh at me.

"I used to talk to God years ago," she says and stunned I stare at her. She breathes deeply, "Can I have your sweatshirt please, I feel cold." I pick it up from where she has thrown it. I hand it to her and she takes it. "Thanks," she pulls it over her ripped top.

She turns and I catch my breath as I see her bruised face for the first time, I recognize her.

I hand the jogging bottoms to her, she pulls them on.

"Do you want to come to my room and clean yourself up?"

She nods.

She winces in pain as I help her up.

"Please don't say anything about this Billie," Sapphire says.

CHAPTER 56

She does not look at me as I press the ice compress against her face. Her cheeks are swollen and her lips bruised. She has a bite mark on her shoulder which has congealed blood on the surface of each tooth incision.

"Good job the show tomorrow will involve us wearing body paint," she makes light of her bruises but I see the pain in her eyes and say nothing. The phone rings in the other room and I ignore it. Jamie and Tony have gone to the theatre already, they will send a car for me in a couple of hours.

"What else did He say?" Sapphire asks and I stare at her not knowing what she is talking about, "you said He told you not to leave me. What else did He say?"

"That you needed Him, you needed Peace."

I hear her gasp, I see astonishment in her eyes, they suddenly fill with tears and she starts crying.

*   *   *   *   *

"My parents got divorced when I was nine. They were always fighting about something. My dad gambled and drank a lot, my mom sought attention from other men to make him jealous. I remember one fight they had when I was eight, they tried to literally split me in half. My dad was pulling one of my arms saying that I was going to live with him and my mom had hold of my other arm and I was crying and screaming, but they wouldn't stop pulling at me and shouting at each other." She stares at the wall and I sit with her quietly. "I went to live with my mom while my dad went to live with his new girlfriend. Overnight my mom became a social outcast, I guess their friends made a choice and my dad and his money won. My paternal grandmother that once loved my mom so much told her that she had to 'support' her son. I never saw her again.

I used to talk to God a lot then. Being an only child I had no one to play with, my mom's mom gave me a Bible. I would read all the stories in there, see how

487

some of the people started off good but ended up doing wrong. I would ask God to help me to do the right things. My friends at school thought I was silly because they used to get up to all sorts of things which I knew were wrong, so I refused to join them. My mom got this new boyfriend when I was about fifteen, and he was bad news, but she couldn't see it. I guess she was lonely and was looking for company," she pauses and stares straight ahead again.

"When did you stop talking to Him?" I ask softly.

"It was a gradual thing. I was always tall and lanky. I never thought myself attractive but people started telling me I was pretty. It was like overnight my lanky duckling body turned into the body of a swan. I started listening to people and they drowned out His voice. Then vanity, pride and greed took over and I thought that I was a paragon of beauty. I started doing beauty competitions, I was the Prom Queen, Miss Dairy Maid, Miss Open Day. I won everything, made money and started trusting in myself. I looked for my self-worth in people. My mom's boyfriend was the worst, he kept on telling me how pretty I was and how he could get me modelling work in New York. My mom was in the middle of making plans to marrying him when I ran away to New York with him. I was eighteen, he was nearly thirty. The rest of the mess snowballed from there."

"Your mum?"

"I like the way you English say mum instead of mom," she smiles and does not answer.

"Where is your mother?" I ask again.

"She died in a car accident, she was on her way to New York to get me. Things didn't work out, her boyfriend got me pregnant, then insisted I get rid of the baby. When I refused he left me penniless." She sighs deeply and then pauses as if guarding what she is about to say. She looks up briefly then bows her head. "Reluctantly, I err..., I umm..., I gave in to all the pressure, I umm..., had an abortion." Her voice falters and I sense a deep regret in her words. She looks up at me, the pain in her eyes is severe. Tears well up in her eyes. She struggles to compose herself. "I worked as an escort for some months then I did a few 'adult' films but that quickly dried up after I was no longer 'fresh meat'. When she heard what I was doing from a friend of mine, she got in her car and drove in really bad weather to come and bring me home. Her car skidded on the ice and hit a tree, she died instantly."

"I'm so sorry," I say gently.

She breathes deeply and nods. I don't think she heard me, she seems far away. Silently I ask God what I can do or say.

Suddenly I know, "She didn't hate you, she loved you."

She looks up startled and shakes her head violently.

"No, no she hated me, I took him away from her. I hurt her and she died hating me. I know she did, that's why I hate myself, that's why I do what I do with men. I've asked for forgiveness so many times but I can't forgive myself and she is not here to forgive me," she starts to sob.

I wait a moment then take her face in my hands and look at her.

"Listen to me Sapphire, when she heard that he had left you and about the things you were doing, she rushed to New York to get you and bring you home. You don't do that for someone you hate. She loved you. The first time you truly asked for forgiveness from God, you were forgiven. You have to stop going back, stop revisiting things, once you pray about something leave it in God's Hands and thank Him as you move forward. Each time you go back and dig up old things either with your mind or physically, like you're doing now by letting men hurt you, you'll get worse and worse."

She shakes her head almost as if refusing to acknowledge my words.

"Sapphire I'm not going to 'sugar coat' things. A lot of people, myself included, may not understand or approve of the things you have done. But nothing gives us the right to judge you, God alone has that right. Yet even He forgives when you are truly sorry."

"How can God forgive me though? How can He? I have sinned, *the wages of sin is death*."

I complete the 23rd verse of Romans chapter 6.

"*But the gift of God is eternal life through Jesus Christ our Lord*. He loves you Sapphire and nothing can separate you, or anyone, from the love God has for them, it's unconditional."

"He still loves me after all the things I've done?"

"There is nothing which God will not forgive, if you are truly sorry and ask Him to forgive you. God promises that: *as far as the east is from the west, so far has He removed our transgressions from us.*"

She gasps, "He forgives! She was coming to get me, she died loving me," Sapphire says as the truth suddenly dawns on her. "Oh my God, she really did love me," I hold her gently as she sobs.

CHAPTER 57

Today's show like yesterday's was great, the audience terrific. Jamie and the dancers did some slight changes to the original performance. I had intended for a few more to be done, but by the time I had taken Sapphire to her room and made sure she was okay, I only had an hour to work. The lights flash in my face as Jamie and I stand with some of the organizers taking pictures.

"This way, look this way please…"

"Billie smile, please…"

"Over here, look over here…"

We are constantly turning this way and that as the flashes continue to go off. Tony holds four fingers up at me. He is standing in the corner talking on the phone. I turn back to the cameras and smile.

"We are going to have to go, we have a radio interview before the next performance here tonight," I say quietly to Mr Shimamoto, one of the executive producers.

He thanks us and we leave. In the car on the way to the number one radio station in Japan I phone the hotel. I ask the receptionist to connect me to Sapphire's room. She answers on the third ring and she tells me she is fine. There is an awkward silence.

"Take care of yourself."

"I will, thank you for…everything Billie," she says softly.

"I left my mobile number by your bed, you can call if you ever need to talk to someone?"

Silence.

"Everything has changed Billie, everything is so…," her voice breaks, she sniffs a few times. "Yes, umm…,I'd really like to call you…, to talk to you, umm…, that is if you really don't mind?"

*　　*　　*　　*　　*

"What would you describe as the most memorable event of your trip so far Jamie?" Ichiro the radio DJ asks.

"Without a doubt the feeling of love I get from the people that come to watch the show. That is closely followed by the welcome Billie and I got at the airport when we arrived in Japan."

"I heard about that, apparently a lot of the other performers saw the crowd and took a back door, but you guys just went up to them and started shaking hands and signing autographs. I think that is what people like about you and Billie, your humility.

I know you have been asked this question so many times, how did you meet Billie?"

"I sang live at her cousin Martin's club in London on the opening night. Prior to that, I had been told by Martin that he had a cousin who wrote really good songs, and that he would introduce her to me after I performed my set on the Friday night, if I was interested. I said I was. That's how we met."

"What were your first impressions of her?"

"From the time I sat down at the table, Billie made me feel comfortable. My first impressions, she was nice, encouraging and very sincere. She really seemed to believe in me as a person and that really mattered."

"Did you have any doubts about her managing you?"

"I made my decision the first night we met and I have never regretted it," Jamie says.

I feel a lump in my throat as I listen to him.

"We are going to take a quick commercial break and then we will be talking to Jamie and his manager Billie Lewis, whom he speaks so highly of," Ichiro says. Music starts to play on the radio.

There is a knock on the door and a lady walks in.

"They are ready for you Miss Lewis."

"Thank you," I get up and follow her.

*   *   *   *   *

492

"We are back and I now have the dynamic duo with me, Jamie Sanders has now been joined by his manager and song-writer Billie Lewis. Billie had to take and make a number of urgent phone calls earlier. Hi Billie, you're welcome. How are you?"

"I'm fine thank you Ichiro, how are you?"

"Well, very well thank you. I have to tell you people listening out there if you have only seen pictures of Billie and Jamie in the newspapers or magazines, believe me these two are much more striking in the flesh. Log on to our studio web camera and see for yourselves. So Billie what inspires you?"

"What inspires me? I think that I am really inspired by things that I see, things that have happened to me or other people."

"I have read somewhere that some of your songs not only deal with important issues, they also have the answers as well, is that why you think they are so popular?"

"I think they are popular because nearly everyone goes through the same problems at one time or another in their lives, and I think that what I do in some of my songs, is share with people how I got through certain things with God's help and wisdom."

"Do you guys have favourite artists, people whom you listen to regardless of what they sing about?"

"No," I say.

"It usually has nothing to do with the artist for me. If a song is lyrically and audibly good, then I will go out and buy it," Jamie says.

"What about when you were young, what kind of music did you listen to then?"

"Soul, Disco, Country," I answer. "I have always had a passion for lyrics and I would listen to *Jim Reeves, Cliff Richard, Tom Jones* and *James Brown* with my mum and *Nat King Cole, Ray Charles* and *Ebenezer Obey* with my dad. I had two different cultures which I combined, and I appreciated and respected both."

"Jamie?"

"A little similar to Billie really, my mum still listens to *Jim Reeves*. I was into *Marvin Gaye, Teddy Pendergrass, Phil Collins.*"

"All strong vocalists," Ichiro comments.

"Okay, it's time for you know what, the chance to ask Billie and Jamie questions, live on the air. I have been told that there are callers already on the phone lines. So let's get this show started."

The producer knocks on the glass window and makes some signs. Ichiro presses a button.

"Caller number one can we have your question please?"

"Hello, my name is Yukihime, I was at the show last night and I think it was fantastic, I want to know if Jamie has a girlfriend?"

"Yes, I have a girlfriend in London?"

"My brother wants to know if Billie has a boyfriend?"

I smile, "Yes I do," I answer.

"Okay thank you caller number one, we now know that they are spoken for. Next caller."

"Hello, my name is Ayaneko, I read in the magazine that Billie and Jamie are very close. Are you going out with each other or have you ever gone out?"

Jamie leans forward, "Billie and I have a very close relationship. When we first started, we were practically living in each other's pockets. A lot of people did think that we were going out. Right from the start we agreed that our relationship would be strictly business. So the answer to your question is no, we are not romantically involved and have never been."

"Thanks for calling," Ichiro says, "I hope that answers your question and any other similar questions that anyone out there might want to ask. Next caller."

"Hello, my name is Cindy Takahara, I have a question for Billy, actually three questions."

"Fire them at her," Ichiro says and I smile at his generosity.

"Billie do you have a best friend? What type of films do you like? And do you have a favourite male actor?"

Laughing I lean towards the microphone, "I have two very close friends and we have different tastes in films, but we go along with each other to watch films. Jen one of my friends really likes the old black and white films, sometimes she takes us to watch foreign films with English sub-titles. Trudi my other friend, can't stand them, she likes all the latest non violent films. I honestly like both types now as well as some of the old comedies.

I tend to distance the actor from the film. For a film to be good in my opinion the whole package has to be good not just a particular actor. There are many good actors out there now, I don't really have a favourite male actor. I like *Denzel Washington* in some films and *Samuel L. Jackson* in some films. I like some of *John Travolta's* films and some of *Keanu Reeves's. Will Smith, Colin Firth, Matthew Modine* and a number of other actors have done some good films. *Jamie Foxx* gave an excellent portrayal of Ray Charles, I think that *Robert De Niro* is a very versatile actor, and *Mel Gibson* is a really good actor and a dexterous director as shown in his film, 'Passion of the Christ'. Can you see why I say I don't have a favourite actor? Does that answer your questions in a round-about-way?" I laugh.

"Yes it does, thank you Billie. I hope you and Jamie have a good time in Japan."

"Thanks," Jamie says.

"Next caller please before we take a break," Ichiro says.

"This question is for Jamie. Which do you prefer, working as a solo artist? Or working in a band?"

Jamie hesitates he seems to be thinking, "They are both really different. In a band you can have a bad day, you can feel tired but because the other guys are there the public may not be able to tell. The down side is you have to put up with a lot of people constantly being around. Half of the time you're not sure who is who, and who is doing what. Decisions have to be approved by so many people before things can get done. As a solo artist, there is a closer knit group. Billie and I work well together and we have two other people who work with us. I don't want to put the whole group thing down, but I know that at this point in my life, I am happier working as I do."

"Thank you Jamie."

"Next caller you're live on air."

"Hello Jamie, I love *Nelson Mandela*, I am inspired by his struggles and victories. Is there a man that has inspired you in the last 100 years?"

"Excellent question," Ichiro says, "Jamie?"

"A man that has inspired me in the last century? *Martin Luther King Jr.* definitely. He stood for what he believed, peace love, unity, equality. He left a legacy inspired by a dream. I have read a number of books about him."

"Thank you Jamie, I have read about him as well, he was a great man," the caller says.

Ichiro presses a button and 'Love Is Not Supposed To Hurt' starts to play in the background. We talk for a few minutes and then the producer knocks on the glass door.

"We're back, next caller."

"Hello Billie, Jamie, I have read all about you both. My questions are for both of you, was it really hard to get into the music business? how did you cope with rejection? and what advice would you give to someone like me trying to do the same thing?"

"Good questions," Ichiro says.

Jamie sits back, so I lean forward and answer the questions.

"It was very hard trying to get in. People didn't want to know that Jamie was a good singer, I don't even think a lot of people even bothered to listen to the demo tapes I sent them. I kept a record of the number of demo tapes/CDs I sent out before Jamie got signed to Digital Records, now McKnight/Digital. I sent out seventy eight altogether, a number of those to the same record company. I never gave up because I couldn't, I believed in what I was doing. I knew that I had to hang in there, keep praying and working hard no matter what I saw happening around me. I got so many rejection letters but, they served a great purpose, they made me more determined. See failure was not an option, it was not in my dictionary of words.

My advice, pray, work hard and never give up despite all odds," I move back and Jamie moves forward.

"I agree with Billie. As an artist I think you need to surround yourself with positive people who tell you the truth. You need to keep working hard. You need to believe you will succeed. Don't sell yourself short. We had offers from independent record companies who wanted us to give them money before they signed me to their label. Billie rejected the idea immediately and we never looked back. Positive people or 'dream makers' as Billie calls them will always lift you up, always make you think that you will succeed. Billie saw the big picture way before me and she took me along until I started to see it. She is my 'dream maker'."

CHAPTER 58

The pounding on the door is persistent, but I am too tired to get up. I hear Jamie's voice and then shouts. I get up and rush into the sitting room. George is standing in the middle of the room talking loudly to Jamie.

"Billie," he shouts and hugs me.

"George," I smile and hug him back thankful that he is here.

We have so much work to do in the next few days.

"I've sorted the private jet out and we should be there and back before the show tonight. What else is there pending?" George asks.

I pick up a pile of papers and place them in his hands.

"I'm so glad you're here George."

* * * * *

The jet lands and after a few minutes we are walking towards a group of people on the tarmac. I can see some cars and a bus parked in the distance.

"Billie, thank you for coming, thank you Jamie. We understand that you are on a very tight schedule, everything has been set up. Please come. The children at the orphanage are waiting to meet you both."

* * * * *

"How have you been managing? These schedules are not humanly possible. They want you in three places at once. I thought New York was bad," George scratches his head as he looks at the papers.

"Hence my happiness to see you George. We need to set up some of those conference interviews you mentioned."

"I'll get on to it."

* * * * *

It has been so busy and each time we have a few minutes to ourselves, the time difference has stopped me from calling Philip. I will be on the road in two hours, if I don't call him now I will have to wait until tomorrow. I pick up the receiver and dial his number.

"Hello," he sounds groggy.

"Hi, did I wake you?"

"Yes."

I laugh.

"Billie?"

"Were you expecting someone else Mr McKnight?"

"Actually…"

I smile. We talk.

*   *   *   *   *

Now, I know why people say that if they want their garden taken care of, they will call a gardener and a plumber if they have a problem with their plumbing. As I watch George organize, plan, re-organise and re-plan the schedules I am really thankful that he is here.

"Sorted," he says loudly to Tony and claps. I smile and turn back to the dancers who are rehearsing for tonight. I feel like I have been here for weeks not just six days.

*   *   *   *   *

Interviews have all been done and photographs taken. Tonight is the last night. It is going to be a spectacular event and there is a big party afterwards. Tony hands me two newspapers and I look at the headlines. *'Jamie Sanders and Billie Lewis travel hundreds of miles to a small town in China; they raise a huge amount of money for orphanage'* - Jamie performed at a private concert where all the proceeds went to a local orphanage from which 18 years ago his sister May Li, was adopted. Billie had two of her signed poems auctioned to raise funds.

'New drop-in Drug Centre opened by Billie Lewis and Jamie Sanders. Centre named 'BenClo', in memory of two friends' – A large donation was made by the couple to help drug addicts and their families.

"If I hadn't met you, I would not have believed people were capable of doing what you two have done. I hear that you are both planning to go to South Africa soon and raise money for the orphanages there. It's so..., it's so.., God bless you both!" Tony says.

* * * * *

Some new acts have come to perform just for tonight. Excitement is in the air for everyone. After tonight's performance Jamie, George and I are not going to the party, we will be rushing to the airport to catch a flight. We have to stop over in France for a show, because Jamie is number one in their national charts. After that, it is home-sweet-home.

The music starts, the concert begins.

CHAPTER 59

The noise is deafening as we walk through Heathrow Airport. There are photographers, television cameras and reporters everywhere. People crowd in on us from both sides as we make our way to the doors. The security men have us enclosed in a human cocoon, we move as one body with them. At the doors we see that there are more people outside. I am told to wait with four of the security men while Jamie and George are escorted to the waiting car by four others. I can feel hands touching my arms and people shouting telling me to smile. I look up and see a man walking away. 'Philip' I think to myself, I know that jacket anywhere. I watch him light a cigarette and stand looking at something. 'Philip doesn't smoke' my brain says as the crowds of people push forward. The security men talk into radio microphones hooked onto their ears. As soon as Jamie and George are safely in the car the other four come back for me. The crowds are shouting and photographers are blinding me with the flash of their cameras. I stumble and feel someone steady me and then hands pick me up by my arms and carry me the short distance to the car. I am placed like luggage unceremoniously in the back of the car. The door slams shut and someone bangs on the roof.

"Move, Go Go Go."

The car moves quickly. After about ten minutes it slows down and then parks behind an identical car.

"You need to all get into that car," the driver says. Jamie, George and I look at each other then at the driver, "it's a precaution, just in case someone saw you get into this car and has decided to follow it. I was careful, no one is behind us now but this is a decoy car. You have to move quickly," he says. He gets out of the car and opens the door. Three people get out of the car in front and walk towards us. Realizing the driver is deadly serious we quickly get out and walk to the car in front, the three people get into the car behind, it turns and drives off. As soon as we climb into the other car and close the door it moves quickly.

"The thing with all this cloak and dagger stuff," George says looking out of the window in a paranoid manner, "is that when you guys get out, I'm going to have to take the train home." The shock of everything must have worn off because despite ourselves Jamie and I start to laugh.

"Thanks for taking me home first. I'll see you both the day after tomorrow."

"Bye George," we say.

The car pulls away from the front of his house and we head towards Jamie's house.

The car phone starts to ring, the driver raises the partition window and picks up the phone. We cannot hear what he says.

* * * * *

"Have you made contact?" The voice on the phone asks.

"Passengers on board now sir," the driver replies.

"Bring them in."

"Roger sir."

* * * * *

Jamie and I look at each other and then the driver who concentrates on navigating the car and does not look at us or lower the window. Ten minutes later we drive down a quiet street and stop in front of a building. The driver lowers the partition window and turns to us.

"Miss Lewis, Mr Sanders, my name is Sergeant Mason. If you would kindly go into that building," he points, "Inspector Freeman is waiting for you."

My heart beats faster, "Sarah?" I ask.

"Inspector Freeman will answer your questions."

"Billie, let's go inside," Jamie says pulling me gently towards the door. He opens it and we climb out.

"Your bags will be taken care of," Sergeant Mason says through the window as we stand on the pavement.

As soon as we walk into the building I see that it is a police station. Wanted pictures are posted on the walls and there is a desk clerk seated behind a glass window. A door opens and Inspector Freeman walks out towards us.

"What's going on? Is Sarah okay?"

"She's fine Miss Lewis so are the children. They are at a safe address now."

"What are we doing here then?"

The Inspector looks at Jamie and then me, "Roger Manning-Smith escaped from the hospital two days after he was admitted. Your house was broken into the next day, we found traces of his blood there."

*   *   *   *   *

Roger was in my house. Why? Was he looking for the answer machine tape? The Inspector said the blood that had been all over Sarah's floor and all over Roger, was not his own. He had self inflicted a stab wound on himself and then poured the blood he had stolen from a hospital everywhere. Why? Something so obvious was missing and I didn't know what.

"Miss Lewis, Mr McKnight is here," Inspector Freeman says interrupting my thoughts. "We have suggested to Mr McKnight that you do not stay at your house until we find Mr Manning-Smith."

Philip walks into the room and rushes towards me. He hugs me and I freeze as I see that he is wearing the same jacket that I had seen at the airport.

"Are you okay?" He asks letting me go.

I nod and stare at the jacket.

"Were you at the airport this afternoon?"

"No," he replies, "come on let's go."

*   *   *   *   *

At my insistence, we drop Jamie at Trudi's house just to be on the safe side. Since Roger was in my house, he probably knows where Jamie lives. Trudi's parents are visiting her for two weeks, I haven't seen them in a while so I spend a few minutes talking to them. I hug Jamie and Trudi and tell them to take care

502

then climb back into Philip's car. I feel strange. It is like I have come down from all the highs of Japan with a sudden rough bumpy landing.

* * * * *

I stand in the doorway and watch Philip make dinner. I have showered and changed, but I still don't feel relaxed. Every single nerve in my body is on edge, every single muscle tense. Su Lee would probably have a field day with me.

Philip turns round, "Billie, how are you feeling?"

"So-so," I reply, "do you need any help?"

"No, I have everything under control. Come and taste this," he holds a wooden spoon up towards me.

"Umm, it tastes good."

"The salt is enough?"

"Yes it's fine."

"You have sauce on your lips, here let me," his fingers are gentle as they hold my face still, he wipes the sauce away with a kitchen towel. His lips replace the towel as they gently kiss mine. I pull back a little and look at him, his eyes are closed and I can see the tension in his jawbone. He pulls me back into his arms and holds me tightly, a little too tightly.

"Philip?" I pull back again and look at him.

"Why don't you sit down and rest, dinner will soon be ready," he looks away.

"Philip is something wrong?"

"No. Err…, no, everything is fine," his eyes say different.

"You are sure you don't want me to do anything?"

"Yes, go and sit down."

I sit at the kitchen table and continue to watch him. He turns and looks in his cupboard for something and I am reminded of the man I had seen earlier at the airport.

"So what did you do today?" I ask.

"Meetings and more meetings. I checked on Sarah and the children, they're fine."

503

He puts dishes on the table. Suddenly I feel drained, empty. My strength seems to have gone on vacation leaving me holding my suitcases at the airport. I just want to eat and sleep, I close my eyes.

"Sleepy head, dinner is served."

I open my eyes, Philip's hand is gently caressing my cheek. I feel like I've slept for an hour not ten minutes. Yawning I get up and wash my hands.

*　*　*　*　*

I stretch and climb out of bed. I have today off and I have decided to go and see Sarah and the children, and then Mr Grace.

I start my morning prayers thanking God for all that He has done for me. I pray for wisdom, discernment and protection for me, my family and friends. I pray that I do His Will and not mine. I finish my prayers, read my Bible, shower then go to make breakfast.

*　*　*　*　*

"Billie, you should be resting, I'm fine with cereal," Philip says. He takes the bowl which I had been about to make pancake batter in, from my hands and sits me down at the table. He kisses the top of my head, "Did you sleep okay?"

I nod.

"You went jogging?" I ask looking at his tracksuit bottoms and sweat stained T-shirt.

He nods.

My mobile phone starts to ring.

"Hello."

"Hello, can I speak to Miss Lewis?" A raspy male voice asks.

"Speaking."

"Miss Billie Lewis?"

"Yes," I reply.

"Things are not right, things are not as they should be. An animal dies and people mourn. A human being dies and no one cares Miss Lewis. That can't be right. Where is the love? Where is the compassion? It's all about money and power. Wars and hate. Money is controlling people instead of people controlling money. We do things, bad things because of our love for money," he mutters something to himself softly.

"Who is this?"

"Things are not what they seem. The picture has become so skewed Miss Lewis. The obvious is now the obtuse. When you look at a person do you really see them or what they want you to see? You can't see the heart Miss Lewis, you can't see the heart. I am sorry, do not be alarmed, do you know anything about Erotomania? Please do not hang up, I am not a pervert. If there is anyone in the room with you do not let them know who I am."

"Who are you?" I ask. Philip stops what he is doing and looks at me. I shrug in answer to the question in his eyes.

"My name is McIntyre, Miss Lewis. Dr McIntyre. I am a psychologist and I treated someone that you know."

"What can I do for you?" I ask.

Philip continues with what he is doing. I turn away slightly.

"Listen," Dr McIntyre replies.

"I'm listening."

"Erotomania is also known as *De Clerambault's syndrome*. It is a rare mental illness, a form of psychosis, a delusional paranoid disorder where the sufferer develops an obsessive infatuation with someone and is convinced they are loved in return. Even when there is no evidence to support this. Sufferers stalk their victims believing the attention is welcomed. In your case the person has been made to believe that you are talking to him through your songs. Are you listening?" His words are rapid and precise.

"Yes, go on."

"In the first stage of the illness the sufferer feels hopeful and excited about being loved by the person. The second stage or the sinister stage is not nice, the sufferer starts to get resentful, writes nasty letters and can actually turn nasty. Have you started to get any nasty letters?"

"No."

"Roger Manning-Smith was a patient of mine, he had his own issues but he used to come to sessions and act out this illness for someone else. Someone dangerous who I think Roger was in the process of 'twinning' with. I don't know the person's name but I have seen him from a distance in a car at night. I have also seen them together at a restaurant called Pertonio's. I think this person might be in the advanced second stage of *De Clerambault's syndrome.* Very dangerous!"

"Pertonio's?" I feel a cold chill. "Why are you telling me this and not the police?" I whisper.

"I've done so many things wrong Miss Lewis, I'm just trying to make things right. I thought I'd warn you first and then go to the police. I saw your picture in the papers this morning and he was there, I panicked and thought I'd better warn you now." He hangs up. I stare at my phone for a few moments then put it back in my pocket.

"Who was that?" Philip asks placing a glass of orange juice in front of me.

"Umm…, someone who knows someone I used to work with," frowning, I take a sip from the glass. "Have you got any of today's newspapers?"

"Probably by the gate," he replies pouring some cereal.

"I'll go and get them," I tell him and put the glass down.

*　*　*　*　*

Everything which I know to be true, is spinning around in my head. I hold on to a tree by the gate for support and stare at the pictures of Philip and I, taken the day I left for Japan with Jamie. 'Philip? Erotomania? De Clerambault's syndrome? Stalker?' The questions make me sick and I cannot fathom the answers. I think hard. Philip had hired a private investigator in America, he saw me years ago and according to him never forgot me. I don't give the wisdom or discernment I had prayed for earlier, a chance to take over. Leaning on my own abilities I start to try and figure things out for myself.

"Billie, it's cold come inside!" Philip shouts from the door. I look down at one of the papers and read the headline: '*Lewis, latest in a long list for McKnight. Will she be the one to tame his wild side.*' I look at a page inside. There are pictures of Philip with a number of different women. Slowly, I walk back to the house.

* * * * *

"What is this?" I ask holding the newspapers up.

"What?" He takes one from me and looks at it. He closes his eyes and says nothing.

"When were you going to tell me?"

"Billie this was years ago, before I met you. I was young, nineteen or twenty, I was stupid. It's not me now."

"It says that I'm just a number on a list. One among the many women that you have dated."

"No, this is rubbish. This is not true now, I have changed, I'm not like that anymore," he holds out a hand to me. I don't take it.

"You said you gave my name to a private investigator and he gave you a picture of me and my phone number."

He looks confused, he nods.

"Why didn't you just get it from Tilly Ann's mother?"

"I..., you had just moved, she didn't have your new number. Look, I don't know why I gave your name to Seymore. It was a spur of the moment thing. I wanted to know..., I umm..."

"And you were not at the airport yesterday?"

"The airport? I was."

I suddenly feel very cold, "You said you weren't."

"In the morning I was, you asked if I was there in the afternoon. What is this all about?"

"I should be asking you. Last night you were acting strange."

"I didn't want to worry you, Inspector Freeman agreed that it was best not to tell you."

"Tell me what?"

"He found a letter at your house while you were in Japan. It arrived two days after you left."

507

"What letter?"

"It was full of rubbish, a nasty, silly, sick love letter. It had some fingerprints on it."

"Roger's?" I ask.

He breathes in deeply then exhales, "No."

"Who's fingerprints Philip?"

"The prints taken from the decomposed body they found."

"So the same person who sent the letter, touched the body?"

"No. A set of fingerprints belonging to the body was found on the letter."

I cannot breathe, I can feel my chest getting tighter as I stare at Philip. I need to breathe, my body is screaming for oxygen.

"Billie!" Philip says loudly. Startled, I start breathing again.

"Steve is back today, I'm going to go and stay at his house."

"Why? What are you thinking?" He steps towards me and I step back. "You're suddenly scared of me? You don't trust me Billie?"

"If I didn't trust you, I wouldn't tell you where I was going," I look down at a newspaper, "I didn't realize you had so much baggage."

"That was then, seven or eight years ago, I've changed. I travel light now. I don't have any baggage."

The phone in the hall starts to ring, Philip answers it. He listens, "Thank you, I'll let her know," he puts the receiver down.

"Roger Manning-Smith just walked into a police station and handed himself in."

CHAPTER 60

I can feel eyes looking at me and I try to avoid them. I try not to look at the other passengers on the train. Thoughts have gone in and out of my head, some of them have taken root, refusing to leave. I don't know what to think anymore. I know that Philip is telling the truth and I can't seem to understand why my mind finds it hard to accept what my heart knows is true. I sit back and stop trying to figure things out by myself. The train stops and some passengers get off and a few get on. A woman pushes a buggy onto the train. I look at the baby inside playing with a yellow ball. I remember sitting in Pertonio's with Philip all night talking about everything. I look at the yellow ball and I wonder why I had let what I read in the newspapers affect me? Why I had reacted the way I did? Why everything had so effortlessly blown out of proportion?

* * * * *

"What?" I ask not able to contain my shock.

"Maybe I should have told you earlier," Steve says.

I stare at him, "You knew Philip when he was seeing all those women and you never told me?"

"I never told you because he has changed. He isn't the same person, and I don't think he went out with half of those women. They were always hanging around him."

"Where and when did you first meet him?"

"In America, I met him on campus at Cornell first and then a few times at law school. He was a young really successful business man. He graduated from Harvard. Kenny and I were at law school together and he introduced Philip to me as his cousin. He always had girls hanging around him, but he suddenly changed, even Kenny was amazed. After my graduation I noticed that whenever we met he was always by himself. He sort of went out of his way to talk to me and be nice to me. When I saw him at Jamie's launch party, I was shocked at first, then I saw the way he behaved towards you. He really has changed."

"So the pictures in the newspaper?" I ask.

"The way I see it, some reporter or person is trying to cause trouble by digging up old history. What is your heart telling you? As grandma used to say *'the heart doesn't lie'*."

*   *   *   *   *

"You used to hate putting your hair in rollers, why did you do it?" Steve asks. He pulls a roller from my hair.

"I still hate it and I don't know why I did it," I reply.

He tugs at more rollers trying to get them free from the curly mass on my head.

"Ow, you're pulling too hard."

"Keep still then, you always fidget," Steve says and laughs. He goes quiet and after a few moments I turn to look up at him. He turns my head back.

"I've met someone," he says quietly.

"Who is she? Have I met her?"

"She's a lawyer, she works in legal aid and her name is Marcia. You have met her in a round-about-way."

"When?"

"You know earlier, umm…, when we were watching the news, the lady talking about human rights and the lack of justice for poor people. The one you were agreeing with. Well you were shouting in agreement, so I guess you were agreeing with her."

"Steve?" I turn and look at him.

"That's her."

"Marcia Richardson?"

He nods.

"The human rights person on the news?"

"She's really nice, maybe one of these days we can all meet up and have dinner?"

He looks shy so I don't overtly tease him. But I do tease him.

"That sounds good, I'd like to meet the lady who has managed to make my brother feel like an introverted extrovert."

He chuckles, turns my head around and pulls out more rollers.

"Keep still," he says.

"I am, you're pulling too hard."

"No I'm not pulling too hard, you are moving around as usual."

"It's not about me keeping still, you used to pull my hair when we were little and you're doing it now."

"No, when we were little you would only cornrow my hair if I put yours in rollers. So I had to do it, you never kept still then and you're not keeping still now."

He pulls a roller free as he talks and pulls my head along in the process. Tactlessly emphasising his point.

* * * * *

He looks through the window and watches as her brother takes the rollers out of her hair. He watches them laughing. He needs to talk to her, he gets out of his car and walks to the front of the house. He is cold and needs his medication, he starts to shiver. As he stands there watching her he remembers how he had felt when he had seen her in her cousin's club, the feelings revisit him. The fear of rejection makes him turn around and walk back to his car. He waits in the cold trying to build up his courage.

* * * * *

"Billie your hair is naturally curly, why try and re-curl it?"

"Because I want the curls to look bigger, I..., that's it! Simon's girlfriend in the picture looked like me, her hair was more curly. Simon said we could have been sisters. They look alike. It's not Philip. The man at the airport, the feet in the restaurant. Newspapers! I need the newspapers."

Steve looks at me strangely, he probably thinks the rollers were too tight and on for too long. He starts to say something then stops and hands me the newspapers. His front door bell rings and he gets up.

Frantically I look through the newspapers.

*   *   *   *   *

"Billie, Philip brought some clothes round for you."

"Where is he?"

"He didn't wait."

I jump up and run to the front door. I pull it open and rush outside. I feel the wind bite into my flesh and my eyes water at the sheer bitterness of the December cold wind.

"Philip wait!" He turns around and stands by his car.

"It's cold Billie, go inside, I'll call you tomorrow," he opens his car door and I rush up to him. I place a hand on his hand, his hand is freezing cold.

"Why are your hands so cold?"

"I've been sitting in my car trying to get the courage to knock on the door."

"Philip, come inside you're freezing," he hesitates. I shiver as the wind bites into my skin, "please Philip."

I shut the front door. I look at his tight woollen hat and matching jumper, the expensive leather jacket he is wearing. It suddenly occurs to me that he is very fashionable in an international sense and someone is actually copying the way he dresses intentionally.

"What is it?" He asks standing in the hallway, not going further into the house, not looking at me.

"When did you change?"

"What?..," he looks at me, "umm.. after I saw you at Steve and Kenny's graduation. I knew you wouldn't have anything to do with me the way I was, and all that stuff back then, the fast life, the money, it wasn't really me. Those pictures were mostly publicity shots, I didn't know or have anything to do with most of those women."

512

"You said you travel light now, did you mean that?"

"Yes," he whispers. I see the answer in his eyes and cover the few steps that are between us quickly. I put my arms around him.

"Are you serious Billie?" Gently he clasps my face in the palms of his hands. His eyes are intense, "I thought you didn't want…," he breathes in deeply and exhales then holds me tightly.

*   *   *   *   *

"That's him," I say pointing at the picture of a man in the newspaper. His face is not visible but his jacket, his dark hair and closeness to where I stood surrounded by the security men are.

"No wonder McIntyre said you were photographed with him," Philip says. I have told both Philip and Steve all that I know. We are in Steve's front room talking about all the different possibilities.

"You're sure it's not this guy Roger who they already have?" Steve asks.

"No, I don't think it is. The person behind this, is intelligent, but pretending to be stupid. Roger is not that intelligent, but he pretends to be."

"I think you should phone Freeman and tell him everything," Philip says.

"Okay," I push all the newspapers to one side knowing there is nothing else we can do.

*   *   *   *   *

"Dr Evan McIntyre or 'Mckee' as he is also known, used to work at a renowned hospital for mentally ill people. He used to have a very good reputation, but from what we have gathered, things went down-hill. He started gambling, drinking, womanizing and acquired debts. He has been treating some well known people privately for some time," Inspector Freeman pauses and looks through some papers. I fidget in my chair and look around his office. The walls are covered with charts and pictures of missing and murdered people. "We think that he may have been selling prescribed medication amongst other things illegally. You said he has called you only once Miss Lewis?"

513

"Yes."

The Inspector exhales slowly and I look at Philip.

"Do you recognise the man in this newspaper picture Miss Lewis?" He holds the paper up.

"No. Does Roger know who he is?"

"Mr Manning-Smith is not talking. I think he actually came here because he is running scared. He asked if Sarah and the children were fine. We told him they were and that was it, he stopped talking."

CHAPTER 61

"I'll be fine in here Philip, Jamie and Aidan are here."

He doesn't look convinced, he looks in the studio then at me.

"No one can get into the building without being checked first and no outsiders are going to use any of the studios until this whole thing has been cleared up."

"Okay." I nod.

"Call me if you suspect anything or anyone."

"I will."

$$* \quad * \quad * \quad * \quad *$$

I concentrate on work. Jamie, Aidan and I work as a team on Jamie's album. We have all the material for his debut album in front of us. It has all been approved and we are adding the finishing touches to a bonus track that Jamie has written. Despite what is happening all around me, life in the company goes on unaffected. 'Love Is Not Supposed To Hurt' is still number one in the charts. Kaleidoscope with 'Only What You Wanna Hear' is number five. In a few days the Christmas number one will be decided.

The promotion people are working overtime to keep Jamie at number one. This of course involves more live performances, record signings, interviews and special appearances. As soon as we finish here and Jamie has written his 'Special Thanks' for the album, he will be going with George and Kofi to promote his album and keep the song at number one. The promotion people have a saying which makes me laugh, but which they believe in: - *'they see you, they love you, they buy you'*. I have tried to tell them that 'good records will always sell', but they feel more comfortable with their galvanizing philosophies.

Someone knocks on the door and both Aidan and I turn and look at the door. The light is on outside the door, so the person should know we are busy and do not want to be disturbed. The person knocks again and Aidan gets up and indicates for me to stay back. Philip must have had a word with him. He opens the door and talks to someone. Thanks the person then closes the door.

"These are for you," he says showing me a box of expensive chocolates.

"Who are they from?"

"I don't know, Bertie, from the post room downstairs, said someone brought them into reception and asked that they be delivered to you."

I take the box from him and look at them, they look like a normal unopened box of chocolates to me. I shake them, they rattle. I put them on the table and continue to go through the credit listings for each song as Jamie sings in the recording booth.

"Do you want them?" Aidan asks.

"No I had a big breakfast this morning. Why?"

"I'm hungry, I haven't eaten anything since last night."

"Do you want me to get you something from the canteen?"

"Only if you're going," he replies.

I laugh, get my purse and go to the canteen.

* * * * *

I balance the three coffees complete with accessories, two sandwiches and three doughnuts on a small tray and walk back to the recording studio. I push the door open with my leg and walk in. The shock of what I see makes me let go of the tray, it falls from my hand and the drinks splash all over the floor. Jamie is on the floor bent over Aidan. He is shouting his name and shaking him. Aidan looks dead!

"What happened?" I ask.

"I don't know, I finished the song and asked him if it was okay, he didn't answer. I came out of the booth and he was clutching his stomach and rolling on the floor."

"We need to call an ambulance, quick."

Jamie pulls his mobile phone out of his pocket.

I kneel down, "Aidan, can you hear me? Aidan it's Billie can you hear me?"

He does not reply, his eyes are closed, his breathing laboured and he is sweating and shivering. I take his jacket from the fallen chair and cover him with it.

"The ambulance is on its way. How is he?"

"I don't know, he was fine when I left to get him something."

"I'm going to see if there is anyone who knows what to do," Jamie says and rushes out of the room.

"Aidan, hang in there, you're going to be okay, please just hang in there. God please help him." He starts to shake violently and I try to hold him down. Jamie rushes back in with Sue and Maxwell, two recording engineers, behind him.

"Billie, Sue has First Aid skills," he says and moves me to one side.

I watch as she takes over.

"He's in shock, we need to roll him on his side, keep him warm and make sure he doesn't bite his tongue. Get me a spoon, please hurry."

Jamie hands her a spoon from the floor which I had just brought in with the coffees and I get up.

"I've know Aidan for years, he's never been sick," Maxwell says standing back.

I move the chair back so Sue has space to work. As I straighten it up by Aidan's mixing table, I notice the box of chocolates by the panel. It is open and about six or so chocolates are missing.

*   *   *   *   *

"I just spoke to the doctor," Jamie says walking into the waiting room. I look up, "Aidan is going to be okay, they say it was a serious bout of food poisoning, possibly toxins that must have been in something he ate this morning."

"Personnel called his wife, she's on her way here, you go with George and do the promotions I'll stay until she gets here."

"Are you sure you'll be okay Billie?"

"I'll be fine, Philip was in a meeting when I called, I left a message with Sally, his secretary, for him to call me when he finishes. I'll get a cab or wait for him to come and get me. You go, there's no point in both of us being here when there is so much work to do."

"I'll see you later then."

*　　*　　*　　*　　*

Philip is dozing on a couch, I walk up to him and look down at him. I turn to leave, his sleepy voice stops me.

"Billie? Where are you going? Why are you dressed like that?"

I look down at my black combat trousers and black jumper. My hair is covered with a black woollen cap. He sits up quickly and I hold the bag in my hand tightly.

"I need you to go along with what I want to do. You don't have to get involved, but I don't want you to try to stop me."

"Tell me?" I sense the urgency in his voice.

*　　*　　*　　*　　*

We are both dressed in black and it is three o'clock in the morning. Philip parks his car in the drive of a school next to the hospital I used to work in and we get out.

"You're sure about this?"

I nod.

"Let's go then."

We walk towards the hospital. I know all the quiet areas and lead Philip through them towards the building I used to work in. I feel his hand pull me back quickly, I look up at him and he raises a finger to his lips and indicates with his eyes. I look in the direction, a security man walks out of the building and down the stairs. He looks around and then walks in the direction of the main hospital. I close my eyes and blow out slowly through my mouth. I feel like I am in some sort of spy movie, I cannot believe I am doing this, but I know that I have to. Aidan could have died and I have to know the truth.

518

I swipe my old ID card, press the numbers, hold my breath and wait. The red light turns green and the door opens, we quickly walk inside. I check the lifts, they are both on the ground floor. I pull out the flashlight from my bag, turn it on, and lead Philip up the stairs. On the ninth floor I pause and look through the glass panel, the lights in the corridor are off. I pull the door open and we walk through.

I move fast, explaining to Philip exactly what I am going to do, as I put disposable gloves on. I take hold of one of his hands and look at it. "Large," I say and hand him a pair of large disposable gloves.

I turn a bench lamp on, one which I know cannot be seen from outside. Nothing has changed in the laboratory and I know where everything is. I get the glass slides I will use. I start by making smears of the chocolates I had retrieved from the box. I place a drop of sterile water on each of the slides and then using a sterile loop from a pack that has been left on the bench, I take pieces of chocolate which look contaminated and emulsify them in the water on the slides. I place the slides on a hot plate to dry. Philip sits on a stool and watches. From time to time he gets up and walks to the door and looks out. When the smears are dry I take them over to the sink. Philip moves towards me.

"What are you going to do?"

"Gram stains. It's a way of staining bacteria so that you can differentiate them."

"Differentiate bacteria?"

"Yes, most bacteria can be differentiated by their Gram reaction. There are other stains but Gram is the most commonly used. Gram positive bacteria have a different cell wall structure compared to that of Gram negative bacteria. Gram positive bacteria have a thicker peptidoglycan layer and stain purple while Gram negative bacteria have a thinner peptidoglycan layer and stain pink."

"Pink? Purple?" He frowns

Old knowledge resurfaces, as I wait for the slides to cool down slightly I explain further.

"Examples of Gram positive bacteria are the bacteria which cause a sore throat, they are called *Streptococci* or the bacteria which cause boils, they are called *Staphylococci*, or the superbug aka MRSA. It's an acronym, it stands for

Methicilin Resistant Staphylococus Aureus and is a bacteria not a virus, they stain purple. Then you have the Gram negative bacteria for example *E.coli* or *Salmonella* species, they can cause food poisoning and they stain pink."

He nods.

I pour the crystal violet stain over the slides and wait for about thirty seconds. I wash the stain off with tap water and then cover the slides with iodine, a mordant, and wait. Next I wash the slides again with tap water and then decolourize them with acetone.

"That smells like nail polish stuff," Philip says.

I raise my eyebrows.

"My sister," he quickly adds.

"It's acetone, it's a decolourizer," I wash the acetone off. My hand hovers between the safranin and carbol fuschin stain bottles. I use the safranin, I pour the stain over the slides. I wait a few seconds and then wash the stain off with the tap water.

I pick the slides up, shake the excess water off them and dry them on blotting paper. I place the slides on the now cooling hot plate and wait for them to dry completely.

"You did this before you went into music?"

I nod.

"I know you know what you are doing, that's why you make it look so easy, but it seems really complicated to me. Do they pay the laboratory workers well?"

"Personally, I don't think so. It's very skilled work which requires a lot of training. Doctors wouldn't be able to function if the laboratory staff were not around. I think that they should be paid more and maybe it would stop people leaving the profession."

"An activist and a Scientist I see," Philip says and smiles.

"Amongst other things."

"What are all those bottles with the different shades of brown stuff in?" He points to a rack containing stool samples. I smile and look at him and then at the words 'Stool bench' written on the side of the bench.

He follows my eyes, "Oh," he says and looks away from the stool samples.

"So on the basis of what you have just done, you will be able to tell if those chocolates were contaminated with bacteria?"

I nod.

I turn the microscope on and place a drop of immersion oil on each slide, then place one slide on the stage of the microscope. I focus and I know. I quickly check the other slides.

"Look at this Philip."

I get up and he moves towards the microscope and sits on the chair. He looks through the eyepiece and back at me.

"The pink things?"

"Yes they're Gram negative rods."

"There are two types, a wiggly one and a straight one."

"The straight one from the symptoms Aidan had, I think is either *Salmonella* or *Vibrio* species and the wiggly one a *Campylobacter* species. If you look at the wiggly ones, they look like seagulls flying."

"Seagulls?"

"Close your eyes think of the beach. See the seagulls flying together in the distance. Can you see them?" He nods. "Okay look now."

He looks through the eyepiece again, "That's right, they do."

"Aidan was poisoned with chocolates meant for me. He could have died."

*   *   *   *   *

We put everything back in place, throw our gloves in the bin and wash our hands.

"The light!" Philip says walking back and turning it off. As we walk towards the stairs I remember a hole in the wall I had seen and a bottle with a bacterial culture in it. I walk towards where I had seen the hole.

"What are you looking for?"

"A hole."

"In the wall?"

"Yes, I saw it once. I'm sure it was here," I touch the wall.

"Where were you when you saw it?"

"Over there, I was looking through that glass panel."

He walks over to the door and looks at the wall.

"It's not possible, look at the wall, look at the thickness. For there to be a hole you need a solid piece of wall like that section," he points to the wall directly opposite. There is an iron sheet standing against the wall, it is being held up by an old fire extinguisher. They have both been there for as long as I can remember. Philip moves the fire extinguisher to one side and pulls the sheet back. My heart begins to thud as I look at the reflective side of the sheet and then the wall.

"You must have seen an image reflected from this," he says. He places the sheet against the opposite wall and I bend and look at a piece of wall that is loosely covering a hole. Philip takes the loose piece of wall down and I look at all the little tubes in racks. I pick one up and read the label. *Salmonella enteritidis, Campylobacter jejuni, Vibrio cholerae.* I show it to him.

"You don't mix bacteria like these together, unless you want to cause colossal damage."

He pulls out his mobile phone and presses some numbers.

"Who are you calling?" I ask.

"Inspector Freeman," he replies.

I listen to him talk on the phone.

"Okay let's go," he says to me as he puts his phone back in his pocket, "we leave everything out on the floor and as we leave the building I'm going to press the fire alarm. Freeman is on his way."

*   *   *   *   *

"..we interrupt the broadcast today with some very important news. A hospital in London has been swarmed upon by police and members of the anti-terrorist force in the early hours of this morning after an amazing discovery by a security guard working at the hospital. The security guard alerted the police when he discovered hundreds of tubes containing 'Super bugs' after a fire alarm went off at the hospital. Police fear that the hospital was being used to manu-facture and store lethal killer bugs for sale to terrorists. A man and a woman working in the hospital are being held for questioning. We will keep you informed as and when we get more information. And now..."

CHAPTER 62

"This is the best way, they will have the chance of a new start," Philip says into my ear as he holds me. I know his words ring true, but for some reason they don't stop the tears from falling or the pain I feel in my heart. I look at Luke, Nick and Maddy all with little rucksacks on their backs and then I look at Sarah and the pain gets worse.

"You can go out and visit, come on you have to be strong."

I cling to him knowing that he is right.

"Okay, I'm okay now."

To keep strong I do not look at the tears in Sarah's eyes.

"Thank you Philip, for this," she holds up the tickets, "thank you for your kindness and help," she hugs him. "I thank God for people like you and Billie, I know I would probably be dead now if He hadn't sent you to help me," she starts crying and Philip holds her.

I walk over to the children.

"Why is mummy crying auntie Billie?" Maddy asks.

"She's happy that you are all going to America. Are you looking forward to it?"

She nods.

"Luke, remember to do what is right okay."

He nods.

"And..?"

"...take care of everyone."

"No take care of yourself, then you can take care of others."

"No one has ever told me to take care of me before."

"Well that's why I'm doing it now," I push the lump in my throat down. "Don't forget what I told you and what Mr Grace said."

"I won't," he whispers, "I'm going to miss you," he adds.

"Not half as much as I'll miss you all," I hug them all to me and kiss them, "God bless and protect you always."

*   *   *   *   *

The tall dark haired woman watches Sarah put the hand luggage in the overhead storage, attend to the children then sit down. She is well disguised and knows that her old friend will not recognise her. Dark sunglasses, a black wig, thick clothes and the onset of her new 'shape-shifting powers' make her invisible. Overconfidence makes her get up and walk past Sarah's row. She turns and walks back to her seat. As she passes Sarah's row a bright light catches her eye. She turns, Luke stares back, he is protected. Her heart beats fast with fear, she quickly looks away and rushes back to her seat.

* * * * *

We drive back to Steve's house. The radio is on, but I do not listen to the music, I pray silently for Sarah, Luke, Nick and Maddy. I pray that they get to California safely and everything works out well for them. My mobile starts to ring and Philip lowers the volume of the radio. I answer it.

"Hello Miss Lewis, are you alone?"

I indicate for Philip to pull over.

"Yes I'm alone, is that Dr. McIntyre?" I ask.

"Did you check?" He ignores my question.

"The newspapers? Yes I checked them."

"Did you see the person I was talking about? Did you recognise him?" He sounds anxious, different.

"I saw the man but I didn't recognise him," I reply.

"Look I can't talk on the phone, I don't trust this phone line. Can you meet me in an hour at-"

"Meet you?" I interrupt him.

Philip shakes his head vehemently. I look away from him.

"Where?" I ask.

He gives me an address then the line goes dead.

"What do you think you're doing, you're not meeting-"

"No," I shake my head, "but I know a man who will."

I dial Inspector Freeman's direct number and tell him.

* * * * *

Two hours later my mobile phone rings, I stop pacing up and down Steve's front room. Philip picks my phone up and hands it to me.

"Hello."

"Hello Miss Lewis, Freeman here."

"What happened?"

"We went to the address he gave you."

"Did you find him?" I ask sensing that something is wrong.

"Yes we found him all right."

"What is it Inspector?"

"He couldn't have made that last call to you. We found him dead, he has been dead for over twenty four hours."

CHAPTER 63

I order a Cappuccino sit back and wait for my cousin Natasha and her American friend Laurel to come. I know that there are two police officers assigned to me who sit watching me as I wait. I feel uncomfortable about it, but they are only doing their job. As I sit in the coffee shop I think about certain things:

Jamie is the national Christmas number one artist. 'Love Is Not Supposed To Hurt' has been at the number one position for four weeks and will go into the New Year. It is one of the fastest selling singles in the history of music. Jamie's album will soon be released.

The police are still investigating things, Roger is still not talking. He does not know Sarah and the children are in America, only that they are safe somewhere. The biological warfare issue is still being investigated. The police arrested a girl who worked in the personnel department of the hospital, and Nigel Elison, on suspicion of growing bacteria for terrorist attacks. They found blackmail letters at both their homes, they were planning to send them to food companies and the government. Nigel is insisting that the letters were 'planted' in his house but he is not saying by whom. Tina is nowhere to be found and the police think she may have slipped out of the country.

The body the police found weeks ago, was confirmed recently to be that of Chloe Davenport. They still don't know who killed her. She had a police record for possession of drugs with the intent to supply. Something I knew nothing about.

"Billie!" I look up and see Natasha walking towards me with a pretty lady. The lady is carrying two packages.

"Hi," I get up and hug Natasha.

"Billie this is Laurel, the painter-"

"Artist," Laurel corrects. I smile at her and shake her hand.

"Have you done them?" I ask.

She lifts the packages up and pulls the wrapping off one. I look at the picture of Philip's grandmother and catch my breath at the sheer elegance of the painting. Laurel has captured something so real in her painting.

"Natasha was right, you really are good. This is fantastic! The other one?"

"Exactly the same, I did them together."

I take the pictures and hand her an envelope with her fee in it. She had said she wanted cash and not a cheque, which surprised me, but I complied. Natasha had mentioned that she and her husband were having problems and she was short of money.

"Ladies I have to run, Laurel these are beautiful, thank you so much," she smiles and I recognize something in her. "You have a gift, don't compromise it, you have it for a reason, don't give it away."

She looks at me stunned, "I was actually thinking of doing something else, like changing professions completely. Why did you just say that Billie?"

"You asked to hear it," I reply.

"You're right! I asked for a sign to know that I'm doing the right thing." I smile at her.

"Natasha, studio tomorrow to work on your collaboration with Jamie and if there's time, I want you to meet LeeBeth, she has just recorded a song with Jamie and wants to do some more collaborations. I'll call you tomorrow."

"Okay. Thanks."

I hug her, "Love you, take care Nat."

"I love you too 'Tubbyless'."

*   *   *   *   *

"Natasha, look, your cousin put too much money in here," Laurel counts the money again and stares at it, "but it's amazing, look it's exactly the amount I needed, right down to the last penny."

*   *   *   *   *

I stand back and look at the Christmas tree. The lights, the colourful objects hanging from it, all make it look beautiful. As I look at the tree and the lights, I am reminded of Luke's Christmas play. The story of the birth of Jesus, 'A Story Of Hope' it was called. The children sang a song that day called 'A Light Came Into The World That Will Never Go Out'. My heart fills with love for God that many people don't understand, I know though that the time is coming when many will.

*   *   *   *   *

"Have you asked her?"

"No," he rubs his forehead nervously, "I will, soon."

"Philip, you got the ring weeks ago."

"I know," smiling he looks at his cousin's face on the screen.

"What are you smiling about?" Kenny asks.

"The way your words come across first and the movement of your lips follow. This videophone is weirdly out of sync."

"Don't try and change the subject."

"I'm not, she has just returned from Japan and Europe, she is really busy right now, I don't want to hold her back."

"Where is she now?"

"In the front room with Danny, you should see her Kay she has Danny on her shoulders and they are both decorating the tree."

"Talk to me Philip."

"Left to me Kay, I would ask her right now, but the thought of her not being ready or not being sure, scares me."

"Ask her. You guys are meant to be. You won't be holding her back. She really loves you, you do know that don't you?"

"I.., she has never said -"

There is a little bang on the door, Philip quickly puts the brochures on the table into his pocket. Danny runs into the room, he looks at the screen, stops and points, "Datsa daddymummy." In his excitement he runs back out of the room.

*   *   *   *   *

"WOU-WOW, WOU-WOW," Danny shouts as he looks at the tree. "Itsa butifu," I laugh at his words and ruffle his hair.

"Okay Danny, let's put a few more things at the bottom. You gonna help me some more?" He nods vigorously.

Together we finish decorating the tree.

I hold his hand and we stand back and look at it.

"Uncle Philip is in his office, go and get him," Danny nods and I watch as his three year old legs run out of the room. He knows Philip's house like the back of his hand.

I make some adjustments.

"Beautiful!" Philip says. I turn round, he walks with Danny towards the tree. He is looking at me, "You are beautiful."

"Me? I thought you were talking about the tree."

"The tree? The tree is nice."

"Nice? One hour, twenty four minutes and," I look at my watch, "tick tock, tick tock, tick, twenty two seconds and I get nice."

He holds his hands up defensively and steps back laughing, I pick up a cushion and walk towards him.

"Did I say nice Billie? What I meant to say was excellent work, well constructed and the way the bells hang, I have never seen bells hang quite like that. Did you do some sort of course in bell hanging? Bell hanging 101 maybe?" He laughs.

I put the cushion down shake my head and laugh with him.

"Where have you been all my life?" I ask playfully.

He stops laughing and looks at me.

*   *   *   *   *

"Tell me what you want to do for your birthday Philip?"

"Spend the day with you, that's more than enough."

Danny runs over to us, he makes a car noise as he drives his toy car along Philip's leg then mine. He runs back to the corner where the rest of his toys are and starts talking to them.

I laugh as I watch him play, "He is so cute."

"It runs in the family," Philip says.

"Does it?"

"Our children will be cute."

"They will?" I smile.

"They will be part of both of us, conceived in love."

I catch my breath as I look into his eyes.

"Billie I need to-"

His front door bell rings, he gets up, "That's Angela."

"Mummydaddy," Danny screams running towards her.

"Hello darling," she hugs him, "have you been a good boy?"

"Yes," he says and claps for himself then proceeds to prattle.

I laugh.

Angela takes hold of my hand then looks at Philip and smiles.

Philip shakes his head.

"What is it?" I ask.

"Nothing, Angela just wanted to know if Danny used his err…, his potty?"

"You picked all that up in a look," I turn to Angela and look at her. She laughs and looks embarrassed. I leave her admiring the Christmas tree and walk into the kitchen, I pick up the two packages that I left behind the door earlier, and carry them to the front room. I hand one to Angela and one to Philip. They both frown and look at each other and then at me. Philip opens his and looks at the portrait of his grandmother. I watch the expressions on his face as he looks at the picture and I am happy that he is happy. He looks at me, I see tears in his eyes which he quickly blinks away.

"Do you like it?" I ask.

He nods.

Angela moves closer and looks at the picture. She gasps.

"You said Kenny is close to his grandmother as well, so I thought he would like a picture too. I had two done, they are exactly the same. You can give it to him for Christmas as a gift from Danny."

She looks at the picture and then me, "He will love this, it's beautiful Billie," she hugs me. "Thank you, thank you so much...," her voice falters. "Pregnancy hormones," she sniffs. "I'd better go."

Philip puts his picture down and takes the one in Angela's hand from her, I help Danny put his coat on and hug him. Philip escorts them to the car.

I tidy up Danny's toys. I put them back in his toy box and place the box against the wall. It is late and I have to go home soon. I hear Angela's car drive off and the front door close.

"I know what I want to do for my birthday," Philip says.

I turn and look at him, "At last! What?"

He walks over to me, pulls me towards the large leather sofa and sits me down. He kneels down in front of me, and a little confused I stare at him.

"Actually it's not just for my birthday, I want something for the rest of my life! Billie I want *you* in the rest of my life!"

"What?" I ask, I'm really confused.

"This is not some spur of the moment thing. I have wanted to ask you for some time, but I was umm..." He reaches inside his shirt pocket, he frowns and pulls some papers out, he puts them on the sofa and puts his hand back into his pocket.

I look at the papers, they are different brochures, "Hawaii? Bahamas? Tahiti?" I ask.

"I was looking at them earlier I must have put them in my pocket." He breathes in deeply, "I wanted to take you somewhere special, I had it all planned out in my head."

"Being here with you is special Philip," I caress his cheek.

He looks at me for a long moment then he pulls a box out of his pocket. I stare as he tries to open the box, his hands are shaking. I hold my breath, he opens the box and reveals the ring inside.

"Will you marry me Billie?" He asks.

I look at the ring and then him. I see the uncertainty in his eyes and smile. Uncertainty is instantly replaced with joy.

"Yes," I say softly. He pulls me into his arms and holds me. I can feel his heart pounding and wrap my arms around him.

CHAPTER 64

W e walk into the building hand-in-hand in total agreement about what we are about to embark on. Philip opens a door and I walk through.

"Good morning," a man says, he smiles his welcome at us. He hands Philip a list of names and a pen. Philip ticks our names and hands the list and pen back to him. I look at the other couples sitting on chairs arranged in a semi-circle.

"Mr McKnight and Miss Lewis, I spoke to you both on the phone, my name is Pastor Daniel McPhearson, welcome to this pre-marriage counselling course, please take a seat," the man says.

Philip and I sit down with the other couples facing Pastor McPhearson.

"Today ladies and gentlemen as you can see, is the first day of the course." He places his list on the table and sits on the table's edge. "I'm on my own today because my wife thinks that I get a little carried away on the first day. She thinks this because the first day with me, unlike a first date, is when I tell it as it is. This is my time to tell you truths which no one wants to talk about. If you go to people now and tell them that you are doing a pre-marriage counselling course, some may laugh, some may wonder, others may think 'you're not even married yet and you're having problems'.

This course is not aimed at telling you that you won't have problems, it's aimed at equipping you to deal with some of them and stopping other problems before they even start, using Godly wisdom and, using it wisely.

I was born and raised in Philadelphia in the USA, I have written a number of books over the years on marriage and how to treat your spouse. Books which have helped a lot of people. Recently I have written books on how to overcome pornography, alcohol and drug addictions through the Grace and Mercy of God and knowing who Jesus Christ is and what He has done for us.

I used to travel and speak at conferences, seminars and in churches about the importance of marriage. I thought I was doing a good job, until two years ago when my wife, whom I love dearly, said that she no longer felt loved by me and she wanted a break. She wanted to move with our children to another state in

America and work with broken families. That was the day I woke up and smelt the 'coffee, the eggs and the toast'. That was the day I also learnt never to speak when you are tired, let alone get into a heated argument.

I will never forget that day, I walked into the house after two whole weeks of travelling and speaking at various conferences. I was tired and my wife had waited up for me to tell me her plans, she knew she wouldn't be able to talk to me the next morning, because of my busy schedule. At first I thought I was being attacked by the devil. Here I was doing the work of God trying to help people and the devil was trying to stop me. In my fear of losing my family coupled with my tiredness, I said some terrible things. My wife never raised her voice, never said a bad word, she just said to me and I quote: *'Go and read the books you have written over the years, pray, wait a while and then we will talk'*. She left the next morning. She went out of her way to make me look good, she made up a story about needing to be closer to her parents for a few months, so no one in the church would suspect. I realized that I wasn't being attacked, the devil had nothing to do with my predicament, I was the cause. You see I loved my wife so much it was like she was a part of me. Yet, I had taken her for granted to the extent she was there but invisible. I would talk to people about respecting their spouse, loving their spouse and showing the love but I didn't practice what I preached. I would get home from conferences and seminars feeling so tired. I would stay in my study working on my next masterpiece and not interact with my family, not relate to them. I even forgot two of my children's birthdays. I was out saving the families of the world and in the process, it nearly cost me my wife and children." He walks over to a stool and sits down.

"Has anyone here heard of the American philanthropist Maxwell Kemp?" Philip and a few other people nod. I have never heard of him. "Umm quite a few of you. Well I won't go into detail about him or his beliefs, but what I want to do, is share something which I read in his autobiography that helped me and I feel is really relevant to the here and now. He says there are many paradoxes in life, things which seem like self contradictory statements, but contain a truth. He says when he was little, he used to wonder why it was that men of valour in the stories he read, would go on long difficult quests in search of one thing or another. They would climb the highest mountain, slay the largest dragon and then come home and not be able to handle the smallest problem. When he was a teenager, men would spend millions upon millions going to the moon or some planet in search of life and not be able the spend anything on the life here, on the war veterans, the homeless, the poor and the needy right under their noses. Not be able to solve the problems in their own country, on their own planet, but ever ready to go to other planets or the moon. He says it is a mystery to him why people readily go out of their way to do great deeds, but can never seem to accomplish the smaller much more important deeds. The more difficult the more easier to do, the less difficult the harder it is to do.

I was so hung-up on teaching people how to make their marriage a success, I travelled the world doing it, yet my own marriage was falling to pieces right before my eyes and I was helpless. The day my wife left I was angry, I turned to pornography and drink. For two weeks I lived in hell, I justified my actions with my predicament. There was a dark hole and despite all the good things I had done in my life, I seemed to be falling deeper and deeper into it. What frightened me afterwards was how quickly it all happened."

He smiles, "God is merciful. He sent my pastor round to my house one evening. You see I had locked myself in my house, I didn't answer the phone, so everyone thought I was away at a conference. My pastor knocked on the door, rang the bell but I refused to open the door. He phoned my wife, she told him where the spare key was and he opened the door and came in. He found me laying on a couch, drained after watching a dirty movie and half drunk. I had not bathed in days. He looked at me and said *'get some things you're coming to my house'*. He and his wife prayed for and with me, they took care of me. I healed. I started to read the books I had written. I prayed and prayed to God for wisdom. Then something amazing happened, everything around me started speaking to me. I heard a song which talks about treating your woman right, it has a couple of lines I like, one of them is *'what's old to you will be new to the next man'* or something to that effect. In my attempt to save other people's relationships I treated my wife like something old and familiar, forgetting that to someone else, she would be new, fresh and exciting."

He picks a paper up, "We will come to this in the next few weeks of this course but I just want to point some things out now. Do you know that the worse thing a spouse can feel is unloved, by the person they love. I counsel a number of people and I often hear things from them like:

My spouse doesn't make love to me very often.

My spouse doesn't find me attractive anymore.

If my spouse is not sleeping with me they must be sleeping with someone else.

My wife could have put me into everyone of those categories. I was intimate with the world through my teaching and counselling but not intimate with my wife. Yet she never threw any of those things in my face but I learnt afterwards that the woman I love felt lonely, hurt, confused and unloved because of my actions. For months she had cried herself to sleep nearly every night. That broke me in pieces," he takes a deep breath and looks at us.

"I learnt how to move forward by being still, praying and listening to God. That's when I decided to do things differently, to fight and save my marriage and help people not to end up like I nearly did. I learnt that it is not the expensive presents, the holidays, the money, which are so important in a real relationship. The simple and tender 'I love you', the physical hug of affection in its pure form, that is not just a prelude to sex for me or a prerequisite set by her, these are the important things.

So now you know why I am here, let me help you to understand why you are here and what you will learn," he opens his folder, pulls some papers out and looks at them.

"Lesson one: Past events. A lot of problems which can happen in marriages, happen as a result of things that we did in the past before we ever met the person we are married to. They are as a result of seeds we have sown in our past because, *whatsoever a man sows so shall he reap.* Some of you are wondering 'what is he talking about', sowing? reaping? are we having a harvest here?" We laugh.

"Everything we do is a seed, if you sow good seed, you will get a good harvest, you sow bad seed, you will get a bad harvest. How does this affect marriage? I'll tell you using my own life as an example.

When I was younger, before I knew God, I was a lad, a 'player', I did everything lads did. I had a number of relationships and a few one-night stands. I didn't know any better, no one talked to me about what was wrong and what was right. I knew the difference, I knew what I was doing was wrong but everyone else was doing it, so I just went with the masses. It was easy for me to get the girls because I learnt from an early age men and women are different. I learnt women want intimacy, affection and love, men on the other hand want sex. So all I had to do was lie and give them what they wanted and I always got what I wanted. Women give sex for intimacy and men give 'pretend' intimacy for sex. In all my relationships the woman got hurt because when I, like most men, got what I wanted I didn't have to pretend anymore, it was there for the taking. I didn't have to lie. So how does this affect marriage?

When you have so many different relationships and you get married, which I hasten to add is usually to someone totally different. You take all the thoughts, all the images from those previous relationships into your marriage. Your sex life with your spouse is affected. You start to compare people. I counsel people who are married and it has amazed me at the numbers that say, when they make love to their husband or wife, they have thoughts and images of past lovers, Soul-ties. Some people even imagine they are with that other person. Am I scaring you?" He pauses. "Good," he says and continues.

"People today are in bondage and because they are also in denial, they don't face their problems, they hide them and dwell on other people's problems to try and make their own look smaller. Instead of facing and dealing with their own problems in marriage they dwell on other people. Some of you are frowning, okay let me make my point a little clearer by confusing you some more. How many of you have been in your car driving somewhere at say eleven in the morning, on a week day and hit traffic and the first thought in your mind is 'what are all these people doing on the road, shouldn't they be at work or at home?'. Do you ever ask, what you are doing there? What makes your reason more valid than anyone else's?

Usually the faults you see in others are a reflection of what is really in you."

He looks at us, it is almost as if he is going from face to face.

"We readily want to see other people's problems and not our own. We look at ourselves as special and everyone else as 'not-as-special-as-me'. Sometimes we can become so self-centred that we lose sight of God and His Will. His Will is that all might be saved not just us. He loves everyone. We sin when we do wrong, and we sin when we don't do what we know is right, sins of commission and sins of omission. My point is, selfishness cannot survive in a good marriage!"

He looks at a piece of paper, "Remember what Jesus said to the people who wanted to stone the woman that had been found committing adultery: '*Whichever one of you that has committed no sin may throw the first stone*'. They all left without throwing any stones because there was no one without sin. Just like today, there is no one without sin. The woman was told to go but commit sin no more. She was given a chance to do the right thing, the chance to change. That was the chance I took. The chance some of you may need to take if you haven't done it already. You need to let go of any old memories and start afresh with the person you are sitting with here today. Some of you may be feeling bad or guilty about your past, you have to realize that God forgives our mistakes when we are truly repentant and ask Him to forgive us. He is the God of second and third and fourth chances but we should never take Him for granted." He stands up.

"I want to show you something," I watch him take off his jacket and his shirt. I look at the different tattoos on his shoulder, muscular upper arms and broad chest. "Before I met my wife, I had the name of each girlfriend I ever had tattooed on me. As you can see I have a number of names. Now, before I could commit fully to my wife, I had to get rid of these," he points at the names. "Each name comes with an image, a thought, something that stopped me getting to the higher level of intimacy which my wife required of me. So I knew if I wanted my marriage to succeed, I had to do something. I had to pull up all the bad seeds I had sown in my past. It was hard, some of those seeds had turned into little bushes, some into trees.

How did I do it? I did what Jesus told the woman to do, I stopped sinning. This meant I had to get rid of all the thoughts, images, desires, lusts, everything that was the old me. I had to ask God to help me uproot all the bad seeds I had sown in my life, deliver me and help me to plant good seeds. I struggled, daily. It was a battle, but it was one which with the help of God I won. I believe before anyone gets married they have to let go completely of the past. It only happens when you pray because you cannot do it by yourself. You know what happened when I prayed? This," he pulls off one of the tattoos. I gasp and watch him as he pulls off all the others realizing that they are all stuck on.

"Oww, that one hurt."

I join everyone else in the room and laugh.

"Did you all understand that?"

We all nod

"By the end of today I'm going to show you that marriage is a good thing. I will show you how to place your expectations in the One who blesses marriage and not in your partner. Unlike God, a partner can disappoint or fail you.

There are so many confusing messages out there nowadays, people say they are liberated high-flyers, moving up the corporate or professional ladder, and they have no time for a mate or marriage, just a 'shag and go'. They are the 'me, me, me' people, the 'me, myself and I' people. These are lonely people and no matter how much they deny it, they are living lonely lives.

Today I will show you ladies and gentlemen that when you trust in God and not yourselves, your marriage will be blessed. Problems will come but by God's Grace they will not stay.

Now I want you to do something, turn to the person you came with and take a good look at their eyes, nose, mouth, ears. Think of everything you did to get to this stage, to get this person to fall in love with you and want to marry you. I want you to work hard at keeping those thoughts, feelings, actions, intimate and alive. Keep the romance and respect alive in your marriage! Never take each other for granted!"

I feel Philip's hand gently rub the back of my neck, I turn, I look at him and smile. Moments pass as we look at each other.

"So let's get started, a good marriage, one that will last must have love, communication, commitment and companionship, or as I say LCCC…"

*   *   *   *   *

"I heard you had a little non-movement of the bowels so I brought you some prune juice," I hold the bottle up and Aidan covers his face with his hands. "You are in hospital Aidan, you're wearing a dress back to front, don't get shy with me now."

538

He starts to laugh and I place the bottle on the table.

"What, no grapes?" He asks.

I reach into my plastic shopping bag and pull out a brown paper bag with grapes. I open the bag, pull a grape out and eat it then pass the bag to Jamie. He takes a hand full and passes it to Charmaine, Aidan's wife.

"They're washed," I tell them. She passes the bag back to me as Aidan reaches for them. I take some more out, pass the bag to Jamie and sit down by the bed. "So how are you doing Aidan?"

"No grapes?"

"I think you need to have some prune juice, get your system up and running," Jamie says.

"Gimme a couple of grapes, I'll have some of the prune juice."

Jamie hands him the bag. A nurse walks by the bed, she picks up Aidan's chart and leaves a plastic bag at the end of the bed. She looks at Jamie, I can tell she recognizes him. She puts the chart back and walks away, not taking the plastic bag.

"Oh no!" I say looking at the bag on the bed, "you know what that's for don't you?"

"No," Aidan says looking at the bag warily.

"It's a constipation bag."

"A what?"

I wink at Charmaine, "It's a bag they insert to help your motion. You have to lay on your stomach and they pump hot water in one end and-"

"Charmaine pass the prune juice," Aidan says.

"Don't worry Aidan they give you an injection to stop the-"

"Prune juice please, I'll drink the whole bottle, go and get me two more I'll drink them…"

Laughing Charmaine reaches for a glass.

CHAPTER 65

Steve, Martin and I look at the enlarged poster-like picture on the wall and smile. The picture is of the three of us taken over twenty years ago: 'Tub', 'Tubby' and 'Tubbyless' and the gigantic tub of ice cream. My mother has displayed this picture as she promised she would many years ago. She said she wanted the person marrying whichever one of us to know exactly what they were letting themselves in for. Exactly what the three of us had done one afternoon when she had left a tub of ice cream out on the kitchen table. She had gone to answer the telephone and two minutes later when she returned this is what she saw.

"She did it," Steve smiles and I see tears in his eyes.

"What your mother says she does," Martin says.

"Arrr.. don't we look cute," I say.

I look at my face covered in ice cream, I had eaten my share of the loot off the table, this is why my nickname is 'Tubbyless'. Martin's hands are covered as well as his face because he had eaten his out of his hands. He had stuck both hands in the tub and scooped the ice cream out, hence his name Tubby. Now Steve was the smart one, he only has ice cream in his hair and on his nose, his hands are clean. He had eaten his directly from the tub by bending and sticking his head in the tub. Hence our nicknames 'Tub', 'Tubby' and 'Tubbyless'. Smiling I turn and look for Philip, he is talking to my parents. I turn back to the picture.

*   *   *   *   *

"Thank you all for coming here tonight to help us celebrate the engagement of Jen and my son Martin of whom I grow prouder day by day. I want you to lift you glasses and make a toast to them now. To Jen and Martin," my uncle says.

"Jen and Martin!" Everyone says.

"And you are all welcome back here in a couple of months to celebrate another joyous occasion, Philip and my lovely niece Billie are also getting married soon." People in the room clap as Philip walks over to me and puts an arm around me. "Here to say a few words is Kenneth Lewis, my dear brother-in-law, Billie's dad."

I stare at my father, I don't have a clue what he is going to say. I glance at Philip, he is smiling, he knows something I don't.

"A number of years ago my daughter aged 11 wrote and recorded her first song in her bedroom, she dedicated it to my mother who a few days prior had told Steve and Billie the story of the good Samaritan. My mother listened to the song nearly every day before she died. She like the rest of our family was so proud of 'Billie the Brave' as she used to call herself. I remember my mother saying that she had read many books written by wise and learned men and women but it took an 11year old girl to show her things not only from the point of the Samaritan and the good he did but also from the view point of the man that had been robbed and beaten and lay dying in the street. Billie homed in on him and his feelings about seeing a priest and a Levi pass him by. Of the pain he must have felt being so rejected by his own and the shock and joy he must have felt when someone came and rescued him, albeit a Samaritan, most likely a stranger to him.

Billie equated this to people hurting in the world, people rejected by those they know and not expecting help from God because they regard Him as a stranger. My mother loved listening to Ray Charles so Billie recorded the song in the memorable melody of Ray Charles, in D flat. The song is called 'I Don't Want To Die'. Philip has managed to get the song onto a CD for us so here it is. Some of the notes are really high so please everyone brace yourself."

I gasp as the song starts:

> *"Oh oh oh ohhhh Lord I don't want to die*
> *Please Father help me, please Lord hear my cry*
> *I'm hurting, I'm bleeding pleassse, please don't let me die*
> *I'm trusting you Father, to send somebody by.*
> *A Priest (a holy man) and a Levi brother*
> *They both passed me by*
> *I can't believe it Lord*
> *They left me here to die.*

A Samaritan man is coming
Um um um I know he won't help me
Send somebody Father
From this pain set me free

I feel a gentle touch, I feel somebody helping me
I open my eyes, see the stranger, Lord I can't believe what I see

Oh oh oh ohhhh, Lord my people abandoned me
But I trusted in You and You came Lord, You set me free.
Oh oh ohhhh Lord I love You yes I do
Oh oh ohhhh, Lord I do love You...

The music stops, people start to clap.
"*Omo mi*, I am proud of you," my father says.
I rush across the room and hug him.

*　　*　　*　　*　　*

The police officer slides the viewer open and looks inside. He unlocks the door and opens it.

"Manning-Smith, phone call, be quick your transport is here to take you back to jail."

"I am on remand, pending further investigation, I'll take as long as I bloody want."

Roger walks out of the cell and follows the officer down the corridor. "Who is it?" He asks.

"Your lawyer."

Roger picks up the receiver says hello and listens.

The police officer watches the volcanic eruption in sheer disbelief and alarm. Roger screams and shouts down the receiver, then he pulls at the phone again and again, ripping it out of the wall. He kicks it, then attacks everything in sight. The officer radios for help and pulls his baton out.

"Mr Manning-Smith, calm down or I will have to restrain you."

Roger does not hear him. He hears no one, only the voice on the phone which is now in his head.

"MY FAMILY!" He screams and continues to kick at the wall, the table and the phone.

*   *   *   *   *

Philip and I stand outside Martin's club and wave to my parents and Martin's parents as they drive off. As we turn to go back inside and help tidy up a police car with flashing lights pulls up next to us.

"Miss Lewis, Mr McKnight, we are very sorry to interrupt your celebrations, can you please come with us to the station? It really is important," Inspector Freeman says. Sergeant Mason is with him.

"What is it?" Philip asks.

"Mr Manning-Smith got a phone call this afternoon and he went berserk, he started smashing everything up. He says he will only talk to you Miss Lewis."

"Why only Billie?"

"We don't know sir, we are hoping she can help us find out. He is still on remand and we have done everything we can to get him to talk. Now suddenly he has agreed, but only to Miss Lewis."

*   *   *   *   *

"Roger?"

"Billie! You came, I knew you would. You look lovely," Roger says attempting to stand up.

"Sit down please," the police officer in the room says.

"I was just telling her how nice she looks?" Roger says angrily, "so sue me why don't you."

"What did you say?" It suddenly clicks, "That day I was in the category 3 laboratory and I heard voices from the office next door, it was you wasn't it?"

"I thought you knew that already, didn't Chloe tell you?"

"Chloe? It was you and Chloe?"

"She was a pest, she thought because I slept with her it meant something to me. You thought it was Tina didn't you?" He starts to clap.

"I thought-"

"See you're not as smart as they think. You thought it was Tina because they wanted you to think that."

"They?" I ask.

He laughs hysterically, the police officer turns and stares at him. I change the subject.

"Roger, I heard that something upset you today. What was it? Why do you want to talk to me?"

"I got a phone call telling me Sarah was in America with the children. Why didn't anyone tell me before? They're my family why didn't anyone tell me?" He demands.

"They didn't tell you because she didn't want you to know."

"They are my family Billie."

He looks at me strangely, I meditate on the words '*I can do all things through Christ Jesus who strengthens me*' and '*God has given me a spirit of boldness not of fear*', the words become a part of me.

"We need to talk officer, can you excuse Miss Lewis and myself?" Roger asks.

The police officer looks at me and I tell him I will be okay. As he leaves he looks at the darkened glass window. His gesture does not go un-noticed.

"So we have peeping Toms in the area?" Roger asks following the officer's eyes.

"What is it you want Roger?"

He turns his head sideways as if listening for something. I watch him and wait for him to talk.

"You're very bold," he says, " just how bold?"

"What do you think?"

"Our eyes are locked, I can feel the battle, I can also feel the victory won by Christ and I am filled with un-imaginable confidence. I continue to look at him. He turns away.

"Someone phoned me and said Sarah was in America, she said she knew where Sarah was. You know we have to protect Luke?"

"Do I?"

He starts to rock backwards and forwards and to whisper to himself, I feel a sense of something bad. I reject it and immediately it goes away. Roger looks at me, I see in his eyes that he is startled.

"You think that where there is good, evil cannot stand?"

"Where there is righteousness, un-righteousness cannot stand and when light comes darkness is dispersed," I say. I see fear in his eyes and I know the truth.

"It was never about your imaginary family was it, all this time, all the lies you told to Sarah. You were trying to get to Luke. Trying to stop him becoming what he is supposed to be. You don't have the power to do that physically, so what you wanted to do was destroy his mind. Let him think there is no right in the world and his only choice is to do wrong. You want to force him freely to do evil by taking away the option of doing right."

"It's not just down to people like me, it starts in most so called 'normal' homes. Parents don't look after their children, just like my parents didn't look after me. Parents let children do what they want when they want. They don't discipline them, they treat them like babies and expect them to act like adults. Parents say one thing and do another, they jump in and out of relationships and have no morals to teach their children. They expose them to pornography at an early age. My parents had dirty magazines and videos in the house which I used to look at when I was eight, they had sex parties in our house, then they wondered why I behaved strange and lustful all the time."

"Some parents are not good parents but that does not give you the right to-"

"The right?" He interjects, "of course it does. The 'teaching' is ours, it is bad but the 'teachers' are parents, relatives, school teachers. They teach and allow racism, bullying, hate, pride, arrogance, knowingly or unknowingly, it makes no difference to us. Our drug pushers tell us it is so easy to get access to children, because they, the drug dealers are always there, while the children's parents are no where to be found. They are busy trying to get more money to buy the latest trainers or video game for the child, while the child rots. In my world we say of parents: *'You have them, do not teach them, leaving them exposed. We expose them, they choose to do wrong, we have them'.*" He starts to laugh.

"The victory has been won Roger. People are becoming more aware that they have to turn away from the bad which they are doing and turn to God, that they have to pray to God for protection for their children and themselves. Evil is roaming the world right now but we know it will not last. This is the final effort of the evil one to try and get as many people on his side, take as many people who are willing, to hell. I and the many like me, have been given a mission to reach out in love and get people to turn back to God. It is working and you are losing."

"YOU THINK SO?" I sense a change and know that Roger did not speak those words. "People? People quote Psalm 23 Verse 1: *'The Lord is my shepherd, I shall not want'*. Sheep are supposed to obey the shepherd yet they don't obey the LORD. That's why they live in want. I satisfy that want. People? Change? YOU THINK SO?"

I feel a warmth spread through me and a surge of power.

"I know so," I say with authority.

"How many people know about the power of prayer? How many people pray over their children, their marriage, their families, themselves, or their home? How many people know God or even want to know God? I offer people luxuries, material things which they can never imagine, I feed the lustful and depraved desires they have. This is my world."

"Only because people with little knowledge of the truth, people who have listened to your lies, have given themselves to you. You know it is finished, Jesus Christ has won, but you don't want anyone else to know. So you turn the truth around, twisting it, perverting it. You are a liar, everything you offer is based on a lie. I know the truth, it has set me free and I have been given authority over you. I use it now," I plead the blood of Jesus. Roger jerks backwards, he moans and tries to sit up. I see a dull mist around him.

"Billie help me…, the voices…, help me please. There is no peace here only pain and… voices."

"Roger fight it, use your free will to fight it. Submit to God, reject the bad that is trying to grow in you and it will flee. Only you can do it." I hear a growling noise, it sounds like a trapped animal. I stand my ground as Roger continues to growl and moves towards me. Suddenly, he falls back on the chair.

"This is not about me, I can do nothing without God, this is about something bigger than you can ever imagine Roger. The price has been paid, blood has been shed, every knee will bow!"

Roger looks at the darkened glass window and calls for an officer to come in. Inspector Freeman rushes in.

"I'm ready to talk now Inspector," he says.

"Billie," Roger says. I turn to him, "They're scared of you, they've tried, but they can't touch you or people like you because of the relationship you people have with God."

I nod.

I understand.

CHAPTER 66

"What just happened in there?"

"Do you believe in God Inspector?" I ask.

"Yes, I go to church on Sundays."

"Sometimes that may not be enough, you have to have a personal relationship with Him, daily. There are many people like Roger, everywhere. They are on a mission to keep people in ignorance so that they perish. The devil is not a man with a red face, tail and horns. He and his workers who come in many forms, are in schools, supermarkets, discos, and in some places of worship. They may be the person who sits next to you on the bus or the train, the person driving in the car next to yours. They work by getting into your heart and mind when you are not protected. The truth is people will only stop perishing when they start praying," I say.

"When they repent of their wrong doings, do them no more and turn completely to God. You shall know the truth and it will set you free," Inspector Freeman says to himself.

"Inspector people know about the truth, they don't do the right things, so they are still in bondage, still not free."

"Are you one of those Evangelicals?" Sergeant Mason asks mockingly. He looks very confused, scared almost.

"I am a person that seeks to know God, I pray every day to know God more and to do His will and not my own with the help of the Holy Spirit."

The Inspector looks at me strangely he seems to be struggling with his thoughts, "There is an increase in crime centred around evil activity. For a while now I have been looking at the senselessness of it all. Stabbings, rapes, shootings, un-provoked violent attacks. It really is like the Bible says about end times, but despite all the bad something else is happening, something good seems to be emerging. It is almost as if there is a struggle going on."

"Oh no, not you as well Inspector Freeman. You're not one of those Evangelicals as well?" Sergeant Mason asks.

Someone knocks loudly on the door.

"COME IN," the Inspector shouts.

"Sir, Manning-Smith has just given and signed his statement in the presence of his brief."

"Excuse me please Miss Lewis."

He quickly gets up and rushes to the door, he turns and looks at the sergeant who is still sitting down, "Mason get out here," he says.

The door closes behind them.

"What did he say?" The Inspector asks.

"He said he got a text message from Nigel Elison telling him to come down to a flat in Dorster Road, Islington, North London. He claims that when he got there Chloe Davenport was already dead and Elison was there with a friend. Elison told him that he thinks it was an accident, that his friend had called him and asked him to come over to the flat. When he got there he was told Chloe had taken an overdose of barbiturates, fallen and hit her head. Roger Manning-Smith says he was forced to help them get rid of the body."

"Who is this friend?"

"He claims he doesn't know his real name only that he is very evil and dangerous. I think he suspects this friend of foul play but is too scared to say anything. He finally broke down and kept going on about ten pounds and Miss Lewis."

"Thank you," the Inspector says and frowns.

*　　*　　*　　*　　*

Philip does not ask me what happened with Roger. I know he had not been in the side room watching through the darkened window. He had been waiting in Inspector Freeman's office. I look at Philip as he drives me home. I don't feel normal, but then again, neither do I feel abnormal. I wonder if I should feel strange.

"What is it?" Philip asks.

"Nothing, really," I reply.

"That usually means something's up, what is it?" He pulls over and turns the ignition off.

"You didn't ask what happened."

"I know what happened and I know how you feel right now because I have felt the same in the past."

"What do you mean?"

"I set up McKnight Records/Entertainments because I wanted to help people fulfill their musical dreams. I prayed for direction and my prayers were answered. I made a substantial amount of profit in the first year. It was an unbelievable amount. I gave 10% of it as tithes and 7% as an offering. I prayed for wisdom and asked that God show me who or where to give the other 33%. I wanted to give half of what I had made. A lot of things started happening around me almost as if to distract me. I kept praying and trusting in God. I opened the Bible one night and I saw the words that I had underlined in the past from Mathew chapter 25 verses 35-40 where Jesus talks about giving to the poor, feeding the hungry, taking care of the homeless and sick and visiting the people in prisons. I knew where to give. I gave out the 33% to various authentic ministries, charities, orphanages, homeless shelters, prison rehabilitation programs and a number of families who were in need and the very next day I got two notes in the mail."

"What did they say?"

"One said *when you are faithful with a little, then you will be blessed with a lot*. The other had a quote from Acts chapter 20 Verse 35. It said: *'The Lord Jesus Himself said 'it is more blessed, there is more happiness in giving than in receiving'. Be blessed, be happy.'*"

"Who sent them?"

"I don't know. That day some shares that I had invested in tripled, in value. I sold them and gave 50% of the money as I was led and the same thing happened. Since then whenever I make more than I expect from something, I know I have to give half of it away, and I know exactly where to give it."

"A willing heart."

"What?"

"You have a willing heart to do the right thing, to be obedient, you're blessed to be a blessing. Did you feel strange initially?"

"I'll be honest at first I did, then I understood. When you are given something you have to use it to help others. It may not be money, it may be a talent, a gift, or your time. If it is not used properly it may become 'used-less' and eventually 'useless'. I know so many rich people who are miserable Billie. People that once boasted in their wealth and strength instead of God, are now constantly looking for things to make them happy, to fulfill them. The love of money is the root of evil, the love of money corrupts anyone it gets hold of. I know men of God, pastors that have forgotten their first love because of money. They have become caught up in the 'lifestyle' and forgotten the 'Life'. Money is supposed to be used as a tool to do a work.

'To whom much is given much is expected'. A rich person is called to help a poor person, rich people to help poor people and rich countries to help poorer countries. Not everyone answers the call, when you don't answer, you can never have real peace or happiness within. Be it person, people or country. As 'light' and 'salt' you cannot say that you love God if you do not love or help those that truly need help.

I realize that I have the ability to make money and use it to help people who really need help. To spread the gospel requires finances. God has done so much in my life and taught me to do for others. Now nothing surprises or scares me, it just reveals to me the awesomeness of God and how when you do His will, seek His Kingdom and Righteousness first, you will be blessed. It can feel a little scary at first but as time goes by it won't."

"That's it, it's like praying for something and then it suddenly appears and everything around you is trying to make you feel daunted, but all you feel is dauntless."

"I know you can handle it Billie, we are not given what we cannot handle," he starts the engine.

Suddenly my feeling of strangeness dissipates and a feeling of lightness takes its place.

CHAPTER 67

A s I look at the people that flank both sides of the street I am reminded of the airport scene. I can't believe how young some of these people are and I hope that they are not here by themselves. We make our way along the red carpet and into the television studio for the Gospel / Inspirational Music awards ceremony. There are reporters and cameramen all over the place. Cables lay everywhere and we have to constantly step over them as we walk into the main foyer. There are so many musical artists here as well as people in the acting, sports and fashion industries.

Jamie's debut album is being heralded as the critically acclaimed album of the year. According to the critics every single song on the album is a winner. He has been nominated for several awards tonight.

*   *   *   *   *

George, Kofi, Dave and I sit at our table while Jamie gets ready for his performance. He has already received an award for Best Inspirational New Song, the crystal plaque sits proudly on our table.

"Hello Miss Lewis, how are you? I have been trying to get hold of you for some time now."

I look up at the man, I have no idea who he is.

"Excuse me?"

"I'm sorry, my name is Freddy Bannister, I'm a DJ and owner of an independent record label. I heard you are responsible for Jamie's collaborations and I just wanted to say well done, you have made some excellent choices. I was hoping that your artist and one of mine could say, collaborate on a song written by you. That my people can talk to your people as they say."

I smile politely.

He pulls a chair out from a nearby table, places it next to mine and sits down.

"So, how does it feel having three songs in the top five? You must be well chuffed?"

"I'm very happy."

He takes a card from his pocket and hands it to me.

"Here's my card, please give me a call." I take the card, "I hope the fact that I rejected Jamie twice when you guys first started and I was the Head of A&R at a major label, will not be held against me. If it's any consolation, in retrospect, not signing Jamie was a big mistake, it is my one regret. You know how it works in this business, you're only as hot as your last record. If you don't have a hit record, no one wants to know you and you become 'the person that used to be so-and-so'. If you are just starting out like Jamie was back then, forget it, right?"

"It's wrong," I say, "but you're right, that is what happens a lot of the time." I look at the card, "I've heard good things about your independent label Mr Bannister, I'll give you a call."

He looks shocked, "You will?"

"Your good reputation has preceded you, yes I will call you."

*　　*　　*　　*　　*

Jamie has sung his songs and received two more awards. I have presented the award for The Best Female Group. Jamie and I have decided to leave, George and Kofi want to stay. Dave shrugs then gets up and decides to leave with us. While Jamie and Dave sort our transport out I stand by the door and I look at the fans, the people who buy the records and make the artist number one, two or three in the charts. They are standing outside in the cold. I watch a reporter talking to the people and a cameraman filming him. Another man, possibly the producer, is standing by the door looking at the monitor screens which are set up; he is recording and replaying different shots. I stand there and look at the screens and listen to what the people have said and are saying.

"...no, no man, Jamie has said so many times that he is not an idol, he does not want to be worshipped. But I see Jamie as a hero. He is a normal guy that has done un-normal things in the midst of normality, a true role model-"

"...yeah, Jamie could have claimed past fame like many others but no he worked hard and started again. He takes care of his family, friends, strangers, he always says 'prayer changes things'-"

"...Billie? She is a walking testimony. I read she was in debt, she tried to do things by herself and failed but when she trusted in God she succeeded. Her faith is her strength and she shares it. She does not hide it or pretend in public just to be cool. Even when people try to make fun of her because she is a Christian she just turns the other cheek. I want to be like that when I grow up-"

"...I agree with what that girl said over there, Billie Lewis is a role model. I read something she said recently and it changed my life. She said that when you give in to fear and defeat you let go of faith and you are saying you don't think that God can do it. That no matter what, always believe, always expect God to answer your prayers, always trust in God. Then get off your behind and do something positive-"

"...together they are different from a lot of the other so called celebrities. They truly have an attitude of gratitude. They make a difference. God has used ordinary people like Jamie and Billie to do extraordinary things-"

"...Have you not heard about all the money and time they invest in young people? The work they do for the 'A Dream Come True' foundation-"

"...They bring that saying 'put your money where your mouth is' to life-"

I look at the reporter as he continues to talk to the crowd, I look at the teenagers, the young adults and the middle aged people that answer his questions, I listen as they all say the same thing in different words and I smile.

"The car is here, are you ready?" Jamie asks.

I shake my head.

"I know that look Billie, what is it?"

I turn back and look at some musical instruments laying just inside the building by a door.

"Let's do something different."

*   *   *   *   *

554

Everything is set and the astonished people watching are quiet.

I pick up the microphone, "Hi everyone."

They start to cheer and I lift my hand up.

"We don't have a lot of time and I don't know if this is legal or not, so I'm going to hand the microphone to Jamie." I smile at Dave who starts playing some amazing riffs on the guitar.

In the cold, in front of the people that have been on the streets for hours, we do something different, Dave plays the guitar, I play the keyboard and Jamie sings.

CHAPTER 68

"It's going to be all right just relax," Jamie says again. I look at him and nod. I still feel my nerves pulling and stretching, especially in my stomach. Philip is in America and I have to present my 'treatment' for the 'Invisible Pain' video, in five minutes. Unconsciously I find myself placing a hand on my tummy breathing in deeply and exhaling completely.

The door to the conference room opens and Francis Wells walks out smiling, "Billie, we're ready," he says.

I pick my storyboards up and walk into the room, Jamie follows. I place the boards down and look around the room, there are ten people in the room staring at me.

"Good morning."

"Good morning Miss Lewis," they reply.

"I wrote the song 'Invisible Pain' some years ago. It is based on things that were happening around me at the time, things which I have since come to realize, have happened and are happening in other people's lives. A lot of people have invisible scars, I want this video to serve as a source of hope, to let people know that no matter what is happening now, tomorrow can and will be a brighter day." I pick up the first story board...

*   *   *   *   *

I am waiting for Francis Wells to let me know the outcome of my 'treatment' for Jamie's next video. There were three other candidates making a total of four 'treatments' to choose from. I know that I will not be given any special considerations because I am Jamie's Manager. The best idea will go through to become the video. I busy myself with looking at the American tour dates that George gave me this morning. The words on the paper become a blur and I pick up Jamie's album cover and scrutinize it.

Someone knocks on the door and I look up.

Francis Wells walks in, "Billie, it was a hard decision. There were a number of really good suggestions made by two of the other candidates."

I nod.

"We were thorough and considered every possibility, costs, time, availability of people, everything," he pauses and I wait, "you got the video."

I scream and jump up.

"You start a few weeks after you get back from America. Some of the people wanted to play 'safe' and release one of the other songs first but I agree with you, so we are going with your idea about using the footage shot in Japan and here for the 'Not From These Lips' video and will put that out in two weeks with the single. How does that sound?"

"Great! Francis, absolutely great, thank you."

* * * * *

I pick up the piece of folded paper which Dave had been looking at a few seconds ago and open it. I frown as I look at the name on the paper.

Dave walks back into Jamie's front room.

"Did you see a piece of paper Billie?"

"Paper? What's written on it?"

He looks really embarrassed, "My shopping list," he replies.

"I haven't seen a shopping list."

* * * * *

As soon as I walk into the building I see people looking at me and I remember the last time I came here; it had been to see Jasmine Peters, I had been unnoticeable then.

"Miss Lewis! Wow!" The receptionist exclaims loudly, "it's so fantastic to see you in person. How can I help you?"

* * * * *

I knock on the door and a familiar voice answers. I walk into the room and Wayne Campbell stands up. I see the surprise in his eyes.

"Billie!"

"Wayne."

"What are you doing here? I mean…, can I help you? How are you? You look good, fantastic."

"Thank you Wayne, I was just passing and I thought I'd stop by and have a word with you."

"What about?"

"Dave Pemberton. He owes you money, you owe me a lot more money for the two songs you stole. I want you to cancel his debts and I'll cancel yours."

"Billie, there must be some mistake, I hardly know Dave Pemberton," he sits down. I sit down, uninvited.

"No? Maybe you don't, but I know that Malcolm Wexley, the guy with the scar does. I've done a little digging, I know Malcolm is your friend, he used to work for McKnight/Digital and he knows Dave very well. As a matter of fact I found out that he tried a number of times to get Troyston back together. I've often wondered who was backing him."

"I…, err…"

"You and your friend keep Dave hooked on drugs then you hassle or threaten him to do your dirty work-"

"The drugs had nothing to do with me!"

"Maybe not but you knew what was going on and you didn't stop it, you used it to your advantage."

"Look I didn't…, I…," he stands, his body language is aggressive.

"Let's cut to the chase, cancel his debts now Wayne. I don't want to have to kick up a lot of fuss about the past, but remember the songs that you claimed were yours?" He leans forward. "You must have known I had proof that I wrote them. I always hoped you would do the right thing." I remain seated and calm.

He looks shocked, "You're joking?"

"Do I look as if I'm joking? How can you sleep at night doing what you do? And don't tell me you drink Horlicks."

He stares at me dumbfounded, I see amusement shimmer in his eyes, I stare back.

"Okay, okay, I'll do it, I'll cancel his debts."

"All of them Wayne. I know you are behind the other people he owes. Phone him now and tell him, then give it to me in writing."

"You've changed Billie."

"No Wayne, I've grown up."

* * * * *

I hand the envelope to Dave and he opens it. I can see from his countenance that he already looks relieved, as if a weight has been lifted from his shoulders. I made sure that Wayne called him with the good news before I left his office.

"Where did you get this?"

"From Wayne Campbell, he asked me to give it to you."

"You know Wayne Campbell?"

I nod but I don't go into detail as to how, when or where.

"I owed him and some other guys so much money and I thought that the only way I could ever repay it, was to get the group back on the road. They threatened to hurt Marcus so I couldn't go to visit him…. It was a big mess and I couldn't tell anyone. Now you, the person I treated badly, stands in front of me and my debts have been cancelled. How did you do this Billie?"

"I didn't. Before I forget, I was told to give this to you by Francis Wells," I hand him the letter. He opens and reads it.

"It's…, It's an offer to work for McKnight/Digital as a record producer. How did he know that this is something I want to do? No one knows, it's something I used to pray about when I was younger."

"Really!" I'm surprised.

"How did he know Billie?"

I shrug, "Maybe you let it slip to Jamie."

"No, no I didn't, nobody knows. I never told anyone. I thought people would laugh. Who wants an ex-drug addict let loose on mixing boards?" He chuckles to himself.

"You said it there Dave, *ex-drug addict*. No one looks at that anymore. A lot of people have heard the re-mix you did on the Kaleidoscope record. They are giving you credit for that, not your past."

He looks at the letter again and I know he feels emotional, I turn to leave.

"Billie.., I know I called you many things in the past..."

"*Bird*," I say and laugh.

"You are someone special, someone that really cares," he says and smiles.

CHAPTER 69

'Madison Square Garden presents Jamie Sanders'

We are here for Jamie's third and final 'sold-out' performance tonight. Trudi, Jen, Martin, Steve, Philip, Jamie's sisters, May Li and Thandanzi, his brother Michael, and I make our way to our seats, Jamie is back stage getting ready. I look around at the crowd of people knowing that we have come a long way. I look at the manifestation of the 'big picture'.

The music for the first song starts and Jamie walks onto the stage. He starts to sing 'The Greatest Love Of All'. I changed a few words of the original song. It sounds great. As soon as he finishes, the crowds start to clap. Jamie runs off the stage as dancers wearing camouflage outfits, caps and large goggles run on. They dance to the extended instrumental introduction of 'Not From These Lips'. Four more dancers run on and the whole audience is captivated by the dance routine. I smile as I watch one of the male dancers move to the centre of the stage on cue. He pulls off his cap and goggles and the crowd go wild as they see that it is Jamie. He starts to sing. Half-way through the song, a rapper walks on, the audience start to clap and cheer as they recognize *K. West*. He starts to rap. They finish the song with a bang, a wonderful pyrotechnic display. Everyone claps.

"Ladies and gentlemen give it up for JAMIE!" *K. West* shouts. The audience continue to clap and cheer. "Jamie is right, I know you have all heard this before, like Jamie just said in his song, it's not about the 'bling bling', the 'ice' or the 'bagets'. It's not about the naked and scantily dressed 'fly' women in videos that make you hip or richer than the next man. If you have no love in your hearts for your fellow human beings, no compassion for anyone else then those things mean nothing, those things are nothing!" The audience cheer their agreement.

One of the show's producers walks onto the stage.

"Ladies and gentlemen," he says. The audience ignore him as they clap and cheer. "Ladies and gentlemen," he tries again, "it is with great pleasure that the sponsors and I present Jamie with these awards." The look on Jamie's face is comical, I feel the excitement in my heart as I watch with pride.

"Billie did you know about this?" Trudi asks.

"Sort of," I reply, "I was asked not to say anything."

"Jamie your first single sold over a million copies here on pre-ordered sales, before it was released. To date it has sold millions. It has been the number one record in twenty five countries that we know of, around the world. Your album is heading the same way. It is with honour that we present you with this, Best Newcomer's award and this triple platinum disc award," he hands him the awards.

"Thank you, thank you. I thank God for everything in my life and I thank you all so much. Thank you."

The audience clap and cheer as Jamie smiles on stage.

"So this is why you wanted everyone to come?" Philip asks.

I nod and smile through my tears.

*   *   *   *   *

We have a plane to catch in three and a half hours, destination: California, where we will attend an awards ceremony. At Martin's request, we have stopped off at a club in Manhattan called 'AM', owned by Jason Alexander and Martin. Soul music from the seventies is playing and Steve is nodding his head and swaying his shoulders to the rhythm reminding me of my dad. Jason comes over to our table and sits down. There is an atmosphere of euphoria here; everyone is talking and laughing. A song starts and I smile as Martin joins Steve, they both dance in their seats. We are all still on a 'high' from the show, I join them and sway in time to the song 'Love train' by the *Ojays*.

*   *   *   *   *

We are waiting to board the flight to California. Philip's mobile phone starts to ring. I turn to Steve who is telling Trudi something about human rights and smile realizing that Marcia is educating him.

"Billie!" I turn to Philip the look on his face scares me.

"What is it?"

He indicates for me to move to the corner of the departure lounge. I follow him.

"Sarah just called me from California, Luke is missing."

*   *   *   *   *

I place the eye shades over my eyes with one hand and pull the elastic over my head with the other hand. I sit back in my seat. Contrary to the 'sweet dreams' message on the front of it, I am not going to sleep. I am in the middle of a battle. I think about everything that has happened. Roger is in jail, Nigel is in jail, so there is a third person. The third person looks like Philip. Same height, same hair colour. Same-

"Excuse me madam can I get you anything?" The female voice interrupts my thoughts. I do not lift my eye shades off.

"No thank you," I reply.

"Are you sure madam?"

"I'm sure, thank you."

"What about something from duty free?"

"No, thank you."

"Are you quite sure madam?"

I lift the shades off my eyes, "Yes, very sure."

The stewardess walks away smiling to herself, her 'shape-shifting powers' have grown. She is not using any disguise and Billie didn't recognise her.

I continue with my thoughts, the stewardess's voice seems to have opened a door. From way in the background of my mind I see a man's face, hear his voice. Same height, same newly dyed hair colour. I know who it is!!

*   *   *   *   *

"That is all he wants?" I ask.

"Everything. As soon as he sees you wearing the ring he says he will release Luke. We have our people placed in strategic positions Miss Lewis. Our RRU is ready."

"RRU?" I query.

"Rapid Response Unit."

I nod and turn to Sarah, "Luke will be okay Sarah."

She looks scared but she nods confidently, "I know."

"Miss Lewis are you ready?"

"Yes, I'm ready," I put the ring on my finger and look at the blue print of the building once more. "Showtime," I whisper to myself and start to pray silently as I walk to the limousine where Jamie is waiting.

CHAPTER 70

The reporter and cameraman rush towards Jamie and I as we are about to enter the building. They are right on time.

"Jamie, Billie, welcome to 'tinsel town' do you have anything to say to the folks back in England rooting for you?"

"Just thank you for your support," Jamie says and smiles.

The camera focuses on me.

"I would just like to say hello to everyone and thank you," I wave. As instructed I turn my hand around quickly so the ring I am wearing is visible.

* * * * *

"-and the winner for the best song is, WOOO-HOOOO, BILLIE LEWIS!"

Instantaneously the hall erupts with cheering and clapping. In shock I watch as people around me stand up and clap. I can't take it in; my mind is on Luke. I turn and grab hold of Philip's hand and shake my head. "I can't go up there, I can't do it."

"It's okay, the police and security are everywhere, go and get your award," he says reassuringly.

I stand in front of the microphone looking down at the people clapping; I wait for the noise to die down.

"Thank you, I really didn't expect this, being nominated was more than enough. Thank you and God bless you." I can't think of anything else to say. The people start to clap again. I turn and walk off the stage with my award.

* * * * *

"Where is she?" Philip asks

"She's probably still making her way back. It's chock-a-block back there," Jamie answers.

Philip starts to tap the table nervously with his hand as he stares at the door waiting for Billie to appear. He glances at his watch, "It's been nearly five minutes, I'm going to see what's keeping her."

"I'll come with you," Jamie says.

They walk towards the back of the stage.

*   *   *   *   *

"Excuse me, why are we going this way?" I ask the hostess that is escorting me back to my table.

"It's quicker Miss Lewis and more secure. We are nearly there, just down these steps and through the door at the bottom. It leads right back to your table. Let me help you carry your award."

I hand her the award and I follow her down the steps, she moves to one side and I walk through the door into pitch darkness. The door slams behind me. I panic, turn and frantically try to open the door.

*   *   *   *   *

"There she is!" Jamie says pointing. He sees that she is surrounded by the security men and holding her award. The strobe lights throw colours everywhere. It is difficult to see who is who. Philip squints, his eyes search frantically for Billie. He spots the lady surrounded by security men and frowns, "That's not her!"

"What!"

"Get the police Jamie, that's not her!"

Philip runs towards the lady that is holding Billie's award.

*   *   *   *   *

It is cold, damp and quiet. There is a show going on upstairs but I can't hear a thing. I think that I am in the basement.

"Hello, is anyone in here?" I feel the panic rise in me, I push it down with the words *'I can do all things through Christ Jesus who strengthens me'*. And, *'I have a spirit of power and not of fear'*. Slowly I walk into the room. I bump into something, it feels like a chair but I can't see what it is. Something warm blows on my face, I freeze then seconds later turn. I can just about see the outline of someone standing in front of me.

"I know who you are," I say, more confident than I feel.

"Do you?"

"Dr. Colin Plowman! If that is your real name!"

He starts to clap. I hear a click and the room is flooded with light. Stunned I blink then look around, every single prop imaginable is scattered all over the place. Colin Plowman walks towards me.

"Always the smart one," he says.

"Yours," I say pulling off the ring and throwing it at him.

He catches it, "I loved you, I wrote you letters, I bought you cards. I watched you sing a song to me in your cousin's club, I stood in the freezing cold outside your brother's house while he took rollers out of your hair. I was there for you Billie, I tried to be your perfect man, all you did was ignore me." He looks at me strangely, "Billie the Brave."

"What!"

"I was there for you-"

"What did you just call me?"

"Billie the Brave. I bought you cards."

"How did you-?" I pause mid-sentence, I force myself to concentrate, not to get distracted or react. "I didn't get any cards."

"That's because I never really sent them," he starts to laugh.

"You don't know the first thing about real love Colin," I watch as Dr Colin Plowman takes off his dark glasses.

"I wanted you, I know you wanted me, you spoke to me in your songs. I didn't understand your behaviour, your lyrics spoke to me, but you ignored me. Why?"

"I never looked at you in that way Colin."

Silence.

I look around wondering where Luke could be.

"So how did you know it was me? I was invisible."

"No you were never invisible, people just didn't look at you."

"You're right those people in the hospital were no different from the children who used to bully me when I was little, the children that ostracized me and took away my dignity," his head starts to twitch. "All those hypocrites in the hospital, they all ignored me, talked down to me, bullied me. I studied medicine but they treated me like I was an idiot. I have more power doing what I do in one day now, than I have had in my entire life." The atmosphere changes suddenly, papers fly around in a swirling motion, distractingly, voices whisper in chant all around.

I concentrate, "It won't last, the power you think you have was given to you by someone who does not have real power. It is only temporal. It will go and you will be lost if you don't reject it."

He laughs coldly, "You think I am like Roger? That idiot who was scared of his own shadow. We may have been 'twinning' but he was the weaker half. I'm simply the best, I don't have an Achilles heel, you can't touch me."

"No, I can't but God Almighty can!"

Immediately the whispering stops and the papers stop moving.

Someone sneezes, I turn in the direction and strain my ears.

"Luke?" I call out.

"Auntie Billie?"

"Luke, are you okay?" I rush towards the voice. Hands grab hold of me and pull me back.

"Oh no you don't Billie, Luke come out here now, no more hiding. Come out now or I will hurt your auntie Billie."

"Let go of me," I try to push him away.

"Stop struggling Billie, stop it or I *will* hurt you."

"Auntie Billie?" I hear the fear in Luke's voice.

"Luke don't do it! Don't come out! Stay where you are, don't-, arrr-," something hard and cold presses sharply into my arm.

"Shut up, shut up, I told you, I warned you, now look what you made me do."

I stop struggling and stare at the blood gushing out of the cut on my arm.

"Luke you're going to have to come out now, I just stabbed auntie Billie, she's bleeding. You have to come out and heal her now."

"Heal me? What are you talking about? Are you crazy?"

"Oh, you didn't know? Luke has a healing and teaching ministry." He turns, "LUKE, don't make me get angry, I will stab her again if you don't come out. COME OUT NOW LUKE!"

The side of my dress is becoming soaked with blood, I feel sick and dizzy. Suddenly the room goes dark.

"What the-?" Colin starts to say. I breathe in deeply and push him away from me with all my strength. I turn and run in the direction I had heard Luke's voice. My foot catches on something and I fall forward, I hit my head hard on the floor. I can't see anything, I can hear Colin swearing. I crawl towards Luke, my head is pounding and I can feel the blood trickling down my arm.

"Please God help me, please help me," I hear myself say over and over again. Something small and warm touches my hand, startled I pull my hand back and freeze.

"Auntie Billie, it's me," he whispers.

"Luke?"

"I'm here," he touches my hand again.

I can hear him, I can feel his hand but I can't see him.

"Luke, I can't see you," I whisper.

"He's hiding me."

"Who?"

"The angel in Psalm 91. Remember when you taught me Psalm 91? It's true auntie Billie, He sent one of His angels to protect me. God sent His angel."

I feel an intense heat and look up; the heat does not burn, it feels un-real. The heat seems to move and amazed I watch as Luke appears in front of me.

"See, I told you, he hid me behind him. He said I would be safe there. Look at his sword of fire, that's what he used to protect me from all those bad things flying around."

I can feel the intense heat move closer to me, I look up, a massive form of light appears. I turn quickly in the direction of Colin, he doesn't appear to be able to see us. He is swearing and stumbling blindly right next to the door.

"You're bleeding," Luke whispers, "by His stripes we are healed." I watch in astonishment as he places a hand on my arm as if to wipe the blood away, warmth spreads across my arm. He removes his hand, the cut has disappeared. I can't breathe properly, my senses are running riot, my head is throbbing. I grab hold of Luke and pull him towards me, I hug him tightly.

*　　*　　*　　*　　*

Panic runs riot, no one knows where Billie Lewis is.

"She has to be in the building," Philip says.

"We have checked everywhere Mr McKnight."

"She has to be here somewhere, check again."

"Basement? Underground car park?" Jamie asks.

"My men are all over the place, we can't go public or we will start a panic," the Detective replies.

"SIR!" One of the officers shouts and points at his head radio set, "lady just spotted heading towards the props room in the basement."

"Miss Lewis?" The Detective asks.

"No sir, but this lady was spotted acting real suspicious."

"Right, let's go!"

*　　*　　*　　*　　*

A door opens and I watch as a woman walks into the room. There is light all around Luke and I, but she does not appear to see us. She stumbles around in the dark a few feet away from Colin. I need to get Luke out of here; I think that he is starting to panic a little.

"Luke, sweetheart listen to me, we need to get out of here. I'm going to try and distract them-"

"No, don't leave me," he clings to me.

"I won't, it's okay Luke I'm not going to leave you."

"Who's there?" Colin asks.

"Me."

570

"Billie, is that you?"

"No, it's me."

I watch as Colin hits the woman, "It's you Billie, it is you."

"No, no it's me."

The woman looks as if she is changing shape, either that or my eyes are deceiving me. I watch as they start to fight each other. I don't understand what is happening. My head is pounding.

Luke slips out of my arms, he moves towards the wall.

"Luke wait, where are you going?"

"I forgot my cards, they are over there."

"Luke wait!" I whisper.

The voices of Colin and the woman get louder.

"I've got them," he says. He starts to crawl back towards me. Suddenly there is a loud bang; a section of wall right next to Luke falls. Stunned, I watch as in slow motion, the wall falls on top of him.

"NO-, LUKE-," I scream.

*　　*　　*　　*　　*

"We're in, GO, GO, GO."

The men storm the basement through the wall they have smashed. They quickly secure the room and restrain Colin .

"I STABBED HER, I STABBED BILLIE, I KNIFED HER, I WON," an hysterical Colin Plowman shouts.

"It's not Miss Lewis," one of the officers says as he bends over the body of the lady.

"What?" Shocked Colin stops struggling.

"You didn't stab Miss Lewis."

"Of course it's her, I saw her face when I stabbed her."

"No, it's Tina Foxton, you stabbed your partner."

"Billie? Are you okay? Are you hurt?" Philip asks.

I breathe deeply; I shake my head but don't look up.

"Billie, give him to me."

"No."

"Billie, give him to me."

I gently place Luke in Philip's arms. When I had grabbed hold of him; after the wall had fallen on him, he was not breathing. I tried CPR and mouth-to-mouth but I couldn't get him to breathe. In amazement I stare as Philip presses down hard on Luke's chest. Luke coughs then opens his eyes and looks up at me. I hear the sob at the back of my throat.

"Luke?" I whisper.

"I'm okay, look I got my cards!"

CHAPTER 71

One month later

"**I** got two gold stars yesterday."

"Two, that's fantastic sweetheart!"

"Oh, and I made it onto the little league baseball team."

"That's great Luke!" I say feeling so proud of him.

His babysitter tells him his snack is ready, he thanks her.

"Are you still going to come down for my next birthday?"

"God willing I'll be there, you just continue to do well."

"I will auntie Billie."

"I love you, say hello to everyone and be good."

"I love you too and I will, I'll tell mummy you called as soon as she gets back from work at the refuge."

"Okay, tell her I'll call her over the weekend. Bye sweetheart."

"Bye."

I finish my lunch and quickly get back to work on my first video.

*   *   *   *   *

"That's it everyone thank you for your work today. See you bright and early tomorrow," I say to the actors, workers and Jamie. We are on the set of the 'Invisible Pain' video. Things are going really well and we are ahead of our schedule.

"Billie, ready to go?" Jamie asks.

"Ready," I reply picking up my story boards and paper work.

"It's looking good," he says

"It's feeling good," I say as we walk to his car.

*   *   *   *   *

I rush around the kitchen as I make dinner. Philip will be here in an hour. I get plates, cutlery and glasses out. My front door bell rings and I glance at my watch and frown. It's early. Smiling I think of something witty to say. I open the door.

"I hope you'll be this keen when we get marri…," the words die on my lips as I stare in shock, "What are you doing here? How did you know where I live?"

"I got your address from Malcolm Wexley, I am sorry for just turning up unannounced like this Billie, I just wanted to talk to you," Wayne says.

"Wait there," I say. I close the door and walk back into the kitchen. I turn the heat off from under the pan containing vegetables which are cooking, check the chicken roasting in the oven, and walk out of the kitchen.

"You have five minutes Wayne, I'm really busy."

"It won't take long," he promises. I don't let him into the house, I shut the door and wait for him to start talking. "We can talk in my car," he says pointing to the Mercedes across the road.

"Fine, give me the keys."

Reluctantly he hands me his car keys.

*   *   *   *   *

"I know you must hate me-"

"Wayne, I don't hate you," I quickly interrupt him, "I forgave you years ago."

He recoils.

Silence.

He fiddles nervously with a chain on his wrist.

"Wayne?"

"My father used to beat my mother up to control her. I never told you. He would get drunk most evenings and my brother and I would run for cover as he 'laid' into our mother. I hated him, I swore that I would never be like him. What is it they say? *The fruit never falls far from the tree.* I did exactly the same. Before I met you, I hit a girl I went out with, because she didn't do what I said. I may never have hit you, but I tried to control you. I hurt you and I am really sorry," his voice breaks and I look at him. He shakes his head. "My dad's 'legacy'; I bully women while my brother 'ticks' slowly like a 'time bomb' as he allows women to bully him. It seems so hopeless, how do we change history?"

"You don't have to continue to make the same mistakes your father made Wayne. Your life starts with 'you' and your choices start with 'you'. Anyone can change if they really want to and if they really believe that with God all things are possible."

Cars drive past, people walk past, as he sits and cries time stands still. I don't know what to do, I lean towards him and touch his arm gently. He turns quickly and places his head on my shoulder and his arm around me, and continues to cry.

"I'm sorry," he finally says and moves away.

"So am I, umm…, I never knew about your parents."

He wipes his tears away with his hands, "It's a lie isn't it?"

"What is?"

"*Treat them mean and keep them keen.* You were the best thing that happened to me, I treated you badly and I lost you. When you broke up with me I went for counselling and anger management. They have helped in a way, not much though. I don't want us to be enemies Billie."

"I don't consider you my enemy. You came into my life when I needed to learn something. At the time I couldn't understand, now I do. I don't hate you, I really wish you well Wayne."

"You have changed so much."

I look at his face, at the striking features of the man I had thought I was in love with many moons ago and smile.

"We both have. Take care Wayne, I have to go. I'm expecting someone soon." I hand him his car keys and get out of his car.

*   *   *   *   *

As soon as I walk into my front room I notice the light on my answer machine flashing. I press the play button:

575

*"Hi Billie, it's Philip. I won't be able to make it tonight......I'm a little umm...
busy tonight."*

I walk into the kitchen and turn the cooker off. I dial Philip's number, it's
engaged.

CHAPTER 72

I hum to myself as I walk towards Philip's office. I am armed with some of his favourite freshly baked croissants.

"Hi Sally, is he in?"

"Hello Billie, yes he is," she frowns, "he doesn't appear to be in a good mood this morning which is very unusual."

Frowning I knock on the door then walk into his office. He is sitting at his desk and turns as I walk in, then looks away. I walk towards him and notice that he has not shaved and is wearing the same clothes I saw him in yesterday.

"Philip," I say softly, "what is it?"

He looks at me but says nothing.

"Is something wrong?" I try again.

"No."

"I got these for you."

"Thanks," he takes the bag from me and puts it down.

"So what happened? Why did you stand me up?" I joke.

He doesn't smile, "I called and left a message, did you go out?"

"No," I reply quickly, maybe a little too quickly.

He looks at me as if he is waiting for me to say more. I don't. Silence appears, it stays a while.

"Look I'm a little busy now and you're supposed to be on the set aren't you?"

I nod as I feel tears sting my eyes at his unusual coldness. I feel like I am being told to leave. I have never been through this with Philip before and I don't know what to do. I look at him and feel locked out, I don't have a key. I tell him I will see him later, he nods and looks away.

I walk out of his office.

"Anything?" Sally asks.

"No. Is Kenny in yet?"

"Yes, he was in with Philip earlier. I think he's in his office."

I knock on Kenny's door and walk into his office.

"Good morning Kenny, what's wrong with Philip?" I ask.

"I was hoping you could tell me. I went across this morning and I couldn't get anything out of him."

"I don't know what's wrong, he practically told me to leave."

"What!"

"Did something happen yesterday? Or this morning?"

"Not that I know of. Yesterday he left early and said he was going round to your house for dinner."

"What time?"

"About five in the evening."

I march back into Philip's office. I can hear Kenny calling me but I don't stop. Philip is talking on the phone.

"I'll call you back," he says and puts the receiver down.

"You came to my house early yesterday evening! Why didn't you tell me?"

"I asked if you went out, you said no," he replies.

"I said no because I didn't go anywhere. I sat in Wayne's car talking, that's all."

"So why didn't you say that earlier?"

"I didn't know that you had come round. I only sat in his car talking to him, because I didn't want you to come to the house and meet him there. I didn't want him to get nasty with you. When I broke up with him, he hounded me for weeks. He would come to my flat, stand outside my front door and make so much noise, he tried to threaten and then embarrass me into taking him back."

"You should have told me this before. We have talked about everything. Why didn't you tell me?"

"The topic never really came up. Anyway that was then, he has changed now, so next time-"

"Next time? What next time? I don't want him anywhere near you, period."

"Why? Because you don't trust me?"

"I never said that."

"No but you're acting that way."

"I care about you-"

"I'm beginning to think you don't even know me."

"What! How can you say that?" He walks over to me.

"All I did was think about your feelings last night, and I come in here this morning, only for you to treat me like some leper. You don't behave that way to someone you know! Someone you care about!"

"You don't sit in your ex-boyfriend's car, hugging him, and then expect your current one to feel nothing! I can't pretend that I don't feel hurt!"

"GUYS!" Kenny says and I realize we have raised our voices.

We both look at him.

I lower my voice, "Wayne came round to apologize, he started crying, I didn't know what to do."

"Okay," he says and I think I hear a nonchalant tone in his voice, I react.

"No it's not okay. If you really knew me you would not feel threatened by Wayne or anyone."

"How am I not supposed to feel threatened by your ex-boyfriend? You loved him once, you were close to him once."

"That's just it, I was never in love with him." I whisper.

"What?"

"He was the first person I went out with, the only person really and I was never in love with him or slept with him."

"What!"

"You know me so well? Do you really? You have nothing to be jealous about."

"Jealous? I wasn't jealous Billie I was hurt."

We stand looking at each other, not reaching out and not letting go. Seconds feel like hours as they slowly pass.

"Billie you need to get to the set, Philip you need to clean yourself up and sort stuff out here," Kenny says.

"But-" Philip and I both protest.

"No 'buts', both of you need to calm down, meet up later and sort this out, today! Don't let the sun go down on this!"

*　　*　　*　　*　　*

579

"..and now after so many phone calls here are the two songs you want to hear listeners. First we have the new song by Lemar, this young man keeps giving us one hit after another each one a classic....After that Daniel Bedingfield and the classic 'If You're Not The One'..."

The hot water pours down on Philip as he stands under the shower. His ears listen to the words on the radio, but his heart hears Billie's words over and over again.

* * * * *

My sunglasses hide my eyes. It is a cold afternoon, yet one the sun refuses to miss, it shines brightly. I give my work a hundred and ten percent of my mind. I must be acting very well, because no one has asked me if anything is wrong.

"And this is my Manager Billie Lewis, she wrote and is directing the video we are making today. She also wrote the song 'Invisible Pain' that we are shooting the video for. Say hello to the viewers of 'The Box' Billie," Jamie says.

"Hello viewers of 'The Box'," I say in my best, 'Teletubby-like' voice. The cameras have followed him around all morning. I smile as he jokes around and generally has a good time.

I turn back to the monitor as Jamie leads the team to the other end of the set. The two people taking part in the next segment are having final touches done to their hair and make-up. I walk over to them just as the make-up artist finishes.

"Everything okay?" I ask smiling.

They both nod.

I turn to the man, he is a professional actor and has done a few 'bit' parts. "I want exactly what you did in the first take, but with just a little bit more character. You are acting the part of a handsome, arrogant, controlling person and you've got a beautiful woman who loves you, but whom you treat like rubbish." I notice his eyebrows rise.

I turn to the woman, "Elaine, you are beautiful, young and a little gullible, you also think that the sun shines out of his backside. You do everything he tells you," she smiles, "you have both got a very short time to portray this message

580

and I want it to be clear to everybody. To get this shot to work we need to get you both to *cheat*. It just means you both have to move closer to each other. The light behind you will frame better in the shot. I know you can both do this, show the others okay."

They both nod. I walk over to the monitor to watch with Raymond Brown who is the producer and editor.

"Quiet please," I say.

"Scene 4, Take 2," one of the assistants says slating with the clapper board. He ducks out of the way clutching the clapper board.

"And action!" I say to the actors.

I watch as this segment like the others, comes alive. I find myself staring critically at the monitor as the actors act.

"Good, very good," I say. I play the segment over and watch.

"Looks good," Raymond concurs.

We finish filming the final scene. I play it over and watch it critically, it is very good and does not need to be shot again.

I turn to Raymond and smile, "Go on, you know you want to."

"Thank you, thank you Billie," I laugh as he claps his hands and jumps up and down. He takes a deep breath and then says, "People that's a wrap."

Someone cheers and a number of people clap.

"Congratulations Billie," Raymond says.

"Congratulations to you Raymond," I say.

*   *   *   *   *

While most of the others are around the canteen trailer celebrating, I tidy up my notes and make sure that I have everything Raymond will need to produce the final cut. I smile to myself as I feel the excitement flood through me, my first video! I put my papers down and a gust of wind sends them flying everywhere. I rush around trying to pick them all up. A man whom I recognize from this morning, rushes over to help me, he works with the cable channel that has been filming us making the video.

"I think that's it," he says handing me the last of my papers.

"Thank you, thanks a lot," I smile in gratitude.

"Err.., excuse me Miss Lewis, Billie, I was wondering if you would like to go out for a drink."

"I…,umm, thank you but no thank you," I reply.

He nods.

I watch him walk back to his van, then I put my papers together. I smile to myself as I look at the papers, my engagement ring catches my eye and I look at it. *'Love keeps no record of wrong'* I think and reach for my mobile phone, I need to talk to Philip.

"I wouldn't blame you if you had said yes." I freeze, I don't look up, I don't say anything. "The way I behaved this morning was bad. I am really sorry I hurt you Billie."

I turn and look at him. He has changed his clothes, he is wearing a suit and has shaved. Dark sunglasses cover his eyes.

"I am not normally a controlling person, but when I saw you in his car, I felt certain things," he takes his sunglasses off, I see vulnerability in his eyes. "There are some things I can do without a second thought, they are like second nature to me. I can talk to some of the richest men in the world about business matters. I can talk to leaders in third world countries about integrity, abolishing corruption and doing the right thing. I can talk to anyone about spreading the gospel, sowing into the Kingdom of God, about helping those less fortunate than themselves." He inhales slowly, "I look at you and my heart melts, you smile at me and I get tongue-tied, nervous, unsure. I find myself constantly thanking God that you are in my life, I…," he looks away.

I tap his arm gently then hold out my hands to him. He looks at my hands, moments pass, he takes hold of them, I squeeze his hands.

"I was just about to call you, you're right, you're not a controlling person, neither are you demanding, mean or hurtful like Wayne was. I should have told you what happened first thing this morning. I also realize that since we've been dating, even after we got engaged, I've never really said how I feel."

"You show it all the time, you always put me first."

"Don't you want to hear the words?" I ask attempting a joke.

"I do," he waits.

Suddenly it becomes clear. With Wayne I was never sure, but I said it all the time, almost as if I was trying to convince myself. With Philip, I know he is the one I prayed for. I know in my heart what I truly feel.

"I love you Philip."

I see the power of my affirmation in his eyes. I feel his hands pull me towards him and his arms hold me tightly.

*   *   *   *   *

"There I was thinking that you had a shower, a shave and put on that expensive aftershave because you were coming to see me," I say as I stand with Philip by Kenny's car. He laughs and gently caresses my cheek with his lips.

"I'll be back in a few days. I just need to get some things sorted out in Florida and then I am going to do what you do."

"Oh, and what is that?"

"Delegate. Since you came back from Japan, I've noticed that you are more relaxed, so it must be working," he smiles, "plus I want to spend some quality intimate time with my new wife."

I smile, "Have I told you lately that I love you Mr McKnight?"

He nods and I see in his eyes what I feel in my heart.

CHAPTER 73

"At last," George says placing a pile of newspapers on my table and standing back. "At last they are giving credit where credit is due. At last they say he enthrals them. They ate the food, drank the wine, finally - they burp!"

I look at the papers. George has used a highlighter pen to bring my attention to certain sections. I read the first story. It is written by Mr Waverly. It is a retract article. Mr Waverly apologizes for saying that Jamie Sanders had the makings of a one hit wonder in a past article. Mr Waverly writes that he admires Jamie's tenacity and complete sense of realism. He gives Jamie's album ten out of ten commenting on the huge success of every single song on the album. He highly recommends the songs he has already heard that will be on Jamie's second album. I read through the rest of the papers, Rinker and Hallen have written a story about how hard working and loyal to his craft Jamie is. They commend him for his humility and say that it was a good thing that he earned the respect of the public and did not cash in on Troyston's previous fame. I smile knowing if things had gone the opposite way, these same people would have no qualms about tearing him down, piece by piece, and feeding him to the lions, and anything left over to the ants.

"Have you thought about the exclusive release of your video?" George asks me.

I nod, "Definitely MTV."

"Good," he says, "that's the right thing to do."

I look at George and smile, happy that some of what I do and say has reached out and touched him.

*　*　*　*　*

The release date for 'I Choose You Lord' has been moved forward by LeeBeth's record label. The movie is out in America in a few weeks and I have

584

heard that it is destined to be a hit. I have been told the song has really impressed and touched a lot of people and I am happy with that. I am happier still that the director for the video has agreed to use a few of my ideas, together with clips from the movie, to bring clarity to the song. Things are moving fast in every direction and each day I thank God for my blessings when I pray. I find that I pray a lot more these days, I am constantly aware of God's goodness and I am so grateful to Him. I do not propose for one minute that because I now have the things I prayed for in the past, I take God for granted and forget Who gave me what I have, Who made it all possible!

*　*　*　*　*

The lights shining on us are hot. I can feel the perspiration on my back building up as I sit with Jamie answering questions. I have tried to cut down on doing these interviews with Jamie, I have actually been successful on a number of occasions, but since the release of the video for 'Invisible Pain' last week, I have had to do quite a few interviews. The video is doing really well. I have read the critical reviews and seen the public opinion polls, the one thing I am happy about is people are not just watching a mini-movie, they are actually taking in the song, visualizing its meaning and understanding it.

"Miss Lewis how does it feel having four songs in the top seven and a video that has been described as the most requested video this year and has only been out for five days?"

"Each day to me is full of new things and I feel so grateful to God for everything. I am happy that people are listening to the songs and relating to them."

"What's it like working with Jamie?"

I smile, "Working with Jamie is like always wanting to go somewhere and one day finally getting there. I know people say I use one description to describe another, but that is how I see things. I try to explain things in a way which everyone can understand. So, for those of you who did not understand that, working with Jamie is like reaching for a flower and picking up a huge bouquet."

I see some smiles and hear a few chuckles.

"I read somewhere Billie, that getting a record deal for Jamie was not easy. Is that true?"

"Yes it is the truth. It's strange looking at it now, back then I couldn't understand why the record companies couldn't see what I saw. The gift Jamie has. We're both happy with McKnight/Digital. We are both thankful that Jamie is signed to the label. They treat their artists with respect and not as 'unit sellers'. I'm not saying all the other record companies do that, so please do not misquote me. I'm just talking as the Manager of an artist who went to other record labels and sensed at the time, they were not right for us and McKnight/Digital was," I see some hands quickly go up. "Before we go into questions which have come up in several other interviews can I just add that Jamie signed up with Digital Records before the merge of the two companies," the hands go down.

"Jamie, you have already done some magnificent collaborations, who will you be collaborating with in the future?"

"I have done a couple of songs with LeeBeth and Natasha Dubree, on my second album. I am in the middle of recording a song with Dave Pemberton, we were in Troyston together and there is talk between my manager and the management of Kaleidoscope."

"We heard that there may soon be wedding bells in the air Jamie, any truth?"

"At some point yes. I have the right lady. That's the first step."

They laugh. I smile with Jamie.

"What is it like working with Billie and what would you say you have learnt over the period that you have worked together Jamie?"

He smiles and looks at me, "I have always wanted to sing, the first night I met Billie she spoke to me with a confidence that no one else ever did. She told me I was unique, I had a gift. She said things which I needed to hear. I have never said this before but I had actually given up on the whole singing thing up until that point. We met, we spoke and we started working together. Billie prays about everything. As a result she has made decisions which have worked when they looked as if they would fail. Things have turned around when I least expected them to. I have learnt how to pray and how to trust in God for everything. How to put God first in everything. I feel that through knowing her, I have become a much better person," I see some heads in the crowd of reporters and cameramen nodding.

"Billie!" I recognize the voice and turn to Pete Wilson, "Billie I know that my old company wanted to sign you both, and offered you a very lucrative contract, apart from Philip McKnight, is there any other reason you didn't sign with Vigil?" I sense malice in his voice. I look at Jamie and he shakes his head indicating that I shouldn't answer. I cover my microphone with my hand and lean towards him.

"It's okay," I reassure him.

"Pete?" Charles says. I turn and look at Charles, "Pete, I thought that was you mate. For the record can I say Jamie is signed to Digital Records. Billie and Jamie signed with us before McKnight Records/Entertainments merged with us, before she had met Mr McKnight. Can I just reiterate that point, so that everything is clear."

"Miss Lewis can *you* shed some more light?" Pete Wilson says ignoring Charles.

"Mr Wilson, how nice to see you again. As I mentioned earlier and as Charles has just said we signed with Digital before they merged with McKnight Records/ Entertainments. I read some time ago that you were the A&R manager at Vigil, sorry to hear that you are no longer there. As you know there were many reasons why we didn't sign with Vigil Records, the main ones were centred around you. We felt that a certain amount of sincerity was missing. I personally sensed an undercurrent of falseness which in the lawsuit that Brian Turner took out against you, and won, shows my instincts were right." He looks as if he is going to explode with embarrassment, "Despite everything Mr Wilson, I sincerely hope your new venture will be successful, and that you are happy now. I hope-"

"Thank you Miss Lewis," he interjects sharply. I watch as he quickly leaves the room.

CHAPTER 74

"**D**o you guys ever disagree or fight?" I smile at the first question of today's interview. We are holding this press conference in the lounge of a big hotel where Jamie will later perform two new songs which are on his second album as well as 'I Choose You Lord' with LeeBeth. I let Jamie answer the question.

"Billie knows how to do *Tae Kawon Do*. So no, we don't fight," Jamie says and I laugh. "A number of people have tried to cause problems between us but we have a good relationship built on trust and we always seem to know when something is a lie, don't we?" Jamie looks at me and I nod my agreement.

"Is it true that wedding bells may soon be ringing?"

George leans forward quickly, "We will announce that."

"Billie, 'Love Is Not Supposed To Hurt', 'Invisible Pain', 'Hurting Heart' and 'Break Up' are songs you have written which deal with mental and physical abuse in relationships, with domestic violence. Is there a reason you wrote these songs? You've said your songs come from life. Were you ever in an abusive relationship?"

Jamie leans towards me, he asks if I want to answer. I smile at him reassuringly and nod.

"I wrote those songs because I wanted people to be aware that abuse within a relationship is real, and happens every day in every area and class of society. I watched a film some time ago, it was based on a true story. A mother was in a relationship with a boyfriend who treated her really badly. She encountered the odd slap and abusive and derogative language. She also had an eighteen year old daughter who used to get so mad and vowed never to get involved with a man like that. Sadly the daughter ended up going out with a person who was worse and eventually killed her," I pause and look around. "If my songs can help one person, the victim or the 'victimizer', understand that it is not right to hurt, bully, mentally or physically abuse another person, then I feel that I have accomplished something. If I can make someone see that love is not an occasional act, but a way of life, then I am thankful because I have done what I am supposed to do.

Sometimes it's not just about the person being abused or the abuser, it's also about the spectators, the bystanders, or the 'rubber-neckers'. People who listen to others tell them a story about falling down a flight of stairs at home, when they know the person lives in a bungalow. They sympathize and move on, never offering help. People very rarely walk into cupboards, doors or walls. I am not saying it cannot happen, but when the bruise is on the neck, leg or stomach?" I look around at the people. "I just hope and pray that in some way the message gets to the people who need to hear it. That we stop getting so caught up in the opening 'credits' of life and miss the bigger 'picture', miss what really is important." Two women reporters take me totally by surprise and start clapping. I watch as others join.

"Any more questions?" George asks.

"Billie, I'm from a Christian television station, we also have a radio station where some of your poems have been read. I know that you are a very strong Christian lady, I read that you like some of the work of *Maya Angelou*, the teaching and preaching of especially: *T.D Jakes, Joyce Meyer, Creflo Dollar, Kenneth Copeland, Benny Hinn, the 700 club* in America and the many wonderful ministries in England like *KICC, Redeemed, KT, PTSM*, etc. You actually said that anywhere where the true Word of God is preached and transformation is taking place got your vote."

I nod.

"You said on my show that you liked some of the songs of *CeCe Winans, BeBe Winans, Helen Baylor, Don Moen, Yolanda Adams, Kirk Franklin, Alvin Slaughter, Darlene Zschech, Rebecca St. James, Mary Mary* and quite a few other Christian singers. I recall we had a phone call from someone in America that day. The female caller asked if there was anyone on 'Prime time' TV in America that you admired. You said that you admired *Oprah Winfrey*, that even though you didn't know her personally you felt that she had a gift of giving and her generousness was something a lot of people should try to emulate as much as they can because giving to others is based on a love for others."

I nod externally, internally I am amazed at her recollection.

"I remember you said that Psalms 34, 51 and 91 were your favourite Psalms. Billie where did you first get your inspiration for your poetry?"

"When I was little, my grandmother used to read to my brother Steve and I, stories from the Bible. I remember her reading about Jesus talking to a Samaritan woman at a well and her explaining the story to us. I fell in love with that story because it showed me the humility of Jesus. He took Himself to the level of the people everywhere He went with love and not discrimination or condemnation. I wrote my first serious poem after I heard that 'inspiring' story. I haven't stopped since then."

"I remember, you were going to read that poem on the show but we ran out of time because we had a lot of phone calls that day."

I nod as I remember.

"Can we hear the poem now?"

I close my eyes and think of the words of the poem I had written years ago called, **'Drink And Thirst No More'**, I say them out aloud.

"A woman came to the well to get water
She brought with her a jar made of mortar
At the well she met the Man of Life
Who told her all about her troubles and strife
They were two different people and so she thought
That she was unworthy to be near Him, but still He taught.
She listened as He taught her the truth that day
Armed with it, she left her jar and went away
To return with her whole village, her whole clan
and drink the life giving water that was this Wonderful Man."

The room erupts with clapping and I am completely taken aback, I smile and look around.

"Thank you," I say.

*   *   *   *   *

I look at the different letters on my desk. Requests from other managers for Jamie to collaborate with their artists. Requests that I write songs for artists and requests that I work on video 'treatments' for several songs. I make a mental note of a couple of movie sound tracks that look promising. I look through all the paperwork for any message from Philip which may have got mixed in with the papers. I have not spoken to him since the day before yesterday when he had driven from my parent's house in Orlando, Florida, back to his hotel in Miami. There is nothing here from him. I make a second mental note to go to Kenny's office later and find out how Philip is. Now I have to read the mail which has been piling up and reply some letters and emails.

*　　*　　*　　*　　*

I cannot take my eyes off the letter in my hand, I stare at the words, tears momentarily blind me, I blink them away and then read the letter again.

> *Dear Billie*
>
> *I hope you get this letter. I am sending it to the record company in hope that they will pass it on to you. I watched your video 'Invisible Pain' on 'The Box' today and I started to cry as I watched my life play before me. I phoned The box's request line and waited for it to be played again. You see I have lived with an abusive husband for five years now, wishing that things would get better, they have got worse. I have a little girl called Amy and I don't want her to grow up thinking that this way of life is right, that abuse is right like I did. (My father abused my mother).*
>
> *I never had the courage before, but I did something the lady in your video did. I prayed and then spoke to my husband. To my amazement he agreed to get help. The message in your video has really touched my life and I thank you for myself but most especially, for Amy and the millions of other little girls and boys that will see that abuse is wrong.*
>
> *Esther*

"George, this letter, when did it come?" He takes the letter from me and reads it.

"I think it is part of the delivery you got this morning. Bertie from the mail room brought up two sack loads."

591

"Where are they?"

"Let me check with Kofi," he walks out of my office and back in again carrying a large sack. Kofi follows behind him with another sack. They open them and tip the letters out. I pick one up and read it.

Dear Miss Lewis

I first heard the song 'Invisible Pain' on my car radio when I was stuck in traffic on the M25. I was on my way to work when I heard it. I am in my forties and very hard-hearted but your words so touched me, that when the traffic eventually started to move I had to pull off the road, because I had tears rolling down my face.

For years I used to deny that I was abusive to my wife and children. I used to drink so much then and get really violent. I put my wife in hospital twice. I used to say that she deserved the 'hiding' she got because she didn't listen to me. She left me some years ago taking our children. They want nothing to do with me now.

I know this sounds strange, but it was not until I listened to the words of your song, that I realized what a monster I was. I hope younger people who listen to your song will take heed and not end up like me. Abuse is abuse and it is wrong.

I won't sign my name, but I will thank you.

PS

I pray that one day my family will forgive me.

"Billie, I don't believe it. Look at these," Kofi says. I can see that he is emotional as he picks up letter after letter and reads them.

George holds up a letter, "This man was going to kill an old girlfriend for hurting him. He read your poem about unforgiveness and he didn't do it. This other one was written by a person who had been emotionally abused by her husband. She was going to poison him. She had even bought the poison and then she heard your song.

This one is from a teacher that had witnessed a murder and other violent acts in her school. She and some parents started praying and claiming the children back from evil after they read your poems *'In God Is All'* and *'Claim Back The Children With Prayer'*. They prayed fervently and after two weeks noticed a dramatic change in the children. Now this teacher and some of the parents go around the country helping others in areas hit by high numbers of child crime. They are praying with parents and teachers in schools. This is absolutely amazing."

"Billie read this please," Kofi says handing me a letter. He shakes his head and visibly shivers.

Dear Billie Lewis

I am writing you this letter with thanks in my heart to God for you and people like you. I was bullied at school from the age of four or five. I put up with it but I used to burn with anger. When I got to secondary school I met a boy who made the rest of my life totally miserable. He used to pick on me, ridicule me and steal from me. He did this for years. I am now twenty seven years old and up until recently I still had nightmares about my school days. I saw this boy recently and he didn't even remember who I was. He had made my life miserable and didn't even know it, didn't even care.

I kidnapped him and was on the verge of killing him. No, this is not a movie script, it really happened. He was whining on the back seat where I had left him, tied and gagged, so I put my car radio on to drown out his noise. That was when I heard your songs, that was when I saw that I was doing wrong and giving in to evil. I listened to the words and started to cry. I removed his gag and we talked. I released him and went to the police and confessed. He did not press charges. He actually apologized for hurting me when we were little, saying that it was a combination of peer pressure and stupidity. The police let me go and I am under-going psychiatric evaluation. I am doing well, because I have come face to face with my demons, battled and won. I know you will understand what I mean.

God bless you and people like you who care.

George hands me a letter, tears are pouring down his face. Shocked I take it from him and read it.

Dear Billie

I am not going to beat about the bush, I grew up a racist, born to a history of White racist people. My family were poor and blamed everyone that was a shade darker than them for their predicament, (not our own laziness or abhorrence of work). We hated Blacks, a number of Whites (mostly rich folk), Hispanics, Asians, Christians, Muslims and Jews (My great granddaddy on my mother's side was Jewish so I didn't understand that but I went along).

I went into the army at an early age armed with a swastika tattoo. I became a racist with a gun doing things that I am now thoroughly ashamed of. After my tour of duty I left the army and joined the police force. I now became a racist with a gun and a badge. Like the military I thrived on the institutional racism that I saw here as well. The first time I read your poem 'The Colour Of God's Love' I laughed and called it crap and worse.

One day my wife and daughter went to the store, they were crossing the road when they were run over by a car driven by White racist youths - joyriding. The boys were caught within hours, they showed no remorse (Hate knows no loyalty).

My wife was in a coma for a couple of days but my daughter was critical, she needed a life saving operation. A number of specialists were called but they refused to come, claiming other commitments. I was desperate, if my daughter didn't get the operation she was going to die. I went crazy, I personally telephoned a number of doctors on a list that the hospital had given me begging them to come and operate, despite the money I offered them, they refused to come.

An Asian nurse saw what I was going through and gave me a card with a doctor's name on it. That was the day that I learnt that racism is evil, sick and has no pride. I called the number and explained everything to the doctor. I can only describe what happened next as a miracle. In two hours the doctor was on his way across the country with his team of experts. They operated on my daughter Molly and she fully recovered. Dr Kola Oluwafemi, the doctor that performed the operation is Black. He saw my racist tattoos and looked past them. He did not take a penny from me and paid for himself and his team to fly out and fly back. He is a Christian and each year performs several life saving operations all over the world free of charge. He had actually just returned from Brazil when I called him. He told me after the operation that something in his heart moved when I called him and that is why he acted so quickly. Incidentally all the other doctors I had called prior to Dr Oluwafemi were White – was this a coincidence? No!

It took a near tragedy for me to see the evil of racism.

594

God touched and changed my life that day. I still work as a police officer but my weapon of choice is no longer a gun but a sword. The living Word of God is a sword. I pray each day that my testimony will touch someone and make them wake up and not have to go through what I went through to see that racism is evil. I read your poems and listen to your songs often and I thank God that I finally understand 'The Colour Of God's Love' I finally understand the unconditional love God has for everyone. I finally understand the scripture:- 'there is no condemnation for those who are in Christ Jesus' written in Romans chapter 8 verse 1. Finally I understand that God forgives us when we repent of our sins and does not hold our past mistakes over us.

God used my 'mess' and made me a 'Messenger'.

Greetings from my wife Carol Ann, my daughter Molly (she is now three years old) and me. We are expecting another baby in the fall.

God Bless you Billie.

Jack Orson

I listen vaguely to George and Kofi as they read letter after letter. As the tears pour down my face, I thank God for what *He* has done.

CHAPTER 75

I knock on the door and walk into Kenny's office. He is sitting in an armchair next to a low table. I notice three mobile phones on the table. I look at him, his head is bent and resting in his hands. I feel my heart start to pound.

"Kenny? What is it? Is everything all right?" He looks up and my thoughts go to Angela as I look at his blood shot eyes.

"Billie, I..., I don't know," he shakes his head, "Philip...,"

I feel my heart sinking and I walk towards him.

"Tell me what's wrong. Where is Philip?"

"There was a tornado yesterday. They've found his car."

"Where is he?" My voice breaks and Kenny shakes his head.

"I've phoned hospitals, the hotel have people looking and so do the police."

"Hospitals! Police?"

I feel hands steady me then push me gently onto a chair.

"I'll get something for her," a female voice says. I turn and stare at Sally. She places a glass in my hand and I look at the brown liquid in it. "Take a sip Billie, just a little one."

I put the glass to my lips and take a sip. The liquid burns my throat and I cough and hand the glass back to Sally.

"I'm going out there in the next few hours. I have a cab coming to take me to the airport," Kenny says.

"What about Angela?" I ask.

"I haven't told her anything yet. I don't want to worry her in her condition," he runs his hands through his hair nervously. "I know you and Angela talk regularly on the phone, can you phone her tonight and tomorrow just to make sure she's okay?"

"Of course I will."

I see the agony in his eyes. Philip and he are more like brothers than cousins.

"It will be okay Kenny, don't worry he'll be okay. You have to believe that," he hugs me and I hug him back, "please bring him back," I whisper.

I hear him blow out slowly, "I will," he says. I watch him pick up his bag and phones, I walk with him to the door.

*   *   *   *   *

I don't go back downstairs to my office or the studios, I don't want to talk to anyone right now. I walk across the corridor and open the door. Sally is not at her desk, I walk into Philip's office and close the door behind me. I push out of my mind the sudden longing I feel for his presence, his smile, the feel of his hand in mine. I don't dwell on them as I look around the room. I walk over to the desk and smile as I remember the argument we had, the croissants I had gotten him, his slept-in clothes and unshaven face. Silly things. I see the shirt which he had worn that day, it's on a hanger at the back of the door. I take the hanger off the door and the shirt off the hanger. I place the hanger back on the door. My mind seems to be doing things in a strange orderly fashion and I wonder why. Something catches my eye, and holding the shirt, I walk over to the large plasma television, there is a framed picture of Philip and me on a stand next to it. I have never seen it before and I look at what I am wearing as I try to remember when it was taken. I smile as recollections come flooding into my mind. It was at Danny's birthday party. We look so in love, so right together. I look at the framed copy of the poem '**Do You Love Me?**...Yes I Do'. I feel tears attempting to fill my eyes and fight to hold them back. The television comes on and I jump back startled. I look at my hand and realize that I have pressed the ON button. I look at the faces of the people laughing on the screen, people oblivious to what I am feeling and I start to cry. I hold the shirt up to my face, it smells clean, there is no aftershave, no smell of Philip. I don't even have that. Emotions take control and I can't seem to stop my tears. Internally I am struggling. I don't need sympathy or kind words. I need encouragement to believe, and not to doubt what I believe. I turn to the only source I know.

"Help me God, please help me. All things are possible with You so please bring him back, please," I can hear loud choking sobs and look around, no one is there, suddenly I realize that I am making the noise. I bury my face in my hands.

"Billie?" I feel arms holding me and a hand patting my back. "there, there Billie. I understand, it's the shock of it all. There, there," I look at Sally. She uses Philip's shirt to dry my tears. "I would say blow, but if I did that," she pauses and I stare at her and wait, "you would probably not be able to look at him quite the same when he wears this shirt." She hands me some tissues and I start to laugh.

"You're laughing, you won't be when he wears this shirt and you and I start laughing and he wants to know why. I'd have to tell him the truth, 'Billie blew her nose on your shirt. I tried to stop her Philip, honest I did'." She starts to laugh and I laugh with her, "That's better Billie. Be positive. My mother had just married my father when the Second World War broke out. He was sent to fight for king and country with the other young men. She used to say that some nights she would get so scared for him and the only way she could get through it was by praying for him and keeping him alive in her heart, no matter what news came over the wireless. He was always alive in her heart Billie. Both my parents are still alive today," she gets up and walks over to the television, she takes something out of a drawer and holds it up. I sit on the couch watching and wondering what she is doing.

"Keep him alive. This came the other day from America. Philip is a speaker at a men's conference. This is a video of the latest one."

I get up and quickly walk over to her and take the video from her hand. I slot it in the player and press the play button.

I turn to Sally, "Thank you, thank you so much."

She reaches out and touches my cheek, "All will be well," she says and walks out of the room gently closing the door behind her. I sit down and watch the video.

"...when you are blessed with something and you don't bless others as you should do you know what can happen? You can either lose what you have very quickly or you may never come to a place in your life where you truly enjoy the things you have. Sometime ago I was shown the difference between being a tube and being a funnel. I chose to be a tube. Picture for a minute a funnel. It has a big

opening and a narrow exit. When you pour something in a funnel it takes a while for it all to come out the other end. Imagine God blessing you with so much but you're a funnel. As your blessings are poured in you are only able to pour a little out. It can get to a point where you can no longer receive any more because your exit is only allowing so much out, stagnation occurs.

If you're a tube, as the blessings pour in they freely flow out, allowing room for more and more to flow in.

Help people! Not people that you know can repay you but those you know can not. We throw millions of Dollars, Pounds, Yens, Euros worth of food away every year, food that people in third world countries will never see. AIDS, Malaria, TB and Poverty, kill hundreds upon hundreds of people in these countries each year. We have the ability to help. Will things change? Or do we make a stand and change things. We are a blessed nation and we have to start blessing others less fortunate or like a funnel, we stagnate...

We say we want our communities, cities, countries and world to change. People make up these places so these places can only change for the better when people change for the better. Bigotry, racism, hate, greed, violence, in short a general lack of love, can only stop when people change. There is no magic wand, there is however Free Will.

Why don't we do something differently, instead of voting for leaders and complaining about them later, why don't we pray for them. There is such a power in prayer that many will never fathom unless they try it. Read 1ˢᵗ Timothy chapter 2 and verses 1-2, pray for leaders and people in authority. Prayer changes things!"

I don't know if respect increases with each new discovery we make about someone else, but I do know that as I watch Philip in the video, as I listen to him talking to the men in the conference, I feel pride, respect and appreciation of and for him. Philip finishes and highlights of the previous conferences are shown. I listen to the different topics which were presented by various men, and wonder why this sort of thing is not done everywhere in the world. Successful men, talking to other men about how to manage their finances, how to be a good husband, how to raise children, how to do the complete will of God. I lean forward as Philip appears on the screen. His name and the topic 'Lust A While Or Love For Life' appears under his name. I listen to him speak to a different much younger audience.

"...I'm only human - is something that a lot of us say when we do something wrong. It's a fact but we use those words as an excuse when we get caught doing the wrong thing, or for an excuse to go ahead and do wrong. For years and years we've chosen to utter those words and over the years they've lost their value. We have been given the ability of choice. We can choose to do right or choose to do wrong. We can choose who we have relationships with, but one thing you must never forget is when you choose to do wrong there is a price that comes attached. It doesn't matter what the wrong is. There is also a reward that is attached when you choose to do the right thing and a much greater reward when you stop doing wrong and start doing right.

Love is right, it can wait, lust is wrong and usually it can't. Guys get a little hazy when it comes to knowing the difference between love and lust. I was like that, until I learnt when you feel that rush of blood and that pounding as it flows, when that tightness is in your heart and not your libido, it's love." I watch as the men clap. Short clips of other speakers follow. As I sit back and stare at the television, I know in my heart that Philip is alive.

*   *   *   *   *

I can hear knocking and voices, I open my eyes, for a few seconds I think that I have dreamt about everything and that Philip is knocking on the door. My eyes feel swollen and tired, worn from my tears, strained from my fitful minutes of sleep. The door opens, I turn around.

"Billie, are you all right?" Jamie asks. I see the concern in his eyes and I know he knows. I am determined to believe that Philip is okay and close my mind to doubt.

"I'm fine. I was watching a video, I must have fallen asleep."

"Come on I'll take you home."

I get up, stretch and follow him. Sally is waiting in the outer office. As I walk past her I touch her hand and smile. She smiles back.

"I'll get the shirt cleaned for him Billie," she says.

"Thank you."

CHAPTER 76

Messages have started pouring in since it was broadcasted on the television and radio two days ago that Philip's rented car was found, but not him. I have sat through broadcast after broadcast with reporter after reporter, all saying the same thing, that they don't think anyone could have survived considering the damage the car had sustained.

A newspaper this morning had the picture of Philip and I taken at the airport on the day I left for Japan.

* * * * *

I sit with Trudi in my front room and look at newspapers. A picture of Sunita catches my eye and I read the story. Sunita talks about how my words inspired her when she was on the verge of giving up her dancing. At the end of her interview she says that her life has changed and she now believes in God and His miracles, she says she now lives a miracle every day. She also says that she is praying for Philip. I smile at her before and after pictures. Her weight loss is evident, but so is the confidence and happiness I see in her face.

"Who is Yvette Marshal?" Trudi asks.

"Yvette Marshal?" I shake my head not recognising the name.

"It says here that your words inspired her when she was at her lowest point. Her debut single 'Standing Strong' is number one in America. According to this newspaper her album 'Faith Did This' is causing waves-"

I gasp, "I remember her, she was at a radio conference in New York." I feel tears sting my eyes, "Thank God, she did it! She did it!" My emotions play havoc, they seem to have difficulty in expressing themselves, for a few seconds they strain dangerously against their reign, self control. The phone rings, Trudi answers it as I quickly wipe my tell-tell tears away.

I walk out of my front room and climb up the stairs. I open the door of the spare bedroom and look inside the room. The newspaper Philip had left, is still laying on the bedside table. I pick up the USA Today newspaper and look at the front page. After a while I put the paper down and kneel down by the side of the bed. I pray.

"Thank You God for looking after me, my family and friends, thank You for protecting us from evil and keeping us all in good health. Thank You for giving me and everyone in the world the knowledge that You love us and nothing can separate us from Your love that is in Christ Jesus. Thank You for Your mercy and favour, please forgive me Lord for anything I have done knowingly or unknowingly that was not right with You. I am truly sorry Lord.

Thank You for the wisdom and understanding that You have brought to my life. I pray that each day I grow stronger in my knowledge of You. I pray that everything I do will be right with You and bring glory and honour to Your name. Let me be the person You want me to be and let Your Will be done in my life. Thank You for true hope, love, protection, forgiveness, direction and joy which can only be found in You.

Mighty Sovereign God, my Awesome Father in Heaven, Omnipotent, Omnipresent, Omniscient, thank You for Your love. I know You hear me and everyone who prays to You and I thank You. I give You all the glory, honour and praise in Jesus' name I pray. Let the words of my mouth and the meditation of my heart be acceptable in thy sight. Amen." I pause for a while, "I know that You have given me the strength that I have right now and I thank You for not leaving me or forsaking me. Without Your strength I would not be able to stand strong. I trust in You completely and I know that Philip will come back soon."

I stay still and wait. I hear the phone ringing downstairs and I ignore it. I remain still and wait. After a while I feel familiar words flood every corner of my mind, they soothe me in such a way I cannot explain. A melody fills my heart as the words of a song my grandmother in Nigeria used to sing plays in my mind. I hum softly to myself and smile. I close my eyes, I can see her sitting in her rocking chair and singing praise worship to God. The intensity of the warmth is so overwhelming. As the words fill my mouth, I sing them:

"Through it all, You have always been my guide
Through it all, You have never left my side

Through it all, through it all, I can truly say
I have You, I'm in You and I'm okay.

Through it all Jehovah, You have always been my guide
Through it all Jesus, You have never left my side
Through it all Holy Spirit, through it all, I can truly say
I have You, I'm in You and I'm okay."

*　*　*　*　*

"No Miss Lewis cannot come to the phone, I can take a message. I'll tell her," she puts the phone down. "Billie, that was Marrebel, she wondered if you were free, they are short staffed at the shelter. She probably hasn't heard yet."

"I'm free," I say.

"We have three events today, do you want me to cancel?" Jamie asks.

"No, why don't you go with Trudi," I suggest.

"No, I don't what to leave you on your own."

"I won't be, I'll be at the shelter. In fact I'm going to make something to take with me now, so you guys please go to the events."

"No," Trudi says, "I'm with Jamie on this one."

"Okay, how about I come with you to the first reception, that's the charity fund raising reception, then, you drop me at the shelter, go to the second and third and then come and pick me up?" They look at each other and as couples in love do, speak without words.

"Okay," they both say and I smile.

*　*　*　*　*

As I wait for the cakes in the oven I look at the notes and flowers that Trudi has arranged on the table in my kitchen. I look at all the names and read some of the short messages. Phoebe, Sarah, Sally, Aidan and Charmaine, Francis Wells and Sofia, Sapphire, George and Kofi, Natasha, Laurel and Jade her husband, Simon, Raj, Charles and so many other people have all sent encouraging messages. Some really colourful flowers are laying wrapped, on the table, a note is still attached. I read it and catch my breath as I stare at the words. *'Hang in there future sis-in-law. We are all praying down here and all will be well'*, Simon Patterson McKnight and Simone McKnight.

I glance at the bin and see Trudi has placed the condolences there. I smile at her thoughtfulness.

*   *   *   *   *

I look around the street, all appears to be calm. As soon as we turn the corner I see the reporters and cameramen standing in front of the hall where the charity fund raising reception is taking place. I take a couple of deep breaths and walk with Trudi and Jamie towards the building. The questions start as soon as we step into the brightly lit foyer of the building.

"Miss Lewis, how are you feeling?"

"I'm fine thank you," I reply. The clicking sound of the cameras grow louder and the flashes have a strobe light effect, they should have a hazard warning placed on them. Jamie holds one arm and Trudi the other as I am escorted past the reporters.

"Miss Lewis-?"

"Miss Lewis please can you-?"

"Miss Lewis have you-?"

I ignore the questions and keep walking. The reporters follow.

"Miss Lewis can you-?"

"Miss Lewis, are you prepared for the worse?"

I look at the man who has asked the question, and turn away.

"He may be dead Billie, you have to accept it," he persists.

I turn back and look at him, I know I have seen him before. I recognise the cold eyes and smile that is just as cold.

"He is not dead and that is what I accept!" I say fiercely.

He looks startled, he backs away.

*   *   *   *   *

I see eyes full of sympathy staring at me and I smile back at them. People point when they think I cannot see them. Heads come together when they think that I am not looking and separate when I turn to look. I feel the words in Psalm 34 verse 4 grow in me; *I sought the Lord and he answered me; he delivered me from all my fears.* My mobile phone starts to vibrate and I quickly answer it, I see more heads turn in my direction.

"Hello."

"Hello, auntie Billie it's me, it's Luke. I just want to tell you that I am believing with you. I'm joining my faith with yours. Uncle Philip is fine. I have to go, bye." I stare at the phone, warmth spreads through me comforting every cell in my body.

CHAPTER 77

Whe drive to the shelter in silence. I am deep in my silent prayers. Trudi turns the radio on and the words 'I miss you like crazy' jump out at us. I catch my breath and Trudi quickly changes the station. I breathe out slowly and stare out of the window.

* * * * *

Wayne looks at Billie's picture and feels the tears in his eyes brim and then fall. He listens to the words on the radio and closes his eyes as he feels a hurt beyond words. Loneliness fills his heart as he sits still and the words 'I miss you like crazy' wash over him. He looks down at the chain on his wrist, the chain which was supposed to give him everything he wanted. His tears continue to fall as he rips the chain off his wrist and throws it into the bin.

* * * * *

After changing radio stations a number of times Trudi finally turns the radio off and turns the television on. I squeeze her arm as she finally sits back and we watch the news as Jamie drives.

"...And now we bring you some amazing news. People all over the world are renouncing violence. We have had messages pouring into this television station and many others all over the country saying that people are listening to the words in the songs of Billie Lewis and the words are touching them. At first we thought this was a ploy, some promotional thing set up by the record company, but I have spoken to several police officers in a number of the London boroughs and other areas of the country, they have all said that people are handing in weapons. People have just literally walked into the stations and left weapons like guns and knives. Notes have been found with these weapons saying things like 'We are sorry', or 'We want to stop the killings, end the violence and do the right thing'.

The thing they are talking about is what Billie Lewis has written about in her songs and poems, the thing that Daniel Bridges and Richard J. Brown depict in their films, the thing that Maurice Web portrays in his musicals, the thing that is now being talked about in communities, in homes and in churches. LOVE!

I'm just getting some information in now from some of our international correspondents. Apparently this amazing thing is not just happening here, it is happening all over the world!"

Stunned I stare at the television screen, at the pictures of the various weapons that have been handed in.

"....News has just come in of the sudden death of Mr Theodore Heevilone. He died suddenly at a charity event an hour ago in London. Mr T. Heevilone, was dubbed the voice of doom, gloom and fear in the eighties and nineties because of his constant reporting of bad news. After suddenly amassing a large fortune in the late nineties, he went on to manage and later take control of several newspapers, radio and television stations. He will be missed by many."

I stare at the picture of the man on the television screen.

"I've seen that man before!"

"Where?" Trudi asks

"I saw him a couple of years ago in a derelict building. He was standing at the window in a suit and bow tie, and I just saw him at the charity event we just left." I don't mention the basement of the record studio, the man in the black suit that had suddenly disappeared.

"Are you sure it was him?"

"I'm positive," I reply. Stunned, I watch the rest of the news.

*   *   *   *   *

"Are you going to be okay?"

"I'll be fine here, come and get me when you've finished."

Trudi hugs me to her, "I love you," she says, "be strong Billie and...," her voice falters and she smiles.

I nod understanding her unsaid words.

607

"Thank you. I'll see you later."

She waits by the car while Jamie helps me carry the cakes I have made, and the ones I took from the charity reception, into the shelter.

*　　*　　*　　*　　*

"Billie, thanks for coming," Marrebel says, she smiles at me then hugs me, "Mr Grace had to be taken to his sister's place by one of the resident workers so we are a person short."

"Mr Grace has a sister?"

"Yes..., err..., I think she lives up north."

"That's nice. I hope he is happy there."

"He will be."

"So Marrebel, how many lunches?"

*　　*　　*　　*　　*

"Isn't it nice that Mr Grace went to his cousin's place?" Mrs Cotterell says.

"Cousin? Marrebel said sister."

"Did she? I thought it was his cousin. Maybe it's his sister."

I look at Mrs Cotterell, she looks away.

"Billie, have you met Mr Kinder? He just came in yesterday, he's in Mr Grace's old room," Marrebel says.

An elderly man extends his hand to me and I reach out and shake it.

"Good afternoon sir," I say. I look into eyes that I have seen before and catch my breath. I blink twice and look at him again. His eyes seem to have changed but only slightly.

"I heard about Philip on the news yesterday Billie. Everyone here was so upset. I am truly sorry that you have to go through this."

"That's okay, we go through trials to make us stronger, everything will be fine."

"You seem calmly confident that everything will be well."

"It has to be."

"I did counselling once, are you sure you're not in denial? It's a common thing to happen Billie?"

"Denial?"

"Yes, anger, denial, depression, are some of the different stages of grief."

"No it's not denial. It's faith. My faith in God is not an occasional act it's my permanent attitude. If I don't have faith, I have nothing. I have made my choice, this is my life. It's taken me a long time to get here and I will not go back."

"You've seen a picture of the car, what if-"

"No, the veracity of Psalm 91 to me does not allow for 'what if'. I claim what is written in the Bible, God's Word and stand on it, I live by it. Not what I see."

He smiles and looks at me, sympathy no longer in his eyes

"Your mustard seed has grown Billie, you do not look at what you see in the natural, you look in faith knowing that it supersedes all. Your mustard seed of faith has grown," he says. I feel a sudden cold rush, I shiver as I look at him, my heart starts to pound. "You know in all things God works for the good of those who love Him, who have been called according to His purpose."

"I love God and I know He has a purpose for my life," I say.

CHAPTER 78

First a flutter then slowly his eyes open. His vision is blurred but he tries to focus. He tries to move but stops immediately as he feels a sharp pain in his leg. He can feel the damp warm ground beneath him. As his vision becomes clearer he can see trees in the distance. The last thing he remembers is seeing a dark destructive wind whirling from afar but coming at him with such unbelievable speed and force. Then being thrown out of the car. He tries to move again and this time succeeds by gritting his teeth at the pain and pulling himself up. He immediately feels light headed and braces himself from falling back down on the ground.

"Mr McKnight!"

He hears his name faintly, it seems to be coming from the wind blowing against the trees.

"Mr McKnight!"

This time it is clearer and a lot nearer. He tries to turn around, but feels a sharp pain and dizziness. He opens his mouth to call for help. A dry raspy voiceless sound comes out. He breathes deeply and tries to clear his throat.

"Help," he finally manages to whisper.

"Mr McKnight," Philip jumps startled by the voice which is right next to him. He turns and looks at a man he has never seen before.

"I hear a lot of people have been praying for you Philip."

"How did you…? Who are you?" Philip asks.

"Me, I was just passing and heard you call for help. I know you hit your head and twisted your leg. Do you think you can walk?"

"My leg really hurts," he looks down at it laying limply on the ground. "It doesn't feel too good."

"Take my hand and see if you can get up."

"I tried just now and I couldn't."

"Can you try again? Can you trust me?"

"Yes," Philip takes hold of the man's hand. Immediately he feels a warmth spread through his body. His leg starts to tingle. He stands up and stares down in amazement at his leg.

"Come with me Philip, hold on to my hand and don't let go. I know the way back," the man leads Philip along a path. Philip looks down as they walk and sees the sheer drop down into the rocky cliffs and murky water below. He also notices that the path they are walking along, is very narrow.

"Philip some people are coming for you. Stay here and wait for them, they will not be long."

"Stay with me, we can get out of here together."

"I will be fine."

"Who are you?"

He turns and smiles, "You already know me."

Philip freezes in shock, "I…"

"I've had many hot showers thanks to you."

"Mr Grace!"

*   *   *   *   *

"We have to go back to the jeep and get the torches. It will get dark soon," one of the three rescue officers says, he looks up at the sky.

"No," Kenny says sensing something. Looking around he feels strange, as if someone is watching him. A soft wind blows, he shivers.

"Okay let's go this way then. That way is a sheer drop to the cliffs below, no one can survive that and the coastguards have checked it already," another rescue officer says. All three of them start to head in the direction of the thick forest.

"No wait, that way!" Kenny says pointing to the cliffs. "Did you feel that soft breeze just then? Did you hear that?"

"No sir," one of the officers replies, he looks at the others they shake their heads. They turn and look at Kenny's back as he runs towards the direction of the wind's source.

"PHILIP! PHILIP!" He shouts at the top of his voice.

"Kenny?" Philip says stunned to the core. "Kenny!" He shouts.

The rescue workers run towards Kenny and the voice they hear calling his name.

"Over here, get the ropes out he's down here!" Kenny shouts.

They look down. Philip is standing on a small ledge of protruding cliff about ten feet below them. He looks calm. They look below him at the sheer drop and instantaneously get to work.

*   *   *   *   *

"Okay Marrebel, the lunch dishes are done shall we start on the dinner?"

"Are you sure you don't want to go home Billie, I can manage now. You need to rest."

"No way, I'm here until Jamie and Trudi come for me."

"Why don't you go and take a rest here then, go to the sitting room, you've been working since you got here, you've mopped the kitchen floor, washed the bedclothes, cooked."

"I'm fine. What are we making for dinner?" I ask. My Mobile phone starts to ring and I pull it out of my pocket and answer it.

"Billie, hi it's me."

"Wayne?"

"Yes, how are you?"

"I'm fine thank you."

"I heard about Philip. I just want you to know that umm.., I'm here for you. Please call me at any time if you need to talk."

"Thanks Wayne, but really I am fine. Thank you. I have to go now I'm a little bit busy." I turn my phone off and put it back in my pocket.

"Why did you turn it off?" Marrebel asks quickly, "turn it back on Billie you may need to…," she stops and I look at her. She does not continue.

"It's okay Marrebel, I'm not expecting any calls," I reassure her, "Jamie and Trudi will come to get me at nine. Besides, once I start with the dinners, I don't want to be distracted. So come on let's get started."

*   *   *   *   *

Wayne picks up his mobile phone and stares at it for a few moments. He is desperate, he needs to tell Billie how he thinks he feels. He punches in her number and holds his phone against his ear. He listens to the automated voice tell him that Billie's mobile phone has been switched off.

*   *   *   *   *

"There you go, one home-made chocolate chip muffin. Low in fat, rich in taste." I place the plate on the table in front of Mr Kinder.

"Sit down Billie."

I look around at the dinner dishes that need clearing and hesitate. He pulls a chair out. I sit down.

"Something happened to you that night?"

"Which night?"

"The night you found Luke."

"How did you know about that?"

"Trust me Billie. I know you haven't told anyone about it, tell me, don't keep it bouncing around in your mind."

"I…"

"Think back Billie, what happened that night?"

"Why?"

"Trust me."

I take a deep breath and close my eyes. When I open them he is staring at me intently.

"The police couldn't get into the basement, they smashed a section of the wall in to gain entrance. A large chunk of it fell on Luke, it crushed him. I pulled the wall off him and checked him, he wasn't breathing. I tried CPR, mouth-to-mouth, nothing worked. Colin and Tina were fighting with each other, the police were shouting, there was so much noise. I kept on trying to get Luke to breathe, I was worried about brain damage. Then suddenly I felt this overwhelming flood of power upon me, it was unimaginable. I felt this rush of anger in me, not at Colin or Tina but at the evil satanic force behind them and their actions. I started screaming, Colin and Tina didn't seem to hear me though. I grabbed hold of

613

Luke and demanded that he come back. I saw the power I had as a child of God. I understood what David felt like when he went up against Goliath. David knew who God was and what God had done for him in the past and acted on that knowledge. I saw who God is, I saw who Jesus is and what He has achieved by laying down His life for us, I saw the power of the Holy Spirit. I saw who I am and Whose I am. God knows how many hairs I have on my head. The Bible says: 'I am the apple of God's Eyes, that I am wonderfully and fearfully made, that my name is written on the Palm of God's Hand, that He would never leave me nor forsake me, that He has given me a spirit of power, love and a sound mind and that with God all things are possible.' This means that I have the power to face the enemy by His Grace. I felt the power of God's Word, it was so strong, so real. As I held Luke, certain scriptures came to mind, they were like *Living Words*. I could see them, feel them around me, touch them.

I was holding Luke and praying when Philip knelt down beside me. He told me to give Luke to him, at first I refused. When I finally did give Luke to him, within seconds, Luke was breathing."

He sighs deeply.

"Show me your heart and I'll show you your faith. A lot of people say they have faith Billie but they sit back and do nothing as a result nothing happens. Faith without works is dead. We are told to have faith and not to doubt. Earlier on I wasn't testing you, I was showing just how much you have changed from the first time you called out for help all those years ago. Change that matters Billie is measured by the difference between the you *then* and the you *now*. Your mustard seed is now a tree.

You see faith does not see the ground shaking all around, it sees that if God says that He will never leave you or forsake you, then He will not. So it does not matter what is happening around you, as long as you do what is right and obey Him, He will remain with you. When you cannot walk He will carry you," he smiles and squeezes my hand, I smile back. "Every experience you have gone through, and will go through, is for a reason Billie. Tests in life, give you a testimony. Things happen to prepare you for the 'knocks' in life and to make you strong."

I smile.

"What is it?"

"What you said about the 'knocks' in life, Philip said something similar once."

"Did he? I've heard a lot of good things about him."

"You will like him when you meet him," I say impulsively.

"I know I will," he smiles at me.

As I sit and listen to him talking about things that have happened, it is as if I am in a daze.

"…The people at the hospital you worked in were planning to contaminate food, mainly baby food, blackmail the government and food companies as well as sell the bacteria to terrorist. If you hadn't seen what you saw, and exposed them, people would have died.

Luke will have a ministry of healing and teaching when he is older. They tried to take it away by corrupting him, but they failed. The songs you have written have touched people's lives as well as stopped people from becoming polluted with the lyrics of other songs. The list is endless Billie and the reasons many, but the gates of hell shall not prevail." I nod calmly as I hold my turmoil thoughts at bay. 'Who is this?', I think but do not ask.

"Now I think I will go and have this in my room," he gets up and lifts the plate up. I smile at him and watch him walk across the room. I have gone through so much, I do not wonder at his knowledge of my life, it does not take me by surprise. I get up and start to collect the used plates. My mobile phone starts to ring; startled I almost drop the plate in my hand, I know I turned my phone off earlier.

I put the plate down and answer my phone, thinking that it is Jamie, calling to tell me they are about to start heading out for me.

"Billie!" the familiar 'West Coast twang' says. Emotions assault me, overpower me, leaving me breathless and dizzy. I collapse onto a chair. "Billie it's me!"

"Philip?" I whisper. Something across the room catches my eye and I look up. Mr Kinder lifts his plate up to me and smiles. I feel tears of gladness and joy sting my eyes. "Philip, where are you? Are you okay?"

"I'm in Miami, I'm fine and I love you."

CHAPTER 79

Tonight's international event is scheduled to last for nearly four hours. It is being shown live tonight on television in various countries across the world. I sit with Jamie and the other nominees and presenters as the producer explains what will happen this evening and how the ushers will come to get us, when the time comes for us to present an award. We are told that if we have been nominated for an award and are not presenting an award immediately before or after, we must try as much as possible to stay at our tables so the cameras can zoom in on us.

I didn't want to come here today. Since Philip's phone call yesterday, I have been trying to get to Miami. Every flight is fully booked. Steve and Jamie think that I should wait for a couple of more days, because they think that by the time I sort my flight out, Philip will be on his way back. They also said that it was important I be here tonight because I have been elected as the 'A Dream Come True' foundation's spokesperson after news broke about my plans to raise money for orphanages in South Africa. As I look around at all the other artists, managers, DJs and actors, I see the odd turn of a celebrity head now and again and I don't know if it's because of what the papers are calling the *'miraculous survival of Philip McKnight'*, or because Jamie was given an award this morning by the book of records for selling millions of copies of his debut single and album.

"It's important that you all please pay attention to the auto-cue monitor as this will also tell you how much time you have to talk," the producer says. "It will also give you the guidelines to follow." His assistant sets up a large monitor and we look at it. Another assistant starts to type and the producer reads:

"Good evening ladies and gentlemen, the nominees for the best international album are: Pause. Read names and album titles. Pause. The large screen will show clips as you speak. Wait for clapping to subside. Long pause, then open the envelope and announce the winner (with as much verbal funfair as you can muster)."

We all laugh.

The producer looks at us, frowns then looks at the monitor.

"Sean!" The assistant looks up, "Funfair?"

"Sorry dad, I meant fanfare," he quickly corrects his mistake.

*   *   *   *   *

"Jamie…, I'm really thinking about going out to Miami tomorrow," I notice something flicker in his eyes.

"Look why not wait until the day after, if you hear nothing from Philip before then, I will personally take you. Deal?"

"No deal, I'll go tomorrow by myself, you stay and plan your wedding."

"It's a deal only if I come with you Billie."

*   *   *   *   *

'McKnight's Ex-Partner Breaks Down and Weeps'

I pick up the newspaper and read. The story is ineptly written, it is not about an ex-girlfriend as the newspaper's headline appears to depict. It is about Philip's old business partner, William Mathias. He broke down and wept because after years of secretly blaming Philip for his predicament, he found out that Philip had paid for all his treatment at a very expensive drug and alcohol rehabilitation clinic, as well as taken care of his parents, siblings, wife and son. The information that he had a secret benefactor had only been divulged to him a few days ago because it was thought Philip was not coming back.

The picture of the narrow ledge of the cliff, where they had found Philip is next to the story. It shows the rugged cliff face and the sheer drop to the murky rocky waters below.

*   *   *   *   *

"Good luck for tonight Billie."

"Thank you."

"All the best Billie and congratulations on South Africa."

617

"Thanks," I say to another singer who walks past me and heads in the direction of the large hall where a lot of people are eating and drinking as they wait for the show to start. I feel like going home, but I know that I am duty bound to stay for Jamie, for Philip, for the record label and most of all for the charity.

*　　*　　*　　*　　*

Jamie is nervous. I watch as he fidgets with the ring that Trudi has given him and how he keeps looking around the hall. Trudi says something to him and he stands up.

"Where are you going?" I ask.

"Err..., to get some fresh air," he replies squeezing my hand. He walks towards one of the many side doors. I turn and look at Trudi and Jen who are both talking in low voices. Martin says something to Steve and they both look around the hall.

"What's going on? Why are you all whispering?" I ask.

"Whispering?" Steve asks looking around the table. "I wasn't whispering. Martin were you?"

"No, I wasn't."

"Trudi and I were just..., err.., admiring your dress," Jen says quickly, a little too quickly. I frown as I look at them. I go from face to face trying to read the different expressions. Music starts meaning that the awards ceremony will soon begin. Jamie walks back to the table. He sits down and I notice that he is smiling. He leans towards Trudi and says something she smiles and says something to Jen.

"That's it, what is going on?" I ask.

"Nothing," Jamie says, "I was just telling Trudi how nice you look tonight."

"Ladies and gentlemen welcome to this international forty ninth awards ceremony..."

*　　*　　*　　*　　*

I watch the various artists perform, I am waiting for two presentations, The Best Male Newcomer and The Best New Group. A number of awards have already been given out. I hold my breath as the band performing finish their song and a male and female presenter walk onto the stage.

"The next category is one which I am honoured to present tonight, it is the award for The Best New Male Artist. The nominees for the best new male artist are," the male presenter reads a list of names. Clips are shown from each video as each name is read. The female presenter opens the envelope and smiles, "The winner is.... Jamie Sanders. YEAHHH JAMIEEE," she shouts.

Jamie sits at the table in total shock. Everyone at our table is silent as the song plays in the background and cameras zoom in.

"Billie?"

"Jamie, you won!"

We all start screaming at once and Martin pulls Jamie to his feet. Jamie hugs me, turns to hug Trudi and shake everyone else's hand. He walks quickly towards the stage. We watch as he collects the award and stands in front of the microphone. The noise is deafening as he waits for it to die down. The fans are clapping and screaming as well as the other artists. Finally the noise starts to die down; Jamie lifts a hand, there is complete silence.

"I thank first and foremost my Heavenly Father. I thank Him for bringing me this far and bringing the people into my life that have helped me achieve this. One of those people, as you know, is Billie Lewis my manager," he blows out slowly. "She never doubted me, she always said right from the beginning that there was a bigger picture. Thank you Billie." The screaming starts up again. Jamie lifts his hand up and continues, "I also want to thank everyone at McKnight/Digital Records and Martin, Jen, Steve and always Trudi. I love you. Thank you all, God bless you all." Clapping and cheering ensue.

Jamie is escorted off the stage with the presenters. I feel a tap on my shoulder and turn around.

"Miss Lewis it's time to get ready," the hostess says. I get up and follow her.

It takes a few minutes to get behind stage because of all the people standing around. I stand where the hostess has asked me to stand and wait for the footballer that I am presenting the award with. As I look around backstage, I notice it is so much more congested than it was earlier. Some celebrities are watching the show on a large screen behind the stage. They are drinking and smoking. Something catches my eye and I turn to an area where some people are standing around a man. I wonder who he is. I try to look around the people.

"Billie, how are you?"

Startled I turn, I smile at the footballer, "I'm fine David, how are you?"

"Good."

"By the way congratulations."

He smiles, "Thank you."

A hostess hands me an envelope and hands David the award.

"-and now to present the award for the best new group or band here are a footballer who definitely has game, and a song writer who is head of her game."

Music starts and David and I walk through the door and onto the stage. We both look at the auto cue. He starts to read.

"The nominees for The Best New Group Or Band are," he reads the list slowly as each video clip is shown.

"And the winner is," I say. I open the envelope. I gasp and hold it up for David to see. He smiles at me.

"KALEIDOSCOPE!" We both shout and clap. The boys jump up and then run towards the stage as the audience clap and scream. The music for 'Only What You Wanna Hear' starts. I smile as I watch them feeling the pride of a mother watching her children do well.

"Thank you, thank you," Ryan says.

He passes the microphone to Greg, "We are so grateful to God for everything. Thank you for supporting us."

He passes the microphone to Leon. Leon holds it up between himself and Dillon. "Thank you everyone," he shouts.

"Tonight is what I can only call a miracle," Dillon says. "Not long ago we were unsigned and struggling then we met a special man, Philip McKnight. He took us under his wing and introduced us to Billie. She wrote the song and gave it to us and here we are fulfilling what six months ago was only a dream. I speak for all of us in Kaleidoscope, when I say that I thank God for everything, every day. Thank you."

The audience clap and to my surprise the boys hug me one by one. I am about to follow David and the boys off the stage, when a hostess takes my arm and guides me down the front steps of the stage to my table. As I approach the table I notice a large bunch of very colourful flowers laying where I had been sitting. My heart starts to beat rapidly and I thank the hostess then quickly pick up the envelope next to the flowers, slowly I open it. I notice my hands shaking as I stare at the words on the card.

I love you so much. Philip.

I feel tears fill my eyes and I know with or without Jamie I will go to Miami tomorrow or as soon as possible. Jamie pulls my chair out and I sit down.

"The next award is one that has been voted by you, the public. It has nothing to do with sales, nothing to do with money. Here is someone special to tell us more about it," the host says.

I stare at the flowers.

I hear a hush but do not look up, the hall is quiet and I wonder why as I read Philip's note again. I look up at Trudi and Jen and see tears in their eyes. Frowning I turn to Jamie to ask him why they are crying. I open my mouth but the words do not come out.

"This award is one voted by you the public. Over twenty million of you registered your votes for the song of the year, for a song that has touched you the most," slowly I turn to the stage. I blink my tears away as I stare at the man talking. My heart is pounding so hard that I have to strain my ears to hear him.

"I have been told that something absolutely unique has happened with this category this year, two songs received exactly the same number of votes, they received just over nine million votes each. These two songs are written by the same person and according to you the public, they have changed the way you think and the things you do. The same person who wrote; 'In Too Deep', 'I Don't Wanna Escape', 'Your Hand Is On My Heart', 'Break Up', 'Only What You Wanna Hear', 'Your Love Takes My Breath Away', 'Dance' and 'I Choose

You Lord' which has been nominated for a Grammy in the Best Song Written For A Film category." The crowds cheer.

"This award goes to Billie Lewis for 'Love Is Not Supposed To Hurt' and 'Invisible Pain', two songs which you say have made a difference in music and an impact on you."

I watch as people stand up and start to clap and cheer. I cannot feel my legs, the blood is pounding loudly in my ears.

"Billie," Jamie says, "you have to go and collect the award."

I turn and stare at him and feel him gently pull me up. He takes my hand and escorts me to the steps at the bottom of the stage. I climb up the steps and find myself standing in front of Philip. I stare at him. He hands me the award as the audience clap and cheer. I place it on the stand and turn to him. I can hear music playing in the background, hear the people clapping. Everything disappears as I walk into Philip's arms and hold him.

"Are you okay?"

"I'm fine, Billie I-"

"I don't think I can let go," I cling to him, "why didn't you tell me you were coming?"

"We wanted to surprise you," he takes hold of my face and wipes my tears away, "will you marry me soon?"

I nod feeling my eyes flood with tears again.

"I love you."

"I love you too Philip," I hug him tightly.

"Now you have a speech to make," he says as he pulls away. I suddenly become aware of the people still clapping and the flashes of the cameras.

"I can't remember.., I haven't ..."

"Yes you have. It's in your heart. Go and say it."

I turn back to the audience and cameras and breathe deeply. I look at the monitor, it tells me I have two and a half minutes to speak. I turn and look at Philip, I am shaking. His smile encourages me.

"Thank you so much," I breathe deeply again and clear my throat, I wait for the clapping to die down. "I have been asked by the 'A Dream Come True' foundation to share with you how my dream has come true and the importance of *you* fulfilling *your* dream. I would be honoured to do that now if I may." I pause for a moment and recollect my thoughts. "When I was little I always dreamt of writing songs and poems that would touch people, help them with whatever it was they were going through," I stop and stare at the award as my eyes fill with tears. "My dream has always been in my heart, over the years it has put up with a lot of criticism, a lot of things have tried to stop me from fulfilling it. But my dream never died.

I know there are many of you in the audience and at home tonight who have a dream. Maybe you want to be a writer, a doctor, a dancer, a singer, you know your dream. You know what it is that burns in your heart. People will try to tell you that you are wasting your time, they said that to me. In the midst of all the adversity, I never let go of what I believed in, I couldn't.

It does not matter what colour you are, where you come from or what you have done in the past. Some people think it does, but that is a lie. Fulfilling your dream can be a battle. The battle is fought in the world but the victory has to start in your mind. You have to have faith, believe, don't dwell on your past mistakes, move forward and take hold of your future success or you may end up success-less."

I look at the award and smile.

"I wrote these songs four nearly five years ago, but I let what people said hold me back. We are all on this earth for a purpose and we all have gifts which will help us to fulfill that purpose. For those of you still trying to figure out what your purpose is - Pray, find out what your gift or gifts are and what your purpose is. Use your gift to do the right thing and your dream will be fulfilled, you will be fulfilled. It's not about luck or chance. It is and has always been about trusting in God and doing your best. I hope and pray that what I write will help people see, no one is better than anyone else in this world, people are just misled to think that they are, we are *all* unique.

It is sad that we still live in a world where people so readily hate and find it so difficult to love. We need 'change' because things can only change when people change. I believe that if you reach out in love to everyone, one day you will touch someone. That someone will touch someone else and things can only get better from there. The fact that music is changing and positive lyrics are being listened to and acted upon, shows there is hope. Thank you for voting for my songs, I pray they continue to do what they are meant to do."

I pick up my award, "For everyone of you with a dream out there, see your dream don't just dream it! Never let the 'dream breakers' hold you back. They told me I could never touch the clouds, I thank God because He helped me to reach the stars. God bless you and thank you."

I wave at the audience as they clap and clap and clap. I reach back and take hold of Philip's hand and squeeze.

CHAPTER 80

"Miss Lewis, Mr McKnight, over here please. Smile please."
"Over here, Billie, Philip, over here."

"Miss Lewis what would you describe as the most memorable event of tonight?"

"Having my prayers answered in front of millions of people," I say and tighten my grip on Philip's hand.

"Mr McKnight, Philip, your being here is a miracle in itself. How do you feel? Lucky?"

Philip looks at me and then back at the reporter, "Luck has nothing to do with it. I feel blessed, truly blessed. I am so grateful for everything, so thankful."

The reporter looks from Philip to me and nods his head. The cameras click constantly in our faces and we smile. Music plays loudly and balloons start to fall down on us. I catch the words of 'I Choose You Lord' and smile as the video plays on a large screen.

Jamie, Trudi, Martin, Jen, Steve, Angela and Kenny join us as the cameras continue to click away.

Everyone knew that Philip had arrived this morning except me, it was Steve's idea that he surprise me. My eyes fill with tears as I watch my brother and Philip hug each other. They set the precedent and we all start hugging each other.

I hug Kenny tightly, "Thank you," I whisper in his ear.

"Okay everyone on three," a photographer taking exclusive pictures for McKnight/Digital says. We all smile, tickled by the invisible happy chord which plays within us. I hold on to Philip's hand. Steve has a hand on his back and Jamie, Trudi, Martin, Jen, Angela and Kenny gather in close. The love amongst us all is intense.

"One two and …"

The flash pops, the camera captures a thousand words.

That love, faith, trust and obedience brings victory, may not be obvious at the first glance but if you look closer, close enough to see the light in our eyes, the love, you will see the victory. Years ago a song was written, the words of the chorus are: *'Count your many blessings name them one by one, count your many blessings see what God has done. Count your many blessings name them one by one and it will surprise you what the LORD has done'*. I know in the days to come, the months, the years, no matter what I go through. This moment, right here, right now, will always be counted.

Two months and one day later

My father takes my hand and places it in Philip's. He has tears in his eyes as he kisses my cheek.

"God bless you darling," he whispers. I watch as he turns and takes hold of my little bride, Tilly Ann's hand, they walk towards their seats. Soft music plays in the background. All Philip's family, all my family and all our friends are here today.

"Marriage is a covenant, when you make your vows today, you do so in the presence of God. This covenant must be taken seriously because today you pledge your commitment to each other for better or worse, in sickness and in health, forsaking all others, till death do you part." He picks up the rings and places them on the Bible.

"We are gathered here to join together in holy matrimony two dear people." My heart is beating rapidly but I feel remarkably calm. I turn and look at my parents. My mother has already started to cry. My aunt hands her a tissue and hugs her. I turn back. I look at my husband to be and smile at him. He lifts my hand to his lips and kisses it.

"Philip and Billie," Pastor McPhearson continues, "in the presence of your family and friends...."

EPILOGUE

A lot of people do not want to believe that there is evil in the world. They close their eyes to it. Others who know, hope like a bad dream, it will go away or disintegrate into a million pieces, never to surface again. Reality, for those who want to know, evil is real, the battle between good and evil is real but God gives us victory over evil satanic forces. When you know and accept this, you will discover like I did, after praying and reading the Bible, that the 'Way' is the 'Truth' which is 'Life'.

The Bible tells us *'God so loved the world that He gave His only begotten son, that whoever believes in Him will have eternal life'*.

People have become complacent, living for the here and now, not caring about the future. They believe the lies which have been told over the years by an evil liar, an enemy of the truth, that has been around for a long time, polluting their minds and the minds of generations before them with empty promises. A liar who says there is no 'right' in the world and readily highlights all the bad in newspapers and on the news. A liar who has perverted 'right', and made it wrong, and then presented the wrong as normal. As a result people who try to do the right thing, are mocked and called abnormal. People who know the truth, are embarrassed and choose not to say it for fear of being mocked.

I do not profess to have read the whole Bible, but from what I have read, I know God is merciful and loves everyone. He has given us a choice. In the book of Revelations, we are told that Jesus stands at the door knocking, waiting for us to invite Him in. He will only come into our lives when we invite Him in. We can choose to invite Him in, or not.

We can choose to do the right thing, or we can choose to do the wrong thing, which is to continue to listen to the lies of the enemy. If we choose the wrong thing, we remain in bondage, tied up in evil ways. We live with hate, hurt, unforgiveness, bitterness, pain, a sense of worthlessness and a lack of true love. I know, because I have lived like that in the past. I would wake like most people currently still do, feeling miserable, unhappy, angry or sad – and not just on a Monday morning!

Then one day I read a Psalm in the Bible and I realized that I had a choice. A choice to say *'This is the day that the Lord has made and I will rejoice and be glad in it'*, thank God for His Mercy and Grace, and, make the best of my day, or choose not to and be miserable. It's all about doing the right thing, making the right choices.

How do you do the right thing? It's not hard, it never was. The lies which have been told over the years, were told to keep you from the truth, keep you ignorant. You see all you have to do is choose to reject what is wrong and do right. How do you know what is right? You will know when you read the Bible daily and pray continuously.

Jesus tells us to *'seek the Kingdom of God first and His righteousness and all other things will be added on to us'*. God loves us so much that He has given us the Bible as a wonderful 'blue print' for our lives. Doing the right thing involves living a life where it is not just about what we can get but about what we can give. We need to 'sow' into God's Kingdom with our finances, time and prayers. We need to mentor, coach, help and encourage others to do the same. When we do this, others will come to a knowledge of God and His Kingdom will increase.

We need to humble ourselves, actively seek God and pray. This is very important, because when we seek God by praying and reading His Word, the Bible, we fill our minds and leave no room for evil to have a hold on our lives. Our minds can become idle if we do not use them properly and I know that you have heard or read at one time in your life that: 'An idle mind is a playground for the devil'. Well if you haven't, you have now!

God's Word is light and it drives out the darkness and gives us 'life'. When I look at my life now, I see that I am truly blessed. If I were to give a piece of solid advice, it would be to take that first step, accept the Truth, let go of the past, follow the Way and live the Life. The life which you will have, as a result of this, will be full of love, joy and peace and you will grow in patience, kindness, goodness, faithfulness, humility and self-control.

You have read my story, you have seen that I, like most people, tried to do things by myself. I failed and stopped trying when I realized it is only with God that all things are possible, not some things but **all** things. I have gone through a lot in my life and I know that if I did not have a relationship with God, if I had not put Him first, if I had not changed the way I thought and acted, I would not be where I am today. If I had let the things which were done to me, or said to and about me, hold me down, I would still be down.

Take a moment and think about your life. Think about the lies you have been told in the past. The:

'You have always failed and always will'
'You have no future'
'You are not up to standard'
'You are not the right colour'
'You will never amount to 'anything' because of your past'
'Your grandfather failed, your father failed, therefore you will fail'
'You always have and always will make the wrong choices'.

Some of you may still be feeling the pain of these negative words that may have been said to you by a parent, a teacher, a friend, a sibling or even a spouse. Let me tell you why I can confidently call these statements lies. I can because I know that your past doesn't matter, your future does, because God forgives the things we have done in the past. He delivers us from our sins, when we ask Him to, when we are sincere and truly repentant.

When we don't do this, when we continue to do wrong and refuse to change, we risk our future by holding on to our past.

There are people who you and I know that started off really well in life, wanting for nothing. Somehow, because they depended on themselves, their own ability, they lost it all.

There are also people that started off with nothing and went through some very difficult times, but today, because they tenaciously trusted in God, renewed their minds, walked in faith and were completely obedient to God, they have a lot. Through their difficult times they constantly said things like:

> **'God will make a way, where there seems to be no way!'**
> **'Jehovah Jireh my provider Your Grace is sufficient for me!'**
> **'I will bless the LORD at all times His praise shall continually be in my mouth!'**
> **'When the devil is messing, prepare for your blessing!'**

'Joy comes in the morning!'
'Why panic when you can Pray!'

Before I knew the truth I used to look at the second set of people and wonder. Then one day I discovered: **God never said it would be easy but He did say that He would never forsake or leave you or me, if we trust and obey Him.**

Some of you may have been led by perfidious people to believe that God is looking for self, 'worldly' perfection in people. With this lie comes the feeling of ineptness, unworthiness to seek Him. The truth is 'worldly' self-perfection, self-strength, self-holiness are not important. What is important is a willing heart full of love for God, others and yourself. God is the Potter and we are the clay. We should have faith in Him and walk in that faith and let Him mould us into perfection using His standards.

I want to pause for a moment here and address the people that have either turned away from God because of things that have happened in their life, or people that do not, and have never, believed in God. People that say 'if God existed, things would have happened differently in their life or in the world'. Life is made up of choices; things we choose to do without God, so when they go wrong how can we blame Him. Maybe it is time to do things differently; walk down a different path. Let go of doubts, disbelief and confusion. Do what I did, try something new. What have you got to lose?

Turn to God, ask Him to reveal His Truth to you. Seek Him by reading the Bible, pray. Try it, I guarantee that you will see what I saw, that God, Jesus and the Holy Spirit are **R.E.A.L,** (**R**eally **E**xist **A**nd **L**ive) .

Before I go, I would like to share something with you that a woman wise in the ways of God once told me. She said there are many levels of 'good' but only one of 'right'. Most of us try to do good, sometimes in our efforts to do good, we do the wrong thing. Over the years I have learnt that when you do what is right, you will not do the wrong thing. You see the right thing and the wrong thing are on opposite ends of say a spectrum, and good in its many levels falls between right and wrong. Sometimes we can become so blinded in our attempts to do good deeds that we lose sight of what we are doing, and end up with a syndrome called *'Arminitis'*. Don't worry it's not fatal. It affects the arm in various degrees, hence the name. It is caused by the constant patting of one's self on the back, usually after we verbally congratulate ourselves on doing good.

630

We take delight in self praise for our good deeds, instead of trusting in God for the provision of His Grace and Mercy to always do the right thing. *A man's ways seems perfect in his own eyes but they may be wrong in God's.* When you are obedient to God, you can be assured that you are not just doing what is good in your eyes, but more importantly, what is right in God's.

Think! We were created to have a wonderful relationship with God so why do we think that we can go-it-alone.

Who am I? - Billie Lewis, a person like you who has been blessed in so many ways. Look at your life, count your blessings, see your potential, use it. For you are unique!

I leave you with a poem which inspires me each time I read it. I have the author's permission to share it with you. I hope that it inspires you.

'A Message'

You are here for a reason!
You are here for a season!

Just for a moment, push everything aside
Just for a moment, forget about pride
Open your heart, set your mind free
Become, you, the person you are meant to be.

You are here for a reason!
You are here for a season!
So recognize your purpose, don't dwell on your mistakes
God chose you for greatness, so go on, be great!
And just for a moment, forget about troubles, hurts and strife
Now take that moment and begin the rest of your life.

End

Gladys Lawson is a writer and a professional Microbiologist/Scientist with management and counselling qualifications. She has written poems and short stories from a tender age and has had a few of her pieces published in the past. She wrote her first novel a few years ago, but put it to one side as she was in the middle of promoting and writing songs for the recording artist she manages.

Gladys believes that the best writers have lived, have experienced or are experiencing what they write about. As Gladys is a scientist and also manages a singer, her debut novel thus encompasses both of her interests – namely music and science – as well as suspense.

Gladys also finds time to manage another writer, who specializes in short humorous stories and is currently working on a novel.

Ultimately, Gladys would like to write more books, at present she is finishing her second one, more songs and short stories.

Despite all odds: A Dream Fulfilled